Behind Closed Doors

BEHIND CLOSED DOORS

Tony Warren

ARROW

First published by Arrow Books in 1996

3 5 7 9 10 8 6 4 2

Copyright © Tony Warren 1996

Tony Warren has asserted his right under the Copyright,
Designs and Patents Act, 1988, to be identified as the author of this work

Arrow Books Limited
20 Vauxhall Bridge Road, London SW1V 2SA

Random House Australia (Pty) Limited
16 Dalmore Drive, Scoresby, Victoria 3179, Australia

Random House New Zealand Limited
18 Poland Road, Glenfield
Auckland 10, New Zealand

Random House South Africa (Pty) Limited
Box 2263, Rosebank 2121, South Africa

Random House UK Limited Reg. No. 954009

Papers used by Random House UK Limited are natural, recyclable
products made from wood grown in sustainable forests. The
manufacturing processes conform to the environmental regulations of
the country of origin.

ISBN: 00 9925171X

Printed and bound in the United Kingdom by
BPC Paperbacks Ltd, a member of The British Printing
Company Ltd

For Tim Justice
with love

1

It was measuring day at the grammar school and nobody wanted to be a misfit. Forty children watched anxiously as the man from Henry Barrie, the official outfitters, sized them up and down. This was so much more public than a shop. They were sitting on hard wooden chairs in the school entrance hall. The letter had read: 'Parents may wish to bring their children to our premises in St Ann's Square, Manchester (hours 9–5.30). Alternatively a representative will be in attendance at Barton Grammar School on Tuesday, 5th August, with large stocks of all boys' and girls' items on the requirements list.' But it was well known in juvenile society that there were always misfits.

'You, you and you.' The man in the winking gold-framed glasses looked just like a performing seal with a tape measure round its neck. He was plainly enjoying the temporary power vested in its stabbing forefinger. 'I'm putting you to one side. There are always three, and you're the misfits of 1947.' A big cheerful girl, a tiny anxious one and a thin boy rose to their feet.

'You're too chubby.' The girl stopped looking happy and went red. 'You've not got the chest for your height.' That was the boy demolished. 'And as for you – ' the performing seal gazed down reproachfully at the smaller girl – 'somebody's not been taking her cod liver oil. There's nothing in my stock boxes for elves.' The rest of the eleven-year-olds, those blessed to be of standard size, obliged the outfitter with contented guffaws. He beamed back at them with 'Girls into the headmaster's study, boys into the office. Parents please follow. You three wait here until I can run my tape measure over you, individually.'

'I only need the gymslip,' said the plump girl. 'My mother sent a note. I'm Vanda Bell.'

'You only need the gymslip?' The official list was shaking indignantly in the official outfitter's hand. 'Only the gym-slip?'

'My mother's getting the rest.' She was the only unaccompanied child in the high-ceilinged entrance hall. Was it the green and yellow half-tiling or the parquet flooring which caused words to echo their way back to you? *'My mother's getting the rest.'*

And now he echoed the echo. 'Your mother's getting the rest? But *we* are the official outfitters.'

'She has *ways*,' said Vanda Bell. *'Ways, ways'* went the echo. If the child was chubby, she was also quite pretty. She looked like one of those cheerful, sawdust-filled dolls with sewn-on faces – the kind that nobody can ever manage to win at a fairground.

Queues had already begun to form outside two varnished wooden doors with handles made of copper water lilies and windows in a depressing shade of olive green.

The anxious 'elf' now spoke. 'Are we meant to stay on our feet or can we sit down again?' Joan Stone was talking to the boy whose chest had been found lacking.

She doesn't have any trace of a Lancashire accent, he thought. Aloud he said, 'All this fuss and my mother doesn't even know if we've got enough clothing coupons.' In 1947 clothes were still strictly rationed. And then he said what was really worrying him: 'I'm not all *that* unusual.'

Elfin Joan Stone did a bit of sizing-up of her own. Beneath his grey flannel shorts the boy's knees were very, well, *kneey* – except that wasn't a proper word. And his feet, at the bottom of the long woollen socks, were a size too big for the rest of him. Thin he certainly was but the face was nice-looking. In fact, 'You're almost pretty,' she said. The moment the words were out she knew she'd said the wrong thing.

'Boys aren't meant to be pretty,' he snorted. 'It leads to trouble.'

'What's your name?' she asked hastily.

'Peter Bird. And if this school's anything like the last one, they'll soon be calling me Tweety-Pie.'

'They will if you tell people.'

'I won't have to. There's boys from the other school coming here.'

He's not as well spoken as me, thought Joan. But he's got much less of an accent than the gymslip girl. Joan wasn't snobbish, she just liked to get people categorised. Joan was also given to drifting off into daydreams and she couldn't have been listening properly to all that went before. 'Haven't you got a mother?' she asked Vanda Bell. The minute she'd said it she felt awful. What if Vanda's mother was dead?

'Oh I've got a mother all right.' Could Vanda really be chewing gum on such a solemn occasion? 'But she's out banging.'

'What's banging?' asked Peter. It sounded like sex and he was making a study of the subject.

'I'm not allowed to say. I've been told not to talk about it.'

Definitely sex, decided Peter. It was the fact that sex was so veiled and mysterious that made it so interesting. He, in his turn, was sizing up his companions. Not in *that* way. No, it was just that it was the kind of afternoon where a good gawp seemed the fashionable thing, and Peter was deeply interested in fashion. He decided that the little dark elf girl was not beautiful, but that she was attractive. 'Attractive' was a big word in the fashion pages of the *Daily Express* in 1947. Sometimes he wondered whether there wasn't a kind of condescending tolerance to it. They were also very fond of the word 'gamine' – he was pretty sure that Joan Stone was that, too. But she looked as though she had old parents. There was a definite look to people with older parents, and the woman sitting murmuring to his own mother, on the brown wooden chairs, was ancient.

'I think we're meant to stay standing up, Granny,' called out Joan.

Another and more interesting figure was marching towards them – a woman with a tight perm in a stockinette suit. Peter immediately had her down as not married. And he was right. 'I'm Miss Barlow, the school secretary,' she announced confidently. 'I take it that you three are this year's rejects.' With this damning phrase she headed towards her own office.

The woman's words filled Joan Stone with rising panic. Rejects? 'Did you two pass your eleven-plus exam?' she asked anxiously.

'Yes' came back from both.

'It's just that we don't seem very *wanted*.' Joan had never felt less valuable in her whole life. But she wasn't one to wallow in self-pity. 'We'll just have to stick together,' she announced firmly. 'The world is full of ordinary people. We'll be the ones who are different.' And the grammar-school echo caught hold of the word and threw it back at them. '*Different, different, different*.'

Going home, Vanda found herself on the same bus as the Peter boy and his mother – who didn't sound as though she came from round here. The prematurely white-haired woman made mysterious reference to somewhere called 'the Five Towns' and spoke of Wedgwood in a reverent voice. Still, she paid Vanda's bus fare, and when the chubbiest of the rejects got off the bus, at the Grotto Lodge development, she was fourpence better off than she'd expected to be.

Grotto Lodge was a council estate. The roads had numbers instead of names. First Drive, Second Drive . . . Imaginative residents said that it was a bit like living in America. Less fanciful souls just saw rows of pre-war, semidetached houses – all pebbledash walls and slate roofs and crazy-paving paths which divided little gardens that were bounded by sooty privet hedges.

As Vanda bounced towards the side door of number 42 Sixth Drive, a black cat scuttled past her. His name was Dick Barton and the only person he liked was Vanda's gran'ma.

The child had her own Yale front door key. Inside the house the smell of dry-cleaning fluid was even stronger than usual. Her mother must have refilled the tanks. This smell was so much a part of their lives that the fact that other people's houses weren't haunted by it made them seem unusual. Not that the Bells were the kind who often got invited inside their neighbours' houses.

'Vanda?' The cry came from upstairs and it was accompanied by a distant creak of protesting bedsprings. Gran'ma Dora was a big woman.

'Yes, it's only me.'

'Come and give yer gran'ma a kiss.'

Come and give her a few answers, more like! 'Is the cat meant to be out?' Vanda began to thump her way up the narrow staircase. There was no carpet on the stairs; some was always going to be put down but it never happened. Next door often dropped unsubtle hints about 'a lot of thudding'.

Dora Doran had lived in bed for so long that people had stopped asking the reason why. On the one occasion when Vanda had dared to ask, her grandmother had replied: 'I stop in bed because I've got a bone in my leg.' Oh she was a big woman! Yards of pale pink, extra-outsize flannelette nightdress covered the great sprawling breasts and the hefty arms which were the size of a wrestler's. Mostly she just lay very still – away in a visionary's dream. Gran'ma Dora's white hair hung over her shoulder in a diminished plait, but you barely noticed that she was going bald because the eyes were so amazing. They were the colour of forget-me-nots seen through hazy mist – that was the cataracts. But you still felt that she could see right into you.

'Where's the gymslip?' Gran'ma Dora could certainly see enough to know that it wasn't there.

'It was awful.' Vanda flopped down onto the orange and turquoise paisley eiderdown. Nothing in the room matched. Come to that, nothing in the whole house matched. It was like living inside a perpetual jumble sale. There were even two old banjos in the bedroom, propped up against an empty teachest. Vanda wouldn't have minded betting that none of the other children had gone home to anything like this.

'Don't mope. Tell your gran'ma.'

'You know those funny chocolates me mother sometimes brings back from the market?'

'Cadbury's Misshapes?'

Vanda nodded gloomily and snuggled closer. 'It felt just like being one of those.' Her grandmother smelt reassuringly of camphor.

5

'As a matter of fact, I've got some wine gums on top of the pot cupboard. Might a chew cheer you up?'

'No. I'll never eat one again. I'm going on lettuce and glasses of water.' Of course, Gran'ma was very good at leaving these long silences so you had to explain more. 'There were three of us. And this posh little titchy girl said we ought to stay friends.'

Gran'ma reached out for the wine gums anyway. Everything important was kept strictly within arm's reach. 'At a new school, there's certainly safety in numbers. Christ!' She let out an agonised moan. 'I trapped me titty against me brooch.' Grandmother and granddaughter sniggered happily. 'In what way was you an oddbody?'

Vanda said it. 'Fat.' This was the only word on earth that was capable of depressing her.

'No!' Gran'ma actually sat bolt upright – a small event in itself. 'Don't decry yourself. You're like me. You're like your mother. The women in our family start off big and they end up big. But they have a beautiful season in between. Not many get what we get. You'll see!'

'I bet you were never this fat.'

'I bet I was fatter. And little girls wore bishop's sleeves in them days. I must have looked like two for the price of one. But I *became* glorious.'

Gran'ma loved rolling out resounding phrases, and she was never afraid to voice the things that other people on the Grotto Lodge Estate only hinted at. 'You'll fine down when your monthly purges start. And that's when the lads will come running. Losing a little show of blood's nothing; not when it's going to see you into your natural inheritance. I'm not like your mother, I've got plenty of time for men. I sometimes think I'll get out of bed and find meself another. If there's one thing I miss it's your grandad's bum in the small of me back in the middle of the night.'

'One of the other misshapes was a boy.'

'Shall we get the cards out and find out about him?'

Vanda hesitated. The tarot cards could lead to trouble. Gran'ma had even been hauled into the police court and charged under the Fraudulent Medium's Act. Old Mrs

Doran had not so much objected to the five-pound fine as to the fact that the word 'fraudulent' had been plastered all over the *Swinton and Pendlebury Journal*. ('The accused was heard to shout from the dock: "The cards do not lie." ') Yes, the tarot could lead to trouble. It was what caused people to refer to the family as 'them gippos on the corner'. Dora Doran charged five shillings for a reading. She only did them in the school holidays because Vanda had to be there to let the clients in and to conduct them upstairs. It goes without saying that Gran'ma only did it in bed.

'Pass me the box.' It was home-made and decorated with a pokerwork design of a human eye coming out from behind some clouds. Dora clawed open the little brass catch and flipped back the lid. She didn't come straight to the cards. They were parcelled up inside a black silk pocket handker-chief.

The tarot pack finally in her hand, Gran'ma Dora became an empress. Extracting one card, which showed a gaudy engraving of the sun, she extended the rest of the stacked cards towards her granddaughter. 'Shuffle!' she commanded.

Vanda didn't need even the slightest of explanations. The tarot had been part of her life since the day she was born. In fact, the Sun, the card Dora Doran was holding, had been chosen for the child on the very day of her birth. It was the card of someone who would always – eventually – get what they wanted. Today Vanda was the querent, the person seeking answers, which was why the Sun had to be isolated from the rest. Suddenly, inexplicably, she didn't want to do it. 'Gran'ma, use your own card. You be the questioner.'

'When I've not met the buggers? Don't be so daft. That's enough shuffling. Hand them to me. Now . . .' She fanned out the cards so that only their chequered backs were in view. 'Take one for the boy and one for the girl.'

And still Vanda hesitated.

'Right,' said Dora 'they're going back in their box . . .'

'No.' Quickly she snatched a card, and then another.

'Give.'

Vanda handed them over without looking.

'Mmm . . .' Dora Doran tightened her mouth. There was a

7

little bit of a grizzled moustache above it. 'You've come up with two strong items here. They're both from the Major Arcana, both what you might call biggies. You're sure this one's the one you want for the boy?'

Vanda nodded. She couldn't understand why she didn't want to do it today but she didn't.

'Well, I like him,' nodded Gran'ma. 'You've pulled out the Magician.'

'Like David Nixon on television?' Vanda's head was filled with visions of a top hat and rabbits.

But from the look in Gran'ma's eyes she was obviously seeing something quite different. 'This is somebody who won't let his right hand know what his left one is doing.' The sense in the old blue eyes became lost behind the fog of the cataracts and her voice began to drone; it was for moments like these that people parted with their five shillings. 'He's not a bad lad. Oh Christ . . .' Tears, real tears. 'God bless the poor little soul. Mind you, all the ones I've known have always been good to their mothers.' She wiped the tears away with the back of her knuckles and treated Vanda to a gummy grin. 'There's nothing here you need know about yet. Not when he doesn't even know himself.'

There would be no point in asking Gran'ma Dora detailed questions; when she was in this mood, you just had to be satisfied with what you were given. 'What about the girl?'

Dora began to snigger. 'You're everything she's not. She's your direct opposite, she's the Moon.' The card showed two wolves howling up into the night sky. They were at the beginning of a long and winding road. 'Always remember that night resents giving way to day. And vice versa. When all comes to all, you'll want what she's got. And sooner or later she'll want what you've got. That should be worth watching! Let's feed some more cards into it . . .'

But their progress was arrested by a loud scream. 'Mother?' a voice came roaring up the staircase. And now it was coming nearer. 'That bloody cat of yours got between my feet again. It's made me rick my ankle. One day, I swear, I'll put Dick Barton in the gas oven and turn on the tap.'

Hastily Gran'ma began to pack up the cards. But not

8

hastily enough. Ethel Bell was already through the door. This was another woman large enough to block out daylight. 'Not those flaming cards again?' she asked indignantly. Ethel Bell looked like a hugely inflated version of Vanda but with extra air pumped around the ankles, and dyed black hair – a great big dolly in a royal-blue coat which was too tightly belted round the middle. 'And I was just going to make you a nice cup of tea, Mother,' she said sorrowfully. 'Oh you are naughty. Those cards get us talked about like nothing on earth.'

Gran'ma assumed a knowing expression. 'Funny how the gift can skip a generation.' It was an old routine. 'What gets us talked about is *you*. And I, for one, have every sympathy with the neighbours. It can't be very nice living side by side with a woman who goes out *banging*!'

The Moon, who only knew herself as Joan Stone, was writing in her diary:

> I haven't told you anything since my birthday and now it is a sunny afternoon in late August. Last week we went to the grammar school to be measured for uniforms and I may have made two new friends. I think the boy could come from quite a good kind of background because he was wearing Clark's sandals. The girl appeared to me to be of the same class as Martha, our apple-cheeked cook, who awaited our return with wholesome stew in the oven. It was packed with nourishing mushrooms which may sound extravagant but is not when money is no object.

Lies. She had returned to one slice of cold corned beef with plain boiled potatoes. And they had not been prepared by any apple-cheeked cook, for Martha was a figment of Joan Stone's imagination.

> Whilst I was at the school with Granny, my mummy was also out shopping at Mrs Critchley's, the most exclusive shop in the neighbourhood. She purchased a

9

charming tailor-made cocktail frock in red astrakhan. She is going to wear it to the golf club garden party.

More lies. Her mother was a subject which was not allowed to be mentioned. 'Don't ask,' was all Granny would say. 'You'll be much happier not knowing.'

Joan's diary was written inside an antique exercise book, bound in marbled cardboard. The label on this cover read *Miss Brent's Seminary for Young Gentlewomen. Ellesmere Park, Eccles, Lancashire.* The book was a leftover from Granny's own childhood – from the days when both sides of the family had lorded it over the rest of the town. And now all that was left was horrible Ingledene. This ramshackle Victorian house was also in Ellesmere Park, a district which had known both ups and downs. By 1947, the larger houses – the villas banded with multicoloured brickwork – had taken a definite plunge towards dereliction. And Ingledene was hidden behind banks of overgrown rhododendrons and stretches of privets which had defied convention by bushing and flowering. After rain, they always smelt much more beautiful than they looked.

But nothing could turn the house into a thing of beauty. Semidetached in a massive way, the front of the building was decorated with rickety little iron balconies. Nobody had ever managed to get out onto them because they were too narrow to afford a foothold. This didn't stop the people next door from trying – over and over again. Granny was always having to erupt into the garden to scream up warnings about rusty ironwork to a series of undesirable new neighbours. Next door had suffered the final indignity: it had been turned into furnished flatlets.

Shabby gentility was the order of the day at Ingledene. Up in the old sewing room (which she thought of as her study) Joan chewed on her pencil and wondered what to write down next. In her own mind there was no question of the diary being untrue. Its pages recorded her *other* existence, the one inside her head – a world where life was more generous than the penny-pinching reality of downstairs.

Instead of writing she spoke aloud: 'I expect it will be

pilchards again for tea.' She was talking to an old dressmaker's dummy in the corner. The knob-headed creature, with its beige cambric body and mahogany stand, was quite a friend. Correction: her only friend. And all because of Granny's stubborn pride. Joan's last six years had been geared towards sitting a scholarship to the grammar school. To that end, her grandmother had found money for the modern equivalent of Miss Brent's seminary – an undistinguished school called Fernbank. Children at the school had made friendly overtures towards Joan, there had even been invitations to tea and to birthday parties. Granny, however, had strict rules: if you accepted an invitation, you were honour-bound to ask the person back. And that would have meant outsiders getting to view the shabby interior of Ingledene. 'Let them remember it as it was' had been Granny's unyielding attitude.

Joan hid her diary in one of the dozens of drawers of the sewing machine and began to make her way downstairs. It was amazing how the smell of damp could vary. Today it struck her as a cross between old hymn books and sweet mothballs. The walls of the staircase were painted olive green to just about her shoulder height, and maroon above that. The two colours were divided by a flaking stencilled dado of once golden sunflower heads. The paint must have been applied when Briggs's Patricroft Foundry (*Iron Bedsteads Our Speciality*) was still a thundering industrial wonder. All that was over. The foundry premises had long since been sold to a manufacturer of wireless valves.

In today's diary entry Joan had even improved the weather; by the time she got to the ground floor she could hardly hear herself think for the sound of rain battering down onto the glass roof of the billiard room. The noise was easily penetrating a locked door. How many years since there'd been a fire in there? Or one in the dining room? Or visitors in the front drawing room where all the furniture was under dust sheets and the American pianola was safety-pinned inside a huge, linen, baglike shroud? Small wonder that the world of the diary was always sunlit.

'Joan? Have you washed your hands?' This was Granny

11

calling from the kitchen. 'And be sure and put the plug in the bowl. Hot water costs money!'

Joan pushed open the door of the downstairs cloakroom and knocked over Uncle Bruno's black sit-up-and-beg bicycle. Granny had not failed to miss the clatter and the child could hear her berating Bruno in the distance. 'When I am grown up,' said Joan to the lavatory pan, 'I shall never ever use carbolic soap again.'

Footsteps were coming down the corridor. 'Hurry up,' said Bruno from outside. 'She's sent me to wash mine.'

'You can come in, I'm quite decent. Is it pilchards?'

Bruno walked through the door laughing. 'No, it's her other rare treat, it's mince and carrots.'

And that was something else Joan would avoid as an adult. But she hoped Uncle Bruno would still be in her life. As if to reinforce this thought she turned round and gave him a hug.

'What was that for?' He was still smiling.

Goodness but he was getting nice-looking. Tall, with dark enough red hair to allow a suntan. And that always made the amused eyes seem greener. 'The hug was for love.' You could say things like that to Bruno. At seventeen he was more like a brother than an uncle. He had arrived late in Granny's married life and she always referred to him as 'that terrible final shock'. Mrs Briggs rated her only son's birth as much more of a tragedy than her husband's sudden death. And she was not above hinting that the one had led to the other: 'No man of sixty-five should have been expected to have to teach a child to bowl overarm.'

'Should you be in your blazer?' asked Joan anxiously. School uniforms were supposed to be 'costly' and not meant for the holidays. His navy-blue blazer, crested with an owl, proclaimed him a pupil of Manchester Grammar School – the only feather in the family's latter-day cap. It was considered streets ahead of the school Joan would be attending. You had to be *really* clever to get a scholarship to MGS. Two bus fares there and two back, every single day! Sometimes it was impossible to avoid thinking like Granny Briggs.

'It's all right. I'm wearing it officially. We went to the

vicarage to collect the parish magazines.' It was the young people's job to deliver these; rather like doing a paper round but not common because no money changed hands.

As Joan rinsed her hands, Bruno took hold of the wet tablet of carbolic soap and stood waiting his turn. 'The vicar's wife asked Gran to go and hear the Carl Rosa Opera Company with them. It's *Madame Butterfly* on Tuesday.'

'I bet she won't go.' Granny Briggs sometimes seemed to *enjoy* denying herself pleasure.

'She says she's nothing to wear.' Bruno took his place at the sink and peered through the little window above it. 'But that's not what she said to the Holy Family. She called it "having my squirrel bridge cape remodelled".' The cloakroom window was decently veiled by a crocheted curtain. It only covered the bottom half and Bruno was looking over the top. 'They're fat uns!' he said.

Joan had to stand on tiptoe to see out. Two heavily mackintoshed female figures were picking their way, in rubber wellingtons, through the puddles of next door's drive. There was something familiar about the smaller one, who was only a girl. But Joan was more interested in something else: 'Why do you think they're carrying sacks?'

'They're almost certainly burglars,' Bruno teased solemnly. And then in altogether more realistic tones he added, 'I just hope they're not thinking of coming here. We've nothing worth pinching.'

'There's the portrait of Flora MacDonald.' She had been brought up to think of this as priceless.

'Too heavy. And much too big to get in a sack. Come on, we don't want burnt mince.'

There were more of the crocheted modesty curtains in the kitchen. It was dominated by a huge cast-iron wall oven with a brass plaque which read *Briggs's Patricroft Foundry*. Joan always wondered whether her grandfather had brought it home from the works in pieces – a bit at a time. ('Guess what I've got for you tonight, Olive? A lovely doorknob!') Nowadays, this great black-lacquered range was just a stone-cold reminder of the past. Cooking was done on a cheap little electric stove in the scullery.

Granny Briggs was already at the table, doling brown slop onto chipped blue and white Spode plates. She was a thin woman with a tired face and pale grey eyes. Her white hair was fighting a losing battle with two tortoiseshell combs, meant to keep it upswept to the top of her head. The big white wraparound overall looked as though it had been bought for some professional cook who had failed to materialise. As Granny Briggs was very flat-chested, the yards of white material brought to mind an ironing board covered in a sheet. 'The Carl Rosa Opera Company!' she snorted. Olive Briggs was plainly enjoying a deep resentment. 'Bring my plate, Bruno. And bring the parsnips.'

'I thought it was carrots,' said Joan innocently.

Too innocently for Granny's liking. 'Are you trying to be funny?' Without so much as a breath's pause she added, 'For what we're about to receive, may the Lord make us truly thankful, amen. I could kill the vicar's wife. What have I got that's fit to wear in the orchestra stalls?'

Joan's mind was immediately filled with visions of A Night at the Opera: white ties and tails, and diamonds shimmering in powdered décolletages. 'You've got wardrobes full of old evening dresses upstairs.'

Granny sniffed and attacked her plate of mince with an old soup spoon, something the young people would never have been permitted to do. 'I wouldn't want to look like something left over from the Delhi durbar.' Briggs's Foundry's Indian connection had once been second to none. 'Since the war it's all semi-evening dress.' She managed to make this sound a second cousin to the Seven Veils.

'Couldn't you shorten something?' Joan was trying to be helpful. She should have known better.

'Shorten something? I'd *know* it had been shortened. Does this mince taste to you of metal polish?' They were not allowed to answer for she continued: 'No, I've got clothes for Government House and perfect outfits for the Ragged School – with nothing in between. What I could really do with is a good wardrobe dealer. Somebody who'd come and take all that junk upstairs off my hands.' Was this really Granny

Briggs's heart's desire? If it was, two unlikely fairy god-mothers were already working their way towards her.

There was a definite art to banging. Vanda knew that much already. On the housing estates you always sidled up to the back door to ask whether they had any old clothes to sell. But posh people like to be *seen* to get rid of their cast-offs, so you did the deal right out on the front step. Ellesmere Park still fell into this second category. It was an area of unadopted roads. This one was little better than a cart track. And the rain was coming down in stair rods.

'Just smell those wet privets.' Vanda was sniffing the pale cream florets appreciatively. 'They're like something that could have been bottled in Paris.' The rag collectors had reached a house with *Ingledene* chiselled into the sandstone gateposts.

Ethel Bell was already sizing up the garden, where a lead nymph danced on a marble pedestal surrounded by flourishing catmint and struggling old stems of bleeding heart. 'Looks as though it could belong to broken-down toffs.' But the sight of lined curtains, whatever their condition, was always enough to send Ethel Bell rolling up a front drive; lined curtains meant there must have been money at some time.

It was Joan Stone who eventually answered the distant ringing. Though she didn't know it, she had a dab of mince on her chin. 'Hello,' she said, recognising Vanda from measuring day.

'Is your mammy in?' rapped out Ethel.

Vanda Bell was not one whit embarrassed at being caught out as a juvenile wardrobe dealer. It was just what she had to do, for the moment. One day all her clothes would be brand-new; she trusted and believed in that. Not for nothing was her tarot card the all-optimistic Sun.

It was the Moon who was covered in confusion. Any question concerning her parentage always caused Joan Stone to blush. Unsupervised reading of adult fiction had led her to believe that she might be illegitimate.

'Your mammy,' repeated Mrs Bell. 'Is she in?'

'I'll get my grandmother,' stammered Joan. But that woman was already hurrying down the olive-green and maroon corridor. As she travelled she whipped off her cook's apron to reveal a faded beige crepe afternoon dress and a pair of aggressive elbows.

Ethel Bell sized up the owner of Ingledene. And Vanda knew that this one glance would equip her mother with an exact valuation of every item on the householder's back – right down to the shoelaces. It was woe betide the woman who answered her own door dressed to kill! Ethel had been known to carry off garments while they were still warm. She wouldn't expend this amount of energy on floppy crepe de Chine, but her professional antennae must have divined some alluring item on the premises because she was already assuming her special wheedling face. 'You look as miserable as I feel,' she said to the woman on the step. This was one of Ethel's standard opening gambits.

Granny Briggs attempted to take charge of the proceedings: 'I don't buy at the door.'

Ethel grabbed them right back with a hand on Granny's arm and 'Would you by any chance have any connection with that red-brick grammar school up the road?'

'My father was once on the board of governors.' Mrs Briggs sounded marginally mollified.

Ethel's eyes became points of jet. 'And I bet you've had a daughter there too. And I bet her old blazer's still hanging in the wardrobe. This poor child . . .' Ethel thrust Vanda in front of her own enormous bulk like a chubby little hostage. 'This poor child has got nothing but one shop-bought gymslip to go to school in.' She pronounced it 'skewel' and the word was delivered in a beggar's whine.

Joan ached with embarrassment for poor Vanda. But she needn't have troubled. The wardrobe dealer's daughter was used to being thrust forward and proclaimed as next-door-to-naked. This was how Ethel got hold of most of the children's clothes she sold on her second-hand stalls on the markets. But for once her mother was telling the truth. They *did* need a school uniform. 'Have you collected yours yet?' she asked Joan interestedly.

'Yes,' whispered Joan. 'Last week.' She didn't dare speak louder because she didn't want the grown-ups to hear the bit that came next. 'Everything would be too little for us to share.'

'You shouldn't *feel* things so much.' Vanda actually succeeded in putting the smaller girl at her ease. 'We'll get one, you'll see. Hockey shorts, the lot! I always get what I need. I don't worry and I get it.'

'That's a very expectant attitude for somebody who's just a child,' said Granny Briggs. 'And I'm afraid I don't believe in dealing on the front doorstep.' Pushing Joan down the hall, she slammed the front door in the Bells' faces.

Outside on the step, Ethel Bell reviewed the situation philosophically: 'I should have saved me legs. They've got dingling-Ginnie growing by the gate. It's always unlucky for me, dingling-Ginnie.' In her own way Ethel was as superstitious as her tarot-spreading mother. Suddenly she stopped being a crafty professional and turned into a portrait of outrage. 'Fancy her slamming the door on us when you was already acquainted with the kiddie! Anyway, I bet I could buy and sell them twice over.'

'Then why can't you buy me a full school uniform?'

'Because it would go against the grain.'

Though the rain hadn't stopped, the sun was trying to break through, and the scent of damp privet was suddenly much stronger. It was almost intoxicating. Ethel Bell's spirits seemed to have taken an abrupt leap, for she smiled as she added, 'Just look how much I spend on your ambitions! I kit you out for *them* in the finest that money can buy.'

Vanda paused in her trudge for the unadopted road. 'They're not my ambitions, they're your own.'

'We'll show the world,' cried Ethel Bell. 'Once we've got twenty thousand in the bank we'll have our halibut and fitted carpets. And stop trailing that bloody sack in the sludge.'

And what of the Magician? What of Peter Bird – known to his enemies as Tweetie-Pie? Was the same rain falling upon him?

Yes. Well, almost. As he lay cocooned under the covers of the narrow iron hospital bed, the rain was battering against the window above his locker. Cronkheit Ward specialised in ear, nose and throat operations, and Peter was now minus his tonsils and adenoids. The operation itself had been just a little prick in the arm, and when you woke up you got all the free ice cream you wanted. But his throat was sore and he was feeling homesick.

Even *Children's Hour* didn't sound the same when it came blaring from a big wireless set in the middle of the high-ceilinged Victorian hospital ward. Was his mother, he wondered, also listening to *The Adventures of Norman and Henry Bones* on the portable in the morning room of number 10 Hawksway? The worst thing about these longings for home was that he could actually see the roof of their own house from where he lay. The Ravensdale Estate backed onto the grounds of the Royal Manchester Children's Hospital. Peter wished he was back in his own bed with the Pelham puppets hanging in the window, instead of being stuck in this one which had an awful memorial plate above it.

> *Sacred to the Memory of Lily*
> *Wadsworth who Went to Join the*
> *Angels on Christmas Eve 1926*

But had she gone to join them from this very bed? Was this where she had died? That's what was worrying Peter. That and the fact that every time he turned over the rubber undersheet creaked as though it was leading a sinister life of its own. Or was the crackling sound really *Lily*? The final words of the inscription were *Only Sleeping*. He was forever having to stifle the thought that her invisible ghost might actually be in bed with him – deathly pale in a green operating gown and little white surgical socks.

The rain outside gave way to more of those bitty shafts of sunlight. And *Children's Hour* was replaced by the shipping forecast. Who cared about what was going on in Crombie, Dogger and Heligoland? He just wanted to be at number 10 Hawksway. Norman and Henry Bones made it Wednesday: and Wednesday was permanent-waving day. Peter's mother ran a small hairdressing business in what should have been their dining room.

Through the window he could see more of Miss Lathom and Miss Parr's house than he could see of their own. They were maiden ladies who lived together, schoolmistresses; but that didn't stop them being his great friends.

Here in hospital he had made a new enemy, Sister Birch, who wore a severely tailored navy-blue dress and a tall white starched cap. It was kept on her head by narrow linen strings which tied in an angry little bow under her chin. She was thin and chilly and very, very cross with him. He didn't really want to think about his crime. Instead, he thought about Miss Lathom and Miss Parr. Grace Lathom was always spoken of as 'mannish' but Iris Parr was much more eau de cologne and nice blouses. They had real antiques in their house; this was unusual on the Ravensdale Estate where interiors tended to be like something out of the catalogue for a pre-war Ideal Homes Exhibition. The maiden ladies had practically every book that was ever printed. And they got round food rationing by having things like Loch Fyne kippers sent down from Scotland by post.

The mastoid boy on one side of Peter's bed, and the sinus girl with the tubes on the other, both had visitors. The girl's mother needed a vase for flowers; nobody brought toys as presents because new toys were still hard to get, and anyway it was well known that, once introduced onto the ward, they would have to be left behind, because of germs.

You couldn't have visitors until you'd been in for a week. But I'd still like one, thought Peter. Yes, I'd like a visitor of my own. The one he got was not at all to his liking. Sister Birch, who moved as though she was on castors, was gliding towards his bed.

'Yes or no?' she asked coldly.

'No.' Peter turned his head away from her. He still didn't want to think about it.

'Have you any idea of the trouble you're causing?' She sounded a little bit Welsh. 'And look at me when I'm speaking to you. If you won't do that, cast your eyes to the top of the ward and see who's talking to Staff Nurse.'

19

It was Mr Doonan the surgeon, the nearest thing Cronkheit Ward had to God. Sister adjusted her starched bow. 'He's going to speak to you, Peter Bird. And I expect he's going to speak to you very severely.'

The surgeon was already coming nearer and a lot of the mothers were burbling 'Good evening, Doctor,' which was not his proper title. But Peter had done something much worse than getting a name wrong.

'This is the little boy,' called out Sister importantly. Peter had already noticed that if Mr Doonan was God, Sister Birch viewed herself as Queen of the Angels. In fact there was definite rivalry as to who was boss. 'This little boy – ' she could have been describing an infant demon – 'this self-willed child has not had a bowel movement for four days. He wantonly deceived me. And you, Mr Doonan. Though you didn't know it, you operated on a boy who was full of bizzie.'

'Well, he lived,' said the surgeon cheerfully. Peter liked him; he was big and Irish and sparklingly handsome, and when they'd first gone to visit him in his consulting rooms he'd shown Peter a picture of his own children, and the adopted one was black.

'He's blocked solid,' said Sister Birch indignantly. 'We might have to consider putting something up his botty.'

Peter decided to trust Mr Doonan. 'She gave me brown stuff to swallow. Twice. I *could* go,' he said carefully. 'In fact it's getting hard not to go . . . '

'Then why don't you?' asked the surgeon politely.

Peter's voice was still croaky from the operation, croaky and indignant. 'There's no toilet paper. They try to make you use cotton wool instead.' His tone made it clear that he had found the idea distinctly creepy.

'Of all the ridiculous . . . ' Sister was snorting so much that her cap quivered.

Mr Doonan's tone was plainly designed to remind her of his Almighty powers. 'I presume that you too were once ten years old, Sister?'

'I'm eleven,' croaked Peter, even more indignantly.

Mr Doonan dismissed this with, 'Ten, eleven, you're still fortunate enough to be living in the years of imagination. And

20

Sister has plainly forgotten how big small things can seem. But it *is* about time that Mafeking was relieved . . . ' Bedside mothers were pretending not to be listening in. 'Send out for lavatory paper, Sister Birch. Peter is coming with me.' The big surgeon led the small boy up the ward by the hand. At eleven, Peter felt he was really too old for this. But he liked the feeling of the warm, dry hand; and he liked Mr Doonan. Liked him? The word wasn't strong enough; at that moment Peter actually *loved* him.

Once Peter had done his duty he felt about a stone lighter and twenty times more cheerful. And to his joy, when he got back to his bed he found he had an illegal unofficial visitor. It wasn't the usual voluntary worker pushing a brush between the beds this evening. Instead, it was Miss Lathom.

'Shh,' she said in conspiratorial tones. 'I persuaded Mrs Clitheroe to let me stand in for her.' The most noticeably mannish things about Grace Lathom were her shoes and the cut of her iron-grey hair. Most of the rest of her was covered in what she would have worn for domestic duties at home – a flowered Liberty smock over a stout tweed skirt.

'Brought you this.' From out of a pocket Mrs Lathom produced a small glass jar. 'Real honey and lemon. Finest thing on earth for easing throats.'

Peter was distinctly impressed. With everything on ration, a whole pot of honey was luxury indeed. 'Where did you get it?'

Miss Lathom winked. 'Let's say I know some black-market bees. Brought you a spoon, too.'

It was one of her plated apostle spoons. Not the best silver ones (Peter knew where every single item lived in her house). No, this was an everyday spoon from the kitchen table drawer. But it brought Hawksway vividly to mind. 'How is everybody – at home?' he gulped.

Miss Lathom seemed to hesitate.

'Go on,' said Peter. This phrase, often used in their conversations, was meant to encourage reluctant revelations. 'Go on.'

'Well, somebody has to tell you.' She shifted her weight

21

from foot to foot. 'You can't just walk straight in on it. Your father has come home again.'

'Oh.' It was just a polite noise, something to say while he considered the situation. But, inside, Peter was feeling far from polite; in fact his thoughts were full of panic.

'Perhaps your father won't be so . . . *exotic* this time.' To cover her gruff embarrassment, Miss Lathom pretended to be doing a bit more of the amateur sweeping up.

'*You*!' It was Sister on her last round of the day; the final inspection before she handed over to the night staff. 'Yes, you.'

'Are you addressing me?' Grace Lathom returned the bullying hospital sister's glare with an all-seeing gaze which she had appropriated, long ago, from the principal of Somerville College, Oxford.

Sister Birch was quite quelled. 'It was just that I didn't know your face.'

'And why should you? I am a *rogue* volunteer – almost a pirate. I am standing in for little Mrs Clitheroe. And there are those who would say that I was taking up altogether more space.'

'This is a very naughty little boy you're talking to.' Sister tried throwing Miss Lathom a different variety of glare.

But Miss Lathom was more than up to it and stared her out. And now she excluded Sister Birch from the conversation altogether with, 'I shouldn't worry too much about your father, Peter. But somebody had to tell you. Maybe, this time, it will be all right.'

And maybe not. In fact, almost certainly not. Why should this time be any different from all the rest?

The children danced in the middle of the room. The mothers sat watching on a row of tubular steel and canvas chairs, ranged against a wall that was opposite to the practice barre.

The accompanying tinkle-tinkle was provided by Mrs Musker on the upright piano. But it was Miss Ashworth who was calling out dance instructions above the thud of sixteen pairs of little feet. '*Glissade*, *changement* . . . *changement*, *glissade*. Stretch that *foot*, Alicia.' Anybody looking for a list of lavish Christian names need seek no further than a provincial suburban ballet class. There were two Alicias, one Tamara, a Tatiana who had been named after the great Russian dancer Riabouchinska, and even a small brunette called Ginger. It was as though the mothers' ambitions for their daughters had been present at their very christenings.

The *glissade* was a travelling movement, the *changement* took the girls up and down. But the one who travelled lightest and soared the highest was Vanda Bell. Fat she might have been but she was in the centre of the front row and she was its indubitable shining star.

The Odette Ashworth Studio School of Dancing was based in a room which had been converted from a brick double garage, built onto the side of a 1930s bungalow. Swan House sat right on the border of Worsley, a district which considered itself a cut above neighbouring Swinton. The mothers were the kind who wore Jaeger camel coats and Jacqmar scarves. All the girls had been shod by England's of Piccadilly in Manchester – stockists of real Anello and Davide ballet shoes. In this instance, even Vanda Bell's white canvas slippers had come from the proper shop and her matching tunic had been made to exactly the same pattern as the rest.

But Ethel Bell didn't look like the rest of the mothers. In this setting she more than ever resembled a bundle of navy-blue bolsters, belted round the middle with a buckled leather strap. And what was she doing rummaging inside an old paper carrier bag? Vanda was certain that this bulging item must have come into her mother's hands since the beginning of class.

The room was walled with mirrors, so it was easy for Miss Ashworth to adjust her lipstick as she taught. She was a woman who had been trained for great things which had never quite happened. As if in memory of this, Odette Ashworth always wore a rough sketch of a stage make-up. If you'd added red dots to the corners of her eyes she could have danced straight onto the centre of the stage of Covent Garden. Her prime had coincided with the war years so that she had been obliged to join ENSA and entertain the troops;

23

and when she escaped from that, it had been only into the chorus of *Perchance to Dream*. A good but uninspired dancer, she was an excellent teacher – the best for miles around. And she was forever looking for one child, just one, who would become the Great English Dancer.

Ethel Bell was quite convinced that this child lived at number 42 Sixth Drive. Hadn't Vanda achieved higher marks in her grade examinations than any other pupil in the history of the school? Hadn't she carried everything before her in the Sunshine Competitions, won all there was to win at Lewis's Festival? Whenever Miss Ashworth murmured the terrible word 'size' (and she didn't murmur it too loudly because the child *was* remarkable), Ethel always countered with, 'She'll fine down. My mother did, I did. The only problem could be her bust. If that gets too voluptuous she'll just have to settle for musicals.'

This statement always managed to annoy the mother of the girl called Ginger. The women on the chairs were much more ambitious than their dancing daughters.

As the music ground to a tinkling halt, Miss Ashworth said, 'Vanda, Ginger and Mary, stay in the centre. I want to see your Grade Three *enchânement*. All other girls to the side.'

Old Mrs Musker adjusted the veil on her hat and struck up with a familiar passage from *The Nutcracker*. And Vanda danced. This time there would be no barked interruptions, the aim was to make the whole thing appear seamless. 'Get it like pure silk,' was the most Miss Ashworth would breathe. And as Vanda travelled across the polished floor she turned into herself-in-her-own-right. I am *me*, she thought (*pas de chat*, *pas de chat*, and don't make them jerky). I am me, and somehow, some day, it will all be all right. It was her grandmother who had instilled this attitude into her. 'If you can dream it, you can have it,' that's what Dora always said.

But what did Vanda want? She negotiated two *pas de basques* and reminded herself that the next bit went '*en arrière*', which was ballet-French for behind. Will my bottom ever get smaller? Will all of me slim down? Yes, it will, it will, it will. Trust and believe, more of Gran'ma Dora's words.

Trust and believe. Sometimes she wondered whether the old woman was in league with the devil. And, ouch, Mrs Musker had just hit a wrong note.

'Needs tuning,' the accompanist called out, as though the sandwich in her hand had nothing to do with it.

Now came the bit that Vanda enjoyed the most. It began like sailing and then you flew on the wind. As she soared up towards the painted Lincrusta ceiling and gazed into the overhead neon lights, the young dancer tried to visualise her ambitions. They were all to do with *things*. All the things she hadn't got. Fitted rose-coloured carpets, and grey and white Regency-striped wallpaper, and a great big crystal chandelier; she saw all of these, plus gilded door handles, in one quick flash of her imagination.

As her feet touched the ground, reality intruded. On the mothers' chairs Ethel Bell was pulling something out of the carrier bag labelled *Paulden's – Well Worth a Bus Ride*. But the contents hadn't come from that shop, they'd come from Henry Barrie's; and from the look of things it was a long time since they'd left the school outfitter's premises. Ethel was shaking out an old grammar-school blazer in triumph. Just one glance was enough for Vanda to be able to tell that it would be half a size too small for her. Her heart sank to her shoes. Why couldn't her mother just go to a shop like anybody else instead of crawling her way through other people's reach-me-downs. Because Ethel was the Cast-off Queen, that was why.

'And rest,' called out Odette Ashworth. 'Something went very wrong in the middle, Vanda. You were suddenly dancing as though the world was an ugly place.' Which only went to show how well Vanda Bell's heart and her feet were linked together.

Ethel, blazer held aloft, was busy miming a demonstration of big seams, which could presumably be let out. Miss Ashworth treated her to a cold glance. 'What I have to say next concerns both you mothers and all the girls. Mona Inglesby is bringing her International Ballet to the Opera House and I think it would be very nice if as many of us as possible could go and see her dance *Coppélia*. I would prefer

25

us to sit in the dress circle so we can study the feet. I'm afraid the seats will be ten shillings and sixpence each.'

'Put me down for two,' bawled out Ethel enthusiastically.

The money would have bought at least the sleeves of a new . . . no. Vanda was sick of the word 'blazer' so she went back to her dreams of rose carpets and a gilded drop-end sofa, and of herself – goodness how skinny and elegant – doing a rather good impression of Madame Récamier. Only the self of today was pushing the vision to one side and what she was seeing now was a dumpy little schoolgirl in a badly altered school uniform.

You can only tell how your own house smells to other people when you've been away from it for a while. Peter returned home from the children's hospital on the morning of the day that he should have been starting at the grammar school. He didn't come back by ambulance. His mother had just walked the length of the high brick wall which bounded the hospital grounds and collected him from a waiting room decorated with a mural of Donald Duck and Mickey Mouse.

When Peter pointed out to her that it said they were 'By Kind Permission of Walt Disney' she hadn't seemed much interested. And when he propounded his new theory that half the children in the neighbourhood probably associated good old Walt with the terrors of hospital, Peggy Bird merely nodded absently. Was this because his father was back home? Or was her mind on the four ladies she'd already said she'd got booked down for shampoos and sets?

Once they were back at Hawksway, Peggy hurried off to check the hot water cistern. The tank had no thermostat and on one occasion it had even blown itself up into the rafters. You couldn't get thermostats, you couldn't get anything – though the war had been over for two years.

Noticing his father's coat hanging on the hallstand, Peter began to anticipate explosions of a different nature. More peacetime deprivations showed in this military greatcoat dyed navy blue. Peter's father always maintained that nothing had gone right for him since he'd been demobbed. Of course they didn't hand out medals so freely in peacetime. Eddie

26

Bird was a holder of the Victoria Cross; Bird VC had once been a name that had made headlines.

Peter sniffed deeply, quite noticeably turning his head away from the greatcoat; *that* would only pong of Woodbines and stale beer. His father always boasted that he'd spilled more down his own tie than most men could drink in a lifetime. The house itself smelt clean, with overtones of ammonia. Somebody must have had their hair bleached recently. But where was this nice whiff of new paint coming from?

'I just got to the cistern in time. It was already rumbling.' Peggy had reappeared at the top of the stairs.

'Why are you whispering?'

'Shh. He's having the morning in bed.' She began to tiptoe down the stairs. 'He's not feeling too good.'

'Is it his old trouble?' Peter had barely bothered to lower his voice, but the phrase he'd used was one that was meant to save both mother and son embarrassment. Now he said something much bolder: 'Why did you let him back into the house?'

'How was I meant to stop him?' When she wasn't worried she was very nice-looking with crinkly laughing eyes. Peggy's hair had gone white in her early twenties, even before she met her husband. It made her look what Peter thought of as young-old. But this morning she just looked old and she sounded worn out. 'He's got every right. He's got the law on his side. I'm every bit as much his possession as the house is. The fact that I'm the one who's paid for the lot doesn't enter into it. Let's stop worrying and have a nice cigarette.'

'I don't smoke.' But Peter found it flattering that she always forgot he was only eleven. 'And you shouldn't smoke so much, either.' They were allies. He loved her as fiercely as he disliked his father. 'Peggy, couldn't we just move somewhere else?'

'You've got two *Children's Newspapers* waiting for you in the lounge.' It had obviously been a mistake to remind her of his juvenile status.

Peggy let out a deep sigh and looked defeated. 'We've tried the moving routine. I sometimes wish we'd stayed in the

27

Potteries where we belonged.' She took off her old Donegal tweed coat and placed it on the furthest side of the hallstand from her husband's. 'The trouble is, people think he's such a hero. Look what happened when we flitted to those furnished rooms! Who else but a VC could have persuaded the *Sunday Chronicle* to track us down?'

'But I thought that he'd gone for good this time. That's what he shouted when he slammed off with your best fibre suitcase.'

'I know he did. But he must have suddenly needed a big row. And that always brings him back to me.' Fishing in the pocket of her navy tailored frock, Peggy Bird produced a packet of Players and a box of matches. She continued to talk as she lit the cigarette which was held between angry lips. 'He landed in last Tuesday midnight, with a taxi ticking away outside and not so much as a farthing in his pocket.' All pretence of whispering had stopped. 'Said it was my wifely duty to pay off the driver. You never heard such a barrack-room lawyer in all your born days! All I can say is, the laws of this country were made by men *for* men.'

'All that cigarette smoke's making the front of your hair go yellow. We could always poison him.' Peter meant it.

'Yes, but they'd put us both in different prisons.' Peggy Bird sounded as though she had considered the idea quite seriously. 'And while I think about it, if you go in the airing cupboard watch what you're doing. We don't want any accidents. He's got a bottle of Gordon's gin tucked behind the clean bedding. It's easier to pretend we don't know it's there.'

Rat-a-tat-tat went the door knocker. The first customer could be seen through the circular stained-glass window in the front door, the one that showed two bluebirds kissing.

As the business of the day was about to begin, Peter supposed he had better check that everything in the house was in its place. He was a boy who was greatly given to rituals. He always prayed as he passed certain places, and there were various household items that he always felt duty-bound to touch for luck.

'Good morning, Mrs Ramsden,' said his mother to the woman on the step. And then she called over her shoulder to

Peter, 'Watch out for the paint on that lounge door. It's only undercoated. We don't want it marked with fingerprints.' Peggy was a dab hand at home decorating. She didn't just slap on the paint any old how, she could achieve fancy effects like pastel-shaded wood grain. And she thought nothing of twiddling her brush to produce a fake knot. She was still calling after Peter: 'There's a surprise for you through that door.'

He pushed it open. The room he remembered as pale beige was now apple green with pink touches. Peggy's voice was coming nearer. 'Come and have a look at my efforts, Mrs Ramsden. I mean you've got to do *something* when the government won't let you have wallpaper. I managed that mottled effect by dabbing it with a sponge.'

'Don't look at the state of my hair,' said Mrs Ramsden – all the customers always said that. 'Your decorating's just done with distemper, is it?' The untidy little woman had already removed a hat which was another tribute to the government's Make-do and Mend campaign.

'Distemper?' Peggy Bird was all mock indignation. 'This is genuine Walpamur. Just like they have at Buckingham Palace.' Peter's mother was a great supporter of royalty and National Savings and the Lifeboat Fund.

Mrs Ramsden was still looking around in wonder. 'I see you've grained the surround of your fireplace, too.'

'And the piano,' said Peggy. 'I'm not one for dwelling on my troubles. I paint them away instead.'

'Have you got problems?' asked Mrs Ramsden, interested.

Peter knew that his mother wouldn't tell. She might come from the Potteries, but she was very well aware of the unwritten rules that governed the Ravensdale Estate. Private matters were never aired in public. That would have been as unthinkable as removing the lace curtains which screened every window.

'This isn't turning you into a beauty queen, Mrs Ramsden.' Peggy stubbed out her cigarette in a Wedgwood ashtray, and then pinched off the end so that she would be able to light it up again later. 'Peter, the varnish on those shelves should have set hard by now. Do me a favour and put all the books back, there's a good lad.'

First she led her customer out, then the door burst open again and in flew an unaccompanied orange duster. Peter was still sizing up the changes. The pink and green paintwork echoed the colours of the stained-glass tulips in the leaded transoms of the bay window. This made the three-piece suite and the carpet look even more pre-war and porridge-shaded than usual.

He picked up the duster and began to attack the pile of books. The third one he came upon was the family photo album, so the duster got dropped to the carpet as interest set in. It was a genuine Victorian album, like a big Bible with a metal clasp. All the earlier sepia photographs sat securely within their gilt-edged mounts, but once you got to the 1930s the pictures stopped fitting inside the mounts. They were mostly snapshots, poked in at the side of the ornate gaps; people in very rudely revealing woollen bathing costumes, and men in plus-fours laughing and playing ukuleles. Nothing that pretended to be overposh, just a contented world of suburban plenty.

The only photograph of his father had not even been poked into a gap. It just floated loose. Not that 'floating' was a word you could associate with Eddie Bird. The snapshot made him look as though he had no clothes on because he was standing behind a collapsible canvas washbasin, grinning. There were tents in the background, and a sign on a distant wall showed him to have been at *Captain Cunningham's Camp for Working-Class Lads*.

Peter suddenly remembered the bit in the Bible about not gazing on your own father's nakedness, so he hastily turned the page. But the Bible hadn't said anything about gazing on Uncle Norman Fairchild's nakedness. Peter always had a good rude look at this picture because Uncle Norman had rolled the top of his swimming costume down so you could see where . . . oh dear. This was leading back to those thought processes he always tried to brush aside. Peter closed the family album and gave it a guilty rub with the orange duster.

The book belonged on the top shelf, which was taller than

the rest. As he carried it over, the boy caught sight of a little watercolour that hung above the bookshelves. It was a picture of the parish church at Stoke-on-Trent. For a moment Peter could have wished that his eyes had lightened on something, anything, else. Even one glimpse of anything remotely resembling a holy image meant that the insecure child felt obliged to pray. The sight of a *real* church had been known to force him to his knees in the street.

These involuntary prayers were meant to be a talisman against all the things that were going to come and get him: his father in a rage, the big brown dog from Dovesway which slavered mad saliva, the gangs of rough lads who shouted 'girlie' after him in the street. Though his fears were many, his prayers had been reduced to one simple plea: an all-purpose entreaty to the Almighty which he had dreamed up for himself. 'Please, thanks, forgiveness; in the past, and in the present, and in the future.'

Even thinking about this caused him to offer up the prayer again for luck. But did God mind you using the word 'luck' when you were talking about prayers? It seemed he did because somebody had suddenly started to lumber around in the room overhead. And that somebody could only be Peter's father.

The book in its place, Peter climbed down from the chair and picked up the *Giles Cartoon Annual* for 1946. This volume was something of a faithful companion. It was soon joined on the shelf by 1,000 Household Hints and *Rebecca of Sunnybrook Farm* by Kate Douglas Wiggin. This last one was meant to be a girl's book but that had never stopped him reading and enjoying it. '*And* I do embroidery!' Peter actually said this, defiantly, aloud. And if God didn't like it, well, God was supposed to have made him, so why had he made a boy who liked sewing? But old worries were quickly replaced by one that was much nearer to the surface: the masculine lumbering noises were now coming from the hall.

'Pete?' The hoarse whisper was just the other side of the door. 'Are you in there, Pete?'

He supposed he'd better open it. 'Did you want me?'

The figure by the cupboard under the stairs was wearing

nothing but a towel. Well, a towel and a bleary expression, and a lot of black body hair. In the years since he was photographed at Captain Cunningham's Camp, Eddie Bird had grown a slack stomach and enough fur to stuff a cushion.

'Has she got women in?' His breath smelt of mustard.

Peter knew that this was what happened to alcohol when it had been to sleep. But a different smell came from his father's body – a sweet sweaty one. And it was always there, even if he'd just got out of the bath; Peter's mother maintained that this was also old alcohol, trying to rise to the surface. 'He's pickled in it,' she would snort.

But in the mornings Eddie Bird was generally a sorry figure. Under the influence of an obvious hangover he somehow seemed apologetic. 'Has she got customers?'

'Only one, so far.' If Peter answered warily it was because his father's apologetic state could quickly turn to nastiness.

'Wouldn't do to let them catch me like this. Wouldn't want to drive the ladies mad with desire.'

And he half means it, marvelled Peter. He also realised that every word was causing his father wincing effort.

'The ladies, God bless them,' muttered Eddie as he began to search behind the vinegar and sauce bottles – the cupboard under the stairs was used as a pantry. 'Have you by any chance seen . . . No, it doesn't matter.'

But it'll matter in a minute, thought Peter. He'll know that I might know where it is, so he'll try being all friendly with me.

'Shouldn't you be back at school?' In the mornings Eddie never remembered anything he'd been told.

And as his father straightened up, Peter noticed that the hair was beginning to wear off the back of his calves – all that was left was snapped-off bits. 'I've been in hospital. I'll be starting at the grammar school a week late.'

'Not easy.' The whites round the blue eyes were very pink. 'Oh dear, oh dear, oh dear.' These mocking words sounded like a gramophone with the needle stuck. And then Eddie Bird went in for the kill: 'So you'll be a new boy on your own, eh?'

Peter determined not to show fear, for that was what his father liked. 'Yes.'

'Oh dear.' Eddie picked a bit of blood off one of yesterday's shaving cuts and then rubbed his thumb against a bristling chin. The blue eyes stared straight into Peter. 'You'll be in for a rough ride. They always give new boys a rough ride. And being new a week late will make you very noticeable.'

'You mean they'll *duck* me?' It was a word Peter had tried not to think about during the long summer holiday. Tried but not succeeded. 'You mean they'll push my head under water?'

'Things like that.' His father had resumed his search and was clanking a hand behind the breadbin. 'Of course I was never at a grammar school but I've heard they have these initiation ceremonies . . .'

'More than ducking?' Peter's panic was now out in the open.

Once again he was treated to the bleary blue gaze. 'Whatever they try, the thing to say is, "Right lads, let's get this over with and then we can all be mates."'

He's trying to be helpful, thought Peter. But he could no more imagine himself saying what his father had said than he could visualise himself in a rugby scrum. Still, the hairy monster *was* trying to be pleasant so why shouldn't he, in his turn, be pleasant back? 'If you're looking for your gin bottle, it's in the airing cupboard – behind the clean bedding.'

Crack! Peter's face went numb and then it began to sting on the spot where his father had landed him one.

'Don't talk to me as though you was some bleedin' critical woman.' The mustard smell was suddenly much nearer, and the sweet one too. 'I hate that cissified voice of yours. Do you know what you're going to grow up to be? If you're not careful you're going to end up as a bloody simpering jessie.'

Suddenly Peter was angry. Blazing. He'd heard the word before from the boys who yelled things after him, but he'd never expected to hear it from his own father. 'What *is* a jessie?' Once and for all he wanted to know.

From the look of things he had plainly landed his father with a question that was beyond answering.

33

Eddie Bird tightened his towel uncomfortably. 'They're men who wear lipstick,' he muttered. 'And the only work they can get is as stewards in the Merchant Navy.' The rheumy eyes filled with self-pity. 'Having a nancy-boy for a son is going to make things very awkward for me, very awkward indeed. In the airing cupboard did you say?' Now he was back in full flood: 'And before you go giving me any more of your girlish impudence, has it ever occurred to you that *you* might be the reason why I sometimes reach for a drink? Yes, you, *Mary*.' And, with this, Bird VC headed upstairs for the bathroom.

Earlier that same morning, more than a hundred apprehensive children had converged upon the grammar school for the first day of the first term. *Omnia gignit industria* – everything comes about through hard work. The school motto was inscribed underneath the golden crests of their maroon blazers and on the boys' caps, and it was embroidered in tiny stitches onto the petersham bands which went round the black schoolgirl felt hats. The first-formers stood out from the rest by the blatant newness of everything they wore. But in that nervous sea of maroon and gold, Vanda Bell was even more noticeable than her peers; and for the opposite reason.

Maroon is a colour that fades shabbily and her second-hand blazer looked as though it had been let out by somebody whose fingers were all thumbs. If the dog-stitches were bad, the hat was even worse. Only Vanda's mother could have laid hand on one with a brim that was distinctly narrower than the regulation style. It looked like a 'Kiss Me Quick' hat, bought on Blackpool promenade.

I feel a joke, she thought as she marched down School Road. Pausing to size up her own reflection in the window of the school tuckshop, which was called Pam's Pantry, she consoled herself with the fact that two quite big boys were giving her interested looks. Perhaps they'd noticed that her bust had started. It had only been there for the past couple of weeks and other girls might have found its presence embarrassing. Not Vanda Bell. She saw these bodily alterations as messengers of change. And quite frankly she could do with all the changes she could get. That was when she noticed the reflection of another new girl who was also staring at her.

Never mind, she thought. I'm a dancer. I know how to move. And I shall move as though I was already in the second year. That way my awful clothes will just look *experienced*. And now the other girl wasn't a reflection; she was reality and she was addressing Vanda.

'Hello.' It was Joan Stone, the elf from Ellesmere Park, and everything she'd got on was at least a size too big for her. 'I'm meant to grow into it all,' she said unhappily. 'I feel just like a posh scarecrow.'

'Don't be so wet.' But Vanda said it quite nicely. 'Who wants to look like a pea in a pod anyway? On measuring day, you were the one that said the three of us were going to be *different*. Where's that boy? Have you seen him anywhere?'

Joan shook her head. 'And all the other boys seem much rougher than he was. I hope they *don't* call him Tweetie-Pie.'

'If they do, we'll sort them out. And would you please stop walking worried. We're noticeable enough without that. Yes, we've definitely got to find that boy. We did promise we'd stick together.'

Before they could start, a bell sounded from within the big red-brick building which was set in a garden like a little corporation park. The school secretary was standing under a heavily berried rowan tree with a list in her hand. 'Would all the new first-formers please go and sit on the front chairs in the big hall. Girls to the right, boys to the left.'

The assembly hall was high-ceilinged with an iron-railed balcony. A high platform stood at the end of the room with a grand piano on it. And behind that was a big green stained-glass window, decorated with a massive version of the school crest in three shades of yellow.

The most noticeable thing of all was the noise. Joan Stone thought it sounded just like a public swimming baths multiplied by ten but minus the splashing. Another bell rang, everybody rose to their feet, and silence fell as a long line of teachers in black academic gowns began to process past the side of the platform. The men joined the boys, and as the line of women teachers came nearer Joan noticed one definite wig and several pairs of gleaming false teeth.

'Ye gods,' breathed Vanda. 'They certainly weren't chosen for their looks!'

'The one in the furnishing-fabric skirt looks all right,' murmured Joan. 'And the two tailor-mades aren't bad.'

'Cop a look at their mean mouths,' was Vanda's covert verdict.

All eyes swivelled back to the platform as a strikingly good-looking boy, almost a man, dark-haired with long legs and broad shoulders, took his place at the piano. In the midst of this cheerless setting, Joan Stone thought that he looked like somebody who'd strayed down from Mount Olympus.

'Wow!' said Vanda Bell, this time quite audibly. And an Indian girl, with her hair in just one plait, turned round from the row in front and said 'Shh' in a way that suggested she belonged to the ranks of born goody-goodies.

The boy on the platform was now joined by a big man in the most tattered academic gown of the lot. The headmaster had barged up the steps as though he was in a bad temper, but when he turned to speak to them the girls both noticed that he had kind eyes. 'We will sing the school hymn,' he announced. 'First-formers may just listen.' But these brown eyes were nothing like as riveting as the amused green ones belonging to the pianist. He looked like somebody who was raring to have fun. Instead, he raised his hands and began to play a solemn dirge. And everybody but the first-formers burst into song:

> 'Land of our birth, we pledge to thee,
> Our love and toil in the years to be.
> When we are grown and take our place,
> As men and women with our race . . .'

Bit hard on the Indian girl, thought Vanda Bell. But her thoughts were really on something much more exciting. So were Joan Stone's. They flickered between the beauty of the pianist and the oddness of the hymn. One minute everybody was singing to God and the next they seemed to be addressing

36

the Motherland. The words put her in mind of newsreels of Hitler's rallies:

> 'Oh Motherland, we pledge to thee
> Head, heart and hand, in the years to be.

'. . . Amen.' As they sat down again, Vanda whispered to Joan: 'See that boy on the piano? Well, I've fallen in love with him.'

'You can't have.' Joan's own whisper was distinctly alarmed.

'Why not?'

'Because . . .'

'Shh,' interrupted the turning-round Indian girl.

But this didn't stop Joan from saying, 'You can't be in love with him because I am too.'

As Vanda swung round the corner of Sixth Drive the straps of her new schoolbag – well, it was *nearly* new – started to cut their way into her shoulders. Still, she thought, it throws my back straight, it's good exercise for the beginnings of my bust. Come to think of it, that was more than a bit sore too, tender and smarting – almost like having two boils on your front. Perhaps the satchel was making it worse? As she walked along, struggling to lift the bag off her back, Vanda noticed a pink-skinned redhead, in a cotton frock and a cardigan, hesitating outside their own house. The stranger had got right up the garden path.

'Did you want something?' called out Vanda.

The woman started guiltily. Could she be a burglar? Or, worse still, was she a plain-clothes policewoman? They were a breed who'd called before; once when Gran'ma got done for fortune-telling, and another time they'd swooped down on Ethel after she got hold of some suspiciously cheap furs.

'What do you want?' Vanda was untrained in niceties.

'Does Mrs . . . er . . . Doran live here?'

Vanda's eyes went straight to the possible policewoman's feet. They didn't *look* flat. And her wedge-heeled shoes were Brevitt Bouncers – surely a bit beyond a copper's pay? 'Tell me what you want her for?' Lace curtains were already beginning to stir along the drive; although a council estate, Grotto Lodge was rated 'superior'.

'Does Mrs Doran still do the, er . . .' As if reading the child's mind, the woman said, 'I've not come to trap her. As a matter of fact,' she sniggered awkwardly, 'I'm a probation officer. The old lady's been the talk of the courthouse. The girls who arrested her were most impressed by what she saw for them. I thought I'd have a go.'

You've certainly taken your time, thought Vanda. It was a good three months since her grandmother had made head-lines. And at the age of eleven, three months is an eternity.

The pink skin made the woman look lightly boiled. 'Does she still do it?' she persisted.

'Yes, but it's gone up. It's not five shillings any more, it's six and six.' Pure invention, but quick-witted blood ran through Vanda's veins. She slid her Yale key into the door.

'Just coming home from school?'

'First day. Mind you don't knock that tank.' Vanda indicated a small cistern which was sitting on the hall floor. 'It's filled to the brim with cleaning fluid. And don't think of smoking, either,' she commanded. 'Not in this house. Not if you don't want to be blown to kingdom come.'

'I was at the grammar school myself.' The woman was plainly trying to get things onto a social basis.

'Did they make you do gym?' Vanda dumped her satchel next to the cistern. 'We had to climb ropes. It plays hell with your muscles. You stop where you are, I'll nip up and see whether she's in the mood.'

Vanda thudded up the bare boards of the staircase. Her grandmother was definitely awake because she could already hear the mattress creaking as the old woman stirred. Dora called out, 'What's going on?'

'You've got a customer.' Vanda crossed the room and pulled back the curtains.

'Where's this sudden rush of energy come from? And spray them flies with the Flit gun. But leave that window alone, Vanda. I *like* a nice fug.'

Vanda, nevertheless, flung it wide open. 'Fug? This is

beyond a fug, it's putrid. Anyway, she deserves fresh air. I've put your price up. She's going to cross your palm with six and sixpence.'

Gran'ma Doran reached for the box decorated with the occult eye and took out the deck of cards wrapped in a black silk handkerchief. 'Pass me my teeth, Vanda. Is she one who's ever been before?'

'No, but she let slip . . . '

'I don't need to know anything she let slip.' The words got clearer as the teeth clacked into place. 'The cards will tell me all that's necessary.'

'Suit yourself.' Vanda felled four bluebottles with one puff of fly-killer.

'How was the new school?' Gran'ma was tightening the little elastic band that fastened the end of her white plait.

'You get different teachers for every subject and they've given me four different lots of homework.'

'I'd rather stop ignorant,' breathed the old woman fervently. 'Would you send the lady up with two Rennies? I've got a pocket of gas trapped underneath me ribs.' As if to prove her point, Gran'ma broke wind lightly.

'You, who didn't even want a window opening!' said Vanda, scandalised.

'I just hope this new school's not going to turn you into a snob. Six and six, eh?' She reached for a cracked cup which was full of loose change. 'Right, wheel 'er up. Let's see what Fate's sent over the doorstep.'

Vanda stopped being bossy and became hesitant. 'Gran'ma Dora, will you do *my* cards, when she's gone?'

'Oh it's Gran'ma Dora now, is it? I'm not sure I like girls who only get loving when they want something. I might do your cards, and I might not.'

'Please. I did get you one and sixpence extra.'

But the balance of power had definitely shifted. 'I'll have to ask the tarot whether I should. Was it this new school as taught you not to give me a kiss when you come in?'

Vanda jumped onto the bed and gave the old woman both a kiss and a hug. In return she was offered a quick cackle of delighted laughter. 'Cupboard love,' smiled Dora Doran. It was a beautiful smile but Vanda didn't hang around to appreciate it. She was already through the door and heading downstairs to look for the Rennies.

Gran'ma Dora had certainly been right about one thing: Vanda was indeed charged with amazing exhilarated energy. If this is being in love, she thought, it's absolutely wonderful. His eyes, those long legs, and the way the hands had caressed the music out of the grand piano! Even the memory of it was better than drinking a whole bottle of cream-soda pop.

'Will she see me?' asked the woman in the hall nervously.

By now Vanda was through the door into the kitchen. 'Yes, as a favour.' Returning to the hall she added, 'But would you give her these tablets?'

The woman took them, yet made no move to climb the stairs. 'I expect all the ladies are a bit nervous, the first time.'

'If you want the toilet, it's up at the bottom of the stairs, on the right. Mind you, I don't know what state you'll find it in. Gran'ma's not very particular.'

'No.' The woman's eyes flickered to the front door and then back to the staircase. 'No, I went before I came.' Now she fiddled nervously with the top button of her cardigan. 'Where will I find the lady who does it?'

'Upstairs. She's behind the only door that's painted black.' This had been done in a fit of Bank Holiday enthusiasm and they had never got round to tackling the rest. The way the woman was climbing the stairs brought Nurse Edith Cavel and the firing squad to mind.

Vanda, left to her own devices, picked up her satchel and carried it into what should have been the sitting room. In reality, it was more like the back room at a dry-cleaner's, with another bigger tank of cleaning fluid and even a Hoffman presser. Only the very best garments were subjected to this. The rest, once cleaned, were either stacked in piles or hung from the picture rail on old wire hangers.

There was also a table, and this would have to serve as a desk. Vanda opened her schoolbag and pulled out a whole pile of brand-new textbooks. The grammar school had handed her enough for a birthday. There was a big blue atlas, a Latin grammar and a French one, *A Midsummer Night's Dream* and

40

Chaucer for Juniors. The maths textbooks were full of diagrams that were as mysterious as alchemists' charts, but these didn't alarm her. Not much alarmed Vanda Bell, though she was beginning to wonder whether there would be enough hours in the evening for four lots of homework and two consecutive dancing classes, tap and national, at Odette Ashworth's.

For English language you were meant to write an essay entitled 'My Mother'. The teacher had particularly said that she didn't want them using Biro, so Vanda scrabbled in the sideboard for a bottle of ink and a dipping pen. How many other sideboards, she wondered, were stuffed with strangers' cast-off stockings?

The wooden pen was already chewed at the end, and she chewed it some more before writing, 'My mother is fat.' And that was all she could think of. It was most odd. Lots of half-formed thoughts about Ethel were buzzing round in her head, but she couldn't grab hold of them and put them into words. It was obviously a knack and she hadn't got it. At her old council school, when they'd wanted you to do composi-tions they'd always pinned a picture up on the blackboard, so you could write down what you saw.

For the moment she turned her attention to mathematics, which struck her as a very fancy name for just five sums. Anybody could cope with a bit of multiplication and division. There were rules to sums. 'My Mother' indeed! That English mistress was nothing but a nosy bugger. It was just a dodge to find out about your home life. Six sevens are forty-two . . .

For a girl who lived in a house of chaos, mathematics was a wonderfully clear-cut and ordered refuge. Vanda was already double-checking the result of the final calculation when the fierce cry came from upstairs. It was a cross between a grasp and a scream followed by 'I have never been so insulted in all my life.' Loud shouting, and it was the probation officer who was doing it.

Vanda was so surprised that she made an ink blot. When it dries I'll cover it with white poster paint, she thought as she dived for the door and opened it so that she could hear better. The Brevitt Bouncers were already clattering down the bare

41

staircase. And then the rest of Gran'ma's client came into view, very flushed and spluttering. 'That woman touched on areas which no lady should mention.'

'I never claimed to be a lady.' The unthinkable had happened: Gran'ma Dora was actually on her feet and shouting from the top of the stairs. 'I saw a rumpled bed and I said it wasn't your own.'

The woman smoothed down her good cotton frock. 'Let me out of here,' she muttered fervently. But she was heading the wrong way. Realising this, she turned agitatedly and brought down a bentwood hatstand laden with assorted ladies and gents' hats, headgear was flying everywhere.

'Mind the cleaning fluid,' called Vanda desperately. A black bowler was already sailing on the liquid surface.

'I saw you having jig-a-jig-jig with a man of God,' bawled Gran'ma.

'Please,' begged the woman. 'Not in front of the child. And anyway, it never went beyond caresses.' With this she attempted to change into somebody who was merely ruffled. 'You might have wrapped it up a bit,' she said.

'That's not my style. Vanda, show the poor soul out, and then come up here yourself – while the fluence is still on me.'

As Vanda reached up to open the door, the probation officer attempted to retrieve the situation with, 'Of course she *is* remarkable. It's just that I wasn't expecting anything so . . . deep.'

'Kick her out and come upstairs,' insisted the oracle on the landing. 'If she thinks she's going to report me, I'll have great pleasure in telling the authorities everything I saw.'

'Now I *do* need the bathroom,' said the erstwhile client desperately.

'Then you'll have to knock next door,' snapped Gran'ma. 'We're very funny about who we let sit on our lav.'

Tut-tutting to herself, the woman gathered together the shreds of her dignity and left the house. Before Vanda could close the door the departing figure called out, 'I could report you to the Sanitary.'

'But she won't,' came from the top of the stairs. 'Not if I got the measure of her. And I did. Right, monkey, do you want a reading or don't you? Up you come. Probation officer? It makes you wonder what you'd see in the cards for a judge!' This last thought was pronounced as big Dora hauled herself back under the paisley bedcover. 'Now then, let's have a look at what we can get for you. Stack them scattered cards and shuffle,' she commanded. 'Would this be in the nature of a query?'

Vanda nodded and shuffled. She was a bit worried about what she was going to have to explain. Taking a deep breath, she announced, 'I'm in love.'

Gran'ma grunted. '*That's* started, has it? OK, let's take your own card out.'

'You'd better take Joan Stone's out too. She's fallen for him as well.'

'Joan Stone?'

'The Moon.'

'Oh, her. What you've got, she'll want. I already told you that. Right, there's you,' down went the Sun, 'and there's her. Take one for him.' Gran'ma fanned the cards.

Vanda closed her eyes and snatched one quickly.

'You're sure?' asked Dora Doran.

'Positive.'

Only now was her choice turned over. 'Oh my God!' exclaimed Dora. 'Sweet Jesus! I could have wished anything for you but this.'

'He's beautiful,' said Vanda indignantly.

'He's trouble. Trouble with a capital T. You've only gone and chosen the Tumbling Tower. This man is chaos.'

The Moon was quite near to the clouds; Joan Stone was up in the old sewing room. Tea was over and she was refilling the Swan fountain pen she'd been given for winning her scholarship. By rights she should have been concentrating on her homework, but Joan's mind was full of thoughts of the pianist with the long fingers and those crazy green eyes which had seemed ready to brim over with mischief – even as he was playing that heavily-patriotic hymn.

Lunchtime detective work had revealed that his name was Toby Eden, that he had come to Lancashire during the war as an evacuee, and that he was supposed to be distantly related to *the* Anthony Eden. In her mind's eye, Joan was already seeing herself being taken to the House of Commons for the first time. They were on the terrace, the *Queen Mary* was sailing past on the River Thames, and Toby was murmuring, 'Mr Churchill, may I introduce my new bride?' This evening, however, imagination had to be put to more practical use. Like all the other children in her form, Joan was obliged to come up with an essay entitled 'My Mother'.

But which mother was she going to write about: the one she'd invented for her diary, or the real person whom nobody would discuss?

You were meant to use your rough book for preliminary notes and then to transfer the polished version into a stiff-backed blue English notebook. For absolute safety's sake, at this experimental stage, Joan decided to draft out her first effort on a piece of scrap paper, which could if necessary be burned in the empty black-leaded fireplace.

'The real one or Mummy of the Diaries?' She actually said this aloud to the dressmaker's dummy.

Truth won. Joan began to write: 'Nobody will ever tell me anything about my mother. I do not know what she looks like. I have no idea where she lives. Sometimes I think I must be the kind of . . . ' she paused, hesitated and then wrote it, 'bastard as those aristocratic people in history whose names begin with Fitz.' But the word she had debated was glaring up from the page as though it had been written in doubly blue-black ink – *bastard*. Did it perhaps demand explanation?

Once again the nib hit the page: 'Bastard is not a swearword when you are one. But it is a funny feeling because you never quite know who you are.' Well, that wouldn't do because you weren't meant to begin a sentence with a conjunction; not in an English language lesson, anyway.

The word 'conjunction' got mixed up with the word conundrum inside her head. And she scrawled down, 'I am a living conundrum.' It was no use. It wouldn't work. Joan glared at the page and the page seemed to glare back at Joan. 'It's going to have to be the other one,' she said to knob-headed Sarah-Jane. The same Swan pen, the one that hadn't seemed to want to write, now began to speed forward with enthusiasm.

My mother

My mother is more like a sister than a parent. She is
always there when I need her. She is my best friend.
When I came home from school today she was dying to
know everything that had gone on and . . .

And what? Reality intruded as Joan remembered the true
sequence of events. As she placed her schoolbag on the
kitchen table, Granny had asked her, 'Well? Are the other
girls as common as I feared?'

'Oh no. One of them's a doctor's daughter. She's called
Ruth Chatterjee.'

'That's an Indian name,' said Granny accusingly. 'Is she
properly Indian or just a chee-chee girl?' Granny Briggs
tightened the sash round her oversized cook's apron. 'We'll
have to watch our step there. And we'll certainly have to keep
your Uncle Bruno under wraps; girls like that are always on
the lookout for a white bridegroom.'

Joan tried retaliating with, 'She says she's related to India's
own Shakespeare.'

Granny remained unimpressed. 'That doesn't change the
colour of her skin. Is she Hindu?'

'I don't know. But I shouldn't think so because she
definitely got to her feet for the school hymn.'

'Christianised, eh?' The idea seemed to have evinced some
grim satisfaction. 'That almost certainly means that she's
very low caste. The missionaries generally got to them first.'

'She *is* very good,' admitted Joan. 'Actually, it's a bit of a
bore.'

'Don't mistake it for *real* goodness.' Granny was dividing
the butcher's slices of ox liver into even thinner slivers.
'Indians can be very sly.'

Up in the old sewing room, Joan Stone cleaned the nib of
her pen on a bit of chamois leather and went back to her own
brand of slyness. Except she wasn't being sly, she was simply
trying to make the best of a bad job. 'My mother spends a lot

45

of money on clothes but this does not stop her giving to charity. She sometimes sells flags on flag days.' This looked ridiculous. Joan crossed it out and substituted, 'She will always rattle a collecting box.' That looked even sillier. It was just more of the same old made-up rubbish. She was trying to use the world of the diary for real-life purposes, and the light of common day was showing it up for the shabby thing it was. Not shabby – sad. And she didn't want to be sad. What's more, she didn't want to be somebody who had to talk to a dressmaker's dummy.

'But I'll tell you what,' she said to Sarah-Jane, 'this is a bit of a bugger!' The influence of Vanda Bell was already beginning to show.

Somebody was knocking at the sewing-room door. 'Can I come in?' called Bruno from the landing.

'Yes.' There wasn't time to hide the written lies so Joan put her forearms over them and leaned forward across the top of the sewing machine which she used as a desk.

As Bruno came in he was laughing. 'She's still muttering away to herself about Indians. Did you ever taste anything like that liver? By the time she'd finished with it, it looked just like the leather tongues on my best brogues. Have you got such a thing as a spare green crayon? I've got to do a map to illustrate my history essay.'

'They're in my pencil box. It's in my satchel.' This was leaning against the base of the dummy. 'Take what you need.'

'Wouldn't that be a bit like going in a lady's handbag?'

Granny was always going on about things like gentlemen not going in ladies' handbags. Not wishing to rob Bruno of one scrap of his tattered birthright, Joan got up and began to cross the room. It was only after she'd taken two paces that she realised she'd left her essay unguarded. She began to hurry. 'Just a green one?'

'Please. It's going to shade in Bosworth Field.'

'Light or dark green?'

'Makes no odds.' Without so much as a breath's pause he added, 'Did you know that I could read things upside-down?'

Even before Joan straightened up she knew where he would be looking. And he was, his kind face frowning as he studied her composition. 'That's worse than going in handbags,' she cried. 'It's much worse.'

Instead of arguing, Bruno just said quietly, 'I don't think you'd better show it to anybody else.'

Joan's cheeks began to burn. And so did her shame and her anger. 'I never showed it to you. You went and pried.'

'No.' He was very definite about this. 'My eyes just wandered over there and . . .'

'And I'm left feeling ashamed. And that's not fair. What was I meant to do? Nobody will ever tell me the truth; there's always a row if I ask. And I *don't* believe you don't know anything.'

It was Bruno's turn to redden. 'I only know bits. And I can't tell you because I was sworn to secrecy.'

'OK, I'll put *that* in my composition. "My mother is a woman of mystery," ' declaimed Joan. ' "Even her own brother is not allowed to speak about her." That should make Miss Titheradge sit up!'

Bruno shook his head. 'I don't think you can do that, either.'

'Then what? You're very good at telling me what I can't do. Tell me what I can.'

The young man in the Manchester Grammar School blazer still refused to be rattled. 'The way I see it, it's not your problem, it's Granny's. She's made it her own by resorting to all this secrecy.'

'Just tell me what you know,' begged Joan. But she knew he wouldn't, knew that he would have been made to give a 'Briggs's Promise'. And Briggs's Promises were not made to be broken.

'She's gone to change her library books,' said Bruno. 'But when she comes back I'll make her tell you the lot.'

And the writer, the second self who had always lived inside Joan Stone, noted that the words which applied to her uncle at this moment were 'handsome' and 'brave'. But why brave? What was so awful that he had to be courageous about it?

Because it was his first day out of hospital, Peter was invited to tea with Miss Lathom and Miss Parr, a high tea in their dining room with his favourite black-market Loch Fyne kippers.

'The best thing to do with kippers is just to stand them in a jug of boiling water.' Miss Lathom always said this and never failed to add, 'No smell, no mess, and in four minutes they're done to perfection.'

Miss Parr looked up from her *Manchester Guardian*. 'Would that we were all on the terrace of a Parisian café,' she twinkled. 'Fouquet's or Les Deux Magots.' She tapped her newspaper with an elegant forefinger. 'It says here that they're going to ban us from travelling abroad, yet again.'

'It's *your* government,' pointed out Miss Lathom, who was rooting in the sideboard for table napkins. Peter came to their house so often that he even had his own silver and bone napkin ring. 'If you wanted foreign travel, you should have voted Conservative.' Grace Lathom was a staunch Tory. But Miss Parr, who originally came from the wicked South (and in Peter's eyes this added greatly to her glamour), Iris Parr was not just Labour: in a pre-war election she had once stood on the back of a bronze lion in Trafalgar Square, campaigning through a megaphone for somebody called George Lansbury.

'And nowadays his daughter is an actress in America,' she would tell Peter, because he was very interested in things like that. And when you went to Miss Lathom and Miss Parr's they always tried to see that you got what you liked.

Just being there was enough for the boy from next door. The schoolmistresses' house was the only detached one on Hawksway. This was simply the result of the way the original estate had been divided up by the builder. But Peter was glad that they had got the unusual one; it seemed entirely suitable. The two maiden ladies were nothing like the rest of the neighbours. If he saw Grace Lathom as a pirate with her iron-grey Eton crop and her clomping shoes, Iris Parr was a pretty gypsy. Could you use the word 'pretty' about somebody of forty-five? Yes, he decided loyally, you could.

Nobody on the better end of the Ravensdale Estate ever spoke aloud about money. That was considered common. This didn't stop people whispering about it behind their lace curtains; and it was generally rumoured that the spinsters

48

were 'not without'. The only person who knew the whole story was Peter Bird. Miss Lathom had inherited the nice watercolours and the silver and good antiques, these and some worthwhile stocks and shares; Miss Parr was the author of a series of French grammar books which brought in royalties twice a year. If you added all of this to their teachers' salaries they were doing what the stouter of the two women described as 'very-nicely-thank-you'.

In Peter's eyes their book-lined house was the safest place on earth. Where there weren't books there were plain white walls and beautiful French chintzes. Though the rooms were always filled with flowers, these didn't stand in water – his hostesses abhorred cut blooms and florist's wire. All their flower arrangements grew up out of moss or peat. Both women had green fingers and neither of them was a martyr to housework. You could make a mess at Miss Lathom and Miss Parr's and nobody minded.

Not many people in Hawksway had a charwoman but the two teachers did. Miss Lathom always spoke of Mrs Pye as 'God's gift to this household'. Although Grace Lathom talked like a person of definite consequence, her vowel sounds were still splendidly rounded and northern. For the moment, she was using these to berate Mr Attlee and his Labour government: 'Yes, you voted some wonderful men in, Iris, wonderful! No foreign travel, two teaspoons of petrol a month, more rationing than wartime . . .'

'And what about the National Health Service?' rejoined Miss Parr indignantly.

'Flawed,' was Miss Lathom's verdict. 'What's to stop the pregnant French from coming over on holiday so that they can have their babies for nothing? They'll probably grab free wigs and dentures while they're at it.' Peter knew that this was a deliberate tease aimed at Iris Parr, who regarded France and the French as sacred. Not Miss Lathom: 'And don't give me "that wonderful General de Gaulle". He's got a look in his eyes I don't trust. One day he'll turn on us. You'll see!'

'*Vive la France!*' cried Miss Parr, quite unperturbed. 'But I do feel so very cut off from Paris. I'd like to do something to

49

express my solidarity. This morning I thought of giving up shaving underneath my arms.'

'God knows why you had to interfere with nature in the first place.' Miss Lathom grabbed one of the kippers by the tail and hauled it from the jug.

They never modified their conversation in front of Peter. He liked that part the best. He even knew that Iris was going through 'a difficult change' which sometimes gave her dizzy spells and had once landed her with a hot flush at the blackboard. Though she taught French she had never attempted to pass that language on to him, maintaining that this wouldn't endear him to his eventual teacher. 'There's nothing worse than somebody in the front row who's two clever jumps ahead of the rest.'

As Miss Lathom placed the kippers on plates, she worried aloud about Peter getting left behind: 'Once you get to school, you'll have to latch onto somebody reliable and copy down every single note they've made.' Crossing herself, but not in a showy fashion, she said, '*Benedictus, benedicat.*' Miss Lathom always pronounced grace in Latin.

'Amen.' Peter reached for a piece of brown bread. 'How will I know who's reliable?'

'You'll know. Look how easily this flesh comes off the bones. You'll know because you've got better instincts than Henry.'

'*Henry!*' Both ladies seized hold of this word and cried the thought out loud. Miss Parr added, 'Fish in the dining room and no sign of him. He must have got out again.'

Henry was a white retriever with a tan burglar's mask. Though he loved his owners lavishly, he loved roaming even more. 'Of course he could have got himself shut behind a door,' ventured Miss Parr.

'Kippers would have set him barking. No, he's probably halfway to the Brontë Country by now.' Because Miss Lathom taught English, a lot of her references were literary. 'Beat the gong, Peter. If he *is* in, he'll bark.' The gong was a brass cannon shell, hanging inside a wooden Corinthian arch. It had been given to Grace Lathom when she was a little girl,

50

for launching a ship. *That's* how different they were from the rest of the neighbours.

Peter always found hitting the gong a very satisfactory experience and now the whole house rang with shimmering sound. But there was no answering bark.

'He's hopped it again,' announced Miss Lathom with grim satisfaction. 'He knows Mrs Pye's short-sighted, he must have sneaked round her legs. Oh he's crafty!' This was said with little short of pride. 'People keep telling me I ought to get him castrated.'

'Don't even think of it,' murmured Miss Parr, who had a romantic nature.

'Why not?' sniffed her friend. 'It's not as though he's any thought of becoming a priest.'

'What's that got to do with it?' asked Peter.

'Eunuchs can't join the priesthood. St Paul said so.' Miss Lathom was very High Church – both ladies were. On Sunday mornings they had to travel miles to find a service exotic enough for them. But Henry had been known to travel even further. He had once followed Miss Lathom to school, the whole way to the other side of town. And he'd done it hours after she'd left Hawksway on her motorbike. 'He must have known the niff of my tyres,' had been her proud explanation. But she wasn't boasting now, she was worried. 'He's so stubborn he could cause an accident.'

'Perhaps he's in the bottom field,' suggested Peter. 'I'll finish this and go and have a look.'

'And would you pick up my prescription?' asked Miss Parr. 'I already phoned Dr Moult. He said he'd leave it on the bench in his little hall.'

'Pudding first,' announced Miss Lathom. Post-war food shortages were much in evidence in the Bakewell tart, its filling improvised from ground semolina and almond essence. People had got so used to weird food that this was eaten without comment. Well, almost without comment; Iris Parr did make some sentimental reference to a patisserie in the Rue des Petits-Champs. She was a former student of the Sorbonne. 'Once the travel ban is lifted,' she always promised

51

Peter, 'we will show you Paris, just like we showed it to the Girl Guides.'

In the days when they lived in London the two teachers had run a Guide troop; Peter could never hear the story of the trip to Paris often enough. 'Did the Guides sleep under canvas?' he enquired innocently.

'No, dear,' shuddered Miss Parr. 'No, we put them up at a very nice little hotel on the Left Bank.'

'It had to be admitted we were not particularly good Guide mistresses.' Miss Lathom was finishing off the rest of the nasty Bakewell tart. 'In fact our girls always said that we handed out proficiency badges as the whim took us.'

'But when we took the girls to Paris,' cried Miss Parr, 'the whim took us in a very happy direction indeed. We'll show it you, one day, Peter. We'll give you the City of Light.' In anybody else this could have sounded silly, but Miss Lathom and Miss Parr were like Joe Gargery in *Great Expectations*, the man who always said 'What larks, eh, Pip? What larks!' They brought colour and hope into Peter's life. And he, in his turn, was always happy to run any small errands they might need.

In search of Henry, he made his way towards the bottom field. You had to cross the main Manchester Road and the field was bounded by the only set of high iron railings for miles around – all the rest had been carted off to help the war effort. These survivors were grubby to the touch, and so was the grass, and so were the elderberry bushes on the crest of a distant slope, as sooty as the trunks of the huge elm trees which rose out of them. Industrial Salford smoke had drifted uphill and cast a grimy pall over everything. Nobody on the Ravensdale Estate left washing on the line for a moment longer than was strictly necessary.

But here in the field, if you half closed your eyes and disallowed the noise of traffic, you could almost imagine you were in the real country. This murky greensward was all that was left of the original grounds of Ravensdale, a Victorian pit-owner's mansion which had been pulled down to make way for the housing estate. Viewed from here, the building development struck Peter as downright deceitful. You could only see the larger type of houses, the kind he lived in; much smaller sunshine-semis, with just a through room, were hidden away at the back. Rough boys lived in the smaller type, and even the thought of them caused him to cross his fingers.

The field must once have been part of a stableyard; all that was left of this was a cast-iron hitching post, next to some stone steps. Could these have been a mounting block? They always brought the poem 'The Highwayman' to mind. But, every time, this thought had to be pushed aside because the iron post was one of the places where Peter felt obliged to pray. Though he knelt down, he kept it silent: 'Please, thanks, forgiveness; in the past, and in the present, and in the future. And if you could help me find Henry I wouldn't half be obliged.'

Perhaps he should try Miss Lathom's method of praying? She was so High Church that she was practically a Catholic. Using the Lathom method, God himself was hardly ever approached. Instead, causes were addressed to appropriate saints who were meant to act as your ambassador. Miss Lathom even knew of one for fishbones stuck in the throat – St Blaize. The animal man was, of course, St Francis of Assisi. There was nobody around, so Peter decided to give the saints a fair chance, but he got to his feet to do it. They couldn't be offered *too* much – he didn't want to get in bad with God.

'Hi, it's me,' he said to St Francis. 'Henry's bunked again. Got any ideas?' This was elevated to nearly proper prayer status by the addition of 'Amen'.

Even at the age of eleven, Peter knew that heavily sacred thoughts would inevitably be followed by equally profane ones. He saw this as the devil pricking him with his toasting fork. It was some days since Peter had added anything to his interested study of sex so he went to look behind the elderberry bushes. The grass was often flattened there; it was the place where good-time girls were said to wrestle with Yanks.

Today there was a little glass tube on the ground. The label

53

read *Rendell's Foaming Pessaries*. Nothing else, no instructions; so what were they? He had certainly seen the name Rendell on showcards in the windows of surgical stores in Manchester – those puzzling window displays where neat fans of Durex packets lay alongside *The History of Corporal Punishment*. Any grown-ups who didn't quicken their steps towards these establishments passed by them with noticeably averted eyes. There was *mystery* to Stewart's Surgical Stores and that's what fascinated him.

Miss Lathom's church also had mystery but in a different way. Peter dropped the glass tube and rubbed his fingers on a dock leaf; he didn't want to catch one of those venereal diseases. *VD – a Shadow on the Nation's Health* was all it said on the secretive posters. But it was definitely sex because, when you asked, people said you didn't need to know yet; shy adults went red. He'd never liked to ask his spinster teacher friends because, not being married, they might not know.

Their church's mystery wasn't like Durex; St Agnes's was very dark with statues in grottos, and flickering candles, and sickly sweet incense which smelt like the sticky stuff that dribbled down the stamens of lilies. You could hardly believe you were in the Church of England at all. But you were: it said so on a board outside.

No sign of Henry yet. 'St Francis, could you have another whistle?'

Peter couldn't whistle, and he couldn't bowl overarm. He wasn't overworried about either, except for the fact that they made him noticeable. And the last thing an eleven-year-old schoolboy wants to be is that.

A gang of rough-looking boys were climbing over the far fence, by the East Lancashire Road. They looked as though they came from 'the Shivers', which was the local nickname for the scruffy end of Irlams o'th' Height. Yes, they *were* from those battered terraced streets. And they were boys who already knew him.

'Let's get the cissie,' one of them yelled. Their scramble turned into a concerted rush towards Peter.

At the same moment the green berry-laden bushes parted and a white streak emerged. It flashed to Peter's feet where it turned into a big white retriever with a tan Burglar Bill mask. It was Henry. 'Thank you, St Francis,' breathed Peter. The rough boys might continue to yell things but they wouldn't actually bash him up – not if he had a dog with him. Being seen to like dogs was part of their puzzling brutal code.

Henry licked Peter's hand and then let off a fiercely defensive bark. Not satisfied with this, he turned back his lip and showed the boys from the Shivers his sharp teeth. But reappearances after bunking were often followed by further dives for freedom. Quickly, Peter pulled off his own tie and attached it to the dog's collar, as a lead.

This caused more derisive noises from the boys in torn jerseys and tumbling socks. But Henry had definitely halted their fire, these jeers just a last feeble arrow. Not for the first time Peter caught himself thinking how easy it must be to be *them*.

Leading Henry away, but still conscious of the gang's eyes on his back, he whispered to the dog, 'We've got to go to Dr Moult's, Henry. We've got to pick up a prescription.' They could already see the doctor's house from the ridge of the hill. Big and gabled and Victorian, it was over on the main Manchester Road. But to get to it you had to go past a dense coppice of hawthorns. This was a definite point of fear because another gang of boys, from the sunshine-semis on Dovesway, sometimes used it as a den. They were the ones who had once hung Peter's trousers in a tree. His whole world was like one of those olde-worlde maps inscribed *Here Be Dragons*. But there was something reminiscent of cosy parchment lampshades about that phrase; Peter's real-life landscape was more shadowed, more full of prickling-haw-thorn terrors.

But they got to the main road without incident. Main roads were OK, his oppressors never tried anything much when there were grown-ups around. Could you take a dog into a doctor's surgery? Would it be good hygiene?

The doctor's garden path was edged with tall butterfly plants. It led through a trellis arch and right round the house to the back door, which was down some steps. The door was already ajar and Peter led Henry into a little hallway with an old oak settle in it. All the prescriptions sat on this; old brass weights kept them from fluttering away. Miss Iris Parr's prescription was under one engraved *4ozs Crown Weight*.

'How's the throat?'

The voice made Peter jump, but Henry was wagging his tail. Dr Moult must have come up behind them, through the garden door. 'Hello, Henry,' he said. The doctor knew everything and everybody on the Ravensdale Estate. 'Come into the surgery.'

'What about . . . . ' Peter indicated the dog.

'Bring him in, bring him in.' The doctor was slim and dark-haired with eyes that looked right into you. The district nurse had once said to Peter's mother, 'I sometimes think he can read my mind.'

'I'll just rinse my hands.' The accent was noticeably Scottish. But the same district nurse had assured them that Scots were the finest doctors. Women were crazy about Dr Moult.

'Let's have a look at what they did to you in hospital. I'll just get my little torch. Say Aaah.'

'Aaah.' Was it Peter's imagination or could he really feel the warmth of the light shining down his throat?

'Very neat, very clean. I'd say you could go back to school tomorrow.'

'Oh.' A new batch of dragons were roaring towards him before he was ready for them.

'Something wrong?'

'No,' lied Peter. He just hoped that the doctor wouldn't start calling him laddie. He liked everything about Dr Moult except for that.

'I think there *is* something wrong, laddie. How's the sewing coming along? Still going to be the next Norman Hartnell?'

Peter could actually feel the progress of a blush as it crept up his face and into his hair. '*You* said that about dressmaking, not me.' The doctor had once caught him sitting up in bed, after measles, making a felt waistcoat for his rabbit.

'What's wrong, Peter?'

How could he tell Dr Moult what he didn't really

56

understand himself? Yet, in a startling flash, Peter suddenly saw the core of it. It all went back to the war. All the ladies had been waiting for a soldier to come home. He'd heard it so often that – somehow – the boy had come to believe that peace would be bringing home a soldier especially for him.

And it had never happened.

'Do you perhaps feel different from the other boys?' The doctor was watching him closely.

He knows! He *can* read minds. 'No. I'm exactly the same as the rest,' protested Peter loudly, too loudly – but he was beyond controlling his voice. 'I'm not different at all.' Was there a special saint for telling God that you were sorry for lying?

Granny Briggs had yet to return from the public library. Joan and Bruno were waiting for her in the front drawing room. 'Why here?' he had asked as he helped her to unlock the door.

'Because I have to ask her an important question. And it needs to be asked in the right setting.' Even at the age of eleven, Joan had a highly developed sense of occasion.

It was thirty years since the drawing room had been painted old rose. When bombs dislodged the chimneystack at Ingledene and damp got into the house, the walls of the room had become blotched with raspberry splodges. The grey-white plasterwork of the ceiling always reminded Joan of grubby cake icing. But the ornate white marble fireplace was still as imposing as the day it had been installed, its pallor echoed in dust sheets draped over all the furniture, and in the linen bag which was safety-pinned round the American pianola. The soulful portrait of Flora MacDonald, holding a piece of lucky heather, gazed down upon the two young people who sat on leather patchwork pouffes on either side of an octagonal Indian fretwork coffee table.

'Shall we wind up the skeleton clock?' asked Joan, suddenly highly nervous and feeling the need of something, anything, to do. 'Did you know that your hair's exactly the same dark red as Flora's?'

Bruno commented only on the clock idea. 'That glass dome's a pig to get off. Anyway, the clock's spring has probably gone by now. This room gives me the willies; it's never been used since my father's coffin was propped up in that corner.'

'I thought coffins always went on dining tables.' Joan had read every Victorian novel in the house.

'Granny was scared there might be woodworm in the legs.'

Silence fell again. How odd it was that he always called his own mother 'Granny'. Joan stopped picking at the thonging which held the pouffe together, and went to look out of the window. Wartime blackout material still hung behind the proper curtains, but evening sunlight was shining through the glass. Outside, a blackbird perched on top of the lead garden nymph suddenly burst into song. As if emboldened by this most confident of sounds, Joan asked, '*Am* I a bastard?'

'Of course you're not. There had to be a Mr Stone for you to be Joan Stone. Talk sense!'

'Then am I adopted?' This was a theory she had often examined but always pushed aside.

'No. No, you're a Briggs, a real Briggs. You're Rhoda's daughter. That much I *can* promise you.'

'So tell me about my father.' The blackbird had stopped singing, flown down and landed beside the catmint; it was trying to pull a worm out of the ground.

'Your father was supposed to have been very ordinary. If you sit on one of these things for long enough, d'you think it stamps its leather pattern on your bottom? Your papa worked for the foundry. There was an awful to-do when she chose to marry "just an employee". So when Rhoda went, he went.'

'Went where? Where did she go?' But the bird had snapped the worm in half. Instinctively, Joan knew that she wasn't going to get a full answer.

And she didn't. 'Went where she went. You know I can't tell you. I would if I could but I can't.'

'She's in prison, isn't she?'

'No. Shush . . .' Granny must have come in by the back door before Joan got to the window because outdoor shoes could be heard making their way along the corridor.

'It's not a day for shushing,' cried Joan. 'It's a day for bringing everything out into the sunlight.'

The door rattled open. 'Who said you two could sit in here?' Granny, in her old tweed shopping coat, was pushing the combs up into her untidy Edwardian hair.

'Nobody.' Joan was all defiance. 'Nobody said we could. We just did it. Who's my mother?'

'Who's your . . . ' Granny sat down with a thud on the sheet-covered sofa. Its old springs protested loudly, though the skinny woman couldn't have been much of a load. 'I think I'd better get up again,' she said. 'Damp could strike through.'

She's only playing for time, thought Joan. 'You haven't answered my question.'

But Granny was already on her feet and fighting back with, 'I don't *have* to answer impudent little girls who trespass where they've been told not to go.'

Easy-going Bruno attempted to play the peacemaker: 'Joan's a bit upset.'

'She's not the only one. Get up off that pouffe, this instant, Bruno. You'll get chin-cough.'

'What's chin-cough?' asked Joan.

'He'll know when he gets it!'

Joan attempted to square up to her grandmother. It wasn't a very impressive attempt; Joan was too small for that. 'I want to know what I've always wanted to know.'

This time Granny was ready for her: 'If you intended to make me very unhappy, you've gone the right way about it. I can't think what I've done to deserve this evening. First the library let the new Netta Musket go to somebody else – even though they'd sent me a postcard. And now this! A drawing room full of questions.'

Bruno was still managing to remain calm. 'It's just one question. She's not trying to meddle, she's got to write an essay entitled "My Mother".'

Wringing off her beige cotton gloves, Granny Briggs paced the full length of the faded Indian carpet. She was plainly deep in thought; Joan could tell that by the way the old lady was chewing her thin bottom lip. She also looked near to tears. Out came the handkerchief but Granny Briggs just blew her nose. 'Right,' she said with sudden decision, 'there's only one answer. She'll have to be sent to school with a note. You can forget this essay, miss. I'll write and say it was impossible for you to do it.'

Bruno spoke up like someone who was better versed in school affairs. 'It's her very first English homework,' he protested.

'And she's not able to do it. I'd have thought that you, at least, would be on my side. Once I tell the child, her innocence is gone. Gone for good. And that's enough on the subject. Let's go and put the kettle on.' She was attempting to return things to normal. '*These You Have Loved* should just be starting on the wireless. I often think of writing in to Doris Arnold for a request but she must get so many that . . .'

'When *will* you tell me?' asked Joan, very quietly.

'Once you become a woman.' Yet again Granny chewed on her lower lip, then she said, 'This has to be got through, once and for all. Bruno, put your hands over your ears. Just do as I say and forget the pained expression.' Taking a deep breath and looking every minute her age, Olive Briggs turned her attention to her granddaughter. 'Joan, I want you to listen to me carefully, very carefully.' Granny looked as though she'd rather be discussing anything else on earth. 'If you ever find blood coming down your leg, from your private parts, it's nothing to be frightened of. Come to me and I'll give you something to wear. And that's when I'll tell you about your mother. It's what I'd always intended, and no bit of school homework is going to make me change my mind.'

All through the summer holidays Peter had pushed thoughts of this particular morning to one side. But now it was here, it was going on all around him; and just like being kept waiting at the dentist's, the bus had failed to materialise.

'I thought you kids started yesterday?' Mrs Slaughter from Dovesway glowered down at Peter in his too new school uniform – it would be the only one in the place that wasn't at least a day old. His wits sharpened by fear of the unknown ('*They have these initiation ceremonies . . .* '), Peter realised that a quarter past eight in the morning was Mrs Slaughter's hour for being Queen of the Ravensdale bus stop.

She didn't wait for a reply. She just marched out into the middle of the sunlit road on legs that were blotched from having been too near the fire. As well as an old mac she was wearing a turban, and she had buck teeth. Glowering towards Irlams o'th' Height, this figure yelled, 'Get a move on!' Did she imagine that her words would lure the bus around the bend? Marching back to the pavement, Mrs Slaughter announced to the other would-be passengers, 'If it doesn't show up soon, we'll have to get one to the depot and change.'

Would that cost extra? Had he got enough money? Peter added a new panic to his fears of being ducked. Not that he was all panic, and he certainly wasn't given to wallowing in self-pity. A good half of him was extremely excited at the thought of going to a new school.

'Bus service?' Mrs Slaughter was stepping off the kerb again. 'They couldn't run a fleet of Dinky cars. What's called for is lady inspectors! We'd soon get things running to time.'

She sounded so like Al Read being a woman on the wireless that Peter replied with the comedian's catch phrase, 'Right, monkey!' He was rather good at imitations. At his last school this had often got him out of potentially dangerous situations; but nobody at the bus stop was impressed, least of all Mrs Slaughter, who looked as though she was considering lecturing him for giving cheek.

Peter shifted his gaze to the other two people who were waiting. The boy and the girl would have passed for grown-ups had they not worn touches of Barton Grammar School uniform; she had just the hat with ordinary clothes and the young man sported a Barton tie. Rules were plainly relaxed as you climbed up the school, and satchels gave way to briefcases.

The pair were not having an animated conversation, more a desultory mutter. 'Did you see who was playing the piano yesterday?' mumbled the boy.

'That evacuee. Toby something.' The girl yawned. 'He'd get where water wouldn't. Nice eyes though. But you wouldn't notice that.'

'I'd like to kick him.'

'Why?' His blank statement appeared to have startled the girl into more vitality. 'What harm's he done you?'

'None. There's just something about Toby Eden that I can't stand.'

Peter had often heard the same sort of thing said about himself, and every school fear he'd ever known came rushing in on him. The sun chose that moment to go behind a cloud, and the double-decker bus finally groaned its way round the Height corner.

There was a brief row about precedence because the two older pupils tried to get on before Mrs Slaughter. Peter went upstairs. This was a matter of pride. The bottom deck would certainly have been safer, with more grown-ups and the conductor more in evidence, but if he went downstairs he would be advertising fear.

Two boys from his old school were already in possession of the back seat and the whistling started straight away. That and cries of 'Tweetie-Pie'. With the first whistle the summer holidays had very definitely come to an end, but Peter was a past master at pretending that the noise wasn't happening.

The bus, which was one of the elderly kind with cut-moquette seats, rolled past the children's hospital. Nobody got on there, nor at the Dell which was safely genteel. Mentally, Peter was preparing to redraw the boundaries of his personal 'Here Be Dragons' map.

At the Grotto Lodge council estate a veritable eruption of schoolchildren bawled their way upstairs. Danger, danger, danger. This tide of maroon and yellow was led by the plump girl he'd already met on measuring day. Boys were swirling all around her. Peter was well versed in the art of spotting a ringleader, and this one, a boy in a crooked cap with reddish hair and acne, was yelling, 'She's getting tits!'

The girl plonked herself down next to him. Peter couldn't half smell dry-cleaning! That and bacon. Vanda was finishing off a bacon sandwich.

'Want a bite?' she asked.

As a matter of fact he didn't, but he took one anyway – grateful for any friendly gesture on this journey into the unknown. A wary glimpse over the shoulder revealed that the

62

ringleader was perched on the edge of the seat behind them, and that the rest of the gang were scattered around the top deck. Peter had often noticed that, once the back of the bus was full, rough lads always made it a point of honour to get a whole seat to themselves.

'Lana Turner.' The voice could only belong to the boy behind them; it was throaty and urgent.

Sex, thought Peter. Lana Turner, 'the sweater girl', was a big Hollywood sex symbol.

'Where were you yesterday?' asked Vanda. The instincts she had inherited from her grandmother had already told her that Peter had no interest in her too tight jersey. If she fastened the blazer round it, would her cheeky admirer think she was taking notice of him? Not that Vanda minded the attention but it was a bit early in the morning for that sort of thing. 'Why're you starting a day late?'

'I was in hospital – tonsils.'

'Lana Turner.' The urgent croak repeated itself without the slightest change of intonation.

'I'm on the waiting list for that, and adenoids,' said Vanda. 'Is it true that after the operation you get National Health ice cream?'

'Have they got milk in them, Lana?' The croaker was at it again.

Peter found himself in something of a quandary. Was he meant to act as a knight in shining armour? Was she expecting him to rebuke her admirer? But Vanda proved to be quite capable of looking after herself. Round went her head. 'Small things amuse small minds,' she snapped.

'They're not that small,' protested the boy, seizing the opportunity to stand up and peer down her front.

'Yes, but I bet I know what *is* small. Sit down, you dirty bugger. My mother always says that boys who talk like you don't have much inside their trousers.'

Having turned the situation right round – Croaker was now the centre of a lot of noisy derision from the rest of the rabble – Vanda returned her attention to Peter. 'Sorry about that,' she said.

But Peter was even sorrier: experience told him, for certain sure, that the matter would not be allowed to rest there, that the boy would come in again from another angle. And Peter was positive that the next object of interest would be himself.

'What a nice new cap,' came menacingly from the seat behind. And before the words had died away Peter felt his hat being twitched off his head. As he swung round to grab it back, he saw that it was already flying towards the lads on the back seat. And from there it sailed forward to two louts across the aisle. One of them looked inside the cap and yelled, 'Peter Bird! His mummy sewed in a nice little nametape.' The wine-coloured cap continued to fly around the bus like a boomerang. But was it ever going to find its way back to Peter? If he arrived without it, he would be in trouble before he started.

'Fares please.' The uniformed conductress was little and snappy. 'And if you lot at the back are still smoking when I get there, you pay full fare.' As the cap described another arc she grabbed it in mid-air. 'Whose?'

'His.' It was Vanda who took it from the conductress; she felt the attack on Peter was probably her fault. 'A fourpenny one, please.'

Peter got the same.

'I'm half-dead,' announced Vanda. 'Two hours' home-work and two hours' dancing.'

Peter tried to appear knowledgeable: 'Tap?'

'I do the lot. I'm an all-rounder.'

This provoked more sniggers. Mindful of Miss Lathom's injunction to find somebody reliable, Peter asked, 'Do you think I could copy your notes from yesterday?'

'You'd be better off asking Joan Stone. You already know her; on measuring day she was the little titchy one. Copy hers. She's more of a swot than me.' As she talked, Vanda was sizing Peter up. 'I know more about you than you think.'

'How?' The bus was descending a hill which led them past the ugly great sheds of the transport depot. 'How do you know more about me?'

'Me gran'ma saw you in the cards.' Her grandmother had said that this would be a boy who needed looking after. Not for the first time, Vanda marvelled at the accuracy of the tarot.

It had also told Dora Doran that Peter was a boy with his own brand of inner strength.

'Cards? Is she a fortune-teller? The Bible's dead against soothsayers.' He only knew this because there'd been a rumpus about a crystal-gazer at Miss Lathom's church bazaar.

Each time the bus halted to take on more passengers there would be a rush of juvenile feet for the top deck and an increase in the decibel level. By the time the 28 groaned its way to School Road the din had become earsplitting. The few grown-ups who'd ventured upstairs looked distinctly relieved as the schoolchildren finally jostled into the aisle and began to clatter their way down to the pavement.

This was the point where division began. Boys and girls noticeably parted company and went off in two separate streams. Both were heading in the same direction and Vanda felt disinclined to ditch Peter. The brief ride had induced feelings she might have had about a stray dog; there was something more than a bit like a young greyhound about him. Was it her imagination or was Peter actually shivering?

'Do they have initiation things for girls, too?' he gulped. The last thing he wanted to do was join that masculine tide. 'Did you get ducked yesterday?'

'No. No, there was nothing like that.'

'There is for boys.' He'd been hearing about it for years, and his head was filled with confused visions of brass taps and of water running into a huge sink – of his head being pushed beneath the surface.

As they walked down School Road, Vanda noticed that Peter had gone bright red in the face. 'What's the matter?'

'Nothing. I'm just practising holding my breath.' Soon they would be at the boys' gate, soon he would have to try to pass as one of Them – the ones who lumbered and roistered and were totally confident inside their own skins.

Would Peter rather have been a girl? No. But, as far as he could see, he was the only one of his kind in the whole world. There wasn't even a proper name for what he was, unless you counted 'cissie' and 'jessie'. He suddenly remembered his father saying, 'They're men who wear lipstick and the only work they can get is as stewards in the Merchant Navy.' That was not how Peter wanted to see his own future.

'Doesn't Tweetie-Pie look *sweet* in his new cap?' It was another boy from his old school, not just one, three of them, the three worst – all ganged-up and grinning. 'He looks a real sweet sweetie.' Before he'd even crossed the doorstep Peter had gained his grammar-school nickname. Somebody else, a stranger, was already yelling it: 'Hiya, Sweetie!'

'Will you be all right?' asked Vanda. With some knowledge of boys' rules, she doubted she was helping him by lingering.

'I shouldn't think so.' There was no wailing in the tone of his voice, it was entirely matter-of-fact. He'd already had whole years of getting used to the idea of being an object of crude interest. 'But I'll survive. I always do.' Except, this time, there were hundreds of them. He'd never been alone in such a big crowd of Them before.

'Listen,' said Vanda. 'See that bit of wall, there. It's where the boys' part meets the girls'. You sit on that at break, and me and Joan'll come and find you.' With this she vanished and so did Peter's satchel.

The leather strap was wrenched from over his shoulder and the schoolbag started to go from hand to hand. 'Gimme that back,' he shouted.

'What have we got here?' Compared with the boys from his old school, this lout was King Kong – dark-haired and already shaving. As Peter brushed aside the thought that the youth was also quite handsome, his attacker repeated, 'What have we got here?'

King Kong had been joined by a tall thin boy with lank hair and a mean little mouth. 'It looks as though it's going to cry,' he sneered at Peter. 'Yes, it *is* going to cry. Let's get him to the downstairs cloakroom. Let's fill the sink and duck him under. Mind you, if it *really* cries for us, we might not do it.'

'It' had other ideas. Mimicry had got Peter out of many a mess at his last school. Perhaps the same thing would work here. Holding up his hands like a lone soldier facing enemy hordes, and grinning crookedly, Peter began to give an excellent imitation of his own father. He even made use of the words which had been suggested by Eddie Bird: 'Right, lads, let's get this over with and then we can all be mates.'

The statement struck him as utterly ridiculous. But at least one of his oppressors was plainly taking it at face value. 'Just trying you out, mate,' said King Kong amicably. 'We've no time for cissies round here.'

The other boy got hold of Peter's arm. 'Yeah, we do this to them!' He emphasised his words with a tug. 'And this and this.' Finger and thumbnails flicked viciously against Peter's cheekbone. The boy was a larger version of a kind Peter had encountered before; they always kept going when the rest had stopped.

'That's enough, Ricky,' decreed the handsome gorilla. And Peter found himself wondering why such a nice-looking boy had chosen such a skinny slob as a friend; this Ricky even had green at the top of his front teeth. Against all odds, Peter was hoping to find a friend in the school for himself – some boy who would just be content to let him be who he was. Peter's fears and phobias were always at war with a broad streak of optimism; if Henry the dog could accept him, why shouldn't a male human being?

Latecomers on bicycles were still tinging their way into the yard. A louder bell reverberated from inside the towering red-brick building. Nobody rushed for the main entrance; they just seemed to drift reluctantly and Peter tagged along behind them.

Once inside that tiled echoing hellhole, he had no idea where to go. The big hall seemed the obvious place but, when he put his head around the door, everybody seemed to be making their way to set places; so he retreated and stood outside in the part where they'd been measured, pretending to be deeply interested in a glass case full of silver trophies.

'If you're caught lingering after the second bell you'll get fifty lines.' It was the woman with the tight perm, the school secretary who'd bossed people around on the August visit. 'Come along, get a move on.'

'I don't know where to go.' Some memory stirred of arriving at private hotels at the seaside with his mother. 'I'm looking for Reception.'

'Are you indeed?' She was not unkind. Peter wondered whether she *always* carried lists. 'You go where you went yesterday.'

'I've come a day late.'

'Name?'

'Peter.'

'Not here.' The woman had turned reproachful. 'Boys have surnames only here. If it's Bird, your absence was noted.'

'I've got a letter, explaining.' Peter fished in his pocket.

Taking the letter, the woman announced: 'You're in the Latin form. One L, room twenty-seven.' She seemed to be looking around for inspiration and her eyes fell upon Joan Stone, who was hurrying towards the door which led into the girls' side of the hall. 'You, new girl! Are you in the Latin form?'

For a wild moment Joan wondered whether she was meant to reply with the Latin for 'yes'. English was already forbidden in anything to do with French lessons. Not knowing the Latin word she merely nodded.

'This is Bird. Go and put him with the rest of the boys in your class.' With this she disappeared into her office.

Peter recognised Joan immediately. 'Hello,' he said, and then he fell back into private-hotel behaviour with, 'How're you enjoying it here?'

'You're always on the trot and there's miles of homework.' Joan's mind was full of thoughts of handing over the note from Granny Briggs, instead of the 'My Mother' essay. And English language was the first lesson on the timetable. 'Follow me.' Very conscious of the fact that Peter's coltish height would emphasise her own lack of stature, she led the way into the noisy assembly hall. At the side of him she felt like a comma next to a capital I. 'You go in with that lot, there.'

At least they didn't look menacing; they didn't look anything, just a load of boys in uniform. Peter pushed his way towards a gap and had another glance down the seated line. He had very definite ideas about what his dream friend was going to look like and he certainly wasn't sitting here.

The bell rang again, as it would do every day of the years of his life at Barton Grammar School, and in came the teachers. Peter decided he would equate them with film stars. As twenty men came towards him, the best he could manage was Spencer Tracy's father and a moth-eaten version of Henry Fonda. A couple of elderly ones looked like minor characters from Ealing comedies but the rest could have been divided into two teams – the balding blobs, and the skinned rabbits whose collars were too wide for their necks.

It was Peter's turn to assimilate everything the girls had seen the previous morning. The first-formers were right up at the front so he had a good view of the tall boy who was mounting the steps of the platform. As this youth turned to make his way towards the grand piano, a ray of sunlight shone through the stained-glass window at the back of the platform, like a spotlight, adding lustre to dark hair and sparkle to a pair of mischievous green eyes. In that moment Peter learned that hearts really could miss a beat. The figure lifting the lid of the piano was a nearly grown-up version of Him – the dream friend.

The headmaster barged in on the moment with clomping feet and furry earholes. Glaring at the assembled school he announced, 'We will now sing hymn number twenty-seven in the school hymnal, "Dear Lord and Father of mankind, forgive our foolish ways".' As he bawled these words he seemed to be looking straight at Peter Bird. No, it was more than that: the headmaster seemed to be looking into Peter's very soul.

And I don't give a monkey's, thought the boy, startled to find himself using one of his own father's favourite expressions. I don't give a tuppenny damn! Barton Grammar School had suddenly become a place filled with glorious possibilities.

As the English teacher was also their form mistress, it was she who marked the register before starting the first class. 'Dorothy Aspinall?'

'Here, Miss Titheradge.'

'Norma Barr?'

'Here, Miss Titheradge.'

'Vanda Bell? Somebody nudge her.' Somebody did.

Vanda came to with a start. She had been right on the edge of falling asleep. 'I could drop off on a clothes line,' she admitted cheerfully. 'Sorry about that.'

'How many hours' sleep did you have last night?' Miss Titheradge was one of the first teachers the girls had spotted the previous day, the one in the furnishing-fabric skirt — chintz wasn't on clothing coupons. 'And please don't yawn in my classroom.' She was quite pretty in a fuzzy-haired way but she was noted for having a beady eye. 'How many hours' sleep?' she repeated.

Vanda calculated. 'Eight,' was her final verdict.

'Have you been in the tropics recently? Have you perhaps contracted sleeping sickness?'

The class thrilled to the sarcasm. Sarky Titheradge's tongue was legendary; most of them had heard about it before they'd so much as set foot in the school. And now they were getting their first real taste of those scorching words, that withering gaze. Vanda was not even remotely nonplussed. 'The furthest I've ever been is Abergele.'

'Then why are you so fatigued? Are you perhaps a marathon runner in your spare time?'

'No, but I do dancing. And last night it was acro. That's acrobatic,' she explained helpfully.

'It will have to stop,' pronounced Miss Titheradge. 'See me at the end of this period.'

But Vanda was not prepared to wait until then. 'It's my mother you'll have to have your fight with. She's a big woman and she's very ambitious.'

'Homework,' rapped Miss Titheradge. 'Did these exertions allow time for homework?'

'Yes.' But Vanda had the feeling that the words 'my mother is fat', followed by a lot of revelations about second-hand clothes and street markets, would only inflame Miss Titheradge to further flights of sarcasm.

Mention of homework had set Joan Stone worrying again. Once the form mistress had finished marking the register she asked them to pass forward their English notebooks. Up went Joan's hand.

'An excuse I presume,' sighed the teacher. 'Were you also preparing to be a ballerina?' Once again the class was eating it up. Everything they'd heard about Sarky Titheradge was coming true.

Joan had also heard these stories. And the ones about the teacher's deadly aim with a blackboard duster. Somewhat nervously she said, 'I couldn't do it. I've been sent with a note.' Joan pulled Granny's blue Basildon Bond envelope from between the pages of her rough book.

'Bring it to me . . . No, don't go back, stay where you are. Stay on the platform while I read it.'

Joan just prayed that it wasn't going to be read aloud. She had no idea of the contents but she didn't want the whole class learning them, not while she was on blushing, public, view.

'Mmm . . .' Miss Titheradge's eyes were running through several paragraphs. 'What an extraordinary set of circumstances. But you wouldn't know about that. You seem to have been trouble from the word go.' The famed sarcasm had fallen away, the note seemed to have charged the woman with genuine interest. 'I think we'd better keep an eye on you and a very close one too. You may return to your place. But in future I'd like you a bit nearer the front.'

Midmorning break arrived, after Scripture, at half past ten. As Peter made his way to Vanda's appointed spot, the place where the boys' wall met up with the girls', he reflected that he might as well forget about redrawing his dragon map; this place was *all* danger spots. Barton Grammar School? They should have named it Dragonville! Yet, apart from a tentative catcall of 'Hello, Sweetie', he was being left gloriously alone.

Could it be that dragons had a pecking order, that he had already faced up to the worst of them – and that word of this had spread? He turned round and looked straight at the one boy who had yelled. The lad hesitated for a moment, then just turned away. As he sloped off he looked like the last person out with a whip and top when the fashion had suddenly swung to roller skates.

Peter didn't have to wait long for the girls. They were already coming into view, chattering indignantly. 'That Miss Titheradge humiliated me,' cried Joan. 'She's got everybody looking at me sideways.'

'She's done me a favour,' said Vanda complacently. 'Up until now I just did dancing because I was made to do it. That old bag's made me see that I *like* it. I might end up dancing till I drop dead. And next time she calls me Anna Pavlova I'm going to ask her why she's dressed in curtains.'

Peter needed no encouragement to put in his two penn'orth on the subject of Miss Titheradge: 'She didn't even like the way I walked. Did you hear what she said when I went up to the blackboard? She said I minced.'

'You do, a bit,' pointed out Vanda, fairly.

'Vanda's going to teach me to walk elegantly,' announced Joan.

A deal must already have been struck for Vanda came back with, 'And Joan's going to learn me to talk proper. Walk up and down, Bird.'

Oddly enough he didn't mind this attention for he sensed that it was kindly meant. He was also very well aware that his walk was more than a bit tripping. He was always trying to take longer strides, but something would generally distract him so that trip-trip-trip he was back to the other. But for the girls' benefit he proceeded to march up and down like two of the dragons rolled into one. 'Call me Peter,' he said.

'You look like Dorothy Ward as Dick Whittington,' laughed Vanda. 'If I were you I'd smile a lot. Did you know that Arabs don't say cheese when they're having their photo took; they go pa-ta-ta instead.' This was a trick she had picked up at Odette Ashworth's.

They all went pa-ta-ta and collapsed on one another in a heap of laughter. 'What's that smell of lighter fluid?' cried Joan. The odour was just like the little ampoules of Ronsonol which Granny pierced when she needed to fill her Dunhill lighter.

'It's probably me,' declared Vanda. 'That's what comes of living in an old-clothes dump.' As she said this aloud, she felt a rush of liberation. She was part of a morning where secrets

72

were being thrown to the winds. It was as though the three of them were already in a union which was beyond the usual conventions. She tried to voice this aloud with, 'We're lucky really – that school outfitter turned us into friends. We're friends and Miss Titheradge is the enemy.'

'*And* we've got somebody in love,' put in Joan. She thought she'd better explain this to Peter. 'Did you notice the boy who plays the piano? He's called Toby Eden and we're madly in love with him.'

'Me too,' declared Peter, enthusiastically, 'me too!' And in later life, both the girls would marvel that they had accepted his unusual statement without so much as one moment's hesitation.

were being thrown to the wind. It was as though the three of them were already in a union which was hers and the usual conventions. She tried to voice this aloud with. 'We're lucky really – that school outfit around us into friends. We're friends and Miss Tibberidge is the enemy'.

And now, would somebody integer out in joint. She thought

2

On the Grotto Lodge Estate, in the kitchen of the Bell household, the wireless was playing. John Snagge was reading the one o'clock news: 'In London, this morning, time went more slowly than usual. A flock of starlings had settled on the minute hand of Big Ben, causing the clock to lose four and a half minutes, its slowest for ninety years.'

To Vanda, preparing her grandmother's lunch, this time-lag seemed entirely appropriate. In everybody's childhood there comes one summer which is remembered as attenuated and golden, and this was being hers. No, it was theirs: by the summer of 1949 the three children had finished their second year at Barton Grammar, and even in the school holidays they were inseparable. Ever afterwards they would recall this break as 'that bicycle summer', as a time when they seemed to be forever pedalling through sunlight to one another's houses.

But before Vanda could go out there was the tray to be taken upstairs. As she left the kitchen she switched off the radio. Gran'ma Dora was on a diet. Her cateracts had got so much worse that the doctor announced they were ready to be skinned. Before this could be done, he decreed that the patient must lose weight. 'Otherwise I might die under the knife,' was how she explained it.

Today, as Dora sat up in bed she said, 'Well, I'm certainly not going to die under the knife and fork! Are you sure you've read the chart right?'

'Hard-boiled egg, watercress, one slice lightly buttered toast. Come on, buck up, it *is* a butter day.'

'It's hardly worth the bother of putting me teeth in.' Nevertheless Dora reached for the cup without a handle, fished out her dentures and clacked them into her mouth. In half a dozen chomps the sparse meal was gone. 'I'm bored,' she said. 'I can't pretend I'm looking forward to that

74

operation. They sandbag you to the bed afterwards. And if you cry the whole thing's ruined. I'm bored.' Out it came again, in the same childish tone. 'And I can't even see to do me cards.'

Vanda reached for the pokerwork box, the one with the occult eye. 'You pick them out and I'll tell you which ones you've got.'

'Who shall I read for?'

'Us.' Vanda was already setting the Sun, the Moon and the Magician into a triangle.

'*Our Gang*!' Gran'ma was referring to a series of comedy films about another group of inseparable children. 'Right, put them down one each from the Minor Arcana.' Barely granting Vanda time to accomplish the task, she snorted, 'What've you got for yourself?'

'The Three of Cups.'

'Three maidens dancing in a circle with goblets upraised,' intoned Gran'ma. 'That means joy, rejoicing and having a bloody good time. Just as I said, *Our Gang*! What's Joan Stone got?'

'Four of Wands.' Vanda tried to see whether she could manage the description herself. 'Two girls with posies and four sticks up in the air – like a maypole.'

'The tarot never lies. That's success and achievement through hard work. Just the card for a girl who's top of her class.'

Dora's granddaughter only hoped that Joan's scholastic triumphs were not going to be rubbed in. These might be the holidays, but in term time Vanda was always trying to balance dancing and schoolwork. While her reports from Odette Ashworth's glowed, at Barton Grammar School she generally hovered somewhere near the bottom of the class.

'And what's my boy got?' For some reason Gran'ma had taken to Peter in a big way.

'Seven of Pentacles.' The pentacles were like Stars of David inside a circle, and the slim young man gazing down at them certainly bore a marked resemblance to Peter Bird, who was well on the way to becoming handsome.

'Seven of Pentacles, eh? That one's a bugger to interpret.'

Dora began twiddling the coarse hairs that grew out of the mole on her chin – always a sign of deep concentration. 'The card's got some contentment in it, but there's itching powder too; I'd say this was the last of his childhood. It won't be long before curiosity gets the better of innocence.' She suddenly began to guffaw to herself. 'In the old days I'd have told him to go to Tommy Duck's! Mind you, those places change . . . .'

'What places?'

'Never you mind. And I want to talk to you very seriously, Vanda. When I go into hospital there's to be no messing about with these cards. Understood? Miss Wilkinson would have been very firm about that.'

Miss Wilkinson, a former employer, now deceased, had been a huge figure in Gran'ma Dora's life. Vanda had grown up on tales of this family legend in the same way that other children learned the stories of Mother Goose or Jack and the Beanstalk. And these were not such unlikely comparisons: Miss Wilkinson was someone who had made a serious study of magic.

'When I first went to her,' Gran'ma would say, 'I was just "the little servant girl". It was Cook who told her that I got premonitions. And that was when Miss Wilkinson started to take an interest in me. She was a funny little woman, sort of scrunched-up with a bit of a hump. All her frocks had to have an antimacassar at the back to cover it. But she had the kindest eyes on earth. They were so wise that they made you forget she dragged one leg.'

In Vanda's mind Miss Wilkinson was an ancient version of the Little Match-girl. And Dora Doran would reinforce this image with, 'There was something sad about her but she burned very bright. And she was always looking for *more*. "There has to be more, Dora," she would say. "There just has to be that extra bit more." That's how the poor soul got mixed up with the Order.'

Vanda could never hear enough about *them*. Dora would always tighten her mouth disapprovingly as she said, 'You'd never have guessed such things were going on in Ellesmere Park. She let them have a room at the top of the house for it.'

'For what?'

'For what they did. At first she just condoned it on the premises. Then, after a bit, she started limping up there herself. It wasn't long before she changed the name of the house. It stopped being Glencora. Magi House she named it – even had the words chiselled into the stone gatepost. And nobody was allowed to clean out that top room but herself.'

'Did you ever go in?' Though Vanda knew the answer she didn't mind going over old ground again because she was always hoping for more details. 'What was inside?'

'Black velvet walls and an *atmosphere*. I think they used to spray the velvet with ether, when she wasn't looking. She'd definitely fallen into bad hands. I don't care if them candlesticks *did* come from Burns, Oates and Washbourne's Catholic Repository. They weren't put to a Catholic purpose! We used to hear clanking. Of course all the impedimenta was kept in a locked wardrobe, but I was the one she trusted to rinse out her mauve veils.

'One day, hellfire broke loose up there. You might think that a solid house couldn't shudder. Magi House did. Cook took hysterics. We had to burn feathers under her nose to bring her round. She packed her things and left that night. Went without so much as asking for a reference, and references was important to a woman in service. Mind you, she might just as well have stopped where she was because, the following Thursday, Miss Wilkinson banished the whole Order.'

Dora's sightless eyes were still turned in on her memories. 'I can see them now, Mr Brocklehurst and Mrs Cairns and the Otway sisters, clanking their way down the drive with a brass sword, and big bound books, and a thing with chains – for burning incense. That was when Madam sent for the Bishop, and the place was blessed, and we all had to receive Holy Communion in the dining room. But the one thing Miss Wilkinson never let on about was the tarot cards. I sometimes think they have their own kind of glue; there was no way she was ever going to part company with *them*.'

And now it was 1949 and blind Gran'ma was groping these same cards back into their black silk handkerchief. 'You've not enough knowledge yet to go messing,' she said as she eased them back into their box. 'And when I'm gone they'll be yours. But that's not to say they're yours while I'm in hospital.'

Vanda was thinking about something else. 'We never asked the tarot about Toby Eden today.'

'Him? That dark sparkler!' Dora Doran had never been impressed by what the cards had to tell her about the Tumbling Tower.

'How can a sparkler be dark?'

'Think of black jet. That's what your young man reminds me of, sparkling black jet.'

As Vanda went out to the back garden to pump up her bicycle tyres, she reflected that Gran'ma's dark hints had told them much more about Toby than real life had revealed. All the trio knew for certain was that next term he would be going into the upper sixth form; and that the one solitary stubborn pimple on the side of his neck had finally subsided. Toby was now a man. Oh yes, there was one other bit – he no longer played the piano on the platform. That had stopped when he was unfrocked as a prefect. This marked him out as a rebel: revolutionaries have always had a definite advantage in the sex-appeal stakes.

Why had his prefect's badge been taken away? It was rumoured to be something to do with playing cards for money in the school library. Joan Stone, who was obsessed with history, said it all sounded 'very King Charles'. And that Cavaliers had much more glamour than Roundheads.

Geographically, Joan's home was the nearest to Toby's. But his adoptive family lived in one of the modern 1930s houses in Ellesmere Park, where old brickwork tended to look down on new. People who dwelt in these labour-saving villas were regarded as 'fast cars and everything on account'. It was the vicar who let slip that Toby Eden had absolutely refused to be confirmed. This raised him to even higher pinnacles in Joan's estimation. She had given up God herself. He had refused to answer her prayers for periods.

Vanda's monthlies had arrived in the first year, in floods. As she cocked her leg over the bicycle seat she wished, not for the first time, that her mother would allow her to use

Tampax. It wasn't true that virgins couldn't, she knew that because she'd already tried one. Peter had maintained that classical ballet must have ruptured her hymen.

He was still reading everything about sex that he could lay his hands on. What might have seemed an unhealthy passion for the subject was in fact a battle with confusion. This ended in the Central Reference Library when he turned a page and read two whole paragraphs which could have been a description of himself and of his desire for somebody of the same sex. It seemed he was *not* the only one in the world, not even one in a million; he was simply one of millions. And the relief was so great that he had been surprised to find himself in tears.

But this sudden infusion of knowledge turned Peter Bird into somebody who would weep much less in the future. 'I'm a homo,' was how he announced it cheerfully to the girls. 'I'm like Alexander the Great and Oscar Wilde.' The three adolescents soon became deeply interested in who 'was' and who wasn't.

It was only a couple of weeks later that, sitting on the school wall, Joan whispered, 'Peter, do you think that your name is already inscribed in the big black book at Scotland Yard?' Uncle Bruno had told her of this ledger; he'd heard about it at the dramatic society where somebody had said, 'The police have got the names of all the homos in England. And the top two are Noël Coward and Ivor Novello.'

'I don't think I'll be in the book yet,' had been Peter's view. 'I think you have to *do* something about it before you get in.'

But in the 1940s 'doing something' was still highly illegal. And, anyway, where was he meant to find somebody to do it *with*? While a certain amount of comparing and touching went on in the boys' bogs, Peter's reading had led him to view these shadowy all-male proceedings as just a stage in his classmates' heterosexual development – something they would grow out of. He had once declined a classmate's offer of sixpence in return for a wank. The idea had been quite tempting, but the heightened atmosphere of the moment was accompanied by much masculine talk of 'juicy tits' and of girls who allowed hands to roam under jumpers. No, this was *their* world. The more he saw of it, the more he realised that he needed to find a route to the world of his own kind.

Peter had not tried to hide his ambition from the two girls. One of the books in the library had hinted at clandestine meeting places and secret handshakes. The young trio were constantly on the lookout for homos; the giveaway signals were generally considered to be suede shoes and corduroy jackets. As Vanda cycled downhill along Manchester Road she spotted a man carrying an umbrella. According to Ethel Bell, that was supposed to be another definite sign of a queer.

Surprisingly, Vanda's bicycle was not at all second-hand. Metallic pink with drop handlebars, it was hard to believe that this had been a present from her mother – who couldn't be right about umbrellas and queers because the man leered at Vanda's legs as she flashed past him. Ethel had bought the bike off a woman who won it in a competition. Sunlight twinkled on the chromium handlebars as the machine reached the flat part by the Dell. That was where Vanda applied her brakes as she noticed another cyclist; Joan Stone was pushing her bicycle up the hawthorn track.

Joan's bike was a black sit-up-and-beg gent's model. Though it looked the kind of machine that could have belonged to a curate, she had in fact inherited it from Bruno. 'I've got a flat front tyre,' she explained as she caught up with Vanda. 'I think the valve must have gone.'

'Miss Lathom's got a puncture outfit.' Miss Lathom and Miss Parr's house was a box of delights with everything needed to make a summer holiday perfect. Only too delighted that Peter had found friends, the teachers were as kind to the two girls as they had always been to their young neighbour.

'Did your grandmother do the cards?' asked Joan as they wheeled their bicycles the length of the hospital's high wall. More accurately, Joan pushed hers while Vanda stayed on the saddle of her own, tap-tapping her way along with her feet, a no-hands proceeding which generally led to disaster.

'Yes, she did them.' Only now did Vanda realise that the cards had said nothing about the forthcoming audition. 'I've got to go to Hulme Hippodrome next week, it's for this year's panto. They're looking for leads for *Babes in the Wood*.'

Reverting to the subject of the tarot, Vanda added, 'She did them but she wouldn't tell me anything about Toby.'

Mention of his name always caused them to sing a few bars of 'Loving Glances'. This was the summer when half the schoolgirls in Great Britain were singing this melancholy Tin Pan Alley refrain.

> I'm not too young for loving glances,
> Quite old enough for fate's romances,
> We'd ride the train to Arizona,
> Then catch a plane for old Paloma . . .

The awful song, made worse by the fact that Joan was tone-deaf, kept them occupied until they came to the turning for Hawksway. As they swung round the corner they were still singing; that was the moment when Vanda's feet, tip-tapping beneath the side of the pedals, failed to negotiate the bend so that she and the bicycle crashed to the ground. 'I just hope it doesn't make me flood,' she observed ruefully.

'Now you've gone and spoiled everything,' cried Joan. 'I was going to save the news until I could tell you and Peter together. I've *started*.'

Vanda was absolutely delighted to hear this menstrual excitement. 'When?'

'This morning – it happened in the bath. I suddenly saw this cloud of red water. Granny was in Eccles but I knew where the Dr White's packet was kept.' She wriggled awkwardly. 'I don't think I can have got the belt on right. I feel just like a badly saddled horse.'

Vanda brushed this aside with, 'But isn't it good news? And, just think, we'll always be on at the same time. Peter will be thrilled to bits.' There were no secrets between the three of them. Within an hour of Peter discovering his first two hairs 'down there' the girls had been informed. They even knew that he'd been sitting on the lav at the time, reading an article in *Picture Post* about Anna Neagle in *Maytime in Mayfair*. And within a matter of days there was the additional news that his voice had started to break. Not that they needed telling, they could already hear the comical wobble.

81

'Vanda, straighten the bell on your bike, you've knocked it skewwhiff,' said Joan. And then she announced in an important voice, 'Our childhood is over. Mind you,' she added more realistically, 'it's not going to stop me taking *Collins' Magazine*.' This publication was as relentlessly middle-class as Clark's sandals or Aertex shirts. It cost two whole shillings per monthly issue; but Granny Briggs never failed to find the money because it was well known that children of consequence read *Collins'*.

Vanda Bell was more a fan of *Girls' Crystal*, which filled the mind with tales of highly improbable boarding schools and left cheap printer's ink on your fingers, but she generally borrowed Joan's glossier publication to read the Molly Wainwright serial. Miss Wainwright was an author who specialised in writing about children who earned their living on the stage; her radio serials always came top of the *Children's Hour* request-week polls.

'It goes all round the world you know, *Collins'*.' Joan Stone was not above a bit of mild swank. 'On this month's letter page an American girl says she wants an English penfriend. Sally Morganstern, she's called. I'm thinking of writing to her. Quick! Grab him.' It was Henry the retriever, and he had the look of a dog who was in the middle of doing a bunk.

'Henry,' called Vanda. 'Good boy, come here.' Much as he loved going over-the-hills-and-far-away, Henry was also partial to pretty girls so he allowed himself to be grabbed. And the girls were pretty, or at least beauty was on its way. Joan was more than ever a stylised pixie; everybody said she looked like a young dancer called Audrey Hepburn who was on all the calamine-lotion adverts. Blonde Vanda was still reminiscent of a doll won on a hoopla stall, but the curves that had piled onto her bust seemed to have been trimmed from her waist.

As they got near to Miss Lathom's house, the front door flew open and Peter emerged looking worried. 'Oh good,' he said when he looked down and saw the white dog which had happily followed the girls home. 'You've nabbed him.'

'Joan's started!' yelled Vanda.

The pixie tried to look prim. 'There's no need to tell the

whole of Ravensdale Estate.' As a matter of fact Joan was so relieved to have caught up with Vanda that she would have cheerfully allowed an announcement in the *Manchester Evening News*.

'You must be thrilled to bits.' Peter's voice was much deeper. 'And listen.' He began to sing a snatch of their favourite, 'Loving Glances'.

> 'Don't call me young,
> My heart can't stand it,
> You are my man,
> You're passion's bandit . . .

'Hear that? It doesn't crack back to soprano any more. It really does sound as though my voice has finally decided to settle down. Did you know that the chap who recorded 'Loving Glances' wears a wig? Bit of a swizz, isn't it?'

Joan pushed Henry through the gate. 'I think it's very odd that a man should sing those words at all.'

'I don't.' As he said this, Peter's voice gave one final squeak and then it settled down forever. No longer the timid first-former, he had grown in confidence to the extent where somebody who didn't know the whole story could have mistaken him for cocksure.

The girls leaned their bikes against the wall and made their way up the path. It was Joan who closed the gate behind them. The gardens of the Ravensdale Estate were not just bounded by privet hedges, they were also constrained by a set of suburban horticultural rules which decreed that every plot must try to pass for its next-door neighbour. This led to a proliferation of poplar trees and of cement paths, and of flowerbeds edged with blue lobelia, white alyssum and miniature French marigolds.

These rules ended at Miss Lathom's front gate. 'I like a garden as much as possible like a birthday card,' was what she always said. It was equally like that song which is full of gentians and lupins and tall hollyhocks. Ravensdale maintained that lupins always 'turn back to blue'. Not Miss Lathom's. But this could have been because Miss Parr had smuggled the original seeds out of Kew Gardens – stashed beneath her hatband.

The aroma of freshly made coffee drifted through the spinsters' front door, where it went into competition with the scent of flowering stocks. Clomp, clomp, clomp – Miss Lathom's big men's shoes were heading down the hall. 'Who's for coffee-dash?' she called out when she reached the top step. This morning her Liberty smock featured a design of tiny parrots. Coffee-dash was an idea she had snitched from the Oxford Kardomah; the beverage contained a small amount of very good coffee infused into boiling milk. Miss Lathom was a great believer in the idea of children developing adult tastes at a gentle pace.

The young people followed her down the hall and into the kitchen. Pretty Miss Parr was at the gas stove, frothing up the hot milky drink with a wire balloon wisk. 'I've substituted honey for sugar, for a change,' she said. And she began to sing:

> 'Where the bee sucks, there suck I,
> In a cowslip's bell I lie . . .'

'Not round here you don't,' grunted Miss Lathom, 'I can never get cowslips to do anything. This seems to be a morning for singing. First Peter, now you. Perhaps we should go the whole hog and have a musical evening!'

Miss Parr took a damp rag to some milky froth which had landed on her navy linen dress. 'I've not heard of anybody having such a thing since before the war.'

These words caused the children to prick up their ears. Anything 'pre-war' generally meant de luxe.

Grace Lathom began to pour the contents of the pan into old willow-pattern mugs. 'I shouldn't think anybody would want to be bothered with musical evenings any more.'

'We would, we would,' protested Peter. 'What were they?'

Miss Lathom smiled in fond memory. 'All a great nonsense, really.' Turning to Iris Parr she said, 'Do you remember how Miss Clay, the geography mistress, used to carry her cello round to anybody who'd have her?'

'Do I not! Didn't she once turn up on us on the wrong night? And we still had to let her play.' Being a teacher she plainly felt that the three children needed more explanation. 'It was before anybody had wireless sets. All we could do was make our own entertainment.'

'Did dancing count?' asked Vanda eagerly.

'Never in my experience.' Miss Parr passed round a plate of home-made shortbreads.

'Of course it counted,' scoffed Miss Lathom. 'You're forgetting Winnie Holt and her Grecian draperies. There was always a great to-do about rolling back the rugs for Winnie.' Miss Lathom took a deep swig of coffee-dash.

Peter's thoughts were already leaping ahead: 'There are no rugs in our hairdressing room – just lino. And we could push the piano in from the lounge.' He turned to Miss Parr. 'D'you think you could still get hold of the woman with the cello?'

'I'd have a job, she was blown up by a landmine.'

Miss Lathom lowered her cup and said reproachfully, 'It's not funny, Iris. They planted a mock-cherry tree to her memory.'

Joan Stone, who had no musical abilities whatsoever, foresaw an adventure taking shape in which she could have no part. 'Does anybody have to write out the programmes?' she asked hesitantly.

'Yes, and somebody always has to turn the pages of the music,' said Miss Parr. 'That's a very important job indeed.'

You could never tell whether Miss Parr was joking or not because her dark eyes always twinkled. But what you could tell was that Joan was right: a stray thought was about to turn into a reality.

As if in confirmation of this Miss Lathom murmured, 'It might be a nice way of getting all your parents together. It's not as though they've really met.'

The girls gradually ceased to make more than a perfunctory contribution to the conversation. They were too busy considering the idea of their families meeting one another. Vanda was not a snob but the gap between council tenants and people with mortgages suddenly loomed wide. If there was going to be music, what if her mother insisted upon doing her

85

usual Grotto Lodge party-piece? How would Hawksway react to big Ethel Bell bawling out 'The Hole in the Elephant's Bottom'?

Vanda never let anything worry her for long. Joan was having a much more lengthy struggle with almost exactly the opposite problem. She was quite sure that Granny Briggs would consider herself a cut above Ravensdale Estate. Bold reference to Miss Lathom's Oxford degree would have to be worked into any invitation. Perhaps the whole idea of this musical evening would fizzle to nothing. But it didn't sound like it; not when Miss Parr was extolling the virtues of piano tuners from Henshaw's Institute for the Blind. And then the conversation turned to party refreshments. No, the musical evening was definitely on.

Still tasting faintly of coffee, Peter walked the girls, who were pushing their bikes, as far as Manchester Road. Henry was also with them but this time he was on his lead.

'I've got to ride up to Odette Asworth's,' announced Vanda. 'She's going to put me through my audition piece for the panto.'

'Joan?' Peter was speaking sternly. 'What's the matter?'

'The elastic of this belt thing is cutting in.'

'It's more than that and you know it.' Two years had got them very used to one another. 'What's up?'

Joan hesitated for a moment and then said, 'I was so excited about getting periods that I'd forgotten something . . .'

Vanda was ahead of her: 'Now your monthlies have started your grandmother's got to tell you about your mother. She's got to. She promised.'

As Joan cycled along the bumpy central unadopted road in Ellesmere Park, she was feeling even more nervous than when she had parted company from the other children; she barely noticed the furniture vans outside an especially ramshackle ivy-clad villa. A brand-new For Sale sign poked out from between the speckled laurels of Magi House.

Half of Joan wanted to get back to Ingledene as quickly as possible, but other thoughts steadied her pedalling. Would she have to tell her grandmother that she had sneaked an extra bath? In summer, hot water meant the immersion heater, and that cost money. For the past half-hour Joan had been remembering that she had left the Dr White's packet on the marble washstand; Granny was bound to ask questions about bloodstained garments. And there weren't any.

Joan swerved sharply to avoid a black cat, and rounded the corner of their own road. Black cats were arguably lucky or unlucky. Oh dear, the superstition was as much in two minds as her pedalling feet. This caused her to start thinking about Victor Sylvester giving a ballroom dancing lesson on television. Slow-slow-quick-quick-slow. Not that they had television at Ingledene. If she wanted to watch something she had to go round to Vanda's. Vanda's mother . . . Oh never mind Vanda's mother. Today was the day when she was going to find out about her own. And what was Granny Briggs doing out in the front garden?

She was rubbing the lead nymph with a damp window leather. 'It's hard to believe that God invented pigeons,' she said distatefully. 'Joan, I hope you've not been out doing anything strenuous?' Granny's tone had turned severe. 'And you can forget any idea of tennis this week. There are special rules for certain times of the month.'

These last words were spoken so darkly that Joan felt they should have left italics on the summer air. 'That's not what the gym mistress says.'

'I *am* a woman, Joan,' said Granny scathingly. 'I do know about such matters.'

Joan decided to crash straight in with it. 'And I want to know about another woman. You always said . . .'

'I know what I said.' Granny's eyes darted to the front of the house next door, the one with all the balconied bedsitting-room windows. 'I couldn't possibly tell you about your mother out here. We could be overheard.' As if to prove her point, somebody threw up one of the windows and the air was flooded with the crackling strains of a radio orchestra playing Elgar's 'Pomp and Circumstance'.

'We'll go inside,' said Granny abruptly. As Joan followed the bony old woman up the marble steps, her feet were keeping time with the mournful music. Once they got into the hall, the tune turned into something that sounded as though it was being produced on a comb and paper. And by the time their progress reached the sitting-room door, the sound was as good as gone. That was where Granny said brightly, too brightly for it to be genuine, 'I don't think you've ever heard the American pianola actually *playing*, have you?'

She's scared to death, thought Joan, absolutely scared to death. 'Just tell me. Tell me and get it over with.'

Granny steadied herself against one of the flaking, silver-painted radiators. 'I've never allowed myself to think it was your fault. Never. How could anyone blame a newborn baby?'

This statement was quite enough to begin to fill Joan with a sense of puzzled guilt. 'Blame me for what?'

'Do you know where babies come out of ladies?'

'Yes.'

'Are you sure? Point to it on yourself.'

Joan did as she was asked.

Granny Briggs blinked, looked away and said: 'As you came into the world she was very badly torn.' Granny glanced back. 'Take that finger away from there, Joan, it looks rude. Rhoda got septicaemia and it turned to puerperal fever. And after that she . . . she stopped being herself.'

Torn – that was the word which had taken control of Joan's mind. The medical terms she found incomprehensible, but *torn* was raising up dreadful images. And how could her mother have 'stopped being herself'? For the first time in years Joan's old stammer came back as she said, 'I d-d-d-don't understand.'

'She went doolally-tap.' Translating this term of the Raj into standard English, Granny rapped out coldly, 'She went mad. Stark raving mad. She tried to eat her own hand. Your mother's a madwoman.' Emotion came back into her voice with, 'Rhoda was everything you will never be. I can't help it, you won't.' Her old face began to grow wet with angry tears. 'She was beautiful. She threw herself away on nobody. And she ended up with a poisoned brain.'

'But where *is* she?'

'Behind a lot of locked doors.'

'Where?' Doubting she would ever be allowed to raise the subject again, Joan had to find out now. 'Where?'

'That's my business.'

'And don't you think it's mine?'

'And don't *you* think you've done enough damage already? Now you're a woman, Joan, I'll tell you something frankly. Life isn't all honey and it isn't all jam.'

As a matter of fact, Granny must have told her that at least twenty times before. But the word 'jam' made Joan think of the colour red. And that brought blood to mind, which revived thoughts of that poor torn flesh. 'I didn't do it on purpose.' The words burst out of her.

'I hope you're not suggesting that I said you did?'

'I want to meet her.'

'Well you can't.'

We'll see about that, thought Joan. That's something we'll definitely have to see about.

Odette Ashworth would never have dared to ask the parents of her posher pupils to allow their children to attend an audition at Hulme Hippodrome. It was definitely not the gleaming Manchester Palace. Neither was it a complete dump. Hulme was an unlovely working-class suburb, a mile from the city centre. By 1949 the Hippodrome had become a number two variety theatre which featured stars of not quite the first rank, and bigger names who had fallen out of favour with the leading theatrical managements.

The party from the dancing school consisted of Miss Ashworth, four mothers and four pupils. A pair of taxis, unversed in theatrical matters, had dropped them outside the front of the early Edwardian music hall. It was cold for the beginning of August and there was rain in the air as Ethel and the other mothers stood tut-tutting under the theatre's iron and glass canopy. The object of their indignation was a set of large posters advertising somebody called Phyllis Dixey in a twice-nightly revue entitled *Peek-a-Boo*.

'She's banned in a lot of places,' said Ethel indignantly. 'Comedians make dirty jokes about Phyllis Dixey.'

The girls had already found their way to the theatre's

glass-fronted display cases. Now they were gazing in disbelief at photographs of a lady-like blonde in pin-up poses. In some she was holding a muff, in others it was a gentleman's top hat – in all of them she was glowingly naked.

Miss Ashworth moved between the girls and the pictures. 'I understand that the censor *does* require her to wear a piece of sticking plaster,' she said. But anybody could tell that the teacher was as shocked as the mothers. She tried to cover this with, 'It's just a touring revue. I expect that Hulme has to take whatever London sends them. The pantomime will be quite different. It's going to be a brand-new production. Hulme's noted for panto.'

The artistes' entrance was down a damp and cobbled side street which smelt of chips that had been fried in ancient fat. Odette Ashworth, very much the old professional, threw open the stage door and instructed her party to keep close behind. Once inside, their progress was halted by the doorman who opened the window of a tiny office hung with keys and signed photographs. 'Names?' He checked them against his list. 'You're to go down to the other side of the stage and wait.'

'I know the way.' Being backstage seemed to have charged Miss Ashworth with even more self-importance than usual.

He was unimpressed. 'You've put on weight.'

It's the musquash jacket that's bulked her out, thought Vanda as they clattered down a set of uncarpeted steps. Musquash in August! But Miss Ashworth always maintained that, when you were in show business, it was your duty to *show*.

This did not just apply to herself. For the purposes of this audition she had fished into the dancing-school wardrobe and produced two gingham dresses for Alicia and Moya to wear – they would be auditioning for the role of Girl Babe.

Boy Babe had not been quite so simple. Vanda and Ginger were kitted out in bright red linen shorts and striped matelot jerseys in black and white. Vanda's was too tight. Even here, in the wings of the stage, Miss Ashworth was having second thoughts. 'You look a bit busty,' she said doubtfully.

'She looks a *lot* busty,' was Ethel Bell's less cautious verdict. 'In fact she looks like puddings boiling over.'

Odette Ashworth undid her own coat. 'We should have flattened her out with a roll-on round the chest.' This observation caused Ginger's mother to smile for the first time since they'd seen the posters. Ginger Lambert was as flat as a plank.

'We've got to get to the other side of the stage,' fussed Miss Ashworth. 'Everybody got their shoe bags?' They had. 'Then follow me.'

The iron safety curtain began to rise as the party started to cross the big stage. 'Halt,' called the dancing teacher as they reached the centre. By now the metal barrier had completely vanished. 'Look at that view!' cried Odette Ashworth.

Across the footlights, the only real light in the auditorium came from one huge naked electric bulb hanging in the centre of a vast crystal chandelier. The exit signs were merely marked by dim flutters of green gaslight. Cleaners with dustpans were working in the stalls where the empty seats made a repeating pattern of red plush blobs. Vanda supposed that the two open-ended golden horseshoes, up on higher levels, must be the circle and the gallery. Yes, they were, because you could see more of the dark ruby blobs; but there were proper little gilt chairs behind the velvet swags of the curtains of the boxes.

'That,' intoned Miss Ashworth, 'is the most beautiful view in the whole wide world.' Her voice continued to ring round the theatre. 'It's what divides *us* from the general public. And they never, ever, get to see it.'

'Excuse me, Sarah Bernhardt . . .' The sibilant male voice came from the auditorium. That was when Vanda noticed three men with their hats on indoors, grouped at the back of the stalls, under the overhang of the circle. 'When you've quite finished reciting your scene from *Trelawney of the Wells*,' continued the nasty voice, 'we've got an audition to take.'

'Good morning, Harry,' beamed Miss Ashworth as she led her troupe towards the opposite wings. The stage was set with scenery from the present show – a backdrop of Piccadilly Circus with side pieces cut to look like the ends of London buildings. Viewed as near as this, it was all a bit daubed and garish. But exciting, thought Vanda, definitely exciting; and she started to feel nervous.

The far wings seemed to be seething with apprehensive figures. As she got nearer to the side of the stage, Vanda recognised faces which were familiar from dance competitions. Some of the other teachers attempted to greet Miss Ashworth but she was already busy calling out, 'Would my mothers please go and sit on the seats by the scene-dock door?' The mothers noticeably swanked their way towards this half-filled row of chairs – the Odette Ashworth School had a very high reputation.

Few of the other girls were in stage costume, most were just in practice outfits; three dozen children in pursuit of only two roles. So far, Vanda's nervousness had been almost pleasant; now it began to turn into something altogether more dithery. Miss Ashworth was already fishing sheet music out of a green tartan briefcase.

As this audition was for leading parts, the girls would be obliged to sing one chorus and then follow it with a dance routine. The side of the stage was already ringing with the sound of metal plates on the soles of tap shoes. 'Girls –' Miss Ashworth gathered her charges conspiratorially around her. 'Just listen to that din. We know better, don't we? We know how to keep our footsteps *muted* until we get to the centre of the stage. And what do we do when we get there?'

'We *smile*, Miss Ashcroft.'

'Eyes and teeth, girls. Eyes and teeth.'

The stage manager was peering into a shorthand notebook; a sallow man in shirt sleeves, he looked as though he could have done with a good meal. 'I believe the girls from the Hester Braid School have got to get a train back to Warrington?' He looked up from his pad. 'We'll see them first.'

The girls from the Hester Braid were nothing special. Their work was as safe and as dull as their teacher's fawn Kangol beret. Vanda's one worry was that somebody would get in first with the song she was planning to use herself, but nobody did. The biggest excitement came in the shape of a girl called Christine Duffy who forgot the words of 'When the Guards Are On Parade' and ran off the stage crying. This definitely added to the overall tension.

'Is it four of yours we're seeing, Miss Ashworth?' The stage manager was running a finger down his pad again.

'Yes. We'll start with Ginger Lambert.' The child's mother rose from her chair and made her way towards the wings. Vanda had already noticed that this maternal surveillance was allowed. Mind you, it would have taken ten stage managers to stop just one of these determined women. As Ginger went into 'The Sun Has Got His Hat On', Vanda could see Mrs Lambert doing the words under her own breath. And when the dance started she also mirrored that, but just in a small way.

A disinterested 'Thank you' came from the auditorium.

Odette nodded towards Ethel Bell, who took Mrs Lambert's place. Vanda needed only one glance at her mother to realise that Ethel was dying to wee. But there was no time to worry about this: her teacher was already striding towards the centre of the stage. 'Vanda Bell,' she announced. 'This year's outright Sunshine champion.'

As Vanda replaced her teacher, she saw that the men in trilby hats had moved to the front of the stalls. The working light was still shining down from the grubby chandelier so she could see them quite clearly. The one who'd made the cracks at Miss Ashworth couldn't have looked more bored. He was filing his fingernails on the edge of a matchbox. But the other two were looking at Vanda in a way that was growing daily more familiar. It confirmed the fact that her striped matelot jersey was at least one size too small. And, oh dear, there was a lot of jogging up and down in the dance chorus of 'Everything's Up To Date in Kansas City'.

The introduction to her music was already starting, and the man in the orchestra pit was going much faster than Mrs Musker had ever done. As previously instructed, Vanda beamed at her small audience, opened her mouth, and let rip. The acoustics of Hulme Hippodrome being excellent, she found it easy to fill the whole theatre with her cheerful voice. She was thoroughly enjoying telling the world that the residents of Kansas had 'gone about as far as they could go'.

As she went into her dance chorus, the man filing his nails watched her as critically as Miss Ashworth would have watched; the older two watched like . . . like men. Vanda had always been taught that she was not to be afraid of spreading herself about, that she should travel across the stage. But as she did, her bust seemed to be leading a life of its own. Step-ball-change went her feet, bounce-bounce-bounce went her top. Perhaps it had always done this, but never before had grown men sat watching. It wasn't just her mother who was going to have to rush for the lav at the end of this ordeal.

The routine finished with an energetic display of bucking and winging. Bounce-bounce-bounce-bounce. That was when the most grinning man, the one with the cigar, said, 'Could we have the dance again?'

Vanda stopped thinking about her bladder and saw red. The look in the man's eye had reminded her of cartoons of wolves. She was just about to give him a mouthful when Miss Ashworth's warning voice came from the wings: 'One more dance chorus, Vanda, if you please.'

Right, thought Vanda, you're no bloody help. These fellers are leering at me. If I've absolutely got to do it again, I'll give them something to look at. I'll *shame* them into looking away. It wasn't that Vanda had any knowledge of men, she was just a natural performer with an inbuilt feel for her audience's needs. It was almost as though the very bricks and mortar of that gilded old wreck of a theatre were telling her what to do.

It is perfectly possible to take a set dance routine and make it mean a dozen different things. As her music crashed out again, Vanda's fast mind turned her body into something that had hints of both Veronica Lake and Lucille Ball. They were two of her heroines and she willed them to come to her aid. All the carefully rehearsed tomboy movements were suddenly charged with sexual promise. Vanda would never have been able to find these words for herself, but natural instinct showed her the style that went with them. This time, when her bust bounced, she looked the man with the cigar right in the eye. Her own eyes said, I am wickedness, I am what you shouldn't be looking at, I am *fun*.

94

Yes, the building was whispering to her. 'Yes. Stay with me,' it seemed to be saying. 'You've come home, Vanda. We'll be all right together. I'll give you everything.'

At its insistence she even changed the end of the dance so that she finished on a throbbing stomp. And the worst of the men bit right through the end of his cigar.

'Can I go now?' asked Vanda, innocently. But it was theatrical innocence; this was not the same girl as the one who had followed Miss Ashworth onto the stage.

'Odette,' bawled the cigar-man. Interested, Vanda stayed where she was until the teacher marched out and joined her. 'That's not a kiddie, Odette.' The man's voice seemed to suggest that Miss Ashworth had been trying to pull a fast one.

'She was thirteen in . . .'

'May,' supplied Vanda.

'Christ,' said the man. And he said it very reverently.

Now the one who'd been busy with his nails spoke up. 'She'll never make a dancer, dear.' His hair was peroxided. 'One part keeps moving when the rest has stopped.'

Miss Ashworth was ready for him: 'We're hoping she'll fine down. Her ballet is very special.'

'It's her charlies that are very special!' He spat on the tips of his fingers and smoothed down plucked eyebrows. 'We could be looking at the next Phyllis Dixey.'

'You dirty bugger!' Another generation of huge theatrical presence had burst onto the stage. It was big Ethel Bell. 'How dare you talk about a stripteaser in front of a young schoolgirl.'

'This *is* show business,' snapped the waspish creature. 'Take it or leave it.'

'So what are you offering?' Ethel snapped her own words right back.

The third man, the one who'd said nothing so far, plainly realised that things were getting out of hand. As he removed his hat to speak to Vanda's mother, a black skullcap of brilliantined hair came into view. His voice was steady and masculine and quietly cockney. 'Just occasionally,' he said, 'just occasionally something remarkable turns up at these general auditions.'

'She's not a something, she's a somebody.' Ethel was only marginally mollified.

The man, who had plainly met Ethel's kind before, offered her an altogether reliable smile. 'She's too young for what she has to offer. There's a Continental quality there.' He fished in a top pocket. 'Could I trouble you to reach down and get this card? When she's seventeen, I want you to bring her to see me in London.'

The card passed from the impresario to the pianist to Ethel. 'Will *he* be there?' She had turned the blaze of her attention onto the cigar-chewer – the man whose behaviour had rendered the startling change in her daughter. 'Will that randy sod be present?'

The impresario refused to be deflected. 'If I'm right, and I'm not used to being wrong, she could fill theatres with men like him. As I said, she's got what we call a *quality*.'

Odette Ashworth must have felt she'd been silent for long enough. 'Do you really think so?' She sounded quite impressed.

But Ethel seemed very far from satisfied. 'I don't know where the kiddie learned to do what she just did.'

The brilliantined impresario silenced these maternal grumbles with, 'Nobody learns it. It's either there or it isn't. Are you really only thirteen?' he said, quite kindly, to Vanda.

'Yes.'

'OK, Odette. Thank you for showing me a future star of the Folies Bergère. And now, have you got anybody up your sleeve who might be suitable for the part of Boy Babe?'

'The old conservatory', that's how Granny Briggs always referred to the cast-iron and glass structure which projected from the back of Ingledene. Her tone seemed to imply that the very purpose of the antique glasshouse had changed. And in a way it had. As Uncle Bruno moved out of his teens, and Joan moved into hers, the pair of them had taken to using this Victorian winter garden as their own sitting room.

By now, Bruno was reading English at Manchester University so he described the conservatory as 'purest Betjeman'. It had a domed ceiling and a slate floor and the windows were inset with panels of bright green glass, painted with a raised design of bunches of white grapes.

If only Granny Briggs had employed the services of a window cleaner all this could have been highly impressive. But their regular man wanted seven and six a time to tackle that amount of glass. And Granny suspected him of planning to fall through her roof – for the compensation. No, in Granny's mind it was the *old* conservatory, so it didn't matter that this winter garden had gradually become as murky as the corner of some abandoned railway station.

Or like Buxton Pavilion after the end of the world, thought Joan as she opened her best writing pad and unscrewed her fountain pen. It was hard to get comfortable on cast iron, and the chair was the wrong height for the ornamental ironwork table which was stacked with back numbers of *Collins' Magazine*. Joan reached for the most recent issue and turned to the page headed 'Your Editor's Postbag'. Not that she needed to read the letter again. She practically knew it by heart.

Dear Sir,
I am thirteen and I am in the ninth grade.
I live in New York City and I am looking for a penfriend. My family are in artistic professions and I am interested in going to the ballet and to ballgames. I am also getting good on the saxophone.
Sincerely,
Sally Morgenstern.
P.S. My mother says 'no boys'.

The door from the house shuddered open and Bruno, dressed for tennis, came down the slate steps. He was carrying a racket, screwed into a heavy wooden press, and the overhead vine patterned his suntanned limbs with leaf-shaped shadows.

'Why are the hairs on your legs blond?' asked Joan. They seemed curiously at variance with the dark auburn hair on his head.

'Don't know, don't care. Have you seen three tennis balls anywhere?'

'Maybe Bowzer had them.' It was out before she realised what she's said.

'Who's Bowzer?'

Joan could feel herself going red. It must have been the uncapped fountain pen in her hand that had caused her to speak out of her 'other' world.

'So now you own a dog in your diaries, do you?' teased Bruno. 'That's news.'

'I've not had him long,' she said primly. Joan was regretting that she had ever ventured to tell her young uncle about this half-world on lined paper.

Bruno moved towards an old oak settle which had been dumped in the conversatory when it was suspected of having woodworm. He lifted the seat and fished inside the recess. 'Don't you think it's about time you gave up all these imaginings and faced up to reality?'

'Don't you think it's about time you learned to mind your own business?'

'Hey, hey, hey,' he said reprovingly as he straightened up, greyish tennis balls in hand. 'There's no need to snap my head off.'

'And there's no need to tell me how to run my life.' In truth, his opinion had come too near to recent thoughts of her own. Now she abandoned them, once and for all. And only because he had chipped in. Bruno was heading off for the tennis club quite unaware that he had scored an own goal.

And if that's a mixed metaphor, I don't care, thought Joan. In recent months she had become much more interested in style and construction. The contents of the diaries had changed, too. Martha 'our apple-cheeked cook' had been given the boot. Joan had come to see that this character was too obviously borrowed from safe, middle-class children's stories.

The character of Mother still featured on the pages, though she had undergone a startling transformation. For a while, Joan had toyed with the idea of mirroring reality by placing her in a mental institution. But the diaries were not meant to heighten pain, they were designed as a release from it. On the written page, Mother, far from being incarcerated, had spread her wings. She had turned into the woman that Joan herself wanted to be when she grew up – a popular novelist.

A recent diary entry read: 'The critics have been a little hard on Mummy's latest book, *Monte Carlo Cocktail*, but her readers are buying it in their thousands. This novel is a subtle blend of high finance and top-class infidelity. Princess Elizabeth is said to be reading it, in secret, at Sandringham.'

All this had gone into the latest of the lined exercise books. The open pad on the iron table in front of Joan was unlined and alluringly blank. The diarist, in preparation for turning herself into a correspondent, shook her pen so as to be sure that the ink would flow freely.

Dear Sally,
Are you still looking for a penfriend? How about me? My name is Joan Stone and I have just had my thirteenth birthday. After the holidays I will be going up into the third form at Barton Grammar School. I do not know how this compares with American grades.
    I was interested to learn that you have artistic parents. My father (deceased) was a painter in oils. He specialised in storms at sea. My mother . . .

The Swan pen glided on and on. The tale Joan was telling was not precisely lifted from the diaries. No, she was altering, editing, adapting – mixing the products of her imagination with touches from real life. Though she didn't know it, Joan was doing what she would eventually do on every morning of her adult working life: the writer within was constructing a complete little world of fiction.

Granny of the diaries was a shadowy figure, but in this letter she emerged as Olive Briggs, 'our housekeeper'.

Have you seen the film *Rebecca*? Old Olive is very like Mrs Danvers. She thinks of Mummy as her queen and gives the rest of us a hard time indeed. However, the food she provides is absolutely delicious.

When it came to the titles of her mother's alleged novels, Joan decided to be guarded. America might be a long way away but people could still check up. She played safe with, 'Mummy does not like me to swank about her literary endeavours.' But the temptation to mention that *Monte Carlo Cocktail* had been smuggled into a royal residence proved too strong. This led to crossing out, which messed up the page, and it had to be torn from the pad and thrown away.

Bowzer, the make-believe dog, grabbed himself a couple of paragraphs. And even Joan was startled to discover that he had a sworn enemy in the shape of her Shetland pony – Miss Pigtails.

Now that *did* sound made up. She changed the pony's name to . . . Joanna. Where was it all coming from? The only people she described absolutely accurately were Vanda, Peter and Uncle Bruno. There was no need to improve on the best things in her life.

The sound of a distant roll of thunder brought the writer back to the surface. Rain was already beginning to speck onto the glazed roof. But would it really rain, would there be a great big downpour? One of Joan's greatest delights was to sit inside this glass room while the rain hammered on the windows. Of course, you had to move pans and vases around to catch the drips where the roof leaked. But what did that matter?

She started to try to list other things which pleased her. All she could come up with was an image of the kitchen at Miss Lathom and Miss Parr's. The two teachers were encouraging the children to learn to cook. Not like in domestic science at school, where you seemed to take a whole afternoon to make gravy. No, the two spinsters had wonderfully untidy cookery books with lots of handwritten recipes, picked up on foreign holidays, which came slipping from between the printed pages. And each recipe seemed to begin with 'Chop an onion'.

Yes, thought Joan happily, it's always best when we're chopping onions. A flash of phospherescent lightning made dirty glass seem clean; and this was followed by another, almost instantaneous, roll of thunder. The storm must be nearly overhead. And here was the rain, real rain, great sheets of it, rolling down the sides of the dome. Oh it was wonderful, it was like being under the very top of the sea.

Joan rushed for a zinc bucket and placed it beneath the drip by the vine. A pan went on top of the radiator. The rest could take care of itself. Not quite. Joan's one horticultural effort, a pot of chives, was getting an unexpected drink. As she moved it, her thoughts returned to onions. Would they be chopping them for the refreshments for the musical evening? Perhaps not, because they might make the guests' breath smell. Miss Parr was writing letters of invitation to all the parents. When would Granny's arrive? Just look at that wonderfully swimming ceiling! And how much would it cost to send fibs across an ocean to America? The next crack of thunder was worthy of Judgment Day.

That bicycle summer included one week that would come to be recalled as patterned with red pillar boxes and variously coloured envelopes. Joan's letter went off to the United States, and Miss Lathom's invitations to the musical evening landed on the front doormat at Ingledene and on the bare boards of the Bells' hallway.

The sight of the postman on Sixth Drive must have stirred the Bells' next-door neighbour into action because, within minutes, brown envelope in hand, she was knocking at their front door. 'I've a confession to make,' she said nervously. 'This must have been lying behind my door for a week. I've been in Blackpool.' It was obvious that the woman was not enjoying being in the wrong; her conversations with Ethel Bell were usually restricted to complaints about the smell of petrol or about the height of unconfined privet hedges.

'Nothing good ever came in a brown envelope.' Ethel snatched it from the quivering hand and slammed the door. The letter was addressed to Mrs Dora Doran, but Gran'ma's eyes were so bad that it was automatically opened by her daughter. 'Oh my God,' cried Ethel, once she'd read the contents.

101

'Oh your God, what?' Vanda was attempting to mend the bentwood hatstand with black insulating tape. 'This thing's had it. It's given up under the weight of years of old coats.'

'Don't talk about weight,' groaned Ethel. 'Has Gran'ma lost enough, that's the question.' It was a warm morning and she fanned herself with the letter. 'They want her in hospital tomorrow. They're going to do her eyes, one at a time. Two separate operations. And just look at this list they've sent. It's worse than when you started at Barton. Nightgowns, towels, soap, toothbrush – that's a laugh.' Nevertheless Ethel looked perturbed. 'Mother's very heavy on nightgowns. What she's got are hanging in tatters. We might have to go out banging for some.'

'No way!' This cry came from the top of the stairs, and Gran'ma's words were heard through the sound of a recently flushed lavatory. 'I'm not without clothing coupons. I'll have new.'

'At your time of life?' Ethel was scandalised. It must have been the expression on the face up on the top landing that caused her to add, 'I'm sorry, Mother. It's just that *new* goes against the grain.'

'Come upstairs, Vanda,' bawled Gran'ma. 'And bring the Airwick. The sun's swelled the little window frame in the bathroom. I couldn't manage to get it open.'

As Vanda went to the kitchen to look for the green bottle the two elder generations continued to argue. Phrases like 'a complete waste of money' and 'I suppose you'd rather see me in some dead woman's winceyette' went flying up and down the narrow staircase.

The bottle of pungent air freshener was standing open, above the cat's dinner. Well, to be strictly accurate, above the remainders of two days of cat's dinners, on old enamel plates. Sometimes Vanda staged a personal fight against this ever-growing tide of chaos. But it was always a losing battle. Not for the first time she reflected that, when she eventually came to leave home, she was going to move herself into a world where nothing was chipped, nothing was broken – a world where everything would be delivered in shining cellophane wrappers. Vanda had a very definite vision of her future surroundings. Even the gilded antiques would look like new, and all her china vases would be filled with pure silk flowers so that never again would she find herself confronted by wither and decay.

And there'll be fitted carpets too, she thought, as she clattered up the bare steps – white fitted carpets.

'Got the bottle?' asked blind Gran'ma. 'I've made a pong that's just like the pong me own mother used to make. You'll be making that smell yourself, one day.'

'They'll have invented something to stop it by then.' Vanda pulled the wick out to its fullest length and the landing was flooded with the aroma of cinemas at opening time.

'Has she gone?' whispered Gran'ma.

'Yes.'

'What?'

Her granddaughter repeated 'Yes' more loudly. Dora must be getting deafer because Ethel was now in the living room, bawling disagreement at the Radio Doctor.

'I'm scared,' said Dora Doran quietly.

'Don't be.' The words seemed inadequate when Gran'ma must be thinking of surgeon's knives, and of being weighted down with sandbags after the operation. 'Shall we go into the bedroom and cut the cards?'

'No we shall not.' Energy had returned to Dora's voice. 'Those cards can be a bit *too* bloody accurate. I'd rather just take me chances. But you can do something for me. You can guide me back into bed. I want to talk to you.'

The only tidiness in the entire house lay on the floor between the bathroom and Dora's bedside. All obstacles had been moved into banks, on either side of an unobstructed blindwoman's pathway. 'I'm not even sure I want to see the world again,' grumbled Dora as she flopped onto the edge of the protesting bed and waited for Vanda to lift her legs. 'Does this room still look like Agecroft tip?'

'Oh no,' laughed Vanda. 'Worse than that, much worse. Whoops-a-daisy . . .' The huge legs were now on the bed. The nightdress was indeed a tattered disgrace.

'I've lost *some* weight,' said the old woman. 'But will it be enough? I want you to listen very carefully. There's a will.

103

You mother doesn't know there is but there is. I used to do the cards for Mr Adcock the solicitor, advised him on stocks and shares. The will's in his office at Swinton.' Gran'ma cocked an ear. 'Can she hear us? Go to the door and listen.'

'I don't need to go to the door. She's just slammed into the kitchen.'

'You're sure?'

'Positive.'

'I didn't bring her up to live like a pig. My house was always a little palace.'

'That's what I'm going to have.' Vanda looked round the bedroom. 'I'd tidy it for you, Dora, if I could. But it's reached the stage where there's nowhere to put anything.'

'Does she still hang onto all the old sauce bottles?'

'She hangs onto everything.'

'I should have let her go on the stage,' sighed Dora. 'I often think about it. I should never have stood in her way. If I'd let her go off to be a dancer she could have spread her trail of rubbish right round the British Isles. Each town could have had its own little bit.'

'You've got that wrong,' laughed Vanda. 'She'd have carried it with her!'

'Eeh I do love you,' said the woman, holding out her arms for a hug. 'I love you and that's why I've left you the lot. There'll be ructions!' It was obvious that the idea did not displease her. 'All I ask is one thing. Live clean. Put your rubbish out for the binmen and change your knickers every day – that's all your gran'ma wants for you. I don't want *you* kicking your way through last week's chip papers. Understood? Live fragrant, Vanda. Live fragrant and go and see the seven wonders of the world.'

'But where will you be?' A silly question because she already knew the answer. 'Please stop talking like this or we'll only end up in tears.' She hugged the mountainous woman. 'I don't want you to die.'

'Double-extra-outsize,' said Gran'ma. 'Women's XXOS, that's the size of nightgown that's called for. And even those'll be a close fit.' She peered sightlessly across the room. 'You'll find some white fivers inside the pocket of the best banjo case. And me clothing coupons used to live behind the electric clock, on the living-room mantelpiece.'

Gran'ma, it transpired, had a whole production worked out. Two everyday nightdresses were to come from Lewis's department store. But an especially good one, in white cambric, was to be purchased from Kendal Milne and Company – Manchester's own Harrods. And this garment was to be reserved for her coffin.

'Now you *are* getting morbid,' said Vanda. 'You could last for years.'

'If that's the case, it can stop in a drawer. But when the time comes, I don't want the Co-op. I want to be carried out of this house by the best. I want Laithwaite's of Pendleton. And I want an elm box with solid brass trimmings.' It was a long time since Vanda had seen Dora Doran enjoying herself as much as this. 'And while we're on the subject of boxes, when you inherit the tarot cards, you must make a box of your own for them. That was one of Miss Wilkinson's strictest rules – own cards, own box. And you must take it to a Catholic church and rub it with holy water. Otherwise demons can get in. I'm deadly serious about that – real demons. Understood? Climb down and get that cash.'

Neither did it finish there. 'I want "Lead, Kindly Light" playing at the funeral. I should think the Church of England would view me as a witch so you'd better try and get the Unitarians to bury me. I've a lot of time for the Unitarians; they're against nothing but closed minds.'

'Vanda!' It was Ethel calling peremptorily from downstairs.

'I've taken twenty pounds.' Vanda put the rest of the money back into the pocket, behind a little booklet entitled *Entertaining Your Friends with the Banjolele*. She didn't want to say the next bit but the words came out anyway. 'You're *not* going to die, are you?'

'I don't know, not for sure.' Dora was remarkably cheerful. 'And I've already told you that I'm not cutting the cards so don't start mithering. When you buy that best nightgown, get one with a bit of real lace round the neck. Brussels lace, not Nottingham. You'd best take another fiver.'

'What do your *instincts* tell you?' persisted Vanda. 'Miss Wilkinson always swore by your instincts, didn't she?'

'I've shut 'em down.' She could have been talking about a furnace.

'*Vanda*!' The repeated screech was loud enough to bring off wallpaper.

'That's a sound I won't miss,' nodded Dora.

Vanda fumbled for her hand. 'I'd miss you.'

'Are you shedding a tear?' asked the blindwoman happily.

'A bit.' It was the truth.

'That *is* nice.' Dora sounded genuinely grateful. 'It's really nice. No gran'ma could ask for more. When you're old yourself you'll understand that.'

'Vanda! How many times do I have to call you?'

'What a bitch!' said Gran'ma fervently. 'If I do live, it'll only be to spite her.'

Vanda blew her nose, got off the edge of the bed and headed for the door.

'I'm glad we had this conversation,' Dora called after her. 'Things could still go either way.'

The staircase seemed dingy after the sunlight of the bedroom but a pink angry moon was gazing up at Vanda. 'What's she rambling on about?' asked Ethel.

'Are her clothing coupons still behind the clock?'

'They could be.' Ethel looked shifty. 'And then again they could have been sold.'

'Well you'd better find some from somewhere. She's sending me shopping. And anyway, why *shouldn't* she have new?'

'Who said she couldn't? Certainly not me.' Ethel lowered her voice. 'Want to know why? I'm doing nothing to thwart her; chances are she's got more money tucked away than Martin's Bank. I don't want her leaving it to the cats' home.' Ethel shook out a huge panne velvet dress; it looked just like a field of pansies. 'I've got plans for that money of hers. You can't know how many times I've bitten my tongue and daydreamed about counting the cash instead.'

How funny when you're not going to get it, thought Vanda. Aloud she said, 'Isn't that velvet dress amazing?'

Ethel draped it across her own huge bulk; it looked like a Spanish shawl on a cooling tower. 'Think it'll suit me?'

Ethel saving a posh frock for herself? This was something new. 'Where do you propose wearing it?'

The other letter was the invitation to the musical evening. 'Now all I've got to do is find the music for "The Hole in the Elephant's Bottom".'

At Ingledene, Granny Briggs looked up from reading her copy of Miss Lathom's letter for the second time. 'Of course you can always tell a lady by her writing paper,' she said. 'And this has most definitely come from a lady. What's more, she was taught the same style of handwriting as I was. I must say that I would never have expected anything like this to come out of one of those little red-brick housing estates.' She managed to make it sound as though Joan had been keeping some delicious secret from her. Granny began to read aloud from Grace Lathom's letter.

'It could be that we are trying to revive something that died with the war. However, when the young people heard about the musical evenings of yesteryear, nothing would suit them but that they must have one of their own. If you would care to bring along music or an instrument, we would be delighted; inability to perform in no way lessens the warmth of this invitation.

'I should never have let the violin go!' cried Granny Briggs with more animation than Joan had heard from her in years. 'I should have kept up with my practising.'

'There are still two violins under the bed in the top attic,' Joan reminded her.

'You could hardly expect me to get to concert pitch in ten days. No, Bruno will have to do the performing for this family.'

'When he can only play the spoons?'

Granny squashed this with, 'There's plenty of time for him to learn a monologue. We've got the complete works of Kipling in the dining room. It wouldn't be a real musical evening without somebody reciting "The Green Eye of the Little Yellow God".'

Bruno chose this moment to return from Manchester. Granny's plan was immediately placed before him. 'It all sounds very jolly,' he said. 'But I can't see myself reciting. I'd rather sing that thing I did at the Harlequin Players party, "Don't Put Your Daughter on the Stage, Mrs Worthington".'

Granny went back to being her usual critical self. 'Isn't that by Noël Coward?'

'One of his best.'

'No thank you, Bruno,' she said coldly. 'I think you'll find they don't want any Noël Cowarding in Swinton. Of course he did sterling service during the war, and the rumours about him might just be rumours, but I don't think Miss Lathom would thank you for bringing them to people's minds.'

'Bringing what to people's minds?' Bruno asked this dangerously quietly.

'You know.' Granny's tone was even quieter and the glance towards Joan had 'Not in front of your niece' written all over it. Joan was amazed. Surely Granny couldn't know about the big black book at Scotland Yard?

'And since we're on the subject, Bruno,' the old critic continued inexorably, 'one of the men from the Harlequin Players was seen in Woolworth's, in Eccles, buying face powder.'

Bruno flushed. 'You have to powder over greasepaint. Even Laurence Olivier powders over greasepaint.'

'Mm,' Granny bit her mouth into a mean little line. 'If it was only for amateur theatricals, why didn't he get his sister, or even his mother, to purchase it?'

'What are you trying to suggest?'

'I'm suggesting we don't like gentlemen in face powder. Is that good enough for you?' Granny must have realised that an already taut atmosphere was tightening. In an attempt to lighten things she assumed her most studiedly arch 'joking' voice and said, 'The next thing you'll be telling me is that you amateur actors trot off for a nice drink with the pansy-boys at Tommy Duck's!'

'How dare you suggest I would be seen in such a pub?' he stormed.

'I dare do a lot of things,' said Granny cheerfully. 'I bet you wouldn't believe that when I played a gypsy czardas on the fiddle I always used to tie ribbons on the end of my bow.' Even the *idea* of a musical evening seemed to be bringing out unusual aspects of people's characters.

Peter Bird put his head round the door of the hairdressing room. One of his mother's clients was strung up to the permanent-waving machine, the other was under the chromium beehive of a dryer. 'I can't find them,' he said.

Peggy removed a cigarette from her mouth before she spoke. 'Did you look properly?' Her own white hair was in definite need of attention. Nicotine had tinted the front wave yellow again.

Noticing where his glance had rested Peggy said, 'Don't worry. I'll get it right for tonight.' She raised her voice so as to include the woman under the whirring dome: 'Won't be a minute, ladies.' To Peter she said, 'Go on, lead the way.'

It led into the front lounge. Peter talked as they travelled: 'I've even looked in the bill drawer. I don't think I've ever seen them.'

'You must have.' Peggy looked round the room for inspiration. 'They're little paper flags. Some have drawings of fish on them and some have a hen. In the old days we used to use them to go on the top of the pyramids of sandwiches. There should be a few blank ones too. I thought I could paint some new designs while Mrs Harrop's hair cooks.' She was struck by a sudden thought. 'They might just have been left inside the big photo album.'

'No. I know that album backwards.' As if to prove his point, Peter took it down from the bookshelves and riffled through the thick cardboard pages. 'See, no flags.' But something else fell to the ground.

Peggy bent down and picked up an old dance programme. It had deckled edges and a silken tassel. 'My God, that takes me back! North Staffs Hotel, 1932. See that exclamation mark against number seventeen – the interval Excuse Me waltz? I got a proposal in the middle of that dance.'

'From my father?'

'Him?' Peggy's tone had turned scathing. 'He proposed in a bus shelter – outside a bankrupt pot-bank. Which was just about his mark. Mind you, he was the best-looking lad for miles around.' She took a drag on her cigarette which led to a violent fit of coughing. It was a while before Peggy managed to gasp, 'How are the mighty fallen, eh?'

Peter was looking at the one photograph of his father inside the album, the one taken at the working lads' camp. 'Why are there no more pictures of him? There used to be all the war ones.'

'His thirst got bigger.'

Peter didn't understand. Peggy enlightened him with, 'People in pubs stopped remembering he was a war hero so the supply of booze dried up. Nowadays he carries all the photos around to remind them. He carts his press cutting around too. I only know that because the landlord of the Dog and Partridge was once good enough to bring them back. They came home before the hero did.' She dimped out her cigarette. 'He'd passed out on that bit of wasteland in front of the Shivers.'

'Is he coming tonight?' The idea of his father lurching between the guests of a musical evening was not one that appealed to him.

'No he is not.' Peggy was very firm about this. 'Now he's out of work again, I control the purse strings. He's going to be handed just enough to keep him boozing till closing time. We'll play "God Save the King" at ten o'clock, the Dog and Partridge closes at half past. Yes, it's carriages at ten tonight.'

'You know how he gets wind of things . . .' Peter was unconvinced.

'All we can do is hope for the best. I did think of asking Miss Lathom to light a candle for it. But how could she go to church and ask God to keep somebody away from a party? I can't find the little silver forks, either.'

Peggy automatically headed for the sideboard where canteens of cutlery were stacked behind one of the doors. But

Peter shook his head: 'Not there. The smallest leather box has gone from the top of the pile.'

'It can't have. They've never been out since the Lifeboat flag day meeting.' Peggy pushed a hand into the dark recess and produced something that Peter must have missed. 'Whatever's this?' It was a piece of cardboard torn from the front of a Woodbine cigarette packet, and it bore a scrawled message which Peggy proceeded to read aloud. ' "IOU one set of forks (boxed) signed Bird VC." ' Hasn't he got a Christian name? What does he think he is, a living newspaper headline? He's even dated it. He took them today.'

'But what does it mean?'

'It means he's popped them,' said Peggy grimly. 'My Auntie Ellen would turn in her grave if she knew that her good pastry forks had ended up in some pawnbroker's safe.' Fury and frustration mingled in her voice. 'And *still* he has to try and be heroic, and do the honourable thing, and leave an IOU. You remember this moment, Peter. You remember it for when I'm had up for murder.'

'Shall I borrow Miss Lathom's set?'

'I suppose you'd better. But don't go telling the whole story.'

It struck Peter as bitterly unfair that his mother was the one who had to sound ashamed. He attempted to reassure her with, 'I'll just say we've mislaid them.' Peter only hoped that this white lie would not bring on another spate of praying. There was too much else to occupy him on this busiest of days.

'Oh my God,' breathed Peggy. 'That shampoo and set's still under the dryer. Miss Harrop's hair must be boiled rigid!' She dived for the hairdressing room and Peter made his way to the front door. 'Try not to let the midges in,' Peggy called over her shoulder.

The relentlessly warm weather had brought late swarms of insects. In Miss Lathom's front garden he could see Joan Stone batting a cloud of hovering transparent wings aside as she attempted to cut parsley with a pair of kitchen scissors; Miss Lathom grew all her herbs in amongst the flowers. 'I'm bitten to bits,' called out Joan. 'And poor Henry's just been doused with flea powder. He's very ambitious this morning so watch what you're doing with that garden gate.'

Peter didn't speak until he was near enough not to be overheard. 'My dad's pinched some silver forks.'

'I know.'

'How?'

'Well, I didn't know they were forks.' Joan straightened up with her bunch of parsley. 'Miss Parr's just come back on the bus from town and I overheard her saying that she saw him sneaking into that Jewish pawnbroker's at Pendleton. This parsley's running a bit to seed. Do you think that Sally Morgenstern could be a Jewish name? I'm still waiting to hear from her.'

But Peter didn't want to think about Joan's American penfriend; if his father had managed to get his hands on money this morning, what sort of condition would he be in by tonight? Solid silver had to be worth quite a bit. When Peggy doled out the cash, she had some control over the extent of his drinking. But now it seemed that Bird VC was floating free. Oh God, whatever state would he roll home in? And I'm *not* going to say my prayer again, thought Peter. Too late, it was already echoing around his head; as it ended he added, 'And please don't let him be sick inside the grate again.'

By late August the nights were starting to draw in, and Peter was determined to brighten up the dusk of this very special evening. 'I've hung our Chinese lanterns in the branches of the big poplar at the end of the garden,' he said to his mother.

'Those old things? They must date back to the ark.' But Peggy didn't really sound critical; Peter could tell that she was enjoying the idea of playing hostess too much for that. The refreshments were all laid out in the lounge, the piano had been moved into the hairdressing room, and the maiden ladies from next door were finishing arranging branches of preserved copper beech in two china umbrella stands. They had copied the idea from their Constance Spry album.

So far, only one guest had arrived – Mrs Musker, the pianist from Odette Ashworth's. She was going to play for Vanda's dancing and Ethel was rumoured to be paying her seven and sixpence for the evening. Nevertheless, the accompanist had come dressed very much as a guest in a flowered silk frock with matching coatee. She also wore big gleaming glasses. 'They're the new bifocals,' she explained. 'It's their first outing. I'll be quite happy to accompany anybody else – that's if I can see. These specs are a bit like wading under water.'

'Where are the matches?' Peter asked his mother. 'I need to light the lanterns.'

'I suppose you're getting too old for me to be able to say you mustn't play with fire. By the gas stove.' Peggy's hair had been washed back to white and she was wearing make-up, which made her look a lot younger. What's more, she'd bought a black grosgrain dress in Mrs Critchley's summer sale, especially for the occasion.

As Peter went through to collect the matches and the kitchen ladders, he reflected that Peggy looked like a woman who didn't have a care in the world. Nobody would have guessed that her husband had been missing since mid morning.

It seemed as though everybody had chosen to arrive at the same moment. Ethel Bell looked just like a jolly corporation flowerbed, and Vanda was in a blouse and skirt but carrying a soft-topped case which promised something more exciting for later. The front door was still open. At the bottom of the path a taxi was disgorging Granny Briggs and Joan and Bruno. Joan's uncle was carrying two bound volumes with parchment bookmarkers sticking out of them.

But Peter wasn't looking at the books. He was much more struck by Bruno himself, now paying off the driver and telling him to keep the change.

You could have all *my* change, thought Peter. You are beautiful. As quickly as he thought this, a mantle of guilt wrapped itself round the idea. It surely couldn't be right to be wondering what his friend's uncle would look like with fewer clothes on? Correction: with no clothes on at all. In the past Bruno had merely been a shadowy Ingledene figure, glimpsed in the distance. Granny Briggs, not being made of hospitality, always insisted that Joan's young visitors must stay in the

113

garden. But here was Bruno in big close-up, looking spruced and gleaming and made of friendliness.

If I was a woman I expect I'd be thinking he'd make a good husband. These variously torrid and romantic notions had thrown Peter's eyes into soft focus. It was only as Joan muttered 'Did you ever see such a bloody awful frock in your whole life?' that his vision sharpened itself up to an extent where he was in a state to notice what she was wearing. 'She got it out of a locked cupboard,' announced Joan. 'I think it must have belonged to my mother.' With its pink taffeta bodice and skimpy net skirt, the dress looked like something on a bridesmaid in a photograph taken in 1936. Joan continued to be outraged: 'And you know how self-conscious I am about my skinny arms. Arms? They look like sticks of rhubarb!'

But two much more self-conscious people were already edging their way up the garden path. Mrs Naylor was one of Peggy's regular clients; she and her husband were big in the Eccles Amateur Operatic Society. In fact they were known as the Anne Ziegler and Webster Booth of Ravensdale Estate. The man, in black jacket and striped trousers, looked like a worried little bank manager. His wife was all finger-waved hair and printed georgette, and she was clutching a tissue-paper parcel. It wasn't a present because you could see the toes of her silver evening shoes poking out of the wrapping.

They hadn't even been introduced when Granny Briggs said, 'Don't I know you from *The Merry Widow*, at the Broadway Theatre, Eccles? It *is* Count Danilo, isn't it?'

'Yes,' said Mr Naylor seriously. 'And this is my leading lady – as in real life.'

Granny treated his wife to an analytical glare. 'Used you not to be in the chemist's at Patricroft? I seem to have some memory of your saying "Your prescription's ready, Mrs Briggs." '

'I only worked there until my marriage. And then I returned to the shop to do my war-work.'

This was a reply that was above reproach. Peter, feeling himself to be the host, was keeping a watchful ear and eye on the proceedings. The guests were already mingling nicely as

114

sherry and fruit cup were served in the lounge – Miss Lathom and Miss Parr were in charge of the refreshments. The room looked much bigger because the piano and the music cabinet had been moved into the hairdressing room. Grace Lathom also appeared larger; she had discarded her usual smock in favour of an Arab-looking garment. 'It's a copy of something Berber tribesmen wear on their visits into town,' she was explaining to a thoroughly approving Granny Briggs.

'Just her cup of tea,' hissed her granddaughter. 'There's nothing she likes better than the *National Geographical* in the doctor's waiting room.' Joan was still smarting at being got up to look like a pink Christmas cracker.

Vanda, who had slipped up to the bathroom to change, now reappeared disguised as a Hungarian peasant. This was for the dance she was going to do in the first half. Peter had said that the programme was to be sherry, entertainment, refreshments, and then more entertainment. For the moment, the piles of sandwiches and vol-au-vents were covered with damp table napkins to keep them moist. It had to be the warmest evening of the year.

'Ladies and gentlemen,' boomed Miss Lathom. 'May I have your attention for a moment please, while I give you a toast. The toast is *joy* – let it be unconfined.'

Everybody raised their glasses, said 'Joy' rather nervously and took a sip of their drinks. Mr Naylor added 'Hear hear,' and Mrs Musker let out a discreet hiccup.

'Joy who?' Vanda asked Peter. But he didn't answer her. He was too busy watching Miss Lathom, who suddenly looked close to tears.

Peter moved swiftly to her side. 'Are you OK?' he asked anxiously.

She attempted to reassure him with, 'I'm absolutely fine. It's just that Father always proposed that particular toast. It brought back such dear, dead times . . . I'm absolutely fine, dear. Let's get them round the piano.'

Miss Parr's arm went protectively round her friend. 'You're sure you'll be all right, Grace? I could easily slip home for the sal volatile.' Tonight, Iris Parr looked more like somebody's mistress than a schoolteacher, in black crepe de

115

Chine and little diamond earrings. 'We don't want you getting into one of your states.'

Miss Lathom shrugged her off gratefully but manfully. 'Get the guests through, get them through.'

The programme opened with Vanda's dance. It was the same kind of czardas that Granny Briggs had once played on her fiddle. This brought Granny into the conversation that followed, and in a very animated way. 'Yes, ribbons on my bow,' she said as she accepted a second glass of sherry. 'And once I even wore brass hoops in my ears, tied on with cotton. But that was at a party in an Indian hill station.'

As Mr and Mrs Naylor took their places at the piano, Peter started to relax. It was all going exactly as he had imagined it. Mr Naylor had one formal hand on the upright grand, the other was placed reverently upon his wife's shoulder. 'Fold Your Wings of Love Around Me': they were singing it in unison. Dusk was really falling now, behind the lanterns glowing in the trees. And against this backdrop the singers looked just like statues.

At the end of the song the couple bowed graciously to enthusiastic applause, and Peggy rushed round with a plate of hot cheese straws, 'To be going on with.'

'For our next number,' announced Mr Naylor, very much the star of the Eccles Amateurs, 'we would like to sing "The Keys of My Heart".'

'Oh dear,' said Miss Parr, perfectly audibly, '*we* were going to do that.'

'If I may make a suggestion . . .' It was obvious that Mrs Naylor, once up on her feet, lost all social apprehension. 'How would it be if we did it as a concerted item? We'll begin, and you and Miss Lathom can take alternate choruses.'

So now there were four statues round the little piano. And on the piano stool Mrs Musker was working up a bead sweat.

'I will give you a coach and six . . .' boomed Miss Lathom when it came to her turn.

'Six black horses, black as pitch.
Madam, will you walk,
Madam, will you talk,

116

Madam, will you walk and talk with me?'

And Miss Parr sang back that no she wouldn't walk, or talk, or indeed follow any of Miss Lathom's vocal suggestions.

The entertainment sped forward happily, and in next to no time they were at the interval, which was all balancing acts with plates, and 'You must try one of these little whist pies,' and 'Could I trouble you for another stick of celery?' Vanda had been upstairs to change her outfit again. This time she was kitted out in a shiny red plastic raincoat, in preparation for 'April Showers' with tap routine to follow.

As Ethel Bell explained to Granny Briggs: 'When she opens the umbrella, it's in all the shades of the rainbow.'

'This dancing must have cost you a pretty penny,' was the munching reply.

'Oh yes,' nodded Ethel. 'But tonight's her swan song.'

'Pardon?' Vanda whirled round on the heels of her red tap shoes. 'Why should tonight be my swan song?'

Ethel chose to address her reply to Mrs Briggs. Was it the refined atmosphere of the evening which had got her talking posh? 'It's something I've given a lot of thought to. Vanda went for an audition at Hulme Hippodrome and men started fancying her titties.' Seemingly unaware of the fact that Granny Briggs was swaying with shock, Ethel continued: 'That audition gave me a glimpse of the shape of things to come. I saw what my own mother must have seen, when I was stage-struck. I'm not going to let any daughter of mine be mauled by men. Not even with their eyes.' Ethel grabbed a passing chicken wing. 'So now I've decided that she's going to go in for the new big glamour occupation. She's going to be an air hostess.'

'Just like that?' This came from a furious Vanda. 'And what about the Folies Bergère?'

'What *about* the Folies Bergère!' was Ethel's heartfelt reply. Returning the conversation towards Granny Briggs's direction she added, 'This dirty old man even suggested there was money to be made from showing her etceteras in Paris. I don't mind telling you it's given me sleepless nights because I *have* invested in her. But if that's all the stage has to offer, she'll be better off going up in aeroplanes.'

Remembering how the old theatre had seemed to whisper to her, Vanda burst out with, 'But that's not what I want.'

Ethel's reply was equally spirited: 'It's not what I had in mind for you, either. I'd got me sights set on Sadler's Wells. But the family bosom got in the way.'

'Ladies and gentlemen,' boomed out Miss Lathom, 'would you please recharge your glasses and move back into the other room?'

The second half began with Bruno Briggs's recitations. Everybody was very startled when this well-spoken young man went into broad Lancashire for 'Albert and the Lion'. But for an encore his voice turned icily posh as he declaimed Robert Browning's chilling description of 'My Last Duchess'.

> 'That's my last Duchess painted on the wall,
> Looking as if she were alive. I call
> That piece a wonder, now . . .'

It's you who's a wonder, thought Peter. After all, there was no harm in just looking. But the gym cloakroom at Barton Grammar had taught him that dark red hair on the head might mean bright ginger elsewhere. I do hope not, his thoughts continued, I can't stand that kind of rude ginger hair. And then his mind split into two voices; one was berating the other for even thinking of Bruno in an erotic light. Guilt was at war with romance. With *lust*, went the left-hand side of his brain. OK, he replied silently, with lust. But he's much sexier than Toby Eden. The two parts of his brain fused back together as he wondered what Joan would make of his having ideas like this about a normal man. Peter turned round to look for her but all he found was Vanda, disconsolate and unhappy.

As the poem ended and warm applause rang round the room, she said to Peter, 'My mother's announced I've got to be an air hostess. I don't want to work for BOAC, I'm going on the stage. Oh she's a contrary old bag! And she doesn't care a bit about Gran'ma Dora. From the way Mum's beaming and smiling, nobody would guess that Dora had her second eye done today.'

'Did you ring the hospital?' asked Peter, as he watched Mrs Musker going through some music which Mrs Naylor had produced from her husband's briefcase.

'The switchboard just said she wasn't round from the anaesthetic yet.'

'She'll be all right.'

' "Bless This House",' announced Mrs Naylor. 'An old one but a good one.' Placing her hands together as though in prayer, she closed her eyes and began to sing in a pious moan.

This is getting boring, thought Peter. It didn't stay boring. *Bang* went the front door. And it was such a loud bang that Mrs Musker's hand froze in mid-air while Mrs Naylor's plea to the Deity to 'keep us pure and free from sin' dwindled to nothing. The sound of unsteady footsteps started to come from the hall. Peggy made a frightened move towards the door. But it was already opening.

'Well, well, well, well.' As Eddie Bird swayed into the room he was dipping into fish and chips, wrapped in newspaper. Peter noted that somewhere along the way his father must have mislaid his sports jacket. And had he been in a fight? There was certainly crusted blood beneath his nose and on the front of his shirt. Trust it to be that awful old striped shirt, the one with the turned front and the shortened sleeves. 'Well, well, well.' He was into his second chorus.

'Change the record, Eddie.' Peggy spoke tensely.

Her husband was almost liquidly relaxed. 'Not invited, eh?' he crooned. And Peter was irresistibly reminded of *The Sleeping Beauty*, though even the Fairy Carabosse could not have had such hairy arms as this.

Eddie's eyes settled on Vanda's bosom. 'Fancy a chip?' he said to her.

'Watch it,' muttered Ethel warningly.

Not much scared, Vanda was nevertheless aware that this was a man who was out of control. 'No thank you.' He looked liable to topple in any direction.

'Anybody going to offer me a drink?'

119

Miss Lathom, very much the commanding officer, stepped forward. 'There's sherry and there's fruit cup, Bird.'

Eddie pulled himself erect and saluted sharply. And in that moment you could see the ghost of former magnificence. 'I'll take the sherry, sir.' Then he went floppy again, and his tone turned mawkish as he said to Peggy, 'I'm sorry, my darling. I didn't know I'd gone and forgot your birthday.'

'It isn't my birthday.'

'Then what the fuck is it?'

Eddie had used the one word none of the guests had ever expected to hear in polite company. 'Come along, Mabel,' said Mr Naylor to his wife. 'I can't permit you to listen to conversation like this.'

'Can't you?' Suddenly charged with angry energy, Eddie slammed the door and barred their way. 'And what did you do in the big war, Daddy?' He looked a giant against Naylor, who could have come off the top of a wedding cake.

'I was assigned to the Inland Revenue at Blackpool.'

'You really *did* fight for your country, didn't you? Blackpool, eh! Was it bed and breakfast or full board?'

Glass of sherry in hand, Miss Lathom interrupted him with, 'Here you are, Mr Bird. We're having a little musical evening.'

Eddie downed the drink in one swallow, then handed back the glass. 'Since you're asking,' he muttered, 'I *will* have the other half. A musical evening, eh?' As he wrapped his lips round the words, Eddie's eyes fell upon his son. 'And what are you going to sing? "There Are Fairies at the Bottom of Our Garden"?'

Peter wished he could just evaporate. As it was, he managed to stammer out, 'I'm not singing anything. My voice hasn't settled down enough for real singing yet.'

'Miracle to me that it ever broke,' muttered Eddie. Beaming at the assembled company he explained, 'I didn't think he'd got any bollocks.'

'Now we *are* leaving, Mabel.' Mr Naylor draped a georgette stole around her shoulders.

'You are going nowhere.' Eddie sounded dangerous. 'This is my house and I give the orders.' His bleary gaze took in

Bruno. 'You! You look as though you've got red blood in your veins; don't tell me they got you to sing a song?'

Peter watched Bruno closely. He was the only person in the room who didn't look embarrassed or scared. He just faced straight up to Eddie and said, 'I did "Albert and the Lion".'

Eddie considered this for a moment. 'I quite like "Albert and the Lion",' he admitted. 'Put it there.' He held out his hand for Bruno to shake. 'And where's that drink?'

'Just coming up.' Miss Lathom put it into his other hand. 'Do be good, Mr Bird.' She could have been speaking to a wayward child. 'When you want to, you can be so nice and entertaining.'

'What are *you* going to sing for us?' It was Mrs Musker piping up from the piano stool. She was addressing Eddie.

'I could recite "The Good Ship *Venus*",' he said, winking wickedly.

'Oh no you couldn't.' Peggy spoke firmly – too firmly.

'Who couldn't?

'Twas on the good ship *Venus*,
Oh boy you should have seen us,
The bosun's head was a pro in bed
And the main mast was a . . . .'

'No . . . stop it.' Peggy was shaking with shame. 'You'd spoil anything. Anything at all. People have gone to real trouble. And you . . . you're just a wrecker.'

'Don't cry, babe.' Eddie's tones were much too intimate for a social gathering. 'Don't break your little heart. I'm not worth it.'

It's like being in a bedroom, thought Peter.

'Let me do something to make you proud of me again, Peg. Tell you what, I'll tell them about when I went to Buckingham Palace to get me VC.'

'For God's sake, not that old chestnut!' No sooner had the words exploded out of Peggy than she must have noticed the circle of expectant faces. Now she qualified her statement with, 'Go on then, if you must.'

'It was like this,' said Eddie importantly. And then a

puzzled look crossed his face. 'I've forgot what I was going to say.'

Peter, well used to this symptom of his father's drinking, had heard the Buckingham Palace story so often that (purely for his mother's sake) he was able to prompt him: 'Four paces forward and salute . . .'

'Oh yes.' Memory must have flooded back through the haze of alcohol. 'Yes, we was conducted into the ballroom at the palace. Four paces forward and salute, was the order. But the King said, "At ease, Bird." And the Queen said, "After all you've done for the country, I should jolly well hope so. After this, we just hope you have a long and happy life." The Queen of England said that to me.' His eyes raked the room and settled on Mr Naylor. 'And what did she say to you?'

'I've never actually met her.'

'Well, I actually have. You're looking at somebody who has. And that somebody wasn't even invited to your fancy party.' Self-pity turned to fury: 'Well, you can sod off, the lot of you. I might be out of work but this is still my house and your dainty party's over.'

Ravensdale Estate was made of unwritten rules but there was none to cover a situation like this; everybody simply filed out as quickly as they could. Peter just thanked God that a warm night meant nobody had coats to collect. And when everybody had gone, the Chinese lanterns – still shining down from the trees – seemed to mock the remains of a nice idea. Perhaps Miss Lathom's letters of invitation had been right; maybe they'd been trying to revive something which had died with the war.

'In a way, I almost felt sorry for Mr Bird.' Ethel Bell was panting her way past the hospital wall. 'And we've left your music behind. But, my God, if your father had ever carried on like that I'd have chucked him out years sooner.'

Vanda's father was a figure who was rarely mentioned. 'Why doesn't Mrs Bird chuck Mr Bird out?'

'He's got the law on his side. And I'm a big strong woman – that's the difference.'

'You're a big bully.' In the exodus from Hawksway, Vanda

122

had managed to grab hold of her little suitcase; the handle was already beginning to feel sweaty under her grip. 'Air hostess? It's not as if you've ever been up in a plane! You're not condemning me to that. Me, who was sick on the Isle of Man ferry.'

Ethel fanned herself with a podgy hand. 'Just think of it, Rome, Paris, Cincinnati. You can always take Kwells until you get used to it.'

Vanda remembered the promised legacy, the one that Gran'ma Dora had said would eventually be hers. 'I'm already planning to see the seven wonders of the world.'

'How? What with?'

It wouldn't do to tell. 'I'll get there.' They were coming within sight of the lights of the council estate.

'Anyway, I bet I could buy and sell those Birds twice over,' said Ethel. 'But I couldn't help feeling for him. Hard to think he's the same hero who was once paid good money to advertise hair cream.'

'But you won't stop me going there.' It was half a question and half a statement. 'I can still go round and play at Peter's, can't I?'

Ethel chose not to react. Instead she said, 'War comes at a terrible price, Vanda. See that house over there? Two drowned at sea. See that one opposite? Her husband bailed out on a parachute and he's never been seen from that day to this.'

'That settles it. I'm definitely not going in for air-hostessing. Have you got any more morbid stories up your sleeve?'

But Ethel returned from the past to the present with, 'What's a policeman doing up our front path? Hey, you,' she called out indignantly. 'Have I been broken into?'

The policeman shook his head and stayed where he was.

'Well, what then?' Ethel quickened her pace. 'I'm not paid to come rushing up to you, you know. It should be the other way round.'

He was old for a policeman and solemn-looking. 'I only stopped here because I want us to go somewhere where we can sit down.'

'Are you after a date?' Ethel nevertheless looked worried.

'Find your key and let's get inside.' His bicycle was propped up against the drainpipe.

Ethel opened the door. 'It's Mother, isn't it? Mrs Doran. Has something happened to her?'

'I'm afraid it has. Look, why don't you go in and sit down?'

'Why don't you cut the cackle? Is she dead?'

The policeman flipped the top of his notebook from under its strap of black elastic and peered at a lined page. 'The hospital say they regret to inform you that she never came round after the anaesthetic. Mrs Doran passed away at a quarter to seven tonight.'

'I knew it was that,' cried Ethel, which struck Vanda as ridiculous because her mother's first thoughts had been of burglars. 'I could have told them it would happen. All that weight should never have gone under the knife.'

'Would you like me to put the kettle on?' asked the policeman.

Ethel was eyeing him up and down. 'Are you a forty-eight-inch chest?' she asked.

'Yes,' was the startled answer.

'Thought so. I can size anybody at a glance. It's a professional knack. I've got a very nice Harris tweed overcoat in your size, going cheap — only fifteen bob. Just suit you. How about it?'

'Not me, love.' He looked appalled. He tried to redeem this with, 'You see, in my job we have to be very careful what we buy and where from.'

'Just what are you suggesting? There's nothing iffy about my overcoats. You heard him, Vanda, you was a witness.'

But Vanda was already overcome with a desolate sense of loss. It was like nothing she'd ever known; a muggy night was suddenly the coldest, emptiest place on earth. 'For God's sake, Mother,' she cried. 'Me gran'ma's dead!'

The policeman seemed grateful to have matters returned to a proper footing. 'That's right. And the lady almoner wants you to go and collect the death certificate in the morning.'

'I don't have to be told what to do when somebody dies,'

snapped Ethel. 'And if you're not going to try that coat on you can sling your hook.'

'Goodnight,' said the policeman, almost falling over Dick Barton, the black cat.

'It's not been very good so far but I suppose we must live in hopes.' Closing the door after him and putting the chain on the lock, Ethel continued her grumbling with, 'I never even got to sing "The Hole in the Elephant's Bottom".' However, she soon brightened up enough to say, 'It's just possible that I might have ended this day a much richer woman than I began it. You can rest assured she'll never have got round to making a will. Now I suppose there'll have to be all the trouble of applying for probate.'

'There *is* a will.' This much Vanda could manage to say. Not trusting herself to deal with more, she fled upstairs. Even as she gained the top landing Vanda realised that this would be a different upstairs – a place where familiar items could suddenly seem haunted. And all because an old woman would never come back to use them.

'Hey, you!' Ethel was calling up from the bottom of the stairs. 'Where is this will?'

'Adcock's at Swinton.'

'That slimy bastard.' Ethel all but spat the words into the air.

'She used to read the cards for him.'

'Yes, and years before she used to do a lot more than that. Come down here.'

Vanda stayed where she was. 'I'm upset.'

'We're both upset. We don't know what's in that will.' Ethel picked up the black cat by the scruff of its neck. Opening the little hall window, she pitched Dick Barton out into the hot black night. 'At least that's the end of pandering to that bloody animal of hers.'

'What if she's watching?' gasped Vanda. 'What if she saw what you just did?' Though she felt upset enough to weep, tears seemed reluctant to come.

'Don't be so daft.' Ethel's voice was full of contempt. 'I'll prove how daft you are. Mother?' she called out. 'If you're here, why don't you knock that trilby off the hatstand?'

125

Nothing happened.

'That's always been my answer to the Spiritualists.' Ethel opened the top button of her flowered frock and blew down the cleavage. 'Phew! You could coddle an egg down there.'

In the midst of heat, Vanda could not stop thinking of cold death. 'Where will Gran'ma be? Will they have kept her in bed with a sheet over her?'

'In this weather? If they've any sense they'll have her on a marble slab in the mortuary.' Ethel plucked at one of her own chins. 'I suppose she didn't happen to mention what was in that will? Flinging the cat out might just have been a bit hasty; she was awkward enough to have made him her sole heir.'

'No, she left it all to me.' It was out before Vanda had given any thought to the consequences of what she was saying.

For once Ethel seemed at a loss for words; she just clung to the bottom banister with her mouth opening and shutting. Finally she managed, 'To you?' With new energy, which seemed to be growing dangerously, she repeated herself: 'To you? You cunning little bitch.'

Up on the top landing, Vanda had been hoping for something, anything, that would unblock her tears; and the word 'bitch' did it. 'You're not a bit sorry she's dead,' she sobbed. 'I want me gran'ma. I want a cuddle off her and I wouldn't care if it did smell of camphorated oil.' The one thing she didn't want to do was even look at horrible Ethel, who had never given her so much as a kiss in her whole life. Vanda just turned away and stumbled through the first door she found.

It led into Gran'ma Dora's room, that haunt of broken banjos and overflowing teachests. Blinded by tears, Vanda followed the path between the heaps of rubbish – the path which had always been kept clear to allow the old woman to reach her bed. As she flung herself down on the mattress, Vanda could smell lingering traces of the camphor. Something uncomfortable was pressing into her face; it was one of the elastic bands that Dora had always used to tie up her skinny plait – perhaps the only skinny thing there'd ever been about this great big generous woman. 'Come back, Dora,'

126

sobbed her granddaughter. 'Come back and prove her wrong. She's the bitch, not me.'

Inside Vanda's head a picture began to form. This image was so strong that it could have been fashioned from thousands of miniature tubes of neon light. What she was seeing was the pack of tarot cards, fanned out across a black silk handkerchief, and they were all but breathing with life.

A message?

Vanda opened her eyes. The real cards were where they had always been, on the Jaffa orange crate stand at the side of Dora's bed. And now the girl remembered having been enjoined to keep the cards but to destroy their box. Something about making one of her own and taking it to a Catholic church and rubbing it with holy water. But all that had been said when Gran'ma was alive. With Dora dead, the last thing the girl wanted to do was throw away anything that had belonged to her. No, she would keep the tarot pack *and* the box.

And that is where Vanda Bell made her big mistake.

Joan wasn't precisely eavesdropping. The morning after the musical evening everybody slept late at Ingledene, their rest having been much disturbed by thunderstorms during the night. Perhaps these had also made the postman late. The mail didn't plop onto the mat until half past eleven. As Joan bent down to pick it up, she could hear Granny rumbling away at Bruno in the front drawing room. She was saying, 'What I don't understand is this: it rains through the attic roof, nothing shows on the level of the bedrooms, and then the damp ends up down here. Your grandfather would have explained it in a minute.'

Joan had picked up one postcard and one envelope with red, white and blue edges. There was a sender's address on the back. And, yes, it was from Sally Morgenstern of East 68th Street, New York City.

Granny was still rattling on in the distance. 'Sometimes I think we'd be better getting out of this leaking wreck of a house and moving to somewhere like that place last night.'

The shudder in her voice was perfectly audible through a closed oak door as she added, 'But what if we got an awful man like that as a neighbour?'

The postcard said that the library were now holding a copy of *Our Dearest Emma*, purchased at Granny Briggs's request. Fancy her asking for that! All of Barton Grammar knew that *Our Dearest Emma* was 'a bit near the knuckle'.

'Bruno, I want you to speak to Joan. It's about Mr Bird's language. I want you to tell her which words she must forget she ever heard.' Joan found herself torn between a desire to open the envelope from America and an urge to put her ear right up against the wood.

'What words were those?'

'You know.'

'Why don't you tell me and then I'll be absolutely sure I've got the right ones?'

The teasing mischief in his voice was obviously wasted on Granny Briggs. 'Nothing would get me to say them out loud. I'll write them down . . .'

'Oh *those* words,' said Bruno after a moment. 'At least, I think I know which ones you mean. It would have helped if you'd put all the letters in, instead of just capitals and dashes. You do mean "bollocks" and . . .'

'You're not too old for a smacking,' said Granny. 'Never let me hear you use that word again.'

'Then how am I meant to tell her?'

'Just do it,' snapped Olive Briggs. 'Of course there can be no question of her being allowed to go back to that place. I don't want the boy here, either.'

'He seemed a perfectly nice little boy.'

'Yes, and what if the pair of them start getting romantic ideas? Hitler was quite right about one thing, blood will out.'

At Ingledene, Hitler was somebody who had never quite gone away. Joan knew that before the war Granny had been a member of an organisation called the British Women's Fascisti. Mind you, to hear Granny tell it, so had half of high society. Not that Olive pretended to be as posh as that. But she plainly considered herself on a higher social plane than the Birds. 'What if that Peter boy ended up wanting to marry her?'

Uncle Bruno was at his most sardonic: 'Somehow I don't see that as a possibility.'

'Well, I see it as my Christian duty to keep them apart.'

Her son began to sound irritated: 'I think the vicar might argue with you there.'

'The fact that Mr Lunn wears his celluloid collar back-to-front does not mean that he knows God any better than I know God.' Without warning, the door opened and Granny Briggs looked straight out at Joan. 'Thought so!' she said triumphantly. 'Listeners never hear any good of themselves. And I don't want you seeing Vanda, either. We don't need to know old-clothes dealers, not socially. Give me that mail.'

'One of them's mine.'

'Which alters nothing; I've every right to know what's coming into this house.'

Joan suddenly saw red. 'Well, you'll be pleased to hear that the library's got your dirty book in.'

Crack. With one hand Granny slapped Joan across the face, with the other she snatched at the letter and the postcard. 'Morgenstern?' she said, peering at the envelope. 'Don't tell me you're corresponding with Jews?'

Bruno raised his hand in a mock-fascist salute: 'Heil Hitler!'

'You can make mock. But Hitler got the roads built, he got the trains running on time. We travelled on the Continent in those days. We saw the changes.'

'This was also the man who murdered millions.'

'I still don't like Jews writing here.' Nevertheless she handed the envelope to Joan. 'I can't help it, I don't. And I don't want them knocking at this front door, either.'

'She lives in New York,' protested Joan.

'Good. Let's hope she stays there. Thank God this weather's beginning to cool down, it's been enough to fray *any*body's temper.' This was the nearest to an apology that Granny Briggs was ever likely to offer. 'Let's try and get things back to normal.' As she marched off down the corridor, she called over her shoulder, 'Your Uncle Bruno's got an etiquette lesson for you – on a piece of paper. It's words we don't say.'

'It's all right,' Joan reassured him. 'I heard that too.'

Seeming to guess at something of her misery and confusion, Bruno said, 'I, for one, had a lovely time last night. I've already written Miss Lathom a thank-you note. I really liked your friends.'

'Only now I can't see them.'

'Oh come on,' he urged her, 'you've got a bike, you've got imagination – of course you can see them.'

'But why does she have to be like that?'

'Because she's very conscious of being shabby-genteel. She was never on her dignity when we *did* have money. She was nice then. You'll have to do what I do, be a bit cunning. I lead a whole life she doesn't know a thing about.' Curiosity entered his voice as he asked, 'Is there really a dirty book waiting for her?'

'*Our Dearest Emma*.'

He had plainly heard of it. 'Aha,' he nodded, 'the bedroom secrets of Lady Hamilton. There you are! We certainly weren't meant to know about that. Even old Olive has her secret nooks and crannies.'

But Joan was more interested in something else: 'What's this private life of yours?'

Picking up his pen and writing pad he said, 'If I told you, it wouldn't be secret any more. And that would reduce the fun. Got any spare stamps?'

Joan indicated her airmail letter. 'I'll need them to answer this. Sorry.'

'I'll leave you to read it in peace. I've got to go and meet some people Granny knows nothing about.' He winked wickedly and went.

Bruno and Granny always laughed at Joan for 'saving her pictures till the last'. This meant that she spun out her pleasures. Confront Joan with a chop and potatoes and peas, and the best bit of meat would always be eaten at the end. Finally free to read her letter from America, Joan decided to take it to the other end of the house where she could savour it in privacy. Granny rarely ventured into 'the old conservatory' because it represented the greatest evidence of the Briggs family's dilapidation.

This morning the pools of water which had leaked onto the slate floor made it look even more abandoned than usual. But the days of relentless heat had done wonders for the woody old vine. Joan could hardly believe her eyes. Though it was the wrong time of the year, the creeper was actually showing signs of flowering.

Dear Joan,

I got three replies to my letter in *Collins'*. The others were from kids who seemed very interested in school things. I am not interested in school things. As your mom is a writer and my dad is a publisher, I have chosen you as my penfriend.

My dad said to ask who is your mother's publisher?

Panic! But wait a minute, something could always be invented. An American couldn't know the names of *all* the English publishers.

I get *Collins' Magazine* because my dad publishes the Molly Wainwright books in the States. She is a friend of ours and comes to visit. My dad says that she only comes to see our dogs! We have a French poodle and a British spaniel.

I was a red diaper baby. Know what that means? It is not true that we are Commies. Molly (I can call her that) says we are 'left of Lenin'. Mostly it just means that I go to school at Dalton and the people we know are writers and artists and jazz musicians. Did you ever hear of a black guy called Leadbelly? We know him. He says that I am going to be pretty hot on my sax.

Modest it wasn't. But Joan's own letter had hardly been retiring. The handwriting began as neat and then got wonderfully crazy and excited. Sally Morgenstern had not hesitated to cross out words, and she had turned two ink blots

131

into drawings of beetles with balloons coming out of their mouths; one said 'Hello Joan' the other 'Hello Sally'. Towards the end of the letter, the handwriting had grown so much in confidence that only about a dozen words covered each of the final pages.

> . . . so hurry up and write back and I will tell you about going to see *Kiss Me Kate* which happens in a circus tent, next Tuesday.

I've met my match, thought Joan. Here's somebody who can write even bigger fantasies than I can. Except, what if they weren't fantasies? No, nobody could be called Leadbelly – grown-ups would never allow you to say that. And all the wrapped-up hints of Communism were just too far-fetched. This is the most tremendous challenge, she thought. I'm going to have to prove I can invent as well as she can.

If the vine was flowering, so were Joan Stone's creative abilities. I'll match you, Sally Morgenstern, she vowed. My way will be subtle and English, but I'll match you word for swanking word. Would it be too much to claim that Dame Joan Barbirolli was going to conduct the Hallé Orchestra in a promenade concert, in the back garden, at half-term?

'Man that is born of a woman hath but a short time to live, and is full of misery.' Even the priest was living proof that Dora was not getting the funeral she wanted. The puny Church of England parson glanced sideways at the three people in the front pew, the only mourners present in the tiled crematorium chapel, and then carried on processing towards the coffin. 'He cometh up, and is cut down, like a flower; he fleeth as it were a shadow, and never continueth in one stay.' Dora's last requests were all being studiously ignored. The coffin had not been lifted onto the catafalque by Laithwaite's men; Ethel had settled for the Co-op because they paid out a dividend on funerals.

At least Gran'ma's wearing the right nightie, thought Vanda. She knew that because she'd taken it to the funeral parlour herself. They'd asked whether she would like to view

132

the body. And now she was feeling guilty for having said that she would prefer to remember Dora as she was. This was something Vanda had often heard other people say, but only in that hushed undertaker's office, where everybody talked so softly that they could have been afraid of disturbing Jesus in the next room, had she really understood what the words meant. The man behind the desk had used the phrase 'clothing the remains'. And the idea of remains had frightened her.

The minister droned on. Everything he was saying about Dora was stuff that Vanda had told him herself when he'd called round with a little notebook the previous evening. This morning, that basic information had been translated into something altogether more fancy: 'Her tender devotion to our dumb friends . . .' Why couldn't he just have said that Dick Barton hated everybody except Dora? And that coffin definitely wasn't elm, it looked much more like the yellowed wood of the big honours boards at Barton Grammar.

My God! What was happening? Had Dora woken up inside the box?

The whole thing had suddenly begun to slide forward. Sacred music was coming from nowhere and the coffin was heading for two little doors – just like the service hatch in Joan Stone's dining room.

'If Dora's trying to sit up, she'll have banged her head,' gasped Vanda.

Mr Adcock placed his hand on her shoulder. 'This is just what happens,' he said quietly.

She didn't like the feel of that hand. 'If it's what happens, why aren't there flames?' The coffin was just gliding into an empty gap. And now the doors were closing behind it, like on the Ghost Train at Blackpool.

'They stockpile them,' murmured Ethel. 'It's all kidology,' she continued in a churchified whisper. 'It's not worth their while lighting the ovens until they've got a whole batch.' Now she reverted to more normal tones. 'Funny how a funeral gets to you, isn't it? I suppose she wasn't *all* bad.'

'She was lovely,' insisted Vanda loyally. 'Is that it? Has she gone?'

'That's it.' And only now did Mr Adcock remove that cushiony hand.

'But it's not right.' Vanda was worried; horrified even at herself. 'Nobody cried. At first I was busy trying not to. And then that man starting making her sound like a stranger. No, it can't all be over like that.' Struck by the sudden thought that maybe she could rectify her own behaviour at the funeral parlour, she said, 'D'you think they'd let me go round the back and say goodbye to the box?'

'Go round the back?' scoffed Dora. 'This isn't Hulme Hippodrome.'

'Well, you said they kept them waiting.'

'Nana's under the crematorium's jurisdiction now,' put in Mr Adcock. His fat and cheerful appearance was belied by sharp little eyes, and he wore the same sort of black jacket and striped trousers as Mr Naylor had worn at the musical evening. 'This is a very good crem, you can rest assured they'll see that Nana gets to God.'

'I never called her Nana in me whole life. And I didn't say goodbye . . .'

Nobody seemed to understand the terrible importance of this omission. Her tones were so frantic and urgent that the clergyman joined in the conversation. 'Shh,' he said soothingly. 'She's with the angels now.'

'No she isn't.' Vanda had no religious faith whatsoever. 'She's parked at the back in a wooden box. Just let me go and talk to her.' Even as she said this, she wondered what she would say.

At least I could tell her that the cards are safe, she thought. At this moment they were in the pocket of the navy-blue raincoat she was wearing. And all because Ethel had tried to find them and burn them. It's all burning and boxes today, she thought. Burning and boxes and boxes and burning. And, Oh God, if you *are* there, just send Dora back for one minute so she can put her big arms round me again.

'Tears are for the best.' The minister nodded approvingly. Then he shook hands with the two adults and pocketed an envelope which Mr Adcock had slipped him.

Everybody started to head towards an open door at the bottom. 'We'd better go and pick up the flowers,' said Ethel.

'What flowers?' Although Vanda had allowed herself to be shepherded out into full daylight, she could hardly believe her ears. 'I said, what flowers?'

'Our own. I told the undertaker to take them off the coffin. We might as well have the benefit of them ourselves.'

And there they were, a spray of chrysanthemums and graveyard fern, lying on a paving stone underneath an official card inscribed *Floral Tributes for the Late Dora Millicent Doran*.

'Not that I've got a vase that's big enough,' said Ethel, ripping off the purple ribbon and dumping it in a wire wastepaper basket. 'Still, they'll split.'

'And now for the baked meats.' The lawyer was speaking in a tone that attempted to be jocular. 'I thought we'd go to the Ellesmere Cinema.' But this bit was not meant as a joke. The Ellesmere Super Cinema de Luxe, on the East Lancs Road, had a café tacked onto its side.

'Who's paying?' asked Ethel, suspiciously.

'My treat,' he assured her. 'Yes, my little treat.' He led the way to his fawn Ford Consul, unlocked it, and then went round to the other side to hold the door open for Ethel. This was the car in which the trio had followed the hearse. By dispensing with a limousine Ethel had managed to get a reduction out of the Co-op.

The Ellesmere café had pale pink basket furniture, flowered tablecloths and a set luncheon at half a crown. As they waited for their orders to arrive, Vanda, who had seen a lot of films at the adjacent picture house, said, 'Is this where you read the will, Mr Adcock?'

'I'm the battered haddock,' he said to the waitress. 'And the two ladies are Prem salads.' Reaching for the ketchup, he turned his attention to Vanda. 'We no longer have an official reading of the will. We just furnish the appropriate parties with the relevant paragraphs.'

'Panyan pickle?' The waitress was offering Ethel a small cut-glass dish with brown slop and a silver spoon in it, held

135

forward so reverently that it could have contained some hitherto unrevealed sacrament.

Ethel waved her away. 'We've got private business to discuss. Now then, Bertie.' It was the first time Vanda had ever heard her mother call him this, and the unexpected use of a shortened version of Mr Adcock's Christian name seemed to speak of previous intimacy. 'Now then, you may be sorry you've decided to pay for my dinner, but there comes a time when all the mourning and the grieving has to stop. Vanda claims that Dora left her the lot. Right or wrong?'

'That is substantially correct.' It could never have been a *cosy* intimacy.

Ethel put down her knife and fork. 'And is that why you've been making yourself so hard to get hold of on the phone?'

'Not at all,' he said through a mouthful of haddock. After he'd swallowed this he continued with, 'It's a big year for me in Rotary. I seem to be forever off out and about.'

'The Rotary Club, eh? Very respectable.' Using her fingers, Ethel picked up a slice of luncheon meat from the plate and sniffed it thoughtfully. 'I've been trying to remember the very first time I saw you, Bertie. Trying to recall the circumstances. Can *you* remember them?' Not taking her eyes off him for a moment, she shoved the Prem into her mouth and began to chew. There was a word for how she was chewing but Vanda couldn't think of it.

Suggestively. That's right, downright suggestively.

'I'm sure, when you put your mind to it, there's more than one way of interpreting a will,' said Ethel cosily.

It couldn't only have been Vanda who was reading hanky-panky into these words because Mr Adcock suddenly turned into a strict professional who snapped, 'No there isn't. Not in wills that I draw up, anyway. A will is a will, and that's that.' His face had gone pink with annoyance.

Ethel seemed far away in a pretty dream: 'The first time I saw you, I couldn't have been much older than Vanda. I was carrying a can of hot water and a towel into a little back room on the top floor, at Mother's old house in Gossamer Street.'

'That's as maybe.' He wasn't pink now, he was bright red.

'No maybe about it. Bertie used to be quite the young

turkey cock, in his day, Vanda. I bet they don't know about *that* at Rotary.'

Could the lawyer have been Gran'ma's boyfriend? No, the ages didn't add up. Even if he was ready for retirement, Dora's death certificate had said she was seventy-nine. But Ethel had certainly got him on a pin. And Vanda had been on enough of her mother's pins to feel sorry for the man. So she thought she would help him out by throwing in a question: 'How much do I get?'

'Mrs Doran was quite a wealthy woman. She had far more assets than . . .'

'Stow it!' Ethel had barged right in on him. 'Cut the cackle, there's no point in building the child up with false hopes. Not when I devoted years of my life to looking after that cantankerous old bag. Naturally I'm going to contest the will . . .'

'It wouldn't do any good.' Mr Adcock, it seemed, had pins of his own. Now it was his turn to gaze happily at the person on the other side of the table, and to speak slowly. 'Your mother anticipated this course of action. There is a clause in this document,' he tapped his breast pocket, 'which says that anybody who contests her will shall be automatically pre-cluded from inheriting anything. You contest it and you won't even get your own bequest.'

'Which is?' Ethel was all suspicion.

'Fifty pounds.' And never can these words have been said with such lip-smacking satisfaction.

'Fifty pounds?' Now all of the Ellesmere had heard them. 'Fifty lousy quid?'

'I understand that it's meant to compensate you for any small inconvenience. Virtually all the rest is to stay in trust until Vanda comes of age.'

'Small inconvenience?' Ethel was spitting with fury. 'Pisspots, and beautiful little meals on trays, and considered and studied – right, left and centre. My husband was the one who was correct about that woman – she *was* a witch.'

Mr Adcock hadn't finished: 'You are also to get five pounds for every week that the cat,' he cleared his throat, 'known as Dick Barton, stays alive.'

'She ranked the bloody cat above her own daughter!' Ethel looked as though she couldn't believe what she was hearing. 'Spit out whatever's in your mouth, Vanda.'

It was a piece of tomato. 'Why?' She swallowed it instead.

'Because we're not breaking bread with this rogue.' Ethel tore at the clasp of her handbag, ripped out her purse and counted four copper pennies onto the tablecloth. 'Go and phone Joan. Say you're going round there for the afternoon. I've got lawyers of me own to see.'

Mr Adcock shook vinegar onto his chips. 'You'll be wasting your money.'

'And don't think I've finished with you, Bertram Adcock. Fortunately I'm blessed with a very long memory. That's the phone box, next to the toilets, Vanda. Bugger off and use it.'

The telephone was in a slanting recess, under some stairs which went up to the ballroom above. Swinton was so crime-free that the phone book shared a shelf with a collecting box for the People's Dispensary for Sick Animals. Vanda didn't dial Joan's number, she knew another way of getting through. This involved tapping the number out on the two metal pins of the phone rest. Most children knew the theory of these illegal proceedings but Vanda had the reality down to a fine art. It was a bit noisy but you got connected for nothing.

'Ingledene.' The voice at the other end belonged to Joan Stone.

'Can I come round?'

The tiny embarrassed pause was almost as imperceptible as a bat's squeak. This didn't stop Vanda from hearing it. And then Joan said, 'I'm still not supposed to be seeing you. Or Peter,' she added hastily. 'We didn't think you'd be around today. How was the funeral?'

'Awful.'

'Are you on your bike?'

'Don't be so daft, Joan. I've just come from the crem. We didn't even bury her with ham. We saw her off with luncheon meat instead. It's all right, forget about me. There's a matinée on at the pictures. It's Greer Garson, I hate her.'

'Of course I won't forget about you,' said Joan sternly. 'Be outside the school gates in half an hour. That's where I'm meeting Peter. I've found a place for us all to go. It's the most . . .' Joan broke off in mid-sentence to say to some invisible third party, 'It's all right, Granny. It's just somebody from the Harlequin Players for Uncle Bruno.' Her voice came back down the line much more loudly with, 'Yes, Miss Yardley, I'm sure he'd love to audition for *The Constant Nymph*.' This was followed by a conspiratorial mumble of 'See you in thirty minutes,' and then a bright 'Goodbye.'

As it was still the holidays, Peter was on the pavement side of the wall and he had brought Henry, the white retriever, to school with him. They had come down the cycle track so the dog was on the end of an old clothes line. 'Sit,' said Peter. Perched on the saddle of his bicycle, he was keeping his balance with feet that touched the ground. When you were in a raincoat you always had to remember to be careful not to get your coat in the spokes. And here came Vanda wearing just such another blue gabardine mac. She was sucking one of those cheap ice lollies from Pam's Pantry. 'Isn't today cold and shivery?' he asked her. 'The only thing that seems to be left over from summer are these dismal brown butterflies.'

'I think they're moths.' Vanda was more interested in the lolly, ten licks and the colour had been almost sucked out of it. And then she noticed something else. 'Peter, why are you wearing a black tie?'

'Respect for the dead.' He said it like somebody who'd been caught out. Even as he'd tied the knot he'd wondered whether the gesture was excessive. 'I'm wearing it for your gran'ma.'

'She'd be really pleased.' Vanda meant this. 'She liked you.' Somehow this small token seemed to have given Dora more of a heartfelt farewell than anything achieved by the undertakers and the hired parson. 'I won't forget you did that for her,' she said solemnly. 'Oh look, they're not all brown, there's a Red Admiral.' Henry began to bark joyfully.

'And there's Joan coming across Pedlar Bridge.' This was a cobbled hump over a railway line. As Joan regained the road, her bicycle was still rattling alarmingly. 'Your lamp's fallen off,' called Peter.

'Your lamp!' shouted Vanda. 'She can't hear us. Just look at the sight of her on that man's bike – she looks like somebody perched on a penny-farthing.'

As Joan arrived and descended from the boneshaker, she was not without criticism of her own: 'Did you have to draw attention to the fact that I was coming?' She looked nervously across the road at a row of neat red-brick villas. 'There's a woman in one of those houses who's on the flower rota at church with Granny. I don't want her seeing me with you. She might say something.'

'If I'd known,' said Peter, 'I'd have brought a bell and shouted "Unclean."'

Joan failed to register the faint hurt inside his joking. 'I half thought of coming in disguise.'

'Nothing could disguise the way you ride that bike.'

Glancing frantically towards the neat villas with their hanging baskets, Joan attempted to stem all this with, 'I've found somewhere for us to go. It's an empty house between here and Ingledene.'

'But is it lowly enough for us?' asked Peter, solemnly.

Vanda adopted a similar attitude: 'Perhaps you'd better just give us the address and we'll make our own way there.'

Peter corrected her: 'Our own *humble* way.'

'I'm sorry.' The girl from Ingledene said this quietly. 'But now you know what it feels like for me. At least it gives you some idea of what it's like to be an outsider.'

'And we're insiders?' Peter was quite proud of his newly discovered ability to raise one eyebrow.

Joan led the way back over Pedlar Bridge. It was Vanda who bent down to pick up her friend's tumbled bicycle lamp. As she handed it over, a passenger train rattled along the track below. 'Here, put this back on its bracket. I wonder if even one of them is?'

'Is what?' Peter had been finishing off Vanda's lolly and now he reached down to allow the dog the final licks. 'Is what, Vanda?'

'I wonder if anybody on that whole train is an insider. Or is everybody on the outside, thinking that it's the rest of the world who've got things straight?'

140

'When I get home I'm going to write that down, Vanda.' Joan Stone was genuinely impressed. 'I didn't think you could be so *deep*.'

'There she blows again,' sighed Peter, 'the great lady passing judgment on the rest of us.' But this time he was laughing enough to confess, 'Guess what? Last night my father was brought home drunk by a hero-worshipping policeman.'

'I thought he'd gone on the wagon after the musical evening.' Joan was making mental notes of these events; she thought that should she ever come to write a drunkard into a book they might prove useful. 'Yes, he was definitely on the wagon.'

'Well he's fallen off it with a bang.'

'And my mother called the lawyer a bad bastard,' swanked Vanda. 'The waitress was so surprised she dropped his college pudding and custard. For my money, that's much more interesting than being on a flower rota.'

This conversation had got them over the bridge and onto one of the unadopted roads of Ellesmere Park. Joan pointed towards a For Sale sign, swinging amidst a bank of unusually tall rhododendrons. 'That's the place. And I've found a way in.'

'I'll bet you anything it's at the back.' Peter was off again. 'I'd stake my life on it being the humble servants' entrance.'

Joan had taken enough. 'My grandmother is every shade of snob there is. There, I've said it; she's a real pig-snob. Does that satisfy you?'

Peter was immediately chastened by the idea of having forced her into admitting this. 'I'm sorry.'

'Good. I'm glad.'

Although Vanda was the only one on foot, she was not lagging behind the pair of bicycles – she was ahead of them. It was as though their bickering was just voices on a wireless that somebody had chosen to turn down. Her hearing was not the only sense which seemed subtly altered, her vision was being taken over too. Something was sharpening it up to a state where the world could have been drawn with a fine mapping pen. And these new eyes craved more than glimpses of the castellated building now appearing, now disappearing, behind dense foliage. She must have passed the place a dozen times previously on her way to Joan's, but never before had it called out to her like this.

She reached the entrance to a drive lined with speckled laurels and giant cow parsley. There was no gate, just more of the dusty brown butterflies hovering over a pair of tall sandstone columns with battlemented tops. The left-hand pillar was incised with two words – *Magi House*.

I've walked into my gran'ma's past, thought Vanda. This is the place where Dora carried coal scuttles and polished grates; it's the building which housed Miss Wilkinson and the Order. But why was it still called Magi House? Wasn't Miss Wilkinson supposed to have changed everything back, after the Bishop had blessed the place?

It was Joan who bent down and retrieved a wooden nameplate with protruding rusty screws from the midst of a clump of bracken. ' "Glencora"!' She read the word aloud. 'Somebody mustn't have liked the other name.'

But it still won, thought Vanda. The Bishop couldn't have blessed it hard enough because Magi House had still fought its way back to the surface.

At the sight of the moths, Peter had tightened his grip on the dog's clothes line. Henry was wont to pant off after butterflies, and that could inspire him with the idea of a major bunk.

Not today. The three of them had already started moving up the drive but Henry's rope tightened as he stayed where he was. 'Come on,' said Peter encouragingly. The dog was not to be encouraged. His usual amiable expression had vanished and he was wearing the face he generally saved for people carrying shopping bags. For some unknown reason, shopping bags always threw Henry into a panic.

Peter dismounted from his bike and gave the rope another tug. All pleading brown eyes, the dog still refused to budge. Suddenly all the hairs on Henry's backbone rose up and he began to growl in the way he generally saved for Alsatians. If shopping bags induced panic, Alsatians brought on brave fury.

Yet there was nothing there. Just a grubby white gravel drive and two stone posts with iron brackets, where gates no longer hung.

'This house has a past,' said Vanda solemnly.

'What sort of past?' Joan threw the Glencora nameplate into a clump of foxgloves which had gone to seed. Something else caught her attention and left her gazing straight up in the air.

'Henry's not going to move,' said Peter. 'Hold my bike, Vanda. If we're going inside we'll have to leave him out here. I'll just tie him to this iron bit. D'you know what I don't like? I don't like the way these shuddery brown moths seem to be following us around.'

'They must have heard you,' laughed Vanda. 'Look, they've darted up the drive, they're ganging up with all those others.'

'But birds won't fly over the place.' Joan was still looking up into the sky. 'I've been watching. They get to the edge of the garden and then they veer off. Watch those pigeons . . . there! It's just as though a magnet pulls them off.'

'Or else something stops them from wanting to go in.' Peter looked perturbed. 'Are we sure that we want to?'

'My gran'ma used to work here.' Vanda was already striding up the drive. She was suddenly very conscious of the tarot pack in its wooden box in her coat pocket; it was banging against her leg.

Vanda had never told them about Dora's days with Miss Wilkinson. When you live in a house that's full of cast-off clothing and dry-cleaning tanks, you think twice before adding to your family's reputation for eccentricity. And now she felt that giving away secrets could somehow diminish the power.

Power? She actually found herself examining this word which had sprung so vigorously into her head. Yes, she decided, *power*. Somehow, from somewhere, I have been given an amazing extra ability . . . and it's all to do with the box of cards. But with this ability came a need for secrecy. Instinctively, she knew that if she told the story her words could disperse some of this new-found energy onto the air.

'What do you know about this house?' This time it was Peter.

'Nothing.' She laughed defiantly. '*Had* you there, didn't I?'

Nevertheless, Peter covertly scratched his forehead, then his chest, then his shoulder. In reality he was making a protective sign of the cross – he'd learned to do it at Anglo-Catholic services with Miss Lathom and Miss Parr. There had to be something odd about a place which frightened off animals and birds.

'Let's go for a walk on the golf course,' suggested Joan.

'When I've got Dora's cards with me?' Vanda knew how to lay bait. 'And you can't do them in the open air. You need a roof over them.'

As they turned a bend in the drive, the high shrubbery ended and they came within sight of Magi House. It was a Victorian cotton magnate's version of a manageably sized castle. But the battlements hid only rain gutters, and the elaborate stone lintels were filled with unromantic sash windows. Time had added genuine antiquity in the shape of cracked cement facing and broken downspouts. Somebody had chalked *Spunkbags Stop You Having Babies* on the fake Tudor front door, where a broken milk bottle lay smashed against an iron boot scraper.

'What awful cheap flowered curtains they've left behind,' said Peter.

'Come on.' Vanda didn't need telling the whereabouts of the cellar door; something or somebody was already pushing her in its direction. You went past the old zinc dustbins and, yes, there were the area steps. 'I'll do the cards for you,' she wheedled again. 'But I can't just do them in any old room. There's a special one for it – right up at the top.'

'I don't think I want to go any further,' said Joan. The stairs from the basement of Magi House had led them up into a dank ground-floor kitchen dominated by an abandoned enamelled gas stove and fraught with rusty mousetraps.

'However many people must it have taken to answer those bells?' Peter sounded awed. The names of all the rooms in the

144

house were gold-lettered on a glass-fronted box with a mahogany surround. A trademark proclaimed the fact that it had been installed by the Electric Housemaid Company.

My grandmother answered them, for one, thought Vanda. Yet again something was warning her to keep the details of this to herself. The importance of the message inside her head was quite clear: tell nothing and the power will build. And now an actual voice had taken over: '*Keep your own counsel, Vanda. Keep your own counsel.*' They were old Dora's brand of words but this wasn't quite old Dora.

'*Ha-ha,*' it laughed, and she felt the need to experiment. Could she drown out the gabble with the sound of her own voice? 'Why are you suddenly scared of the place?' she asked Joan. 'You were the one who found it.' Yes, the inner voice had cut out.

'I don't know . . .' Joan's words tailed away because she didn't want to tell the truth. Twice she'd been to Magi House before, and never had so much as a qualm. But introducing her friends onto the premises had – somehow – changed its atmosphere.

Vanda missed the other girl's silence. Greatly daring she asked, 'Are you by any chance hearing a voice inside your head?'

'No, just my own thoughts.' I'm right, and it's something to do with Vanda, she thought triumphantly. But the triumph was overlaid with panic. 'I want to get out,' she said.

'Don't be so soft,' scoffed Vanda. '*Upstairs,*' said the voice. '*Top of the house.*' 'Are you scared?' she asked Peter.

He was just glad that he'd had the foresight to cross himself. 'Maybe a bit,' was all he would admit. 'What did you mean about hearing voices?'

'*Careful,*' it went. '*Don't dim me down.*' Realising that the other two were gazing at her expectantly, Vanda decided to laugh. 'I was only acting spooky,' she giggled.

Joan was not quite convinced. 'Perhaps it's just that I'm due for my period,' she reasoned aloud. 'That means you're due too,' she said to Vanda.

'Well I'm certainly not,' snorted Peter. He was speaking much more bravely than he felt. It was no use, he was going to have to admit it: 'I'm with Joan. There's something here I don't like. I vote we get out.'

'When I'm going to look into the future? You want to know what's going to happen to Toby Eden, don't you?'

Joan Stone, in the cause of gaining information about Toby Eden, would willingly have sat down to tea with the devil. 'Yes, I do want to know that.'

'Then we have to go upstairs.'

Peter was in like a knife: 'Why upstairs? That's the second time you've mentioned it.'

Vanda improvised quickly: 'Because it's nearer to the stars.' She went on to explain that her grandmother had always told her that the tarot and astrology were the ivy and the tree. '*Not bad.*' The inner voice was speaking in tones of grudging admiration. '*An explanation not to be sniffed at.*' But who was it? There were shades of Dora in its speech patterns, and overtones of somebody much posher. In fact it was hard to tell whether it was even female.

'*Careful,*' warned her hidden colleague.

'Wax,' Vanda jiggled a finger inside her earhole. 'I've been plagued with wax in my ear for days.' '*Good girl. And now get up those stairs.*'

Vanda pushed open the door covered in old green baize and peered out. 'Come and have a look at the hall. It's posh gone musty.'

'I know,' said Joan. 'I mean I *am* the one who found the place.' And now I wish I hadn't, was what she was thinking. Nevertheless she stepped into a bare-boarded entrance hall which smelt of cats.

'It's practically baronial.' Peter had followed the two girls. The hall was lined with dark mahogany panelling. The only remaining furniture was a ramshackle bamboo umbrella stand, and the house must have slipped a long way down the social hill because somebody had drawing-pinned a complimentary calender from Vernon's Football Pools into a shadowy recess that was wired up for a candlestick telephone.

'I thought the Post Office always took their instruments back,' said Peter.

'There's no point in trying it.' Joan was talking to Vanda. 'I already did, last week. The line's dead.'

But it might not be dead for me, thought the girl with the cards in her pocket – odd how the idea of those cards kept pressing itself into her mind. On this strange day, if I lift up the receiver will there be somebody waiting for me at the other end?

There wasn't. All she could hear was the extra voice inside her skull. '*Stop messing around*,' it said. '*Get where you've got to go.*'

Albeit reluctantly, the other two followed her. 'Isn't the echo of clomping feet weird?' Peter suddenly felt the need to really pray. I can't, I won't, kneel down here, he thought. But I do need to get God in on this. Struck by a sudden golden inspiration he began to sing:

> 'No goblin nor foul fiend
>   Can daunt his spirit.
> He knows he at the end
>   Shall life inherit.
>   Then, fancies, fly away . . .'

The air was rent by a terrible distant howl. Henry the dog must also have felt frightened by the idea of being a pilgrim, and out in the garden he too was singing for safety.

The most awesome thing was the confident way in which Vanda all but stormed the staircase. She seemed to know exactly where she was going. How could the others be expected to understand that she felt as though she was walking towards the promise of an embrace?

On she went, past the first floor where one of the doors was half wrenched from its hinges. Joan and Peter were still panting behind her as she reached the second landing: the woodwork was not quite of such good quality here, and the panelling had been replaced by wallpaper covered in a sinister design of ratlike hares hiding in olive-green undergrowth. Nothing would satisfy Vanda but that she must reach the attics.

147

These didn't cover the whole of the house, they just ran under the battlemented part at the front. This was the point where Joan volunteered, 'The room on the left must have belonged to their cook. There are still bits of an old uniform dumped on a peg behind the door.'

But that's not the door I'm looking for, thought Vanda. And neither is the one on the far right. No, it's this middle one – the one with its own little staircase.

No effort went into mounting these final three steps. She was up them and over the threshold as though borne forward by invisible hands. '*Yes. You're finally here.*' But how could the voice be flooding her with this feeling of having come home?

And what a home! Tattered shreds of old black velvet hung from patches of dirty brown glue on a glass skylight. What she was hearing now was ordinary everyday memory: Dora talking about everything being covered in black velvet in the room belonging to the Order.

'They must have pasted that stuff up for blackout, during the war,' said Peter.

Vanda didn't bother to reply; she was tentatively sniffing the air, wondering whether there could be any lingering trace of that intoxicating chemical her grandmother had mentioned – ether. Yes, that was right, ether. But there wasn't. The only other remaining shreds of velvet stuck out from round the edge of the brass mounting of the light switch. '*Get a bit.*' The voice was more masculine now and deeply insistent. '*Get a little piece and put it in the box with the cards. It's like charging a battery.*'

Vanda did as she was bid: she ripped one of the tiny remaining fragments from under the light switch. It was odd how precious it was managing to make itself feel; she was reminded of her own mother holding up an especially valuable item on the second-hand stall – Ethel had a trick of handling old Italian shoes as though they were caskets of rare spices.

'Go in my raincoat pocket,' Vanda instructed Peter. 'Get the box out.' Even as she said this, she was wondering whether somebody else should really be handling it. But he

148

was already extracting the decorated wooden coffer with its design of an eye emerging from behind clouds.

'Don't open it, Peter. I'm the one who has to do that.'

As she took the box, he experienced mild relief. The feel of the thing had been making him wonder whether he needed to start praying again.

Vanda undid the brass catch, flipped back the lid and put the velvet fragment into the folds of the black silk handkerchief which was already swathed around the tarot cards.

'Whatever are you doing?' asked Joan.

'*Say you're having them on.*' 'I'm having you on,' she announced as instructed. 'I'm trying to make it a bit more interesting.' These last words she'd improvised for herself.

'*It is done,*' said the voice. As Vanda began to unwrap the cards, she realised that the plushy little black snippet was now totally devalued, that whatever power it had contained had passed into the cards. 'OK, Peter, shuffle them – hard. Take your time over it.'

Reluctantly he did as she asked. 'There you are. Oh goodness, I've dropped some.'

'No.' Vanda was speaking urgently. 'Leave them where they are. Dropped cards can mean the most.' So they stayed on the floor while Vanda took the Sun and the Moon and the Tumbling Tower from the pack. But where was Peter's card, where was the Magician? The voice inside her head began to snigger, and Vanda knew exactly where to look.

Bending down, she turned over the ones which had fallen to the ground. Yes, the Magician. And next to it was the World.

'There's something you've not been telling us,' she said to Peter, sternly. 'You don't care about Toby Eden any more, do you?' Even as she said this, a picture started forming in her mind. '*Yes,*' breathed the secret voice. '*Yes, it is who you think it is.*' Glowing inside her brain a young man's face was forming. But if she told Peter who she was seeing, Joan would hear the name too. And that could only lead to trouble. 'You've got a new outside interest,' she said to him in matter-of-fact tones.

'*Good girl, you'll be able to use that later.*' But why should

149

she want to use this vision of Bruno against her friends? It was as though the voice was trying to turn her into somebody else.

Using Dora's method, Vanda began to spread the cards. '*It's between you and Joan now. It's turned into a two-way battle.*' The voice was only confirming what the spread had to tell.

'Everything's altered,' was what Vanda chose to announce aloud. She also felt free to add something else. 'Toby's drawing much closer to us. We'll be seeing a lot more of him next term.' She paused and gave the spread her further consideration. 'Mmm . . . he'll know our names. And it'll involve us using our legs.'

'Like dancing?' asked Joan, worried.

'Like I don't know.' But she did know. She was being shown pictures of them running around with pieces of paper in their hands. When Dora was teaching her to read the tarot, nothing like this had ever happened. You were just meant to know the meaning of each card and to interpret them accordingly. This new way of doing them was more like sitting in a seat at a silent picture show while somebody played Chinese Whispers in your earhole.

As she got Joan to count more cards into the design, Peter tried to distance himself from these too revealing proceedings. 'Fancy somebody leaving a carpet behind,' he said. 'Black too, it must have shown every thread of cotton.' Idly, he pulled back a corner of this ancient floor covering. 'There's something on the boards underneath,' he said. 'Lift up the cards, while I look.'

'This is serious business,' protested Vanda.

'So's this. There are funny markings on the floor.'

'What sort of funny?' asked Joan. Ignoring Vanda's outraged protestations, she started to move the cards to one side.

'Ouch!' Vanda had actually felt the pain of Joan's touch inside her own head.

By now, Peter had the carpet hauled halfway across the room. Yes, somebody had burnt an outline into the floorboards in bold pokerwork – the same kind of pokerwork that had been used to decorate Vanda's eerie box. But the design

150

on the floor was infinitely bolder and much more evil than that. The only time Peter had ever seen anything similar had been in a book by some pagan from the Isle of Man, a book called *The History of Witches and Witchcraft*. What the three children were gazing down at was a huge charred pentagram.

Vanda Bell wasn't the only one with instincts; Peter had plenty of his own. 'I'm getting out of here.' He announced it firmly but his voice was shaded with fear. And this same emotion was echoed by Henry, the dog, who suddenly began baying from the garden gate.

'Run,' said Peter, suiting the deed to the word; both he and Joan were panicking their way towards the top of the staircase. But nothing on this earth would have stopped Vanda Bell from pausing to pick up the scattered tarot cards.

There was no sound of traffic coming from the Manchester Road, so it must have been well past midnight when Peter found himself hauled to the surface – from his dreams.

Not that he was completely awake, just near enough to reality to register the fact that somebody had pulled the lavatory chain. And that the bouncing clanking noise was the sound of the empty Cussons Imperial Leather talcum powder tin tumbling into the bath. If a clumsy hand set the rubber knob on the end of the lavatory chain swinging, the talcum canister always went flying. The only clumsy hand at number 10 Hawksway belonged to Eddie Bird.

A further little crash meant that the china denture bath must also have taken a tumble. It lived on the same windowsill as the talc. Eddie must be really rolling around tonight! And now the former hero farted. 'Beg your pardon, Field-Marshal Smuts,' he said smartly. For some unknown reason he always said that when he farted.

Nothing pleasant was holding Peter this near to the surface. Yet for some reason he didn't want to snuggle back into his dream. And 'snuggle' was the wrong word, for it had not been a comfortable dream. He had been in a place it would have been better to leave. But *where* had he been? He could either wake up properly and consider the matter, or allow sleep to lure him back to this unhappy location.

151

Magi House: the answer came in these two words, not in a mental picture. Peter was neither more awake nor asleep than he had been before. Yes, the words were 'Magi House' and 'smothering'. The dream broke back into his consciousness: he had been in that room at the top of the abandoned villa, and showers of tarot cards had rained down on his face. The Sun, the Moon, the World . . . just like falling leaves but made of flannel. He'd fought them off because they were choking out his breathing. They'd been all over his face, throbbing with a life of their own.

And now remembering turned into reality as the dream sucked him back into himself. The woollen cards across his eyes and nose and mouth were not the worst part – the worst part was the stench. It reminded him of the odour that rose up from the orange-coloured crust at the bottom of the white china urinals in the boys' lavatories at school. But never before had he encountered a smell that contained an emotion. Hatred, that's what it was made of – hatred.

And now he understood what he was smelling. This was the stench of evil. As the strangely woollen cards moved closer across his face like a balaclava without eyeholes, the gaseous odour was almost shrieking at him. But Peter was not entirely defenceless. With the one bit of breath that had not been taken away he managed to gasp, 'Please, thanks, forgiveness; in the past, and in the present, and in the future.'

The demonic smell did not grow less but neither did it increase. Very definitely possessed of a life of its own, it was hovering, musing, waiting.

I need a sword, thought Peter wildly. But no shining blade came to his rescue. Instead, his head was flooded with some words he had heard in Miss Lathom's church. These weren't words he'd consciously learned but, nevertheless, there they were, waiting for him: '*O Everlasting God, who hast ordained and constituted the services of Angels and men in a wonderful order: mercifully grant, that as thy holy Angels always do thee service in heaven, so by thy appointment they may succour and defend us on earth.*'

As he added a heartful 'Amen', horror was replaced by peace, and the air was as fresh as a crisp morning on

Fleetwood front. But Peter was left knowing one thing —
some battle between good and evil was firmly under way.

3

On the surface, life was going on just as though nothing unusual had happened. But Vanda kept asking herself whether she could have imagined that voice. And had it told her anything she couldn't have dreamed up for herself? One thing she did know, the whole experience had left her distinctly wary of the tarot pack. For the time being she'd hidden them, box and all, inside one of the old banjo cases in the front bedroom. She had made up her mind that, in future, she was only going to ask the cards about things she really needed to know.

Ethel Bell and her daughter were standing behind the second-hand stall on Cross Lane Market in Salford. 'School starts again next Tuesday,' said Ethel with grim satisfaction. 'You could do worse than try this on for size.' Third-formers were allowed to dispense with gymslips in favour of grey flannel skirts. It goes without saying that Ethel Bell was proffering a garment that was just subtly wrong.

'I don't need to try it on.' Vanda had inherited her mother's eye for instant sizing. 'The waist's an inch too big but I can gather it up, under a belt.' She didn't bother mentioning the non-regulation patch pocket. She needed to keep Ethel sweet because she was about to tackle her on the subject of another, and bigger, problem.

This year the market superintendent had allocated them a much better Saturday site. It was near to the entrance, in the same row as the man who perpetually slammed his hand against pieces of linoleum, declaring, 'Not a break, not a tear, not a blemish.' And they were just a bit further down than Barmy Mick, who could attract a crowd in seconds by throwing free rolls of fly-catcher at passers-by. 'Mick's gone mad today, grab your bargains before the men in white coats arrive!' There was another second-hand clothes dealer in the same row – the famous Salford Mary. A lessser spirit than

Ethel might have baulked at going into competition with this popular rag-picker. But Ethel Bell had a gimmick: not only did she use her stall as a wooden stage, she also expected Vanda to act as a mannequin.

Noting that Mary had a gang of customers around her, Big Ethel put down her mug of tea, hauled herself up onto the boards and went into action. 'Here you are, ladies, here you are! A big tweed autumn stroller. Get it on, Vanda, don't keep your public waiting. Isn't she lovely? This garment would set you back ten guineas at Kengal Mills.'

She can't even pronounce Kendal Milne properly, thought Vanda as she buried herself in the raglan-sleeved coat, assumed a smile which did not come from the heart, and began to swank around the makeshift stage against a backdrop of beaded evening dresses on wire coathangers.

'Are you expecting again, Lily?' Ethel Bell knew all the regular faces in the crowd by name. 'This'll be just the thing to keep it quiet till Christmas.' Now she assumed the tones of a fashion commère: 'And as our Vanda turns, you ladies will note that the coat features the elegant new saddleback.' Ethel always took her time in getting to the actual price. 'Two minutes with a needle and cotton will soon take care of that bit of droopy lining.' Her voice began to rise passionately: 'I'm not asking five pounds, or four, or three . . .' Ethel clapped her fat hands sharply together. 'Seven and sixpence – that's my price. Seven and a kick. Go on, six bob then. Sold to the lady in the rabbit hat.'

The money was taken by a self-effacing male helper called Mo. Ethel only used him on the bigger markets. He had one eye and a leather bag like a bus conductor's for the cash.

'It's cocktail time,' bawled Ethel. Her daughter was not expected to struggle into dresses. Vanda just held them in front of herself, indicated details like revers and pockets, and swayed alluringly. There were always stray men at the back of the crowd, waiting for nothing more than these moments. Mindful of her theatrical future, Vanda always used these men as an audience for her most beguiling smiles. It was like Hulme Hippodrome in a small way.

I am wickedness, she would think to herself as she turned

155

her bust into upthrusting profile. I'm what you sweet old bastards shouldn't be looking at.

Sometimes her male admirers even clapped, and this was always a cue for Ethel to glare and move on to ancient bed linen. Pillowcases, bolsters, raggy old blankets – today they must have moved a ton by closing time. As they packed unsold items back into the hessian sacks, Vanda took a deep breath and finally got round to mentioning the one thing she really needed.

'Tights. I need new ballet tights. And I'm low on pointe shoes, too.' Until recently, these would have been provided without her having to ask; Ethel had even gone to proper shops for anything to do with dancing. 'It isn't just school that starts again next week. Odette Ashworth's does too.'

Ethel was gripping the top of a washed-out chintz loose cover between her teeth. 'Not for you it doesn't.' Her big arms were waving wildly as she attempted to manhandle the rest of the material into a shape which would pack. 'Hulme Hip was the end of that. No mother in her right mind would have her daughter trained up for men to ogle at.' She pronounced it 'oggle'.

'They gawp at me here,' pointed out Vanda, reasonably.

'That's in the way of business.'

'But what I want to do is in the way of business, too,' argued her daughter.

'It was your feet I had trained,' said Ethel darkly. 'But that wasn't the part they were interested in auditioning. I was there. I saw. Men are weak reeds, it doesn't take much to start them playing pocket billiards. Pass me them vests and underpants.' Ethel treated her daughter to a cold look and a critical sniff. 'There's a lot of your grandmother in you, Vanda. She made that money of hers out of men's weakness.'

Greatly daring, Vanda ventured to ask something she'd been dying to ask for weeks: 'Was she a pro?'

The half-expected smack across the face did not materialise. Instead, Ethel paused from her folding and considered the matter to the count of five. 'She was worse,' she said eventually, 'a lot worse. You could try asking your friend Mr Adcock.'

'But what did she do?'

'Would you mind lowering your voice, please? I'm very well thought of round 'ere.' But the crowds had thinned to almost nothing. Nevertheless, Ethel waited until two lingerers had moved out of earshot before she continued. 'Your grandmother lived off prostitutes' backs.'

Vanda was more astonished than shocked. 'Dora?'

Ethel nodded. 'Dora. You're inheriting mucky money.'

'You'd have had it,' retorted Vanda.

Indignation had set in: 'I earned it. I had whole years of it. Oh, a lot's been kept from you. We put all that behind us when we moved to Grotto Lodge.'

'All what?'

A last straggler edged towards the stall. 'Have you any ladies' combinations?' she asked nervously. Ethel Bell, when packing up, was famous for being fratchy.

'Combinations? They're things of the past. Have you thought of trying cami-knickers?' Ethel snatched a flimsy garment from the top of one of the overflowing sacks. 'It's the same principle. You've still got the flap for convenience.'

'No, I'm old-fashioned,' explained the woman. 'Them was better days,' she sighed, 'much better days.'

'Were they?' barked Ethel, so violently that the customer backed away. 'Better days my arse!' she said under her breath. And again she waited until there was no chance of being overheard. 'We lived in Chorlton-on-Medlock,' she said eventually. 'Gossamer Street was back-or-beyond of Manchester University. Big house, three floors, and your grandmother took in the other sort of pros – variety artistes. But the talkies did away with the variety theatres. That's when the house turned into something else. Your gran'ma always varnished it over with a French name. She called it a *place de passage*. Which is a very fancy way of saying knocking shop. Those girls used to rent the rooms off her by the hour. Nice girls some of them, even if they did have their price chalked on the soles of their high-heeled shoes.'

'You're joking,' gasped Vanda.

'It's not a joking matter. Those were the cheaper girls, off the scruffy end of Oxford Street. And when times was bad

157

they used to cross out one price and put another underneath.'
Ethel was shaking her head as though she could hardly credit
her own memories. 'Why d'you think I was so dead set
against your being a stripteaser? What's the difference
between one of them and the chalky girls? I'll tell you the
difference: Phyllis Dixey promises and a tart delivers. And
what happens when just a promise isn't enough? No, milady,
your dancing shoes are hung up for good. You're going up in
aeroplanes.'

Something warned Vanda not to argue. This wasn't
clairvoyance, it was common sense. Besides, a plan was half
forming in her mind. But first she would need more
information. 'How did Mr Adcock fit into all of this?'

'Dirty Bertie? He wore out more than his fair share of
staircarpet. Dora didn't just let in the chalky girls at half a
crown a throw, she had two permanents on the top floor –
Lena McGrath and Josie Pickles. I'm talking about an
altogether better class of whore here. They didn't walk the
street, they entertained regulars. Did it with the gas fire on,
and accepted chocolates on top of the agreed sum.'

Ethel began to tie all the unsold bedding inside a big tartan
motoring rug. 'Spoiled, that's what Dirty Bertie was. You
could tell he came from moneyed people because he didn't
come round for it on pay day. Tuesday was Bertie's night for
jig-a-jig-jig. Naturally, he got the taste for it more often.
They do. That's when he brought Gossamer Street to a
standstill by making a decent woman of Lena McGrath.'
Ethel hurled the bundle on top of the pile of sacks. 'And she
had the nerve to get married in white with a wreath and veil.'

'I bet they don't know about that at his Rotary Club,' said
Vanda. And she said it very thoughtfully indeed.

The night before term started, the Birds didn't get back from
Stoke-on-Trent until late. They had been to a family
reunion, and as their taxi passed through Irlams o'th' Height
and came within sight of the Ravensdale Estate the parish
church clock was chiming midnight.

Now it was the next morning, and Peter found himself

woken from not enough sleep with, 'Hurry up, Joan Stone's on the phone.' It was his mother. 'From the sound of things, she's ringing from a box. And put your dressing gown on – your breakfast's nearly ready.'

Still only half-awake, Peter made his way downstairs to the telephone which lived on the hall windowsill. 'This is too early, Joan,' he said without any preamble whatsoever.

Neither did she bother with niceties: 'Have you got a film in your camera?'

'Yes, but there are only two goes left on it. I used up the rest in the Potteries.'

'I've been trying and trying to get you. I thought you were only going for the day.' Joan's tone was almost accusing, but that was only an indication of how well they had grown to know one another.

Peter yawned. 'My father got arrested for breaking up the Liberal Club. It was a weekend so they kept him in the cells. That's why we had to stay.'

Peggy interrupted him from the kitchenette: 'I don't think you should be telling people that.'

It was too early in the morning for Peter to do anything but ignore this. 'Why do you want my camera?'

'To take a picture of Magi House.'

This was a name that was potent enough to bring him wide awake. 'Are you mad?' he asked. 'Nothing on earth would get me to set foot in that hellhole again.'

'You'd have a job,' snorted Joan. 'It's burned to the ground. It happened the very night we were there. The fire people are calling it "a holocaust of unknown origin". It just burst into flames.'

'Since when did you know firemen?'

Joan assumed almost maddeningly patient tones: 'I phoned them because I needed to know. One day I'm going to use the whole thing in a story. I need the pictures of the remains for reference.'

'Sometimes you can make yourself sound very important, Joan.' And he wasn't being flattering.

Joan chose to ignore this. 'Will you bring your camera?'

159

'I've wrecked your egg,' grumbled Peggy in the back-ground. 'You've no business discussing private matters with outsiders.'

As Peter paused briefly to listen to what his mother was saying, Joan took his silence for a refusal: 'Please bring it, Peter. I'm sorry if I sounded bossy.'

'OK, OK.' But as he replaced the receiver he found himself wondering whether the demons of Magi House would be able to work their way into his Box Brownie.

'There's something very deceitful about coming back to school after the summer holidays,' said Joan Stone. 'The smell of all those brand-new books deceives you into thinking that something exciting is about to happen. And then the smell of school dinners brings you back to reality. Wasn't that fish pie dreadful?' It was still dinnertime, and Joan and Vanda and Peter had automatically assumed their usual seats on the front wall.

There was something different about the school garden this year. A sundial had been erected to the memory of a teacher called Mr Jenkins-Jones. 'Did you know that people always said that he used to grope boys?' asked Peter. Somewhat gloomily he added, 'He never tried to grope me. Sooner or later I'm going to have to find that pub called Tommy Duck's.'

'You want to watch out.' Vanda spoke sternly. 'What you've got in mind could bring the police round to your house.' She wondered whether to tell them the next bit. 'I've got an appointment with a lawyer. I phoned through to Adcock's offices yesterday. I'm going to see him after school on Thursday.'

'What about?' asked Joan.

At one time Vanda would have replied with the whole story. But she'd risked doing the cards again and that voice had warned her to keep her own counsel. 'Just about my trust fund,' she said loftily.

This managed to irritate Joan. If anybody was going to have a trust fund it ought to be her – trust funds were much more Ellesmere Park than Grotto Lodge Estate. She decided

160

to keep up her own end by taking the conversation in an international direction. 'I've had another letter from New York.' Fishing in her blazer pocket she produced the airmail envelope as evidence. She didn't actually read from the letter, she just said, 'Sally Morgenstern's been to see Elizabeth Taylor in *Little Women*.'

'It's coming to the Broadway, Eccles, next week,' said Vanda. 'We get stuff a lot faster these days.'

Joan wondered whether the girl with the lawyer and the trust fund was trying to cut her down to size. 'Sally's got a cashmere coat with a mink collar, from a shop called Bergdorf's, for Rosh Hashanah,' she swanked. 'Jewish people always have something new for their New Year.' When Vanda failed to react the other girl ploughed on with, 'Sally's mother sounds very sophisticated. She says that when she dies she's going to have her ashes scattered at Bergdorf's.'

Vanda started scratching her forearm. 'I think that fish pie might have given me food poisoning,' she announced. 'You scratch a bit too, Joan. If we could both work up a rash we could get ourselves excused domestic science.'

Peter joined in with, 'And I could get off manual.'

'You never go anyway,' pointed out Vanda. It was no secret that Peter was so bad at woodwork the teacher was happy to pretend not to notice his absence.

'If all three of us bunked off next Tuesday,' said Joan, 'we could go to the afternoon matinée of *Little Women*.'

From within the school building a grating electric bell recalled them to thoughts of the present afternoon. 'Have you got my camera safe?' Peter asked Joan.

'Yes, it's in my desk. Bruno gave me one of those new combination padlocks for this term.'

Vanda got down off the wall. 'Do you know why Magi House burst into flames?' She asked this question impressively. 'It did it because its job was done. It wouldn't do to tell you more than that,' she continued loftily.

'Are you practising being dramatic for when you see your lawyer?' Joan was still a bit narked that nobody had seemed impressed by her news from New York.

Peter too was climbing off the wall. 'Here's where I have to try to make myself invisible. If that woodwork master actually sees me, he gets a conscience and feels he has to haul me off to the manual room. I wouldn't care but I'm still making the same teapot stand I started in the first form.'

As he parted company from his closest friends and headed for the boys' entrance, Peter considered his solo situation. As long as he kept himself in groups where there were girls present, he could almost pass as just another lad in a maroon blazer. Almost, but not quite. And five minutes alone with the boys of his own form left him feeling like a visitor from another planet. He knew his presence rendered them puzzled and unaccountably wary. That was the main reason he avoided all-male subjects like woodwork and gym.

As Peter walked into the building he caught sight of two of his classmates heading for the manual room. On the face of things, he looked like these people; the subtle variations came in the way he moved, the way he spoke. Even his sense of humour did not come from the same direction as theirs. And the biggest joke of all was that these confident creatures marching off to manual were beginning to envy his ability to get on with girls. His close friendships with Joan Stone and 'Tits' Bell were starting to gain him a reputation as quite a devil with the ladies. Though the schoolboys of 1949 knew how to yell 'cissie', they had little understanding of the full meaning of their jibe.

These days, for the most part, they left him alone. New boys, out to make a reputation for themselves, could be a bit dangerous. Last year's intake had taken great pleasure in reviving the nickname 'Sweetie'. But experience had taught their intended victim that no reaction was the best fire extinguisher. And this term Peter had height on his side – he could easily have passed for sixteen.

Pale autumn sunlight shone through the words *Omnia Gignit Industria* in the stained-glass window of the main hall. Upstairs, on the iron balcony, girls from his own form were scurrying towards the domestic science room. They were all clutching sewing bags in maroon linen, items they'd made in the first year. Whatever they made then had to serve them for the rest of their school careers. It was the same with art folders

– you lettered your name on the front when you were eleven and you carried it round till the end of the fifth form.

Come to that, it was more or less the same with your reputation with teachers. Peter's first report had labelled him 'sensitive'. At Barton Grammar School that was a dirty word – a euphemism for girlish. If they wanted to think that, they were more than welcome. But why, Peter wondered, were the gender rules so rigid? Why were all boys meant to enjoy going down into the bowels of the school to learn how to make a cross-halving joint in a glue-laden atmosphere? Personally, he would have far preferred to join Joan and Vanda for three-quarters of an hour's needlework, followed by Mrs Waterworth's lesson in stuffing a tomato.

His truant footsteps led him past the geography room where a zealous monitor was already placing a globe on the teacher's desk. Of course the globe represented the world; but Peter was thinking of the noun with a capital letter, the World – the card which had tumbled onto the black carpet of Magi House with his own. How odd it was that Vanda had known he was keeping a secret passion from her and Joan. But he could hardly have announced 'I'm absolutely batty about Joan's Uncle Bruno. I meet him regularly in my dreams. We've already slept in a leaking tent together.' The World was definitely Bruno Briggs.

Where should he hide from the woodwork class? The school library was a possibility; but sometimes you got asked questions there, and overconscientious teachers were quite capable of checking as to whether you really had a free period. Anyway he already had a book to read and he could read that anywhere, now that he'd made a brown paper cover for it. At home, the volume had also inspired a special hidey-hole behind a pile of nutty slack inside the coal shed. It was a good job that the women behind the counter at Pendlebury Library never looked at what they were stamping.

Peter had reached the corridor that fronted the school gymnasium, which had to be the most echoing room in the whole school. But today, this first period after dinner, it stood silent. This meant that the gym cloakroom would be empty

163

too, the perfect place for three-quarters of an hour with his book – *The Trials of Oscar Wilde*.

He pushed open the boys' changing room door and breathed in that smell of sweat and gym shoes and the leather-topped changing benches. This was an inner shrine of mysterious masculinity.

Shrine? Yes, shrine. Here's where they took their clothes off and stood unconcernedly naked. He had no sexual interest in the boys of his own form because they were just that – boys. But some of the sixth-formers had stood here naked too. And they were men. Peter's thoughts were as undressed as the men he was thinking about.

I'd like to really look at them, he thought. Touching came into it, too. And then an image of the Bible and the words from that bit where Leviticus spoke out against things like that. Something about not lying with men like you would with women. And there was that other forbidding bit in St Paul. But even the smell of the room was arousing.

Wondering whether there were moments when God *wasn't* listening to what you were thinking, Peter headed guiltily for a corner where two of the benches joined together. It was only as he plonked himself down that he registered a change in the noise levels. His own echoing footsteps must have covered the fact that one of the showers was running; they were down a step and round a corner, in a tiled area of their own.

Who could it be? The only person Peter could think of was the gym master. And that wouldn't be any great thrill because he was beefy and hairy and altogether too reminiscent of Eddie Bird. Not that Peter had any intention of staying. Not now.

Too late. The naked figure who walked up the step and into the cloakroom was not hairy. He was Rodin's bronze statue of a soldier, in Manchester City Art Gallery, come to life. The statue's dick was much lighter bronze than all the rest; an art student had told Peter that this was because people couldn't resist touching it.

And Peter couldn't resist looking at that area on the living version. He'd never realised that they could be so . . . fleshy.

Mind you, warm water could act as an enlarger. Not that it was in a *rude* state . . . what was he thinking of! His guilty eyes went up the flat stomach, beyond the navel, went between two dark red nipples on a broad wet chest, took in a strong neck, and registered a face.

Last term this would have been dreams-come-true time. The face belonged to Toby Eden. Peeping Peter could not pretend to himself that he was having anything other than an erotic experience. But he was a boy of generous instincts and he just wished that Joan and Vanda had been there to share the naked magnificence of the moment.

'Hello,' said Toby. His voice was as dark as his hair, and he was laughing. 'You bunking off something?'

'Manual.' He watched as Toby started to towel himself vigorously. 'Are you playing wag, too?' God, that schoolboy word for truancy could be misinterpreted; it sounded terrible!

'I've not got a lesson till three o'clock. I went running at lunchtime so I was a bit sweaty.'

He knows I'm looking, thought Peter. And he doesn't care. Anyway, I can't swivel my eyes to the window, that would seem even odder. As Toby rubbed his chest, the dark nipples seemed to become more prominent.

'I've noticed you before,' said the smiling statue. 'You're the one who's always with those two girls. I wonder if you'd like to help me?'

Will it involve touching? wondered Peter wildly. 'In what way?' he stammered aloud.

'We're going to have a mock election this term. I'm a candidate. I need leg-workers. People to rush round with pamphlets.'

Peter would have thought that nothing could have blotted out the sight of his first, fully grown, naked man. But these words did. They transported him back to Magi House where he was hearing Vanda predict that Toby Eden was coming nearer, saying that it would involve pieces of paper and their legs. If she'd already managed to see that much, what might she be able to tell him about himself and his new passion for Joan's Uncle Bruno?

165

'So do you think the three of you can help me?' The towel was down again and everything was on view.

'I'm sure we can.'

'What's your book?'

When Vanda's monthly period arrived her psychic abilities vanished. She knew they'd not gone away forever because, when she spread the cards, she could still hear a distant mutter. But it was as indistinct as the murmur of conversation overheard through a double-brick wall. And the inner eye, the one inside her head, seemed temporarily veiled in muslin.

In this state, all she could do was read the cards by the rules. The spread suggested that her forthcoming meeting with Mr Adcock would have a far from foregone conclusion. But two cards kept coming up together – the Nine of Wands and the Nine of Swords. And that combination belonged to somebody who would, if necessary, walk over broken glass to get her own way.

And I only want tights, she thought. And two pairs of Anello's pointe shoes . . . and perhaps some green character shoes with Cuban heels. And maybe a new examination tunic . . . Let's face it, I want what I can get.

That's why she had taken the bus up to Swinton instead of the one that got her straight home. Her meeting with Adcock was due to take place at four fifteen, which meant she still had ten minutes to kill. In the late 1940s, Swinton town centre was just a long drab row of Victorian shops facing a modern town hall with a Superman tower with a neon clock on it. The design had won a prize but Swintonians could not see why. 'It's just like a bloody brick mill' was the general consensus of opinion.

Swinton was not short of cotton mills. Those and the stands of a bleak rugby football ground were about the only things that broke above all the slate rooftops. The elaborate Victorian parish church was in a style which had not yet come to be admired again. In 1949 it was still smoke-blackened and surrounded by a graveyard full of decaying monumental masonry. Most people just thought of Swinton church as a trolley-bus stop.

Vanda darted under the overhead wires and through the traffic. On impulse, she had decided to kill some time by looking at the display of photographs in the shop window of the *Swinton and Pendlebury Journal*. As Ethel baulked at paying fourpence a week for the newspaper, Vanda always caught up with local events and activities by studying these pictures and reading the captions underneath.

The first one to catch her eye said: 'Local girl Ginger Lambert, who is to play the role of Boy Babe in the forthcoming Xmas panto at Hulme Hippodrome.' And all because she hasn't got a bust, thought Vanda. Ginger Lambert, whose left foot was nothing like as talented as her right one! But the sight of this photograph had served a purpose. It had strengthened Vanda's resolution to screw some money out of Mr Adcock. After all, it was her own money. The lawyer was nothing more than her living money box.

The premises of Adcock, Little and Carr were not in an office block. Instead, their names were lettered in gold on the bay window of a house which was midway between the *Journal* offices and the dearest cakeshop. This house had once had elaborate fretwork gables but these had been replaced by plain wooden boarding and the garden had been cemented over.

More gold lettering on the window of the front door said *Please Enter*. And the first door on the right was marked *Mrs Meeson – Official Spirella Corsetière*. There was no carpet on the hall and staircase, just highly polished brown linoleum. Vanda had time to notice all this because, being early, she was dawdling her way into the building.

I shall start off like a social visit, she told herself. And then I'll get to the business part. But only if it's absolutely necessary will I remove my raincoat. Anyway, I'll probably get further by leaving him guessing.

By now Vanda had reached the first-floor landing. Before she had time to ring the solicitor's bell, his door opened and a woman burst out. 'Got you,' she cried triumphantly. 'Oh dear, sorry. I thought you were boys.' The speaker was like a bony 1920s remnant with brown hair coiled into earphones.

167

'They creep up the stairs and shout. It's the echo that attracts them.' She had glittering eyes and a nervous manner. 'We can't have the front door shut because some of Mrs Meeson's customers don't care to draw attention to their visits.' The woman was all in beige with pleating at the bottom of her skirt. 'I am Miss Prince,' she announced.

'And I am Miss Bell.' After all, one way or another she expected that Gran'ma Dora's estate would be paying for this visit.

'He's not back yet. He's been speaking at another of these lunchtime functions. Some weeks Mr A's all over the county.' She had led the way into an outer office, and Vanda knew for certain sure that all the 'touches', the Scottie dog pencil holder, the pierrot and pierrette biscuit tin and the collection of cacti, had been added by Miss Prince. 'He's a wonderful man,' continued the secretary. 'Did you know that he was recommended for the British Empire Medal? When all came to all, he didn't get it. There's a lot of jealousy in the world of good works.' Miss Prince plainly had the world's biggest crush on her boss, so it should be easy to gain information from her.

The woman returned to her desk and continued with an interrupted task. She was attacking a red tartan necktie with Thawpit, the stain remover, applying it with a little orange cloth. 'I love the fumes of Thawpit,' she said enthusiastically. 'But one has to watch out, they can make you go quite giddy!'

While the woman was, as it were, drugged-up, Vanda decided to press home her advantage. 'How's Mrs Adcock these days?'

'She is, of course, a very good woman.' Almost reluctantly, Miss Prince replaced the cork in the Thawpit bottle. 'And there are altar cloths galore to prove it. You never saw such tiny stitches. Of course, Mrs Adcock was taught by nuns.' She didn't actually say 'nuns', she mouthed it instead, as though the word was not quite suitable for Protestant premises. 'Just sometimes, I think she's a little bit too sedate for him. I feel he could do with somebody with a bit more daring.' Miss Prince placed the red tie underneath her own collar and began to knot it. 'Not too jazzy?' she asked anxiously.

'No . . . no, no.' But you are more than a little bit batty, Vanda thought. Perhaps he gets you to work for him very cheap.

Miss Prince stabbed at the red tartan with a tiepin decorated with yet another Scottie dog. 'Where were we? Mrs Adcock: it's not for me to criticise but sometimes their house is just like the Vatican. Priests? Go to afternoon tea there and you fall over them like footstools. I hope you just saw what I did, Miss Bell?'

'No. No, I didn't.' Vanda was nevertheless quite thrilled at being accepted as Miss Bell for the very first time.

'I bit my own tongue,' said Miss Prince. 'And I did it on purpose. It's not my place to criticise Mrs Adcock. Prayers before meals are one thing but she has them said in Latin. She's the kind who won't let little children have their ball back.'

'This is Mrs Lena Adcock?' asked Vanda, fascinated.

'There's only ever been one. You've surely noticed her letters to the editor of the *Journal*? She's always writing to him about dog dirt. And Mr Adcock's such a sport,' sighed his employee. 'It makes you wonder where he found her.'

It was Vanda's turn to bite her own tongue. But before she could find out more, Miss Prince hid the Thawpit bottle and began tidying her desk because unmistakably masculine footsteps could be heard mounting the staircase. 'I'd know his tread anywhere,' she breathed.

The door opened and in he came, in his black jacket and striped trousers. 'Good afternoon, Mr Adcock.' With these words she turned into another person – a dim subservient mouse. Only the tartan tie gave the lie to her performance. 'Miss Bell to see you.'

'Could you find me a mint, Miss Prince?' he beamed. 'I wouldn't want to go breathing table wine over the young lady.'

You're not getting that near, the young lady thought indignantly. The exertions of the staircase had left him just a little bit flushed, and there were tiny beads of perspiration below his brilliantined hairline. He really was a very pink and meaty man.

'I'm afraid it will have to be a digestive mint, Mr Adcock,' said his secretary respectfully. 'But your lunch could probably do with settling, anyway.'

'And it was chicken again.' He spoke the words mock tragically. This was obviously a long-standing office joke because Miss Prince smiled gratefully.

'To business, to business, to business.' He pushed open the door of his inner sanctum. Vanda wondered whether he was a bit tipsy. 'Not that you need a business excuse to come and see Uncle.'

Uncle?

Perhaps he, too, felt that this needed explanation. 'You are now fourteen.'

'Not till next May.'

'Only thirteen?' The idea seemed to fascinate him. 'Thirteen, eh? That means we have eight years before you' – he treated her to a big show of beaming dentures – 'before you get your hands on the swag. So I thought that perhaps you might like to call me Uncle Bertie. Our families go back a long way.'

Further than you think I know about, Uncle Bertie. A lot further back than tarot readings at Sixth Drive. But she didn't say anything.

Miss Prince was hovering in the doorway; his over-cosy suggestion that Vanda should call him Uncle had plainly changed his adoring secretary's attitude. 'Will you require tea for her, Mr Adcock?' Her tone was icy.

'I think she's a little young to actually enjoy tea. How about pop?'

'It's not something we've got in,' the secretary said tightly.

'I expect you'll be glad of a bit of fresh air, Miss Prince. You could nip to the temperance bar.'

'Dandelion and burdock?' she asked Vanda, with lightly veiled hatred.

There were no two ways about it, the woman was dippy. 'I'll have tea.' Vanda was none too keen on being left absolutely alone with Adcock. In fact, as Miss Prince stomped from the room, the lawyer's youngest client found herself wishing that the woman had left the door ajar. Adcock's eyes were at their most leery.

'This is nice.' His big bulk went down to light the gas fire. It had a saucer of water in front of it. 'This is really very nice indeed.' Which was more than the office was. Big and bare, with a roll-topped desk in the middle, Vanda could easily imagine herself tearing round the linoleum while he panted after her, trying not to bump into the two chairs. Perhaps not, because people would be able to see in from the tops of passing buses.

'Vanderella eh?' he said. 'Vanderella. The little girl who had nothing, and overnight discovered she'd come into a fortune.'

All I've come into so far is a lot of heavy breathing, thought the heiress.

'It's quite warm in here, isn't it?' he asked too innocently. 'Would you like to take off your coat?'

'No thanks.'

The lawyer changed tack: 'How's your lady-mother?' he asked. His upward inflexion made him sound like a budgerigar. 'How is she, eh?' Vanda was coming to realise that he had two voices, a deeply sentimental one and the feathered sergeant major. The sloppy one came back into action for: 'Ethel was once a little belter.'

'She's fine. How's Mrs Adcock?' Vanda had taken enough of the social occasion, now she was going in for the kill. Copying his style, she repeated herself: 'Yes, how's Mrs Adcock?' And without pausing she added, 'I'm a bit short of ready money.'

Mr Adcock, who had been moving towards the seat behind his desk, paused in his tracks and turned to face Vanda. 'You look a lot older than thirteen. So you're a little bit short of the readies?' His feet began to bring him back in her direction.

My God, men do lick their lips in anticipation, thought Vanda. And it's something you hardly ever see a woman do. But in anticipation of what? How much would he be prepared to risk in a room without curtains?

That cushiony hand, the one she remembered from the

171

funeral, landed on her shoulder. Squeeze. 'I'm sure we could reach some arrangement.' Squeeze.

'It would have to be strictly businesslike.' The hand didn't move. 'Wasn't Mrs Adcock Lena McGrath?' Not just the hand moved, his whole body shot across the room. 'Well, wasn't she?'

'In a different life.' It was hard to tell whether his voice was shocked or pleading. He looked ten years older and extremely frightened. 'Just goes to show you can't trust anybody,' he muttered. 'Your grandmother always swore she'd never say a word.'

He mustn't be allowed to malign Dora. 'She didn't. I got it elsewhere. Gossamer Street, the chalky girls, white wreath and veil – I got the lot.' Each revelation had hit him like a punch, shaken him to an extent where Vanda was left wondering whether this was how strokes started.

Eventually he breathed, 'What's your game?'

'I told you. I need some cash.'

'And I think you should know that this office is equipped with a new invention,' he said wildly. 'It's called a Dicta-phone. It can record every word you say. I'm very well known at Swinton police station.'

Vanda knew all about tape recorders. They had one at Odette Ashworth's. Inside her own head she quickly played back all she'd said so far.

He was watching her closely. 'You're the first juvenile blackmailer I've ever come across.'

It was all right. She'd said nothing criminal. All he'd done was jump to conclusions. Mind you, they were the conclusions he'd been meant to jump to.

Obviously thinking that he was in a position to press home some advantage, Bertram Adcock continued with, 'Have you any idea what life is like inside a girls' reformatory?'

'Switch your machine on.' He didn't. 'Go on, switch it on and let it hear this. You've got a hundred thousand quid of mine . . .'

'That's not the precise sum,' he protested. 'But near enough, near enough.'

Vanda had decided to be dead straight with him. 'I'm

somebody who's going to have a big career. I've been told I could end at the Folies Bergère. But I need to go on with me dancing and I want singing lessons too. And Ethel's cut off the cash. You've still not switched your thing on.'

Mr Adcock waved that last thought aside with an airy gesture. 'So we're actually talking in terms of investment.' Relief and curiosity were blended with the remains of fear. 'Why did you think you had to bring Lena into this? Certainly we can sort something out, financially. But whatever possessed you to rake up the past?'

For the first time since she'd met him, Bertram Adcock had ceased to behave like an overripe character from *Dandy* or *Beano*. He had just sounded like a puzzled human being. '*Have* you got that thing on?' she asked him.

'No. This is just between the two of us.'

Vanda was still giving his question about raking up the past her full consideration. She was more than startled by the answers she was getting back. 'I thought it might help you to see things my way,' was the nearest she was prepared to admit to blackmail. 'But now I think about it, there was something else. Can I meet her?'

Of all the things she'd said, this seemed to surprise him the most. 'Meet Lena? But why?'

Out it came. 'Because she knew me gran'ma in the olden days and there's nobody left who did. Me mother's dead awful about Dora. And I miss her . . .' As she looked through the window, a number 38 bus went past. It was no use; all Vanda could do was repeat the same thought in the same unhappy manner: 'I miss her. And it's not as if there's even a grave to go to. And me mother flung her cat out and he's never coming back.' But if Adcock moves to put a comforting arm round me, she thought, I'll scream blue murder.

He did not make that mistake. Instead he said, 'I knew Mrs Doran. And I had very considerable respect for her. Have you thought of advertising for the cat?'

'You can't advertise for a cat that doesn't want to come back.' One thing had to be settled: 'Mr Adcock, I don't like it when I feel you're going to pounce. There'll be no need to call me Miss Bell but I am a customer.'

173

'Quite so.' The smile he offered was hesitant, but it belonged to a much more likeable man – one who was capable of being friendly and concerned. 'Tell me something: is your mother totally against this . . . er . . . step-dancing?'

'Only against finding the money for it. And then there's shoes and tights and bus-fares. You didn't mind me mentioning the pouncing?'

'Not at all,' he reassured her. 'Not at all.' You could see how he'd got on in Rotary, he was quite nice really. 'What we need to do is to approximate an annual figure. Mrs Doran's will is couched in terms that would allow for that. To be quite honest, Nana's main concern was in making sure that you would be the sole beneficiary. You and' – he smiled – 'Dick Barton. So he's gone missing, has he?' Mr Adcock sounded thoughtful. 'That's something your mother should have reported to me. That should give us power to our elbow. Yes, our elbow is definitely not without power.' He obviously couldn't quite resist the temptation to revert to his former self: 'So one day we'll be seeing you at the Folies Bergère, eh?'

'Yes.' Vanda was searching round for some statement that would retain her control over the situation. 'And anybody who wants to have a look will have to buy a ticket.'

'You're Dora Doran's granddaughter all right.' And for the very first time ever he sounded like a genuine friend of the family.

Joan Stone sailed over Pedlar Bridge on her bicycle in a joyful daze. She knew something that Vanda didn't know. As Mr Adcock's youngest client was heading self-importantly for the Swinton bus, Peter had lingered behind to reveal some of the steamy mysteries of the gym cloakroom. Naked, he'd seen him absolutely naked! But Joan was the kind of romantic who cared less for thoughts of the body than for the idea of the soul. In her dreams she knew exactly what she wanted from Toby Eden – she wanted to *merge* with him. She saw herself and Toby as pastel-shaded mists which would roll into one another and co-mingle.

'Bit clammy!' had been Peter's reaction. But this had taken nothing away from Joan's excitement at the thought of being a leg-worker in a mock election. The co-mingling would come later. And to add to her near ecstasy, somebody was burning leaves on a bonfire at the bottom of a garden on Ellesmere Road. Autumn leaf-smoke was her favourite scent on earth.

Pebbles scattered from underneath her tyres as she increased the speed of her pedalling. All Joan wanted to do was get home, get up to the old sewing room and put her news into a letter destined for Sally Morgenstern. But how would fact meet fiction on the subject of Toby Eden? He had already been described as 'a distant kinsman of a leading politician, a young man with pianoforte accomplishments'. She decided she would remain a bit Jane Austen, something along the lines of, 'The gentleman has today revealed that he would like our paths to cross more closely.' In real life, perhaps Sally Morgenstern could be invited to come over for the wedding.

Joan rounded the corner debating lilac versus lemon for bridesmaids' dresses. As she turned into the drive of Ingledene, she saw a battered Riley motor car parked at the foot of the steps of the house. Somebody was passing out books and odd-looking cardboard tubes to Bruno, who was standing on the path.

'You've forgotten the Wedding March,' said a man's voice from inside the Riley. Out came another of the tubes.

'I'll say I have! Hello.' Bruno had registered Joan. 'We've been to the second-hand barrows on Shudehill. I've managed to get hold of some rolls for the American pianola.'

Joan resisted the temptation to bend down and peer inside the car. But it had that kind of pre-war glass which had turned brown with age. 'Who is it?' she whispered.

'Just a friend. Can you take some of these books? They were dirt-cheap but why do they have to chalk the prices on the front? It ruins the bindings.'

The mystery man inside the car called out, 'See you on the steps of the Free Trade Hall. Watch out for Luminol Lil!'

Luminol was a popular sedative, a sleeping draught. 'What's he talking about?' asked Joan.

'He's crazy,' laughed Bruno as the car rolled away and just missed the gatepost. 'Nicely, outrageously, crazy. Look, I even managed to get you a copy of *William Does His Bit*. You've not got that one.'

By now Granny Briggs had appeared at the top of the steps. 'Who's your friend?' she asked Bruno. 'He's driven right over my dingling-Ginnie.'

'Somebody from Bowden,' he replied evasively.

But she plainly considered this to be quite enough of an answer. 'We had a Riley once,' she said. Bowden was a very posh district.

'Let's go and try these.' Bruno was waving one of the cardboard tubes.

Granny Briggs had other ideas. 'I need to talk to Joan.'

'Don't be such a spoilsport,' laughed Bruno. 'There's still a plug on the electric piano, isn't there?'

Granny refused to be mollified. 'We've got a whole cabinetful of those tubes of tunes.'

'Yes, but ours won't play properly. Not since they got damp in them.'

It was no use, Joan simply had to impart her news to somebody: 'Toby Eden's going to be an election candidate and I'm going to be a leg-worker.'

'Oh dear,' said Granny as they all began to troop up the steps. 'He's supposed to have bad blood.'

Bruno immediately rushed to Toby's defence: 'Just because he got himself chucked out of the Unitarian youth club . . .'

'It was hardly the place to try and introduce a roulette wheel.' Granny allowed herself to be shepherded into the front drawing room. 'I'm not at all sure that he's a real Eden. Orphans are often prone to making up stories about themselves.'

How true, thought Joan fervently. How very, very true. The idea of co-mingling seemed more beautifully alluring than ever.

Bruno began to unfasten the safety pins that held the linen shroud around the pianola. Granny Briggs let out a deep sigh. 'It was always a beautiful piece of furniture,' she said as inlaid rosewood came into view. 'Rhoda was the one who really appreciated it. Mind you, she could use it as a real piano too. I remember her teacher telling me that she never had to be taught how to play cross-hands – it just came naturally.' But Granny was obviously thinking of something else, and all the time she'd been talking her gaze had stayed fixed on Joan. 'Another new term, eh? And has this year's English teacher asked you to write another essay about your family?'

'No.' What was coming? 'No, we have to do "How I Would Spend Five Pounds" by Thursday.'

'She's been moved.' Granny was talking to Bruno, who already had the little doors open, the ones which revealed the recess meant for the pianola rolls. 'That's the National Health Service for you. Not so much as a by-your-leave. And I bet they put her in a restraining garment to do it.'

'Are you talking about my mother?' asked Joan, fascinated.

'It's still a locked ward, but apparently they can choose what they want to wear for themselves.'

'She's not a they,' said Joan indignantly, 'she's a she.'

'Don't you dare speak to your own grandmother like that,' snapped Olive Briggs. 'I don't need reminding what she is – or was.' The conversation was now directed towards Bruno. 'It seems it's a lot more relaxed there. When they phoned through, they were even talking about tennis and a perm. I'm afraid I was a bit too straight with them. I said I didn't want that lovely hair ruined by harsh chemicals.'

'Where is this place?' asked Bruno. The paper-covered roller was now in position and he was stretching the tissue, holey as a doyley, across to meet another empty tube. 'Where is it?'

'Two buses away. It's beyond Bolton. I imagine it's where that watery part starts. All gloom and fir trees.' Granny paused but she obviously hadn't finished. 'They go in for treatment there. They think it might do her good to meet Joan.' Suddenly she began to weep. 'I can't take her, Bruno. I can't do it. That poor thing, shunted out of where they understood her. She's nothing more than National Health cargo.'

For years Joan had dreamed of the possibility of such a meeting. So why did she feel hesitant about it now, why did the thought fill her with unexpected shyness?

Granny was talking to Bruno again. 'You'll have to take her.'

'Me?' He almost ripped the flimsy paper in astonishment. But one last fiddle got it stretched into place. 'Why me?'

'Because she pushed your pram when you were little,' snapped Granny. 'And she bought you all those Beatrix Potter books. You're her brother. It's your duty.'

'But you said she attacked you.'

'Oh no I didn't.' Granny had visibly stiffened. 'I said there was an incident. You're the one who's put that complexion onto it. Anyway, they've got her on something new. It's something they developed for shell-shocked soldiers. Never mind the details, will you take Joan or won't you?'

He turned kind but worried eyes towards his niece. 'Do you want to go?'

'I think so. But I feel peculiar about it, Bruno. Should I, or is that awful of me?'

'Well, if it is, it's awful of me too.' He pressed a little brass switch above the keyboard and the room was flooded with the curiously artificial strains of 'There's No Place Like Home'.

On Sunday afternoons Peter generally did his weekend homework, and then he read the *Sunday Graphic* from cover to cover. Today he couldn't decide between the newspaper and Miss Lathom's copy of *Little Women*. Because she was a schoolmistress, he hadn't told her that they intended to play wag this coming Tuesday in order to see the film. But he was interested in seeing how the book would compare with the movie. That was before he noticed the block advertisement on the front page of the newspaper. EVIL MEN it read, and then in smaller lettering, *Britain's Homosexual Menace — See page 4.*

And that was the end of Louisa M. Alcott's chances. Peter got up and closed the lounge door before he so much as dared to open the paper. The *Sunday Graphic* wasn't much given to photo-illustration; mostly it was just pages of dense grey text. And what a tale they had to tell!

There were, it seemed, in every major British city, clandestine meeting places where 'evil men', who called one

178

another by girls' names, gathered together for 'beastly purposes'.

Girls' names? He wasn't at all keen on the idea of that. Would it be obligatory? But nothing on earth would have stopped him from reading on. The article, which was couched in terms of high moral indignation, featured a panel with a black band round it. Inside this, the writer had felt it his duty to list what he called 'the premier cesspits'. Manchester was credited with a pub called the Ogden Arms in Sackville Street. Where was Sackville Street? He could look that up later. First there was the main article to be studied.

It filled him with terror. This piece did not view homosexuality in the same way that the books in the Central Reference Library had done. People like him were, it seemed, 'cursed with abnormality' and 'unrepentant deviates'. As if that wasn't bad enough, he could hear his father lumbering up the hall. Should he shove the paper under a cushion?

Too late – the door had already opened and Eddie was weaving his way into the room. The pubs only sold beer for two hours on Sunday lunchtimes so he wouldn't be really drunk. Peter knew that Eddie would just be restless for seven o'clock when licensed premises would open again, restless and conversational. And probably ready to pick an argument.

'Reading?'

'Er . . . not really.'

'Don't "not really" me.' Eddie's glance had fallen upon the open newspaper. 'The whole Dog and Partridge was talking about that bloody article. We had people like that in the army during the war.' Eddie flopped into an armchair. Two of his trouser buttons were undone. 'I knew a colour sergeant who went under the name of Shirley. Fiercest word of command I've ever heard in any man, but he still called himself Shirley Temple. You could always spot them in the NAAFI; they sat in little groups, snatching *Picturegoer* off one another. Are you one?'

Peter couldn't be sure that he'd heard his father properly. 'Pardon?' he gulped.

'I'd think twice before you answer me. I'm somebody

who's never handed in his service revolver.' Eddie looked bitter. 'Shooting's too good for poofs. Well? Are you one?'

'No.' As Peter blurted it out, he asked God to forgive him for the lie, and for being something so awful that it could provoke this amount of hatred.

'Just checking up,' said Eddie easily. 'Just doing me fatherly duty. What's your book?'

'*Little Women*.' It was out before he realised what he was saying.

'*Little*-fucking-*Women*? What sort of a book is that for a lad to be reading? Where's the Biggles I bought you?' Now it seemed that Eddie was trying to explain things to himself, 'I know, I know. It's just that you're too artistic for war stories. But *Little Women* . . . that's a bit strong for a father to stomach. And stop shaking like a bloody girl.' He relented clumsily with, 'You see, son, these pansies we've been talking about, they'd be all right if they could just bring themselves to 'ave a go with a bint. Once they'd tried a woman, they'd soon forget the other. Tell you what, as soon as you're sixteen I'll take you to town and treat you to one.' Eddie winked conspiratorially. 'We might even 'ave one each.' His eyes were filled with real and friendly concern as he said, 'There's something else that's worrying me.'

'What?' If only there was cooking sherry in the pantry he could volunteer to get him a glass of that. But there wasn't. Anything to get out of the room and away from these awful speeches.

Eddie, however, did not make a speech. He just said one word. 'Church.'

'What about church?' Recently, Peter had taken to going to High Mass with Miss Lathom and Miss Parr.

'I never had anything against Church Parade, we all had to go on it. Except for the Yids, that is. No, what I'm talking about is taking it too serious. I knew a bloody good gunner who was forever hanging round churches – even behind the lines. And do you know what happened to him?' Eddie paused impressively. 'He stopped being able to get the horn.'

'Oh.' Peter could feel himself going bright red.

'I've never told you the facts of life . . .'

'You don't have to. We did them in biology.' It wasn't true but something had to stem this unexpected intimacy.

'All right, Professor,' smiled Eddie. 'What *is* the horn?'

'It's getting an erection,' mumbled Peter.

'And can you?' Eddie was pointing an accusing finger at him.

'Yes.'

His father let out a deep sigh of relief. 'Thank God for small mercies. You can't be all jessie if you can get the 'orn.' Seizing hold of the copy of the *Sunday Graphic* he scrumpled it into the ball. 'I'm going to put this on the back of the fire. I didn't think they should have even been allowed to write down where it goes on.'

As Eddie held the paper in the glowing cinders with a poker, his son caught himself thinking of a name and an address. The Ogden Arms, Sackville Street, Manchester.

It was the perfect day for playing wag – clear sunlight and an autumn breeze. The trio had made their separate ways to Eccles. As Peter put it, 'If we're on our own, and somebody stops us, we can always claim that we're going to the dentist. Three of us together would never get away with that.'

They finally met up on the high stools of Redman's snack counter. Redman's was a chain of grocery stores whose windows displays always featured lentils and haricot beans and little hillocks of dried fruits. And the reputation of Redman's potato cakes stretched right across Lancashire.

'I'm buying,' announced Vanda. 'Three Bovrils and three hot potato cakes with best butter,' she said to the woman behind the counter.

The assistant's hygienic dairymaid's cap extended as far as her eyebrows. 'Shouldn't you all be at school?'

Vanda assumed a fake-ashamed expression for her impro-vised answer. 'We're on our way to the nit clinic,' she said.

Joan Stone was not going to be left out of any game that involved imagination. 'Yes, we've been singled out for special treatment.'

Almost involuntarily the woman moved further back behind the counter so that she had to stretch out a hand to

181

slap the cold potato cakes onto the hot griddle. Noticing another and much younger woman doing nothing, she called out, 'Would you look after this order, Jean?' Unable to resist the temptation to scratch her mobcapped scalp, she moved well away from the truanting trio.

'How come you're so rich?' Peter asked Vanda.

'Adcock coughed up. Odette Ashworth has to send him bills for tuition. But I got cash, for shoes and things, out of him. And you know men, they've no idea.'

'The big picture starts at five past two,' said Joan. She hadn't even bothered to lower her voice because Jean, on the griddle, didn't look the kind who took much interest. But the other woman had come back and, standing ostentatiously away from the Barton Grammar School pupils, she whispered something in Jean's ear.

'Poor little sods,' said Jean quite audibly. 'It's always the same after warm weather, our dog's flecky too.'

'I wish we'd had the sense to dump these.' Vanda was clutching her maroon linen sewing bag. So was Joan, and both had satchels on their backs. This term Peter was using a leather shopping bag which looked a bit, but not a lot, like a briefcase.

'Separate or together?' asked Jean the counter assistant. Vanda was already holding out a ten-shilling note. Jean hadn't finished. 'Sometimes the stuff from the clinic doesn't shift them,' she said. 'What you want to ask your mothers to get is Rankin's Ointment.'

And the funny thing was that all three truants were overcome by a terrible urge to scratch their heads. Peter was the only one who actually gave way to it. 'Be sure your sins will find you out,' he murmured. But they soon forgot any imaginary itching as they gave themselves up to the luxury of the world's finest buttered potato cakes.

Traces of the butter were still being wiped from chins as they emerged into the sunlight where Joan said, 'All get your books out.' She had instructed them to carry copies of *Little Women*. If questioned at the box office, they were to wave the books about and claim that their visit was purely in the cause of study.

Actually, Vanda had forgotten hers. But it didn't matter because when they got to the ticket desk the two women inside the glass rabbit hutch were deep in an argument. 'James Mason doesn't but Stewart Granger does,' one of them announced mysteriously.

'A one and sixpenny please,' said Peter.

He handed over the exact money and a ticket emerged from the automatic dispenser. The cashier continued talking over her shoulder to her friend, who was sitting at the other opening. 'Stewart Granger definitely does because you can see his tongue go right in.'

'They're showing more and more,' said the other one. You could tell she didn't like whatever it was. So concerned was she with the matter that she clanked out Vanda and Joan's tickets without making any comment at all about school uniforms.

'Now we only have to get past the man on the door,' breathed Joan. But he was old and short-sighted and having trouble with his torch batteries. 'Anywhere after the first gangway,' he told them.

The floor of the cinema sloped quite sharply downhill. *British Movietone News* was already flickering across the screen in black and white. The commentator, who sounded like a duck quacking, was saying that growing world mistrust of Britain's currency meant that Sir Stafford Cripps had been obliged to devalue the pound by thirty per cent.

'He certainly wasn't made Chancellor of the Exchequer for his looks,' said Vanda. As they sat down, the scene changed to the South of France. 'It's festival time in Cannes,' announced the weirdly over-enthusiastic voice, 'and all the starlets are sunning themselves *sur la plage*.'

Joan made a mental note of the crowds of people in furs and diamonds and white dinner jackets arriving at the première of *Une Nuit Chez Zou-Zou*. She actually caught herself looking for 'Mummy' in this worldly throng. Joan knew exactly what that fantasy figure would look like, and she immediately began to compose sentences for her next letter to Sally Morgenstern: 'Mummy had to be at the festival because one of her books is being made into a film – by Italians.' Italy was surely far enough away for safety?

Bolton, of course, was much nearer; but the trip to see her mother had yet to take place. Granny was forever hiding in the shadows of phrases like 'Give Rhoda time to settle in' and 'The whole idea could be a big shock to more than one system.'

'French kissing,' murmured Peter.

'Eh?' Vanda was more interested in two women who were making their way along the row in front.

'That's what those ladies in the box office were talking about. I've worked it out.' Sitting there in the darkness he reflected that, with the aid of a street map, he had also worked out the whereabouts of the Ogden Arms, Sackville Street, Manchester. You went right down to the gloomy end of Princess Street and up a turning. The pub was at the side of a dank canal.

He expected that once you got inside it would be exactly like the Café Royal in *The Picture of Dorian Gray*. Oh yes, there'd be people sipping absinthe (whatever that was) beneath gilded Egyptian mirrors. Clothes: they would be the problem. As a third-former he was out of flannel shorts and into long pants. But these were still, unmistakably, grey flannel school uniform. He expected that the habitués of the Ogden Arms would all be got up like the illustration of Lord Alfred Douglas in the book of famous homosexuals.

There was an old spotted scarf at home; Peter had already tried tying it inside the neck of his school gaberdine. It had made him look a bit more exotic but it hadn't made him look eighteen – that's how old you had to be to get inside pubs. Peter tried to imagine himself sniffing fine old cognac but reality intruded with the smell of the Broadway's scented disinfectant.

'Of all places!' Vanda was full of indignation. The women groping their way along the next row had finally settled for seats which directly blocked her view of the screen. 'Excuse me, but could I trouble you to remove your hat?' This standard request was far from unreasonable as the hat was both high-crowned and wide-brimmed.

The offender did not even bother to turn round. 'You could always move.'

Vanda got to her feet. 'Come on,' she said to the others.

'Sit down!' came from the row behind them.

It was Joan who leant forward and explained. 'Sorry to trouble you again,' she said, 'but patrons to the rear of us don't want us to move.'

With much tut-tutting, the woman consented to remove her headgear. 'It would probably be the same wherever we sat,' she grumbled to her companion.

'Give me your hatpins.' Her friend spoke in a soothing singsong voice. 'This sari of mine makes a jolly good pincushion.'

'Oh my God!' whispered Joan. 'It's Ruth Chatterjee's mother. You see her round Monton with a shopping basket and a dusty hem.'

Up on the screen the news had been replaced by the advertisements. They were just slides: 'Fowne's for Gloves' and 'After the Film, Why Not Try a Tasty Tea in the Broadway Café?' These and others were accompanied by a tango played on an invisible Mighty Wurlitzer. The organist must have been skilled because he even joined in with the beginning of the orchestra music under the opening titles of the big picture.

Little Women began to weave its spell. The film seemed to make more of the character of Amy than the book had done; perhaps this was because Elizabeth Taylor was playing the part. When Peter Lawford strode onto the screen as Laurie, the girls at either side of Peter let out little moans of pleasure – the actor could have been Toby Eden's brother.

'But Toby's taller,' breathed Vanda. Joan just went 'Oooh' over and over again. 'Oooh, oooh, oooh.'

'Shush!' came indignantly from the row in front.

There's a lot of crying to *Little Women*. They'd all brought handkerchiefs but these were wringing wet before the story was halfway told. 'And Beth's got to nearly die yet,' sniffled Joan Stone. 'I'm awash. Whatever are we going to do?'

Not taking her eyes from the screen, Vanda undid her maroon needlework and handed out portions of half-finished

185

sewing. She and Joan had a knicker leg each. Peter was allocated something smaller. Although the three of them knew the story well, Hollywood was well known for changing things. And for several terrible minutes it really did look as though Beth was genuinely going to heaven.

But the fever turned, the patient's breathing eased, and the three youngest members of the audience gave their noses a final blow on sections of sprigged cotton which should really have been at Mrs Waterworth's domestic science lesson.

'What am I blowing on?' asked Peter.

'It's the gusset,' whispered Vanda. And she began to chink with laughter. It was that kind of suppressed amusement that is highly infectious and soon the three of them were shaking enough to make the seats creak.

The End came on the screen and double fury glared round at them from the row in front. The one with the straying hair said to the Indian woman, 'Give me my hatpins, Mrs Chatterjee. And you three children, don't think you can just slope off like that because you can't.'

They couldn't anyway because the lights had turned toffee pink, the Mighty Wurlitzer had risen up through the floor of the stage, and 'God Save the King' was playing. In 1949 everybody froze to attention for the National Anthem. The two women were the kind who even sang the words. The moment they were ended, they stopped facing the front and turned round again. 'I know you, girlie,' said Mrs Chatterjee.

For an awful minute Peter thought she was talking to him. But she wasn't, she was addressing to Joan Stone. 'You're the snob's granddaughter.' Turning to her companion she explained: 'Her grandmother had the infernal cheek to refer to me as a native. And that was straight after we'd knelt together at the Communion rail.'

The other woman was stabbing her hat into place. 'You're a disgrace to the uniform,' she told them. This sounded extra grim because she still had one of the hatpins between her teeth. Now she held it aloft like an avenging sword. 'Do you know who I am?'

Joan managed 'No' but the other two just stood transfixed.

'I am Mrs Cotter. I used to be Miss Platt – senior history mistress at Barton.'

'She's an old girl of the school too,' put in fidgety Mrs Chatterjee. 'She's on the honours boards, twice.'

'And I am ashamed.' Despite all her efforts the hat was not quite straight. 'Deeply, bitterly ashamed. I am going straight from this cinema to a telephone box. Names: I want your names and your form number.'

Retribution came swiftly. School assembly was always taken by the headmaster, Pixie Picton. Even his wife used the nickname Pixie though he was six foot tall with huge feet and a thundering voice. Wednesdays was his morning for preaching a short sermon. 'God is love and putting milk bottles down the boys' bogs is not entertaining. The offenders will kindly desist. We would do well to remember that our heavenly Father gave his only begotten Son to come down to an ungrateful earth where some sixth-formers seem to be under the impression that their common room is a Mississippi gambling hell: Toby Eden, see me after assembly. The face of the risen Lord must surely be wearing an aghast expression as it gazes down on the perfidies of the younger end of this school: Vanda Bell, Joan Stone and Bird of Three L to see Miss Staff immediately this service is over.'

As far as Peter was concerned, the announcement was subtle punishment in itself – only girls were sent to see Miss Staff the senior mistress. Never before had he heard of a boy being handed over to her mercies. She was a short squat woman who taught geography and a bit of English. Perhaps it was this latter interest which caused Miss Staff to weigh her every word most carefully.

'The three of you have brought the entire school into disrepute.' By now they were in her study with its feeble coal fire and the oak furniture which looked as though it had been brought in from a good middle-class home. A curiously sickly reproduction of a painting of fairies, by Margaret Tarrant, hung beside the door to Miss Staff's personal washroom. That extra facility, more than anything else, underlined the fact that you were in the presence of a person of consequence.

Though she was wearing a Cambridge BA gown over a rust-coloured frock, both her hairstyle and her profile brought Julius Caesar to mind.

Miss Staff continued playing weights and measures with words: 'Mrs Cotter was frankly appalled. Setting the question of truancy to one side for the moment, how could you bring yourselves to waft around . . . er . . . undergarments? Joan Stone, you at least did not lie about your identity.' But the beady eyes had swivelled to Vanda. 'Did you seriously think that anybody was going to believe that you and Bird were Phyllis Dixey and Stanley Matthews?'

'It was just a joke.'

'Explain the humour to me.'

Vanda couldn't. 'It seemed funny at the time.'

'Well, it didn't take Scotland Yard to work out your true identities. Come!' Somebody had knocked at the door.

Quite a big girl called Glenys Griffiths walked into the room. She was already proferring three pennies. 'Excuse me Miss Staff but could I buy . . .'

Miss Staff became highly agitated. 'No, no, no.' With her thumb she was indicating the presence of Peter. But the girl refused to be silenced: 'It's a real emergency, Miss Staff. In fact . . .'

'Bird,' boomed the senior mistress, 'look out of the window.'

'What at?'

'Never mind what at. Just do as I say.'

As Peter gazed through the glass and towards the sundial erected to the memory of Mr Jenkins-Jones, Vanda and Joan watched the teacher unlock a stock cupboard and take out a sanitary towel which she proceeded to wrap up in a sheet of graph paper. Threepence changed hands, and a curt nod dismissed Glenys from the room.

Obviously I'm not regarded as a full girl, thought Peter, who had already worked out what was happening. First I'm sent here and now I'm just a bloody in-between. For a mad moment he contemplated saying, 'Although I'm a homosexual, Miss Staff, I still know how women's bodies work, and you're much more embarrassed about it than I am.'

188

'You may turn round, Stanley Matthews.'

Joan Stone decided to put in her two penn'orth. 'The thing is, Miss Staff, we went on what you might call a literary pilgrimage.'

'You might. I don't. You will each write a thousand lines: "An appreciation of literature is better gained from the printed page than from a seat at the Broadway Cinema." '

'It won't all go on one line,' protested Vanda.

'Then put it on two. And I haven't finished. All three of you are also on detention for a week. You may go to your classroom.'

Her study led out into a small, tunnel-like hallway. As they emerged from its gloom into the main entrance hall, Joan Stone said, 'I wouldn't care but there's no Court of Appeal; I wasn't supposed to be as bad as you two but she lands me with just the same punishment.'

Somebody else was emerging from another shadowy tunnel, one which led to the headmaster's study. It was Toby Eden. 'Hello,' he said to Peter. 'So you're in the doghouse too.'

'Did he beat you?' Peter asked. Visits to the headmaster's study often ended with the swish of the cane.

'Worse than that,' laughed Toby. 'Far worse. He's gone and landed me with running the detention class for a whole week.'

Detention was always held after school in the geography room. *Shall We Journey to Africa or the Antarctic?* queried a poster by the side of the blackboard. The walls of the room were covered with pictures and diagrams with creases down their middles and the words *Teachers' World Supplement* printed in the bottom right-hand corner. You had plenty of time to notice things like that because detention was about doing absolutely nothing but sitting still – for three-quarters of an hour.

Today there were just the three of them at desks, and Toby was behind the teacher's table on the platform. Rain was hurling itself against the windowpanes. The only other sounds were distant voices coming from the boys' cycle sheds and the noise of home going bicycle wheels swishing their way through puddles in the playground.

As Joan gazed up at Toby on the platform she thought, I expect heaven will be a lot like this; we'll just be content to sit in the presence of Jesus. The idea of a week of detention with Toby Eden had quite restored her faith in God.

Vanda's thoughts were much more prosaic. Say it was just me and him, the two of us, here together. What would I want to do with him? Kissing was definitely part of it, and she quite fancied the idea of nuzzling him – the way horses did. Beyond that she wasn't too sure. Vanda's body caused people to think of her as a sexual lighthouse but, unlike Joan, her inner self had no great interest in the idea of physical passion. I bet he'd make a belting pal, she thought. We could go to a cricket match at Old Trafford together, and we'd laugh a lot on the bus afterwards. But increasing rain on the windows reminded her that the cricket season was over.

He looked better with no clothes on, thought Peter. I just wish Joan was allowed to ask us to her house again so I could catch a glimpse of her Uncle Bruno – fully clothed would be more than sufficient. He took a penknife from his pencil box. Somebody had already carved a capital P on the desk and Peter began to turn it into a B.

Noticing what he was doing, and that nobody had stopped him, Vanda raised her hand.

'Yes?' Toby lowered his copy of the *National Geographic*. 'What can I do for you?'

'We've got a thousand lines to write. Would it be OK if we did them here?'

'I bet you sixpence you can't do three hundred by a quarter past four.' That was when detention was due to end.

'Sixpence?' asked Vanda. 'You're on.'

Joan wasn't at all sure that he ought to be encouraged to gamble. Hadn't it got him into trouble in the past? 'Are we allowed to write our lines if we don't take part in the bet?'

'Suit yourself,' he replied disinterestedly.

'Well, I will have a little wager,' she decided.

Peter got out his rough notebook and began writing. And it was to him that Toby spoke next – which Joan considered

190

very unfair. 'Don't you know about special pens for lines?' Toby asked Peter. 'You wire two together, just the right width apart; that way the job's done in half the time. But you need an ink bottle with a wide opening – Parker Quink's the best.'

'I'm gambling sixpence like Vanda,' said Joan, just to be sure he knew.

'Did Bird tell you about the mock elections?' asked Toby.

Joan paused from scribbling; this was much more interesting. 'What party will you represent?' It would be well worth losing sixpence for the chance of talking to him.

'I'm to be an Independent.' He smiled ruefully. 'Pixie's under the mistaken impression that it will give me a sense of responsibility.'

Vanda was looking at his nice friendly face. Yes, he would make a very good pal. But business was business: 'What will you give us for working for you?'

'The honour's enough,' protested Joan. Then she wished she hadn't because it had sounded like crawling.

'What will you give us?' persisted Vanda.

'Three jumps at the cupboard door and a bite at the knob.' Lancashire children were more used to being given this reply when they asked what there was to eat.

The door rattled open, all the posters on the wall fluttered, and in stomped Miss Staff. 'We are not accustomed to sounds of hilarity emerging from the detention room.' This pronoucement was directed towards Toby Eden. 'Why are these children writing?'

'Aren't they meant to be?' he asked innocently. Toby suddenly looked too much of a man for a school blazer.

'They are meant to be meditating on their misdemeanours.'

'I'm sorry, Miss Staff.' He sounded quite relaxed. 'It's years since I was put on detention myself.'

'Your recent crimes have been too grave, Eden, for such mild punishment.'

Thank goodness we hadn't started to make those cheating pens, thought Joan. Peter was wondering why he'd never noticed before that Miss Staff went in for almost exactly the same kind of heroic footwear as his friend Miss Lathom. The idea opened up some startling thought processes.

Vanda was the only one who actually said anything: 'It was our fault. We took advantage.' And Joan could have killed her. Why hadn't she thought of the line herself? And why had she never realised that she and Vanda were fated to be deadly rivals? Even with old Miss Staff in the room, Toby's eyes had momentarily rested on Vanda's bust. Except he must have sensed that Joan was studying him so he treated her to an almost imperceptible wink. A common wink! Oh the whole situation was dreadful, dreadful. But it also had to be admitted that it was wonderfully exciting.

Vanda went straight home and counted out the tarot cards. As the pattern of the spread began to emerge, she realised that the guiding voice was back inside her head. '*Look at Joan's card*,' it sniggered. The Moon was upside-down.

'*Doesn't bode well for young Miss Stone*,' gurgled the voice. It was nothing like as distinct or revealing as it had been at Magi House. In fact, today, it sounded as though it was coming up through a grid over a drain. Vanda couldn't have put a definite gender on the sound to save her life. It reminded her of an illustration Peter had shown her in one of Pendlebury Library's bound volumes of *The Yellow Book*, a drawing of a gnarled and dwarfish eunuch. '*Cheek!*' it giggled, so it must have been able to read her mind. '*Bloody impertinence. But I can't resist telling you that a little friend of yours is not going to be at tomorrow's detention party.*' Even as Vanda began to wonder whether she was going barmy, she was forced to admit to herself that the voice might just know what it was talking about. The Moon dealt upside-down did not bode well for Joan Stone.

Joan had cycled home to Ingledene in a state of heightened awareness. Love does that to some people. Even the touch of the rain on her cheek reminded her that life was about all the basic elements – wind, air, fire, water. But mostly she was thinking that her own life would rise to another glorious climax at half past three tomorrow afternoon. Detention, detention, magical, painful detention!

Painful? She was trying to remember what Peter had said when they finally left the geography room: 'Did you notice how his eyes kept flickering over to Vanda's front?' Joan's own bust was just two faint swellings. Tomorrow, perhaps she could stuff a couple of artfully folded handkerchiefs down the front of her Junior Miss size one brassière. Joan always pretended that she was already into a size two. Anyway, once she had shown Toby her soul, the lack of wobbly mounds would cease to matter. When he saw how much she loved him, the great golden light of her devotion would be enough to enthral him into her arms. It took a snapping corgi to bring her back to reality. The animal rushed out of the garden of a dormer bungalow called Cosy Nook and tried to attach itself to her ankles.

When she reached home, Joan flung down her bicycle by the kitchen railings and rushed into the house to see whether the dog's teeth had broken her skin. How long, she wondered, did hydrophobia take to set in? No, it hadn't even left a mark. So now she was free to luxuriate in more thoughts of Toby Eden.

Not for long. In her imagination he was just handing her a single gardenia and saying 'May I have the pleasure of the next kiss?' when Granny Briggs marched in, umbrella in hand and weighed down under a load of paper carrier bags marked *Brough's the Cleaners*.

'What's that bike doing where somebody could break a leg?' Before Joan had time to answer, Granny continued with, 'Don't move from this spot. I want to see whether Brough's have shrunk your best frock.'

They hadn't. The tartan might have been a shade less aggressively blue than before, and the Peter Pan collar fractionally more droopy, but apart from that it was the same old best frock it had been for two long years.

Outside, a car began to roll up the drive. 'I don't know why he has to choose friends with sports cars,' grumbled Granny. 'They play havoc with my potholes. You notice he never invites the drivers in?'

Joan felt obliged to come to Bruno's defence. 'You've never exactly encouraged us to invite people in.'

'I'd still like to know what sort of fast crowd he's running around with.' Granny ripped another of the cleaner's carrier bags asunder and began a minute examination of a jumper suit of her own. 'There are too many mystery acquaintances and not enough studying done for my liking.' She sniffed the jacket of her newly cleaned outfit. 'Good heavens! This smells exactly like Vanda Bell's mother did at that benighted musical evening. Have you done your homework yet?'

Joan debated mentioning detention. A whole week of it was going to take some explaining. She was saved from immediate trouble by a loud crashing sound and a yell from outside. 'What did I tell you?' said Granny with happy satisfaction. 'He's gone and fallen over that bike.'

Joan moved towards the door but before she got there Bruno burst into the room with, 'I've got oil off your chain all over my new riding mac.'

'A thoroughly affected garment too, when you haven't got a horse,' sniffed Granny. 'And to think that in India we once went round literally begging people to take polo ponies off our hands at the end of the season. If that coat needs cleaning you'll have to sing in the streets for the money. Brough's have already had a fortune off me today.' She took out a flowered dress, one that Joan had never seen before, out of another of her carriers. It was of a pre-war design, the inverted pleats in the skirt lined with apple green. 'What d'you think?' she asked Bruno.

He studied the dress helplessly for a moment. In the end he managed, 'Are they going to let her out to go to tango teas?'

'Let who out?' asked Joan. Even as she said it, she knew that they must be talking about her own mother. 'Is she coming home?'

'Are you mad?' snorted Granny. Under the circumstances, Joan felt that the old woman could have chosen her words more carefully. 'The last time they tried letting her home she deliberately pushed your pram into a duckpond.'

This hurt. 'Didn't she like me?'

'I can't pretend she was much struck. She wasn't much

struck on anything at the time. She even shouted the bandleader down at a flannel dance at Monton Cricket Club.' Granny shook out another garment. This was a white linen frock with a genuine sailor's collar.

'It's straight out of *No, No, Nanette*,' protested Bruno.

'They said "some of her clothes",' retorted Granny. 'And these are they. Don't think my own heart doesn't bleed, Bruno, because it does. Nothing would please me more than to go to Kendal's and get her everything new. The money isn't there.' She pushed angrily at the tortoiseshell combs in her very clean white hair. 'It just isn't there. I wasn't born to go round switching off electric lights and worrying about the cost of bathwater.' Her voice filled up with undisguised yearning as she said, 'Just for once I'd love something brand-new, something totally frivolous in a Kendal's carrier bag. I've not even had a new winter coat since the end of the war.'

Joan experienced a fiercely protective rush of emotion. Suddenly her arms were round Granny Briggs. 'I'll buy you one,' she promised. It was a bit like hugging a wooden plank but she ploughed on with, 'You'll get one out of the very first money I earn.'

'You?' The heavy scorn was worse than a cup of cold water in the face. 'And how do you propose to earn that sort of money?'

Fragile belief in herself took an unhappy plunge. 'With s-s-stories.' But real self-belief is made of cork and Joan's bobbed back to the surface with the words, 'I'm going to be a famous writer.' It was the first time she'd ever said them aloud at Ingledene.

And the first time Granny had been given the chance to react. 'A famous writer?' she scoffed. 'And this comes from the girl who can't even spell necessary! If it's you I've got to rely on, I'd better look after this coat; it's plainly going to have to last me till my dying day.' Again she picked up the *No, No, Nanette* frock and gazed at it unhappily. 'I'll put these dresses in a little attaché case with a tin of peaches and a jar of Marmite. Funny how she still remembers she likes Marmite.'

'Did you ring up Joan's school?' enquired Bruno.

'The secretary was very understanding. They know Joan's a special case.'

She didn't like this. 'Why am I a special case?'

'Because of where your mother is,' snapped Granny. 'You've got to have tomorrow off to go and see her.'

'But I'll miss detention,' protested Joan wildly. 'I can't miss detention.'

'Joan,' Granny Briggs was at her most severe, 'I just hope you don't go round saying silly things like that in public. What girl minds missing detention? And what have you been up to? Never mind that, I've enough on my mind as it is. But watch out for making stupid statements when you get to the mental hospital. They're trained to look for signs like that. I don't want them phoning me up to say they've decided to keep you there.'

It wasn't two buses to the hospital, altogether it was three. But Granny had been quite right about it being near reservoirs and ringed round by dismal fir trees.

'It's the fact that they're all exactly the same height which makes them so sinister,' observed Joan as they dismounted from the last bus, a single-decker.

'Probably because they were all planted at the same time.' Bruno was carrying the little attaché case. Joan had hold of a bunch of flowers, yellow antirrhinums, pinched from the garden of the bedsitting-room house next door and wrapped in once used but specially ironed Kendal's paper. 'At least it's stopped raining,' added Bruno.

'Yes, but there's something creepy about the way those fir trees are going drip-drip-drip.'

Other people had also got off the bus. They too were making their way up the wide tarmacadam driveway, towards the red-brick mansion on the hill. Nobody acknowledged anybody else. Well, not beyond the merest of nods; then they seemed to cast their eyes down again. 'It's as though they're ashamed,' whispered Joan.

'It's getting better than it used to be.' Bruno was refusing to speak in anything other than normal tones. 'When I was little I was made to pretend that Rhoda didn't exist.'

By now they were nearer to the house, which could easily have been a great big Queen Anne Barclay's Bank. It had an imposing pedimented portico and a lot of bow windows. 'Christ!' cried Joan. She'd never said that in her life before, but this was her first experience of heavily barred windows. 'It *is* a loony bin. I mean, I always knew it was but . . . Slow down a minute, Bruno.' She couldn't remember a time when she hadn't wanted this moment, yet now it was here she felt distinctly nervous. Nervous? Frightened. 'What's it going to be like inside?'

'You're as wise as I am.'

'Well, what was the last one like?'

'Don't know.'

'You mean to tell me that Granny's throwing the pair of us in at the deep end? There's a man waving at me through one of the windows. What shall I do?'

'Wave back. Come on, there are a whole lot of people on the steps. Let's get in with them.'

Under cover of the portico the other visitors seemed released to mumble. They were half whispering drab phrases like 'He's been on that electric shock treatment' and 'Not quite so many locked doors as they have at Prestwich Asylum.'

Locked doors: Joan had forgotten about those. This one was opened by a middle-aged man in a porter's uniform who allowed everybody to enter. He was actually smiling, which struck Joan as being more sinister than friendly. 'Have you got a visiting docket?' he asked Bruno. The other visitors were already proffering slips of buff paper. Joan's uncle produced just such another from his wallet. 'To see Rhoda Stone,' he said.

The man examined the docket. 'Oh, she's on Primrose,' he murmured darkly. 'You need an escort to get to Primrose.' Joan had already noticed a line of uniformed nurses standing waiting in the panelled hall, which was like a bigger version of the one at Magi House. 'Stop here.' Still holding onto the docket, the porter began to move towards these women. He had a funny walk; one leg dragged behind him. He got to the line, addressed one of the nurses and, limping painfully, led

197

her back to Bruno and Joan. 'Nurse Whelan will take you along.'

Hers was a nurse's uniform with a difference: a huge bunch of keys hung from a chain round her waist. 'We did try phoning,' she said with an Irish accent, 'but you'd already left.' Nurse Whelan had look-into-you eyes. She was a burly woman of indeterminate years. Her age was further blurred by the fact that her hair had been dyed aggressively black. Joan supposed that, when it came to staff, places like this had to take what they could get.

'I'm afraid Rhoda worked herself up into a bit of a lather this morning. It ended up with her pouring a jigsaw puzzle into the big milk jug. Bless her.' She added this in a way that left Joan wondering whether Nurse Whelan said 'Bless her' after every transgression. She was leading the way towards a heavy wooden door. 'Follow me.' Up came the bunch of keys. Click. The door was unlocked.

A long corridor didn't smell of hospitals, it smelt of institutional gravy. The windows were covered with screens made of that heavy wire netting that goes round tennis courts. In the distance somebody screamed. 'Lottie, at it again,' muttered Nurse Whelan, 'bless her.' She raised the jangling chatelaine from her waist and, click, another door was open. 'A few more before we get to Rhoda. You should really have brought your climbing boots.' Steep uncarpeted stairs lay ahead of them. 'We thought you'd like privacy so I've put her in a special little room, up at the back.'

Will it be padded? wondered Joan wildly. Bruno must have sensed her panic because she suddenly felt him take her hand.

Nurse Whelan had not missed this. 'Nervous?' She beamed at Joan.

'Just a bit.'

'They're only people who are away in little worlds of their own.'

The big nurse began the steep ascent, the other two followed behind. 'Rhoda's a lot calmer than she was this morning. The chemical cosh is a wonderful thing. Before we had it, all we could do was hose them down with jets of ice-cold water. Up one more flight and we're there.' She was obviously used to the stairs but the visitors were panting a bit. Over her shoulder, the nurse said to Bruno, 'How long is it since you've seen her?'

'Years. Umpteen years.'

Nurse Whelan brought the procession to a halt by stopping and turning round. 'You do know she's regressed, don't you? Dr Shultz made us all read through her case notes when they unloaded her here – bless her. She's regressed very considerably. How old are you, dear?' It was Joan she was addressing now.

'Me? I'm going towards fourteen.'

'Rhoda's much younger than that.'

Joan was doing mental arithmetic. 'She's got to be at least thirty-seven.'

'She's been shut away for an awful long time,' sighed the nurse. As she showed them her back again and carried on climbing, she was already reaching for her keys; it took two of them to unlock the final door.

The room could have been somewhere that was used by a government department for interviewing members of the general public. There was a barred window, high up on one wall, and the only furniture was a table and two tubular aluminium and canvas chairs.

'Where is she?' Joan was all but whispering again.

'Where's my little love?' laughed Nurse Whelan. But it wasn't Joan she was talking to. 'I know your games, Rhoda Stone. You're playing hide-and-seek behind the door again.' She beckoned the visitors to follow her into the room. The feel of the bunch of flowers in Joan's hand made her wonder whether this cell contained a vase; and if it did, was it about to come crashing down on her own head?

'There you are!' As Nurse Whelan pushed the door back into place, she revealed a figure standing behind it. Could a grown-up really be obliged to wear a 1920s bobbed hairstyle with a pale blue ribbon-bow tied at an angle above the fringe. But this grown-up, in a shapeless institutional dress made of material that looked like mattress ticking, this grown-up was hugging a balding teddy bear.

'I'd forgotten how alike you look,' murmured Bruno. He

sounded just like somebody keeping his voice down at the cinema. Recollecting himself, he managed, 'Hello, Rhoda.' He didn't kiss her, which Joan thought was odd; normally, Bruno was a very hugging sort of person. But there was something set apart about the creature with the teddy. Her skin was waxy and her eyes perturbed.

'You know Bruno, don't you?' coaxed Nurse Whelan.

Rhoda ignored her visitors. 'Bruno's just a little boy. He goes to the kindergarten at Miss Frame's.'

'I grew up.' He was attempting to be his usual cheerful self.

She wasn't reacting to him. 'Where's Bruno?' she asked the nurse, puzzled.

'And this is Joan.' Nurse Whelan pushed the woman's daughter forward. 'Take your coat off, Joan, or you'll have us thinking you're not stopping.'

Joan didn't want to remove her gaberdine, she wanted to run. But she did as she was asked and thought of all the locked doors between here and the main road.

Rhoda Stone was also behaving as though she was watching a movie. 'She's got a nicer dress than I have.' It was the blue tartan one. Joan had put it on specially. But specially for what? Everything seemed in slow motion; it was like walking under water.

Bruno held up the attaché case. 'We've brought you some dresses.' Placing the soft-topped case on the table he clicked open the rusty brass locks. All-seeing Nurse Whelan moved across the room in a kind of deft way that made you wonder whether she was good at ballroom dancing. Seizing hold of the jar of Marmite and the tin of peaches, she said, 'It wouldn't do to tempt Providence. I wouldn't want to be responsible for either of you getting brained.'

'Marmite,' smiled Rhoda. 'Lovely Marmite.'

'She still loves her belly,' laughed the nurse. 'Look at these nice frocks, Rhoda. You're going to be quite the society lady.'

Putting her teddy bear to sit on one of the tubular chairs – 'Nobody touch Mr Teddy' – Rhoda approached the case.

As if to encourage her, Bruno lifted up the white dress with the sailor collar. 'Look!'

The voice which answered him was no longer childlike. It

belonged to an embittered middle-aged woman. 'Sid Stone bought me that. It was always cheap and awful, just like he was himself.' The snarl vanished and the face went back to being waxily drugged.

'She comes and goes,' sighed the Irish nurse.

Rhoda began to clap her hands. 'Peaches. Rhoda wants peaches and custard.' The clapping stopped as she gazed suspiciously at Joan. 'If it's a party, why haven't you brought me a present?'

'But I have.' If I can invent letters to America, I ought to be able to go along with this charade, thought Joan. 'I've brought you a beautiful bunch of flowers.'

'Now don't you be destructive, Rhoda,' warned Nurse Whelan. 'We don't like little girls who are destructive, do we?'

'I like you.' The child-woman was addressing her nurse. 'And I think I like you too.' She looked at Joan and sniffed the flowers. 'But I really wanted Happy Families.'

'She's always going on about this happy family of hers.' Nurse Whelan shook her head sadly.

'No,' Joan was all eagerness, 'it's a card game.' She turned to her mother. 'It lives in the games cabinet, next to the American pianola, doesn't it?'

Rhoda beckoned Joan to come closer. Her mother smelt of school cloakroom soap. 'Who's that?' whispered Rhoda. She was nodding towards her own brother.

'It's Bruno. We told you.'

'No.' Rhoda shook her head. She plainly enjoyed doing this so she did it some more. 'No, no, no. They're having you on. There's a lot of that goes on round here. I want to go home,' she confided. 'Only I can't remember where home is.' This was the moment when Joan noticed that Bruno was crying.

'Bless him,' said Nurse Whelan automatically, as she moved across the room to tighten the mad ribbon in Joan's mother's hair.

There was a clublike atmosphere in the geography room after school that day. Even though Joan was absent, the rest of them had been through the experience of getting copped misbehaving in detention the previous afternoon – everybody except Quinn of 1C. A small indignant boy in spectacles, he kept reiterating varying versions of 'It wasn't me who did it. I shouldn't be here.'

'Oh shut up,' said Toby eventually.

'Aren't you the one they call Sweetie?' Quinn was addressing Peter.

It was Toby who took it upon himself to answer. 'You can stop that before you start.' So Quinn just sat back, leaning against the varnished pine partition which could be pushed back to throw this room and the next into one.

Since yesterday afternoon, Peter had experimented with two penholders and a bit of wire. He had also brought a bottle of Quink to school from home. Now he dipped the invention into the ink, opened his rough notebook and tried writing with it for the first time: *An appreciation of literature is . . .* 'Hey, it works.' Every word had appeared twice, perfectly formed.

'But you've got to get the left-hand margin absolutely straight or the deception shows,' warned Toby.

'If she comes in and cops him again, he'll get *two* thousand lines.' Vanda was eating a Mars Bar.

'Lightning never strikes twice in the same place,' said Toby.

Vanda's next words came out a bit chewy: 'Our new television aerial's supposed to have a lightning conductor on it.'

'How long have you had a new aerial?' asked Peter, surprised.

'Since me mother swapped a bacon slicer for it.'

This method of writing lines made your fingers inky. 'Where did she get the bacon slicer?'

'In exchange for a box full of old zinc washers and some adjustable spanners.'

'This is fascinating.' Toby, who was already sitting on the teacher's table, tried to get his legs into the lotus position. 'Come on. Tell us some more.'

Vanda screwed up the Mars wrapper. 'No, it's boring. Have you got television yet?'

'Yep.' Toby had hold of his own toes.

'Do you ever watch *Picture Page*?' This was the big interview programme. 'Tell you what, I'll be Joan Gilbert and you be a guest.' Vanda started talking posh: 'Well then, Mr Eden, you wasn't born round here, was you?'

Toby elected to take her quite seriously. 'No, I was born in London. Camden Town. We were what is known as London Irish. That was my real parents. The people who adopted me are purest Eccles.'

'And are you really related to Anthony Eden?' asked Peter.

'I'm the one who's being Joan Gilbert,' protested Vanda. 'But it's not a bad question. *Are* you?'

'Could be.'

'We're all Labour at our house,' called out Quinn from his position against the partition.

Toby called the gathering to order with, 'OK, I'll be Leslie Michelmore.' He was the other interviewer on *Picture Page*. 'Tell me Miss Bell, what are your ambitions?'

'I'm going to be the next Phyllis Dixey.'

Toby just missed falling off the table. 'You're joking!' he said. But there was a new kind of respect in his voice. 'Do you know what Phyllis Dixey does?'

'She strips and she teases.' Vanda had given the matter very considerable thought and had reached the conclusion that Miss Dixey must remove her clothes to music. 'She's the girl the Lord Chamberlain banned.' This bit had come off one of the posters outside Hulme Hippodrome.

Well, well, well, thought Peter, who had been watching Toby closely. The idea's getting him quite worked up.

'Where do you do it?' asked Toby. His voice was a bit too eager.

'I don't do it anywhere, yet. Well, I practise a bit – in front of the wardrobe mirror.'

'You mean . . . dancing?' Toby was trying to appear casual but his fingers were gripping his toecaps hard.

'It's more swaying, actually. It's a bit like the hula-hula.'

You couldn't do this to him, Joan Stone, thought Vanda. Not even if you *were* here.

Toby's next words came out in a rush: 'I bet you a shilling you couldn't do it now.'

Here was a chance to make a profit on the sixpence he'd won off her yesterday, when she hadn't been able to write three hundred lines by the end of detention. 'I could give you a sketchy idea,' she said. What was that creaking noise? 'But the only thing I'll actually take off is me cardigan.'

'That'll do,' he said eagerly.

'Oh no it won't!' The muffled voice belonged to Pixie Picton. Quinn of 1C let out a cry of indignation as the partition behind him was wrenched back to reveal the headmaster and Miss Staff. You could also see into the history room where they had obviously been experimenting with a new epidiascope, a kind of magic lantern which was resting upon a similar table to the one that Toby was sitting on.

Miss Staff was the next person to speak. 'You may go home, Quinn.'

He wasn't prepared to leave it at that. 'I'd like it understood that I shouldn't really be in detention.'

Miss Staff chose to ignore this. 'And you will tell nobody, repeat nobody, what you have heard here this afternoon.'

Quinn reached for his schoolbag, got to his feet and headed for the door. Awe-inspiring silence was maintained until he had left the room. As the door closed, Miss Staff made a deferential hand movement to indicate that the headmaster should have the first word.

Pixie glared at Toby Eden. 'You'd have *let* her remove that cardigan, wouldn't you? This is the final straw, Eden. My God but your bottom's going to burn. And then your feet are going to take you out of this school, once and forever.'

Toby got down from his table and walked fearlessly up to the headmaster. They were exactly the same height. 'If you're proposing to chuck me out you can beat your own arse, you're laying no cane on mine.' In this moment he was not without dignity. 'It was a bit of fun, that's all, a bit of fun. But being a joyless bastard, you wouldn't understand that. And you sock me and I'll sock you right back. And *then* what will you do? There's no way you can double-expel me.' Turning to Vanda he said, 'Sorry for getting you into this. Once you're old enough, I owe you a night out.'

'How old's old enough?' she asked him eagerly.

Toby, Toby, Toby – Peter was sick of the sound of his name. The formal announcement that the sixth-former had been expelled was not made until Friday morning's school assembly. Once Pixie Picton proved that he had not relented, his words eclipsed Joan's news of Rhoda and the hospital, eclipsed the fact that Miss Staff had sent for Ethel Bell to tell her that Vanda had only one more chance; they totally overshadowed everything.

And the school was rife with rumours. The most persistent one was that Vanda Bell had been discovered in the geography room wearing nothing but her bra and pants. Considering she hadn't so much as removed her maroon cardigan, the three young people felt that this was distinctly unfair. Vanda squared up to Quinn of 1C at the homegoing bus stop: 'What have you been saying to people about me?'

He was as indignant as he had been in detention. 'I never said nothing. We're Christadelphians at our house, we're not allowed to gossip.'

Vanda was inclined to believe him, but somebody had obviously said something. Suspicion fell on Pixie and Miss Staff. Had staffroom comments of theirs been embroidered to a point where they were becoming the stuff of school legends? By Friday lunchtime, Peter was refusing to join in further discussions of the subject because they inevitably ended with Joan and Vanda assuming tragic attitudes and wailing that, with Toby gone, their lives would not be worth living.

At least they could talk about it. And they'd had him there, to look at, every day for years. In his whole life, Peter had caught no more than five glimpses of his own dream idol – Bruno Briggs. Common sense intervened: Bruno was a perfectly normal young man who had never shown more than polite interest in his niece's friend. The time had come when

205

Peter was going to have to go off and find his way to the *Sunday Graphic*'s world of Evil Men.

Except that brought the Bible to mind. Evil led to the pit; and Peter didn't want to go down into the fiery pit. But it was becoming more and more obvious that he was going to have to take all his confusions to town. The only boy he'd ever seen of his own kind was himself, reflected in mirrors. And it wasn't enough.

Long before pornography was generally available, the backs of doors in the cubicles of gentlemen's lavatories were plastered with lurid indelible pencil and ballpoint accounts of sexual adventures. And with handwritten advertisements. *Wanted Other Young Lads for Good Times. Leave Time and Place.* The penmanship varied from the neatly educated (*Is there anybody else who needs a friend?*) to the bizarre and berserk, who went in for crude cartoon illustrations. But they were proof that the psychology textbooks had been right about one thing: homosexuals did indeed come from all walks of life.

Peter couldn't really visualise himself finding love against a background of glazed brick and flushing cisterns. Anyway, the police kept watch on the lavs with the most adverts. The *Manchester Evening News* was full of accounts of their swoops and raids. He couldn't imagine that Noël Coward and Ivor Novello hung around such places. Mind you, neither could he see them boozing in a canal-side pub called the Ogden Arms.

Tommy Duck's – that was the name of a bar in Manchester that always cropped up when people made cracks about 'queers'. It hadn't been listed as one of the *Graphic*'s premier cesspits and it wasn't in the phone book either. This had led Peter to suppose that it might be a bit more discreet and respectable, some altogether nicer way of going about things. Barton Grammar School was much given to instilling 'standards' into its children.

There was an aching and lonely part of Peter's mind which dwelt a lot on thoughts of such places. All he wanted was a friend. And if he had to go to peculiar places to find one, he supposed that this was just the way things were. He couldn't for one moment imagine that it all went on in the daytime. As this world was spoken about only in whispers, he envisaged it as dark and shadowy, with fedora hats pulled down over one eyebrow, and coat collars turned up against prying eyes.

That Saturday afternoon he said to his mother, 'Can I go to town tonight? *Sous les Toits de Paris* is on at the Continental on Market Street. It would be good for my French.'

In 1949 parents did not worry unduly about teenagers going into the city centre. Peggy had larger reservations about the subject matter of the film. A telephone call to Miss Parr, who was after all a French teacher, removed these. 'It's supposed to be old but excellent,' said Peggy as she replaced the receiver. She even seemed impressed by his enterprise. 'Find me my bag,' she said. 'I'll treat you.'

'No, I've got the money.' He hoped his reaction hadn't sounded ungrateful. But he couldn't compound whatever sin he was about to commit by taking money from his mother.

'You know where the town bus stops are, don't you, Peter? Rather than hang around afterwards, you'll probably do better to go to Victoria and get an express bus from underneath the arches.'

Buses were not the problem; the problem was the whereabouts of Tommy Duck's. But Peter had a plan. He was so anxious to put it into operation that he even paid tuppence extra to get to town on one of the express buses Peggy had talked about. If I'm going to hell, he thought, I'm doing it in style!

Yet even as the bus swayed past Salford Cathedral he automatically prayed, 'Please, thanks, forgiveness; in the past, and in the present, and in the future.' For the moment the Bible was at war with the names in that alluring black book at New Scotland Yard. But only for a moment. Peter had searched the New Testament carefully; Jesus hadn't said anything about homos, not a word, it was only St Paul. And he was a saint who had only gone into business when Christ left off. In fact, come to think about it, there wasn't much to choose between St Paul and the Mormon missionaries who delivered sermons on a blitzed site at the corner of Deansgate. Though maybe there *was* something to choose between them

207

because the Mormon men were always spectacularly attractive.

Late September mist was already rising from the River Irwell as the bus reached the echoing terminal, which was under a railway bridge and illuminated by gaslight. At this time of year, mist could turn quickly to fog – fog which was so thick that you couldn't see the face of the person in front of you. And Peter needed to see faces tonight: it was all part of the plan.

The streetlighting turned to electric as he walked over soot-blackened Victoria Bridge. And it stayed electric all the way to the Central Reference Library. This was a circular white granite building with a pillared canopy and steps up to heavy bronze doors which wouldn't close until nine o'clock.

The doors weren't part of the plan but the steps were. Indeed they were the whole plan. It was said that if you stood on them for a quarter of an hour you were bound to see somebody you recognised. Peter was hoping to recognise another homosexual.

'Ship ahoy!' cried the female news vendor who had her tin tray of change on the base of one of the white stone columns. 'Everything's going up and nothing's coming down. Ship ahoy!' She always shouted the same thing to get people's attention. Peter's was caught by the sight of a black man coming out of the library with a packet of Churchman cigarettes in his hand. Students often dived out of the building for a quick smoke on the steps.

As the man lit up, Peter noticed that the palms of his hands weren't black like the rest, they were pale pink. You never saw negros on the Ravensdale Estate so this alone marked the evening out as special. West Indian calypsos were just starting to be heard on the wireless and Peter's favourite one consisted of little more than the same four words, repeated over and over again – 'Everybody likes Saturday night.'

The people beyond the limits of the portico all seemed to be trooping past in their best clothes. There was finally enough clothing material available for the younger women of Manchester to have been able to catch up with Dior's 'New Look'. Their autumn coats had nipped-in waists and vast sweeping skirts, just like technicoloured highwaymen. Their menfolk, having finally escaped from military uniform, still seemed anxious to look as much like one another as possible, with short-back-and-sides haircuts and clothes in all the most anonymous shades of brown and grey and navy blue.

It was quite cold up on the steps. After a while it was also a little bit boring. Peter shoved his hands deeper into his raincoat pockets, where he encountered his folded school cap. He gazed in the direction of Boots all-night chemist's; their neon sign had turned into a blue blur – fog was erasing the edges of everything.

'Ship ahoy!'

Most people seemed to tell the old woman to keep the change. She must be onto quite a good thing. Maybe not: she had to be out in all weathers and the fog was turning into the kind you could taste. And that was the moment when Peter started to feel that somebody was watching him.

Straight away his eyes followed the direction of the instinct. And a man – not on the steps but down on the pavement – turned round and began to walk away. Only now he was turning back again and retracing his steps. He wasn't so much walking as patrolling. But this was definitely not a policeman.

For a start his hair was too long. And because he was going a bit bald at the front, it looked as though it was slipping off the back of his head and onto the collar of his too tightly belted raincoat. Now he was circling the steps. Correction: he was circling Peter Bird. The man's eyes kept flickering towards him in the same way that Toby's had been drawn to Vanda's bust.

For just one moment Peter's attention was distracted by the sight of a marmalade cat making its way purposefully along the pavement; a cat which seemed to know exactly what it was doing, right in the middle of Manchester. Was it true that all ginger cats were toms? As the question entered his mind, something crossed his line of vision. The man had fluttered up the steps and was standing next to him.

Fluttered? If that seemed a funny word to use for a man, this was a funny man. For a start, he smelt like Woolworth's

209

scent department; Phulnana, that was the name of the perfume he was wearing. He was wearing mascara too, and his eyelashes were as spiky as park railings. Not wanting to be caught staring, Peter looked down and caught sight of a pair of club-toed suede shoes, the kind that teddy boys bought from Stead and Simpson.

Would it speak? It was hard to think of the creature as 'he'.

It spoke. 'Town's dead, isn't it?' The prim voice was all hissing s's.

Peter had very definite ideas about the kind of dream friend he was seeking, and this was definitely not him. But the man might know where he was to be found. 'Yes it is rather quiet,' replied the schoolboy, cautiously. Greatly daring, he added, 'Could you tell me whereabouts Tommy Duck's is?'

'Tommy Duck's? My dear, Tommy Duck's is *over*. I mean it's still there but it's gone – if you know what I mean. But it once had the *reputation*, so the memory's lingered on.' Some of the words were overemphasised: it was as though he wanted to be sure that you would get the very finest point of his meaning.

And he's trying to talk posher than he really is, decided Peter. 'Has it all moved to the Ogden Arms then?'

'What would a little chicken like you know about the Ogden?' Though the man used his eyelashes like a woman, there was definitely five o'clock shadow beneath the pancake make-up on his chin. 'Anyway, it's gone from there *too*.' Obviously sure that his audience was ensnared, the painted man produced a silver cigarette case, lit a cigarette and blew out the smoke like Bette Davis. He even sounded a bit like her as he said, 'First they took our money, then they called us names, then they barred us.' Realistic Manchester crept back into his voice: 'There was a bit of trouble with Lily.'

'Lily who?'

'Lily Law. My sister in a blue two-piece with silver buttons. The police.' Mention of this word had set his eyes raking the foggy horizon. Peter had already marked them down as hungry eyes. Eyes that were never still. The stranger had stopped looking for policemen and was treating the negro

210

student to covert glances. 'Makes me feel just like Tondelayo in *White Cargo!*'

'Who's he?' Peter was torn between fascination and distaste.

'Tondelayo? He's a she. Just like me. My name's Hetty. What's yours?'

I don't want to tell you, thought Peter. But you're the only person who's going to be able to tell me what I need to know.

Hetty started coming up with information anyway: 'My dear, all those chicken-hawks at the Union would just *love* you.'

Peter was in like a hawk himself: 'Where's the Union?'

A group of young men in Salford Tech scarves emerged from between the bronze doors and Hetty ate them up with his eyes. Waiting until they were down the steps and out of earshot, he said, 'It's just down from the Ogden. Corner of Princess Street. Oh my God,' he breathed. 'Don't look now but plain-clothes Lily have just rolled round the corner from Bootle Street.' This time the eyelashes were batting in fear. 'Can you tell I've got slap on?'

Peter supposed this to mean make-up. 'Yes.'

'It's too much for a white lady to bear!' The men were already advancing towards them as Hetty darted down the steps and disappeared into the fog.

The two men who had dislodged this nocturnal dragonfly were almost his exact opposites – all trilby hats and crombie overcoats and clomping feet. One was pointing a stubby gloved finger after Hetty and both of them treated Peter to a glance – a *memorising* kind of glance. Five minutes of Hetty had been enough to set his own mind into a pattern of overemphasised words.

He only hoped the rest wasn't catching! But it had shown Peter how the boys at school must feel about *him*. The gap between him and them was as wide as the one between himself and Hetty. It certainly wouldn't be fair to hand on the Barton brand of derision to somebody who was only trying to be friendly.

'Ship ahoy!' For a change the news vendor chose to shout out a genuine headline: 'Tokyo Rose convicted of treason!'

211

Her efforts were rewarded by the sale of a newspaper to a man in an oily boiler suit. As she took his money the little woman glared at Peter. 'Come 'ere.' She said it quite sharply.

'Me?'

'You.' She was wearing one coat on top of another and years of exposure to the elements had left her with a seamed old face which was like dried chamois leather. 'What was you doing talking to George King?'

Could she mean Hetty? 'I didn't know that was his name.'

'Well-known town character. Used to wear high-heeled shoes behind the counter of an ironmonger's in Ardwick. What did he want you for?' Her teeth were even more battered than her torn pixie hood, but her barking manner failed to disguise something grandmotherly and protective. 'Did he want you to go off with him?'

'No.'

'What's a nice lad like you doing hanging around on public steps?' As she sized him up and down, Peter was pretty sure that her experienced city eye was judging him to be made of similar material to Hetty. 'Did he ask you to go to the Snake Pit with him?'

'No, honestly. What's the Snake Pit?' He only hoped he didn't sound too eager.

'That crumby café near the bus station. You want to steer clear of the Snake Pit.'

Which bus station? he was wondering wildly: Piccadilly or Lower Mosley Street? The latter was nearer but he could hardly head off in that direction while she was still watching.

'Tokyo Rose convicted of high treason!'

A foreign-looking gent wearing a cheap raincoat over formal evening clothes interrupted her with, 'Have you got a Football Final?'

She snatched a pink newspaper out of her upturned orange box at the base of the pillar. Under cover of this transaction Peter bid her a hasty 'Goodnight' and began heading towards Princess Street. The weather seemed to have emptied the streets. As he crossed the road a sports car roared up out of the fog and just missed his ankle.

To keep his spirits up, Peter began quoting Oscar Wilde to

himself. 'Lying back in the hansom, with his hat pulled over his forehead, Dorian Gray watched with listless eyes the sordid shame of the great city . . .' He'd read the book so often that he could recite whole chunks of it by heart. But there was nothing particularly sordid about Princess Street, unless you counted the fog which was the drifting, rolling kind; it turned the huge Victorian cotton warehouses back into the Venetian palazzos which had originally inspired their design. Under the weirdly diffused orange streetlight, the deserted roadway could have been the Grand Canal.

And still there wasn't another soul in sight. It was like walking through a dream. In a moment he half expected to see the Bridge of Sighs. He could almost believe that if he threw a stone into the shadowy roadway he would hear a watery Venetian splosh. The side street showed up as alleyways of muted green gaslight. And now he was coming towards a real canal, where the ghostly road turned into an ordinary Manchester bridge.

Peter snapped out of his dream and into reality. Somebody was bawling into a crackling microphone; it was meant to be an imitation of Frankie Laine singing 'Ghost Riders in the Sky'. But this wasn't really a man's voice at all, it belonged to some woman trying to be a baritone. The noise was coming out of a double-fronted canal-side pub with a Georgian front door and stained-glass windows – the New Union Hotel.

He had finally arrived.

Twenty minutes later Peter was still hovering outside the building, infinitely colder and not much the wiser. Although he had money in his pocket he had not dared to go inside because you had to be eighteen to get served in pubs. All thoughts of Venice had vanished. This was sooty Manchester with a vengeance. But he'd been right about one thing: everybody arrived at the pub as furtively as though they were entering one of Dorian Gray's opium dens. ('Dens of horror where the memory of old sins could be destroyed by the madness of sins that were new.') It was all collars-up and a quick look round to see whether anybody was watching.

The fake man's voice on the microphone had given way to

somebody who was genuinely masculine. But after one basso-profundo chorus of 'Bless This House', the singer had warbled the second one in a voice which was piercingly falsetto. It was all a far cry from the musical evening. Some of the men going into the pub had looked reassuringly normal, but he had been a little intimidated by the sight of peroxided hair on others, and by the appearance of two women in drape suits who had persuaded a barber to give them Tony Curtis haircuts.

A fluffy-looking girl, in a short fur-fabric jacket over a lace cocktail frock, suddenly burst out of the Union's side door and headed for the low wall at the side of the canal. She was hotly pursued by another woman dressed as a teddy boy. 'There's no need to be like that,' roared the tough one.

'There's every need.' Only now did Peter realise that the younger woman was more than a little drunk. As she swayed on her platform soles she still had a half-pint glass in one hand. 'You've shown me up in front of all the others. One gill of mild, that's what you bought me. One bloody gill of mild.' Still keeping against the wall, the girl began to totter up the street in the direction of the police courts. She was muttering to herself: 'And that Angela's had whatever she wanted from the top shelf.'

'Calm down,' bawled the other as she marched behind her. 'I've told you, it's not what it seems. She's only me cousin.'

'Which changes nothing. You're a disgrace to every lesbian at the telephone exchange and I'm bloody furious.' Taking a final swig from her glass the girl flung it across the road at a wall, then scrambled up on top of the parapet of the canal. 'I've had enough.' A curious crowd had started streaming out of the building; she was gathering quite a sizeable audience. 'I'm going to jump.'

Her friend was suddenly all tender concern. 'You're not going to jump, love.'

'I am. And what do you lot think you're looking at? I'm going to jump,' she repeated defiantly.

'No you're not.' The other one's temper suddenly snapped. 'You're not because I'm going to bloody well push you!' And she did.

214

The girl vanished from sight. And this time the sound of splashing canal waters was not in Peter's imagination. All around him hell broke loose as women divided into rival factions and started fighting. Tough souls handed jackets over to the more nervous to hold. One Eton-cropped woman actually stripped to the waist, or rather to a man's interlock singlet and a pair of escaping breasts. Within two minutes three more tomboys were in the canal and a police siren was howling its way along Princess Street.

Some of the real boys had also streamed out of the pub to swell the audience, but at the sound of the siren they deposited their glasses on the Union's stone windowsills and began to melt into the mist.

Peter judged it sensible to follow their example. Even in flight he couldn't help noticing a couple of men dressed as the sort of spivs who sold black-market nylons. They were nothing like the idealised friend of his dreams but neither was there anything cissyish about them; in fact they were almost overmasculine. The same was true of another figure in a motorbike jacket. He looked very conscious of resembling Marlon Brando but he sounded purest Salford as he said to his worried blond companion, 'If you get caught in a raid they always ask where you work . . .'

One moment the night was patterned with dozens of agitated figures, the next they were swallowed up by a fog which muffled fleeing footsteps.

A merciful fog, thought Peter as he took refuge in a deep doorway. Three figures were sheltering there already but the smell of cheap perfume reassured him that they were on the right side. The scent was Phulnana again. 'Hello, little chicken,' whispered Hetty. 'Oh my God,' this was in more audible tones, 'they're even coming after us by *water*.' Fierce spotlights had begun to play from the canal, accompanied by a noise which sounded second cousin to an air-raid warning. 'It's the police launch!'

'Lily must think she's Esther Williams,' hissed a voice with an over-refined accent.

As the motor launch slid past them and headed towards the Union, the doorhole was illuminated by another, smaller, light – the young man with the genteel voice was nervously lighting a cigarette. He had plucked eyebrows and a dark Burton's suit with an artificial silk scarf tied in the neck. The other newcomer was buried inside a big raincoat with heavily padded shoulders; somehow he was managing to wear it like a lady's winter stroller. 'I'm sure I saw Waddilove in that police car,' he said. 'The bastard swore that if he caught me on the town again I'd be eating my Christmas dinner in Strangeways.'

'Why?' asked Peter, not caring in this company if he did sound innocent.

'Why? For being me. They don't need *reasons* to hate us.'

'We're less than lice,' said Hetty quietly.

These were words that left Peter chastened. Just because these people had not lived up to his dreams of meeting latter-day Oscar Wildes and Alexander the Greats, he was in no position to criticise them. Mind you, the Marlon Brando one and the spivs had looked more interesting: rough but interesting.

The boy in the big coat moved onto the pavement and peered down the street. 'I think the cop car's gone but it still wouldn't be safe to risk going back in the Union.'

'Even if they'd have us,' sighed Hetty. 'The law's probably been in and warned them about allowing us to congregate. Look how they threatened to do the Ogden as a disorderly house. And what was going on? Six queens were discussing the price of floral chintz, that's what was going on! Oh well,' another sigh, 'I suppose we'd better stroll off down to the Snake Pit.'

'Where exactly is it?' asked Peter quickly.

'Opposite Lower Mosley Street bus station. It's where queers meet whores. And why? Because it's the only place that's allowed to have us. Coming?'

'No thank you. I'd better be getting home.'

Hetty must have sensed some prim reserve in Peter's reply. 'You'll be back,' he said, 'I'd stake my sugar-daddy on it.' As he walked away he took each of the others by an arm. There was nothing sexual in this; they looked like a breakaway group of Tiller Girls, and the fog wrapped itself round the trio like floating chiffon veils.

For the moment, Peter lingered where he was. He felt the need to think about all he'd seen. He was not to know that he had found his way into this queer half-world at a time when it was still hugely gender-confused: that it would take his own generation to uncover the differences between homosexuals and transvestites and transsexuals.

Peter had only walked twenty yards in the general direction of the Grand Hotel when two figures materialised and barred his way. They were the same plain-clothes policemen he had seen outside the Central Reference Library – the ones in trilby hats and heavy overcoats.

'Where d'you think you're going?' The detective who spoke looked just like the woodwork teacher at school, the same heavy moustache and eyebrows that almost met in the middle.

'Home. I'm going home.'

The other one said, 'And where've you been?' He wasn't at all bad-looking. Peter just hoped that the fact that he'd noticed this was not showing in his eyes. The man repeated his question: 'Where've you been?'

Panicked, Peter sought for some innocuous answer. 'Just out and about.'

'And how old are you?'

'Sixteen,' he lied, mentally apologising to God and asking for protection in the same silent prayer.

The first one was back in like a knife. 'Have you been in the Union?'

'No.' Could they arrest you for just being near the place?

The detective must have sensed something of Peter's boiling fears. 'But you know what the Union is, don't you?'

'It's a pub.'

'It's a running sore. What's your name?'

Should he give a false one? No, that was a crime in itself. 'Peter Bird.'

'And where do you live, Peter Bird?' The good-looking one had the same kind of mean mouth as Richard Widmark, the film star.

'It's sort of beyond Irlams o'th' Height.'

'And has it got a "sort of" address?'

On closer examination he wasn't good-looking at all; his skin was too tight over the bones. 'Ten Hawksway, Ravensdale Estate, Swinton.'

The older one took over. 'Peter Bird, that's a name we'll have to remember. We're policemen, so we can guess what you are and we can guess what you're after. I'm going to give you a bit of advice. Fuck off back to Swinton. There's enough shite on these streets without you making more.' They were still barring Peter's path. 'Understood?'

'Yes.'

'Good. Because if we see you again we'll take you straight down to Bootle Street faster than you can say Vaseline. And we've got a doctor down there who'll be able to tell us whether you do know what the Union's about. Go on, on yer bike, Mary!'

4

One of the least noted changes of adolescence is the effect it has upon young people's watches. Time suddenly seemed to be going much more quickly. One moment, Joan and Peter and Vanda were third-formers with barely a responsibility on earth, the next it was as though the fourth year had passed in a rapid blur, and the young grammar-school pupils were now obliged to concentrate on the newly introduced O-level examinations.

The marking standard was said to be much higher than it had been for the old School Certificate, where allowances had been made for the educational disruptions caused by a world war. This was 1951, rationing was finally over, and pupils were meant to be capable of learning the contents of textbooks from cover to cover.

From the moment she could read, Joan Stone had embarked upon a love affair with the printed page. But she had grown to hate English literature lessons at school. Her teacher, Miss Titheradge, was absolutely determined that everybody was going to achieve a pass mark. To this end, she forced the whole form to learn her own opinions of the set books, equipping her pupils to write safe and solid answers to any conceivable examination question. In the process, Miss Titheradge ruined *The Merry Wives of Windsor* and *Paradise Lost* for Joan, forever.

English language was a different matter. Sarky Titheradge taught that subject with an iron rod of superb quality. Even in the first year she had spotted Joan's way with words. As a result, the teacher watched over the girl from Ingledene even more strictly than the rest: a fancy word was never allowed to pass where a simple one could be just as effective, red ink question marks were always placed against excessive adjectives, war was declared upon any flight of imagination which was not brought to a satisfactory conclusion.

For the rest of her life, Joan would be grateful to Miss Titheradge for all this. For the moment, the teacher's influence was most reflected in the girl's diaries and in her letters to Sally Morgenstern.

These days, in the winter months, Joan was allowed a paraffin stove in the old sewing room which still served her as a study. The stove was called the Briggs Patent Cathedral Heater. Knee-high, it was the same shape as Big Ben but made of lacy black-leaded ironwork. The pink light which shone out of its red glass doors cast a twinkling pattern across the grey walls of the little attic. The only other illumination came from a bare fifty-watt bulb hanging on a flex from the ceiling. The 'desk' was still that same old sewing machine, her pen the same Swan she had got for passing the scholarship; the only thing that was different were her words. These days Joan's letters were much more guarded.

They weren't the exact truth. That would have ruined the whole point of this escapist penfriendship. But they were a bit nearer reality than those early second-form extravagances. 'Mummy' was the biggest problem; sophisticated and elegant Mummy with her string of alleged best-sellers. On several occasions Joan had seriously debated killing her off. But a superstitious streak kept telling the more sensible side of her brain that, should she murder the novelist, something awful might happen to her real mother.

Nowadays, Joan was considered old enough to visit the hospital outside Bolton on her own. Sometimes Rhoda could be encouraged to play dolls' tea parties and Happy Families and Snakes and Ladders, sometimes she just sulked. And she was a baleful sulker! On one terrible occasion a fight had nearly broken out, over the ownership of the blue sweets in a box of Bassett's Liquorice Allsorts. When it got beyond hair-pulling, Nurse Whelan had restrained her patient with a startlingly expert half-nelson wrestling hold.

By the time the next visiting day came round, Rhoda must have been given something to calm down – the eyes that gazed at Joan looked as dead as glue. And the pair of them were never left alone together after that.

Eventually, Joan despatched Mummy to the South of

France. She was supposed to be living in a big white house on the edge of a cliff – the Villa du Chic. The cliff was there against the day when Joan got up enough nerve to push her over

> Dear Sally,
> You last letter gave me a real shock. When I opened the envelope and that paper butterfly shot out, and flew around the room, I let out a loud scream.

Would this have brought Old Olive, the dreadful but faithful housekeeper, to the rescue? Like many another dragon in fiction, the character of 'Olive Briggs' had seized hold of its audience's imagination; Sally was always begging for further stories of the servant-monster. This meant that Granny, the *real* Olive, was just a falsely lavender-scented shadow in the pages of her granddaughter's letters.

Joan shuddered to think what Granny would say if she knew that a character bearing her name was supposed to be more than a little bit fond of the bottle and given to light pilfering. Once created, this other Olive had taken on a whole life of her own: her favourite foods were pickles and rhubarb, her drink was gin, and she had a gentleman friend called Dan Worthington.

In one of her letters, Joan tried announcing that the housekeeper had been given the sack. When this news reached New York, her penfriend's distress was so genuine that Joan relented. In just seven words the old fraud was reinstated.

Over the last two years Sally Morgenstern's letters had revealed a girl with a kind heart and a curiously adult lifestyle. Joan had long ceased to imagine that her penfriend was making up what she wrote. Photographs and newspaper cuttings proved that Mr Morgenstern was indeed a publisher and that his wife's collection of paintings, and her friendships with artists and writers got her into the New York gossip columns. When word of the British post-war food crisis reached America, the Morgensterns despatched a massive parcel of provisions to Ingledene.

'But why so many pickles?' wondered Granny. She was all set to write a leter of thanks until Joan pointed out that the accompanying card had said 'For Joan with love from Sally'. This kept it between penfriend and penfriend. That had been a close shave! A letter of thanks from the wrong Olive could have brought the whole house of cards tumbling down.

Thoughts of her narrow escape reminded Joan to stick to reality in this present letter. And the mental image of a house of cards brought Vanda to mind. Sally was absolutely fascinated by the idea of a girl who wanted to be a striptease artiste. She was equally intrigued by references to a fifteen-year-old boy who made no bones about being a homo. 'We talk about them quite openly in our house,' she wrote back. 'My Uncle Walt is one. As a result, he can get seats for any show on Broadway. Please send more news of Pete.'

Joan refilled her pen before continuing.

> Peter and I have started going to church on Sundays with Miss Lathom and Miss Parr. The Church of England comes in three kinds – High, Low and Broad. I was brought up Broad which is about what the King and Queen are. Miss Lathom's church is so High that they behave as though the Reformation never happened. They have Mass, just like Catholics, and there are three priests on the altar and clouds of incense. Bells go off in the middle of the service and people cross themselves like billyo. Peter definitely believes in God but I am only open to conviction.
>
> Vanda is still an atheist. This is probably beause she is very materialistic and only interested in getting money out of her trustee, Mr Adcock. Recently she has had a permanent wave and commenced singing lessons.

Joan crossed out 'commenced', inserted 'started', and thought about Vanda. Self-contained, that was the new word for her. Everything was geared towards her coming career; her life seemed to be nothing but training and diets and calcium tablets to strengthen her fingernails. The single-mindedness was almost eerie.

Peter too had changed. While the trio which had been formed on the day they were measured for school uniforms was still very much a trio against the rest of the world, it was as though it had developed three strong and separate branches. Branches which blew in different winds. Peter Bird was nothing like as forthcoming as he'd been at one time. These days he was always 'going somewhere'. And he seemed disinclined to explain where that somewhere was. And how could you put that in a letter without sounding disloyal?

Joan Stone was made of loyalty. Her passion for Toby Eden had never diminished. But he had become a student at Liverpool during term time, and somebody who was said to go to London for the university vacations. And Joan knew for a fact that cunning Vanda had taken to hanging around outside his house. Not that it would have got her anywhere: Joan Stone had also done her fair share of loitering.

'Three times I've called you, Joan. Three times and I didn't get so much as one word of acknowledgment.' Most unusually, Granny Briggs had walked into the old sewing room. She was bearing a letter. 'That American friend of yours must be made of money. This has come Airmail Express. Never mind reaching and grabbing, I want you to slip to the newsagent's before they close. They've not delivered my *Lady*.'

'Can I see the letter first?'

'*May* I, not can I. If you must. They've sent the evening paper but they forgot to put the magazine inside. That's the second time this month. And while you're there, I could do with a stick of sealing wax.' She paused for breath. 'Joan? Would you mind telling me what I just said? You see, you've no idea! I'm not kidding, you live in a world of your own.'

'I heard, I heard.'

'And stop repeating yourself like that. It sounds Jewish. What's the matter? Whatever can a penfriend have written to make you go so white?'

Sally's letter was short, just two paragraphs. And it was the nearest thing to dynamite that Joan Stone had ever handled.

Changes had been made on the Grotto Lodge Estate. As paint

and timber gradually became more available, the borough council instituted a programme of refurbishment. But first there was a general inspection of all their properties. And that was when Ethel Bell nearly found herself out on her ear.

The clerk of works did not mince his words. Sniffing the petrol fumes in the hall, and hastily opening the front door to throw a lighted cigarette into the garden, he said, 'Dwelling house? It's more like a branch of Sketchley's!' His glance took in a heap of old clothes which had yet to be put through Ethel's cleaning tanks. Unfortunately, something smaller than a pinhead, something black with agitated legs, chose that moment to leap into the air. 'Do I spy a flea?' he asked, with grim satisfaction.

There was still fight left in Ethel: 'Well if you do, you must have brought it in yourself.'

The letter from the council arrived a week later. Once the cleaning tanks had gone, and the old clothes were disposed of, the house must be fumigated. Thereafter, structural alterations and some redecoration could take place.

'All this fuss,' raged Ethel. 'And what are we promised at the end of it? A nasty little bungalow range on the living-room wall, that's what we're promised!' Grumbling even more, she hired a shed behind Swinton Palais for her stock and her tanks. Then workmen moved into the house and stayed so long that they even hung their own calendar on one of the replastered walls.

All that had taken place last year. Once the men had finally left, Vanda moved into Dora Doran's old bedroom. It was much less of a tip than it had been during the blind woman's occupancy. As of old, no two items matched; but at least Vanda had been allowed to choose the apple-green distemper and the cream paintwork. She regarded this as a step in the right direction. One day she would have everything colour-toned and of the finest quality. The workman who had proffered the shade card had also asked her to marry him. He was the one whom his colleagues always described as 'just a little bit simple'. But if the proposal did nothing else, it reinforced her belief in her own ability to fascinate grown men.

Not that Vanda really needed proof. Male teachers went red when she looked up from her desk at them. And Peter Bird had told her that she was the subject of some of the wildest fantasies ever written up behind the doors of the cubicles in the local public lavatory.

And if that doesn't make me a nice girl I don't care, she thought. You can only do your best with what you're given, and I've been given curves, and Vaseline seems to be making my eyelashes grow thicker. She tried not to think of Joan Stone's legs; their owner seemed to be supremely unaware of their slim magnificence. Vanda hitched up her skirt and studied her own in Gran'ma Dora's long mirror. If Joan Stone's legs brought *Vogue* to mind, Vanda's were much more like the saucy limbs displayed on the front cover of *Reveille*.

But how soon will I be able to show them off for money? she wondered. And how do I cross the gap between dancing school and the stage? Seaside shows, pantomimes, musicals: the Odette Ashworth School fed girls into all of these. Whenever Vanda mentioned her ambition to fulfil the prophecy that she would be 'the next Phyllis Dixey', the dancing teacher always led her out of the hearing of the Jaeger and Aquascutum mothers and said things like 'It's a very sordid branch of the business' and 'You'd be far better off teaching.' Vanda was blowed if she was going to waste a thirty-nine-inch bust on teaching middle-class infants to dance the Highland fling.

Thoughts like these always led to her reaching for the tape measure. For the third time since Christmas she tightened it round herself. Correction: a thirty-nine and three-quarter-inch bust. Her thoughts returned to the same old question, how she could set about displaying it in theatres. Reaching for the box of tarot cards, Vanda held it to her forehead and said to the power within, 'What do I have to do?'

As she lowered the little wooden coffer, the pokerwork eye on the lid seemed to be looking right into her. Vanda began to spread the cards. Like her grandmother before her, she had devised her own methods. Today she slammed down one card, with its face to the eiderdown, to represent the problem.

The next pair to land on the orange and turquoise paisley quilting were meant to give her some indications of an answer. Already, inside her head, that sexless guiding voice had begun to snigger contentedly – a sure sign that she was on her way to something accurate.

She turned the 'problem' card over. The Sun – her own card – that made sense. The other two were both Pentacles. The King of Pentacles was certainly a man who could solve business problems. And the Ace – a hand holding a star – generally provided a fruitful outcome. Even as she was wondering what tied the pair of them together, the nasty tittering inside her head turned to real words.

'*You already know him.*'

And the King's face seemed to be rearranging its own features. Even his crown had misted away, to be replaced by a cap of hair, like black patent leather. She did know him! It was the boss-man from that audition at Hulme Hippodrome. The impresario who'd given her mother his visiting card.

'Vanda? Could you start me a bath going?' Ethel's voice, coming from the bottom of the stairs, cut across the inward vision. Ethel demanding a bath when it wasn't even a Friday night? That was an event in itself. 'Did you hear what I said, Vanda? A gentleman's going to carry a load of glass bottles up.'

This mysterious statement was enough to get her daughter out onto the landing. The man was already mounting the staircase, panting under the weight of two zinc crates which – if everybody had their own – belonged to Allied Dairies. Vanda recognised him immediately. He was the binman, the corporation refuse collector; and the crates were piled high with clanking Victorian bottles.

'Dump them in the bathroom, John,' bawled Ethel, who was already putting a lot of weight on the banister and causing the stairs to creak in protest as she made her way to the first floor. 'Get that tap running,' she gasped at her daughter.

John had already got the crates into the poky bathroom. Now he was smiling expectantly at Ethel; in fact one hand was halfway out. But she dashed any hopes of a tip with, 'I'll see

226

you right, son, when you bring me another load. Try to get the ones with the most raised writing on.'

'She's a character, isn't she?' John had risked a look at Vanda. And he wasn't smiling at her eyes.

'If you want a thing doing, do it yourself!' Ethel had dropped the bathplug in place and set the water running.

'You can't wash those old bottles in that new bath,' protested Vanda. 'You'll chip the enamel.'

'It's the corporation's enamel, not mine.'

'Yes, and it's my bare bum that'll get nicked.' She shouldn't have said that – the binman had gone quite pink with joy.

Ethel, who never missed a trick, treated him to a cold look. 'My mother was right about one thing: man is an animal. The sooner you're back with more glassware, the sooner you'll get your beer money.'

As this idea hurried him out of the bathroom, Ethel shook the last of the contents of a box of Oxydol into the water. 'Whoever would have thought there was dollars to be had from antique bottles!' Since clothes rationing had ended, Ethel's stalls were patronised by only the poorest of the poor. But a new breed of second-hand purchaser had begun to sniff around the northern markets; antique dealers from the United States were already beginning to ship out Lancashire junk. Their scavenging had begun with old guns and swords, then moved on to ancient brass and copperware. In recent months they had started swooping down upon Staffordshire figurines and pot dogs.

'But old bottles?' Vanda found the idea almost incomprehensible.

'My Mr Yankee says that the name of the game is keeping ahead of the market,' sniffed Ethel. The soapy suds caused her to sneeze. Once she'd blown her nose on a towel she continued with, 'He says he's going to store this lot up in his warehouse in Brooklyn, for when the craze starts. Don't knock it, I get a tanner for each one that's clean and washed.' She rinsed out a bottle embossed with the words *Burdekin's Infant Elixir*. 'Yer gran'ma used to talk about being doped down with this when she was a little girl.'

227

The Oxydol had caused foam to rise up on the water, just like the bubble baths which Jane of the *Daily Mirror* was to be seen taking in the photographs displayed outside Salford Hippodrome. 'Ethel?' That's what she called her mother these days. 'Ethel, d'you remember that audition at Hulme?'

The question had plainly been a mistake because Ethel was already bridling with indignation. 'Will I ever forget it!'

Nevertheless Vanda pressed ahead: 'What was the name of the man who gave us his card?'

'Gave me his card, lady. *Me*.'

Swishing a bottle through the suds, Vanda tried to sound casual: 'Have you still got it?'

'We need a clean rag to dry this lot.'

'I'll go for one.'

'You're very helpful all of a sudden. I'll go meself.'

This was, to say the least of it, unusual. Normally Ethel would do anything to save her own legs. Yet she was already out of the bathroom and moving towards the top of the stairs. On the rare occasions when she strode out like this there was always something nastily triumphant about it.

Vanda decided to follow her. Big Ethel was better at getting down the stairs than she was at ascending. In next to no time she had reached the bentwood hatstand in the hall – an item which had survived the council's purge. Her podgy fingers grabbed at an old handbag dangling from one of the bottom pegs.

'You don't keep clean rags in there,' protested Vanda.

The bag had already been snapped open. 'No, but it's where I do keep this.' Ethel was holding aloft a pasteboard visiting card. 'Souvenir of Hulme Hippodrome. And d'you know what I'm going to do with it?'

'I hope you're going to give it to me.' But in her heart of hearts she knew that this would not be the case.

And she was right. Card held aloft triumphantly, Ethel headed for the living room where a coal fire was burning in the new bungalow grate.

'No,' shouted Vanda.

'Don't you even dare to think of striking your own mother.'

228

'I wasn't going to.'

'Well don't. D'you know what Adcock's done to you? He's turned you into a spoilt young madam.' The fat little fingers tore the card in two.

'That's my future,' shouted Vanda.

'And this is where it's going.' Two pieces became four, which were summarily despatched into the flames. 'You take one step towards me and I'll push you on the fire with the card.'

'But it was my future,' wept Vanda as she watched the white pasteboard fragments turn black. 'It was my whole future.' Blue flames had already risen up and licked it into ashes.

While Vanda was gazing at ashes, Joan had removed herself to the coldest corner of Ingledene – the conservatory. Which of the poets said that hell would have icy regions? Joan couldn't remember. But whoever he was, he was right.

If this latest letter from Sally was dynamite, it had blasted her English penfriend into a living hell on earth.

And that's *not* too dramatic, she said to herself, ever conscious of her own words. I have landed myself in a Hades of my own making. It began inside my head and now I'm trapped between my own words. Oh those letters to America! Those fanciful letters. Those *lies*.

There was just enough of the grey afternoon light left to penetrate the ice that covered both sides of the windows. Just enough to read the letter from New York again. And if it had arrived on the hottest day in August, its contents would still have caused Joan to shiver.

Dear Joan,
Guess what? We are coming to England! By the time you get this we should have already set sail for Europe. We are coming over on a liner called the *Île de France*. It is supposed to be très de luxe. Somebody at the steamship office told Dad that Franchot Tone and Merle Oberon will be on the same trip.

229

I'm the one who writes stuff like this, protested Joan's mind. But the absolute reality of Sally's words was even emphasised by the quality of her envelope, by the maker's name embossed underneath the flap – Cartier.

They get their writing paper from a real crown jeweller's, thought Joan wildly. And I wrote her fibs on Basildon Bond. Why, when it was freezing cold, did she feel so clammy? She was absolutely sweating. And the idea of reading the next paragraph again gave Joan some faint inkling of how a swoon might start. Breathe deeply, she told herself. Take deep breaths and just read it.

> Soon I will be knocking at your door.
> Isn't that wild? We dock at Le Havre
> which is in France. Then we go to Paris
> and Florence and maybe Rome . . .

If only she'd given me actual addresses, I could have written to put her off; I could have said we'd got illness in the house. In Joan's mind's eye she could actually see a printed notice affixed to the front door of Ingledene – *Scarlet Fever – No Admittance*. But it was imagination that had got her into this mess. She forced aside sudden and frenzied thoughts of swallowing all Granny's sleeping tablets. God forbid that the Americans should arrive on the day of her own funeral!

'Bruno? Is that you in there?' It was Granny's voice and her footsteps were coming nearer. As Joan didn't have any pockets she hitched up her skirt and stuffed the letter and the envelope down her knickers. An invisible Granny was still talking. 'It's so cold that fieldmice have come into the kitchen from the garden.'

Yes, and I'm so panicked that it feels as though mice are gnawing at the pit of my stomach. Nevertheless, Joan tried to appear nonchalant as her grandmother walked into the room.

'However hard I stamp, I can't keep my feet warm.' Granny was zipped up against the weather in her wartime siren suit, with an old windjammer of Bruno's pulled over the top. 'This house has gone beyond redemption. But I can't bring myself to kill fieldmice. She's brought her babies with her. I just can't do it.'

And this considerate person is the woman I've turned into a gorgon called Old Olive the housekeeper; that's what her granddaughter was thinking. Aloud, she said, 'If they're only babies we could put bread and milk out for them.' Joan had always hankered after pets.

Granny shot her a withering glance. 'I'll have to ring the town hall. They'll send somebody round with the proper poison.'

Poisoning young things? Joan found the idea horrifying. 'You couldn't!'

'Sometimes I think you're not all there. We'd be overrun in a fortnight. I'm beginning to wonder whether all of this isn't a judgment on me. In the days when I was waited on hand and foot by all those Indian servants I was never very nice to them.' She let out a deep sigh. 'The vicar said something I didn't want to hear last Sunday. He said, "The mills of God grind slow but they grind exceeding fine." Did a goose just walk over your grave, Joan? Why are you shuddering?'

The tea they sold in the bus station café was exceedingly weak but nobody complained; nobody in the Snake Pit was in a *position* to complain. It wasn't the official refreshment room. In truth, it didn't even boast a proper name. Somebody had simply turned the ground floor of a decaying warehouse into a fly-by-night café, and then tacked up a sign outside the door which said *Thermos Flasks Filled*.

Few bona-fide passengers lingered within this cigarette-smoke-filled establishment. The walnut-veneered counter looked as though it had been stolen from somewhere altogether more posh, and the chromium plate was peeling off the giant cylinder of a tea urn. If the curling sandwiches, under their greasy plastic dome, failed to deter genuine travellers, a second glance at the clientele was usually enough to send them heading back for the safety of the pavement.

Once outside, they almost invariably risked a second, and disbelieving, peep through the window.

The Snake Pit was the haunt of some of the most painted queers in Manchester.

That's how it had seemed to Peter, the first time he summoned up the courage to enter. But that had been two years ago. Nowadays, the faces behind the Max Factor masks had identities and names. Not, of course, the names they were given in baptism. What vicar would have christened a man Belsen Betty? Or Norma Dawn, or Cottage Kate? There was a Lana and an Amber, and an Ava with a Birkenhead accent, who dressed as much like a woman as the law allowed. 'As long as I'm wearing trousers, Lily can't do me for masquerading' was how he'd explained it to Peter. And this was not a particularly kindly world: less attractive boys could find themselves referred to as Bertha or Gladys.

'I wouldn't have one of those nicknames for anything,' said Peter Bird stoutly. It was a Friday evening, and he and Hetty King, the roving-eyed youth he had first encountered outside the Central Library, were making two cups of the weak tea last as long as possible.

'We've already given you a name.' Hetty tapped his cup with a varnished fingernail. 'I swear they put bicarb in this to spark up the colour. Yes, we call you Ladybird.'

'I won't answer to it.'

'Then you'll get kettled.'

Peter didn't have to be told that this meant he would be cut dead, ignored. 'Getting kettled' belonged to the secret language known as Polari, which the boys who called themselves queens used constantly. Bits of near Latin were mixed indiscriminately with backslang; the whole vocabulary totalled little more than a hundred words, but by weaving them in and out of ordinary conversation it was easy to outwit an eavesdropper.

A homi was a man, and a palone was a woman. Hetty King viewed himself as a homi-palone. And this was the part that Peter didn't like. He didn't see himself as any kind of half-woman. He was just a young homi who happened to fancy other homis.

In later years a lot of the Polari would be embraced into standard English. But in 1951 only people who hid in places like the Snake Pit knew that naff meant bad, that bonar was good, and that tatty was reserved for anything which was deemed beyond the pale.

Many of the words were sexual. Though Peter understood their meaning, in practice he was still the complete innocent. He refused to believe that the attitudes held in the tatty café were those of the whole homosexual world. But until he was old enough to get onto licensed premises ('My dear, you should get a load of some of those big butch homis in the Union!') all he'd got was Hetty King and her 'sisters', with their tantalising tales and their endless language lessons. These boys feminised everything; they could even feminise a steamroller – it became a steamrollerette.

'Name me the parts of the body.' Hetty sounded just like Miss Littler who'd taught him in the infants. 'What's your face?'

'My eek.'

'And your eyes?'

'Ogles.'

'And what do poor short-sighted queens have to wear?'

'Ogle-fakes.'

But Hetty's attention had been caught by something else. 'Quick, varder! It's Mother Macree and Blondie Jack.' The pair must have rated highly in this unusual social register because Hetty produced a powder compact and gave his own reflection a quick glance in the mirror inside the lid.

Peter recognised Blondie Jack immediately, though not by name. He was the big, tough-looking man who always collected the money on the Bobs – the roller-coaster ride at Belle Vue Amusement Gardens. Legend had it, amongst Manchester schoolchildren, that this giant had once done the whole ride standing up in the leading coach. So what was he doing here? Except, under the Snake Pit's unshaded light bulbs, the blond hair looked as though it had known the attentions of a peroxide bottle.

'Hello, Hetty, who's the chicken?' The other man had leering eyes. Except for too much brilliantine, he was extremely well dressed. In fact he looked like a wax dummy from out of Burton's window – pencil moustache and all.

Peter couldn't help feeling that they'd met before; in a shop, where the man had had a tape measure slung round his neck. Queens always maintained that if all the queers were thrown out of Kendal's department store, there'd be nobody left to serve the customers.

The pair sat down at the table. The blond one was squashed up against Peter. 'The chicken is called Ladybird,' said Hetty.

Peter felt he had to speak out. 'I'm not called Ladybird at all. My name is Peter.'

'Course it is,' said the blond man. 'And don't you go letting them give you a camp name. Not if you don't want one. There's butch and there's bitch. I've always stood out against a camp name myself.' His breath smelt of milk stout and, somehow, he was just too friendly.

'Oh you've stuck out, dear!' snorted the wax dummy. 'You want to watch yourself with this one,' he said to Peter. 'She thinks she's a man.'

'Take no notice,' said Blondie Jack easily.

'Big excitement's coming to town,' announced his brilliantined companion.

'You mean the show?' Hetty King had produced the compact again and was doing things to his eyebrows with spit and a forefinger, as he gazed at his own reflection. Moments like this always caused Peter to want to run. However, if there was excitement in the air he wanted to be in on it. 'I know all about the show,' continued Hetty, importantly. 'The poster's been up near the CWS on Balloon Street since dinnertime.'

'What show?' asked Peter.

'Big drag show coming to Hulme Hip.' Blondie Jack smiled at him. 'Should be camp.' And without so much as a second's pause he seized hold of Peter's hand underneath the table and attempted to transfer it to his own lap.

'Stop that!'

'Stop it, I like it,' rejoined the man in a silly voice.

'I *don't* like it.'

'Then what are you doing here?'

Looking for something better, thought Peter as he pulled

234

his hand free. There has to be something better for me than men wearing not very discreet rouge.

He was all set to leave until Hetty King said, 'Every queer in Manchester will be there. You mark my words: all the ones who never came out on the town will start crawling out of the woodwork. Men who you'd never think were like us in a million years . . . they'll all turn out to see *Forces in Frills*.'

And they're the ones I want to meet, thought Peter. But why should these men whom nobody would guess were queer want to go and see a show called *Forces in Frills*? Peter already knew the answer. Because there were so few places where they could relax with their own kind – that was why.

Ever since Sally's letter arrived, Joan had known what it was like to go through life with a lead weight fastened to her innards. And sleeping was worse than being awake. When she wasn't having nightmares full of scornful American laughter, Joan was dreaming things which didn't have stories. It was as though emotions, like shame and remorse and fear, had actual personalities; and they took it in turn to wrap her in their terrifying embraces.

During her waking hours, Joan, who had never had much interest in mathematics, found herself caught up in obsessive counting games: five days to cross the Atlantic, three in Paris and three in Florence and *maybe* three in Rome . . . That means they could be banging on the door next Tuesday. But if they spend a week in each city . . . It was no use, her head always ended up spinning.

That Saturday morning the fire was burning in the Briggs Patent Range in the kitchen and Joan was helping Granny to clean the silver. Whenever the Duraglit wadding came out, Granny always insisted that they wear old gloves. 'It's more like a lick and a promise than the days when we used to go to all that trouble with proper plate powder,' she said. 'Would you do these silver pheasants from the dining room, Joan? I'm a bit superstitious about silver gamebirds. Did you know that some people won't have them in the house?'

'I don't need bad luck.' Joan got up and backed away from the table in horror.

235

'Don't be so silly. You're too young to be affected.' Olive Briggs moved over to the window and picked up a clean duster which had got left on the sill. Peering through the crocheted curtains she said, 'Oh hello, here he comes again – ever hopeful. Have you noticed that he keeps pretending to save me trouble by coming to the back door?'

Joan didn't have to be told that Granny was talking about the postman.

'Mid-January and I think he's convinced himself that I've simply forgotten his Christmas tip.'

'Post, Mrs Briggs.' The owner of the muffled voice was also banging at the door.

Granny headed for the passageway, muttering, 'Nobody tips me so why should I tip them?' She called back, over her shoulder, 'Don't just look at that pheasant, polish it.'

Applying Duraglit with crossed fingers is not easy, but Joan did her best. A new adding-up game took over her thoughts; this one allowed the Morgenstern family a week in each of the European cities. How many days would it take on a train from Rome to Manchester? And would something terrible happen to her for half-visualising a railway accident somewhere in the Alps?

In the background Joan could hear a muttered exchange of conversation and the sound of the back door being closed. This still left a draught blowing through the open kitchen door. Whatever was keeping Granny out in the passageway?

'Well of all the bloody cheek!' Granny Briggs stormed back into the room with a picture postcard in her hand. 'I'm not given to strong language but this is enough to make a saint swear.' In furious tones she began to read out the message on the back of the card. ' "Paris is certainly très gay. The shops are wonderful. I have even managed to find some pickled mushrooms for Old Olive." You do realise that the postman saw that, don't you? "Old Olive" indeed! In next to no time it'll be all round Eccles. And that cheeky friend of yours has got pickles on the brain!'

'She's American,' said Joan, weakly. 'They're not like us.' And even as she said it, the weight of guilt grew greater. Now she had managed to get Sally – who was only trying to be

236

generous – into trouble. 'It's this bloody pheasant's fault,' she said, bursting into tears. As she flung the offending bird onto the newspaper-covered table, its hinged wings let out a protesting clank.

'Don't you dare swear at me,' fumed her grandmother.

'You just swore yourself.'

'Do as I say, not as I do. Go to your room this instant.' Granny was still hopping mad. 'No pushy Jewish child is going to call me names.'

'I'm sure she didn't mean any harm.' The last place Joan wanted to go was her bedroom. Recently it had turned into a place where she did nothing but march up and down, and visualise awful things, and count. 'I'm sorry for swearing. Don't make me go to my room. Couldn't I go out on my bike instead?'

'I don't care what you do, just as long as you get out of my sight. You've been moody enough for ten girls, recently. Oh yes, that postman's armed with all he needs to get his revenge. They'll soon be calling me Old Olive behind my back, in the shops! That child would do well to remember that she'll be old herself one day.'

Joan reached for her raincoat which was hanging on a hook behind the door. 'She's nice really.'

'I'll "nice" her if I ever clap eyes on the precocious little madam!'

Those mills of God are obviously grinding away again, thought Joan as she went down the corridor to get her bicycle out of the downstairs cloakroom. That was where she encountered Bruno, who was struggling into an unfamiliar duffle coat.

'Where did you get that?' She was just trying to delay him while she got up the courage to spill out the whole story. Her head felt ready to explode, and she had suddenly realised that she would have to share her secret with somebody, anybody.

'Borrowed it off a friend of mine.'

What was he talking about? Oh, the coat. 'What friend?' This was just another delaying tactic. Bruno looked all set for off.

All he replied was, 'You can't get your bike out till I've moved mine.'

'Don't do it for a minute. I need to tell you something.'

'I'm in a rush. I've promised to cycle down to town to book some cheap tickets.' In the same breath he flung his university scarf over his shoulder.

Somebody who was in this kind of a hurry would be no sort of audience for her lengthy tale of woe. 'It's OK,' she said, almost relieved.

'Sure?'

'Positive.' But I'll have to tell somebody, she thought. It's either that or my head's going to burst.

They cycled together as far as the end of the road. Then Bruno pointed his bicycle towards the city and Joan pedalled her solitary way along the track that led across Swinton Fields. They weren't really fields at all, just some spare land which had been allowed to lie fallow between suburban housing developments. But mist and frost had rendered them magical, though Joan felt she had no right to enjoy this.

By now she had reached the Dogdene Estate of semide-tached houses. In Joan's eyes these were only made remark-able by the fact that a boy called Mickey Grimshaw, who was on *Children's Hour* on the wireless, was said to live in one of them. He was supposed to be a big friend of another young radio performer called Sheila Starkey, who lived behind Peter Bird. That was the direction in which Joan was heading.

As she pedalled across the East Lancashire Road, she thought she saw the first flitterings of snow in the air. By the time the cyclist got to Hawksway, the ground beneath her wheels was carpeted in white. It seemed almost a shame to have to make footprints up to the Birds' front door. She'd left her bike out on the pavement, propped up against the garden wall.

'He's out.' Peggy had answered Joan's knock wearing a nylon overall in mauve, and orange rubber gloves. 'And I'm in the middle of trying to rescue an amateur bleaching job. I mustn't linger or the poor lady might find herself bald. I never know where Peter is these days,' she sighed. 'It might just be worth your while asking Miss Lathom.'

238

The snow was suddenly the kind that got into your eyelashes, but Grace Lathom answered her doorbell quite quickly. 'I do hope you've come to invite yourself to lunch, Joan. Stamp your feet to get rid of the snow. I've made kedgeree, and Miss Parr says that I've done enough for the five thousand! You couldn't have arrived at a better moment; she's having difficulty in threading a fine needle. No, not in there. In the dining room. But let me take your coat and I'll give it a good shaking.'

A log fire was burning in the dining-room grate; the scent of woodsmoke made Joan's eyes smart for a moment, so she started to rub them.

'That's just what it's done to mine,' exclaimed Iris Parr, who was still struggling to get cotton through the eye of a needle. 'See if you can do better.' She was sitting at the dining table with a little heap of lingerie in front of her. You always thought 'lingerie' for Miss Parr because she made a point of getting her underclothes abroad. 'Nuns made this lace.' She was indicating a petticoat. 'I've had it on three different slips. It's lasted since long before the war.'

As the visitor took charge of the needle and thread, Grace Lathom's head came round the door. 'Joan? You're not allergic to mussels, are you?'

'No.' The cotton was already through the hole.

'Good. Don't get too involved in that mending, Iris. Lunch will be through in a moment.' She'd had her grey hair trimmed until it almost resembled a crew cut. 'Lay an extra place for yourself, dear.'

It was nice to be in a house where they knew you well enough to let you go into the sideboard. Had both the maiden ladies been to the hairdresser's? she wondered. Pretty Miss Parr's gypsy curls looked a bit darker than usual. 'Peter's mother's rescuing a blonde who's gone wrong,' said Joan.

'And I too have been at the dye bottle. I saw where you were looking. Is it that obvious?'

'No, no.' Joan hastily transferred her gaze to the table to see whether kedgeree called for fish knives and forks. Apparently it did. Guilt at having been caught staring joined up with all the old Sally Morgenstern guilt. It was something that never left her alone for more than five minutes.

Miss Parr managed to erase it temporarily with, 'This summer we're hoping to make an old dream come true. When you've finished with your exams, we're going to take you three young people to France. That's if your parents agree. Good marks won't enter into it; we're not *that* much schoolmistresses!'

'But won't it cost the earth?' For a moment Joan forgot Sally's Europe in the excitement of thoughts of an abroad of her own.

'I've had two books published for these new O- and A-levels. I'm afraid I've done disgracefully well out of them.'

Joan, who rarely got the opportunity to hug anybody, flung her arms round Miss Parr. 'Paris, like you always promised?' Why oh why did anguished thoughts of the Morgensterns rise up to haunt this most exciting of moments?

'Something wrong?' asked Miss Parr.

'No, nothing. And you smell marvellous.'

'It's L'Heure Bleu by Guerlain. Their shop in the Champs-Élysées is just as it was at the turn of the century. All polished mahogany and mirrors and wonderful old glass cases. You'll be able to see it for yourself in July.'

Another smell was coming into the room, something halfway to curry. Miss Lathom had entered holding a steaming dish against her blue and white smock. Peter Bird always maintained that these garments covered an asbestos front, for she never seemed to feel the heat.

'Proper Patna rice, and real saffron, and smoked haddock. I'm afraid I've had to fake the cream with the top of the milk. But just look at those juicy mussels!'

The kedgeree tasted as good as it looked. And the conversation ranged from what could be achieved in one day at Versailles to the wonders they could expect to encounter in the Salle des Illusions at the Musée Grévin.

'It's a waxworks, really,' explained Miss Lathom. 'But hidden in the middle is this octagonal room, lined with mirrors. And when they dim the lights, something quite magical happens.'

240

'But don't tell,' Miss Parr implored her friend. 'Don't tell what happens or you'll spoil it for her. It must have cost a king's ransom to build; nobody could afford to do it these days.'

'Joan?' Miss Lathom spoke sternly. 'Whatever ails you?'

Their guest had been wondering whether Sally would have seen the same place. And the thought had cloaked her in gloom. 'I'm a bit bothered about something.' Should she – dare she – tell? Instead she asked, 'Do you think confession is good for the soul?'

'Naturally,' pronounced Miss Parr. 'We are, after all, Anglo-Catholics.'

That wasn't what Joan had in mind at all. But the moment when she might have blurted out the whole story had passed. The spinsters had priests who listened to their dark secrets; not that Joan could imagine them having any.

Henry, the retriever, wandered into the room, sniffing hopefully. 'Poor Henry,' said Miss Parr. 'We were out all morning being beautified, and now we have to be out again. He does so look forward to a bit of company at the weekends. It's a pity dogs can't have baby-sitters.'

'I'd do it,' volunteered Joan. Even as she spoke she was wondering whether Miss Parr had invented the idea to keep her occupied.

Iris Parr confirmed Joan's thought with, 'Well, if you *are* down in the dumps . . . Tell you what, there's a lovely new guidebook to Paris up in the study. You'll find it on the desk, next to that carrierbag full of knitted blanket squares. The ones we really ought to sew together. A couple of hours with that guidebook will be just like being in France.'

'Ought you to ring your grandmother?' asked Miss Lathom.

'She's a bit off me at the moment.'

'These things never last.' Grace Lathom passed the cheese. 'Just let her know where you are.'

'Where's Peter, do you know?' Joan had finally remembered what she'd come for.

'Gone to town to spend his Christmas book tokens.' Grace Lathom looked troubled. 'At one time he would definitely

241

have been the first person we'd have told about the French idea. But these days we hardly seem to see him. Joan, and there's no criticism in this, have you noticed him getting a bit . . . well . . . mysterious?'

'Yes, and he uses words that aren't in any dictionary.' The moment her own words were spoken, she worried that they might have sounded like ratting on him.

'Being fifteen isn't easy,' said Miss Lathom philosophically. 'I was absolutely appalling at it.'

'I seem to remember weeping a lot,' put in Miss Parr. 'I imagined myself to be in love with Byron. And he was dead. So everything seemed hopeless.'

Once the washing-up was done and the teachers were bundled into their coats, Joan was obliged to put on her own raincoat so that she could help Miss Parr push the bull-nosed Morris, which was refusing to start in the cold weather. Miss Lathom, behind the wheel, looked a bit like General Rommel. As their car chugged off in a haze of blue exhaust, Joan noticed that her own bicycle was still leaning against the Birds' wall. Snow had piled up on the saddle so she moved it into the teachers' garage.

Henry had never stopped barking through the window since the car had left. She hurried indoors to keep him company. That, after all, was why she was meant to be here. He was a most affectionate animal and in two minutes he'd rushed round the house to bring her a whole selection of rubber toys. After treating Joan to a searching look, he even dived under the stairs and came out with a disgraceful old bone.

'I don't think we'd better take that up to the study.'

This was a book-lined boxroom, right above the front door. The snow outside was coming down heavily again. Joan switched on a table lamp and a small electric fire. 'Don't go near that with your tail, Henry.' This was something he seemed to know about already, and he also seemed well used to the idea of somebody reading. Henry just liked being with people. The only interruption he made was when he placed his head on Joan's feet, then lifted it again to give one of her ankles an affectionate lick.

242

'You really *do* look like a burglar with that brown mask,' she said to the white retriever. And then she let the guidebook transport her back to Paris. Le Ritz, it revealed, was so exclusive that it didn't even have a lobby. Wasn't a 'lobby' the name that people who lived in back streets gave to the entrance passage from their front door? No wonder Le Ritz was too posh to have the same thing! It was also described as 'much favoured by high-spending American tourists'.

All the excitement induced by thoughts of Paris evaporated. Joan went back to feeling heavy and guilty and frightened. Why oh why hadn't she told the teachers what was worrying her? Because they took their own guilt to professionals, they unloaded it on priests, that was why.

A new idea began to ring louder than her problems. What was to stop her doing the same thing? The nearest church with a confessional was round the corner from Teapot Hall at Irlams o'th' Height. But that one's proper Catholic, she thought. And there could be somebody local, sitting waiting to go into the priest's box, who'd know I was a fake.

This didn't rule out a trip to one of the High Church kind. They might be exotic but they were still Church of England. She only knew how to get to St Hilda's, in Prestwich, in Miss Lathom's car. But the two schoolmistresses didn't consider themselves to be solely attached to one parish. 'We shop around for God,' was their unabashed motto. And Joan suddenly remembered a sermon she'd heard preached about six months previously, a sermon on the very subject of confession. '*All may, some should, a few must.*'

'I've got myself into the *must* lot.' She actually said it aloud, and Henry sat up expectantly.

The thought of doing something practical about her sins raised Joan's spirits to an extent where she borrowed a red scarf from the hallstand, tied it round Henry's neck and bundled him up the stairs of the next bus for Manchester. Once they got to town, she led him into Piccadilly Gardens for a quick pee, then sought out another bus, for Gorton.

The weather seemed to have reminded the double-decker of its age. It groaned its way down to Ardwick Green, then shuddered past the Speedway entrance to the amusement grounds. By the time the skeleton outline of Belle Vue's roller-coaster came up on the right-hand side, the bus was literally inching its way through the snow. It was so unlike a usual day that the conductor hadn't even bothered to come upstairs to take their fares. 'It's just to be hoped they've had the sense to get the animals from the zoo inside,' Joan said to Henry. But he was more interested in trying to beg a second piece of chocolate off a man on the seat in front of them. 'Is there a public baths just after this?' she asked Henry's friend. If she'd remembered it properly, that was where they ought to be getting off.

'Two stops further on. Just look how it's coming down now. It'll only have to get a mite deeper for them to stop the buses.'

Would she be able to find the church again? She only remembered its name because it was so odd – Our Lady of Mercy and St Thomas of Canterbury. Two for the price of one, she thought. That should be enough for even my sins.

'Gorton Baths,' called the conductor from downstairs. 'Don't leave your towels on the seat.'

Russet-brick council houses lined the road to the church. But did it definitely have a priest who heard confessions on a Saturday afternoon? Some boys chose that moment to dodge out of a side street and throw snowballs at them. Henry replied with a burst of the extra-excited barking which dogs always seem to save for snowy weather.

The building coming into view was almost as extraordinary as its name. With neither tower nor steeple, it looked like the kind of grandiose, single-storey music room that can sometimes be seen sticking out of the side of a stately home. But this edifice sat on a piece of spare ground in the middle of the corporation housing estate, with soot-blackened weeds poking their way through the snow. The church had the look of having been half-finished for a long time. The painted sign on legs in the garden mentioned Mass and Benediction and – yes Sacramental Confession on Saturdays from 4 p.m.

'I think you'll have to wait outside,' she said to Henry. She decided to tie him to one of the uprights that held the notice board in place. She hadn't even finished knotting his leash

244

when Henry began to sing. Well, that's what his owners called the extraordinary noise he emitted when he felt distressed. This sound, halfway between the ring of an insistent telephone and the song of a maddened blackbird, was so eerie that it had once lost Miss Lathom and Miss Parr the services of a cleaner who was of a nervous disposition. 'It doesn't sound like a dog at all,' she'd said, prior to taking flight. 'It sounds for all the world like somebody possessed.'

'*Brr-brr, brr-brr, ah-eeh, ooh.*'

'Not outside a place of worship, Henry,' said Joan desperately. It was no use, she would just have to sneak him inside. The door on the end wall was nothing special, but it pushed open into magnificence.

A most helpful little sign above a stone holy water stoup explained that, contrary to all outward appearances, you *were* in the Church of England. And would visitors please remember that they were also in the True Presence of the Most Holy Sacrament of the Altar. It seemed that the building had been designed by somebody called Walter Tapper. The printed notice went on to ask you to be sure to notice the choir loft, which divided the nave from the sanctuary. There was a lot more about something called the baldaquin.

Joan supposed this to be the pale orange marble canopy over the coffin-shaped high altar. It was a bit hard to see things properly because it was getting dark outside, and the only real light inside the cold, incence-scented church came from a few penny candles flickering in front of baroque statues in the shrines along the side walls. The confessional looked like an antique Spanish shed, standing darkly against the whitewashed wall. Up until now, simply getting here had filled Joan's thoughts. Standing beneath a painted plaster-of-Paris wall-relief, inscribed *Jesus Falls the Second Time*, she finally began to think about the true purpose of her visit.

She'd seen Bing Crosby as a priest in a film, so she knew that the man in the dog collar would sit in one half of the shed while she knelt in the other, with just a poky little hole to whisper through. Oh dear . . . Still leading an interested

Henry on his leash, Joan tiptoed towards the shed as though she was expecting it to explode.

A red light glowed above the door. Did this indicate that the confessional was occupied? That was the moment she thought she heard somebody murmur, 'With a man or with a woman?' Whatever it was they were saying, she knew she oughtn't to be listening. Joan backed hastily away. Somebody – not in the confessional – cleared their throat behind her. Henry growled softly.

The church didn't have pews. It had rush-seated chairs instead. That's where the throat-clearer was kneeling. The figure was female, her hair covered in a black lace scarf. She was fingering rosary beads. Was this, Joan wondered, a holy occupation in itself? Or was the woman simply waiting her turn?

She decided to take a seat, two discreet rows behind the black lace mantilla. Of course! You weren't meant to come in without your head covered. Joan untied the red scarf from around Henry's neck and draped it over her own hair. Wasn't it supposed to be something to do with St Paul having said that your hair mustn't tempt the angels?

The door of the confessional clanked open in a very unholy way, a thin man came out, and the woman in front got to her feet and walked over to the forbidding Spanish shed.

'Please God, when it's my turn, just let me find the right words,' prayed Joan. Henry distracted her by sniffing at the leg of the chair in front. Cats, that's what he must be smelling. Joan was smelling them too. Yes, a tomcat must have got into the church and sprayed. Singularly unaware of where he was, Henry lifted his leg.

'Not here,' hissed Joan in anguish.

Too late. Old habits die hard and Henry had proceeded to mask out the offending odour. It was only a token gesture but he'd still left a small puddle. And Joan hadn't even got a handkerchief on her.

The woman with the rosary beads couldn't have been much of a sinner because she was out of the confessional inside three minutes. Now it was Joan's turn. And Henry had no intention of being left behind. 'OK, but keep quiet,' she hissed at him.

There was very little room inside the penitent's half of the box. It was almost filled by a wooden pri-dieu, where you were obviously meant to kneel. A pale orange strip light shone above an iron grille. Joan could just about make out the outline of the priest. He was already reciting in a polite monotone, 'The Lord be in your heart and upon your lips that you may truly and humbly confess your sins. In the name of the Father and of the Son and of the Holy Ghost.' There was a pause and then he said, 'Aren't you going to read the words on the card?'

That's what the light was for! So you could see to read what was typed on the bit of paper that rested on the shelf part of the praying desk. Feeling like Mary Queen of Scots just before execution, Joan peered forward and dutifully read out: ' "I confess to Almighty God, to Blessed Mary and all the saints, and to you, Father, that I have sinned, in thought, word and deed, through my own fault. Especially since my last confession which was . . ." ' Here came a gap in the typewritten text so Joan just made a pause and then read out the final sentence. ' "I have committed these sins." Do I just whirl right into them?' she asked anxiously.

'Close the door,' came the voice from the other side.

Joan obeyed, though she had her doubts about the wisdom of following this instruction – Henry didn't even like being confined inside the car. It was a good thing that the priest seemed to be sitting sideways on, and that the dog had hidden himself beneath the ledge.

'I suspect,' the voice was quite kind, 'I suspect that you may be a first-time penitent. Forget that I am a human being. Think of me as a telephone to God. Have you given the matter of making your Life Confession serious thought?'

It was Henry, down in the shadows, who chose to answer: *Brr-brr, brr-brr, ah-eeh, ooh*. Joan immediately thought of the fleeing cleaner saying that it didn't sound like a dog at all, it sounded like somebody possessed.

'Try putting it into words,' urged the priest.

That was the point when Joan decided to give up. 'Come

on,' she said to the retriever as she flung the door open again. 'Sorry about this,' she called over her shoulder. 'I'll send you a postal order for your building fund.' Henry was already tugging her towards the street. 'We've committed desecration,' she said to him as they got outside. 'And no wonder it was so dark in the church, just look at all this new snow.'

As they made their way back towards the public baths, the streetlights flashed on. Motor cars, their windscreens blinded, were moving cautiously. One or two had even given up the struggle and parked by the kerb.

'It's a judgment on us.' Henry wagged his tail in reply. A wind was getting into the big flakes of snow and blowing them into spirals. The weather was no longer pretty, it had become menacing. Joan's thoughts, just as they'd done on the day when Sally's letter arrived, turned to visions of Dante's icy sections of hell. Redoubled guilt was stinging down upon her in cold wet flakes. Would confessing to a dog count as the real thing? Joan didn't think it would.

Twenty frozen minutes later, the pair of them were still standing at the bus stop. The wind had dropped but the snow had continued to fall, and it was lying so thickly that you couldn't tell where the road ended and the pavement began. Passing cars had petered away to nothing when a man in an oilskin suit and goggles, pushing a motorbike, struggled into view. 'If you're waiting for a bus,' he said, 'they're all parked up on the side of the road, about a mile back.'

Henry must have decided that the man's intentions towards Joan were not entirely honourable because, after first growling warningly, he pulled back his upper lip to reveal a set of gleaming teeth.

'You've scared off the only other person left alive on earth,' moaned Joan. But there were still animals around; from behind the wall of Belle Vue Zoo a distant elephant trumpeted, and some exotic bird screeched a frantic reply. 'I wouldn't mind howling myself,' muttered Joan. 'Whatever are we going to do? We'll have to start walking.'

All afternoon she had been conscious of the fact that her school shoes were not really up to this weather. They were the kind that had a narrow strap going over her white socks, to meet a little round button. The right-hand shoe suddenly seemed unaccountably loose. Loose? It was flapping!

'Oh no,' she groaned. Somewhere along the way the button must have come off. 'Now we are in a mess,' she said to the retriever. Experimentally, she kicked off the shoe and tried a couple of steps in just her sock. In next to no time her foot was soaking wet and her toes were stinging as hard as the end of her nose. How long did frostbite take to set in?

Suddenly Henry pricked up his ears. Joan was still experiencing nothing but muffled silence. And then, in the distance, she began to hear a curious sound like a grinding tractor. Way down the road a blue sports car, a Sunbeam Talbot, was edging into view. As it ground its way past them, Joan finally got to see what was causing the strange noise – the car's wheels were ringed with snow chains.

'Bully for him!' she said bitterly. Except the car had stopped and the driver was reversing. As he drew level with them again, he wound down the nearside window. The face which looked out was familiar. She *had* to be hallucinating. These days, the only place she ever encountered those green eyes and that dark hair was in her dreams.

'Hello,' smiled Toby Eden. 'Need a lift?'

'I've got a dog with me,' she said, somewhat unnecessarily.

'I wasn't about to suggest that we put him over the wall of the zoo.' Toby opened the passenger door from inside. 'It'll be a tight squeeze but there's room for both of you.'

A tight squeeze with Toby Eden! Could there be any greater joy on earth? Joan had overlooked Henry's aversion to confined spaces. Once inside the car, he transformed himself from a dog into a giant ferret. He even tried to scrabble his way through the wound-down window.

Toby, who had begun to encourage the car towards Ardwick, brought it to a halt. 'He's making things a bit too dangerous. Don't you know any dodge for calming him down?'

'He's all right in his owner's car if you sing to him.'

'We can do better than that. Hold onto him for a minute, just until I get the engine going again. There!' He turned a knob on the wooden dashboard and the car was flooded with the strains of Delia Murphy singing 'The Spinning Wheel'.

> There's a form at the casement,
> The form of her true love,
> And he whispers, with face bent,
> I'm waiting for you, love.
> And there, by the fire,
> Blind Grandmother's sitting . . .

'My own grandmother must be wondering where on earth I am.' She had never got round to telephoning.

'Whatever were you doing in the middle of darkest Gorton?'

Henry was chirruping along with the song, but quite happily. It was a companionable little sound. And Joan felt relaxed enough to say, 'I went to confess something to somebody, but it didn't work out that way.'

Toby didn't press her for an explanation. He just said, 'So you're still weighted down with guilt?'

Just fancy his understanding that! 'The thing was, I had to tell *some*body.' An exotic idea was beginning to take shape in Joan's mind. Goodness but Toby's hands looked very safe on that steering wheel – such nice, long, strong fingers. No, it was a mad idea, and she'd better forget it before she went and made a fool of herself – again. Except, ever since the first form, Toby Eden had been raised way above the saints in Joan's estimation. So maybe, just maybe, she could unload her guilt by confessing to him.

'I've got this penfriend,' she began, warily. She could still call a halt to the story before it got too revealing. But now she'd started she didn't want to stop. And by the time they reached London Road Station the whole story had been spilled to the accompaniment of Delia Murphy's Celtic harp.

'And is that it?' asked Toby, as though he heard accounts of black lies and mad mothers every day of the week. 'That's the lot?'

'What do you think I should *do*?' she asked him.

'Oh I never tell people what to do,' he replied easily. 'Don't believe in that. But at least you've got it out of your system. And if you want forgiving, I'll forgive you.' Barely taking his eyes from the road, he leant across and gave her a reasssuring kiss on the cheek.

I am in heaven, thought Joan. And if I want to stay here, I'd better behave as though people are always kissing me. I'll act nonchalant, pretend it's nothing. As if to reinforce this, she said, 'That's a remarkably fine car wireless you've got there.'

'Yes, and I generally keep it tuned to Radio Eireann.' The music had changed again to 'Believe Me for All Those Endearing Young Charms' sung by a passionate tenor. 'That's Count John McCormack singing,' smiled Toby. 'Particular favourite of mine. Of course that's the Irish in me coming out.'

'How can you afford a car with all these fancy trimmings?'

'Won it playing poker.'

Joan tried not to sound shocked. 'Isn't that illegal?'

'I do believe it is,' he said, grinning. 'That's a law that needs changing. How's that friend of yours who got me into all that trouble in detention at Barton Grammar? The one with the big frontage.'

Men! It was her he'd just kissed, not Vanda Bell. 'She's concentrating on her training.'

'It's a rum ambition she's got!' Toby braked to allow a nervous pedestrian to pick her way across Blackfriars Bridge. And the swaying of the sports car brought his arm into contact with Joan's. She went straight back to heaven.

'You don't live far from me, do you?' he asked.

'No. But I've got to take this dog back to Swinton.'

'Suits me. I'm heading for Bolton. I'm supposed to be playing squash at six o'clock.'

You couldn't play squash with women. Or could you? Joan told herself that this jealousy was something she was going to have to watch.

As they passed through Salford, somebody on the radio started to sing 'I Know Where I'm Going' and Toby joined in.

I know where I'm going,

I know who's going with me,
I know who I love
But the dear knows who I'll marry.

He didn't sound English any more, he sounded Irish. And Salford looked like Iceland in the moonlight.

They reached Hawksway in near silence. He'd switched off the radio when 'Danny Boy' started – said it was unlucky for him. 'Which house?' he asked.

'The detached one.' She didn't want it to be over, but Henry, recognising home, was scrabbling to get out. 'I wonder when I'll see you again?' she said quietly.

'Oh, I'll find you,' he replied easily.

'But how will you know where to look?'

'It'll just happen. They don't call me Lucky Eden for nothing.'

He didn't make the slightest move towards kissing her again. Joan tried to tell herself that this showed respect. Tried and failed. Greatly daring, she leaned across and kissed him instead. And then she followed Henry out of the car and heaven turned back into a cold Saturday.

Once again Vanda had consulted the cards. And once again she'd found herself confronted by the King of Pentacles. And just like last time the printed face had misted into the man from Hulme Hippodrome. The wheedling voice inside her head was refusing to speak today, a sure sign that it expected her to act for herself. But how? She didn't even know the impresario's name.

'*Miss Ashworth does.*' It finally, grudgingly, scratched its way to the surface of her brain. '*Odette Ashworth knows his name.*' When the voice came through as reluctantly as this, Vanda was always left with some knowledge of how gramophone records must feel about gramophone needles.

Her head was still hurting inside as she piled the cards back into their box. One fell out. The tumbled card was the Magician. What the hell could Peter Bird have to do with her ambitions? She slipped the box of cards inside the old banjo case, slid that under the bed and slammed downstairs to see whether her tyres were still pumped up.

The snow, which had lain around for five days, had finally melted. It would only take her ten minutes to cycle to Miss Ashworth's. Once you got to Swinton Marketplace you barely had to pedal. The rest of the route was downhill all the way.

The streetlights on this stretch of road were the pre-war kind which gave off a bluish-white light. They turned the colour red into deep purple and made lipstick look almost black. This did nothing to flatter Odette Ashworth who was standing outside Swan House with the collar of her fur coat turned up. Whatever could have happened to make her stare so disconsolately at the built-on garage – the annexe that served as her dance studio.

'Subsidence?' asked Vanda. This was the standard local response to anyone caught gazing at brickwork. The whole district was crisscrossed with underground coal mines.

'I wish it *was* subsidence,' said the teacher. 'At least I'd be due for compensation. No, I've been reassessed at the town hall. They're counting the garage as business premises, and that puts my ratable value up.'

'But it's been a dance studio since I was six,' protested Vanda. People from Grotto Lodge regarded the town hall as one of life's natural enemies. 'Why have they suddenly swooped?'

'Because Bunty Anderson has failed her Elementary.' Bunty Anderson was the town clerk's daughter. 'She's pipped her exam, her mother's marched her off to Muriel Tweedie's school on Deansgate, and my rates have gone up. It's bureaucracy run riot!' Miss Ashworth slipped her key into the front door of the proper house entrance to the bungalow. 'Come in. What brings you here on a Friday evening?'

'I've got something I need to discuss.'

The entrance hall of Swan House had its own settee and three occasional tables. These were crammed with framed theatrical photographs. Ivor Novello was the only one who rated a frame of solid silver. But a display of artificial flowers had been arranged so cunningly that the head of a big floppy peony covered the words he had written on the picture. Vanda had once snatched the opportunity of having a good look when she'd been sent to answer the front door. The inscription read, *For Odette, as sweet a chorus girl as ever danced for me.*

'Spill it out, Vanda.' Miss Ashworth, heavily made-up as usual, was snatching the opportunity to repair an eyebrow with a narrow stick of brown greasepaint. 'I'm due to give a private lesson at seven o'clock.'

Vanda began to improvise: 'I was wondering about some extra private lessons for myself.' Any questions about the man from Hulme Hippodrome would need wrapping up a bit. 'I thought maybe you could teach me to do toe-tap on pointe.'

'Well you thought wrong.' Miss Ashworth was outraged. 'My ratable value hasn't gone up *that* much. I'd have my legs cut off at the knees before I'd stoop to teaching anybody such vulgar circus tricks.'

'Oh,' said Vanda. Actually, she'd taught herself to toe-tap already. She'd thought it might look quite spectacular done on the top of a drum.

Her teacher was still fuming. 'You've upset me very much by even suggesting such a coarse idea. How long have you been in this school, Vanda? Nine years, ten? Has no feeling for beauty rubbed off on you?' She throbbed this so dramatically that a collection of glass animals started to make tinkling noises on the mantelpiece.

And her fur coat's going bald at the elbows, thought Vanda. Well, if she wants beauty, I'll just have to give her a performance of it. 'I'd always thought I'd dance at Sadler's Wells,' she said in a sad little voice. 'That was always the aim.' Absolutely untrue: if it had been anybody's aim, it had been her mother's. But Vanda Bell had been born with an instinctive feel for her audience.

'Don't think I don't sympathise.' The teacher actually took hold of her hand. 'I had high hopes for you myself.'

'But you've got to do the best with what you've got, haven't you?' Vanda had switched to speaking in altogether more practical tones. 'So could you give me the name of that man with the shiny black hair, the one at the audition?'

'Why?' The teacher let go of her hand. 'Your mother was dead set against him.'

'Mr Adcock pays the bills these days.'

Miss Ashworth looked genuinely concerned. 'I still don't think . . .'

Vanda cut in with, 'You were the one who took us there.'

'And I made a mistake. A big mistake. Can't you just accept that for what it was?'

'No. Ginger and the others can get jobs in the chorus and work their way up from there. I'm stuck with this,' she banged her bust hard enough to make it hurt, 'so I've got to make me own way as best I can.'

'*My* own way,' Miss Ashworth corrected. 'Vanda, you never took all that silly talk about striptease seriously?' You could tell she was thinking of her school's reputation.

'I took it deadly seriously.' Vanda took a deep breath: 'I'll give you ten pounds in cash to tell me that man's name and address. I'll bring it to the musical comedy class on Tuesday. Ten quid's not to be sniffed at. At least it'll help you with your rates.'

'Don't be so impertinent. I wouldn't lower myself to do such a thing for *twenty* pounds.'

'Then how much?' Adcock allowed her pocket money and she never got round to spending it. 'I'm a girl with a post office savings book – how much do you want?'

Miss Ashworth looked like a woman who was seeing her pupil through new eyes. 'I want nothing. And I'm beginning to think that I want you out of my school.'

'I already left. It happened five minutes ago. Didn't you realise?' It was Vanda's turn to be furious. 'Toe-tap may be everything that's flashy, but at least it'll get me to centre of the stage. And I'll be there in my own right. I won't be like some people – tagging along with a line of other girls who could be just anybody.'

Odette Ashworth's painted eyes narrowed. 'I hope you're not suggesting that's what I did. I performed for the troops

255

under gunfire. I understudied the leading dancer in the number one tour of *Perchance to Dream*.'

'That's not what Ivor Novello wrote on his photo.' To prove her point, Vanda swept back the artificial peony which concealed the shaming inscription. 'He said you were just in the chorus.'

'What I really did was too complicated for him to put into just one sentence,' mumbled Odette. The tips of her ears had gone bright scarlet. 'I think you'd better leave this house.'

'Is the number for Muriel Tweedie's school in the phone book?' asked Vanda. But suddenly she had stopped seeing Miss Ashworth as silly; the woman just looked defeated and sad.

'I taught you everything I know,' she was saying quietly. 'I had the highest hopes of what you might have brought to British ballet. You've had the kind of attention money couldn't buy. Even when it became obvious that you were filling out, I still taught you to the very best of my ability.'

Vanda refused to allow herself to feel ashamed. 'All I'm asking for is one name and address.' Her voice was as quiet as the teacher's had been.

'You won't get it from me. You really won't.' Odette had regained her composure. 'You may sneer at what I achieved on the stage, Vanda, and it probably wasn't very much. But I was around long enough to see a lot of big stars in action. The public have no idea. Big stars aren't nice. It doesn't go with the territory.' She moved the artificial flower back into place. 'Tonight's been a revelation to me. You *will* find your way to centre stage, you're made of just the right stuff. You'll charm people, and you'll bribe them, and you'll wheedle. And when you've got what you want, you'll get the big star's bonus – you won't know what it is to have a single moment of contentment. I've seen. They don't.'

But Vanda was remembering that old wreck of a theatre which had seemed to promise to give her everything. And the woman who was criticising her had never smelt the inside of the house on Grotto Lodge Estate. 'Goodbye, Miss Ashworth. And thank you for teaching me properly.'

'Good luck. I really mean that.' But Vanda had already

sped into the night outside, a place where bright lights would dye her peculiar colours.

'Where does he go?' bawled Eddie Bird; you could hear him quite clearly from the garden. 'Where does he slope off to?'

Out in the darkness, Vanda, who had come straight from Miss Ashworth's, hesitated on the doorstep. Should she knock or should she continue to listen?

Peggy's voice was the one raised next: 'You simply refuse to see any good in him.' The curtains weren't drawn and, quite unexpectedly, her outline appeared at the window.

Eddie was still at it: 'Well, he's not leaving this house till I get a satisfactory explanation.'

His wife must have registered Vanda's presence because she suddenly assumed social tones to call out, 'Peter, go and open the front door. You've got a visitor.' And then she went 'Shush' to her husband.

As Vanda waited to be admitted, she wondered what she was doing here. Fallen tarot cards were certainly significant, but how could Peter Bird be expected to lead her to the audition man?

The door opened to reveal Peter dressed as though ready for out. 'Oh hell!' He didn't sound very welcoming.

'That's a nice overcoat!'

It was loose-fitting with raglan sleeves. 'Genuine Donegal tweed. Two of my aunties in Stoke gave it to me for Christmas. Only I might just as well take it off again, he's no intention of letting me go out.'

'So will it be all right if I come in?' Her foot was already on the doormat.

'Let's go through to the hairdressing room,' sighed Peter. 'The big barney's still going on in the front.' At that precise moment the phrase 'police here if he's not careful' arose out of the urgent mumbling coming from behind the lounge door.

'What's caused it?' asked Vanda.

'My big mouth. Last night I said I'd been at a free BBC concert. Only, tonight's *Evening News* went and announced that the whole thing was cancelled. Apparently the fire

257

sprinklers went off, they flooded out the Holdsworth Hall. And I'm the one who came home saying that Joan Hammond had never sung better!'

'I never thought of you as telling lies.' Vanda was quite impressed.

'I hate having to do it.' There was no mistaking the fervour of his reply. 'Loathe it.'

They'd reached the hairdressing room. It looked very different from the night of the musical evening. The green washbasin was no longer disguised by a plywood cover, and the towering permanent-waving machine and the rexine-covered hairdressing chair looked as though they were awaiting the arrival of the Ugly Sisters from *Cinderella*.

'I was going to a show tonight,' said Peter. 'But he practically wants to see the birth certificates of all the people I'm going with. As a matter of fact I was going on my own. But will anybody believe me?' For the first time since the days of bullies in the first form Vanda was seeing him close to tears. 'I'm allowed no privacy,' he muttered. 'There's not even a lock on the bathroom door.'

'You could always say you were going to the show with me.' Vanda picked up one of the professional tail combs and began to attack her hair. Reflected in the wall mirror, she could see Peter looking thoughtful. This outing obviously had something to do with those men he met in town. 'Where's it on at?'

'Hulme Hip.'

'*Told you so*!' It was the first time the voice inside her head had ever spoken when she hadn't got the tarot cards in her hand. '*What did I tell you?*'

'You are going to the show, Peter Bird.' It was just like Cinderella again. 'And what's more, I'm coming with you.'

Vanda at a drag show? 'I'm not sure that that would be a good idea.' Peter lowered his voice: 'It's an all-male revue. The audience could be a bit' – he tried to find the right word – 'specialised.'

'When did I ever say I minded queers?' Vanda was attempting to pile her hair on top of her head.

Peter watched her efforts critically. 'You'll never get that up without a brush.' With one hand he pushed her into the hairdressing chair, the other was fiddling inside a tin box. 'You need some of these curved combs to hold it in place. Keep still, I'll do it. Lift your feet up, I'm going to wheel you nearer to the mirror.' Moving the chair made such a squealing noise that they didn't hear the door opening.

'Oh,' said Eddie Bird, registering Vanda. 'It *is* you.' His shirt was open to the waist, revealing a large surgical dressing, surrounded by chest hair. It goes without saying that his eyes were busy taking the clothes off the girl in the chair. 'Excuse my Elastoplast,' he said. 'I had a bit of an argument with a swing door.' Eddie suddenly began to brim with ghastly bonhomie. 'Why didn't you *say* you'd got a date with Vanda? You make mysteries when there's no need. I see he's given you some of our combs,' he added genially.

Peter's blood boiled as he coaxed the hair into an Edwardian shape. They weren't 'our' combs, they were his mother's.

Peggy had followed her husband into the room. 'I can't see why you couldn't have said it was Vanda,' she grumbled indignantly. But the voice was also tinged with relief. 'Do you want me to finish that?' She reached for the brush and then took her hand away. 'Actually, he's every bit as good as I am. He seems to have been born with a flair for it.'

'Look, it's three shades of blonde,' Peter was talking to his mother, 'and all of them natural.'

'Just as long as it gets him the ladies!' Eddie grinned broadly at Peter and left the room.

'And I bet that'll be an excuse for a drink,' Peggy murmured to herself. 'Pantry door opening: what did I tell you?' Now she did take hold of the brush. 'That top bit wants to go into a couple of big swoops.'

'Too tarty.' He seized back the brush and turned the hair into a classical pompadour.

'Vanda, I would never have believed it,' exclaimed Peggy. 'You look fully nineteen and a perfect lady.'

Vanda's altered reflection was doing a great deal for her ego. 'Would it be a cheek to ask for a dab of pink lippy, Mrs Bird? Just a discreet touch.'

'Does your mother let you?'

'She doesn't care either way.'

'Well, as long as it is a discreet dab.' Peggy left the room, presumably to find the lipstick. As she went, she called to her husband, 'Don't think I'm not counting how many you've had.'

'Would you believe he's begged her to mark the bottle? I tell you, he's beyond me!' Now the tail comb did come into play. After a couple of final adjustments, Peter stood back to view his work. 'I'm dead bucked with this,' he said. 'My mother's right. You look downright aristocratic, but with wicked fires burning underneath.'

Some women spend a lifetime trying to achieve a style of their own. In less than five minutes Peter had shown Vanda possibilities that would be enough to see her through a whole career. 'You're a bloody genius,' she said gratefully. 'When you start doing this for money, you'll make a fortune.'

'Hairdressing's not what I'm going to do.' Peter sounded almost shocked at the idea.

'Then what?'

'I'm not telling anybody.'

His parents were right about one thing: his secrecy could be downright infuriating. 'What time does the show start?' she asked.

'It's twice nightly. The second house is eight thirty.'

'Well at least the men in that audience won't gawp at my bosoms.'

'I sometimes think you bring them into the conversation too much. Anyway, they won't call them your bosoms; where we're going, they'll call them your willits.'

Peggy returned wearing glasses; she was screwing a lipstick out of its gilt case. 'This one's called "First Romance",' she said. 'Don't be heavy-handed with it.'

'Here, let me.' It was Peter who drew a new mouth on Vanda's lips.

She rubbed them together and mumbled, 'How about a bit of black mascara?'

'You're about as subtle as a lav brush,' he snorted.

'I don't know where he gets these expressions from. That

260

was a terrible thing to say,' laughed Peggy. 'Still, the pair of you make a very handsome young couple.' But it has to be admitted that she didn't sound as though she'd convinced herself.

Peter was not about to make an issue of it; his head was full of other things. The show, the show, any moment now they would be off to see *Forces in Frills*.

'Get a load of the willits on the palone with Peter Ladybird!' The night was alive with Polari. At Hulme Hippodrome you went straight from the street into the stalls bar. Almost as big and lofty as the theatre itself, the bar even had its own dress circle, a balcony which went round three sides of the room. Both levels featured men with adjusted hair colouring. And they were just the audience.

Peter had been planning to sit right up in the gallery, but Vanda wanted to be as near to the warm glow of the stage as possible. It was she who had paid for the tickets that would eventually admit them to the orchestra stalls, right down at the front. Inherited caution in money matters never prevented Vanda from spending to get her own way. But she made Peter buy the drinks. 'Get me a dry ginger,' she said. 'It looks like champagne.'

As he pushed his way through to the bar, Peter was not surprised to encounter Hetty King. It was Hetty who had told him that Friday night, second house, was guaranteed to reveal the biggest queer turnout. 'Didn't I promise you that the Gin and Tonic Brigade would be here in force?' he breathed rapturously. 'When did you ever see so many tightly rolled umbrellas in one place? Enough to stage the big sword fight from *The Count of Monte Cristo*! There are queens here tonight who haven't been out since VJ Day. Get a quick varder at that toupee, the one drawn on with the eyebrow pencil. The poor bitch looks as though she's held together with florist's wire!'

But many of the groups of men in this buzzing crowd would have passed unnoticed in the Midland, Manchester's best hotel. Unnoticed until you looked again, and saw that each party contained at least one figure gesticulating beyond the norm, or talking with mannered over-emphasis. Yes, the giveaway was the company they kept.

But they're all of them Us, thought Peter. We're all made of the same basic stuff, even if the ingredients are assembled a bit differently. And there are a few here that I wouldn't half mind getting to know better. It was well known that the Gin and Tonic Brigade had a whole circuit of licensed haunts of their own. The only times they visited the Snake Pit was when they were consciously slumming.

'Two dry gingers,' said Peter to the barmaid. He was pretty sure he would have got away asking for real booze. The self he saw reflected in the etched glass mirror behind the bar could easily have been a young eighteen. Peter decided that next time he went to Stoke-on-Trent he would let his generous aunties know that he'd like an umbrella for his birthday.

'Noël Coward is definitely having a thing with Graham,' announced a drawling voice behind him. 'A friend of mine says that the pair of them have set up house together. And he should know; after all, he *does* work in the bedding department at Gorringe's.'

Debating whether this kind of conversation was one up on Snake Pit discussions of the price of taffeta, Peter carried the drinks over to Vanda. As he travelled, he caught sight of two married men from Irlams o'th' Height; they seemed to be on more than nodding terms with a youth known as Ten-bob Terry.

'What does *camp* mean?' asked Vanda.

'Why?'

'That made-up friend of yours has just told me that I'm ever so camp.'

What *did* it mean? This word, then unknown to the general public (Peter had just noticed a smattering of bewildered-looking married couples), this word covered a multitude of sins. It meant outrageous. It could also mean comical. Dorothy Squires, a highly dramatic ballad singer with a devout queer following, was definitely camp; Vera Lynn wasn't. But Miss Lynn's singing style was already becoming a–glimpse–over–the–shoulder–to–yesteryear, so it wouldn't be long before she was.

Peter didn't have to answer Vanda's question himself. One of the Gin and Tonic Brigade, self-consciously clutching a book with a photograph of Marlene Dietrich on the cover, took it upon himself to join in the conversation. 'Camp means "to stand out against an already theatrical background",' he said. The book looked as though it had been chosen as a fashion accessory.

Vanda was delighted with his definition. 'That's me,' she said happily. 'I like that.'

The man, a cut-price version of Michael Wilding, was giving Peter a bold stare – a look known in these circles as the old–one–two. He was somebody who had definitely taken advantage of the January sales. Peter recognised the suit as having come straight out of Austin Reed's window.

Obviously mistaking sartorial interest for something else, the man followed up his stare with a smile. Austin Reed's? He would have done himself a bigger favour by investing in better dentures. When I do take the plunge, thought Peter, I'll make sure it's with somebody who's got their own hair and teeth. What I'd really like is a queer version of Bruno Briggs.

A bell rang and everybody began to move towards the entrance to the stalls. Out on this side corridor, the crowd was swollen by more of the theatre's regular patrons, including some old Hulme grannies, chuckling away at the sight of the massed umbrellas. Perhaps I'll get a walking stick instead, thought Peter.

As they passed into the battered plush and gilt auditorium, Vanda was momentarily disorientated. Being in the audience is like seeing it the wrong way round, she told herself. And then she breathed in the well-remembered scent of stale cigarette smoke and harsh disinfectant, and she knew it for home.

As they took their seats, the orchestra was already belting out 'When the Midnight Choo-Choo Leaves for Alabam', and amber footlights were doing wonders for old red velvet. 'We never got a programme,' said Peter. Vanda didn't bother to reply because the curtain was going up, and that was the closest she ever got to a mystical experience.

On the stage there wasn't a female impersonator in sight, just a barber's-shop quartet of men, dressed as porters, and singing against a backdrop of a railway station.

'Alarming, disarming, but more than ever charming,
  The girls are due in town.
  Deceiving, misleading . . .'

As this refrain built up the excitment, lights started to shine behind the backcloth. It must have been painted on gauze because – suddenly – you could see inside the station, and cymbals were crashing, and on they came. There was a Rita Hayworth look-alike and an overvivacious Betty Grable, and then a crinolined Alice Faye and a remarkably convincing Hedy Lamarr and . . .

'Bette Davis has even got the *shoes* right,' gasped Vanda 'They're fantastic. If I'd not been told I'd never have guessed.'

The porter rushed in again from the wings with a lot of black patent-leather luggage. That was the cue for the arrival of the principals. You could tell they were more important than the rest by the width of their skirts and the great crusts of sparkle on their beaded bodices. 'But too much hair in the wigs.' Vanda was getting critical. 'That one with the beautiful shoulders has got enough hair for two real women.'

And enough nerve for ten! Vanda didn't understand why the audience rocked at the leading lady's reference to her sequins being 'a bit underdressed for the Snake Pit'. But Peter was howling with the rest. And he was experiencing an amazing sense of freedom. This is what being normal must be like, he thought; just for a glorious change there are more of Us than there are of Them.

If the show was brash, it was also brave. Bright limelight was playing on all the outrageous style which usually had to hide itself away in dismal dumps that nobody else wanted. This was like being told that you did have a right to your own place in the sun. Peter suddenly felt a great rush of warmth towards the very kind of queens he'd criticised. Without them, there would never have been anything like this.

But it wasn't just *their* night out: all of the audience, the married couples, the old grandmothers, everybody was swept along by the wicked energy of *Forces in Frills*. Even the female trapeze artiste was a man, though God alone knew where he'd hidden his muscles. And the spectacular fashion parade down a glitter-dusted staircase, which ended the first half, seemed to be a contest as to which of the performers could gain enough applause to blow the very roof off Hulme Hippodrome.

In the interval Peter and Vanda went to stretch their legs in the big bar. Here they discovered that the boys dressed as girls had come down from the stage to mingle with the audience. They were selling glossy souvenir brochures.

'It's a neat little earner but it ruins the illusion,' said a voice behind Vanda. This was so exactly what she was thinking herself (Alice Faye's five o'clock shadow was showing through a mask of greasepaint) that Vanda turned round to see who had spoken.

It was the King of Pentacles. But not a picture on a tarot card misting into a human face. His dark overcoat looked a bit more worn and his hair could have done with a trim, but this was the man himself – the real thing.

'Hello,' she said. 'Remember me?'

The faintest flicker of recognition passed across the sallow face. His features were so chiselled that he reminded her of a sandstone gargoyle of an ancient saint. 'Aren't you the young lady I put into *Mother Goose* at Cardiff? The one who came to grief with the educated geese.'

Thrilled to be taken for grown up and already established in show business, she said to Peter, 'Could you excuse me a minute. This is serious business.' Summoning up her most brilliant smile for the King of Pentacles, she attempted to refresh his memory with, 'You said I was going to be the next Phyllis Dixey.'

'My God,' he exclaimed. 'It's Odette's bouncing Boy Babe. How old are you now?'

How old was he? Forty-five, fifty? Their memories went at that age. 'Seventeen,' she lied happily.

'And never been kissed, kicked or run over.'

All too true. Not that she was going to admit it. The King seemed to feel the need to explain his return to Hulme. 'I'm still in London but I don't just book acts these days. Often as not we're booking shows into theatres. I've been sent up to see whether this is ready for the number ones.'

'Oo-er, she's been sent up!' shrieked a perfumed eaves-dropper.

The gargoyle steered Vanda into a corner. 'Got yourself an act together yet?'

'Well . . .'

'I see, just one you do in front of the bedroom mirror.'

This was so accurate that Vanda started to feel herself going red.

'Everybody has to start somewhere. I expect that Phyllis was once just hopes and dreams in front of a looking glass. Did you see that she's already got double-crown posters up on the side of the theatre? And she's not due back for a fortnight.'

What about *me*? That's what Vanda's soul was singing. Never mind her, take some notice of me. Determined to help her own cause, she said, 'Isn't it getting hot in here?' and removed her school raincoat.

The gesture was not wasted on him. His eyes flickered back to her face. 'Get yourself a bit of experience. And when you come to London, come and see me.' Out came his wallet and she was handed the twin to the visiting card that Ethel had destroyed. But other cards were coming to mind – tarot cards. This was the most accurate they'd ever been.

'What's your name, darling?' On his lips the endearment didn't sound as though it had anything to do with sex, it was just theatrical.

'Vanda Bell.'

'There's a big American stripper called Virginia Ding-Dong Bell. Once you've found your way round a stage, you might just be the English answer.' He didn't seem much enlivened by the thought. But he did add, 'I've known stranger things happen in this business. If you're really bent on stripping,' he sighed, 'come here again and watch Phyllis. She's getting a bit long in the tooth but she still knows how to carry corn.'

While all this was going on, Peter had moved across to look at the old framed poster on the wall. Old Mother Riley 'with her beautiful daughter Kitty' and *Randle*'s *Scandals* and *This Is the Show*, which had the first letter of every word in big Day-Glo letters so that, from a distance, it just spelled *TITS*. Somebody was looking at him. And in *that* way, too. He'd learned to recognise the feeling of eyes on the back of his neck. But when he turned his head, the man looked hastily away.

And Peter Bird knew why.

In the kitchen at Ingledene the Briggs Patent Range was no longer quite so gleaming. In fact, parts of it were entirely obscured under a fall of soot. And the chimney sweep was refusing to do anything about it.

'You've only to look at the state of the mortar between your bricks outside,' he said disparagingly. He wasn't soot-blackened himself; presumably he sent others to do that part of the job. No, he was just a drab man, all gaberdine raincoat and Ford Popular, someone who only leapt into prominence at times when other people were in despair.

The kitchen had been in a state of chaos since breakfast time. And since then Joan had been to school and come back. Now dusk was beginning to fall, and Granny Briggs looked like a survivor from a colliery disaster. This surely had to be the end of her big wrap around overall; no bleach on earth would be strong enough to get it back to white.

'It's just a good job that your fire wasn't lit at the time,' said Eccles's own Napoleon. He even had one hand held self-importantly inside his coat.

Granny bit her lip for a moment, then she must have decided to throw herself upon his mercy because she said, 'Please do something about it – *please*.' Joan did not like to see her begging.

The man didn't even give the range a second glance. 'No

can do. I wouldn't let a brush of mine up those complicated flues. Not when they're in that neglected state. More could come down than you're bargaining for.'

'Well if it does, I'm insured. They've been having a fortune off me for years. It's about time I had something back.'

'I'll pretend I never heard that,' he said reproachfully. 'You do realise that you just asked me to stage a fiddle? That's no way to get your house repaired, madam. I'm afraid you've come to the wrong man for an insurance swindle. And your driveway's a danger to other people's cars. Good afternoon.' And that was that: he picked up his trilby and showed himself out.

Granny gazed at Joan in disbelief. 'Did *you* hear me attempt to compound a felony?' She began to make little spitting noises. 'I can even taste this stuff.'

'What you need is a cup of tea.'

'With the stove out and the cooker clogged with soot?'

'There's still the electric kettle in the front drawing room.' This was generally kept sacred for those days when the vicar came in for a cup of tea. He didn't come often. 'Last time I looked there was a caddy there, and sugar and everything. I'll just bring the milk.'

Granny must have reached that state of despair where even helpful suggestions have to be picked to bits. 'How can I sit down when I'm in this filthy state?'

Joan virtually frog-marched her out of the room: goodness but she was bony. 'That's what dust sheets are for. Everything's well covered and the sheets will wash.'

The drawing-room door seemed to have swelled in its frame, so Joan tried putting her shoulder against it. She was feeling a bit like that scene in *Little Women* where Meg takes the reins of the household into her own hands. The door gave way with a protesting cracking sound.

But what was that other noise, the one coming from the inside of the room? It sounded like several women sighing.

Joan felt for the light switch; four bulbs went on in the overhead electrolier. There should have been five, but Joan was more concerned with trying to trace the sighs to their source.

'Ye gods, more filth!' Granny had beaten her to it; the gasping sighs were being made by fall after fall of soot which was piling up, in black waves, in the hearth of the white marble fireplace. 'Thank God we couldn't afford a fire in here.' Her voice began to rise hysterically. 'He tried telling me that the flues could all be interconnected. He told me and I said it was impossible. You see, I don't know about these things. I left all that to your grandfather. Anything mechanical and he was a whiz, an absolute whiz. Oh, Freddie,' she sobbed at somebody who wasn't there, 'why did you have to go away and leave me to cope?' She fished blindly in her apron pocket, took out her handkerchief and blew her nose.

Joan was not surprised to see that more soot seemed to come down it than snot. But Granny must have blown herself into better control because she sounded almost herself again as she said, 'When they carried that coffin out of this house, I was a woman who didn't know what you did with fuse wire. Well, I know now!' Her gaze shifted back to the fireplace. 'But I'm not up to coping with this. I shouldn't think a civil engineer could cope with this.'

'Let's have a cup of tea and a think. Where's that kettle gone?'

'It's got put with the other things, in the Chinese cupboard. A serious gardener would give a fortune for that amount of soot. They *do* something with it. Ye gods, there must be enough here to fertilise Chatsworth!'

As Joan reached the orange lacquer cupboard on the wall by the bay window, she thought she heard a car turning into the drive. 'Where's Bruno?'

'A late lecture and then rehearsals for *Medea*.' Granny was rummaging in the soot with a poker. 'There are clinkers in here the size of cricket balls. They're really creepy, there's no proper weight to them.'

Who could be in the car? It was just about to stop at the front door. Because light from inside the room was reflecting on the windowpane, Joan really had to peer out to see. Wasn't that a Daimler? It was certainly a black limousine, and definitely a uniformed chauffeur behind the wheel.

'If that's a motor car,' said Granny weakly, 'maybe it's that first sweep I rang. The one who said he was booked solid. Perhaps he's had a change of heart.' But she didn't sound much convinced of this theory.

Horror mounting inside her, Joan hastened to pull faded shot-silk curtains over the scene outside. But not before she'd seen a girl of her own age push open one of the passenger doors, while the chauffeur leapt out to undo the other.

This couldn't be anybody but the Morgensterns.

'I'll see to it, Granny. You stay where you are.' The words flew out of her on a much higher note than she'd intended. And if Joan's voice was out of control, so were her limbs. The hand that reached to close the drawing-room door behind her was shaking in terror. And that was nothing compared with the panic inside her head. Her brain seemed to have split up into several different caverns of thought ('Will they?' 'Might they?' 'Could I?'). And these warring spaces were all frantic with agitation. She could feel her heart thumping like it had never thumped before. And somebody was playing a different rhythm on the front doorbell: *Hi-diddley-aye-ti-pom-pom*. Granny Briggs couldn't stand people who did that.

'Anybody home?' The man peering through the plain part of the glass had dark hair, big soulful eyes and a wide mouth. Under any other circumstances Joan would have thought that he looked wonderfully intelligent and interesting. 'Please forgive the War of Independence and let us come in from the cold. We're sorry we threw your tea into Boston Bay.'

'*Is* it the other sweep?' Granny had stepped hopefully into the hall.

As the old woman headed towards the front door, her granddaughter attempted to bar her way. 'You'll find it's all a terrible mistake,' was the best she could come up with. One of the blobs of soot had left Granny looking as though she'd got a black eye.

'Joan,' she said in sarcastically patient tones, 'there's a man outside singing "Transatlantic Lullaby". Would you please let me get to my own front door?'

She got there and opened it. 'Yes?'

The singing stopped. 'My name is Herbie Morgenstern and this is my daughter, Sally.' At the bottom of the steps a slim blonde girl was looking up at Joan. The face was as clever as her father's. And Joan was intuitive enough to realise that one glimpse of tumbledown Ingledene had been enough to cause the girl in the pink coat to assume a politely wary expression. After all, this was *not* the same house as the one that Joan had described in her letters.

It was Granny Briggs who took control of the proceedings. 'I was hoping you were the chimney sweep. I'm afraid we're in a bit of a pickle.'

'We should have called you first, but Sally wanted to surprise Joan.'

'You don't by any chance know anything about chimneys, do you?' asked Granny wildly.

'A fireplace problem?' He sounded deeply interested. 'I love fireplaces. I refused to let the builder block them up at our place in the Hamptons.'

Whatever these Hamptons were, they were obviously a passport to Granny's favour because she said, 'The worst of the damage is in the kitchen. Perhaps you would be kind enough to take a look.'

Granny inviting somebody into the kitchen? It hadn't seen a lick of new paint since 1939. But Olive Briggs proved herself more than equal to the situation. As she led everybody down the dank hallway she said, 'You see before you the results of a world war. England has suffered enormous financial reversals.'

Joan couldn't think of the blonde girl with the dark eyelashes as Sally. 'Sally' was somebody she knew from the pages of hundreds of letters. This stranger was obviously having great difficulty disguising her surprise at finding herself inside a cold building which was, literally, falling apart. But Mr Morgenstern was like somebody who had stumbled in on an adventure.

The tall, loose-limbed man walked into the kitchen, ignored the fact that there was soot everywhere, and actually stroked the door of the Briggs Patent Range. There was something very near to reverence in his voice as he said, 'That's the handsomest stove I ever saw.'

'We made them ourselves.' Granny Briggs spoke with simple pride. 'You'll find the same item in royal palaces.'

'It is superb.'

'Yes, but the flues have gone phut! And a very low kind of workman has just refused to touch them.'

'I'll touch them.' Herbie Morgenstern's mouth had spread into a delighted grin. He was already swinging a beautiful new grey flannel jacket onto the back of an old chair. 'I was getting bored with playing at being a tourist.' In a moment he was across the room and poking his head right inside the chimney. 'We need a lamp.'

Granny hesitated. 'What if the whole thing comes down from inside?'

Herbie's head came back into view. 'You have insurance?'

'Yes, but . . .'

'That's what insurance companies are for.'

'Precisely my own sentiments.' When had Granny Briggs last smiled so beautifully? Her granddaughter couldn't remember. 'Joan, go and get Mr Morgenstern a flashlight. I think there's one by the lead urn in the old conservatory.'

'May I come with you?' asked Sally politely.

'I suppose so.' Joan hadn't meant to sound unfriendly, she was just dreading being left alone with her. Perhaps, if she kept moving, Sally wouldn't get a chance to say anything. But sooner or later Joan knew that she was going to have to face up to the girl with the searching hazel eyes. 'Mind the steps, they're made of slate. Sometimes they get icy in the winter.' It was dark in the conservatory. Would the dreaded conversation be better held here and now? She took a deep breath, let it out and said, 'I made it all up.'

'I know. And I think it's wild!'

Hardly able to believe the admiration in Sally's voice, Joan reached up and tugged at the bobbin on the cord that pulled on the light. Sally was all but fizzing with pleasure. 'You mean you don't mind?' Joan was staggered.

'Mind? When you invented a whole world for me? You must have as good an imagination as your mother.'

'*No.*' It was more a cry of pain than an actual word. 'You

see you've *not* understood. First of all there's no Old Olive. Well, there is, but it's Granny.'

'I already worked that out.'

'Well, you wouldn't be able to work out my mother.' Joan was close to angry tears. 'It took me years and years. She's in a loony bin.'

'Excuse me?'

'She's mad. They've locked her up.'

Sally's eyes widened. 'Like Mrs Rochester in *Jane Eyre*?'

If Sally was going to behave as though this too was wonderful, then Joan was going to hit her: no joking.

But she had misjudged her penfriend: 'That must be awful for you.'

'You get used to it.' Joan Stone was finally telling Sally Morgenstern the unvarnished truth.

'Are you decent, Peter? Can I come in?' At least his mother had asked. An uninvited Eddie Bird, all brand-new haircut and knife-edge creases, had been barging in and out of Peter's bedroom since half past five. Nobody had eaten yet, and the Birds were teatime people – they weren't used to late dinner.

'Yes, come in,' called Peter. 'It's a shop!'

'Don't be so cheeky.' She was still in her underslip. 'I've decided against the silk frock – too chilly. I'll settle for that little two-piece I had for your Auntie Nora's wedding. It's at the back of your wardrobe.'

Peter's room was jam-packed with a massive walnut bedroom suite which had been passed on to Peggy Bird by a well-meaning cousin. 'It's not my wardrobe at all,' he said, 'it's just a public cloakroom.'

Peggy stopped rattling through hangers; she had found what she was looking for. And old pyjama top was fastened round the outfit, to keep it clean. 'I'm all thumbs tonight. You undo it and see what you think.' She always asked his advice about clothes.

'I think there's altogether too much fuss. And if that's what you're going to wear, you'll need a brighter lipstick.'

'Navy and white's always nice and safe.'

'Red lipstick, white hair, and navy blue: you'll probably get mistaken for a Festival of Britain souvenir.' He was in the mood for a row with somebody.

Peggy wasn't about to offer him the opportunity. 'You look nice.'

'You're sure this chalk stripe doesn't shout out the Fifty Shilling Tailors?' The suit might have been bought especially for tonight, but he intended to wear it to launch himself on the Gin and Tonic Brigade's circuit. Since his visit to Hulme, there was somebody Peter was hoping to see again. And that was putting it mildly.

'You don't look like my little boy any more.' For a brief moment Peggy had looked sad. Now she plunged ahead with, 'You've got good-looking. And just for once, could I ask you to *behave* grown-up, too.' She'd climbed into the navy skirt. 'If you can't do it for your father's sake, do it for mine.'

'I don't see why I've got to go at all. Can I get to the mirror? This parting in my hair is just like a dog's hind leg.'

'You've got to go because Major Shadwell is a very big figure in your father's life. Find me my marcasite brooch from the middle drawer.'

Peter was in no mood for fetching and carrying. 'All these bracelets lying loose,' he grumbled. 'If the police ever searched my bedroom they'd mistake me for a dra . . . for a female impersonator.'

'Why should the police search your bedroom?' she asked sharply, as she snatched the glittering brooch out of his hand. 'And keep your voice down. We don't want a row about things like that with your father, not tonight.' For the first time ever, Peter realised that she *did* know what he was talking about. 'Peter, you can be really nice when you try. Couldn't you just try tonight?'

'The taxi's here,' bawled Eddie Bird from the bottom of the stairs.

'Two dabs of Yardley's Lavender and I'll be all yours,' she called back.

In the car, Eddie sat next to the driver and dominated the journey into the town with a rambling monologue about the wondrous Major Shadwell. Peter had heard it all before, heard it too many times to be even remotely interested.

'Tripoli . . . Battle of Messina . . . threw back the Afrika Korps's own hand grenade . . . decorated by the King on the same day.' It was all as boringly familiar as Latin declensions.

'Where to in town?' asked the driver.

'Nothing but the best for Major Shadwell, the Prince's Bar and Grill.'

Peter stopped lolling in the back and sat up with a start. The Prince's? Dear God in heaven! While gathering information in the Snake Pit, he had learned that the Gin and Tonic Brigade stuck to a fixed list of watering holes. They began at the Café Royal in Peter Street, moved on to a discreet side bar at the Midland, then pointed their umbrellas in the direction of (could he have heard his father correctly?) the Prince's.

'Yes, it's one of Willoughby's establishments,' swanked Eddie.

It *was*, it was the same place. Peter's head was filled with memories of a conversation with Hetty King: 'That Prince's Bar! My dear, the ground floor is camp as a row of tents. And upstairs is nothing but normal people feeding their faces with mixed grills. And they have to walk right through the bar to get to the restaurant!'

Homosexuals had an elastic attitude towards social hierarchy; gin and tonic drinkers thought nothing of looking for rough trade at the Snake Pit, Union customers sometimes lashed out the tuppence extra on drinks at the Prince's. And the people who used the Union were the same ones who haunted the bus station café – there was *bound* to be somebody who knew him. Peter could already imagine the cries of 'Good evening Miss Ladybird'.

'This is it,' announced the driver. 'And if you need a hangover cure afterwards, Eddie, you're very conveniently placed for the all-night chemist's.'

'It's not going to be that sort of evening,' sniffed Peggy. Peter could tell that she was nervous. But nothing like as nervous as he was feeling himself. The bar was hidden away behind stained-glass windows. The only thing that stood between Peter and exposure was a heavy wooden door.

'Give it a push and let your mother go in first,' ordered

Eddie. Peter did as he was told. 'Well, go on, get a move on, we've not got all night.'

As Peter crossed the threshold of licensed premises for the first time, he was startled by the sheer blast of the smell of beer and spirits. And by the sight of Blondie Jack and Mother Macree, half-pint pots in hand, leaning against a pillar. But he needn't have worried: that half-world of 1951 had rules to cover every imaginable situation.

The two men totally ignored him; in fact they looked *through* him. Peter was obviously out with his family so no hint of previous acquaintance must be allowed to show. And now he recognised several of the others, but all of them studiously avoided catching his eye.

'The arrow for the restaurant is pointing up those stairs.' Eddie was visibly brightening at the sight of beer pumps and bottled stock.

As they mounted the staircase, Peter's thoughts were at war with themselves. Half of him was almost numb with the relief of having got away with it, but the other half was rebelling at the idea of people having to erase themselves. It was as though they were putting down their own value and he couldn't pretend to like it. One day, he thought, one day we've got to be able to say hello – just like everybody else.

The first-floor restaurant was a throwback to the turn of the century. It was an old-fashioned grill room with dark panelling and starched white tablecloths. Great big joints of meat were being wheeled around on dinner wagons by waiters who looked like character actors out of British films. 'Have you a reservation, sir?' the headwaiter asked Eddie. Peter had never imagined that a suit of tails could get as threadbare as this, but it only added to the Edwardian distinction of the Prince's Grill. This place was posh.

'We're here to meet Major Shadwell.' Eddie didn't need any further assistance; over in an alcove, beyond a row of hunting prints, a tall good-looking man was already getting to his feet. If he'd had a beard and long hair he could have been Franz Hals's Laughing Cavalier. As it was, his brown curls were clipped as for battle, but the generous mouth was smiling.

Good teeth, thought Peter as the man said, 'Evening, Bird, hello, Peggy . . . and this must be Peter.'

Peter was entirely familiar with the look he was getting. It was the old-one-two. Crikey, he thought, we *are* everywhere.

Not a hundred yards away, in fact right across the street, a very different party, a gathering of four, was already three-quarters of the way through their meal. 'The last place on earth I expected to be tonight was in the French Restaurant of the Midland Hotel.' No longer soot-bedaubed, Granny Briggs looked a changed woman – she was even wearing her squirrel bridge cape.

And Joan was another eye-opener. Clothes being the most important single detail in any suburban outing, it was fortunate that Sally had been under the impression that they were still rationed in Britain. That's why she had persuaded her mother to buy a complete outfit from Bergdorf's, no less, for her penfriend.

'Such a pity your wife can't be with us tonight,' Granny said as the waiter filled up her glass. 'It's years since I had a good Sauternes with dessert.'

Her granddaughter had never known that such desserts existed, that rococo whirls of hot meringue could be baked around freezing cold ice cream. And there was real cream to pour on the top, too.

'You really do pay for dressing, Joan.' Granny was continuing to be expansive. 'All that lovely baby blue! Tell me the American names for those garments again, Sally.'

'That's a sweater set, and that's a felt circle skirt, and the shoes are white bucks.' Sally was dressed almost identically, but in pink. 'Wouldn't Joan's hair look great in a pageboy fluff like mine?' she enthused.

'It wouldn't suit Joan at all. She'd look like the Renaissance gone barmy,' snorted Olive Briggs. She had gone back to being everyday-Granny for a moment. Mr Morgenstern, who plainly regarded her as a collector's item, greeted this last remark with a delighted guffaw. 'Now stop that!' She actually dealt him a reproving slap on the wrist. Joan had never known Granny Briggs to take to *any*body like this before.

The French Restaurant was all rose brocade wallpaper and banks of flowers and twinkling candlelight. There were even candles in the old Waterford crystal chandeliers, which were still untouched by electricity. Customers were very much bowed in and out of the restaurant, and Joan had noticed that Granny Briggs was being treated with, if anything, even more deference than the rest. Granny didn't look a frump here, she looked mildly eccentric but definitely distinguished; somebody who'd been around, knew the rules.

'That's Catherine of Braganza,' she said, nodding towards a big portrait on one wall. 'My husband always used to raise his glass to her. What a pity Bruno isn't here to carry on the tradition.'

'Perhaps I could do it for him,' suggested Mr Morgenstern. Up went his glass. 'Catherine,' he said.

'Catherine,' they all joined in happily. The girls had been allowed to try a little of each of the wines, but the waiters had been told to top up their second glasses with sparkling mineral water.

'I bet Mom isn't having this kind of great time at Renishaw,' said Sally. Herbie Morgenstern had already explained that his wife was spending a couple of days with some poets called the Sitwells.

'And where will your son be this evening?' he enquired.

'Rehearsing for an amateur production of *Medea*.' The Morgensterns might have the Sitwells but the Briggses had got Euripides

Granny, whose wine had *not* been diluted with mineral water, proceeded to enlarge upon the theme of Bruno and *Medea*. 'Personally,' she said, 'I'm not convinced he's up to the role of Jason. I think they only gave it to him because he inherited his father's legs. My husband always had much better legs than I,' she confided to Mr Morgenstern. 'In fact, for a lark, we once persuaded him to try on a pair of my . . .'. Registering the fact that Joan was all agog, she concluded the sentence with '. . . well, it *was* fancy dress. And Bruno's legs are rather more masculine and muscled than his daddy's were.'

278

Sally got to her feet. 'Could we have change for the powder room?' she asked her father.

'How much should they tip?' he enquired of Granny.

'Not a farthing more than a shilling,' she decreed. 'You don't want to go spoiling things for people who come afterwards.'

As Joan got up to leave, Granny said, 'Those matching outfits bring the Andrews Sisters to mind. You look as though you should be singing in close harmony.'

The archway at the end of the restaurant led into an octagonal cocktail bar. As the girls crossed the thick dove-grey carpet, a man at a white grand piano was playing 'Loving Glances'.

'Guess what?' said Sally. 'That pianist just winked at me.'

'Guess what? Toby Eden kissed me last Saturday! Only nobody knows but you,' she added hastily.

'So he *is* real.' If somebody had just given her a present, Sally could not have sounded more delighted. 'I usually talk much more than I did at the table but I was scared to ask questions because . . .' Her voice tailed off.

'Because everything I'd written could have been make-believe.'

'What about Peter and Vanda?'

'Real. Alive as anything. Did you really want to go to the cloakroom?'

'No, I just need the change. He'll buy me anything but I can never get my hands on nickels and dimes. Molly Wainwright says she's going to talk to him about it.'

For Joan, hearing her favourite *Collins' Magazine* author spoken about as though she was just anybody was definitely one of the highspots of the evening. 'What's she like?' she asked eagerly.

'She's OK. She's my friend. Did you know that she does all her writing in bed? Molly says that if she doesn't get up she doesn't have to answer the phone. My dad says that she's only as successful as she is because she's still got a child's imagination.'

A terrible thought occurred to Joan. They had reached the

magazine stall but it was closed, with an iron grille pulled over its front. 'Does your father know about *my* imagination?'

There was an awkward pause. 'Bits,' was the most that Sally seemed prepared to admit.

'Oh no,' groaned Joan. She was so furious with herself that she could have stamped one of her new white buckskin shoes. 'Did you tell him?'

'I didn't have to. I'd already told that chauffeur from Daimler Hire to look out for a house that was a bit like Balmoral Castle. We were also looking out for your flock of peacocks.' She changed the subject: 'Will you take me to meet your mother?'

'It's all locked doors and she thinks she's still about eight.'

'I don't care. She's your mother. You're my friend. I want to meet her.'

'What must Mr Morgenstern be thinking of me?' Joan all but whispered this.

'He only knows the bits he worked out for himself. Sneaky I ain't. He said he wondered if he ought to put you under contract right now. He was just joking,' she added hastily. 'But he understands writers; he knows they live inside their own heads.'

'Do you really think I'm going to be a proper writer?' Joan had never dared to ask anybody this before.

Sally treated her to an old-fashioned look. 'Per-lease!' she cried. 'With that head on your shoulders, what else could you be?' And they both burst out laughing. 'Where will Peter be tonight? Out homoing?'

'No, he doesn't do it all the time. He said his parents were taking him to meet the most boring man on earth. Wasn't it brilliant of your father to vacuum all that soot out and then find a chimney sweep?' Herbie Morgenstern had only one Manchester contact, an art dealer named Kalman. But after a few telephone calls to and fro a sweep had been promised for the following morning. 'Usually you can never get them to turn out.'

'This one will turn out,' said Sally proudly. 'He's a kosher chimney sweep. Joan, what's so funny? Why are you laughing?'

280

'I can't tell you.'

'You must.'

'Promise you won't be annoyed?' Joan was still having difficulty in controlling her amusement. 'It's just that Granny thinks she doesn't like Jews. And there she is, eating out of your father's hand like . . .' All laughter subsided as she caught the expression on Sally's face. 'I'm sorry,' she said. 'Really sorry. You know I don't think like that. And Granny only thought she didn't like them because she'd never met any.'

Sally repeated some words that Joan had used earlier in the day. 'You get used to it,' she said. 'Yes, you get used to it.'

Under the watchful eye of Major Shadwell, Eddie Bird had reverted to military discipline. The nearest thing he came to stepping out of line was when he suddenly blurted out, 'I wonder whether it would be possible for me to have another pint of mixed?' In truth, the major's watchful eye was paying more attention to Eddie's son. Peter had been encouraged to have a Dover sole, pressed to try a glass of hock, and found himself being drawn into the conversation at every turn.

The major, it transpired, collected antiques. He was in Manchester for a big sale at Capes Dunn's auction rooms. He wasn't staying at an hotel, he was at the Reform Club. 'It's an amazing Victorian building, right here in your own city; it's something you really ought to see.' All the invitation in his eyes was directed towards Peter. 'How old are you?'

'Sixteen in June.'

'Good Gordon Highlanders,' the man exclaimed involuntarily. 'I took you for much older than that.' Major Shadwell began to talk about a recent trip to Berlin. Describing a pre-war German film star's attempt at making a comeback in cabaret, he said, 'She was really rather . . .' He seemed to be lost for the right word.

'Camp?' suggested Peter quietly.

'What does that mean?' his mother asked, puzzled.

'Probably something Continental.' Eddie never liked it when the spotlight was off himself for too long.

One word had changed the whole atmosphere. The major

was no longer flirtatious, he was worried, frightened even. Very soon afterwards he called for the bill and settled it quickly.

There was no real cloakroom at the Prince's so Eddie went across to the coatstand and began rummaging ineffectively. Probably because he was famous for knocking things over, Peggy hurried across to help him.

Major Shadwell began to speak in a voice which was little above a murmur. 'You wouldn't say anything, would you?'

'No, I won't if you don't.'

'Your father once saved my life.'

'Well, he wouldn't have done if he'd known you were queer.'

His parents returned and began distributing overcoats. Once they were all buttoned up, they began their descent into the bar. As before, custody of eyes was studiously observed. And one young man, standing alone by the counter, was avoiding looking at Peter even more assiduously than the rest. In a way it was understandable, just as it had been understandable at Hulme Hippodrome. Because that young man was Bruno Briggs.

'Joan, wake up.' The voice belonged to Bruno. 'It's a madhouse downstairs and you've got visitors.'

The next thing she heard was the curtains going back with a terrible rattle of wooden rings. Daylight was trying to shine through her eyelids and she could feel the edges of a headache beginning to close in. Why did her tongue feel like a flap of suede? 'I think I might have a hangover,' she murmured. Though the symptoms were less than pleasant, the idea was sophisticated enough to have a certain appeal. 'Are my eyes bloodshot?'

'I can't tell till you sit up and open them . . . No. But your grandmother's had to have bicarb and hot water. I've never seen so many people in this house since Father's funeral.'

'Who's here?' she yawned.

'That American, and workmen, and a blonde American daughter who's just like a Catherine wheel on bonfire night.'

'Sally's not round,' cried Joan indignantly. Raising her voice had made the inside of her head hurt even more.

'No, but she revolves a lot and it wouldn't surprise me if she exploded.'

Joan knew her uncle so well that she realised all this criticism was just a front, that he was worried – really worried. 'You're not jealous, are you? I'm sorry you missed out on all the . . .'

'I'm not jealous.' He said it absolutely blankly, then he moved across to the bedroom door and turned the big old iron key in the lock.

'Bruno,' said Joan, 'look at me. What's the matter?'

He didn't turn round. 'I'd rather just say it facing the wall,' was all he offered.

This brought back memories of going into that awful confessional in Gorton. 'Blurt it out and get it over with,' she urged him.

Now he did turn round. He was very white in the face. 'It's what other people could blurt out.'

'What people?'

'Somebody you know.' He was searching her face to see whether his words had prompted any reaction. 'So nothing's been said? It's all right.' His words began tumbling over one another. 'Forget it. If you *had* heard something, you'd know what I was talking about.'

'This isn't fair.' Half a story was absolutely against their rules. 'You've started now, you have to tell me.'

'No I don't.' There was absolute certainty in his voice. 'You're better off not knowing. It's just that the same person's had the chance to suspect something twice.'

Would silence get more out of him than further questioning? Eventually it did. 'I'm sorry about locking the door,' he said wretchedly. 'It's just this constant bloody fear of being discovered.'

'What have you done?'

His reply was more to himself than to her. 'Done? I've not done anything yet. But they're always watching. They know who we are.'

Never before had she known him to be this cryptic.

283

Neither had she heard him sound so neurotic. 'Shouldn't you think about seeing a doctor?' This was, after all, a man whose sister had spent the past fifteen years in a mental institution.

'Doctors? What can they do to help anybody? They're useless. Absolutely bloody useless.'

A terrible thought was beginning to gather momentum. 'Have you got TB?' Medicine had yet to supply the answer to this disease. At least, that's what Joan thought.

It seemed she was wrong. 'They can treat that now. If that's all that was wrong they could do something. Joan, I didn't sleep at all last night so I've said too much. I don't know what's got into me; I shouldn't have said anything at all. Do me a favour, wipe the whole thing from your mind.'

'Can it kill you?'

'No. It can't do that. Just promise me one thing . . .' For the first time that morning he was looking her straight in the eye. 'If anybody ever comes to you with stories, will you come straight and tell me? I want to be able to give you my version. It's not something I chose, believe you me.'

It could only be one thing. VD – veneral disease. 'Aren't there posters in gents' lavatories?' she asked. 'There are special clinics. I could go into a ladies and write down their addresses.'

'You would too!' His eyes filled with tears. 'It's OK, I do know about those places.' It was years since she'd seen him cry, but Bruno's tears were falling so uncontrollably that she jumped out of bed and flung her arms round him. Her uncle was twenty-one and he looked about twelve. 'It's just that I didn't get any sleep,' he repeated. 'I couldn't bear it if you hated me.'

'I couldn't hate you, not even if you'd murdered somebody.' Oh she did love him!

'That friend of yours . . .' Bruno stopped before he'd really started. He had obviously thought better of the idea. 'Never mind.' He blew his nose and began to laugh in an embarrassed way. 'Sorry about all this. I was only asked to come and let you know that Sally's waiting downstairs.'

'Sally the Catherine wheel.' She smiled back. 'Have

284

another hug for luck. And listen, you tell me when you want to tell me. But whatever it is won't change anything.'

'Like to bet?' English families not being given to falling into one another's arms, Bruno obviously felt the need to change the subject. 'Granny's phoned school. She's talked them into giving you a day off.' He went across to the door. 'I suppose locking this *was* a bit dramatic.'

Though he tried to sound cheerful, Joan was not deceived.

'Joan, Joanie? Which one's Joan's room?' The voice was coming from outside in the corridor.

'Here she blows!' laughed Bruno. 'In here, Sally,' he called out. 'Mind she doesn't singe the curtains.'

Sally did not erupt into the room; instead she came gliding in with a cup of tea in her hand. It was a bit like somebody on silent roller skates. 'Room service,' she said proudly. And then she tripped over the fringe of the Indian rug, and the cup and its contents went flying.

This sent the two girls to the bathroom, Joan to wash her face and brush her teeth and Sally to look for something to mop up the spilt tea. Joan spat out a mouthful of water, coloured bright pink by Gibbs's Dentifrice. 'I've got the day off school,' she said, starting to climb into clean knickers beneath the protective cover of her kimono. She supposed she must look just like a 1920s photograph of somebody changing on a beach.

'I know you don't have to go to school. You're taking me to meet your mother instead.'

'It's not as easy as that.' She reached into the airing cupboard for a fresh bra. 'Granny would never let it happen.' It was now a battle between modesty and strangulation, so off came the kimono.

'You still wear a brassière?' asked Sally, interested. 'I rebelled, I only wear undershirts. Your grandmother kind of knows it's happening.' She reached for a loofah. 'Could I use this to mop up those tea leaves? I asked Mrs Briggs whether you could take me out, and could I choose where. And she said of course I could because I was "the stranger within the gate".'

285

'Mop up with this instead.' Joan had reached under the bath for a floorcloth.

'You think I'm being pushy – about going to see you mother?' Sally sounded genuinely concerned.

If she hadn't, Joan would probably have vetoed the whole idea, there and then. As it was, well, maybe a fresh face would be just the thing her mother needed. 'OK,' she conceded. 'But we'll just call it "going sight seeing".'

Over the years the journey to the hospital, those bus rides where narrow streets and mill chimneys gave way to pine forest and corporation reservoir, had become so familiar to Joan that she had stopped noticing them. But Sally was seeing novelty in everything. 'Can we go on the top floor again?' she asked as they climbed onto the second bus. 'What are those little mountains?' They were slagheaps. By the time they clambered into the single-decker her excitement was plainly giving way to anxiety.

It hadn't taken Joan long to realise that Sally was a girl without half-measures, that she dealt either in joy or despair. 'What's the matter?'

'This.' It was a long narrow package wrapped in the sort of pretty gift paper you never saw in England. Since their journey to the hospital had begun, the narrow grey and mauve parcel had developed a little waist – the result of Sally's worried clutching. 'It's the present I bought in Paris for your mother. Trouble is I brought it for your *other* mother.'

'We have to dive off at the next stop. Hurry up or he'll sail right past it.' There were no hospital visitors on the bus; the only other pasenger was a man with a clanking paraffin stove between his knees.

'You know they've reduced the service on this route, don't you?' the conductor said to Joan. She hadn't known but it didn't surprise her; these visits were invariably accompanied by something which lowered the spirits.

As they descended to the pavement, Sally looked around and said, 'It's just like that poem by Keats, "La Belle Dame Sans Merci".

  ' "O what can ail thee, knight-at-arms,
    Alone and palely loitering?
   The sedge is withered from the lake,
    And no birds sing." '

Joan, who had joined in on the last line, brought the recitation to a halt, with, 'What's in the parcel? Don't spoil it, there's no need to undo it.'

Sally had already pulled back the paper to reveal a scarlet ostrich feather. 'I bought it in Paris. It's got a ballpoint pen running down the middle. I thought she could use it to write her next book.'

'I don't think Rhoda even remembers how to write her own name.'

Sally snatched an alternative plan out of the air: 'You could have it. It would do for your first novel.'

Except I'd have got it by deception, thought Joan. And that might bring me bad luck. This doom-laden idea was overtaken by one which was much more urgent. 'I don't think we'd better take it inside,' she said. 'It's got a stabby point. You never quite know what kind of mood she's going to be in.'

'I could fasten it back up in the paper.'

Joan shook her head. 'She snatches.'

'OK, we'll hide it in this bush.' Sally was referring to one of the hawthorn hedges which ran either side of the drive.

'Poke it in good and hard or somebody'll notice it and nick it. You don't get a lot of pretty things round here. We'll pick it up on the way back. And listen, we'd better hurry up. Those nursing escorts only wait in the hall for the first quarter of an hour of visiting.' They had come within sight of the hospital building.

Sally, who had a literary reference for every occasion, had two for this. 'Is it the House of Usher or Dotheboys Hall?'

'It's somewhere where I'm going to have to hand out a load of old flannel.'

'Excuse me?'

'I'm going to have to tell lies to get you in.' Worried that she might have appeared to announce this too easily, Joan said, 'That stuff I wrote to you wasn't *really* lies; it was just my other life.'

'I already know that. Please don't feel you have to keep on explaining.'

'Well, now you're going to see the most of the truth with your own eyes.' Joan rapped hard on the big iron knocker.

'Those steps coming from inside sound just like Quasimodo,' whispered Sally.

The door opened. 'Hello, Cyril,' said Joan to the porter. She'd known him for so long that she'd stopped registering that he dragged a leg. In the years since her first visit he'd turned into a whole person with a wife called Lily who always took her glasses off for snapshots, but still kept them gripped in her hand. Joan even knew where he took her for her holidays – Barmouth. But would he believe her when she said that she'd mislaid her visiting docket?

He did. 'But is the young lady a relative?' he asked anxiously. 'I can stretch a point if she's a relative; it's what we call "outside influences" that the patients find disturbing.'

The 'outside influence' looked a mite worried at this, but her expression turned to surprise as Joan said, 'This is Mother's Cousin Lucy from Idaho.'

The porter limped away to talk to the nursing escorts who were waiting by a hatch marked *Office*. 'Why Cousin Lucy?' asked Sally in amazement.

'Once I start, I can't stop. I'm already thinking up extra bits to tell the nurse. It's terrible, isn't it?' She meant this.

'It won't be terrible when you're turning it into dollars. We have to ask my dad how you get started. I do *not* care for the faces on those nurses. They make me think of lampshades made of human skin. Sorry, that was a very Jewish thought. We never quite forget the Holocaust.' Nervousness was causing her to talk like an automaton. 'Oh look, he's chosen us one who looks like a wishy-washy pencil drawing.'

'They do a wonderful job.' Even as she said the words, Joan knew they sounded overpious.

'Oh yeah? Ever seen Olivia de Havilland in *The Snake Pit*?'

'Nurse Whelan's off today.' The porter was back. 'This is little Nurse Carter. She's so new that you'll be able to show *her* the ropes. Joan's quite a favourite round here,' he said proprietorially. 'She was even chosen to present the bouquet at the garden party.'

'I'm glad somebody knows what's what.' The young nurse had already begun the unlocking process. 'Do you have supervised visits?'

'Oh no.' Untrue. But Joan had been banking on the presence of Nurse Whelan who was always begging to be addressed as Ursula. This change of heart had only come about because Joan had never said anything to anybody about her scrap with Rhoda. And that had only been allowed to happen because the Irish nurse had nipped out to watch the end of a horse race on television. Nurse Whelan definitely owed Joan a favour. She could even have been trusted with the knowledge of Sally's true identity and been warned not to tell Granny. The presence of this nursing substitute would call for a wholly different approach. 'How is Rhoda?' Joan began tentatively.

'Did you know they decided against shock treatment?'

Was it this that caused Sally to hesitate in her progress up the stairs, or was it the fact that somebody was repeating, 'He touched me,' over and over again. As the nurse selected another key, the recitation changed to 'He touched me *there*. Yes, he touched me there.'

Intimacy had grown quickly between Joan and Sally, grown to an extent where they even had the beginnings of a private language. As yet another elderly female cry of 'He felt me all over' rose up on the air, Joan turned to her friend and observed wryly, 'You get used to it.'

But Sally didn't even smile, she just looked scared. And Joan worried about herself, worried whether life was desensitising her, making her hard. That last glib comment about getting used to things had not been meant as a joke. It was just that nobody had lightened the horror of her own first climb to the visiting room; she had wanted to make it easier for her friend.

'Your mother's mood swings have been terrible just recently,' observed her temporary keeper. 'You never know the minute!' Click: the visiting-room door was unlocked. Down went her keys. 'You wait here and I'll bring her.'

It was the usual drab room, the one with the lightweight chairs and the table that was little heavier than balsawood. It was Sally who broke the silence. 'I shouldn't have made you do this,' she said in a small voice. 'I'm sorry. I feel just like one of those people who used to go and watch Monsieur Mesmer hypnotise the lunatics in Paris on Sunday afternoons.'

'There'll be nothing like that today,' Joan assured her. 'It's OK. I do understand. Every time I come here I find myself worrying about what makes my own mind work.'

'Let's go.' Sally sounded panicked.

And Joan's next words could not have eased any fear: 'We can't. We're locked in on this wing.'

For the next three minutes they went back to silence. Eventually, Sally cut through it again with, 'All this creepy place needed was that dreadful feather pen.'

'No, it's a nice pen.'

Sally shook her head in disagreement. 'I'd no right to barge in here. I'm ashamed.'

'Here we are.' Nurse Carter had returned quietly. 'Come along in, Rhoda.' The patient came hesitantly over the threshold. Dutch-doll haircut, the blue and white *No, No, Nanette* frock, white ankle socks and very new gym shoes – all these added to the air of antique childhood. 'I'll leave you to it,' said Nurse Carter. 'When you're ready for off, just touch that bell.' Click.

'She's locked us even more in,' breathed the American girl involuntarily.

'This is Sally,' said Joan.

'Only we said I was Cousin Lucy from Idaho – to get me in,' chirruped the unexpected visitor. There was no response. 'I thought I'd better just mention it,' she added lamely, to Joan.

Joan was watching her mother closely. She wasn't wearing the dead glue eyes today. And you could never tell, until she spoke, whether you were meeting Rhoda the adult or Rhoda the child. 'Didn't you think to bring any games down with you?' she asked.

290

Totally ignoring Sally, Joan's mother came up to her daughter and said in tones that were quite new, 'I'm too old for games.' But it wasn't the adult voice.

Joan tried again. 'How old are you?'

'Fourteen.'

'Oh.' What on earth was she meant to say next? '*Is it nice being fourteen?*' would only sound ridiculous.

Rhoda saved her daughter from further conjecture by suddenly turning round and glaring at Sally, and asking in a voice like the crack of a whip: 'Who's that?'

Joan's own eyes went to the bell. No, she thought. Let's give her a chance. 'It's Sally. She's my new friend.'

Rhoda glared at Sally again and then slumped herself down into one of the flimsy chairs. 'Well, that's that,' she said wearily. The incredible thing was that Rhoda was managing to make herself sound exactly like a shopworn version of adolescence. 'I knew it was too good to last.'

'What was?'

'You were *my* friend.' The pain in her eyes was much older than the rest of her.

'But I *am* your friend.'

Rhoda thought about this for a minute and then said, 'No. You've got her now. She's got a coat on. That means she can go outside. Joan,' she asked worriedly, 'what am I doing here? When the visiting bell rings, why am I always the one who has to stay behind? If you really *are* my friend, will you be the one who stays behind today? Then I could come and see you next visiting day. We could take turns.'

The only answer Joan could think of was, 'That's not how it works.'

'It's not fair.' The tones could have been adolescence distilled. 'The days take so long to go down. It's not as if I want much – I only want a coat and some bus fare.'

'But where would you go?'

'*Home!*' The cry sounded as though it was torn from deep down inside her. 'I'd go home.' The second time she used the word it was wrapped in love. And then all the light went from behind her eyes. 'But I can't remember where home *is*.' She began to weep, like all her ages wrapped into one, childish

291

sobs mixed with adult moans as she rocked herself backwards and forwards in the chair. The only words that made sense were: 'Even a fox has got its own hole.'

It was Sally who took control of the situation. Extending her hand towards the bell, she looked questioningly at Joan.

Joan shoved out a stabbing finger to indicate that she should press it. Nurse Carter must have been only just outside the door because, one click of the lock later, she came smartly over the threshold. 'What's all this?' she said to her patient. 'What are we doing getting ourselves distressed? Nurse Fishwick,' she called out to a white blur who was passing the door. 'I think Rhoda had better go back to the ward. I'll discharge her visitors.'

Nurse Fishwick was a big woman but she seemed quite kindly. 'Rhoda, Rhoda, Rhoda,' she said soothingly. 'Whatever's happened to put that old black dog back on your shoulder?'

Rhoda treated Sally to one last look. 'She stole my friend,' was all she said before they took her back to whatever sort of life it was she led.

Staircase, door, click; corridor, door, click. Another door ... 'Could you please let us out, Cyril?' asked Joan breathlessly. 'It wasn't a good visit.'

'They all have their ups and their downs.' He led the way to the front door. 'Wouldn't be here otherwise. See you soon, Joan.' The last door had closed behind them.

'I can't look back,' said Joan. 'I daren't. She sometimes waves from one of the top windows and I couldn't look her in the eye.'

'It's all my fault.'

'No.' Joan's voice was filled with urgency. 'She was different today. She was somebody new. She'd never shown real feelings before. Dolls' tea-party stuff and silly tantrums, but not real feelings. You've not done any harm at all. You've unlocked something. But she's got to be given a chance. I've got to get her out of here.'

'Where can Joan be?' This was the question Vanda was asking as she and Peter made their way along the main road to

292

Eccles. It was lunchtime, but now they were in the fifth form they had given up bothering with school dinners. Instead, they generally sneaked down to a confectioner's shop which sold buttered barmcakes. 'Two burnt offerings,' said Vanda to the woman behind the counter. She and Peter had already clubbed their money together.

'That'll be eightpence and don't be so cheeky,' was the snapped-out reply.

Vanda viewed the idea of extending charm towards other women as a complete waste of time. Women did not like her. But in her own way she was quite fond of Joan. 'I suppose we could always walk round there and see if she's all right.'

'What, and get our heads snapped off by Granny Briggs?' Peter regarded his barmcake balefully, 'They're sneaking marge on these again. Are we sitting?'

They settled themselves down on a public bench at the side of a traffic roundabout. Vanda had to raise her voice to be heard. 'Did you know that Mrs Briggs calls us "people of that class"?'

'I was the one who told you. I suppose we could always phone.' And Bruno might just be at home to answer the telephone. Bruno, Bruno: two sightings in half-world locales had been enough to revive all the old fantasies about Joan's uncle. Oh Bruno. (Oh boy!)

'You're never thinking of phoning from the main road?' Vanda sounded scandalised. 'You couldn't risk tapping the number out, you'd be too much on view. And you're surely not thinking of paying?'

I'd pay pounds, he thought. I'd sell my bike and insert all the money into the phone box if it guaranteed that I would get to know him better. But Vanda was normal; and however sympathetic normal people were, it didn't do to tell them too much. That's why he was glad that she had failed to notice Bruno at Hulme. Normals didn't know what it was like to go cold inside at the sight of Strangeways Jail on the skyline. They didn't know about dreams haunted by iron bars and the feel of prison uniform.

'I'm not going halves on that phone call,' said Vanda. 'Fair's fair, I lashed out on theatre tickets the other night.'

And tonight she was going to the theatre again. She wouldn't have to wait until next week to see Phyllis Dixey because her framed photographs were already hanging outside Salford Hippodrome. In the 1950s, most Manchester working-class districts still boasted a decaying music hall. Shows toured round the area in a circle, and this week the stripper was disrobing in a dank little theatre next to the old cattle market.

Vanda did not, for one moment, think of suggesting that Peter should accompany her on this outing. She'd waited years to see the woman whom the tarot cards had constantly revealed as the High Priestess. Gran'ma Dora's name for this card had always been 'Pope Joan'. The moment was going to be sacred.

'I think I *will* ring.' Peter munched down the last bit of barmcake and licked his fingers. 'Can you give me three pennies for a threepenny bit?'

'Want me to come with you?'

No, he didn't. Should Bruno answer the phone, that would be Peter's sacred moment. 'Just give me the change.'

The last person to use the telephone box must have been wearing very strong scent. The interior of the rusting red-painted kiosk smelt like Kendal Milne's ground floor. Peter, surprised to find that his heart was beating faster, dialled the number.

Brr-brr, brr-brr. And then, 'Hello,' said a voice at the other end.

'Bruno?'

'Who's that?'

'It's Peter,' he said joyfully. 'Joan's friend. The one you saw last night in the Prince's Bar.'

'You didn't see me there. Have you got that? You didn't see me.'

'It's OK.' Peter attempted to reassure him. Would Bruno understand how to speak in Polari or would that be too common for a Gin and Tonicker? Peter lowered his voice. 'I'm queer too.'

'You mustn't ring me like this. Understood? Maybe I'll see you around, in town. But don't even think of phoning me here again.'

'But I only wanted to know . . .'

'Goodbye.'

Peter found himself listening to the dialling tone. Overcome by a sense of deep hurt, he replaced the receiver, pushed open the door of the box and returned to Vanda who was still waiting on the bench.

'So what's wrong?'

Was it written all over his face? And then he realised that she must be asking about Joan. Had he dialled with his back to the bench? Yes he had. So it would be OK to say 'There was no reply'. And what sort of life is this? he thought, when he'd said it. It's nothing but whispers and lies. The girls can talk about Toby Eden till the cows come home; I can't even dial a telephone number without causing somebody at the other end to fly into a panic.

That evening Vanda put her hair up on top again. Not that she proposed going in the best seats. She'd had trouble in the past with the box-office manager at Salford Hippodrome, the man who'd said she was too young to be admitted to a stripshow. But there was another entrance at the side of the theatre, one with its own little booking window marked *Gallery – Fourpence*. Vanda poked her hand through this hatchway and exchanged the correct money for a mauve ticket, one that was just torn off a roll. Then she began to climb the stone staircase up to the gods.

On the top floor her ticket was taken by an old man with short white hair and a military manner. He even managed to invest authority into a uniform which was as shabby as the peeling interior of the theatre; the gold braid on his epaulettes was as faded as the gold paint on the stage boxes way down below. These protruding boxes had roofs made in the shape of dusty seashells; they were held up by bare-breasted mermaids. From this height the stage only looked the size of a picture postcard. The show had already started. Six girls were doing a French can-can which was all untidy high kicks with bent legs – not at all the way Vanda had been taught to do it.

For the moment she was more interested in the audience

around her. The gallery didn't have separate seats, just curved rows of benches, like seating at a circus. And you couldn't really call it an audience; there were just a few knots of old women who looked the kind who patronised Ethel's stall, and a solitary man standing behind the rail at the side, on a kind of catwalk where people could walk about.

The only person who looked really alive was a boy seated behind a drawing board, with a jam jar of thick black pencils with quite muscular arms; you only noticed them because he'd pushed up the sleeves of a French sailor's jersey.

The music changed to 'Everybody's Doing it Now'. And the boy turned round and said to Vanda, 'Watch what happens.' He was pointing to the solitary figure in the shadows, on the walking-about part at the side of the gallery.

Very slowly this man started to tap-dance. He could only do it on one foot at a time, but he did it with grim determination. 'Stage-struck,' whispered the boy. 'I've talked to him. You watch, in a minute he'll start smiling at an imaginary audience.' The smile, when it came, was mad and filled with pain.

I could go like that, thought Vanda, and I probably will if I don't get on a proper stage soon.

Two more men came into the gallery, sat ostentatiously apart and placed raincoats over their knees. At the sight of this, one of the toffee-sucking old women began to make reproving tutting noises. The door to the gents' urinal was open, it was your nostrils that led your eyes in that direction. But when was Phyllis going to appear? They certainly knew how to keep you waiting. 'Are you an artist?' Vanda asked the boy.

'Student.'

Was he treating this place as a life class? 'Have you come because Phyllis is nude?'

'Hardly. Anyway, she's older than time.'

'Don't be so bloody cheeky,' called out the toffee-sucker. 'She's still a beautiful woman.'

But it was a man down on the stage who was doing a striptease. He had half-coconuts for breasts, and a grass skirt, and pan lids for a brassière. By no stretch of the imagination was this a female impersonation. It was just a red-nosed comic acting daft.

'That's her husband,' said the boy. But what he was drawing was the shambling amateur tap dancer in the shadows. And he was turning the shadows into a dreamland of applauding hands and exploding champagne bottles.

Salford Hippodrome being a number three theatre, the drumrolls were not of the same quality as they were at Hulme. And it was the microphone that coughed, not the invisible man who owned the voice which was saying, 'Ladies and gentlemen, here she is in person, the girl the Lord Chamberlain banned. The one and only, the incomparable . . . Phyllis Dixey.' Dreadful old velvet curtains parted to reveal yards of creased peach satin swagged up into great swoops to form a backdrop. But the stage was empty of any kind of performer.

'Look over the edge,' suggested the artist.

A woman was making her way down the centre aisle of the stalls. 'Good evening,' she was cooing. 'Good evening, good evening.'

She climbed a short staircase from the auditorium to the stage and turned to confront her meagre audience. Vanda let out a gasp. Britain's most famous striptease artiste was so *ladylike*. Upswept natural blonde hair, neat figure, tiny waist, expensive strapless dress with a full tulle skirt – it could have been Anna Neagle.

'So you've come to see Phyllis Dixey, the old cow.' This was said in tones that could have belonged to a Sunday School teacher. 'She must be ninety, nearly a hundred. She's not. She's thirty-eight, nearly thirty-nine. Don't bite your nails, dear – that part comes later!'

Absolutely refusing to take herself seriously, the dainty creature proceeded to recite a little monologue. It was all about having gone on the stage with the very best of intentions. But it seemed that every audition had ended with the same request: 'Take off a little bit more.'

Miss Dixey sang a bit and removed elbow-length gloves. She recited part of 'The quality of mercy is not strained . . .' and stepped out of her frock. Sixteen bars of dance chorus (Vanda was forced to admit that she had been very well trained) led Phyllis's hands up to the fastenings of her brassière. For the briefest of moments you saw two pale pink blobs, and then the lights went out and it was the interval.

The men with raincoats on their knees blinked a bit, but the women in the sparse little audience were all but cheering. *That* was the clever part. She'd excited the men – after all, it must have been like watching one of their former schoolmistresses undress – but Phyllis Dixey had also managed to entertain the women.

Well, well, well, thought Vanda. I've got a lot to learn. Tomorrow I won't ask the woman in the cakeshop for a burnt offering; I'll be nice, and I'll smile, and I'll see whether I can get her to smile back at me.

'I think I've seen you before,' said the art student. 'Aren't you a friend of that tall slim boy who goes into town a lot – Peter somebody?'

So that's why you didn't stare at my bust, thought Vanda Bell, who was already thinking of changing her name to something more classy. Mind you, Dixey wasn't particularly high-class so maybe you needed something to contrast with the appearance. 'Are you queer?' she said to him, unconcernedly.

'Isn't everybody?' he asked with a wicked grin.

Vanda considered the question seriously. 'I don't think I'm anything,' she decided aloud. A carefree boy who could draw like this was proving easy to talk to. 'I've been in love with the same man since I was eleven. But I just want to *be* with him. I'm not one of those girls who needs to roll around on top of a mattress.'

'That will give you great power.' He was now drawing one of the sculptured mermaids. 'Oh my goodness, what power that lack of interest is going to give you.' The mermaid had suddenly sprouted a vicious riding crop.

'Welcome.' Miss Lathom had just opened her front door to Joan and Sally. 'You must be our American visitor. But I'm afraid I can't shake hands because mine are covered in flour. I'm making bread. Come in and don't slam the front door or the dough will drop.'

'Give me your coat,' said Joan to Sally. 'We generally hang them under the stairs.' You couldn't smell the new bread as yet, but there was an inviting Saturday morning aroma of Kenya coffee.

Sally was looking at the black and white engravings of views of Oxford, the ones that hung along the hall corridor. 'It's exactly as you described it in your letters,' she said shyly. In fact she was much more shy than Joan had ever known her. Mind you, this was understandable when you considered that Sally was about to meet the others for the first time.

Miss Lathom, more than used to young people, took charge of the proceedings: 'Such a pity this is to be hail and farewell in one visit. How did you enjoy your trip to Edinburgh?' In the past week the Americans had been on a whistle-stop tour of North British landmarks.

'I found Edinburgh a bit sinister,' admitted Sally. 'Beautiful but kind of haunted.'

'My sentiments exactly,' agreed Miss Lathom. 'Did you see that patch of blood at Holyrood House? I'm sure they renew it – it *couldn't* have lasted that long.' By now they were in the kitchen where Peter was cutting a piece of bloody steak into cubes.

So this is the famous Sally, he thought. She's got eyes that don't miss a trick, but they twinkle, too, so I bet she's quite a camp palone. Vanda's eyes were running with tears. This was because she was peeling shallots. But she could still see clearly enough to register the fact that Sally's tailored tartan dress had 'class' sewn right into it. One day I'll have a green dress like that, she thought – only better. Vanda, of course, viewed everything and everybody in the light of how they could affect herself.

'You really do chop onions,' exclaimed Sally delightedly. 'Joan always wrote that it was the best when you were chopping onions.'

'Strictly speaking these are *échalotes*.' Miss Parr, spectacles on the end of her nose, was peering into a cookery-stained copy of a *Larousse Gastronomique*. 'What a dark and dismal morning. We're making Boeuf à la mode de Caen to warm

299

ourselves up. And I hope nobody minds a late luncheon because this one is going to take hours.'

'All the more chance to talk.' Miss Lathom walked towards a bowl that was sitting in the hearth and gingerly raised a corner of the pudding cloth which covered it. 'Rising nicely,' she said.

Miss Parr continued to peer into the thick cookery book. 'Can't find it. We'll have to have it Bourgignon instead. Either I need new glasses or you only put a fifty-watt bulb in that overhead light, Grace.'

'That's possible,' conceded Miss Lathom. 'I changed it without my reading glasses. There are no compensations to advancing years. You're nearly sixteen, like the others, aren't you, Sally? Reach for those blue and white mugs and pour us all some coffee.'

'Joan, would you go into the washhouse and get us a bottle of that cheap red cooking wine out of the bottom of the rack?' Iris Parr put down her book while the coffee was being passed around, sat back in her Windsor chair and began to wax philosophical. 'When one is very young, each day is like a perfect little medallion, it has its very own identity. After the age of sixteen the medallions began to run into one another. They blur. Instead of being separate, they're like a lot of cameos on a bracelet.'

'She will read these French philosophers,' snorted Miss Lathom, who was rummaging through a drawer of new light bulbs in cardboard covers.

'This is nothing to do with anything I've read.' Miss Parr was refusing to be rattled. 'It's my own idea. After sixteen it blurs into a bracelet. And when you get to twenty-one . . .'

'Will a hundred and fifty watts be strong enough for you?' enquired her friend.

'It will probably burn the ceiling but at least we'll be able to see. After twenty-one, life becomes like those endless bead necklaces which hang round Christmas trees. The days just run one into another into another.'

Miss Lathom treated her to a cynical look. 'I wouldn't try publishing those *pensées*,' she said. 'People might mistake you for Beverley Nichols or Godfrey Winn.'

300

Peter's ears pricked up at the mention of these names. Both men wrote hugely popular columns in women's magazines; and both were said to be high up on the list in that big black book at Scotland Yard.

Miss Lathom began to clamber up onto the kitchen table. For a brief moment the assembled company was treated to a glimpse of serviceable knee-length directoire knickers; they must have come from a military surplus store because they were in a pastal shade of khaki. 'Easy does it.' She eased out the offending light bulb. 'When do you sail, Sally?'

'On Monday. From Southampton.'

Down on the ground, Miss Parr half rose from her chair, said, 'Grace, do be . . .' Instead of finishing the sentence she suddenly stopped, looking puzzled. One hand went up to snatch at something invisible in the air, and then she pitched forward and landed on the floor. 'Done,' said Miss Lathom, who had been concentrating on the dangerous job in hand.

It was Peter who rushed forward to Miss Parr's aid. Joan chose that moment to return with the bottle of wine. 'What's happened?' she asked, alarmed.

'What's happened?' also came, like an echo on high, from Miss Lathom.

'She's conked out. I'll get her pills.' Vanda was moving towards the kitchen dresser drawer.

'Pills. Oh dear God.' Miss Lathom was helped down by Sally. 'Peter, your legs are faster than mine, go and ring Dr Moult.'

Surprisingly, Peter stayed where he was, down by the figure on the floor. He was holding onto Iris Parr's wrist. 'I think I'm feeling in the right place' he said, plainly panicked. 'But I don't seem to be able to find her pulse. You have a go, Joan.' Girls did first aid in domestic science.

'She must have a pulse,' cried Miss Lathom, 'she must, she must. Let me get to her.'

'I'll phone the doctor.' Vanda headed for the door.

'His number's at the top of the memo pad,' called Peter.

'Iris?' Miss Lathom crouched down and gave her friend's face a little slap. 'Iris?' She too reached for a wrist. 'Nothing. Tell him to hurry,' she called after Vanda. 'And if it's his wife,

301

tell her it's an emergency.' She turned her attention back to the figure sprawled on the polished linoleum. 'Iris? Sweetheart . . .? She can't be gone,' she said in disbelief. 'She can't. I won't let her be.' Again she tried to find a pulse; and then she collapsed, sobbing, on top of the body. 'She has gone, she has. And it's just the way her father went.'

Out in the hall, Vanda dialled the doctor's number. I bet we never get to Paris now, she thought. And a terrible cry of 'Whatever will I do without you?' confirmed it from the kitchen.

Miss Lathom was the only official mourner in the front pew. But she was not alone. She was accompanied by Henry the dog. Peter had wanted to make him a black crepe bow but Miss Lathom had said, 'I know you mean it kindly, Peter, but, please, no little "touches". I don't know how I'm going to get through it as it is.'

The service was at St Benedict's, Ardwick, the most Catholic of the High Anglican churches. The coffin, under its purple brocaded pall, was flanked by huge yellow beeswax candles, each one as tall as a soldier. All these death furnishings were grouped at the end of the centre aisle, in front of the high altar.

The printed programme said that the requiem was being sung to a setting by Fauré. The whole thing was sumptuous enough for Miss Parr's favourite French king, Louis XV. And just as Peter was thinking it was a pity she was missing the event herself, somebody in the row behind muttered in a disapproving voice, 'There's such a thing as *too* High Church. I don't know how the Bishop lets them get away with all this incense.' Former staffroom colleagues were obviously being made restless by the unexpected length of the proceedings.

Although Miss Lathom and Henry were the solitary occupants of the front row on the right-hand side, the same seats to the left of the aisle were filled with people who bore faint resemblances to Miss Parr. Peter kept on recognising the aristocractic set of a pretty head, the angle of eyebrows and the tilt of a nose. And he remembered the year he was seven, when Miss Parr had taken him to see Father Christmas come down the golden ladder. It had stretched all the way from the ground floor of Lewis's department store to the top of the dome. And the thought made him cry. He was crying because more of Fauré's music was speeding Iris Parr up her own golden ladder, and because it would be a long time before he saw her again.

I'll never see her again, thought Vanda. And I'd no idea I could look as good as this in black.

Joan Stone was every bit as much awash as Peter. Something was over. The two teachers had enriched her life immeasurably. And now there was only one of them, so things could never ever be the same.

There were three priests taking the service. It was the one in the largest quantity of purple brocade who doused the matching pall with holy water for the umpteenth time, then moved to the side of the bier. He left the silver water bucket on a little stool in front of the coffin. The bucket had a shiny metal stick in it, with a top like a pomander.

The music had finished. After clearing his throat the priest said, 'I see many unfamiliar faces in the church today. Some of you may not be conversant with the intricacies of a Requiem Mass.' He was definitely trying to be kind. 'It is usual, and indeed traditional, for mourners to make their final farewells by sprinkling the coffin with a small quantity of holy water. You may also care to say a prayer at one of the shrines, and to light a candle for the repose of the soul of Iris Naomi Parr.'

Miss Lathom, who had been kneeling on a hassock, praying, got to her feet. She began to lead Henry, who was on his very best behaviour, towards the silver bucket. But two other women were already hurrying across to be first; they had come from the front row on the other side.

Miss Lathom genuflected towards the tabernacle on the altar and took the silver stick in her hand. 'No,' she said implacably to the women who were challenging her right to be chief mourner. 'You chose to disapprove of us while she was alive; don't think you can take over now.' She said it loud enough for the whole church to hear. And then she splashed three goes of the water – in the names of the Father and of the Son and of the Holy Ghost – over the purple brocade. She hadn't finished: her eyes went down to Henry, and she splashed three lots on it for him, too.

'I've forgiven you,' she said to the women, 'but nothing will ever persuade me to forget.' And in that moment, nobody in the church would have dared to question Grace Lathom's right to have the last word.

5

Joan and Peter got eight O levels each, Vanda scraped through with four including Domestic Science, which was almost unheard of as a scholastic subject. But one day she intended to keep her promise to Gran'ma Dora by having a home 'like a little palace', so she'd studied the subject closely and begged to be allowed to sit the examination. Joan won the English prize and Peter got a five-shilling book token for Religious Knowledge.

All three young people were now in the lower sixth form and the days had indeed started to go much more quickly. The girls were allowed to wear ordinary clothes, just as long as they were plain; the only item of school uniform Peter was obliged to wear was the maroon and yellow tie.

Because Miss Parr's theory about the shape of the days of their lives had been the very last thing she'd said, Peter often thought about it. He agreed with the idea of each day in early childhood being a perfect little medallion. But, although the weeks were definitely speeding by, he wasn't sure that his life had turned into 'a bracelet of cameos'. He had his own theory about this, and it was a slightly outrageous one.

He didn't think he would really move into the next stage of life until he'd had his first proper orgasm. Wet dreams didn't count. And he had the feeling that, should he start masturbating, he would be in danger of settling for that, forever. Actually, he'd tried it once and caused himself to swell in a way that was definitely not sexual. Bright red and three days to go down. No, he'd thought about it, and he wanted sex with somebody else.

Though his libido was at war with his religious scruples, he had started getting critical of St Paul, who had criticised homosexuals. Hadn't Jesus said that you weren't to bother about what you wore? Then why was St Paul forever writing letters to Timothy about a missing cloak? If the saint was

305

wrong about one thing, he could be wrong about another. These thoughts just hung around the edges of the long-established fact that, sooner or later, Peter was going to do it.

Hetty King had taken to calling him 'Miss Virgin Untouched'. But it was also Hetty who had warned him not to think about venturing into the Gin and Tonic Brigade's bars. 'Some of these ritzy queens go to Blackpool at weekends,' he said. 'And the Blackpool police keep coming to Manchester. It'll all be to do with the Clifton snowball.'

The Clifton was a hotel opposite the North Pier. One bar, facing the promenade, was frequented by queers. Two men from that one bar got themselves arrested. Both kept address books with dozens of names in them. Dozens of enquiries were made which led to more address books and scores more enquiries. 'God alone knows where it's going to end,' quavered Hetty. 'They're supposed to have taken one man in because they found a powder puff in his bedroom. It's got so I jump every time I hear a knock at the front door.'

How much of this was rumour and panic, and how much the truth? Peter didn't know. But he did know that Lily Law's presence in the half-world seemed to have intensified, and that the police were said to be forever asking young homosexuals on licensed premises for proof of their age.

Joan was in the lower sixth because Granny Briggs thought that this was where a young lady belonged: it was as simple as that. Vanda was only there because Mr Adcock had said that, in law, she couldn't leave home until she was seventeen; and even then she could be obliged to prove that she was capable of keeping herself. Never one to dash into a brick wall when she could eventually walk round it, Vanda Bell was just biding her time. What's more, she was thoroughly enjoying doing it. But this was something she didn't talk about. Above all else, it had to be kept from Joan Stone.

These days, Sally wasn't the only person who was writing letters to Ingledene. Herbie Morgenstern was famed for the width of his correspondence (a joke he often made against himself) and he was forever dashing off little notes to his unlikely new friend, Granny Briggs. 'Of course he's a great joker,' she said proudly to Joan and Bruno. 'Some of the things he sends me are absolutely killing. I bet our postman doesn't know he's handled the American Communist Party manifesto. I've even been forwarded a leaflet begging me to be buried in a processed-cardboard coffin.' Nevertheless, most Sunday afternoons Granny was to be found at the kitchen table, fountain pen in hand, confronting an airweight Basildon Bond writing pad. She put considerable value on the fact that she had found a friend.

Joan wasn't quite sure of her own feelings in this matter. Letters to America had been her personal province for so long that she almost resented being asked to post an extra one to East 68th Street. Yet it had to be admitted that whenever Herbie Morgenstern forgot the jokes (he had recently sent Granny a membership form for the Ku Klux Klan) and wrote seriously, Granny Briggs accorded him a very fair hearing.

'Has it ever struck you that he might be looking for a co-respondent for a divorce?' asked Bruno mischievously. 'You could end up as Britain's oldest GI bride.'

'And has it ever struck you that you're not too old to get a good swipe?' Granny, spectacles on the end of her nose, was perusing a newly arrived letter from New York. 'There's a message for you in this one, Joan. Listen: "Joan is a great fan of the English author Molly Wainwright. Molly writes me that she is doing a tour of provincial English bookshops, to coincide with the next school holidays. She has enclosed her British publisher's schedule of these events and I see that she will be in Manchester, at Sherratt and Hughes, on April 7. Tell Joan to go and get herself a ticket from the store (they are free) and I will write Molly that your granddaughter will make contact with her immediately after the lecture. In fact I'll ask her to take Joan to tea. Even you would approve of Molly, Olive . . ." Well, there's no need for you to hear all that part. Joan, where d'you think you're rushing off to?'

'The bookshop.'

'All this impetuosity is very wearing,' sighed Granny. But Joan was already halfway down the back steps.

In 1952 Sherratt and Hughes were still on the corner of Cross Street, by the turning for the taxi rank in St Ann's Square. Two rambling shops thrown into one, this was an old-fashioned establishment lined with tall oak bookcases. There were ornate plaster ceilings and creaking floorboards underfoot, but the best thing about the place was the smell of thousands of brand-new books – Joan would willingly have bought it bottled.

They didn't just keep books on shelves, there were more piled high on trestle tables, and big volumes like atlases were kept heaped on the floor. And hanging in the middle of the children's section was a hand-lettered sign which read *Meet the Authors – Tickets at Cash Desk*.

'Could I have one for Molly Wainwright?' Joan asked excitedly.

The cash desk had a polished oak fence around it and was manned by a woman assistant who had known Joan since she was seven. 'Aren't you getting a bit old for her?'

'I don't think I'll ever be too old for Molly Wainwright.' The books were already becoming juvenile classics. Ticket in hand, the thought of classics set Joan's feet in the direction of the second-hand department. You had to go down a twisting, protesting staircase to get into the basement. Here the smell was subtly different because sweet mildew and old leather bindings got mixed into it. But that wasn't what caused Joan's heart to miss a beat.

Sitting on a high stool behind the wooden counter, making notes in a ledger, was a new assistant. She'd often seen him before but never here. It was Toby Eden.

'Hello,' he said. 'I told you I'd find you again.'

'But how long have you been in the bookshop?'

'Ages. Ever since I got sent down from Liverpool. Didn't Vanda say anything?'

Why did a soft tweed jacket make him look even more desirable than before? 'No. Vanda Bell did *not* say anything.' But she's been smiling to herself a lot, thought Joan. And now I know why.

The Snake Pit was not the only unlicensed gathering place, the basement café of Lewis's department store was another. It was all self-service and idle gossip. 'I spent the whole of Tuesday in town, searching the dress shops,' said a Welsh queen known as Edith Evans. 'And then I found exactly what I wanted, not two minutes from home.'

'It's always the same,' sighed little Amber, who was cursed with chubbiness. Lana nodded in agreement. They could have been their own mothers talking. And Peter wasn't sure he believed half of what they said. Taxis to the Labour Exchange, yes. But was there any truth in all their tales of big homis and sugar-daddies? He still found it hard to believe that men who were attracted to men could be interested in these betwixts and betweens.

Mind you, Edith Evans always maintained that if a man was queer she wasn't interested. From his reading in the Central Library, Peter knew that Sigmund Freud had described this viewpoint as 'the homosexual tragedy'.

'Tragedy?' Edith, who always reminded Peter of a long thin hissing snake, was scandalised. 'Miss Sigmund Freud should have been lucky enough to have entertained as much married cock as I've entertained. They may be normal but they still prefer the all-round fit.'

What am I doing here? wondered Peter. Rising to his feet he said, 'I've got to go to the toilets.' As he walked across the basement, the Saturday morning air was filled with the sound of Edith Piaf singing 'If you loved me, really loved me . . .' You had to go past the record department to get to the public lavatory.

'Ladybird! Miss Ladybird, dear? My God but you need an Ardente hearing aid!' It was Hetty King, in no make-up and a brown warehouse coat, calling from behind the electrical appliance counter. A lot of the bitches worked in Lewis's. And that was the worst name they called themselves — bitches. Peter only needed to think of this word to know he should be looking for pastures new.

'Fancy a nice electric kettle, dear?' Hetty was holding up a box marked Swan Brand. 'Some silly cunt's left her receipt behind, so you'd have no trouble with the store detective.'

Peter reflected that Sigmund Freud seemed to have missed out on this carefree attitude towards shoplifting. A window dresser known as the Thief of Baghdad was even said to have got a grand piano out of Lewis's. 'No thank you.'

'You're such a gloomy girl,' sighed Hetty. 'It's time you made your debut and came out properly on the town. Lily Law's lost interest in us. They're trying to clear the vice girls out of Lewis's Arcade. They might just as well try and turn back the sea because . . .'

'Do you sell electric kettles?' asked a genuine female customer.

'No, dear, and I'm busy talking. If they move the whores from the arcade, they'll simple peddle their parts on the 'dilly.' Though the genuine customer had fled in horror, Hetty still looked to left and right before asking Peter, 'Did you hear that Cosy Nellie's been out on the game, in drag? All that's on offer is a hand job; the clients must think she lives with rag on. You *must* make your debut, Peter. You don't know what you're missing.'

I'm missing Bruno Briggs, he thought; he's the part that's missing. All this might be a bit more like real life if Bruno was in it too. 'You never know, I might just come into town tonight.'

But not to your end of town, Hetty. Even as he thought this, he caught himself worrying at his own disloyalty. The same people who called themselves bitches had called him 'sister'. And that was the most they had to offer anybody in the way of acceptance. Peter didn't ponder on this for more than a second; he was already visualising himself sliding a bread knife into his post office savings box, and he was wondering what gin and tonic would taste like.

Oh my God . . . did planning to rob his own money box mean that, deep down, he was made of exactly the same stuff as the rest of them? If it did, it did. But at least he had the sense to realise that no assumed girl's name, nor any of the products of Mr Max Factor of Hollywood, were going to find favour with Joan Stone's uncle.

I'm an uncle-snatcher, he thought cheerfully. He rather like the idea. Well, that was that. The only thing he'd got to do now was snatch the uncle. Tonight's the night, he thought; tonight is very definitely the night.

Vanda never allowed Toby Eden to pick her up at home. One

glance at the state of the dingy lace curtains would have given anybody with imagination a fair idea of what lay behind. And why does our garden always have to be the one with somebody else's scrumpled up Mars bar paper in it? wondered Vanda, as she headed down the path.

One set of Nottingham lace curtains was always much cleaner than the rest. These belonged to her own bedroom. Over that, at least, she had some control. On Saturday mornings she always gave it a thorough bottoming. Today she had even taken a window leather to the old tarot cards.

'*Ouch!*' went the voice in her head as she wiped their faces. 'Oh shut up, I'm only improving your looks.' She had actually answered it out loud. But when she spread the cards, the inner voice must have taken umbrage because it refused to co-operate. All she could do was interpret them with inherited information. She'd laid down the Tumbling Tower for Toby Eden but she didn't like the combination of the cards he'd got on either side. Five of Swords meant that he'd had an attack on his good fortune, and Six of Pentacles, upside-down, would be more than a brake on anybody's ambitions.

The funny side of this only occurred to her as she got on the bus. A brake on his ambitions? She was wearing a new bra which she could hardly manage to undo herself. Toby was great company; sometimes he made her feel as though she was another of the lads – a mate – and she liked that. But there were two Tobys, and the second one had wandering hands.

As the bus bounced into Manchester, Vanda started thinking about how she'd met him again. She'd gone into Sherratt and Hughes to see whether it would be possible to buy her own copy of poor dead Miss Parr's *Larousse Gastronomique*. And they'd directed her down to the second-hand department in the basement. One glimpse at the assistant behind the counter had turned that cellar into paradise. And that very same Saturday, Toby Eden had started taking her out.

On Saturday afternoons the shops at the posh end of town, St Ann's Square and King Street, closed sharply at one o'clock. Vanda always waited for Toby across the road from

Sherratt and Hughes, under the clock of the *Manchester Guardian* building – waited for him to pick her up in his blue sports car.

Today he arrived on foot saying, 'Sorry I'm a bit late.'

'Where are you parked?' In many ways the Sunbeam Talbot was as important as his own presence. It was tangible proof that she was turning into the person she intended to be.

Not today she wasn't because Toby replied, 'It could be parked anywhere. I've no idea.'

'You must have *some* idea.'

'It's not mine any more.' He was trying to appear unconcerned. 'I lost it the same way I got it.'

'Not in another bloody card game?'

'Something like that. Anyway, they weren't bloody card games when I won it.'

'That was before we got together.' Even though she was furious, Vanda couldn't help admiring the sound of that last phrase, 'got together'.

It obviously wasn't lost on him either because he said hopefully, 'We can still go to the pictures.'

The pictures generally meant the back row, and that always led to struggles in the dark. 'I'm not sure that I want to be seen at the cinema with somebody who's not got a car.' She began to move off in the direction of Albert Square. Walking ahead of him proved who had the upper hand.

Toby seemed quite happy to follow. '*Singing in the Rain* is on at the Gaumont. You'll like that, you'll be able to watch Gene Kelly's feet.'

'How can I watch his feet when I'm fighting off your hands?' Anyway, that particular film was classed as Work. She'd every intention of studying it like a textbook, on her own.

'We'll do whatever you want to do.'

He was like a stray puppy dog who wouldn't go away. Not that Vanda wanted him to. She liked him in daylight. 'We could go for a walk.'

'Where to?'

'Does it matter? A walk's a walk.' She led the way across the road and they turned down King Street.

312

'Nice shops here,' he said. 'All I need is new luck.'

Vanda was just hoping that the Salmon sisters wouldn't have finished emptying their windows for the weekend. Salmon's was the most expensive shop of all. Their beading was like something in a jeweller's, and some of their clothes were elaborate enough to be stage gowns. Good, they hadn't stripped the display. And in fact, yes: 'Vanessa Lee wore exactly that same frock on *Music for You*, on television last week.'

'I'll buy you something like that, one day,' he said.

His tone of voice struck her as almost too devoted and obedient. 'You won't need to,' she snapped as she tightened the belt of her school raincoat. 'I'll earn my own. Come on . . .'

But he was refusing to move. 'Sometimes I'm left wondering what you do want me for.'

'We've had this out before. I want you to be my pal.' The tight bra had not left her with a lot of wind to spare and all this striding out meant that her big front was heaving a bit. 'What you staring at?' Trust him to notice!

'I *am* a man, you know.'

And the best-looking for miles around – so a definite asset. Mind you, he wasn't such an asset without a car. But he *looked* like a man with wheels so she was still somebody who would make other women jealous.

'Joan Stone came into the shop this morning,' Toby remarked.

This time it was Vanda's turn to freeze. 'You never said you were meeting me?'

'No but . . .'

'But what?'

'Well I did say I'd seen you.'

'Trust you,' she blazed. 'Just trust you. She's the only girlfriend I've got, and you have to go and come between us. I suppose you know she's barmy about you?' That, she reflected, would have been better left unsaid.

'I love it when you get angry.' He laughed gleefully.

'You mean you love it when I breathe hard.' And just that moment a car came roaring along the street so she had to bounce her way to the opposite pavement. But the idea of another woman taking an interest in him had made Vanda feel proprietorial. She actually linked her arm through his. 'Come on,' she said. 'Let's walk down to Salford Hip and have a look at the pictures outside.'

Quarter of an hour's walk was nothing for a trained dancer's legs, but Toby got a bit fractious along the way and started talking hopefully about cups of coffee and 'a nice sit-down'.

This week the pictures outside the theatre were of a semi-naked brunette called Pauline Penny. By now Vanda was an expert on touring strippers. Many were the fourpences she'd pressed through the hatchway in exchange for a mauve ticket to the gods. 'She's one of the very best,' she said. 'She smacks her own bottom on the stage. Don't laugh, Pauline Penny always keeps it very tasteful. She does it through a green chiffon negligée with monkey fur over the bust.' Oddly enough, Vanda found herself minding the fact that he was looking at the pin-up photographs. 'We could get that cup of coffee at the market café.' But we'll have to dodge Ethel on her stall was a thought she kept to herself.

Dodging her mother was more easily imagined than done. Since the days when Vanda had helped her out, Ethel had graduated to the stall nearest the entrance. Although she dealt in junk for Americans, on Saturdays she still shifted old clothes on Cross Lane.

'A beautiful fur coat.' She was already to be heard singing the praises of her own wares. 'Come into my hands from a lady of quality whose name I'm not at liberty to divulge. But if you work at the raincoat factory, her name begins with an M and ends with a G.' Ethel blew on the fur. 'We're not talking bunny rabbit here, you're looking at imperial sable.' It wasn't bad but, to judge by its antique cut, the coat must have belonged to Mrs Mandelberg's grandmother – if indeed it had ever come from that household.

As Vanda paused for the moment it took to think this, her mother spotted her. 'It's a coat that calls for a mannequin,' Ethel announced. 'And my own beautiful daughter has chosen to favour us with her presence.'

'That's your mother?' Toby looked as though he was trying to stifle both astonishment and amusement.

'Come on up here, darling.' This was the first time Ethel had called her that since the advent of Mr Adcock. 'Let the ladies see what's on offer.'

'If I come up there I'll do a bloody striptease for them!' yelled Vanda Bell. Furious with everybody, she decided to put the threat into action. There were the usual old men at the back of the crowd, and as Vanda clambered up onto the boards of the stall she treated them to her most dazzling smile. Music? What should she use for music? 'Ladies and gentlemen,' she announced imperiously, 'I would like you all to hum the Blue Tango.' Grabbing the fur coat from Ethel, she pushed her arms through the sleeves and swung it on over the top of her raincoat. And then she began to la-la-la the suggestive tune.

Two or maybe three people joined in. No, the last one was just pretending. The rest were watching as open-mouthed as Ethel because – right in front of their eyes – Vanda was turning into somebody who loved the world and was out to shock it.

Sinuously she raised the front edges of the coat all the way up to her chin, so that the gleaming pelts were shaped into a tumbling waterfall. But what do I do next? she wondered. There was a terrible smell of mothballs and her bra was killing her.

Why not? I can kill two birds with one stone. Under cover of the vast furs she slipped her hand beneath her raincoat, found her jumper, pushed it up and began to fiddle with the impossible fastening at the back.

'Oh my God!' screamed a woman on the front row.

At precisely the same moment something gave way. It felt as though a hook and eye had exploded. But the bra was undone. It was one of the new strapless ones. Even so, sliding it out artistically was going to present problems; exposed pink blobs would be enough to get you arrested on Cross Lane. 'La-la-la, it's the tango of love,' chirruped Vanda gaily.

'I'll tango of love you!' Ethel was advancing upon her with a big white sheet.

But the brassière was now completely free; Vanda produced it with a flourish, then waved it round her head like a football rattle. At this point she ran out of inspiration.

'Finished?' asked Ethel dangerously. 'Quite finished?' She must have known her daughter well enough to realise that the jig was over. 'You're quite sure you wouldn't like to show us you knickers?'

'It was just a bit of fun,' said Vanda quietly.

'You mean a bit of filth!' stormed Ethel. 'As God is my judge . . . No, as these good people are my judge, I'll never speak to you again. Now button yourself up underneath and bugger off.'

'It was only a bit of fun.' Vanda repeated the words to Toby. By now she had climbed down to the ground.

'My coat please,' called Ethel. 'Not that anybody'll want it, not after it's been used for prostitution.' It was Toby who handed up the furs.

'And who are you?' asked Vanda's mother. 'Her pimp?'

Before he could reply, a woman bawled out, 'How much for the coat, Ethel?'

'Two pounds, take it or leave it. But if you're planning on repeating that performance I just hope there aren't any gaps in your curtains.'

The woman was already fiddling in her purse for the money. 'At least I managed to sell it,' Vanda shouted defiantly at Ethel. But her mother simply turned away and called, 'Take two quid, over there,' to her male assistant, the one with the leather cash bag and the pebble glasses. He must have been able to see well enough to form an opinion because, as he walked past Vanda, he chose to cut her dead.

And that was the moment when she realised that Toby had seen too much. Not of her body; nobody had seen much of that. Too much of her background, which up until now she had always managed to keep vague and shadowy.

'Anyway, I don't care if she doesn't speak to me,' she said defiantly. 'One day she'll come knocking on the dressing-room door, wanting something.'

'You amaze me,' he said happily, 'absolutely amaze me.' This time he was the one who linked arms proprietorially.

And the men in the crowd were looking at him as though they were wondering what he'd got that made him so special.

Very conscious that her front was bouncing unrestrainedly, Vanda allowed herself to be led as far as the corner of Cross Lane in near silence. He'd seen Ethel in full flood, he'd seen stuff he could use against her. If Vanda was judging him by her own standards, they were the only ones she'd got.

'We could get ice creams at that place by the bus stop,' he suggested.

'Not any more. They got done for having rats in the sugar.'

'Hi, Toby . . . hello!' A car had already slowed down. It was Toby's erstwhile Sunbeam Talbot; Vanda recognised a familiar scratch on the door. The man leaning out of the window had a big grin on his face. 'Is this the famous girlfriend?'

Toby, looking embarrassed, said, 'Yes.'

The driver let out a low whistle. 'Everything you boasted about was true.' So that was why his eyes were glued to her chest. 'Fancy a chance to win the car back?' he said to Toby. 'I'll toss you for it.'

'Against what?'

'A date with the girlfriend.'

Toby hesitated for a moment, then his eyes began to shine. 'Are you game?' he asked Vanda.

Never before had she seen him as animated as this. He was a different person. 'Why not?' she said. Even if Toby lost, fighting one man off would be little different to fighting off another.

'Are you serious?' The other gambler was already getting out of the car. Fuzzy red hair and a cheap tie and short legs.

'Yes,' she said coldly, 'I'm serious. Are you?'

'I'll toss you for it,' he said to Toby. 'You call.'

'Heads I win.'

Half a crown spun in the air. And when it fell to the ground Toby Eden had got his car back. 'I'll never let you go now,' he said to Vanda. 'I couldn't. You're the new luck I've been looking for.'

The town hall clock was shivering out eight as Peter hesitated

317

outside the Café Royal. The four-storey building looked as though it had been given a face-lift in the 1930s. He couldn't pause for too long in the bright lights underneath the scalloped glass canopy. There was a uniformed commissionaire on duty, and Peter didn't want to draw attention to himself. He was only armed with word-of-mouth information. Did 'downstairs at the Café Royal' mean the ground floor or the basement? Bars on both levels were listed in gilt lettering on a board outside.

'Can I help you, sir?'

'No thank-you.' Peter had decided to live out Hetty King's motto: 'When in doubt, Follow Another Queen.' For good measure, Peter followed two. The only thing which had revealed them as 'that way' was sliding eyes. As Peter pursued them down the stairs and into the bowels of the building, he felt as though he'd been stock-checked and marked down as new.

Cigarette smoke and chatter and music were drifting up to meet them. Was there anybody here he already knew? It was a long narrow room with a curving thirties counter undulating right down the left-hand side. The pianist was tucked away in a corner; he had several glasses of gin, each one accompanied by a little bottle of tonic, lined up on top of the grand piano. Behind the pianist, opposite the counter, was a wall full of alcoves. Peter had to look twice to be sure that he was seeing properly. The alcoves were full of fairly posh-looking couples – men and women. Could he be in the right place? Another quick glance round the whole cocktail bar and he had the ground rules straight. They were a bit like life itself: queer people were standing warily on their feet while normal ones were sitting down.

But even these rules were elastic because by the counter, on swivelling chromium bar stools, sat a row of elegant older men. And one of them, a man with thinning white hair, was beckoning Peter with a sinuous forefinger.

Yet he was doing it in a cheerful way. In fact there was amusement in the old eyes. Peter hesitated. The man nodded as if to say, 'Yes, you.' Not much could happen in a public place. Besides, the man looked quite interesting. His suit was cut in the Edwardian style with narrow pants and slanting pockets, but he didn't bring teddy boys to mind. He looked much more like a stage version of a guards officer.

'Did you want me?' asked Peter nervously.

'I did.' The voice was as amused as the eyes. 'I am your Dutch uncle. That is just an expression which signifies that I mean you no harm.'

Peter had been around enough to know that this was indeed the case: the man's eyes had already slid past him and were sizing up other members of this rolling, restless crowd. A crowd that seemed to be perpetually reshaping itself.

'My name is Charles.' The grey gaze was directed back to Peter. 'What would you like to drink?'

'If you don't mind, I'll buy my own.' That meant he would be his own master.

It seemed, however, to have been the right answer because the man beamed approvingly, caught the barman's attention with one summoning gesture of that elegant forefinger and said, 'This young man needs service.'

Was the barman queer or not? If he was, he was wearing 'on duty' eyes. 'What's it to be?' he asked Peter in a bored voice.

Not gin and tonic. Thirty seconds of the Café Royal had been long enough for Peter to realise that he ought to try to keep his wits about him. 'A plain dry ginger, please.'

'Now that was a very sensible choice,' said his Dutch uncle in a low voice as the bartender moved along the counter to reach below for Peter's drink. 'Under the age of eighteen you should really be accompanied by somebody of years of discretion. Please feel free to tell anybody that you are with me. My full name is Charles Penrose.'

Just as Peter was thinking that all this was a very far cry from the Snake Pit, the man added, 'Yes, Charles Penrose, spinister of the parish.' So perhaps it wasn't all that different after all.

'Ice?' asked the barman.

'Yes please.'

'That'll be elevenpence ha'penny.'

It was daylight robbery. As Peter slid a shilling across the counter he only hoped the shock wasn't showing on his face.

But his new friend was the kind who missed nothing. 'That's what it costs when you venture out to see how the world turns. You could get draught champagne for tuppence when I started.' Tonight he was drinking brandy; Miss Lathom had the same-shaped brandy balloons. 'Tell me your name.'

'Peter, Peter Bird.'

'Well, Master Peter, I'm going to give you a little lecture,' announced Charles Penrose. 'And then you must feel free to roam.' He measured out his next words as though he'd been considering them for a long time: 'This place is a palace of piss-elegance. Everybody here is busy shoring themselves up with a new haircut or the latest story from London. Do not be deceived. In their heart of hearts they all know themselves for what they are – old books in new jackets. And you have something they would kill to have back – you have youth.'

I bet you're making it sound much worse than it really is, thought Peter. If it's that bad, why are you so kind? Aloud he said, 'I've just seen somebody I think I know.' It was Mickey Grimshaw, the boy actor from *Chidren's Hour*, that friend of Sheila Starkey's, the girl from Rookswood Avenue.

'Don't sleep with everybody,' enjoined his new friend. 'It will only take the gleam off you.' The awful thing was he sounded as though he meant it. 'And come back if you run into trouble. That's what Dutch uncles are for.'

'Thanks.' Peter began to edge his way towards Mickey Grimshaw, a young man of about his own age and height but with lighter colouring. This was somebody who had confidence written into his every gesture. Mickey Grimshaw's hands were going round like windmills as he emphasised points in a conversation with a man with blond hair but no hint of the peroxide bottle. This other youth was thickset, with a face that looked though it enjoyed laughing.

Peter's own bit of confidence evaporated. He could hardly just walk up and say 'Hello, I'm me.'

He didn't have to do anything. Noticing him hovering, the Grimshaw boy said, 'Well, well, well. I've been waiting for you to turn up.'

'Me? Why?'

320

'You live on the Ravensdale Estate. I spotted you for gay when I was about twelve.'

Hoping it didn't sound fawning Peter said, 'Aren't you on the wireless with Sheila Starkey?'

'I'm at RADA now. I'm just up for the weekend to do a quick broadcast. We're not supposed to work during term, but I need the money.'

'You wouldn't believe what *I'm* doing for money,' laughed the fair-haired man. He really did have a very nice, compact body. It seemed all right to think like this in a place where every newcomer's entrance was greeted by fifty sets of swivelling eyes.

But there was something Peter wanted to know. 'What's "gay"?' he asked Mickey. He thought he knew but wasn't sure.

'It's American for queer.'

'Mick's mad about the boys from Burtonwood,' explained the other one. Burtonwood was the local United States air base. 'I'm Ted Sterling.' Only now did Peter notice that he was carrying an old cardboard portfolio. Ted was still talking. 'I think I know somebody you know.'

'Who?'

Instead of replying, Ted Sterling heaved his portfolio onto a shelf meant for glasses and began undoing its tapes. 'Hang on,' he said. Out came a big sheet of cartridge paper. It was a bold pencil drawing of Vanda Bell, gazing down at a stage from the gallery of a theatre. 'One way or another, everybody interesting in this town is connected. Or if they aren't, they should start putting themselves about a bit.'

Greatly daring, Peter said, 'Do you by any chance know a very good-looking man called Bruno Briggs?' There was luxury in even being able to speak the name aloud.

'Bruno?' laughed the other. 'You'd only have to come round to our house to see whether I know Bruno Briggs. He's making money the same weird way that I am.'

The second lesson on Monday morning was a free period. And there was a definite atmosphere surrounding one table in the school library. Joan and Vanda were both wondering how much Toby Eden had said to the other. Peter only wanted to know what was going on: 'The pair of you are so polite that it's eerie. Would somebody please explain?'

'There's nothing to explain,' said Joan primly. But anybody could tell that she was not really reading that copy of *How to Win Friends and Influence People*. And that Vanda was devoting far more attention than was strictly necessary to munching on a forbidden apple.

'We're due to have a row.' Vanda threw the apple core into the wastepaper basket.

'But it isn't one we can have in library whispers.' Joan Stone closed her book. 'You could have said something, Vanda. You could have mentioned that you'd started seeing him again.'

Vanda, who had abandoned all pretence of whispering, came out with the simple statement 'Kisses in the snow.'

'I beg your pardon.' Joan wasn't begging her friend's pardon at all, she was just waiting to hear what came next.

'You never said anything about having kissed him in the snow.'

'Did he tell you that?'

Snow had been mentioned but not kissing. Vanda had worked that part out for herself. 'You'd be surprised at what I know.'

'Well, why don't you tell me?' Joan turned to Peter. 'Did you know that she goes wobbling round bookshops on Saturdays?'

'Me, I know nothing,' was his hasty reply.

'What did you mean by wobbling?' asked Vanda dangerously. 'In this life we've all got to use what we've been given.' It was her turn to try to get Peter onto her side. 'Did you know that she's been passing herself off as Little Orphan Annie, in a blizzard with a borrowed dog?'

'And I thought I was the one who was obliged to lead a secret life,' said Peter.

'Half of me is very sympathetic, Joan. I mean to say it can't be very nice being as flat as a board.' Vanda was still smarting at the word 'wobbling'.

But Joan still had *How to Win Friends and Influence People*

322

in her hand. And – *crack* – she smacked it down on Vanda's head.

'I'll bleeding well scrag you for that,' stormed Vanda Bell.

'Ladies,' protested Peter. 'Please!' He was surprised at how much like Hetty King he'd sounded. But there wasn't time to think about this because the two girls were tangling like all-in wrestlers. Vanda had brute strength on her side, but anger appeared to have charged Joan Stone with a terrible vitality; she answered every one of Vanda's thumps with a bite or a clawing scratch.

'*Fight, fight, fight!*' As this traditional Barton Grammar School cry rang round the library, Peter reflected that this was the first time he'd ever heard it used to draw attention to a scrap between two girls. Was that really a hank of blonde hair lying on the ground? No wonder Joan Stone was bleeding from the mouth! '*Fight, fight, fight.*' As quickly as these words had risen up again they froze on the air as Miss Staff, the senior mistress, all horn-rimmed spectacles and black academic gown, came clomping across the library floor in her serviceable men's shoes.

This noise acted on the two contestants like the sound of the bell at the end of the first round. But even as they broke apart, both were very conscious of the fact that this *was* only the first round. Vanda rolled off her opponent and lay back to recover her breath. Joan, also on her back and gazing upwards, thought, it's all a bit like coming round after a bad dream – except I can taste blood and there are fifty faces looking down at me.

One face was a lot older than the rest. 'This is disgraceful behaviour,' spluttered Miss Staff. 'Who struck the first blow?'

'Actually, it wasn't struck in this room.' Joan had already started to get her breath back.

'That's right.' Vanda heaved herself up on one elbow. 'It's an outside matter.' She was still fuming with Joan Stone but the pair of them had been allied against Miss Staff for so long that nothing could change that.

Peter decided he ought to try to be helpful. 'I think you'll

323

find it's a private affair,' he said to the senior mistress. And once again there were shades of Hetty King in his voice.

'Yes, it's about a man,' Vanda called up from the floor.

Ignoring the girls, Miss Staff advanced upon Peter. 'And are you that alleged man?'

He would have expected a woman whose feet were in drag to have known better. 'No, Miss Staff.'

'But I'll bet you're in on it. The three of you have been nothing but trouble since the first form.'

All this statement did was further reunite the girls. Peter, feeling he hadn't acquitted himself very well, decided to try again. 'It was bound to happen, sooner or later – in a mixed school,' he observed.

From behind her thick glasses Miss Staff treated him to a glare. 'And was someone like you bound to happen, in a mixed school, Bird?'

That was below the belt, decided Peter, as the onlookers giggled at Miss Staff's remark. One minute women are supposed to be fighting over me, and the next she's resorting to sly digs. She can't have it both ways. 'Aren't those men's shoes, Miss Staff?' he asked overinnocently.

'Bruno Briggs is making money the same weird way that I am.'
The words kept echoing round Peter's brain. He had hoped to be able to question Vanda about Ted Sterling, her Salford Hippodrome artist. But the fight in the library took the girls away to First Aid and then to Miss Staff's study. And after that, Joan and Vanda were both sent home to simmer down. Peter doubted whether actual murder would have got them expelled from the sixth form because Barton Grammar School was distinctly short of senior pupils.

Their absence left Peter with the whole of the rest of the day to wonder about Bruno Briggs and that funny money. Vanda's artist had even suggested that Peter might like to earn some, too. 'But what do you do?' Peter had asked.

The only reply had been a quick glance round the Café Royal, plus a stern injunction to lower his voice. And then Ted had written down an address in thick black pencil on a cardboard beer mat. His handwriting was an elegant little drawing in itself, but the address was far from fancy: 53 Slattery Street, off Regent Road.

Regent Road was a district near to the docks. The inland port of Manchester was actually in Salford, and you could always tell you were near the Ship Canal by the sound of melancholy sirens and the sight of ocean-going liners sailing past the ends of terraced streets. It was dark tonight, so all you could make out at the end of Slattery Street were lights shining through dozens of portholes, like something at Blackpool illuminations but on the move to and fro from Liverpool.

Peter began to walk down the street. Odd numbers were on the left-hand side, where the row of identical houses was only broken by the high wooden fence of a timber yard. Its gates suddenly rattled violently. An Alsatian guard dog had thrown itself against them from inside. All you could see of the animal was a snarling snout. Two inches nearer and it could have got him. A crescent moon came out from behind the clouds and cast bright highlights onto the leaded tops of identical bay windows. Almost all the curtains were drawn and not a lot of lights were on. Few people lived in their front parlours. This cobbled street was on the edge of a district known as the Barbary Coast. Because it catered to foreign seamen, you were said to be able to buy anything down there, anything at all.

Peter's mind went back to the time when he'd thought of surgical stores as mysterious. Everything down here was going on behind closed doors.

But what was going on at number 53? The lights in its front parlour were lit, and they were shining through something that looked suspiciously like sacking. No, it was hessian – artistic hessian. And Ravel's 'Bolero' was playing on a tinny gramophone. Peter recognised the tune because they sometimes had it on *Housewives Choice*, and he was always left wondering whether the BBC knew how much it had to do with sex. All Peter's knowledge of that subject was, of course, still theoretical.

Had he finally reached a place where theory was being put into practice? And for money?

The front door opened and somebody threw the contents of a bucket of dirty water across the pavement. A dumpy female figure peered down at him from the top step. 'Did I splash you?' She had a hoarse voice and compelling dark eyes and dyed red hair which was white at the parting.

'No, no, you didn't splash me.' He had to say this hastily, after realising that he'd been too busy staring to speak.

'What are you doing lingering on pavements?' she croaked.

'I'm looking for somebody.'

'Who?'

Did he want to go in? He wasn't sure. 'Ted Sterling.'

'Are you a new recruit?'

Would this commit him to something awful? 'I might be' was the most he was prepared to admit.

'They're all at it in the front,' she said. 'Come in.'

The hall didn't look as though it had anything to do with her. It was painted white, with big unframed drawings – Peter recognised them as more of Ted's work – tacked to the walls. One of them was of a man with nothing on. 'They do it to music now,' she continued, 'and I get nothing for the extra electric.' The man in the drawing was Bruno Briggs, and he was big all over.

The door to the front room was already ajar so the woman only had to kick it open. She announced Peter with, ' 'ere's a new un. He looks a bit too young to me.'

Three figures turned to look at Peter. They were doing something he found to be, somehow, shocking. They all had dripping paintbrushes in their hands and they were busy colouring plaster-of-Paris statues of the Virgin Mary.

'You've come to God's own country,' said the woman wryly. 'I suppose everybody fancies a cup of tea?'

Everybody did. Ted was obviously the boss of this dining-table production line, and both his assistants were girls. One was beautiful, with a mass of black hair and the same kind of green eyes as a cat. The other was a little bit chubby and breathing asthmatically. But as she sat on her high kitchen stool Peter noticed that her legs were as good as Joan Stone's, and that she was also blessed with a pair of clever eyes.

'Miss Legs is Norma Oldham,' said Ted. 'And the Welsh

326

beauty is Miss Megan Proctor. She's a sulky girl and very heavy-handed with the cobalt blue.'

There was no sign of Bruno.

'Want to have a go?' Ted was indicating the figurines on the newspaper-covered table. 'The routine is that you lot do the clothes and I do the faces. This is Peter Bird.'

'Start him off on her rosary,' suggested the breathless girl.

'He's too young,' protested the one with green eyes. 'I come here to get away from brothers that age. Here.' She handed Peter a paintbrush. It wasn't a very good one; in fact its bedraggled squirrel hairs looked as though somebody had been chewing them.

'Copy that finished figurine,' said Ted. 'All you need to do for her holy beads is little black blobs. We use water paint, and then the man who owns the factory takes them away and sprays them with clear vanish.'

'And I'm thinking of charging for use of the water closet.' It was the croaky-voiced woman again, calling out from the kitchen. Somewhere in the background you could hear the sound of a flushing lavatory cistern.

'That's Mother,' said Ted. 'Follow any gay man home and you'll find a fierce mother ruling the roost.'

'I'm not to bloody blame,' came from the kitchen.

'Does your mother know?' asked Peter, amazed.

'Yes, and she's got ears like Mata Hari.'

'Do you take sugar?' Her head had come round the door.

'Yes please,' said Peter.

Though her head had disappeared again, the door was opening wider. Bruno Briggs walked into the room, pressing down the top catch of the zipper on a pair of American jeans. Peter's thoughts immediately went to the naked picture in the hall.

'See if you can manage the black.' Norma Oldham was tapping a red fingernail against a half-coloured statuette. 'The knack is not to get too much paint on your brush.'

'The candle in the yard lavatory's blown out,' said Bruno as Ravel's 'Bolero' finally ground to a halt. And when he greeted Peter with a guarded 'Hello' he sounded little warmer than the Welsh girl had done.

'D'you want a cigarette, Bruno?' Megan Proctor was a different person in the presence of the man with dark red hair. 'I can easily light the toilet candle again with my lighter.'

She loves him, thought Peter. She's absolutely batty about him.

'Oh, the next person to pee can do that,' said Ted easily. 'We've got money to make. I had to be a bit guarded in the Café Royal,' he explained to Peter, 'it's all cash in hand. If you're any good you can make about fifteen bob a night. I'm the one who decides who gets what.'

'If he's any good,' put in Megan Proctor nastily. 'I don't see him making much effort. Come on, let's see what you can do.'

'Who gave him that brush?' Bruno leant over and took it from Peter's hand. For the brief moment that he'd come closer the air had gone warmer. 'It's the worst paintbrush in the world. Here . . . ' His fingers were wonderfully long and well shaped. 'Try this one.'

While Peter gloried in this first friendly move, Miss Megan Proctor was looking very much put out.

'If I don't get out of bed in the morning, nobody can interrupt me and I can get on with my writing.' Molly Wainwright was proving to be exactly as Sally had described her. The young people on the rows of chairs in Sherratt and Hughes's juvenile book department were gazing up at a woman in her early fifties. She was wearing a good tweed suit and she had well-cut hair and highly polished leather shoes.

Twinkling, that's her adjective, thought Joan. Ladylike but fun. And although it says on the back flap of her books that she's never been married, she doesn't look one bit spinsterish – this is definitely a woman who's known the joy. Joan was distinctly older than most of the rest of the audience. Miss Wainwright's books were recommended 'for bright children of eight and upwards'.

Joan Stone felt about thirty-two and jaded. Prior to the lecture, she had been down in the basement to see whether she could catch a glimpse of Toby. Instead, she'd found a completely new assistant behind the counter, a young man with exploding hair and spectacles and almost too much to say for himself. 'Toby Eden? He got Sherratt and Hughes's petty cash mixed up with his own. He left under a bit of a cloud.'

Though she had hardly liked to ask whether this had become a matter for the police, the new assistant's attitude seemed to suggest that Toby was someone who had got off lightly. The bespectacled man had further startled Joan by suggesting that she might like to meet him, in half an hour's time, for a cup of coffee.

'Oh no, I'm going to Molly Wainwright's lecture.' She couldn't quite believe that she'd heard him properly. Vanda's crack about 'flat as a board' had left Joan feeling very unattractive. In fact she had even sold some of her stamp collection to buy a pair of pink rubber pyramids which had come in a box labelled *Hollywood Cuties*. Their effect was so awe-inspiring that Joan had never worn them beyond her bedroom. Anyway, they called for a bigger bra; she had a complete set of pre-war Czechoslovakian stamps earmarked to pay for one.

'. . . and then at about four o'clock my secretary brings down the work she's typed up, and I correct it.'

This is more important than bosoms, thought Joan. Mind you, it was all right for rounded Miss Wainwright – Joan judged her to be at least a size forty-two, with a deep cup into the bargain.

I bet she was a perfect Venus when she was my age, Joan thought wistfully. 'Flat as a board' was definitely haunting everything. That and thoughts of Toby's ignominious dismissal.

Drawing her lecture to a close, Molly Wainwright asked for questions from her audience, answered them, then sat down behind a green-baize-covered card table while children queued up for her to sign their copies of her books. Some had arrived with well-thumbed copies, others had purchased the very latest *Susannah Goes on the Stage* from a pile by the cash register.

A couple of the children had only brought autograph books, and Joan couldn't decide whether this was a cheek or just sad. Mind you, they probably weren't as lucky as she was. She had already been sent a prepublication copy of the American edition of the new book – a present from Mr Morgenstern.

As the queue dwindled down to just two young people and one pushy mother, Joan suddenly felt shy. What should she say to introduce herself?

There had been no need to worry. Screwing the top back on her fountain pen, Molly Wainwright announced 'You'll have to excuse me' to her trio of adoring readers. 'I have to find a friend I've never met. And it's got to be you.' She was beaming at Joan. 'You're exactly as Sally described you. She said you had eyes like a young deer and it's no less than the truth.'

Joan suppressed a wild desire to ask whether Sally had mentioned anything about a flat chest. An assistant was already helping the authoress into a spectacular mink coat. This showed a side of Miss Wainwright Joan had not been expecting. And the mother of the lingering children was burbling her appreciation of the quality of the furs. 'Please feel free to stroke them,' commanded their owner. 'After all, it's you, my readers, who paid for the coat.' Within ten seconds she had shaken hands with the manager of the shop, bidden the lingering fans farewell and swept Joan out into the street, only pausing to look at her own photograph in the window display. 'Oh dear,' she said. 'They're still using that one. I always think it makes me look a bit like Lady Baden-Powell. Taxi!'

Inside the cab, on the way to her hotel, Molly Wainwright proceeded to talk to Joan as though she'd known her forever. And she was just as warm and friendly as one of her own books. 'Fur coats worry me and I'm not at all sure about eating meat. But we cannot deny that Our Lord partook of the paschal lamb, and I can't visualise myself in plastic court shoes.'

Miss Wainwright was not staying at the Midland, which surprised Joan. Yet when she came to think about it, the Queen's was far more suitable. This old-established hotel, facing the side of Piccadilly Gardens, was Manchester's equivalent of Brown's in London. The public rooms were dark, all the woodwork was deeply polished, and the hotel servants were heard to breathe 'milady' almost as often as they intoned 'madam'. If the Midland betokened fame and money, the Queen's attracted old-style breeding.

As the children's novelist sat in the lounge ordering tea ('And not cucumber sandwiches, Gentleman's Relish instead'), Molly Wainwright looked entirely at home.

'But there is something theatrical about you.' Joan actually said it out loud because she felt so relaxed she could have been talking to an old friend.

'How perceptive. I was on the stage for years. I suppose that this kind of hotel is what I knew in my childhood, but I've been a terrible rebel in my time.'

'Oh good,' said Joan happily.

'Yes, we were definitely landed gentry on my father's side,' laughed the writer, 'but all that's left of that is two family portraits and a bit of battered silver. It's certainly nothing to get excited about. I've always had to earn my own living. Could we have an ashtray?' she asked a passing waiter. 'My dear, these hotel servants are straight out of Dickens,' she whispered to Joan.

'Yes. It's like something in *Pickwick Papers* but quieter.' The conversation which had started was one that was due to go on, with interruption, for many years.

Molly, for that's what she'd already told Joan to call her, dived straight back in with, 'Tell me about your mother. Sally didn't split on you,' she added hastily. 'I sensed a mystery so I wormed the story out of her.'

Joan didn't mind. 'She's still where she was. I'm trying to persuade Granny to have her home. Only for an afternoon, just to see how she fits in.'

'Which she might not.' Molly nodded wisely. 'Do be prepared for failure. Accept that, and anything else will come as a bonus. Those poor Morgensterns,' she sighed. 'Thank you.' The waiter had brought the ashtray. 'My poor, poor Morgensterns . . .' She proceeded to fit a cigarette into a holder which was a stick of gold wire, bent into a circular loop at the top.

'But they're not poor,' cried Joan, watching fascinated. It was the loop that held the Du Maurier cigarette in place. 'They're the richest people I know.'

'Haven't you heard?' Molly Wainwright proceeded to light up, then blew out one perfect smoke ring. 'You obviously haven't.'

In an attempt to urge her new friend on, Joan asked, 'Have they lost all their money?'

'Oh, worse than that. I know that your grandmother is in correspondence with Herbie. Hasn't she said anything?'

'Only that his letters have stopped.'

'That's understandable.' Molly was nodding wisely again. And Joan noticed for the first time that the authoress had more than one chin. 'He probably doesn't want to involve her.'

'In what?' Party manners had vanished and Joan was all but screeching with impatience.

Two women at the next table glared, got to their feet and moved across to a sofa. 'I see we've managed to clear the room already.' Molly did not sound one bit annoyed. 'The Morgensterns are under house arrest.'

'Whatever for?' gasped Joan.

'Un-American activities. Herbie's joked once too often about being one of nature's Communists. And then he refused to testify in front of some committee. You must have heard of Senator McCarthy? It's all to do with that.'

'But Herbie's Granny Briggs's penfriend!' said Joan in dazed wonder.

'And my American publisher.' A waiter appeared with a laden silver tray. 'Tea. How nice. But you didn't bring lemon.' Leaning forward conspiratorially, she said to Joan, 'I've even had a visitor from the American Embassy – a most nosy bit of work! And he made it very obvious that they'd been reading my letters to New York.'

'Are you a Communist?' breathed Joan. What a good job the two women had moved away.

'Of course I'm not,' laughed Molly. 'And neither is Herbie. But they *are* friends of that negro singer, Paul Robeson.'

332

'And Leadbelly,' put in Joan.

'And sweet Leadbelly. Herbert and his wife just happen to believe that black people should have the same rights as white ones. Of course my family were always dead set against the slave trade . . .'

'But what will happen to them?' demanded Joan.

'Who knows?' Molly began pouring the tea. 'Who can forecast?'

An hour passed in no time. After that, Molly gave orders for her luggage to be brought downstairs. The same porter was asked to wait, prior to carrying the suitcases to London Road Station, only just over the street. 'So now I fear I must leave you,' she said to Joan. 'Such a nice ending to this little book tour. I feel I've made a definite friend.'

Joan would really have liked to go to the station to wave Molly off. Besides, there was something else she needed to discuss . . .

But the famous author had already anticipated this. 'Send me some of that stuff you've written,' she said. 'And that's not something I often say. I'll let you know what I think. But don't expect yards of compliments because they wouldn't do you any good.'

The porter was still standing behind her on the pavement, ready for departure. 'This most obliging man is my reward for all those mornings that I stayed in bed writing,' she beamed. 'Herbie swears you'll make a writer too. Let's not say goodbye, my dear. We're not the sort of people who enjoy doing that.'

Holding up a stubby umbrella to halt the traffic, Molly Wainwright began to march out of Joan Stone's life.

But only for a little while, thought the girl left standing waving on the kerb. I'm going to go straight home and copy out my two best short stories, and maybe that essay which helped to get me the English language prize. And Molly will be so impressed that she'll write back and say 'Come to London immediately.'

At Ingledene, Granny was busy preparing a stew – everything chopped big and two Oxo cubes. Bruno was also at the

333

kitchen table, studying. This was because it was cold for early April and they were still keeping only one room heated. 'How was your literary luncheon?' he said, a bit loftily.

'Actually, it was tea. At the Queen's,' she swanked. 'Guess what, Granny? Mr Morgenstern's under arrest. And the American Secret Service are reading all the letters anybody's ever sent to him.'

'All the letters?' Granny dropped a carrot and sat down with a bang. 'They couldn't read mine. I mean, surely to goodness they . . .'

'They read Molly Wainwright's.'

Granny had gone even paler than usual. 'But I put everything in those letters, everything. Once I even asked for his opinion on my gas bill. I put my fears in them too. America's so far away that it seemed safe. Oh my God . . . you did say the police?' Though the question was addressed to Joan, her eyes had rested upon her son. And they were filled with panic.

Waiting for Toby Eden beneath the *Manchester Guardian* clock had lost its novelty. These days it was just part of Vanda's Saturday routine.

This always began at nine thirty in the morning with a visit to Mr Adcock's office. Over the years she had grown genuinely fond of the plump solicitor. He always settled all her accounts, for items like dance training, by cheque. But each Saturday Vanda was obliged to sign a receipt for her pocket money and in exchange she was handed a proper brown pay packet. These days the contents amounted to a pound a week – Adcock knew that she was more of a saver than a spender. Vanda also took a wholehearted interest in the progress of her own investments. Wise handling had almost doubled their value since Gran'ma Dora's death, but she never talked about this to anybody other than Bertram Adcock.

Regularly at half past ten on Saturdays, Vanda had a classical ballet lesson at Muriel Tweedie's school on Deansgate. Tap and musical comedy were learned on weekday evenings at the Monton equivalent of Odette Ashworth's.

Training was still as necessary to her as food and drink, and an ordered routine compensated for Ethel's eternal untidiness.

After Vanda's Saturday class, where she had made no friends, she always ate a ham sandwich and drank a glass of Tizer at the same milk bar, near Knott Mill Station. And then she had a systematic wander round the posh shops, invariably visiting them in the same order, until it was time to meet Toby.

And today he was late.

It really irritated her that a man without a job couldn't even be bothered to be punctual. Not that Toby was going to stay without a job. Not now that she had spotted the interesting advertisement. And of course it was well known that some men would always need a woman to give them that extra shove.

'Aren't you going to get in?' The car must have driven up while she was busy thinking. Even the Sunbeam Talbot had an out-of-work look. A bucket of hot water wouldn't have done it any harm!

Not in the best of moods, Vanda climbed into the passenger seat. Nevertheless, spring was in the air and pale sunlight was shining onto the blue bonnet of the car. 'Got a job yet?'

'These things take time.'

In 1952, in Manchester, this wasn't quite the truth. In fact the *Evening News* was always solid with columns of advertisements for Situations Vacant. Somebody sacked at four o'clock in the afternoon could be working again by the next morning. 'I've seen a job that would suit you down to the ground,' said Vanda. 'On a card in a shop window.'

'I'm not sure that's the sort of job I'm looking for.' In contrast to the dusty car, he looked like somebody who had taken the trouble to shave twice.

'It's in a bookshop window. Shaw's on John Dalton Street.'

'That's second-hand books again.' The idea did not seem to suit.

'Have you tried the other bookshops?'

'You're beginning to sound like the Fiddlers!' These were his adoptive parents. 'I'm not interested in books. I only went to Sherratt's as a stopgap.'

'What are you interested in?'

'All I need is a proper chance.' He switched on the car radio. It was tuned as usual to Radio Eireann. And one of their eternal Irish tenors was singing 'Believe Me for All Those Endearing Young Charms'.

Vanda switched it off. 'What do you want to do with your life?' Nobody would have guessed that she was several years his junior.

'Do you really want to know?' he asked eagerly. 'I'm working on this plan. It's going to make me a mint. Mind you, I'll need investors.'

'So tell me the plan.'

'Sorry, no can do.' He had suddenly assumed an 'important' expression. 'No offence meant, but the idea's too dynamic to reveal. We're going to be rolling in it,' he added gleefully.

'Who's we?' asked Vanda.

'Me and the investors.'

'Why's the car coughing?'

'Now you mention it, it is coughing, isn't it? I think we might be just about to run out of petrol.'

She was ahead of him: 'And you've no money to buy more.'

As he treated her to a lopsided smile, she saw the little boy who must have endeared himself to the Fiddlers. 'I am a bit low on cash,' he admitted. 'Actually, I've got three ha'pence.' The car was starting to come to a halt.

In years to come, Vanda's thoughts would often go back to this moment. If she'd just got out – there and then – her whole life would have been completely different. But there was something about that crooked smile which was highly appealing. For a start it had absolutely nothing to do with the Toby who couldn't keep his hands to himself. This was just the pal she had always wanted. 'How the hell did you get yourself into this mess?' she asked him.

Vanda had not only grown up on a diet of *Girls' Crystal*, she had also been greatly influenced by *Beano* and *Hotspur*. The serials in these comics were all about loyalty: Lord Snooty never let his pals down, and Baldy Hogan would do anything for another member of the football team. 'Is there anything I can do to help?' she asked.

'You could lend me a quid,' he said hopefully. They were sitting in a street at the side of the town hall. 'That way we could at least get some petrol.'

'OK, but I'm going to write down that you borrowed it.' Mr Adcock had never had to teach Vanda Bell to keep strict accounts. 'Here's a pound. And I need your pen.' She made a note of the loan on the back of a theatrical shoe catalogue from out of her shoulder bag.

Toby said, 'I can't wait to be on my own two feet again.' The sun was really shining now; he was looking out of the window at two young boys standing at a bus stop. 'They're just about the same size that Mark and I were, when they shunted us on that train to get away from the Blitz.'

'What, you were the same size as the little one?'

'No such luck. Little evacuees were the ones who got picked first. I was always tall for my age.' He made no move to go off for petrol. 'When we got to Manchester they lined us up in this school hall. People were practically fighting over the cute-looking kids.' Toby was away in a dream of reminiscence. 'My brother, Mark, got given a teddy bear before he even left the room. In the end, all that was left was me and a girl in glasses. I'll always remember her: she was very pale, with grubby pink sticking plaster over one of the lenses.'

'But what was wrong with *you*?' asked Vanda, fascinated. He had never opened up like this before.

'I was very thin and my knees stuck out. And I was self-conscious about being knobby round the wrists and the ankles. Funny what worries kids, isn't it?'

Vanda was looking at the two boys at the 42 bus stop and trying to imagine Toby at the same age. 'Somebody must have chosen you. They couldn't just leave you standing there.' She was remembering old newsreels of evacuees with gas masks slung across their fronts and luggage labels round their necks.

337

'Somebody chose us all right.' Toby's tones had turned bitter. 'Two pigs who were only in it for the money. They came after everybody else had gone, and took me and Sandra Webb home. If you could call it home. It was right down by Barton Bridge.'

Vanda suddenly remembered something. They hadn't been able to get in to see *Two Tickets to Broadway* in town, but it had been shown again the next week, at the Curzon in Urmston. And Toby had absolutely refused to drive over Barton Bridge. Rather than take this short cut he'd motored miles to avoid it.

He pulled out a packet of Players. 'I could still get them sent to prison. Nobody's ever heard the whole story. Smith they were called.' Toby lit a cigarette. 'Plain Smith. Bloody ugly if you ask me. But one night they got too drunk and the police broke in. Mr Fiddler was a special constable during the war so that's how I ended up there.'

'You never still call him Mr Fiddler?' Vanda took the cigarette from Toby and attempted a cautious draw on it. 'I thought they'd adopted you?' For once the smoke hadn't made her cough.

'They wanted to take out adoption papers. Don't get me wrong, the Fiddlers are all right. But they wanted me to change my name too. And I'm Toby Eden.'

A 42 had finally arrived and the two small boys were clambering aboard. 'Where's your brother now?'

'Dead. Went off to his beautiful home and got himself blitzed to smithereens. Christmas 1940.'

While he was in the mood to tell this much, Vanda wanted to know more. 'And where are your real family?'

'God knows. I don't.'

'You must.'

His voice began to rise: 'I don't! It's my life and I don't.' Looking almost ashamed, he calmed down enough to say, 'Letters started coming back marked "Gone Away". That didn't help the adoption either. But Toby Eden's a lucky name and that's definite.' The strain of unloading all this had left him looking close to tears. 'And if it isn't lucky, I'll make it lucky.'

'Course you will.' She was pleased to hear that she sounded very much the true pal.

'I'll get a jerry can out of the back,' he said. 'And you take this quid. There's a petrol station just through the third set of lights.'

'You can keep my quid and get walking yourself,' she snapped. Pal or no pal, her reading of *The Adventures of Baldy Hogan* had also taught her the rules of fair play. 'And don't forget I've written that pound down.'

They were no longer painting holy statues, they'd graduated to wall plaques. Still in plaster of Paris and bigger than a circular dinner plate, the plaques featured an old rustic bridge over a stream. All Ted Sterling's helpers had been assigned a segment. Peter had an easy job: he had to paint the broad span of the bridge in sepia. Megan Proctor had already indicated moving water with several flourishes of olive green. It was she who said, 'I'm sure we're making them too subtle. Granelli's an Italian, he likes things bright.' Granelli was the man who owned the factory. It was he who delivered the plasterware to the house, and with it came great clouds of off-white powder.

'This is no good for my bloody asthma.' Norma Oldham paused to have a wheezing cough. And then she must have remembered another of her ailments because she reached for the black Bakelite box which contained her hypodermic. Norma was diabetic.

Peter could never look while she injected herself. Instead, he concentrated on the sound of the record on the old wind-up portable. It was Betty Hutton singing 'You Can't Get a Man with a Gun'.

'And who the hell brought that?' roared Ted, whose tastes were more classical.

'I did.' Megan Proctor was busy swirling more green strokes onto palest grey plaster.

'You should have brought one that says you can't get a man who's queer.' Having to inject herself often made Norma Oldham ratty. Peter had noticed that before.

'I refuse to believe that Bruno is queer.' Megan was now using the green to indicate the stems of bulrushes. Peter's

339

other job was to colour their tops, after he'd completed the bridge. Megan was still talking: 'Bruno's just not met the right woman.'

'There is no right woman,' snorted Ted. 'Can't you get that into your thick skull? He's as gay as I am. And where is he?' The record had ground to a halt, so Ted began to make music of his own. His tastes were not purely classical because to the tune of 'Sparrow in the Treetop' he began to sing:

'Hoyna–hoyna clinyert,
Hoyna–hoyna clinyert,
Hoyna, hoyna, clit . . .'

Peter Bird loved being in this freewheeling household, which even had its own nonsense songs. The place was filled with creative energy and excitement and Art School gossip. And Bruno. Only where was he?

He chose just that moment to arrive. 'Somebody's left the door open again,' he said as he walked in.

'It's open on purpose,' came the croaking voice from the kitchen. 'I'm trying to let out some of that grey dust.'

'My mother could eavesdrop for England,' said Ted cheerfully. 'I wonder whether she knows that Mickey Grimshaw's introduced me to an American?'

'I just hope he's white,' was the shouted response. And then Mrs Sterling kicked the parlour door open again and came in with a big plate of tinned crab sandwiches. 'No wonder your father stops at sea,' she said to Ted. 'It must be like coming home to bedlam.'

As far as Peter was concerned, it was all gloriously different from life in the semidetached house on Hawksway. His parents knew that he'd got himself some spare-time work but they'd no idea how much he was earning. Last week it had been just under two pounds – a big step up from four and sixpence pocket money.

As Mrs Sterling carried Bruno's white riding mackintosh out into the lobby, Bruno said, 'My mother's driving me mad. She keeps on asking me when I'm going to get a girlfriend. I'm beginning to wonder whether she knows. My

God, these things are awful.' He was looking at one of the almost completed plaques. Ted was performing the final function, which involved rubbing off some of the paint to achieve highlights.

Bruno hadn't finished: 'She even suggested I took a girl to the parish dance "for the look of it". I swear it's all got something to do with this man she writes to in America.'

'You could always take me,' put in Megan, hopefully.

If he does take her, I'll stop loving him, thought Peter. He hated Megan Proctor. And she wasn't any keener on him. Those discontented eyes were forever watching; she was the kind who kept scores, clocked up points. And she couldn't have failed to observe that Bruno Briggs had started to take notice of Peter. Nothing beyond common-or-garden politeness. And yet ... It wasn't imagination because it was happening at this moment. Sometimes Bruno would glance over, like he was doing now, just to see how Peter was getting on.

'Girlfriend indeed!' Olive Briggs's son was still at it. 'I know I'm queer. I'm certain of it. The only thing is, I've not done anything about it.'

Ho-ho, thought Peter. Ted Sterling began to sing 'She Had to Go and Lose It at The Astor'. And Megan took Bruno's announcement of virginity as a cue to wail, 'Do you really want to doom yourself to a lonely old age?'

'Well, thanks a bundle!' Ted's rubbing had become distinctly indignant. 'I know some old queens who've been with the same man for thirty years.'

'Yes, and I know some who've been with thirty men in four weeks.' Bruno was still looking unhappy. 'That whole Gin and Tonic circuit gives me the willies. There has to be a better way of doing things than that. The minute I've got my degree I'm going to get away.'

Peter just wished he had the nerve to stand up and say, 'Don't go. There's no need. You could stay here and let me love you.' They were all of them, always, talking about going away: London, St Ives, the Greek Islands ... it never stopped.

'Val says that her mother and father are going away for

341

Easter.' Valerie was Norma Oldham's cousin who sometimes helped out with the plaster painting. But not often, because Val lived in the country, outside Buxton. 'She wants to have a party.'

'Isn't it a bit far for getting back?' asked Peter. Though he was sometimes allowed a front door key, there was always trouble if he got home after half past ten.

Norma was ready with the answer: 'We could all stay.'

Peter waited for somebody to say 'Except you because you're too young' but nobody did. Megan was obviously slipping! He risked looking at Bruno and found that Bruno was already looking at him. Only when their glances met, the older boy looked hastily away again.

Ho—ho!

They'd broken up early for Easter and Joan Stone was not enjoying this school holiday. For the first time in years she felt friendless. The writer inside her considered this word and changed it to a phrase – bereft of friends. Not that anybody had died; it was just as though everyone Joan was fond of had moved one pace away from her. And, in some instances, two paces.

First there was Vanda. Although the two girls had arrived at a truce where it was agreed that the name of Toby Eden was not to be mentioned, previous intimacy had taken a bruising. Peter Bird was up to something again: it was as simple as that. And this 'something' had rendered him absent-minded, and brought a curious new reserve into his conversation. Neither was there any comfort on offer at Ingledene. For a start, Bruno was hardly ever there. He was even going to be away on Saturday night, at some party. Granny had been much upset to think that he would miss Holy Communion in the parish church on Easter Day.

But Joan's uncle had said, 'If you want the truth, I feel an outsider in the Church of England these days.' And this had caused Granny to retreat even further into her worried shell. Perhaps she was missing hearing from Mr Morgenstern. Joan was certainly missing Sally's letters.

'And Molly Wainwright's still not said what she thinks of

the stories I sent her.' Lacking any other company, Joan had reverted to talking to the dressmaker's dummy in the corner of the old sewing room. Only these days she despised herself for doing it. Could that really be Granny singing?

'Easter flowers are blooming bright,
Easter hymns pour radiant light,
Alleluia, alleluia, alleluia.'

Not only was she singing, there was almost a smile on her face as she walked into the room. 'You've got a letter from America,' she said. She was holding several envelopes; the one she passed to Joan had airmail edges.

'Thanks.' Joan scanned the envelope for a return address. She half expected Sally to be in the State Penitentiary. No, it had come from East 68th Street as usual.

'Aren't you going to open it?'

Yes, just as soon as you've gone, thought Joan. One glance at Granny's eager face was enough to make her relent.

'It's just that *any* news has got to be better than this awful not knowing.' Granny Briggs sounded curiously apologetic.

'Have you got a crush on Herbie Morgenstern?' The thought had only just occurred to Joan so it came out in a surprised voice. She only hoped it hadn't sounded impolite. God knows, I'm a martyr to unrequited love myself, she thought as she undid the envelope.

Surprisingly, Granny had not taken offence. 'No, I've not got a pash on him, though his friendship has certainly brightened my life.' She hesitated for a moment and then volunteered: 'I put some indiscreet theories in a letter to Herbert. It was something or nothing – about Bruno. I'm just terrified that it could have fallen into the wrong hands.' You could tell that even the act of admitting this had taken some sort of weight off her mind. 'Just don't ask me what I wrote because I shan't tell you.'

Joan was more interested in what Sally had written. 'I don't think I can read it out loud because it's got swearwords in it.' The word BASTARD, in big bold letters, stared out from the page.

'I expect she's upset,' said Granny equably. That was the size of miracle the Morgensterns had wrought at Ingledene.

Joan skimmed through the letter. 'You'll have heard swearing before,' she said to her grandmother. 'Listen:

> Dear Joan,
> And any snoopy FBI BASTARD who is reading this. Molly Wainwright called us and said she'd given you the lowdown on our situation.
>
> Dad is in Washington this week. He had to answer questions put to him by the Committee for Un-American Activities. On the stand he took the Fifth Amendment. This means he refused to testify. That way you can't incriminate yourself. Not that he is a proper Pinko but we do know some. He refused to name names.'

'Thoroughly honourable,' said Granny Briggs to Joan's amazement. Obviously feeling that some explanation was necessary, Granny added, 'Even Rudyard Kipling said: "Of what shall a man be proud if he be not proud of his friends?" And their friend Paul Robeson certainly has a most beautiful singing voice.'

'Listen to the rest,' said Joan.

> 'He may have to appear again and they have taken away our passports. They also tried to subpoena my mother. A process-server followed her round a store named Lane Bryant but she gave him the slip in the Stout Stylish department, and now she is in hiding.
> Write me soon, I'm lonesome.
>   Love,
>   Sally'

There was a postscript: 'If Senator McCarthy is reading this, I hope his eyes fall out.'

'So letters *are* being read.' Granny had gone back to looking antique again. 'What an indiscreet old woman I am! Forget I said that, Joan. And, please, I beg of you, not a word

344

of this to Bruno. One's just left wondering how much liaison there is between the American authorities and the British.'

Joan sought for a helpful reply: 'Well it wasn't Inspector Fabian of the Yard who went round to see Molly; it was just some bastard from the American Embassy.'

'You've got more post.' Granny handed her a typewritten envelope and another one with Joan's name and address in handwriting. 'I think I'll go downstairs and drop Herbie a guarded note.'

When Joan opened the official-looking envelope, she was glad that Granny had left the room. It was a brochure, one she'd sent for before she bought the Hollywood Cuties; she'd answered a mail-order advertisement for an inflatable bra. My goodness, the illustration showed there was even a place to tuck the little tube after you'd blown it up. 'Entirely natural to the touch,' it boasted. But could you end up with this being mentioned in the divorce court?

The second letter was addressed in generous handwriting on a bright blue envelope. And the writing paper inside was die-stamped with a heavily encrusted address.

> 22 Shotter Street,
> off Belgrave Square,
> London SW1
>
> 15 April 1952

My dear Joan,
Thank you very much for giving me the privilege of being the first person to read your stories. The one I liked best was the story about the girl who intends to become a striptease artiste. I felt that the character of the mother, the old-clothes dealer, was particularly well drawn. The child's hopes and dreams make for interesting reading but I would really like to know what happens to her when she actually gets on the stage.

But I don't know that myself, not yet, thought Joan.

I was less keen on the tale of Fiona the debutante.

Moygashel is not a suitable fabric for a ballgown. This story struck me as 'made up', and your idea of the London Season was very far from accurate. Either write what you know about or research your subject thoroughly.

God has given you a nice little talent. Let us see whether you can polish it. And when you have a moment from your writing (every day please, except for Sundays) perhaps you would let me have your news?

Love,
Molly

This time it was Joan Stone who was singing early Easter alleluiahs.

Eddie Bird was having the raving abdabs again. It wasn't that he'd been drinking too much, it was the exact opposite. Struck down by influenza, he had been unable to get to the pub, and his body had gone into a state of mental and physical resentment. Not to put too fine a point on it, Eddie was upstairs hallucinating. And downstairs, in the kitchen, Peggy Bird was refusing point-blank to send out for alcohol.

'A drink's the only thing that's going to calm him down.' Peter was anxious for peace because he needed to broach the subject of staying out for the night. Not some night in the abstract – that night. It was now Easter Saturday morning so the situation needed settling quickly.

'He's steeped in it,' said Peggy angrily. 'Absolutely steeped in it. Why should I be expected to use my hard-earned money to buy him more?' In the distance Eddie could be heard yelling something panicky about the Temple of Karnak. It was only fortunate that the hairdressing room was closed down for the public holiday. 'No, I'm letting him dry out. Maybe it'll make him face up to the state he's got himself into. I've already spoken to Miss Lathom, she'll have you till it's over.'

'It' generally took three days. How many times, over the years, had Peter been sent out of earshot of delirium tremens? 'It's not as though I'm still a little boy,' he protested.

'No, but if there are two of us here, it's two people he can try and manipulate. Your father's not dangerous in this state, he's just pathetic. Do as I say, get your pyjamas and things together and move over there.'

Could he – dare he? – suggest he went to Buxton instead? It would take tactful phrasing. Peter had been rehearsing the speech for days but there'd never been a suitable moment to deliver it. 'The thing is . . .' he ventured. But any attention was drawn away from himself by more shouting – something muffled about Cairo – from upstairs.

'The thing is, you're getting on my nerves,' snapped Peggy. 'Just go to Miss Lathom's, Peter. I've not got the time to study you. You're not in Egypt', she yelled at the ceiling. 'And if that sounds hard, he's made me hard,' she muttered to nobody in particular. This was not the Peggy who granted favours.

Peter climbed the stairs and walked into the bathroom to get his razor. For years there had been a big bottle of 4711 eau de cologne on top of the bathroom cabinet. It had been there so long that the gold on the green label was turned black. Now, the opened bottle was in his father's hand, and Eddie was swigging down the contents.

'Needs must when the devil drives,' he said wildly. 'Watch your step out there, son. There's Wogs everywhere.'

'I'll be all right,' said Peter, 'I've got a tin hat.' When Eddie was in this state, it was best to humour him and get out of the way. Crossing the landing to his own bedroom, Peter tried to decide what to take to Miss Lathom's. Why was that little canvas holdall coming into it? Because he'd not quite abandoned thoughts of going to Buxton, that was why. He put his pyjamas into the bottom of the bag, and then threw in a pair of good grey flannels and the black jersey he'd bought in Jaeger's sale. And he'd need clean underpants. But not that pair because they'd got a hole in an embarrassing place.

Not than anybody was going to see them. But if he wasn't going to Buxton, why was he already getting physically excited? This was awful, terrible!

Zipping up the bag, he carried it downstairs and collected

347

his best Donegal tweed overcoat from the hall. 'See you,' he called out to Peggy.

'You'll be nice company for her,' she called back from the kitchen.

Peter doubted this. Grace Lathom minus Iris Parr was a much-reduced personality. In fact she reminded Peter of one of her own more washed-out smocks. She too had faded a little and become less crisp.

As he let himself into her house with his own front door key, Henry bounded out of the sitting room to meet him. The retriever hadn't done a bunk for months. Was the dog somebody else who had lost heart? This year there were no daffodils or cottage tulips flowering in the hall, just empty bulb bowls instead.

'It's only me,' he called out. Henry was already dancing towards the sitting room so Peter knew that Miss Lathom must be in there.

'How nice,' she said as he walked in. They were the same words she would always have used, it was just that there was less energy behind them. 'I've put a bottle in your bed. It must be ages since you slept in the little study.'

Having finished welcoming Peter, Henry had crossed the room and placed his head on his mistress's knee. This move was always accompanied by an anxious gaze. 'Darling, don't,' she said to him, helplessly. 'I'm afraid we've been having rather a funny morning,' Miss Lathom explained. 'Most of the time he accepts that she's gone. And then he obviously gets it into his head that Iris wouldn't just go off and leave him, so he goes and sits outside the bathroom door. That was the only place she wouldn't let him follow her, so he decides she must be in there. And of course she isn't. And that's when we get him puzzled like this. How's your father?'

'Off his head.'

'They do say that the wisest words on earth can be written on the head of a pin. They're supposed to be "This too shall pass". Personally, I'd like to smack the person who said it.'

Peter wondered whether he should encourage her to talk about Miss Parr.

The decision was taken out of his hands: 'Did I ever tell

you how we met? It was at the beginning of term, in the staffroom. She was always, noticeably, much better dressed than the rest. And she was, as it were, the new girl in town. So she asked me to tea at her digs.'

Had Miss Lathom forgotten that he'd heard the story so often that he could have recited it himself? Or was she finding comfort in telling it again? Either way, it was one of his favourite tales so it didn't matter.

'When I got to her lodgings, the landlady sent me upstairs to knock on the door of Iris's room. She was an awful landlady – the kind who behaved as if parsley sandwiches were normal fare. Anyway, there I was, outside the door, and I knocked.' Grace Lathom smiled at the memory. 'The only answer was a lot of creaking and rustling and banging. Of course she was rushing round tidying up, to make a good impression I suppose. And when she finally let me in, the first thing I noticed was a bunch of spring onions, trapped in the dressing-table drawer. Such a small thing, yet so like her.' Miss Lathom's eyes were suddenly dangerously bright and Henry was looking even more worried than before. Any moment now the retriever would start trying to climb on her knee, his favourite method of consolation.

Peter finally dared to say something that he'd been thinking for years. It dated right back to the night of the musical evening. 'You were a married couple, weren't you?'

Miss Lathom, who had been reaching into the pocket of her smock for a handkerchief, froze. 'I cannot think I heard you properly,' she said icily.

He had never heard her use such a tone in his whole life. 'It wasn't meant as criticism,' he said awkwardly. What Peter longed to say was: 'I'm the same, I'm the same.'

But he hadn't said that, so Miss Lathom continued to sound frosty: 'I'm very surprised to hear you venture such an idea. Down, Henry! We had to put up with years of talk like that in staffrooms. That's why we ended up teaching in separate schools.' She had obviously decided to relent: her tone softened as she offered, 'I don't think you knew what you were saying, Peter.'

He could have left it at that. But he didn't. 'I'd like somebody too.'

There was a pause. And then, 'I know,' she said gently. 'I think I've always known. But some things are better not talked about.'

'Why?' It was a real cry from the heart. 'Please tell me why.'

Instead of answering directly, she said to him, 'When anything happens to me I want some words adding to the gravestone. You're the person I'm asking to make sure that it's done. There'll be money left for the purpose. I've left a nice little bit of something for you as well.'

He didn't like the graveyard turn the conversation was taking. 'What words?'

'Underneath Iris's name, I want: "And her friend Grace Lathom". That much I am prepared to tell the world.' And now she did blow her nose. And there was defiance in the gesture. 'Oh dear, your face! I'm not dead yet, even if I am awful company. Are you sure there isn't somewhere you'd be happier?'

A heaven-sent opportunity? 'Not happier,' he said carefully.

'But?' She knew him very well.

'There *is* somewhere I'd like to go. I was going to ask at home,' he assured her, 'but you know what it's like when he's got the abdabs.'

'And I am, as it were, *in loco parentis*. Go on,' she encouraged him.

There was nobody else on earth like her, nobody. 'Well,' he said, relieved that it was finally out, 'there's this party. And it's in Buxton. But it would mean staying overnight.'

'I'm only going to ask you one question.' Miss Lathom looked stern. 'Are these *good* people?'

As Peter thought about it, he could feel her studying him, hard. 'Yes,' he said. 'There's one girl I don't like but the rest are very good people.'

Walls, woodwork, antique furniture: 1950s art students were never satisfied until they'd painted them all white. Peter had

350

already witnessed this tide of snowy emulsion at Ted Sterling's, where the entrance hall and the front parlour were pristine as a dairy. And Norma Oldham's cousin was an indulged only child so her parents denied her nothing; Mr and Mrs Rimmer had even handed over the stables of their sandstone villa and allowed Valerie to turn them into a studio. White paint? There was nearly enough to blind you!

Peter thought the result was wonderful. But Norma Oldham, who already had a diploma in design, was inclined to be more critical. 'She's used every cliché in the book,' she grumbled. 'Her and her sanded floorboards and her Cornish fishing-net curtains! Take no notice of me, I'm probably just jealous.' The Rimmers were Norma's rich relations. 'No I'm not, she copies everything we do. Where did she first see candles in Chianti bottles? My bedroom! And we wouldn't be listening to Ravel's "Bolero" if she hadn't heard it at Ted's first. I'm very fond of Valerie but she wouldn't hesitate to steal a good idea from God himself!'

Valerie Rimmer was a classic example of the artistic temperament without any real accompanying talent. Part Spanish on her mother's side, and obviously aware that her limbs resembled two sets of knitting needles, she always covered them in a way that managed to suggest the ballet. And she had heightened this effect by scraping her dark hair back into a bun, and by outlining her eyes in imitation of Margot Fonteyn. Peter already knew something of her past history: the year at a dubious stage school, the modelling course at Lucy Clayton . . . These days there was said to be a potter's kiln in an outhouse. It was also said to be permanently stone-cold.

'But she has got one genuine talent.' Norma must have felt she'd been sounding disloyal. 'She's got a genius for friendship. God alone knows how often she's reinvented herself, but all along the way she's picked up interesting people.'

And they had all converged on Buxton that night. Even two members of Berto Pasuka's *Ballets Nègres* had been collected from Buxton Opera House and brought out to the stables on the hillside. Anybody out in the courtyard, peering through the stone archways of the windows, might have mistaken the proceedings for an orgy. The professional dancers, improvising to Ravel, had removed their shirts; black muscles gleamed in the flickering light of the candles and of a big log fire. But this wasn't a bacchanalia, it was a bottle party.

Where are we all going to sleep? wondered Peter. The plaque-painting contingent had been brought out to the country in a hired car, driven by Ted Sterling's American airman. The journey had been a tremendous squeeze. Peter had found himself squashed between Bruno Briggs and Megan Proctor – heaven on one side and hell on the other. They'd stopped at an off-licence in Stockport to buy Merrydown cider, and the American serviceman had insisted upon purchasing two bottles of Gordon's gin.

'But you don't have to get me drunk,' protested Ted. 'I am very, very willing.'

Cousin Valerie didn't seem to know many normal men. 'They bore me, darling,' was how she'd explained it to Peter. She said 'darling' a lot – it was a big feature of her acquired persona. She even used bits of borrowed Polari.

But she's kind, thought Peter. 'And the food is wonderful,' he said to Norma Oldham.

'She had every crumb of it brought out from Black's delicatessen warehouse in Manchester.'

Peter could never decide whether Norma was proud of her rich relations or embarrassed by them. He decided to change the subject. 'Just look at the way Megan Proctor's carrying on,' he said.

'I'd rather not. She must have drunk half a bottle of Ted's friend's gin. And she's all over the black dancer. A child of two could see that it's Bruno he really fancies.'

The impromptu cabaret was over and the dancers had merged into the rest of the party. And, yes, the one Norma was talking about *had* got an arm draped over Bruno Briggs's shoulder.

This awful feeling has to be jealousy, thought Peter as Megan began to lurch towards him. 'Put some Merrydown in that,' she said belligerently.

'Does cider mix with gin?'

'I don't want a penny lecture, I want some Merrydown.' She was well away. 'Norma,' she said solemnly. 'I do hope you're watching how much you're drinking. We don't want you going off into a diabetic coma.' Megan downed the cider in two gulps. 'Tonight's breaking my heart.' She sounded much more Welsh than usual. 'Absolutely breaking it in two. Bruno must know what I feel about him, God knows I've made it obvious enough. And what do I get in return? I get ignoredom.'

'I don't think that's a proper word.' Norma reached across and grabbed a cheese straw.

'Thank you.' Megan took it from her and began munching thoughtfully. 'Mind you,' she said to Peter, spitting crumbs everywhere, 'if he goes off with the black man, at least he can't go off with you.'

This was exactly what Peter was thinking himself, and he wasn't enjoying the thought. But he had no time to ruminate on it because the proceedings were interrupted by a man standing in the open doorway yelling, 'Quiet! Let's have some bloody hush in here.' He didn't look like a guest, he looked like a farmer. 'Who let my cows out?' he yelled. 'Who parked a jeep in my field at the side and left the gate open?'

'Mr Millington!' Their hostess had rushed up to him. 'Darling, I'm so sorry. Who's got a jeepette?' she called out.

'She was giving parties when she was five,' said Norma Oldham as her cousin led a guest away to move his vehicle. 'And they're always brilliantly organised. The only trouble is, you have to do things her way. When we were about fifteen, she was the kind who used to switch the lights back on to say "Now we're going to play some guessing games."'

But that's not what Cousin Valerie said when she returned from coping with Mr Millington's problem. 'Sleeping arrrangements,' she began briskly. 'Not that I'm expecting anybody to go to bye-byes before dawn. Peter, you won't mind sharing a bed with Bruno Briggs, will you?'

That same Saturday night, Vanda was somebody who simply couldn't get to sleep. And as she lay in the darkness, she was beyond caring whether it was reasonable to blame it on Toby Eden. In celebration of the end of the first week in a new job with a shipping company, he had taken her to a Chinese restaurant called the Ping Hong. The unaccustomed food, eaten in a basement beneath Mosley Street, had left Vanda feeling distinctly queasy. Even now, here in bed, those sweet-and-sour prawns still seemed to be leading a life of their own.

Perhaps a drink of water would help? She still kept Gran'ma Dora's carafe and glass on the bedside orange box. Not bothering to switch on the light, Vanda stretched out a hand and caused clattering chaos.

The table lamp had gone flying, and so had the carafe; her groping hand was encountering water everywhere. The only sensible thing to do would be to get out of bed and pad over to the main light switch by the door. Pad? The first couple of steps were more like paddling.

On went the main light. How could one single hand movement have caused all this mess? She'd been expecting to see water, but the biggest noise must have come from the box of tumbled tarot cards. They'd gone with such a bang that the lid had burst open and the cards had flown out of their silken wrapping.

'*Not to be missed!*' squawked the voice inside her head. '*Very important.*' She'd been hearing this quavering treble for so long that she had a definite idea of what the speaker must look like – an angry dwarf in a tarnished tinselled-brocade turban. 'Oh shut up,' she said. He was very real to her.

'*It matters*,' he piped. '*Four cards in the night. Four cards in the night.*'

This was precisely how many had landed face-upwards. Two together and two more to one side. Her own Sun and Toby Eden's Tumbling Tower. And then Peter Bird's card and the World. She'd seen the World next to Peter once before . . . A picture of Joan's uncle began to grow inside her head. 'Not that it makes sense,' she said to the empty room.

'*Take a card, any card.*'

'You're off again,' she grumbled, 'you're worse than *It's Magic.*' Nevertheless, she did as he'd told her and got the Star, reversed. Too sexy for her liking, although the fact that

354

it was upside-down could mean delayed fulfilment. 'For me and for Toby, or for them?' She more thought this than said it.

'*For all of you.*' And then he began to sing in a voice that sounded a bit like an old recording of Marie Lloyd. But the song was much more up to date. How on earth could this antiquated midget have learned the words of 'Making Whoopee'?

He stopped singing to say '*Only . . .*'

'Only what?'

'*Take a card,*' he chirruped irritatingly. '*Take a card, take a card.*'

'You can bugger off,' she said stoutly. 'Prawn balls rolling around are bad enough without your gramophone needle getting stuck! And please don't come into the toilet with me.'

'*Poor Peter,*' sighed her tormentor. '*I thought you were his friend.*'

That did it. Now she'd have to take another bloody card! And she didn't like the one she got. Gran'ma Dora had always maintained that the Eight of Swords was a sure sign of approaching scandal.

'*Tee-hee!*'

Oh it was a nasty, self-satisfied giggle, it was horrible. Mind you, she'd first heard it in Magi House, which had hardly been a pleasant meeting place. Miss Wilkinson and the Order; how long was it since they'd last crossed her mind? But she thought about them now, and she remembered the story of the Bishop having to come and bless the place. All these cobwebbed memories left Vanda wondering about the little demon within the cards. Did he merely predict the future, or was there more to it than that? Sometimes it felt as though he exerted his gloating influence over everything that was happening.

'Are you the one that's running the whole show?' she asked aloud. All she got back was the empty silence of the night.

6

The dimly lit interior of Valerie Rimmer's parents' house was as lavish as their daughter's studio was stark. Wilton carpets and velvet curtains and tasselled sofas and too much polished cut glass . . . It was all so like Waring and Gillow's show-rooms that nobody could be blamed for taking stock.

'And here's us in the holy of holies,' laughed Bruno. He and Peter had been allocated the master bedroom, where twin lamps were shining across a great expanse of quilted satin eiderdown – pale beige to go with all the blonde bird's-eye maple furniture. 'And every stick of it fake Queen Anne. Those bow legs make that dressing table look as though it's trying to walk towards us.'

But Peter had stopped sizing up what the Rimmers had got. All he could think now was, There's a bed and there's us. 'Did you bother to bring pyjamas?' he asked Bruno, as he placed his holdall on a stool which had button-studded upholstery.

'I brought myself and two bottles of Merrydown.'

'I didn't bring my pyjamas either,' lied Peter. (*Please, thanks, forgiveness, in the past, and in the present, and in the future.*) Who would be the first one to take some clothes off, and what was he going to do about kneeling down to say his proper prayers?

Bruno slung his jacket over the end of the bed. This left them about equal, in polo-necked jerseys and trousers. Bruno kicked off his shoes and Peter did the same. Off came two separate pairs of socks, simultaneously. But if I pull my jersey over my head, thought Peter, I've got no vest on and I might look a bit thin and put him off.

Bruno could have had no such qualms because the end of last year's suntan came into view, and a pair of dark red nipples were suddenly looking Peter in the eye. The trousers

were coming off too – white underpants and legs good
enough for Wimbledon.

Darkness closed around Peter as he tugged his new Jaeger
jersey over his head, and he could hear his heart beating.
Once he was out in the light again, he ripped off his pants and
draped them and the sweater across the holdall on the stool.

Bruno had already jumped under the covers. Peter got in at
the other side. The bed was so wide that he could have been in
Hawksway and Joan's uncle in Ellesmere Park. Peter
wondered whether to switch off the lamp on his own side. But
the other young man, hands behind his head on the pillow
and gazing up at the ceiling, seemed inclined to talk. 'I
wonder whether this house will fall apart like Ingledene's
fallen apart? We've got earlier versions of everything they've
got, but ours has all gone to rack and ruin.'

You've not gone to rack and ruin, thought Peter. You've
not gone to rack and ruin at all. But 'I don't know' was all he
managed to say out loud. And it sounded so boring that he
switched off his bedside lamp in mild shame.

'If I turn off my light . . .' Bruno didn't finish the sentence.

Peter could hear people talking somewhere in the house
but they sounded a long way off. 'If you turn off your light,
what?'

'I'm not sure I could trust myself.'

Could Bruno hear his heart knocking? 'Turn it off
anyway.'

Bruno did. 'Well here we are,' he said, still a mile away in
the darkness.

'Yes, here we are.' Why has my breathing gone funny?
Peter wondered.

'Goodnight.'

'No.' He was surprised at the determination in his own
voice.

'No, what?'

I'm obviously going to have to be the one to make the first
move, thought Peter. With this he humped himself straight
across the bed, still under the covers, and his arms went
around Bruno Briggs.

'What are you doing?' If Bruno sounded panicked his body

357

felt wonderful. This was nothing like being in bed with your mother or your auntie when you were little – their bodies were all floppy and yielding. This was as though the strong soldier, the one he'd waited for in his childhood, had finally come home from the war. 'Nothing's going to make me let go of you,' he said as he held Bruno even closer. 'Nothing.' Even the smell of clean skin was transporting Peter into an excitement that felt like soaring through space.

'Have you done this before?' asked the other boy in amazement.

'No, but I want to do it now.' This can't be wicked, he thought. It can't be wrong, it feels too good. And then Peter remembered something: he hadn't said his prayers. 'Could you excuse me for a minute? There's something I've got to do.'

'Like what?'

'I'll only be a minute.' Peter jumped out of bed and knelt down in the darkness. 'Thank you,' he said silently. 'And if St Paul's upset, would you explain?' Before he could add Amen the light had flashed on at the far side of the bed.

'You're never down on your benders?' Bruno sounded full of wonder. 'Well, that settles it.' Reaching beneath the pillows, he pulled out the long bolster. 'This is going down the middle of the bed.'

'Why?' It was a cry from a heart which had been happy.

'You're too young, that's why. Anyway it's not yesterday any more, it's Easter Sunday now.' The improvised barrier was already in place.

Peter got back into bed feeling a fool. Out went the light again. He was close to tears.

'I'm sorry,' came through the darkness. 'Where's your hand?'

'Why?'

'I'm holding out mine.'

Peter found it on top of the bolster. He supposed it was something.

'Let's go to sleep like this.' Bruno gave Peter's fingers an affectionate squeeze. 'I do like you. I like you too much.'

Peter tried to snuggle closer but the long cushion of barrier seemed to know its job. 'You felt amazing,' he said.

'You felt pretty amazing yourself.' The bedroom door opened, light flooded in from the corridor, and then more blinding brightness — somebody had switched on the overhead light.

It was Megan Proctor, not quite so drunk as before but twice as nasty. 'This is pretty,' she snarled. 'This is really pretty. Holding hands afterwards, like the Babes in the Wood.'

Bruno snatched his hand away from Peter and sat up. 'You've got it wrong,' he protested.

'You're the one who's got it wrong,' she snapped. 'You must have known I was on offer, and you sneaked off and settled for *that*. Well, I'll get you for it, Bruno Briggs, just you wait and see. And that's Valerie's mother's good bed you did it in, too,' she cried indignantly.

'We didn't,' shouted Bruno.

'Oh no? I saw. I'll remember. You'll be sorry.' She didn't even have the grace to turn out the light before she stumbled from the room.

'And the door's still open,' said Bruno. Wearily he clambered out of bed and began to climb into his trousers.

'What are you doing?' asked Peter, alarmed.

'Going to find somewhere else to sleep.'

'But why?'

'If I stay here something *will* happen.'

And that, it seemed, was that.

The Easter holidays were over and this was the first day of the new term. Midmorning break had arrived but sixth-formers were not obliged to go out into the playground.

'Look over there.' Joan Stone was pointing through their classroom window, 'It could be us, all over again.' Three children were sitting on that bit of the wall where the boys' part met the girls'. 'I know the two in gymslips but I've never seen him before.'

'Poor little sod.' At least I wasn't fat, thought Peter. 'He's new. He only turned up at the end of last term. The day

359

before we broke up they were shouting Mary after him on the manual-room steps.'

'And you didn't stop them?' Vanda sounded full of righteous indignation.

How could you explain to somebody who'd not been through it? Explain that interfering would have only turned the taunts into something bigger, that noticeably gay little boys are Mary every day. And that after a while you simply learn to tune it out. Except, on a day when you were feeling low about something else, the taunts could suddenly hit home harder than the first time they ever happened. 'He'll survive,' was all Peter was prepared to offer to somebody normal.

I'm going to ask him, thought Vanda. It was in the cards so I'm going to come right out and say it. 'Have you been having a bit of how's-your-father with somebody?'

The three children on the wall would still be at the age when they would share every secret. Things were not the same in the lower-sixth-form room. 'Not really,' said Peter. Honesty took over. 'Well . . . it was something or nothing.'

'Who was it?' asked Joan, thrilled.

You wouldn't be so thrilled if I told you, he thought. 'Just somebody,' he said vaguely.

'I'm supposed to be due for a bit, too.' The idea did not seem to have left Vanda Bell excited. 'Not sex itself, just something to do with it.'

Peter began to understand. 'You've been at those awful cards again, haven't you?' Ever since that claustrophobic nightmare, the one accompanied by the appalling stench, he had been wary of anything to do with the tarot. Still, it had to be admitted . . .

Vanda had been watching his face. 'So they were right again, were they?' He would have been surprised to discover how little the idea enthused her.

'Did they say anything about me?' asked Joan.

'Nothing.' And she didn't think of making anything up, either. Gran'ma Dora had always been strictly against invented prophecy.

'Vanda . . .' Peter couldn't stop himself from saying

360

something. 'Do you ever think those cards could be demonic?'

Instead of answering, she looked through the window again, past the mock-cherry trees, past the cracked sundial, to the children on the wall. 'It was all so easy when we were their age.'

'It didn't seem easy at the time.' Joan had the writer's gift of recall. But it led her into remembering the days when they had unhesitatingly discussed everything, without constraint. And just for a minute she could have been eleven again as she dared to ask the one thing she needed to know: 'How's Toby?'

'Got a new job but he doesn't like it.' Vanda did not resent Joan's question. She was still her friend, and they'd both spent years dreaming about the boy who had played the school piano. Vanda could even afford to be magnanimous: 'He said he'd seen you on the other side of John Dalton Street. He said your figure had blossomed.' Personally she couldn't see the difference.

But I'm not wearing the Hollywood Cuties today, thought Joan. They must even poke through my light raincoat! Just as an experiment, she had worn them all the way from Kendal's powder room to Albert Square ladies' lavatories.

The bell rang to signify that break was over. Schoolwork was not as frantic this year as it had been last. Their A-level examinations were not due for another twelve months. Nowadays the three of them were concentrating on detailed study of fewer subjects.

The last lesson of the day was English, and when it was over Peter walked through Ellesmere Park with Joan. He was on his way to Eccles Library where he was reading the new novel *Hemlock and After* as a serial. They didn't have a copy of this story of homosexual life at Pendlebury, and he didn't have a borrower's ticket for Eccles. All he could do was soak up one wonderfully waspish chapter at a time, and then justify each trip by doing a bit of homework at one of the library tables.

'Do you think she's got Toby Eden for keeps?' asked Joan suddenly. Up until then they'd been walking in silence. Spring was really starting to show in all the front gardens.

361

'How can she keep him when she's going on the stage? What Vanda wants is going to take her all over the place.'

Joan had been banking on similar thoughts herself. 'I can't help it. I love him.'

Peter was dying to ask after Bruno. He hadn't seen him since the party, and neither had any of the plaque-painters. But just as he started to phrase a question they passed the bungalow called Cosy Nook, the house where the corgi always flew out and did a lot of barking. And today was no exception.

'There's no point in trying to stroke him,' said Joan. 'He's guarding his territory. Aren't those lilies in his garden early? Peter, where did you make your Easter Communion?'

'I didn't go till last Sunday.' Miss Lathom, who always knew these things, had said it still counted as long as it was done 'within the octave'.

'Where were you on Easter Sunday?'

Getting over being in bed with your uncle. And it was wonderful and awful because he could hardly bear to talk to me at breakfast. 'I was away.'

'Did you see that? He jumped up and gave me a quick lick.' Joan was full of delight. 'That's the first time it's happened in all the years I've been at Barton. Have you really had a bit of how's-your-father?'

'Only a very little bit.' Now there could be no question of bringing Bruno's name into the conversation, not before they got to the corner of her road.

Once they'd parted, Peter carried on trudging into Eccles. Did all the Andrew Carnegie public libraries look like red-brick grammar schools? he wondered. The interior of this one was even half-tiled like Barton, and it had exactly the same high ceilings and ugly panels of stained glass in the windows.

Leaving his leather shopping bag at the desk, Peter headed straight for the fiction department. A familiar figure was standing between the stacks of books, in front of the W's. *Hemlock and After* was by Angus Wilson. And Charles Penrose, the man who'd appointed himself Peter's Dutch uncle, already had the novel in his hand. 'Hello,' he said pleasantly.

Seen in this setting, Charles looked more than ever like an Osbert Lancaster cartoon of a gentleman on his way to a club in St James's. He was even wearing one of those short Edwardian overcoats with a half-velvet collar and several rows of stitching round the hem. 'If I take this naughty volume home, I'll certainly have to conceal it from Mother.'

On his visits to the Café Royal, Peter had been told a great deal about Mother. Charles was long retired from work so the old lady had to be well over ninety.

'Speaking of mothers,' said Charles, 'I've just seen the most extraordinary sight. I'll show you in a moment.'

A woman assistant in rimless glasses poked her head round the corner of the end bookcase and went 'Shh. This is a library.'

'And there was me thinking it was a knocking shop,' whispered Charles merrily. 'I'm glad I've seen you, Peter, dear. I want to issue you with a little warning.' He paused to flick a speck of dust from one of his lapels. 'Do you ever go cottaging?'

Peter knew that Charles was talking about men who combed public lavatories looking for sex partners. 'No.'

'There's no need to look so prim. It's the only place the poor can find friends. Mind you, that doesn't stop the rich from trolling around them, too.' He glanced to both left and right before he spoke again. 'The cottages are being watched by the police. They're supposed to be pulling people in every night.'

The woman assistant's head appeared again. 'I've told you once . . .'

'And you won't have to tell us again.' Charles could have been thanking a duchess for tea. 'Follow me, Peter,' he murmured gleefully. 'I'll show you something comical.'

The other end of the bookstacks led into an open space, with readers' tables in the middle. 'Edge forward and have a look at what that old woman is reading.'

Peter didn't dare to edge too far forward because, wire-framed spectacles on the end of her nose, the woman was

Granny Briggs. Being long-sighted she was holding the book at arm's length. It was entitled *Understanding the Homosexual*.

'It was only the prawn balls I objected to last time,' said Vanda. 'I was quite prepared to give that chop suey another go.'

He had brought her, instead, to an Indian restaurant at All Saints. 'The trouble with the Chinese,' he said, 'is that they like playing fan-tan.'

'I wonder if we'd be all right in a fire?' Dusk was beginning to fall outside, and a fire engine was roaring its way through a red traffic light; the restaurant was on a first floor, the rickety staircase had been lined with varnished plywood which would be highly inflammable.

'And the trouble with me is that I like playing fan-tan too.' Toby placed a camera on the cheap damask tablecloth.

Vanda was still acclimatising. She had already told him that the menu didn't mean a thing to her and then there were Indian toilets to be considered. In a place like this, you could never be sure who'd sat on them before you.

Toby continued to go on about games of chance: 'It's a mistake to go losing money to the Chinese. They can come after you with axes.'

Mind you, she thought, if I *am* forced to go to the petty, I can always line the seat with paper. 'I do like this end of town,' she said in social tones. 'Have you noticed how stagy it is round here?'

'Stagy?'

'Theatrical. There are two theatrical costumiers, and that hairdresser's – Carroll Arden, "Stylist to the Stars". Even the milk bar's got a signed photo of Billy Daniels on the wall.'

'I didn't dare risk leaving this in the car.' He was stroking the camera. 'It's Mr Fiddler's, it's a Kodak Sensor.'

'What are you doing with it?'

'I thought I might get a few shots of you. I should really have done something about it before the light started going.'

'If I'm ever to get started on the stage, I'll want some proper pin-up pictures.'

'I could take them,' he said eagerly. 'All I'd need would be a flash attachment.'

'You'd need more than that. You'd need somewhere to do it.'

Car brakes screamed outside. 'We *are* talking partially draped?' asked Toby knowledgeably.

She found 'partially draped' quite impressive. 'I was thinking of bikini poses, and maybe I could peep out from behind a parasol.'

'Oh yes,' he was all enthusiasm, 'definitely a parasol.'

'And then I could be in the middle of a bunch of balloons . . .'

'And we could get hold of some of that bubble mixture and let a bit of that off too.'

They must both have been studying the same issue of *Lilliput*, the pocket-sized magazine for men.

'Fur's erotic,' he said in the tones of one who knew.

Perhaps he had a point. Phyllis, Pauline Penny and Denise Vane had all been photographed swathed in white foxes.

'Of course I'd have to get hold of a studio,' he put in.

The waiter chose that moment to creak back up the stairs. 'Ah there you are.' Toby was suddenly a much more confident customer. 'We'd like you to take us through the Indian side of this menu, dish by dish.' Toby was actually licking his lips in anticipation.

As Norma Oldham dipped her paintbrush into sky blue, she was singing a song about a golden coach, with a heart of gold in it, driving through old London town. They had finished their run of Old Mill by the Stream plaques, and moved on to coronation souvenirs. These were still three-dimensional wall plates. They featured the Queen-to-be, in profile.

Ted's mother must also have been busy with some colour; today her hair was titian all the way to the parting. She was watching their efforts critically. 'You're a bad bastard,' she said to her son. He had just chosen to give Princess Elizabeth a black moustache.

'I'm keeping this one for myself.'

'You are naughty,' giggled Valerie Rimmer. 'Granelli

wants them for tomorrow.' Turning to her Cousin Norma she said, 'Wouldn't you just know that the others would go and disappear when there's a big rush on?'

'I bet I can tell you where Bruno Briggs is.' With a few deft strokes of his brush Ted had placed a half-smoked cigarette between the royal lips.

'Where?' asked Peter, only hoping he didn't sound too eager. It was over a fortnight since Bruno had been down to Slattery Street. He had never lifted a paintbrush since the party.

'Nante polari,' muttered Ted.

This must mean he wasn't prepared to discuss it with his mother in the room. Peter tried asking a safer question: 'Where's Megan?' She was somebody else he'd not seen since Buxton.

'I expect she's been to the doctor's,' said Norma. 'A nose out of joint takes quite some putting back.'

'Did somebody finally bash her?' asked Mrs Sterling eagerly.

'Life bashed her,' pronounced Norma. 'Or rather the finer points of the facts of life.'

Peter liked Norma; he had always admired her candour. But if she knew about him and Bruno, how many other people had heard the story?

'Bovril?' Mrs Sterling asked the three painters.

'Anything to keep us going,' sighed Norma.

Mrs Sterling began to stomp out of the room in flapping carpet slippers. 'I could always let you have a De Witt's pill.'

'Pink pills for pale people,' intoned Ted. And then he smiled at Peter and said, 'You haven't half started something.'

'Me?'

'You. Get painting. At the end of this lot we're all going to be rich. If we get them done on time, it's double gin and tonics on me, in the Café Royal on Saturday night.'

'I've almost forgotten what the place looks like,' sighed Valerie. Like many women who hung around with gay men, she also went into their bars. Valerie blobbed red onto the rubies of yet another royal crown and said, 'I see this bloody woman's face in my dreams. Does anybody know an old queen called Charles Penrose?'

Peter stopped painting black dashes – for ermine – to say, 'He's my Dutch uncle.'

'Was your Dutch uncle, you mean.' Valerie dipped her brush back into the red. 'He's gone and hung himself.' Registering the expression on Peter's face she said, 'Sorry, I'm afraid tact's not my middle name. Are you all right?'

'It's just that he always went out of his way to be nice to me.' A dreadful picture had already formed in his mind of the gentle soul in the exaggerated clothes swinging from a beam, his side-buttoned boots dangling. 'Why? What made him do it?'

'Something about the police having come round to talk to him.'

'There's another snowball,' sighed Ted. 'It's Blackpool all over again. Bruno must be out of his Chinese mind.'

Norma Oldham stopped working. 'Bruno? What are you talking about?' Peter had stopped too.

'You must be very good at it.' Ted was outlining flames coming from Westminster Abbey as he grinned across at Peter. 'You've really given him the taste for sex.'

'We didn't do anything,' protested Peter.

'Oh come on . . .' Muscular Ted was all twinkling jocularity.

'We didn't . . .'

'He's telling the truth, Ted.' Norma had gone back to her plaque. 'Leave him alone.'

Peter was grateful for her support. 'We honestly didn't. Well, not beyond . . .'

Norma surprised him by cutting in again: 'I know how little went on, I was the one who had to calm Bruno down afterwards. The whole thing left him wondering about himself.' Sometimes she was like the head hen.

'If the stories I've heard are true, he's not wondering any more.' Ted was not malicious but he did like gossip. 'And Bruno couldn't have chosen a worse time to spread his wings. He's supposed to be out on the prowl, in that dangerous Manchester, every single night.'

367

But if he's going to do that, why isn't he doing it with me? was the thought that was running round Peter's head. 'I wish we *had* done something now,' he said.

'Forget it,' advised Norma. 'He definitely thinks you're too young.'

'Did you know that Charles Penrose had a wife?' Valerie had come back into the conversation.

'Don't you mean a mother?' asked Peter.

'There was a wife too, living apart. She's supposed to have spoken very nicely about him at the inquest.'

'There's a wife too often.' Ted was sighing again. 'People think they've got to try and be like everybody else. It never really works, it only leads to misery.'

'Somebody should try telling that to Megan Proctor.' Norma's brush was going full tilt. 'She swears she's got something on Bruno. And she's a vengeful bitch at the best of times.'

'Is this snowball going to be like the Clifton snowball?' asked Peter.

'Worse,' pronounced Ted. 'Stands to sense: the bigger the town, the more the address books.'

The candlestick telephone on the hall windowsill at number 10 Hawksway had been replaced by a more modern model. But it had such a loud and insistent bell that the Bird family always felt obliged to answer it at a gallop. 'Hello,' panted Peter who had dived in from planting nasturtium seeds.

'I never seem to see you these days.' It was Vanda.

And she wants something, thought Peter.

'Are you doing anything in particular?' she asked in wheedling tones. It was Saturday. Time was valuable.

'Why? And why aren't you at ballet?'

'The baby class are using the studio for their spring display. Listen, Peter, could you come into town with me? I'll pay the fares. I really need your help.' She then proceeded to prey on Peter's conscience by telling him that he was the only person on earth who could help. So, reluctantly, he agreed to meet her midway between their respective houses, at Hospital Road bus stop.

368

When he got there, Vanda was already posing against the shelter in a brand-new bottle-green coat with a fake-fur collar. 'Like it?' She sketched a mannequin's turn. 'They had it in burgundy as well, but that put me in mind of school uniform.'

Although he was paying her the reluctant compliment of thinking how beautifully she moved, Peter hesitated to offer an opinion on this latest addition to her ever-growing wardrobe.

'Go on,' she commanded. 'Whatever it is, say it.'

'I don't like phoney fur.'

'This is genuine Minkalene,' she said proudly. 'No, be honest, Peter. I'm only paying your bus fare because I want your taste.'

'The coat's fine, the collar's a bugger.' So she wanted his taste for the price of a bus fare, did she? Honestly, she'd use anybody!

But Vanda was ahead of him; she wasn't daft. 'I'll buy us lunch in Lewis's basement.' The bus had arrived and they were already getting on.

'Why there?' Of all places!

'Because I need to go to that end of town. I'm having some pictures done and we need to choose a bikini and some floaty material.'

'For a frock?'

'For the Seven Veils.'

The conductor was so startled he dropped a big handful of coppers. And by the time he'd gathered up every last ha'penny Vanda had noticed another bus coming along behind – one that was going all the way to Piccadilly. Urging Peter down the stairs, she congratulated herself on having got all that way without paying.

On the second bus the first thing she said was, 'Lady Godiva.'

'What about her?'

'You know about hair. If I hired a great big long wig, could you make me look like Lady Godiva?'

'You'd need to hire a carthorse too!'

'Or Eve,' she suggested thoughtfully. Her ideas for the

369

photo session had grown more ambitious in the seven days since she'd learned how to eat in an Indian restaurant. 'Except where do you find artificial fig leaves?'

'You can get little plastic mats like vine leaves, they'd do. Who's going to be taking these photos?'

'Only Toby.' This time she did have to pay the fares.

Once the conductress had moved down the aisle, Peter said, 'You're going to take all your clothes off in front of Toby Eden?'

I want your taste, not your criticism, she thought. In an attempt to change the subject she said, 'The cards were very definite about you being in bed with somebody. Who was it?' Mind you, Peter might have had a point about the undressing. 'I'll insist on a screen.'

He was blowed if he was going to tell her about Buxton, so he too changed the direction of the conversation: 'Great big long wigs always make hair look dead.' Peter knew that Vanda was only really interested in herself.

Once inside Lewis's she elevated self-interest to new heights. The store had yet to allow customers to try on swimwear. 'It's a matter of *hygiene*,' whispered the assistant. This in no way stopped Vanda: she simply bought a pair of cheap knickers, said she'd wear those underneath, and then insisted that the manageress should cart half the bikinis in the shop up the stairs to Ladies Model Gowns, where there were changing cubicles.

The Salomé outfit posed fewer problems. She just bought fourteen yards of nun's veiling and tried to get a reduction for cash.

Peter had done the real choosing. 'And I think you ought to get a few big spangles to go on the very last veil of all. If you sewed them in strategic places you'd probably save yourself a lot of trouble with the censor.'

'I knew you'd come in useful.' Vanda had no hesitation in buying him pie and chips at the self-service counter in the basement. 'And I'm not mean,' she said earnestly. 'You'd be more than welcome to a dessert.' That would be money in the bank towards an eventual hairdo.

As they moved away from the cashier with their trays,

Hetty King was waving and making motioning gestures from one of the tables. He was wearing his official brown warehouse coat; staff weren't meant to eat in the cafeteria, but a little rule like that was no barrier against a determined queen.

'Well, if it isn't the camp palone you had with you at the Hulme Hip,' he said to Peter. 'Hello, Miss Willits,' he oozed at Vanda.

In that moment, Peter saw Hetty King as somebody who wilfully set himself up as a coconut shy; it was as though Hetty knew people were going to throw things at him, so he got his own bit of taunting in first.

But Vanda had chosen to regard the greeting as a friendly overture, so she just said, 'What a wonderful perfume.'

'It's called Endearing.' Hetty produced a tiny sample bottle from his pocket. 'Haven't you heard the commercials on Radio Luxembourg?' His voice became more vampish than any real woman's as he intoned, ' "Endearing – the perfume that makes you want to fall in lerve." ' Hetty gave a sniff. 'I'm more for having honest-to-goodness trade, myself.' Trade was the Polari word for sex.

'What's the latest on the snowball?' Peter asked.

'My dear, they've pulled the Thief of Baghdad. She's got more stolen goods than a magpie in that house. And what do they charge her with? Gross indecency.'

'But what's that?' asked Vanda, who had often seen the words in newspapers. 'What do you have to do?'

'Place one finger on another man's cartse – that's all you have to do. Where'd you think you're going, Peter? Eat your dinner, it'll get cold.'

Peter had risen to his feet. 'I'm bursting for a pee.'

'Well, I'm sorry to be the one to tell you, but you'll find the Wishing Well empty,' sighed Hetty. 'Our basement cottage used to be like Rome at its height,' he explained to Vanda. 'The Wishing Well was world-famous. And what's it like now? Dead, that's what it's like now – dead as Southern Cemetery.'

'Who cares?' said Peter. 'Anyway I'm bursting.' But when he got to the public convenience it wasn't deserted at all.

Somebody was just leaving. And that somebody was Bruno Briggs. Peter could hardly believe his eyes. 'You must be mad, hanging around here,' he said without any preamble.

'So what are you doing?'

'Going to pee.'

'And I'm supposed to have been doing something else?'

Peter knew that he'd already said too much, but he couldn't stop himself from adding, 'People are talking about you.'

Bruno just turned up his coat collar and walked away without another word. He looked tired, and very far from happy.

That Saturday night was not the same as other Saturday nights: there was tension in the air, business in the Café Royal basement was down by half, and the pianist was playing 'I'm Heading for the Last Round-Up'. And he was normal.

Valerie Rimmer waved from one of the heterosexual alcoves. She was with her cousin Norma and a young man whose scarf advertised him as being a student from Salford Tech. 'If you're looking for Ted,' she said to Peter when he got to their table, 'I'm to tell you he'll be in the Union.'

'I've still never been in there.' Peter couldn't decide whether to have a dry ginger here or not. 'What's the Union like inside?'

'There are limits!' she cried in tones of feigned horror.

Norma chipped in with, 'And that comes from a woman who's just queued up at Madame Tussaud's in Blackpool for the museum of anatomy.'

'Sit down.' Valerie was already moving up to make room for him.

No Bruno, no point. 'Thanks but I think I'll be on my way. See you.' The musical accompaniment changed to 'Strange Fruit' as Peter headed for the stairs. Before he could begin to climb them he felt a hand on his shoulder.

It belonged to Valerie Rimmer. 'I didn't want to say too much in front of my young man.' She pronounced 'my young man' in mock cockney. 'Watch yourself out there. It's a bit like war.'

'Are the roughs back on the town?' Queer-bashing always rose up, like the sap, in the spring.

'I don't know about roughs but there's panic about the arrests. I think all the lads have gone up to the Union to be together.'

'All of them?'

'Those who've risked venturing out. Mind what you're doing.'

From sheer force of habit Peter looked in at the side bar of the Midland where the Gin and Tonic Brigade generally added their own discreet froth to an atmosphere of conventional boozing. Not tonight. And the Prince's Bar was deserted, save for one man at the counter on a high stool. This was Eccles Edward who had already been to prison for homosexual offences. He was a world-ranking scientist. But at a time like this he must have been feeling only too aware that anybody who'd already been caught was marked – that other people could view being seen with him as dangerous.

And that's wrong, thought Peter. 'Hello,' he said, though he'd never spoken to the man before. 'Where did everybody go?' The pariah just shrugged his shoulders.

As Peter got to the door, Eccles Edwards called out, 'Watch your step. I'd *wet* myself tonight before I'd go into a cottage.' And that loud warning was brave because the barmen weren't supposed to know that anybody was queer – the fact that they turned a blind eye was something that was meant to be solemnly respected.

Peter walked down Oxford Street. It was no use, Valerie seemed to be right, it would have to be the pub by the canal. He couldn't pretend he was keen on the idea. In fact he was recalling a bit of overheard conversation: 'You must know Dirty Dorothy, she's so low she's barred from the Union.' It was the place he'd only seen from outside, on that first expedition into hidden Manchester.

Eventually he worked his way up to Princess Street. The Union looked small and squat in the dusk. There was just enough light left for the canal to reveal reflections of tall warehouses, some of them still derelict from wartime bombing. But if rumour was right there was another war going on. And true to battle tradition, somebody was singing. The song was 'I Believe'. Some tortured tenor behind a microphone was crying out that he believed, above the storm, the smallest prayer would still be heard.

Peter didn't know whether to laugh or to cry. Instead he prayed. 'Just let me find Bruno,' was his silent plea. 'Just let me find him so I can put things right.' On 'Amen' he pushed open the front door of the pub.

There was a room to the left and a long mahogany and stained-glass bar to the right. 'I Believe' was coming from behind a closed door at the end of the corridor. But a second and softer theme, 'The Wheel of Fortune', was flooding into Peter's left ear from a jukebox in the side room. This was full of American airmen, and girls who made the professionals in Lewis's Arcade look like royal courtesans. Peter had often heard the disparaging expression 'good-time girls' and he supposed he was finally seeing the reality.

The closed door at the end opened and 'I Believe' got louder for an instant as Edith Evans appeared. Noticing Peter he called out, 'At least this is one cottage that's not being watched.' Then he disappeared into the gents.

The song burst forth again as Belsen Betty materialised. 'Who just went in that cot?' he demanded.

'Edith.'

'I think I'll honour her with a visit. Mind you, she's safe enough. Bread and bread never made a sandwich.'

Not much sex happened on licensed premises: nobody wanted to get themselves barred by the few landlords who would run the risk of being prosecuted for allowing queers to congregate. There was a curiously social side to more systematic cottaging. Some men, lacking the price of admission to a bar, did the round of half the urinals in Manchester purely to see who was out on the town. This sort generally went around in caterwauling pairs. Those seriously seeking contacts always operated on their own.

As Peter walked down the corridor, the near hymn ended to a faint spatter of applause. The door must have been on a spring; it had closed shut again and he really had to push to get it open.

There were far more people inside the end room than the applause had led him to expect; it seemed as though a hundred pairs of wary eyes were looking at him. Once they clocked him for queer, the momentary tension relaxed. The first thing he heard anybody say was, 'It's the same in London. They raided the Fitzroy again last week. And the Marquis of Granby.' Another man said, 'Manchester's half-dead; even Diamond and Miss Lewis must have stopped at home with their crochetwork.'

But there weren't just men here, there were collar-and-tie women too, and a few girls who had gone to the other extreme. Peter was inside an old-fashioned concert room where people sat on stuffed leather seats around the walls and on little stools at Britannia tables. Fading Christmas decorations still hung over a low platform with a tatty piano on it. An old ragbag of a grandmother, whom no other establishment would have suffered, grabbed hold of the microphone and began to sing new words to the tune of 'Ma, He's Making Eyes at Me'.

> 'Now he's leaning on the fender,
> Now he's feeling my suspender,
> Ma, he's inside me.'

'You dirty melt!' shouted a statuesque queen named Ava. It was well known, in this world, that she was looking for a doctor to transform her into a real woman. Sunday newspaper stories about the sex-changed Roberta Cowell had unleashed a whole crop of similar ambitions. Suddenly it seemed as though there were queers, and there were people who were something quite different. It was impossible to think of Ava as any kind of 'he'.

Seizing the microphone from the woman tramp, Miss Ava turned limpid eyes on her audience and managed to create the effect of drag, even though she was wearing a pinstripe suit – albeit with a diamanté brooch in the lapel. Queens being hugely competitive, Ava began to sing a parody of her own. This time the pianist picked up the tune; it was 'The Girl that I Marry'.

'The baby I carry will have to be
Left on the steps of a nunnery,
The boy I called my own,
He has taken to laces and smells of cologne.
His nails he has polished . . .'

'Hi.' Ted Sterling had pushed his way through the crowd and
joined Peter. 'What about this place? Oh God, doesn't it make
you wish we had laws like Holland? This sort of tat's
entertaining enough in its own way, but in Amsterdam at
least you've got civilised alternatives. I'm on my way down
the road. Listen, I promised you a drink. What are you
having?'

'You're not going?' asked Peter, alarmed.

'Got to. My American daren't come in here because of all
his normal buddies in the other room. Dry ginger?'

'Please.'

'I'll be back.'

'My dear, they should be playing "Here Comes the
Bride". Ladybird's finally hit the Union!' Hetty King had
plainly had a few. 'Do you know Cosy Nellie?'

The abundant auburn hair was so artfully waved, the face
so skilfully painted and the white raincoat pulled into such a
tight waist that no outsider could have settled on a definite
gender.

'Because the heat's on, she's come out as a big butch homi
tonight.' Hetty said this as though it was meant to be taken
seriously. And his own eyeshadow was down to a bare
minimum.

'Shift, Sandy!' bawled one of the tougher women. 'OK,
don't shift.' She sat down again. 'But that means I'm not
getting any drinks in.'

'I see our lesbian sisters are out in force, lending support,'
said Hetty disparagingly. 'It's all right for them. They've
never been against the law.'

Cosy Nellie finally spoke: 'What I don't understand is, why
are half of them married ladies?' Her voice was as much done
with mirrors as her appearance. Except for the Adam's apple,
nobody would have guessed.

'I'll explain lesbians to you,' pronounced Hetty. 'We know what we are because we're guided by our dicks. You've got one, Nellie, whether you like it or not. And it responds to what you see. It's like having a barometer in your trousers.'

'She's such a fucking philosopher,' cooed Nellie.

Hetty was not to be deflected: 'Women are built different. They only get stirred very deep down. They're like walking coal mines – waiting for the emotional train to come through. And when it doesn't, they marry a man and think life's a bitch.'

Peter's one worry was that this sweeping judgment would be overheard by the girls at the nearby table and that a fight would break out. Hetty could have had no such qualms. 'One fine morning, two children later, these same women wake up to find they've got a new postwoman. And suddenly that underground train comes to life, the scales fall from their eyes, and the next thing they know they're in here, flinging pint pots around.'

'Yes, but they could give us lessons in true love.' You could tell why Nellie was called Cosy. Then she spoiled it by adding, 'And *somebody* has to keep the tattoo parlours going.'

Their criticism was not even veiled, thought Peter. He found himself wondering whether experience of intolerance had bred more within them. Except he was criticising too. Oh God, there had to be a better way of going about being queer than this. Perhaps he should save up his plaque money and run away to Amsterdam.

'Stead of sitting,
He's just knitting,
With a sailor he met from Thames Ditton . . .'

Ava was still at it and the cigarette smoke in the room was like an engine shed. 'Your drink.' Ted had returned. 'I got you a double pop for being a good little worker. *And* your heart is going to sing: Bruno's just walked in. He's skulking by the bar in the passage. I'm off to meet GI Jack at the Old Garett.'

'Poor Miss Ladybird's lost her homi,' said Hetty as Ted

vanished. 'If you're looking for another, I'd keep my eyes off that teddy boy in electric blue – he's strictly rent.'

'I'm just going somewhere.'

'And we know where.' Cosy Nellie adjusted a diamanté ring.

You don't, thought Peter as he carried his drink past the gents' cloakroom. God heard my prayer, and I'm going to talk to Bruno.

He was leaning against the counter, looking morose. And his opening words were not promising: 'Should you be on licensed premises?'

'I get away with it.'

'Hang around with that lot in there for long enough and you'll end up like them.'

Could that be taken to mean that he cared? 'No I won't.' Greatly daring, Peter added, 'I just want to be a man who loves another man.' You, Bruno, you. 'I'm sorry if I annoyed you in Lewis's.'

'You did sound a bit prissy. It's OK, I know you meant well. I've been thinking about it all afternoon. Couldn't stop. It kept going round and round in my brain. *Are* people talking about me?'

Peter looked across to see whether the barmaid was listening. What you didn't let them hear they didn't worry about. 'Have you been doing those things?'

'Maybe.'

He had. 'Oh.' There was a lot to feel but not much to say.

Bruno must have sensed something of this: 'I just had to find out, once and for all, whether I'm queer. Well, more than once if I'm going to be absolutely honest.'

'Didn't you know in bed with me?'

'You're just a kid . . .'

'I'm not.'

'You are. You're all that's right, but you might not know your own mind yet.'

If the barmaid hadn't come back to spread beer mats on the counter, Peter would have come right out and said 'I love you.' As it was he just said, 'Nante polari.'

'I hate that shoddy language.' Bruno started to speak very

378

quickly. 'Don't get like the rest of them. Stay yourself.' Now he looked like somebody who felt he might have said too much. 'Let's talk about something – anything – else. Joan's driving us mad at home. She's absolutely determined to bring her mother out of that place for a day.'

Peter had also had to listen to a lot of impassioned speeches on the subject. 'If she doesn't try she'll never know.'

'I've got a long memory.' Bruno downed the remains of his glass of beer. 'I remember the last time Rhoda came home. Can I buy you a drink?'

'It's OK. I've not touched this one yet.'

'Right. I'm off.'

That couldn't be it. It couldn't. 'When will I see you again?'

'I've given up doing the plaques. I never enjoyed it and Megan was the final straw. I'll ring you.'

'You've not got my number.'

Bruno pulled out his pen and reached for a beer mat. 'What is it?' He wrote the number down and then added the words Peter Bird. In his firm handwriting it looked quite a nice name.

'Take care,' said Peter. This wasn't just a standard farewell. Tonight was the kind of night when men really meant it.

'And you.' Bruno put up his coat collar and walked out by the side door.

'So your little moment's over,' said the barmaid sympathetically. It seemed they did choose to listen after all. 'Mind you, he's right about one thing: you don't want to go getting like some of those in the end room. The devil gelds 'em and never tells 'em.'

'You still take their money though, don't you? You're talking about my sisters,' Peter said indignantly. And even as the words came out he wanted to change the last one to 'brothers'. And we will, he thought. You wait, some of us will.

Joan was busy rooting in one of the deep cupboards which stood against the walls of the long entrance corridor at

Ingledene. 'I don't know why we call it the vase cupboard,' she said to Granny Briggs, who was standing there watching her in the manner of some official inspector. 'It's just like a jumble sale waiting to happen.' Joan had already fished out an unwieldy pile of ping-pong bats, an oversized ball of rainbow wool and half a dozen of those green glass jars meant for growing hyacinths in.

'If you'd just tell me what you're looking for . . .'

The whole subject needed broaching carefully. Mind you, Granny was in a good mood because she'd finally heard from Mr Morgenstern. He and his family were no longer being shadowed by the FBI but they had yet to get their passports back. In the depths of the middle shelf, Joan's fingers encountered a squarish box, but this felt like cardboard and she knew that the one she wanted was covered in leatherette.

'You've always been obstinate,' grumbled Granny. 'Always had to do it the hard way. If you'd just tell me . . .'

'It's something Molly Wainwright mentioned.' The author's letters to Joan could have been published under the title *How to Turn Yourself into a Professional Writer*. 'She says that if she'd just learnt to touch-type properly when she started out, she'd have saved herself a fortune in time and secretaries.'

Quietly triumphant, Granny announced: 'The old type-writer is beneath the bottom shelf. Unless it's been moved, it should be next to that wonky radiant-heat lamp.'

It was exactly where Granny had said. 'Only I can't get it open. Where are the keys?'

'With all the other keys, in the ginger jar, up at the top. You see. If you'd just ask me, Joan . . .'

But Joan needed to ask an altogether bigger question. She dived straight in with, 'Can I have typing lessons?' All the keys had luggage labels on them and she soon had the case of the typewriter open. It was a bit like a little church organ. Faded gold lettering on the black enamel announced it to be *The Bar-Let Portable*.

'Surely they teach typing at the grammar school?'

Joan had already had this one out with Miss Staff. 'If you

do typing you have to do shorthand and commercial Spanish too. And that means I'd have to drop English.'

'You'll just have to teach yourself.'

'But that's what I've not got to do,' protested Joan. 'I've not got to get into bad habits.'

Granny laid a finger on the machine and stroked the worn enamel. 'I've not thought about this typewriter for years; it came home after he was shot dead.'

'Who was shot dead?'

'Your Cousin Wilfred. Well, my cousin really. I don't know what that makes him to you – something very distant. He was a war correspondent with *The Times*.'

'And you're only just telling me now?'

'I've had bigger things on my mind, Joan.'

The idea of another writer in the family was, to say the least of it, stimulating. 'Was he any good?'

'*The Times* would hardly have employed a dud. He was a confirmed bachelor.' Quite inexplicably, that worried look, the one she'd been wearing so often recently, pulled down the corners of Granny's mouth again.

'There's a woman in Swinton who teaches touch-typing in her front room,' said Joan. 'It's a detached house,' she added, as though this might carry some extra weight with Granny Briggs.

'I'll have to think about it. Any other requests while we're on the subject?'

Granny had been speaking sarcastically but Joan chose to take her quite seriously: 'When can my mother come home for the day?'

'I asked for requests, Joan, not the Chinese water torture.' Granny softened a little as she said, 'It was Cousin Wilfred who taught Rhoda to play battledore and shuttlecock. They don't seem to play that any more. Oh well, he's dead, everybody's dead.'

'Rhoda isn't.'

'We'll have to see,' said Granny firmly. But there was more hope in 'We'll have to see' than there had ever been in all her previous refusals.

'I've already been there earlier, to set some photographic lights up.' There certainly wouldn't have been room for them in Toby's sports car. Stuffed behind the two bucket seats was a blue weekend case, a Chinese sunshade and a varnished cardboard box with an impressive if ancient label which read: *Hulme – Wigmakers to the Theatrical Profession.*

'What's the studio like?' asked Vanda.

'Well . . . how shall I put it? Most of the time it's what could be termed somebody's bedsitting room. With kitchenette.'

'You can stop this bloody car, now.'

He did. They were opposite Salford Cathedral. 'Are you thinking of going in to pray for inspiration?' he asked cheerfully. 'Because if you are, I should warn you that I've searched the length and breadth of this town for proper premises.' He certainly sounded genuine enough. 'And when the words "artistic poses" were mentioned, I was very quickly shown the door.'

'You should have cracked on we were doing something else.'

'And what if they'd barged in?'

'Barged in?' she fumed. 'This job calls for privacy.'

'Which is what you'll get on Barr Hill.'

'All right.' She was marginally mollified. She never knew whether the district counted as Irlams o'th' Height or not. She'd always thought of it as the middle of nowhere. And by the time they arrived, sudden rain was not adding any glamour to a side road which looked as though it was just about to fall on hard times. Modern families had got too small for these tall, narrow terraced houses set back behind privet hedges and four feet of garden. Some of the front doors had more than one bell push.

'There's a Chinese lives on the second floor, at the back,' said Toby. 'That's not where we're going,' he added hastily, 'but it's where I learnt fan-tan.' He was already putting a key in the front door.

The first thing Vanda saw when they'd climbed the stairs to the flat was a green and cream kitchen cabinet standing between two lace-curtained windows. The second thing was a divan bed. A white sheet was drawing-pinned up against one wall, and Vanda recognised the same camera she'd seen the previous week. Today it was sitting on top of a tripod.

Toby began fiddling with plugs. ' "Let there be light," ' he quoted. ' "And there was light." ' If the arc lamp was on the small side, at least it was the genuine article. But that wardrobe was about ten times too big for the room. And dilapidated? Even the silver was peeling from behind the mirrors in the doors. Rain was now really battering against the windows.

Vanda put the wig box on an enamel-topped table. 'Where's me screen?'

Toby made almost too much of clapping a hand to his forehead. 'I knew I'd forgotten something.'

'I'll bet you did.' She checked her own reflection in the mirrored wardrobe. She'd been to Peter's to get her make-up done. The black eyeliner still looked a treat, but he'd instructed her to apply a second coat of lipstick on arrival; and then she was supposed to paint glycerine over the top. It was all in her tin make-up box, inside the suitcase. The glycerine gloss wasn't meant to go on until there was no risk of it being smeared by clothes going over her head – everything was properly thought out. 'I'm afraid you're going to have to step outside,' she said.

'What if somebody sees me?' he asked, alarmed. 'I mean, I've only got the place on a borrow. Couldn't I just turn my back?'

'No you couldn't.' She wouldn't mind being partially undressed for the actual photographs but she was blowed if she was going to stage an unrehearsed striptease in close-up. She knew men, she'd watched their faces at Salford Hippodrome. She was determined to keep the whole thing . . . Vanda sought for the right word. Pally. No more than pally. 'Out,' she said. 'This won't take long.'

As Toby left the room, Vanda wondered whether she might not have been a bit too harsh. After all, she'd already got the bikini on underneath her sweater and skirt. No, it was the act of removing clothes which got men going. You only had to watch Phyllis at it! Humming the Blue Tango, Vanda stripped down to the white two-piece bathing suit and slipped on the matching high-heeled shoes. Though she said it herself, she looked bloody good in that old mirror. 'You can come in now,' she called out, as she rooted for the glycerine bottle. 'You won't see any more than you'd see on Blackpool sands.'

'I've never seen anything as beautiful at Blackpool,' he said fervently.

Too fervently? 'Blow some rubber balloons up.' Things needed keeping on a businesslike footing.

They couldn't find the balloons. Vanda searched her suitcase, and the make-up box, but they weren't there. 'I had a complete plan,' she wailed. 'I had a proper order worked out and everything.'

And things went from bad to worse as Toby refused to be satisfied by the effects she was creating with the Oriental sunshade. 'I don't know why,' he said, 'but it reminds me of a little kid in a Sunday School concert. Not your figure,' he added hastily. 'Not that. The rest of it makes me think of tap-dancing shoes with big bows on them.'

'We'll try the wig,' she snapped. Off came the lid of the box and she lifted the false hair from its tissue paper nest. The wig was so big that this took two hands. It was several minutes before she got it arranged on her head to her satisfaction. 'Well?' Vanda turned to face him. 'Will I do?' She already knew the answer. 'No. I won't do. I look like a cavewoman.'

'Whip it off,' he said. 'Your own hair's much nicer. That's right, just smooth it down a bit. And grab that umbrella again.' He was looking at her through the viewfinder. 'Right. Open it and peer over the edge as if you've got nothing on underneath. Lower it . . . further still . . . more . . . No, it's no use. What are those white pointed bits? Can you roll them down?'

'I can't. They've got bones in them. They're what holds it up.'

'Well that's it then,' he said resignedly. 'I've done all I know. If we were going to get a proper cleavage effect you'd have to take the top off. I'd turn my back till you got behind the brolly again,' he added hastily.

'You most certainly would. Go on, get turning.' As the bra came off she was looking in the wardrobe mirror. The bones had cut in on the sides of her breasts and made red and white marks. As she gave one of these an experimental rub, Vanda could have sworn she heard someone breathing heavily. It was too near for it to be Toby. She stopped looking at her reflection in the glass and examined its peeling mirrored surface.

That was when she saw the eye.

Somebody was looking out from inside the wardrobe. 'Police,' she screamed. 'Get the police!'

'Stop it, Vanda! Calm down,' pleaded Toby.

'No I won't calm down. There's somebody in there.' Toby tried to put his hand over her mouth and she bit it, hard. 'Don't think you can maul me when I've got me tits out.' She struggled back into the brassière. 'Who is it? What's his bloody game?' Now she felt covered up enough to fling open the door.

Standing inside the end section of the wardrobe, like a corpse in a coffin, was the little fat man who had once won Toby's sports car – the man with the fuzzy hair and glasses. He seemed almost prepared for being unmasked: he was waving big five-pound notes around like white flags. 'You win,' he gibbered. 'You win, Toby. You win.'

A terrible silence fell. It was so awful that Toby didn't even seem to have worked up the nerve to reach for the money. 'What was the bet?' demanded Vanda. 'Go on, tell me. I'm prepared for mucky.'

'You like a bit of fun yourself,' Toby mumbled.

'Yes, and I like to choose the company I have it with. What was the bet?' She shouldn't have been wearing high heels against naked feet; she could feel a blister starting. Yet again she repeated, 'What was the bet?'

'That I'd get to see your charlies,' said Toby in a small voice.

'And he'd get to see them too? A free show? On no.' She was very definite about this. 'No, I haven't spent all these years in training to go giving it away.' It was Vanda who took the money off the gambler in the wardrobe. 'I'll stuff this in a Red Cross box. That way it's not prostitution.'

'You're a real sport,' said Toby gratefully.

It had taken until now for the full enormity of the situation to dawn on Vanda. 'You saw *everything*,' she screamed at the man in the wardrobe. 'Every bloody detail. He saw much more than you did,' she cried at Toby. 'Doesn't that bother you?' With sudden inspiration she reached up and snatched the man's glasses off his nose, threw them on the floor and ground them under the sole of her shoe.

'Those glasses are my eyes,' he gasped in horror. 'I can't see a thing without them.'

'Good. I'm glad. Because the next thing I'm going to do is push you down the stairs.'

Toby must have felt obliged to try to call the proceedings to order. 'You've got next to no clothes on, Vanda,' he said stuffily. 'And you're in a strange house.'

'When the police come, you're the one who will have to explain that.'

'You wouldn't?'

'Try me. If I don't get these photos by this time next week I'll have you, and I'll have him. Photos and negatives.' She had to risk this because she'd no idea where she could get pin-up pictures processed. Boots Cash Chemists wouldn't touch them with a barge pole.

'I'll bring them next Saturday.'

'You won't bring anything. You'll post them. And make sure you stick the envelope down properly. You've gone your length, Toby Eden.' Vanda was already climbing into her skirt. 'I'm finished with you.'

'Those glasses are my eyes,' repeated the unlucky punter.

'God knew what he was doing when he made you short-sighted.' Her jumper hadn't even smeared the glycerine. And when she thought about it, one thing really annoyed her. The afternoon had been a complete waste of seven veils.

Although Miss Lathom only lived next door, she always telephoned when she wanted something. 'Peter? I've got a pigeon trapped in the boxroom. I'm going to have one more

386

go at trying to coax him out. If that fails, I'll come and give your father a knock. He is in isn't he?'

'Yes, he's in.' Miss Lathom wouldn't have needed reminding that Peter was hopeless with trapped birds. He'd reach, they'd flutter, he'd panic. In his father's favour it had to be said that Bird VC was wonderful with birds and animals. As a young man he'd worked with horses and he'd even had a short-lived post-war job at a dogs' home. When it came to dumb creatures, nothing was too much trouble for Eddie Bird.

The same could not be said of human beings. As Peter walked into the lounge, Eddie was reading aloud to Peggy from the *Manchester Evening News*: ' "Twenty-eight men arrested in one police operation." ' The evening meal was over and Peter's father was going through a period of semi-controlled drinking. This always left him edgy and highly judgmental. 'This Home Secretary's got the right idea: round 'em up and shove 'em inside! It says here that there are more enquiries pending. What they all need is a taste of the birch.' Registering Peter's arrival he said, 'I hope you never go for a piss in those toilets underneath London Road Station.'

'Store Street?' Peter had spoken before he'd thought: Store Street was somewhere he'd heard much discussed in the Snake Pit.

'Not "piss", Eddie, please.' Peggy sounded pained. 'Let's try and maintain a few standards.'

But her husband was more interested in what their son had said. 'That name came very quick to your lips.'

'What name?' Peter knew, but all he wanted to do was get his hands on the *Evening News* and see whether it said who had been arrested.

'Store Street. How come you know Store Street?'

Peggy deflected his suspicion with, 'It's opposite the fire station, underneath those railway arches. Even I know that and I'm from Stoke.'

How much more did she know? Peter never liked to think too hard about it. Who had the police pulled in? That was more important at the moment.

Eddie wasn't about to let things rest. 'Where do you disappear to in town?'

'Leave him alone,' said Peggy.

'He's got money in his pocket from that cissy painting job. Where does he spend it?'

'On clothes,' she said.

'Not at night he doesn't. Where d'you go? Don't look like that, Peggy. He's bought something called antishave lotion.'

Peter coped with this one by himself: 'Honestly, your eyes! It's aftershave lotion.' Old Spice was something which had only recently come on the market.

'Real men don't use that. And you never put it on and come in and talk to us. Oh no, once you're nancied up you slide off out. That bathroom smells like a Cairo brothel.'

'I am here,' said Peggy. 'I am present. And I don't like talk like that. Anyway, how do you know what those places smell like?'

'One night I'll follow you,' Eddie snapped at Peter. 'And if you go where I think you go, I'll knock seven shades of shit out of you. And now you've made me swear in front of your mother.'

Further discussion was interrupted by one loud rap on the front door knocker.

'It's Miss Lathom,' remembered Peter. 'She's got a bird in her boxroom.'

'Coming,' yelled Eddie. And he marched out of the room.

'Where *do* you go?' asked Peggy, quietly.

'Out.'

'Mmm. Oh well, what I don't know I can't worry about. I'd better go and see whether he needs a pole.'

Once she too was out of the room, Peter seized hold of the newspaper. 'Undercover operation . . . detectives kept the convenience under observation over a long period . . . sundry arrests.' And then, in heavier type, came a long list of names. It only served to emphasise the secrecy of the half-world. Peter knew a hundred nicknames but . . . George Henry King: here at least was one he recognised. Hetty had been accused of importuning, which wasn't as serious as some of the other charges. He'd pleaded guilty in the police court and had been fined ten pounds. Most of the other cases were going to be heard at the Quarter Sessions. Under the names came the bit about more enquires pending.

'Peter.' His mother had returned. 'Your father wants you to take this packet of seeds to Miss Lathom's.'

'But they're my night-scented stock,' he protested. 'By rights they should be in by now.'

'He thinks they might tempt the bird better than bread. Don't be so mean. It's in a terrible panic.'

If that was the case, the bird was more than welcome to four penn'orth of seeds. He knew how it must be feeling. He was in a bit of a panic himself. Where was this police purge going to end?

As Peter got out into the garden he could hear his father's voice coming from next door's open upstairs window. 'Come on,' he was saying. 'Come to Eddie, come on, love. Nobody's going to hurt you.' Peter's mind went right back to his early childhood, to the days when Eddie had still been kind. And he realised that he'd once loved his father, and that his father had once loved him.

Not any more.

The man who presented the prizes at last year's Speech Day had been an Old Bartonian. So, when it came to the traditional speechmaker's request for 'a whole day's holiday for the school', he had endeared himself to the present pupils by saying, 'And not just an extra day, tacked on at the end of the school holidays. One on its own. One when the weather should be nice. Shall we say May the seventh?'

Prize-giving had taken place in the Ellesmere Cinema. Sitting in her front stall, Vanda had felt almost singled out for favour – the date he had chosen would be her seventeenth birthday. But now the day had dawned and the clock had touched nine and she didn't feel especially blessed at all.

In the months since Speech Day Vanda had grown to fear the tarot, come to see it as something which had a life of its own. She could not shake off the feeling that it was capable of interfering with life itself. But on her birthday she always had to spread the cards; this was a ceremony which had been initiated by Gran'ma Dora, and that made it sacred.

The cards had to be arranged into an elaborate lacy pattern, known as Amanda's Fan. One card, for the questioner, represented the ring that held the fan together. The big triangular spread above the ring was supposed to reveal the influences and events of the coming year.

There's no law that says I've got to believe in it, thought Vanda defiantly. But one thing was interesting: Toby Eden's card was not there at all. And why were Joan and Peter so far out on the edges? Right next to Peter's card was the World again – Joan's uncle. He and Peter were being threatened by the dreadful Ten of Wands. Taken at face value, it meant that they had bitten off more than they could chew.

'What's going on?' She phrased the question silently. And answer came there none. Vanda decided that it had been a mistake to pretend she was not going to believe the spread. Experience should have told her that the dwarf inside would take offence. And last time she'd consulted the cards she'd shouted at him. Could it be that he'd gone away forever? There was no point in pretending that she would be anything but glad about that.

> *'Happy birthday to you,*
> *Happy birthday to you,*
> *Happy birthday, Miss Ungrateful,*
> *Happy birthday to you.'*

He was still there – down a tunnel but present. 'So tell me?' she said. All she got back was another derisive burst of 'Happy Birthday to You'. Mr Midget was obviously out to punish her.

Anyway, I don't need you, she thought. I'm only doing it because of Gran'ma Dora and birthdays. Bang in the middle of Amanda's Fan was the King of Pentacles, the brilliantined impresario from Hulme Hippodrome – Mr Alf Blatt. His visiting card hadn't said 'Alfred', just plain Alf, and his tarot card was surrounded by symbols of travel and change and opportunity.

390

'*You will note that they are in very small doses.*' The little tormentor could dodge back when he had something nasty to say. Gran'ma Dora had always maintained that if you gazed for long enough at Amanda's Fan your eyes would start to see some of it more vividly than the rest. And it was true: the impresario's area and Peter's troubles were beginning to look almost three-dimensional.

'*I could tell you, I could tell you. But I won't. Many happy returns, Miss Vanda Bell. And may all your Christmases be white.*'

I don't want another year of the midget, she thought. I don't, I don't. I can't even stand the feel of the cards any more, even if they did belong to Gran'ma Dora. Why can't I just put them in the bin? Because she couldn't. It was as simple as that.

'Only why?' This was voiced aloud to the four walls. What would Dora Doran have done? She would have consulted the cards, that's what she'd have done. Vanda was trapped – trapped. Except . . . maybe she could fight fire with fire. Amanda's Fan allowed for one significant question. You could only have the one and you really had to need to know the answer.

'Vanda?' It was Ethel calling from downstairs. 'Vanda?'

'It's OK,' she called back. 'I'm up.' Sweeping the fan back into a pile, she began to shuffle again. 'What do I have to do to get rid of you?' she whispered. With this she chose a card.

'*Ooo-er,*' screamed the voice within. '*Ooh, ooh, ooh.*' The card was the Ace of Swords – a hand issuing from darkness with one silver blade held aloft. It represented the triumph of some great outside force.

But another force was coming through the bedroom door in the shape of Ethel Bell. She must have just finished eating breakfast because the vast promontory of her front was spattered with damp cornflakes.

Is that my real future? wondered the more realistic side of her daugher. Will I bloat out like that? All I can say is I'd better get a bit of living in first!

Ever since the afternoon of the impromptu striptease on the market, Ethel had been as good as her word; silence had

391

been the order of the ensuing days on Sixth Avenue. Mind you, she was another one who could bring herself to speak when there was something unpleasant to say. 'You've got post. But don't think I've come upstairs to dance attendance on you – I'm on me way to a shite.'

Ethel had handed over three white envelopes and was opening a big brown one herself. Well, trying to open it; the brown manila package was sealed with a lot of Sellotape.

Vanda's first birthday card was from Miss Lathom, a reproduction of Frith's painting of Derby Day. Peter's was abstract with 'Gordon Fraser Gallery' on the back.

'Oh my God, blue photos!' Ethel had got the big envelope open and pulled out a set of glossy prints. 'I don't believe it,' she breathed. 'They're you – doing a titty show.' Now her voice began to gather strength: 'You dirty mare. You're filth, you're nothing else.'

'Wasn't that addressed to me?' asked Vanda dangerously.

Ethel still had one fat paw within the envelope. 'No letter inside. Just photos and these.' She threw two strips of negatives onto the bed. 'Mind you, nobody *would* sign their name to filth through the post.'

'I said, weren't they addressed to me?'

'Don't you bloody snatch or I'll land you one.'

But Vanda had already seized hold of the pictures. They looked what they were: somebody with next to no clothes on, in a scruffy back bedroom.

Her mother was still ranting. 'I've every right to open anything that comes into this house.' This was an old and familiar argument. 'I only let you have the others because it was your birthday.'

'So you did remember?'

'Naturally I remember the day you were born. A woman doesn't forget pain like that in a hurry. *And* it's something you'll soon know about; girls who go around thrusting their titties at cameras soon end up with a midwife in attendance!'

The look of the photographs had really depressed Vanda. 'I'll just have to get some done professionally,' she said. 'These are like a hopeful beauty queen.'

'You get more done and you don't stop in this house.'

'Then I'll go.' She was seventeen now, Ethel couldn't stop her. 'And don't think you can haul me back. Because if you do I'll argue the toss in court. I've got money, I can earn a living. I'm not without.'

'I just hope my mother's looking down on this. I just hope she can see what she's done. Haul you back? So you can hang a red light in the front window? You don't hear me shouting after the binmen "I want my rubbish back".'

'No, because you never put anything in the bin. You've got a tip of your own. It's called forty-two Sixth Drive.'

'That does it! You leave this house today. And you can die on a doorstep before I'll have you back. And by the way, Vanda, happy birthday.' Ethel's eyes suddenly lighted on the pokerwork box. 'So that's where those cards have been all these years. Now I understand things a bit more clearly. Do you know who lives inside that box? Shall I tell you? The devil, that's who lives inside it – the devil.'

Peter replaced the receiver of the new phone in the hall. Vanda had been ringing from a kiosk near the long-distance bus station, and she'd asked him to pass on the news of her sudden departure to Joan. This wouldn't be the best of days for ringing Ingledene because Joan's mother was due home for the afternoon.

'I'll write to you from London.' Vanda's last words were still ringing round his head. And now the phone began to shrill again. Had she changed her mind or had she forgotten something?

It wasn't Vanda. It was Bruno Briggs and he sounded agitated: 'Peter? That is you, isn't it? I wasn't sure I remembered the number.'

'Did you lose the beer mat?' Peter's world was suddenly brighter, sharper, happier.

'No.' There was a awkward pause and then Bruno said, 'Somebody else has got it.'

'Who?'

Bruno didn't answer directly. Instead, in lowered tones, he asked, 'Do you remember that night at Buxton?'

'I'll never forget it.'

'Nothing happened. Do you understand me? Look, I'm in a corridor, it's a public phone. I'm only supposed to make one call but they've gone to the canteen.'

'Who?' And why was Bruno's voice so shaky?

'Nothing happened. And nobody touched anybody *there*.'

'Where? Oh I see. But we didn't,' said Peter ruefully.

'Nobody touched anybody.' The line went dead.

The Gentlewoman's Compendium contained no advice on entertaining somebody who was coming home for the day from a mental institution. Granny Briggs had been flustered about the niceties of the visit since Sunday.

'We don't have to collect,' Joan had said. 'They bring her.' An ambulance, with portholes instead of windows, had duly rattled its way up the drive of Ingledene. But when the uniformed driver climbed out and went round to fling open the rear doors, not one but two women emerged. Rhoda was accompanied by an unexpected escort – Nurse Whelan. The Irish nurse was not in uniform; her flowered two-piece and the neat straw boater could have been an advertisement for the slimmer end of Evans the Outsize Shop.

'And poor Rhoda's got the same coat on that she wore to go into the nursing home to have you.' Granny and Joan were peering through the clear part of the stained glass in the front door. 'Is one meant to tip the driver?'

'It would be more to the point if we opened the door.' Joan was feeling almost as nervous as Granny sounded. Down at the bottom of the steps, gazing around like somebody halfway out of a trance, Rhoda looked extraordinary. Her navy-blue coat was in the style known as 'edge to edge', and these edges were droopily scalloped.

As Joan darted down to greet her, she reflected that she had last seen a similar garment illustrated in one of the old newspapers which lined the sewing machine drawers. Rhoda, gazing round the garden, must also have been looking into the past. 'Where are the lilacs?' she asked. 'And what happened to the potentilla?'

'We're quite grown-up today.' Nurse Whelan confided this in an aside to Joan.

'Hello, Rhoda,' said Granny.

'A little confusion is only to be expected,' warned the nurse.

It arrived immediately. 'We'd better call the police,' announced Rhoda. 'The lead nymph's gone too.'

Joan tried to act naturally: 'We think some men who came round banging, asking for scrap, might have taken it.' This had happened fully eighteen months previously.

But it seemed that Rhoda was stuck in 1936. 'You go out for ten minutes,' she grumbled, 'and you come back to chaos. What's happened to the paint on the front door? I never knew that paint could wither.'

Joan remembered that Granny had been intending to keep this trial visit to a picnic round the kitchen table. But she suspected Nurse Whelan's presence would alter that. And it did: Olive Briggs led the visitors straight into the front drawing room. 'Whip those dust sheets off,' she hissed at Joan.

'Oh my God!' bawled Rhoda. 'It's not just the paintwork that's withered, this whole room has curled up and died.'

'You've been away for a long time.' Granny looked rattled; she was plainly not enjoying being caught on the hop. 'Sherry, Nurse Whelan? Get the glasses out of the Chinese cabinet, Joan.'

'I see you have a pianner,' observed the nurse.

Rhoda was still giving forth protests: 'This settee is damp. And why does everything smell musty?'

'Come along, sweetheart,' purred Nurse Whelan. 'You can't expect things to be as . . . antiseptic as they are on the ward.'

Joan didn't dare look at Granny. Instead she poured out four glasses of amontillado.

'Not sherry for the mammy.' Nurse Whelan had come up behind her. 'It could clash with the medication.'

But Rhoda had seen what was going on at the other end of the room and she walked across and took a glass from the tray. 'Who the hell is the woman in the fishmonger's hat?' She was nodding towards Nurse Whelan as she talked to her mother.

'Oh dear,' sighed the nurse, 'this can happen. Seeing the

old surroundings again must have cancelled me out of her little brain.'

'Is she stark raving mad?' asked Rhoda interestedly. Today the whole tone of her voice and the way she moved were like something out of pre-war British films. 'Chin-chin,' she said as she raised her glass. 'Where's my boy?'

Granny was ahead of the others: 'Bruno's out.'

And he's meant to be here, thought Joan. He swore blind he'd be back by twelve o'clock. But Bruno was somebody who had taken to going around in his own species of daze. For the last week it had been very hard to guarantee that you had really caught his attention.

Glass in hand, Rhoda walked back across the room and examined the portrait of Flora MacDonald. 'At least you're still the same.' Rounding on Joan she asked, 'Why aren't you in uniform, Elsie? Where's your cap and apron? Never mind that, get me a pencil and paper. I have to make a list of what's missing. There's the lead statue, and my wedding group in the silver frame, and the embroidered bell pull has gone too. What's this?' Nurse Whelan, who had been fishing in her handbag, had produced two tablets.

'Just swallow them,' the nurse said as she snatched the sherry glass from her charge. 'A big girl like you doesn't need water.'

The authority in the voice must have recalled Rhoda to her other existence, and she downed the pills without a murmur. The nurse mouthed the words 'little sedative' at Joan.

It didn't act straight away. 'I know I just slipped out for a short while,' said Rhoda to her mother, 'but where did I go?'

'Probably down to the tennis club.' Granny sounded purposely vague. 'Or you could have nipped to see Mr Nash's kittens.'

Mr Nash was a vicar who'd retired when Joan was ten. She had contributed sixpence towards an engraved inkstand for him. But Granny's answer seemed to have satisfied Rhoda. 'Yes,' she said, 'that's more than likely. Not the club, Mr Nash.'

'Matron would go berserk if she knew I'd given her those after a mouthful of sherry wine,' observed Nurse Whelan.

Was this a reminder that she had not yet received her own drink? Joan handed it across to her and a couple of refined sips seemed to restore the proceedings to something almost out of Granny's etiquette book. By way of dainty conversation Nurse Whelan remarked, 'The daddy's death was very sudden, wasn't it?'

'Whose daddy?' asked Joan, wondering whether she was still the maid in the mother's mind and therefore not really entitled to speak. But Rhoda stayed quiet; she'd settled down on one of the leather pouffes and was playing with its fringing.

'Have I put my size seven in it?' Nurse Whelan said to Granny.

'I'm as lost as Joan is.'

'Well, seemingly . . .' The nurse was speaking very confidentially. 'Seemingly,' she repeated, 'our lady almoner has had a letter from a lawyer. I can tell by your face, Mrs Briggs, you've not had yours yet. Oh dear . . .' She looked flustered. 'The fact of the matter is that Mr Stone has gone to God.'

'My father?' asked Joan, astonished.

The telephone began to ring in the hall. 'What a moment for somebody to choose!' Granny headed for the door.

'Why does Mummy look seventy?' asked Rhoda. Her voice was just interested and nothing like as frenzied as before.

'Your mammy's had a little shock.' Nurse Whelan was more interested in talking to Joan: 'I lit a candle for the poor soul. Not that we ever saw him. I only got to know about it because I oblige the lady almoner by doing her bits of darning. She did just happen to mention what was in the letter . . .' This was offered in the kind of wheedling tones which suggested that, given encouragement, she was in a position to reveal more.

Joan obliged her with, 'Do tell. Let's have the lot.'

'No provision has been made for Rhoda because she's under state jurisdiction. I understand that what there is will go to you.'

'Joan!' The cry from the hall was more than urgent.

'Excuse me.' Heading for the door Joan tried to imagine what coming into money could do for her. Touch-typing lessons would no longer be a problem, and she supposed she would be able to afford a more up-to-date machine. She had only got as far as this when she took in the sight of Granny leaning against one of the hall cupboards looking even older than when she'd left the room. 'Are you all right?' In the background her mother was repeating, 'Where's Bruno, where's Bruno?'

'No I'm not all right. Get me a chair. Oh God . . . and close that door.'

'You're OK, here's the chair. Just lower yourself down into it. I didn't think you even liked my father.'

'It's not him.' Granny was like a rag doll with the sawdust knocked out of it. 'I've got to stand surety. I'll have to find bail. That was Bruno. He's at Bootle Street police station. I'm going to have to go down there to get him out.'

'But what's he done?' cried Joan.

'Don't ask me to tell you, I'm too ashamed. And I can't help feeling I'm to blame.' Granny made to get out of the chair and then sank back again. 'I don't think you'll be able to go back to school, Joan. Not if this gets in the papers. They're very serious charges.'

As Joan put her arms round Granny and held her close, she could hear her mother bawling excitedly in the background: 'I bet young Bruno's somewhere up a tree, Nurse Whelan. He'll be out on his own, he always plays on his own.'

'He *was* always on his own, too.' Granny let out a deep sigh. 'I blame myself, Joan. I blame myself.'

Peter was just finishing his tea when the policeman called. Peggy led him into the kitchen where they were eating rissoles and chips round the little folding table. He was a uniformed policeman and he hadn't taken off his bicycle clips. 'Hello, Eddie,' he said uneasily. The war hero was something of a tarnished local celebrity.

'What's he done this time?' demanded Peggy.

'No, it's not him, it's the lad. Just a query.' For some reason that last word seemed to have left him feeling uncomfortable. 'Is he seventeen yet?'

Again it was Peggy who took control: 'Next month.'

'That makes him still a juvenile. His dad will have to attend with him.'

'Attend where?' Eddie was suddenly straight-backed and looking shocked. 'What's he done?'

'Now it could be nothing,' said the policeman. 'They just phoned through and said could we get him there for tomorrow morning at ten o'clock. It's enquiries, that's all. They just need some help with their enquiries.'

'What sort of bloody enquiries?' Though the question was addressed to the policeman, Eddie's eyes were boring into Peter.

The constable said, 'I couldn't say. It can't be all that much or they'd've come for him themselves. Ten o'clock at Bootle Street, and the detective you want to see is – ' he flipped open his notebook – 'Sergeant Waddilove of the Plain Clothes Division.' This was a name that was guaranteed to make queer blood run cold.

Sleep wouldn't come. Peter was still turning his pillow over and trying to thump it comfortable when every last garage door on Hawksway had rattled shut and the traffic on the main road had died away to nothing. In the silence of the night you could sometimes catch the rhythmic clicking of underground colliery trains. But this distant sound only sneaked into the consciousness of peaceful minds. And Peter's mind was in ferment. He could only hear one thing: he could hear Bruno saying, over and over again, 'Nobody touched anybody.' 'Nobody touched anybody.' 'Nobody touched anybody.'

Once the policeman had climbed onto his bicycle and left, the questions had started. 'What've you done?' 'What have you been up to?' He didn't know for sure so he wasn't saying anything. This hadn't stopped Eddie Bird from shouting that he had a damned good idea, hadn't stopped the ringing cries of 'nancy-boy' and 'queer'.

In the end Peter had escaped upstairs, where he tried to reread Arthur Ransome's *We Didn't Mean to Go to Sea*. Even there Eddie didn't leave him alone. First he pulled the lavatory chain so violently that the rubber knob came off and had to be put back to the accompaniment of more muttered cursing about jessies. Next he marched into Peter's bedroom, turned reproachful eyes on his son and said, 'To think we took you out to dinner with Major Shadwell!'

Great had been the temptation to break the news that the major was as one with Oscar Wilde. But Peter had resisted it. And it was only now that he'd managed to render the thought into a neat sentence. Clever phrases don't come to mind when your head is ringing with 'Nobody touched anybody, nobody touched anybody'.

Somewhere in the far distance a dog began to bark. One of the Alsatians from the police kennels in Oakwood Park? Peter could read the police into everything tonight. And when he finally surrendered himself into a shattered version of sleep, there they were again, in plain clothes, surrounding the edges of all his dreams.

He could smell that evil stench again: the one he'd dreamed the night after Vanda read the cards in Magi House. He'd never smelt it since, but it was here now. And so were emotions which were rising up like dank shadows. Eddie had told him he was bad, bad, bad, to an extent where his supposed sins were assuming personalities, physical shapes. Here a disembodied head with a piglike face, there a single yellow tooth . . .

'I'm not bad,' Peter shouted in his dreams. 'I'm not. And the only reason I didn't say my prayers tonight was because I felt left outside. I felt I'd forfeited all my rights. I've lost touch with you, God. I've lost touch with you!'

The stench cut right out. It was gone. And the whole of Peter's mind was flooded with golden light. And not just his mind was being affected, something was happening to his body. Myriad pairs of arms were embracing him, and they felt as though they belonged to everybody he had ever loved. And now they were carrying him off to that place in the night where sleep refreshes, restores . . . The last thought he could hang onto was: 'There *is* a God, there is. And he's still on my side.'

Bootle Street police station brought Gestapo films to mind.

The handsome white Portland stone building was set around a courtyard which rang to the echo of policemen's voices, and to the noise of the engines of squad cars and Black Marias.

The inside of the police station was full of varnished oak woodwork, until you came to the desks and the brass-handled filing cabinets, which were just cheaply stained pine. And there was nothing to do but look at them. Behind a closed door Eddie was talking to the dreaded Waddilove. Peter had been startled to find that he'd already met the plain-clothes policeman.

Now the boy just sat and waited and began to eavesdrop on the conversation of two uniformed coppers with no helmets on. They were trying to forecast the outcome of a forthcoming table tennis match. For some people life was going on as usual. Just half Peter's attention was on this conversation, the other half was still going over and over Bruno's telephone call of the previous day. It had reached the stage where it was as etched on his mind as the occult eye was burned into Vanda's box. Now he started wondering whether Waddilove had recognised him.

The closed door opened, making Peter privy to the end of the conversation within the interview room. Waddilove, who looked more than ever like a suburban version of Richard Widmark, was saying to Eddie '. . . a woman scorned. We've already got enough to send the bastard down for four years, but she laid this extra bit of information after we'd charged him.' It was all very man-to-man. 'So we're duty-bound to follow it through.' They could have been in a saloon bar. Waddilove's voice changed abruptly: 'Right, you.' He was addressing Peter. 'In here, Bird. Sit.'

I speak to dogs more civilly, thought the boy, who was suddenly thinking of himself as 'the accused'. There was another plain-clothes man leaning against one of the dun-coloured walls. The room had a window covered in the kind of frosted glass you generally found in old bathrooms.

Waddilove sat down opposite Peter. 'We've met before, haven't we? I once had reason to warn you off town.' Eddie was still hovering on the threshold, neither in nor out of the room. Peter was more conscious of his father's presence than he was of the detective's question. 'Remember?' Waddilove didn't wait for an answer. 'One foggy night. We had the launch out on the canal. I don't forget these things.'

Only now did Peter recognise the second policeman. He was the other one from that same night, the one with the heavy eyebrows like the manual master at Barton. This was the detective who'd told him to 'fuck off back to Swinton'. Peter wished, with all his heart, that he had listened to this advice. Their very faces could make you feel guilty about even being alive.

Waddilove, all blond hair and shiny skin, was still trying to stare Peter out: 'You've been at parties at Buxton, haven't you, Bird?'

'Only one party,' he gulped.

'And you ended up in bed with a man called Briggs.'

'Nothing happened.'

'What sort of nothing?'

'That sort.'

'I don't know what you mean. Explain yourself.'

'The sort that ends up in the *Evening News*.'

Waddilove appeared to relax. 'Do you know a lady called Megan Proctor?'

'Yes.'

'She says you and Briggs were like the Babes in the Wood, all tucked up together nicely.'

'We just had to share a bed,' said Peter desperately. 'That's all, we just shared a bed. Ask Valerie Rimmer. It was her party, ask her. She was the one who chose the bedrooms.'

'Look, Peter,' said the other one, 'we know what kind of pervert Bruno Briggs is. Did he try anything on? He's older, he's the one who should have known better. He tried to touch your John Thomas, didn't he?'

'No.' Honesty was shining out of Peter. 'He didn't try anything. Nothing at all. He's not like that.'

'Oh he's "like that" all right,' Waddilove said wryly. 'It just seems you've been bloody lucky.' Glancing across to the other policeman, he rattled out something that could have been in code: 'Stories tally, too circumstantial to stick.'

'We could still have the youth as being in need of care and protection.'

'*No*.' The fear in Eddie Bird's voice was terrible to hear. 'Please lads, no. It's just that he's got in with the wrong lot. But he does know women as well. You heard him mention this Valerie. He does know bints, give him a chance.'

'All right, Eddie,' said Waddilove quietly. 'But only for you.' Now he turned a gaze of deepest contempt on Peter. 'You're bloody lucky your dad's a hero. By God, you're heading down the right road for Borstal! Eddie's right about one thing; you've got yourself involved with scum. Get shut of them – fast. Hear me?' The voice he used to speak to Peter's father was totally different: 'Get him down to the Adelphi lads' club, Eddie. Get him taught boxing. He's your son, so there's got to be a real man in there, somewhere.'

As Vanda crossed St Martin's Lane she had to remind herself that she was made of flesh and blood, that taxicabs could knock you down, and that this was not a dream. She really was in London. She'd only arrived yesterday evening, so this had been the first morning of waking to the unfamiliar sounds of the capital.

She was staying in Soho at the Theatre Girls' Club. Most would-be performers in serious training had heard of this historic establishment; many an eventual star had gone off to her first audition from the ramshackle old building on Greek Street. A highly dubious Mr Adcock had insisted upon telephoning the matron of the club, but once he heard Miss Ross's eminently sane and Scottish tones, he felt reassured enough to advance the money which was financing this adventure.

The girls slept in cubicles known as horseboxes, and they all seemed to wear their hair in ponytails. None of them used handbags, they carried around little vanity cases instead. The atmosphere was very like that of a dancing school, except that there were no classes. You ate and slept there instead.

Straight after breakfast Vanda had begun to explore the actors' square mile. St Martin's Lane was bang in its centre. Once she'd got over the thrill of actually seeing the London

Coliseum and Freed's theatrical shoeshop, she began to wander up a narrow passageway called Cecil Court. It was lined with bookshops; most of them seemed to have some link with the stage: two sold nothing but books about the ballet.

Then she noticed the word 'Magi' on a dustjacket in another bookshop window. And when she looked more closely, the window had a mystical eye painted on it – exactly the same kind of eye as the one on her box.

Vanda's cards were safely stored within her vanity case. As she rested it on the window ledge, something seemed to be almost beckoning to her from between the books. '*Tee-hee*,' giggled the voice within her brain, despite the fact that it had not been bidden to speak. '*Tee-hee, tee-hee*.' The whole display was dotted with packs of tarot cards, none of them in the same design as her own. She would never have believed there could be so many variations.

The packs of cards only served to emphasise a major problem. Something had started that day in Magi House. And she needed to put an end to it. '*Ooo-er!*' went the inner voice.

Yes, you bastard, she thought. I summoned you up and now I've got to get rid of you. And this might be just the shop to tell me how. Except could going in a place like this get her in deeper? The man gazing out over the tops of the books looked harmless enough: thirtyish with greyhound's eyes and lank hair.

When she pushed the door open, a bell let out a very down-to-earth ping. 'Would it be all right if I just had a look round?'

'Feel free.' Though the eyes didn't flicker to her bust she didn't think he was queer; more nothing really. The first shelf Vanda came to was labelled *Vegetarianism*. This immediately made her feel guilty. She was on her way to present herself at Alf Blatt's office so she was wearing her bottle-green coat. Never one to ignore free advice, Vanda had swapped the fur-fabric collar for a bit of real ocelot. She couldn't imagine them approving of that in a vegetarian shop.

But this was an astrology shop too, and a flying saucer shop, and they were also purveyors of Egyptian amulets. These were kept in a low glass case on the counter. They were next to some little wooden tops on pieces of string, described on a handwritten card as 'Pendulums for Divination'.

'Would you happen to know anything about summoning something up?' Feeling that this needed more explanation she said, 'Like a genie out of a bottle. Except it's only a voice.'

'You seem to be describing clairaudience.' Now that she'd got him interested, he seemed to be a much more lively person. 'Are you the clairaudient?'

'I suppose I must be.'

'And did you achieve these results in a group circle, or were you on your own?'

'It was a group,' Vanda said. 'It was all a long time ago. And now I'm on my own and I need to get rid of it.'

'Were any of you pubescent at the time?'

'More or less,' Vanda said.

'Thought so.' The man let out a low whistle. Nothing like a wolf whistle, it made him sound impressed and filled with wonder.

Vanda came right out and said it: 'I want to get rid of him.'

'And the group is disbanded?'

Manchester suddenly seemed a million miles away. 'Yes.'

'Not easy,' he said solemnly. 'Not easy at all. Any banishing ritual would really call for the same people.'

He was so busy being an authority that Vanda felt the need to establish her own credentials. Opening her vanity case she brought out the pokerwork box, lifted the lid and took out the silk-wrapped cards. Folding back the handkerchief she saw her own card, the Sun, was on top.

The sight she'd revealed had caused the man to take one almost superstitious step backwards. 'Have you any idea what you've got there?'

'Tarot cards.'

'It's the design I'm talking about. Those are Black Mendoza's.' They seemed to have made him distinctly uneasy. 'Would you please just wrap them up and take them out of here – we don't have anything to do with the Dark Path in this shop. Please cover them up and go.' One of his own hands had slid inside the glass case on the counter and he was trying not to let her see that he was touching an Egyptian good luck charm.

Feeling a bit like one of the Lancashire witches, Vanda packed up and left. As she got to the top of Cecil Court, she found herself outside a gentlemen's outfitters called West End Misfits. And she supposed that all this had really started on the day when they first got together, that afternoon when the official school outfitter had called them the misfits of 1947. Or had it waited to begin at Magi House?

Either way, there was no chance of it being over until all three of them got together again. And how long would that be? Weeks, months, years? For the moment she had a career to launch, and licking her lips to make them shine Vanda turned into Charing Cross Road and began to look for Alf Blatt's office. The last vestiges of her childhood were over.

7

Land of our birth, our faith, our pride,
For whose dear sake our fathers died,
O Motherland we pledge to thee,
Head, heart and hand, in the years to be.

Joan had been the only one of them left to sing the Barton Grammar School hymn at the leaving service for the year of 1954. Vanda had turned into somebody who was just messages scrawled on the back of picture postcards from a series of provincial touring dates. And Peter? All Joan knew was that Peter's mother and father had had a blinding row which culminated in Mrs Bird taking her son back to Stoke-on-Trent. But why didn't he write?

Bruno's case came to trial and he got four years. Once she left school, Joan Stone was somebody else who started to learn about time. Miss Parr had been quite right; the days began to slide into one another until months sped by in the time that had once taken a week.

It still seemed to take forever to settle her father's estate. Sid Stone might never have amounted to much in Granny Briggs's eyes but he'd been a plodder and a saver who'd always lived quietly in lodgings. And Mr Adcock said that, once an argument over some outstanding debt was settled, Joan would be quite comfortably off: 'Enough for you to think of investing in bricks and mortar.'

Bertram Adcock had first come into their lives at the time of Bruno's trial – Granny had refused point-blank to allow any Eccles solicitor to know of her shame. When Bruno's case came up at the Quarter Sessions the newspapers told the story to the whole world: puzzled sexual experiment was recounted in terms that made Manchester sound like biblical Sodom. And after that, Bruno had refused to put his family through the further indignities of prison visits. He just became somebody else who never put pen to paper.

But life went on and Joan's shorthand and typing lessons were soon earning their own living. She left school with the senior English prize and landed herself a job at the *Eccles Journal*. These were the most boring two and a half years of her life. Local journalism was still at the stage where everything she wrote went through the subeditor's sausage machine and came out to an antiquated formula: 'The usual pleasant time was had at last week's meeting of the Patricroft Methodist Women's Bright Hour. Mrs Stanley entertained with songs at and away from the piano. Refreshments were in the capable hands of Mesdames Glover and Price.' Joan only had to write it like that for the editor to be quite happy.

When she first carried her shorthand reporter's notebook into the local police court, she had imagined she was going to be served up with possible plots for a whole series of novels. But court reporting promised more than it ever delivered. There was a curious sameness to all the motoring and drink-related offences. Peter's father showed up once in the dock and was fined two pounds for being drunk in charge of a bicycle, and Joan wondered whether it had been Peter's old bike. It made her long to hear from him.

A more memorable case was brought against a Mr Herbert George Wallace who was accused of behaviour likely to cause a breach of the peace. A policeman gave evidence that he had been called upon to break up a dispute in Woolworth's between Mr Wallace and an elderly Elim Pentecostalist minister. Noticing the accused examining a pair of patent eyelash curlers, the old pastor had seen fit to deliver an impromptu sermon on the evils of men taking unto themselves the raiment of women. Mr Herbert George Wallace had called the preacher an interfering old cunt. And when a woman customer protested, she had been informed that a night with a sailor wouldn't do her any harm.

Joan recognised the prisoner immediately. Peter had twice pointed him out to her in Manchester. It was the Thief of Baghdad. When the magistrate asked the clerk of the court,

'Anything known?' it took fully five minutes to read out the list of previous convictions.

'I've gone straight,' screamed the accused, who was tiny with big eyes like Hedy Lamarr and a blue chin. 'I've gone straight, well, straight*ish*,' he corrected himself as he smiled winningly at a startled policeman. For all his loud mouth and his petty crimes, there was something buoyant and irrepressible about the Thief of Baghdad, and the magistrates chose to fine him a token ten shillings. The chairman of the Bench even attempted to introduce a little humour of his own. 'Go away and sin no more,' he quoted.

When Joan came out of the court the Thief had not gone away. He was standing on the pavement, underneath a cast-iron lamp bracket. 'Just like Lily Marlene,' was how he chose to put it. 'I've seen you in town with Peter Ladybird. I need a favour.' But before he could explain he was overtaken by fury: 'I hope you noted that nobody charged the Elim Pentecostalist? I hope you wrote that down in your notebook. I was going to *buy* those bloody curlers! Could you fancy a cup of tea in the covered market café?'

There was an underwater quality to this snack bar; it had a frosted-glass roof and everything was painted pale green. The Thief of Baghdad insisted that Joan should sit down while he went up to the counter. When he returned with two slopping cups he said, 'I've just resisted a very grave temptation. There was a slice of slabcake behind one of those little glass windows, it had the word *Lift* on it. But I'm trying to be a good little queen.'

Joan couldn't decide whether he was very wicked or very brave. The Thief was still talking: 'Did Peter ever mention the snowball?'

'No, but I know about it.' Was he going to say something about Bruno next?

He didn't, so he couldn't have been aware of the connection. Instead he announced, 'They hauled me into court for that too, but I got off. Insufficient evidence. That didn't stop Lewis's sacking me. After you with the sugar, dear. Nowadays I've got a nice little job doing windows for the Co-op.' He took so much sugar himself that Joan decided that the gleaming white teeth could only be false. 'But it won't stay a nice little job, not if this morning's campalari gets into the papers. So it's up to you.' The beautiful eyes were pleading and he smelt of old face powder and stale cigarette smoke.

Joan remembered their own awful wait for the newspapers after Bruno's trial, remembered the people who'd crossed over the road to avoid speaking to them. 'OK.' She opened her pad and ripped out the relevant pages. 'Here.' She handed them to him.

'Don't put your pad away. One good turn deserves another. Write down my address. You never know, one day I might be able to do something for you. I'm wonderful at beading and sequining, and my prices are highly competitive.'

Joan wrote down, to his dictation, an address in Monton. 'Are you known as Herbert or George?' she enquired.

'You know bloody well what I'm known as! But the Thief of Baghdad's out of date, I've given myself a new camp name. In future I shall be known as Doris de Vere – the Girl of Many Hands.'

'I thought you'd reformed.'

'So did I. But that piece of slabcake is calling to me, dear. It's literally calling!'

Joan thought she'd better get up and go before she ended up in court herself, as an accomplice. She walked up to Church Street and got her bicycle out of the *Journal* yard. She was due to have lunch with Mr Adcock and he had hinted on the telephone that he might have some news of Vanda Bell.

Bertram Adcock was still partial to the set luncheons at the Ellesmere Cinema café. The decor of the place was unchanged, though the basket chairs were beginning to show their age, and the patterned tablecloths had been laundered many shades paler. Nevertheless his favourite battered haddock was still on the menu, and Joan settled for a Vienna steak and chips. The 'steak' turned out to be a rissole. Two cafés in one morning and both of them crumby!

But the news Mr Adcock had to impart was worthy of the

French Restaurant at the Midland. He began with a question: 'How's the conversion coming along?'

Encouraged at long distance by Herbie Morgenstern, Granny was turning Ingledene into an exact replica of somewhere she'd always hated – the student rooming house next door. The portrait of Flora MacDonald had been sold to pay for Bruno's unsuccessful defence, but one sniff of the auction rooms had given Olive Briggs a taste for capitalising her assets. A Hepplewhite sideboard, some Regency bedroom furniture, a mountain of Georgian silver: all of these and more had been sent off to Capes Dunn in Manchester where they had fetched enough to set her rushing round the house for further saleworthy items.

When Granny got to the bottom of that barrel she had decided to part with a whole lot of stocks and shares. And then in came the builders. 'It's chaos,' said Joan, 'chaos. And the part she's earmarked for us isn't going to be anything like big enough. I'm not kidding, she's in love with partitions.'

'We're handling a very easy estate at the moment.' Mr Adcock reached for the tomato ketchup. 'Nothing like as complicated as your father's.' He seemed as fond of sauce as the Thief of Baghdad had been of sugar. 'The main asset is a very solid little cottage. One of those half-timbered ones on Worsley Green. Needs a few bob spending on it, but you're not going to be short of a few bob.'

As far as Joan was concerned, Worsley Green's main attraction was in its literary associations. Virginia Cowles, the woman who wrote *Michael in Bookland*, had once lived there. Maybe at Worsley she could get down to some of the proper writing Molly Wainwright was still encouraging her to try. 'Say I got the house, could I afford to chuck my job in and try a year of going freelance? I can't write a word at Ingledene. It's nothing but workmen going clatter-bang-crash.'

'What an independent generation you all are! Evelyn, this fish is off,' he called out.

The waitress was old and brawny and looked as though she had been there as long as the fixtures and fittings. 'We wouldn't be daft enough to try and poison a lawyer.' She lifted the plate to her nose and gave it a dubious sniff. 'You

411

should've spoken up before you wasted all that sauce, Mr Adcock. Would you settle for a nice Prem salad? You like Prem.'

'I like it very much. That will do splendidly. I'm a great one for the tried and trusted. But your generation . . .' He was addressing Joan again and she couldn't decide whether he was criticising or acting awestruck. 'Take a look at this.' A plump hand had already gone into his wallet.

'Have I got enough money to try the freelance thing?' she persisted.

'You have.' Out of the wallet he produced a carefully folded press cutting. Maddeningly slowly, he began to straighten it out. 'This comes from a publication called *The Stage*.'

One glance was enough to tell Joan that the newspaper went in for precisely the kind of journalism she was trying to escape. The clipping was a review of a production called *Naughty But Nice*. The show was described as 'an all-glamour spectacle with comedy in the capable hands of Bud ("It Must Have Been the Cat") Entwistle'. Elaine DuBarry was 'that scintillating soubrette'. And the supple dexterity of the Duo Benali was said to have produced gasps from the audience at Collins Music Hall, Islington.

'She's right at the bottom,' murmured Mr Adcock. 'Only at the bottom but at least she's there.' Joan's eyes jumped to the end of the article where she saw the words '. . . not forgetting the alluring nude posing of Vanda Bell the Oriental lovely'. 'But she's not Oriental,' she protested, 'she's from Swinton.'

'I understand there used to be two of them,' said Mr Adcock enigmatically. 'The other one was a Chink. I expect it's a throwback to that.'

'So have you seen her?' cried Joan.

'No, but she writes to me about money. She's much more interested in money than you are.'

Joan suddenly remembered something that Vanda had once told her: Gran'ma Dora had always said they would each want what the other had got. And now Joan came to think about it, she realised that she had always envied Vanda's role of heiress. Oh well, she thought philosophically, I suppose I can afford to admit that now that we're level-pegging.

But Mr Adcock ruined the moment by saying, 'Vanda Bell's out of the chorus and on her way. She's definitely on her way.'

That did it. 'I will have that house,' she announced. 'And give me a year and you'll see somebody else who's on their way.' Except Vanda got Toby and I didn't; that was the bit she would never have been prepared to admit out loud. Neither was she prepared to let go of incautious dreams of finding Toby Eden again.

The Planet Cinema didn't run to usherettes at the matinées. The man with the torch by the velveteen-covered entrance to the auditorium had said, 'Just sit anywhere.' From her seat halfway back in the stalls, Vanda glanced round to see whether any members of the company had also passed in. She kept her clandestine affair very much to herself. No, it was OK – nobody. The lights would soon be dimming and eventually he would join her in the darkness.

For the moment, the only entertainment on offer was a blank screen which kept changing from red to green and back again, to the accompaniment of recorded xylophone music. 'How Much Is that Doggie in the Window?' was followed by 'She Wears Red Feathers'. It was the same tune they had danced on to, in the opening of *Naughty But Nice*, when she'd still been in the chorus. Danced? The other girls were barely trained at all. They could just about manage a few untidy high kicks and some ragged-time steps.

But Alf Blatt had simply shoved Vanda into *Naughty But Nice* to gain experience. 'Keep your eyes skinned,' he'd said. 'Watch everything.' She'd watched all right, she'd watched for an opportunity! And it had come at Nottingham, where one of the *Naughty But Nice* Oriental nudes had run off with a boy from the Goose Fair. The Chow Sisters were half-Chinese and came from Liverpool. The pair of them already had fairground connections; they had appeared as 'The Girls Who Are Strangely Different from All Other Girls' in a sideshow on Blackpool's Golden Mile.

'I can't blame her for going,' Kimi Chow would say of her sister, as she sat in the dressing room reading *World's Fair*. 'It was all much more free-and-easy in the sideshows.'

Strict rules governed the appearance of nudes in revue. For a start they were not allowed to move. Neither were they meant to have pubic hair. A safety razor and a modest strip of sticking plaster were the answer to that. And Vanda had to paint her eyes slanted and Oriental because that's what the posters outside the theatres promised, and they had been printed six months ahead.

When Kimi finally walked out of the show at the City Varieties in Leeds, Vanda was stuck with the slant-eyed make-up because her solo poses were done in front of a painted canvas willow-pattern plate. And her music was very tinka-tonk. Different towns meant different drummers, so the gong rarely sounded in the right place before the second house on a Tuesday night.

In the Planet Cinema, the recorded music faded as a cockerel started crowing on the screen. This heralded the start of the newsreel. And it brought Vanda much closer to her secret assignation. There was still nobody she knew in the cinema. On the screen Grace Kelly was getting married to Prince Rainier. It was all right for some!

But he was on his way to her. And that made the cartoon and the trailers, and the advertising film for Stergene and the slides for the local shops, bearable. Vanda suddenly felt the urge for popcorn. She'd noticed packets of Butterkist on sale at the paybox, and she decided to nip out and treat herself.

When she got back into the cinema he was already there. It really annoyed Vanda to think that she'd missed his arrival. Up on the screen he was having an argument with Gina Lollobrigida. Vanda Bell was deeply and totally in love with Burt Lancaster.

The purchase of Joan's house on Worsley Green was completed long before the builders left Ingledene. The original plan had been that Granny would move into Thistle Cottage with Joan. Now she was dithering: 'You could call the spare bedroom my bedroom and I'll come over and stay with you when I get time.' This would have been satisfactory enough if Granny had not added a rider: 'But I'm not having a girl of twenty living on a busy village green on her own. The best thing to do would be to let it and get the income.'

In the end Joan simply used the cottage as an office during the daytime. She was writing a novel, but that was sacred territory and she refused to talk about it. She was less secretive about the magazine articles she was writing for publications like *Titbits* and *Weekend*. 'Twenty Things You Didn't Know About British Earthquakes' and 'The Truth About the Martyr's Skull' were just a couple of her successes. Joan bought pulp magazines, studied them closely, then tried to come up with ideas that were ahead of the market. It wasn't so much writing as revamping material researched in public libraries.

Molly Wainwright was hugely entertained by these efforts: 'I swear you'd rewrite the Lord's Prayer for four guineas!' Her letters were still sources of great encouragement. And when Joan sent her some first efforts at romantic fiction – short stories aimed at the women's magazines – Molly passed them on to her own literary agent.

He was much too important to think of representing Joan. But one of his young assistants, a girl called May Evans, rang Thistle Cottage and began her conversation with, 'I could never sell a story called "More Than Kisses" to *Woman's Own*. But give it another title and we might be able to get you a start, lower down the fiction market.' She had a breathy and enthusiastic voice and a tendency to boss. But May Evans knew what she was talking about, and she was interested in Joan's talent – she was definitely interested.

The aspiring writer kept office hours during the week, but on Saturday mornings Joan would go into Manchester and buy herself a few treats for the Worsley storecupboard and for her new refrigerator.

It was Miss Parr who had, long ago, introduced all the children to the delights of John Marks in St Ann's Square. This was a grocer's shop on the grand manner. Customers didn't stand at the counter, they sat at little chairs, and they were served by assistants whose snow-white overalls went right down to the ground, just like French waiters. The shop was all polished panelling and high ceilings and delicacies from every corner of the globe.

Joan always waited to be served by Mr Potter, who had known her since she was in a school blazer. 'How's Miss Lathom?' he enquired as he sliced Parma ham into the thinnest wafers. 'We hardly ever see her since she retired. She just phones her orders in.'

'It's the rheumatism. Miss Lathom doesn't get out much these days.'

'She wants to try rubbing herself with neat's-foot oil,' he said as he began to pack Joan's groceries into a stout brown paper carrier bag. 'It's an old remedy. You'll get it at any tripe shop.'

Joan always felt slightly guilty about dealing at John Marks. It was dearer than anywhere else. But the items she bought from her earnings were meant to act as carrots, meant to keep her donkeying on for an extra couple of hours each day.

Neat's-foot oil: if she could spoil herself, she could buy a present for Miss Lathom. Joan got a number 19 bus for Pendleton, where there was still a branch of UCP – United Cattle Products. But the bottle of oil looked so gooey and repulsive that she had to search Broad Street for a potted plant to go with it.

Joan spent the next bus ride counting off the flowers on the potted begonia. 'I'll find Toby again, I won't find him, I'll find him again, I won't . . .' By the time she reached Ravensdale Estate the plant had told her that her search would not be in vain. But did a bud really count?

The garden of Miss Lathom's house was much changed. The familiar riot of cottage flowers had been replaced by flat concrete. Just a few terracotta pots had new-looking shrubs planted up in them. 'I can hardly bear to look at it,' Grace Lathom said after she opened the front door. 'But the thing is, it looks after itself.' As she limped up the hall, she added, 'I'm not having a very good day. They talk about sending a man to the moon yet they can't find a cure for rheumatoid arthritis.'

'I've brought something that might help.' Joan had

followed her into the sitting room. This was as cheerfully welcoming as ever – Miss Lathom had always inspired great devotion in her cleaners.

'Everybody's coming up with remedies.' She lowered herself, with difficulty, into one of the chintz-covered armchairs. These days there were two extra cushions on the seat. 'I don't mean to sound ungrateful,' she grunted. 'The latest brainwave to arrive through the post was wax-filled gloves!'

'Is it in your hands again?'

'It's everywhere. And Dr Moult's painkillers make me feel as though I'm thinking through fog. Enough, enough, enough! Have you been sent one of these?' She had reached across to the occasional table by her chair and was holding out a glossy photograph of Vanda Bell posing between two ostrich-feather fans. 'Inflaming passion must be a very odd occupation! Oh well, she's a good girl, she never fails to write.'

This kind of statement invariably led to conjecture about Peter. Not, it seemed, today. Pointing towards the bottle of oil Grace Lathom said, 'It was most kind of you to think of me, and the plant is beautiful.' Most unusually, she seemed to have gone off into a daydream.

'Come back,' joked Joan.

'Sorry, my dear. I was wondering whether to tell you something . . . I've finally had a card from Peter. That long silence hurt. I can't pretend it didn't. But I think he must have been having some sort of struggle with himself. The message was just "Love from Peter". But the picture on the front of the card might have been a clue as to how he's resolved it.'

Joan was all eagerness: 'What was it?'

'On the other hand I could be quite wrong.' The headmistress in Miss Lathom always let you know when you weren't meant to ask further questions. 'I know that half a story is absolutely infuriating and you will just have to blame it on Dr Moult's woozy-pills.' She had recently grown very much older in every way; her crew cut was almost white. 'I have such a job with the buttons on my smock,' she grumbled. 'Here he comes, the Phantom of The Opera!' Henry had burst into the room and was showering Joan with licks. 'Have you moved into your little house yet?'

'Granny's still being funny about me being there on my own.'

'I might just have the answer . . .' Grace Lathom looked like somebody who was sorry she'd started saying something.

'Is this going to be another half-story?' laughed Joan.

'Quite possibly.' She had always been capable of sudden hauteur. Now she relented as she said, 'Two young girls and both of you of independent means. I find the whole idea quite extraordinary.'

'The thing I find extraordinary is that I know nothing about my father. Nothing. There isn't so much as a snapshot in existence. Why on earth did he leave everything to me? I could have meant no more to him than the dogs' home!'

'Please don't mention that word in front of Henry. It's where he came from and they never forget. Oh dear . . .' Tears were falling. 'Joan, it's lovely of you to try to hug me but don't. It hurts too much. It's right in my shoulder, like toothache.'

The tears continued to roll unchecked. 'I took Henry down into the field this morning, and he was in a boisterous mood and pulled me over. And I had to wait till Mrs Mottershead came by with Scamp before I could get up. And Henry was so good . . . he didn't run away at all. He just stood there with his lead dangling and his head on one side, looking puzzled.' She fished in her pocket and produced a handkerchief. Wiping her face she said, 'Mr Bird tries to do what he can, but he never wakes up until midday, and that's too long for a dog. Whatever am I going to do?' All this had caused Henry's head to go to one side again.

'You want me to have him, don't you?' said Joan.

'It's not what I want at all. But I have to admit, I did just wonder . . .'

'I'd have him like a shot. I've always loved him, we all did. And there'd be the green for his walks.'

'I feel like a blackmailer,' sniffed Miss Lathom as she set to again with the sodden handkerchief. Her distress cued Henry to climb up onto her knees. Pain or no pain, she hugged the middle-aged retriever. 'Maybe your grandmother *would* let you live there with him for company? But Joan, if you are going to have him, could you take him today? I couldn't bear to live with it hanging over me. You see he's the last of "us".'

And again she broke down, just about managing to say, 'I'll send you both home in a taxi. But you will remember to sing to him inside the car, won't you? Otherwise he gets himself worked up.' She was still holding Henry close and he was licking her swollen fingers. 'It's finally come to it,' she said. 'This is old age with a vengeance.'

Vanda saw a lot of Burt that autumn. *Trapeze* was showing in every other town they visited. And when *Naughty But Nice* returned to London, for a week at the Metropolitan Theatre of Varieties on the Edgware Road, Vanda found herself not far from Baker Street, where the Classic Cinema was having a Burt Lancaster retrospective season.

The posters for *Naughty But Nice* had finally been reprinted. She appeared on them twice. Once as Vanda Bell, with 'Little Miss Sex Appeal' in brackets underneath, and again as La Shalimar ('Queen of Fans'). She'd pinched the name from the label on her best scent bottle, and she just hoped that Guerlain weren't having a fit about it in Paris.

That six-day Burt Lancaster season caused Vanda to question what she wanted from the film star. It was a straight case of the same old story: she wanted him to be her pal. Life on that tatty tour was curiously friendless. As Vanda's role in the show became more prominent, the other girls grew wary of her. And the men only wanted one thing. It was creaking Jack Vesta who said, 'You've not got the right kind of come-hither with those fans. There's never been a virgin yet who could twirl them convincingly.'

It was an old line, though she didn't know it. What Vanda did know was that she wasn't about to jump into bed with a dilapidated failure who had nicotine-stained fingernails. She had always aimed high, and if anybody was going to get her hymen it would be Burt. But Vanda Bell's strong streak of common sense told her that this was just a dream which had

419

grown up in cinemas scented with Zoflora disinfectant. And yet . . . striptease was said to be very big in America. It was the home of the queen of them all, Gypsy Rose Lee.

What's more, Vanda could afford the trip to the United States; her inheritance had remained virtually untouched. She lived out of her pay packet. And these days, every Saturday night, it contained almost seven pounds. While straight actors were paid on a Friday, variety artistes didn't get a farthing until they'd finished their last show of the week – in case they decamped.

Should she set sail for America? There was only one way to find out: she would have to consult the cards.

Vanda's digs for that week at the Met were down a side street near Paddington Station. The building had a flaking stucco frontage, and inside the house the stairwell was lined with fading, signed theatrical photographs. False smiles which had been frozen forever, at a time when the bob and the shingle and the ukulele had still been in fashion, were now sealed under flyblown glass, with black passe-partout edgings. And Vanda didn't recognise one single name. It was for all the world like the staircase of lost dreams.

But I always make mine come true, she thought as she let herself into a room dominated by a drunken-looking brass bedstead. Her vanity case was on the washstand, next to the jug and basin. Through the cream Nottingham lace curtains she could see trains, three floors below, rattling to and from the West Country. It's a glamorous life, she thought grimly as she unlocked the vanity case to see whether the tarot cards could offer her a brighter future.

As Vanda opened the box with the all-seeing eye, she realised just how much she had grown to hate the pack of Black Mendoza's. But she knew she was stuck with them until such time as she could get together with Joan and Peter again. She was always telling herself that she had consulted the tarot for the last time, and forever running back to it in times of crisis. Even the sliding sound the cards made as she shuffled them filled her with renewed guilt. 'I only want to ask you one question,' she said aloud. 'One card for one answer. What are my chances with Burt?'

She closed her eyes to make her choice and opened them again to discover that the card she'd picked was the most unusual one of all – it was completely blank. And inside her head Mr Midget began to sing 'Little Dolly Daydream'.

'OK I can't have Burt!' She actually shouted it at the ugly flowered wallpaper. 'But I'll have my other dreams. I'll be the biggest. I'll be the best.' Three floors down another train rattled along the track. 'That's right, bugger off to Cornwall,' she bawled after it. And then she started wondering what the landlady must be making of all the noise. The woman might even imagine that Vanda had got a man in her room.

And if she had to go to bed with one to get good at her job, she'd do that too. *Trapeze* had haunted her life for so many months that it would have to be an acrobat. Vanda's mind was already examining the outline of one of the Duo Benali, the acrobatic speciality act in *Naughty But Nice*.

Telephone in hand, Joan was practically dancing with worry and impatience. 'I thought you were never going to answer, Granny. Listen, I'm at Worsley and I'm going to have to stay . . .' Yet again she peeped through the hall window but to no avail. 'Miss Lathom gave me Henry and he's done a bunk. He's been gone three hours already. She thinks he might be heading back there. We're going frantic.'

Dusk was beginning to fall outside. October meant that it was getting dark earlier and earlier, and tonight the clocks were due to go back an hour. A white streak sped across the green, but Joan had been deceived by that once before: it was only the poodle belonging to awful June Gee from next door. Where could Henry be? She'd already rung the police station twice.

Oh but he was an artful little soul! Henry had allowed himself to be led into Thistle Cottage, eaten a good dinner, and then bold as brass he had marched up to the front door, lifted a paw to the latch and bolted. It had been quite a cheerful bolt; he had even paused at the corner where the houses ended to wag his tail.

How could he sniff his way back to Hawksway when they'd come by taxi? Joan had been stuck with this same thought ever since he'd vanished, but Miss Lathom had said, 'He will, you'll see. I know my Henry.' She had sounded more guilty than worried.

Joan didn't dare ring her again; she didn't know what to do. And the lost dogs' home were not answering their telephone. She wandered back into the kitchen and cut herself a piece of the game pie she'd bought at John Marks. But worry made the first mouthful seem to grow enormous and she had a job to swallow it.

It was no use, she would have to go to bed. And because of the clocks the night was going to be an hour longer than usual. One last call to Miss Lathom, another to the police, and then she flung herself on top of the striped mattress of one of the divans she'd bought with Granny at an auction. Joan hadn't got round to bringing bedding over from Ingledene, so the only thing she could use to cover herself was a tartan travelling rug which normally disguised a battered armchair.

Her dreams were full of the white dog with the tan mask. His bright eyes were shining and he was barking his head off. As Joan struggled to get more comfortable on the itchy mattress, the barking increased. Except this couldn't be a dream because next door's poodle was joining in the chorus. Henry was outside in the garden – he'd come back.

Joan opened the front door to a vision of filthy dirty good cheer. Oh but he was pleased to see her! Lavish licks, quick corkscrew twists in the air, an eager dive for his dinner bowl . . . The only thing to do was to telephone Miss Lathom. She never slept soundly at the best of times so Joan knew the call would be welcomed. 'He's back,' she said. 'He's here and he's drunk about a gallon of water.'

'Praise God!' cried Miss Lathom. 'I've been praying to St Anthony and St Francis since teatime. Now I feel so much better about having let him go.' Her voice took on much more serious tones: 'You know what this means, don't you? Henry could easily have found his way back here. This means that he has chosen you for himself.'

On his afternoon off from the college, Peter could either strike out for Huddersfield or for Dewsbury. There was little to choose between the two Dale towns. The bus would wind its way between bleak expanses of moorland, which could not have changed since the Victorian landscape painters had depicted the tumbledown dry-stone walls and the flocks of aimless sheep. Even the mist on the crags managed to look as though it was waiting for Landseer to return. And the grandiose mills that heralded the outskirts of Dewsbury had been there since the great days of the wool trade.

The town was blessed with excellent if old-fashioned shops. Peter couldn't even begin to afford the fine tweeds and handmade shoes on display in their windows, but he could still admire them as he made his way downhill towards Bennett's, the second-hand bookseller's. En route he had to pass a junk shop, and right in the middle of the window was an item that could have come right out of his own past. In fact he could even have been the very person who'd painted the black ermine tails onto the coronation souvenir plaque.

It was late in the afternoon; children were already flooding out of the schools. And many of them were heading for newsagents and toyshops because today was November the fifth.

Peter was still gazing through the murky window at the plaque and his mind went back to evenings spent round the table at Ted Sterling's. And to Norma Oldham and her swanky cousin, and to terrible Megan Proctor. But most of all they went back to Bruno. That was a youthful passion which had been effectively destroyed by shockwaves.

Memories of Bootle Street police station still haunted Peter's dreams. And, strictly speaking, they *had* broken the finer letter of the law. But Peter had got away with it and Bruno hadn't. This filled him with guilt. That was the reason he couldn't bring himself to write to Joan Stone. And because he didn't write to her, he didn't feel he could get in touch with Vanda. Even thinking about it weighed him down with care as he hurried along the street towards Bennett's.

Percival Bennett had first come into his life in the Café Royal, where Peter had vaguely registered him as a fringe member of the Gin and Tonic Brigade: many men had felt it safer to cross into another county to meet fellow homosexuals. These days Peter knew him well enough to address him by name, but he always called him Mr Bennett. This wasn't, strictly speaking, deferential – more a barrier against any attempts at pouncing.

Mr Bennett was small and fat with little white dimpled hands. He also had wildly rolling eyes and a hank of hair plastered across a balding head. When he spoke his voice sounded like Yorkshire-and-elocution. 'I've found you a copy of *The Heart in Exile*. Been keeping it. Half a crown and still got its dustjacket.'

The main reason Peter worried about the pouncing was because the shop was down steep steps, and he would have a job getting out unscathed. It wasn't that Mr Bennett had ever tried to touch, but everything he said contained leering innuendo. He could make words like 'big' and 'throbbing' sound positively obscene.

Today he came in from another angle. As he handed over the novel and dropped Peter's half-crown piece into a metal cashbox, Percy Bennett said, 'Why do you never come in on a Thursday? I could run you over to the Turkish baths in Manchester. Normal people have no idea what's going on underneath Sunlight House!'

Manchester was Peter's past. And he couldn't help feeling that if he ever crossed the city boundaries Sergeant Waddilove would be waiting for him. 'I have lectures on Thursday afternoons.'

'You don't know what you're missing!'

I do, thought Peter as he climbed up the stone steps into the darkening streets. I do, and it's not love. Mind you, it could lead to love . . . His thoughts were interrupted by an early rocket, climbing into the sky and exploding into a cluster of stars.

It was cold, so he began to hurry along the pavement. He was still wearing that Donegal tweed overcoat, the one he had worn to launch himself on the Café Royal. All that seemed in another existence when he compared it with what he was doing these days. His mother had first been startled and then highly dubious about his plans for his life. 'Are you sure it's not just a passing phase?' she had asked. But it wasn't. Of that he was certain.

Outside the Empire Theatre, electric light bulbs were already shining in the glass-fronted display cabinets at either side of the padlocked entrance. These showcases were filled with posters for a production called *Naughty But Nice* and with photographs of its 'stars'. Peter had only paused because there was a picture of two men, stripped to the waist. They were called the Duo Benali. One was like a walrus-moustached Edwardian wrestler, but the other was young and blond and handsome, with a spectacularly defined chest.

Peter's attention was suddenly distracted by the sight of a photo of Vanda Bell, wearing nothing but a smile and a strategically placed hand. With no clothes on, her waist was much smaller than he remembered. But – goodness – she was top-heavy!

If her photograph was here, presumably she could eventually be found in the locked theatre. Now he came to examine the display more closely, there was another picture of her too. But the black wig and the name La Shalimar were obviously meant to kid you that it was somebody else.

Should he try going round to the stage door? No. In their final year together at Barton, it had to be admitted that he'd grown closer to Joan than to Vanda. And as he wasn't writing to one, how could he call on the other? Yet still he lingered in front of the showcase, by now quite oblivious to the attractions of the muscleman. It would be good to see Vanda again . . .

No. His original argument against it was insurmountable. It was a pity, but that was going to have to be that. Loud bangs were going off in the distance and he could already smell fireworks. He could taste them too, and this made Peter realise that he was thirsty. Just past the theatre he had often noticed a scruffy café, up a side street. But when he got there it was too scruffy, so he decided to contain his thirst until he found somewhere a bit more civilised.

Had Peter Bird but ventured through the door of the Kit-Kat Café the first person he'd have seen would have been Vanda Bell. She was sitting at a Formica-topped table with big blond Alan Tate, the young man whose photograph Peter had just been admiring. Alan Tate bore a faint – a very faint – resemblance to Burt Lancaster. That's what had first given Vanda the idea.

With no knowledge of her designs upon him, the young tumbler was explaining why they had to go Dutch. 'The thing is, there's me and me dad in the act . . .' he said.

For all the Duo Benali's exotic name, he had a marked Lancashire accent. 'But there's four mouths to feed. I might have taken over from Uncle Al but he's still driving for us. And me mother expects to be paid for diving on and off with the apparatus.' The climax of their act involved Alan revolving around on his father's head. It was Mrs Tate who burst onto the stage, in a time-defying make-up, spangled leotard and mended fishnet tights, to hand over the metal headplate.

'I certainly wouldn't expect you to buy me my egg and chips, Alan.' Life on tour, she reflected, was all something-and-chips and tinned processed peas. Landladies were meant to provide three meals a day, but what you got was rarely enough – not when you were performing in a twice-nightly revue.

The Duo Benali had circus connections so they toured in their own caravan. 'I wouldn't be doing this if I wasn't born into it,' grumbled Alan. 'It gives me nothing. Nothing at all.'

'It's given you a beautiful body.' She wasn't having him downgrading that. She had definite designs on his physique. Emotions didn't enter into it: there had been more snide talk about 'the virgin stripper' from the girls backstage. When it came to her career, nothing was too much trouble for Vanda Bell, and she always had to have the best. 'Do your mother and father ever go out in the afternoon?' she enquired. Theatrical landladies were dead set against men in bedrooms, and a caravan would afford definite privacy. Only would it rock? This was the one thing about losing her virginity that was worrying Vanda Bell. Would the caravan rock?

'Joan?' It was Granny on the telephone and she sounded out of control. 'Has he been there?'

'Who?' Joan had slept late that Saturday morning; she still had her breakfast toast under the grill.

'Bruno.'

The name acted on Joan like smelling salts: suddenly she was wide-awake. 'Bruno? Don't tell me he's gone and broken out of prison?'

'Don't be so stupid.' Distressed or not, Olive Briggs could still be scathing. 'Apparently he got remission, for good behaviour. They let him out first thing this morning. He's been here and I just wondered whether he'd come to you.'

'He doesn't even know the address. Shut up, Henry.' The dog had begun to bark excitedly.

'He does have your address because I gave it to him. Oh dear . . .'

'Granny, I can smell toast burning and there's somebody ringing the bell. All right, Henry, I hear it, I hear it. I'll call you back,' she said into the receiver.

And again the front doorbell went. Whoever it was had obviously never owned a dog. Henry's barking rose to a crescendo and through the wall Mrs Gee's poodle joined in.

'I'm coming,' bawled Joan. If it was the postman with a rejected manuscript from May Evans, he was going to get a piece of her mind. The bolts were still locked and drawing back the bottom one she nicked her thumb. 'All this and blood too,' Joan grumbled as she opened the door.

Outside on the step, with the milk in his hand and a little suitcase at his feet, stood Bruno. 'It sounds just like a dogs' home,' he said.

'You mustn't say that.' She flung her arms round him. 'It's supposed to get Henry upset.' She was crying herself but they were happy tears. 'I'm sorry,' she sniffed, 'but it's all such a shock. Give me that bottle and bring your case inside.' As he handed over the milk she noticed his chewed fingernails – that was something new.

'What's burning?'

'Oh God, the toast! Come into the kitchen. The coffee's already bubbling.'

'Real coffee.' He sniffed appreciatively. 'The best thing

about being out is the smells. Did you know that prison smells of dry cleaning?'

'Let's have a good look at you.' He was pale, but she would have expected the haircut to be worse. Henry was already offering Bruno a paw. They seemed to have taken to one another with remarkable speed. Joan began to pour the coffee. 'Still black with no sugar? Granny's just been on the phone.'

'Strong words have been exchanged.' He took the mug. 'Actually, I do have sugar these days. Thanks. Nothing would persuade me to live at Ingledene again, nothing. She's turned the place into a bloody dosshouse.'

'Have you come to live with me?' Joan asked eagerly.

'You'd have me, too.'

She was surprised to see the beginning of tears in his eyes. 'Are you OK?' she asked him.

'I'm too near the surface. Traffic makes me jump.' Bruno stroked the dog. 'May I open the back door?'

'You can *have* the back door! Say you'll come and live here.'

'Don't be too kind to me or I *will* weep.'

'Maybe you need to. Come and look at the cottage. OK, Henry, you can come too.' Joan led the way across the hall. 'This is the sitting room.' Following Granny's example Joan had developed a passion for auctions, and the room was furnished with chairs covered in Victorian needlework. There was more cross-stitch in the framed samplers that hung on the wall. 'Too twee?'

'What the fuck else could you do with a stockbroker-Tudor cottage?'

Joan reflected that he'd never used that word before he went to prison. 'Want to see the bedrooms?'

'No. Even that log fire's tempting me to stay. I walked through Ellesmere Park this morning . . .'

Joan didn't try to say anything because he had obviously paused to weigh his words.

Out they came. 'The people who did force themselves to speak were practically dripping with Christian charity.'

'We went through a lot of that at the time of the trial.'

'Yes, I heard all about it from Granny, in her lodging

house.' There was bitterness in his voice. 'Well, nobody's going to have to go through any more. I'm off. What happened to Peter Bird?'

'They did a moonlight. They're supposed to have gone to Stoke-on-Trent. I think Mrs Bird wanted to start a new life.' Henry growled but Joan could see that it was only the postman coming up the path.

'I can't stay around here,' said Bruno, 'I can't. When I was little there was a man in Patricroft who went to prison for what I did. I never knew him, but I knew his name, everybody knew his name. Dobson. I'm not hanging around here to be the new Dobson.'

'Where will you go?'

'Does it matter?' There was an awkward pause. 'The dog's nice.' He put down his cup. 'Thanks for the coffee.'

When he had gone, Joan was left wondering why he had ever bothered to come at all. Except, in her heart of hearts, she knew. Bruno had only sought her out to try to get news of Peter. But at least it proved that he wasn't completely dead inside.

Write Your Troubles Away: this had always been Joan's motto. And the post had brought a cheque from May Evans who had managed to sell another of Joan's stories to *The People's Friend*. Now, it seemed, their editor was interested in the idea of Joan attempting a three-part serial. But first he had asked for an outline.

This took Joan until lunchtime. She had never got round to buying a new typewriter. She always drafted her work in pencil, and then she used the Bar-let Portable to turn it into typescript. Once the story outline was in an envelope, Joan felt the need to speed it on its way. By now she would have missed the Saturday morning post, but at least she could get it into the pillar box.

As Henry led her round the green, she supposed that the houses *were* just stockbroker-Tudor. But they were already over a hundred years old, each little row was in a different style, and time had gnarled them into something romantic. Or should that romantic have a 'k' to prove their Victorian associations? The fact that the cover was on the typewriter did not mean that words were leaving her alone. She was already experimenting with dialogue for *The Heart Has Its Hiding Place* – the serial outlined within the envelope in her hand.

'*I have always loved him, Jenny,*' she said. '*Loved him from the first day I saw him.*' At that precise moment Joan noticed the man leaning against the parapet of the humpback bridge over the canal. It was Toby Eden and he was throwing stones into the water.

'Hello,' he called out.

'Hello.' Henry was already tugging her towards the bridge where he always paused to lift a leg. 'You don't look very cheerful,' she said to Toby.

'I don't feel very cheerful.'

'Why?' The sight of him had set her heart singing like somebody in one of her own stories.

'You couldn't by any chance lend me five hundred pounds?' asked Toby jokingly.

Yet she could tell that he really meant it, so she chose to answer the question seriously. 'I'm not without money,' she said. Joan Stone was not to know that this was the most dangerous statement she had ever made.

The caravan did rock.

And that ceiling could do with a coat of paint, thought Vanda. Is this it, is this what all the fuss is about? Had she but comprehended the finer details beforehand Vanda would have chosen somebody who weighed a bit less. Now she knew what the chorus girls meant when they talked about being hammered into the mattress.

The ceiling apart, Alan's mother had turned the home on wheels into a gypsy palace. If Vanda had a criticism, it was that Mrs Tate had been a bit heavy-handed with the silk fringing. Dear God, when would this huffing and puffing stop?

Still, it was nice to think that Burt was a kind of godfather to these proceedings. Alan's family had finally got round to going to see *Trapeze*; that's why the caravan could be used as a temporary love nest. Not that love had anything to do with it.

430

Vanda about rated the experience with dyeing her hair – it was simply meant to effect a change in her stage persona.

Everybody had said it would hurt, and it did. She felt as though she was being invaded by a clothes peg. The first part had been the worst, the part where he'd gone at her bosom like somebody trying to eat two ice-cream cornets at the same time. 'Just do as much of that as is strictly necessary,' she'd said. The funny thing was that she'd heard her mother in her own voice. Would this jabbing, jabbing, jabbing never end? 'Alan? Are you sure you've not missed something out?' Vanda could have been talking about assembling an item which had been delivered packed flat.

'Just a minute, just a minute . . . a, a, ah, aah.' He collapsed on top of her like someone doing a belly-flop into a swimming pool. She only hoped that those Durex things were as reliable as the pharmacist had promised her.

'You're wonderful,' he said.

He was a nice enough lad, there could be no denying that. Only it didn't take long for him to get his breath back and for those hands of his to start stroking her again. 'That'll be all, thank you.' Whatever did people see in it? 'I've got cramp,' she lied. 'I need to get off the bunk.'

As Vanda struggled into her knickers he smiled happily and said, 'When I watched you from the side of the stage I never thought I'd get to touch.'

'Then we've both done one another a favour.'

'Don't put your clothes on, come back to bed for a cuddle.'

She could now see why blokes called that peg thing their old man. It was getting visibly wrinkled before her eyes. 'I've got to nip to the cobbler's for my white peeptoes.' The private part of him might look old but his face was younger than she had ever seen it. No wonder some of the cast still called him Baby Benali.

He was watching, fasincated, as she leant over to get herself into her brassière. 'I'd no idea you felt the same way about me,' he smiled. 'If you're not careful you'll get me going again.'

I mustn't let him see the suspenders a second time, thought Vanda. She knew from stage experience that they were a sure-fire aphrodisiac, so she just stuffed her suspender belt and her stockings into her handbag. Less than twenty seconds later she was already dressed for off and running a comb through her fringe.

'Is something wrong?' he asked.

'No.'

'After the second house tonight we might just be able to snatch a quick drink. And then it's only ten minutes and you're up on the moors.'

'Get one thing straight.' These days her lipstick went on in three neat strokes. 'That jump was a one-off. And if I never do it again it'll be too soon. I got sick of the cracks about the virgin stripper.' She was still looking at herself in his mother's hanging mirror – she couldn't see that the events of the afternoon had effected any visible change.

'So you just used me.' Still naked and sprawled across the bunk, it was Baby Benali's turn to gaze up at the ceiling. 'Plenty of girls want this body, you know, plenty.'

'Good for them.' She headed for the door. With her hand on the handle she added, 'I can't pretend to know a lot about these things, but I suspect you should develop a bit of finesse.' Having delivered this review of his performance Vanda stepped out into the daylight of Dewsbury.

The caravan was parked on some wasteland by the theatre. As she made her way towards the cobbler's she reflected that, under a pink spotlight, her instinctive knowledge of sex was of far more use to her than anything she'd learned from the actual act. Yet, come to think of it, snatched sexual intercourse had unlocked something surprising and hidden. And it wasn't something she wanted to dwell upon. No, she didn't want to dwell on it at all. Still, the events of the afternoon would be something to drop into the conversation, backstage. In fact she felt like telling somebody about it right now. She felt the need to discuss the whole thing with another woman. That was when she spied the red public telephone kiosk.

Vanda belonged to the generation that regarded long-distance telephone calls as an event in themselves. You had to get through to the operator and, if you were in a box, you needed to have the exact change ready. 'Are you there, caller? The number is ringing for you now.' Joan Stone wouldn't be shocked but she would almost certainly be jealous, so the experience wouldn't be entirely wasted.

'Swinton 4500,' said Joan's voice at the other end. Worsley residents were always complaining about being lumbered wtih Swinton numbers.

'It's me.'

Vanda phoning in the afternoon when it was still the expensive rate? 'Just a minute.' Joan threw a rubber bone out into the hall, Henry bounced after it and she closed the door on him. 'If he hears your voice, he'll want to go through all that growling-into-the-receiver routine.'

'I've only got three minutes.' Vanda sounded a long way off. 'I've just done it.'

'Done what?' Light dawned: the three of them had often sat on the school wall discussing doing *it*. 'You haven't! Was it very, very wonderful?'

'I got more thrill out of staying upright on my first two-wheeler bike.'

Henry was already scratching to be let back in. 'Perhaps it wasn't true love, Vanda.' But she was bursting to ask something else: '*Did* it hurt?'

'Only at first. But you should hear the noise it makes!'

Henry was also making a noise. 'It's no use, he must know who it is. I'll have to let him in.' She opened the door and the retriever put his paw on the flat part of the Welsh dresser and tried to get his head to the phone. 'He'll have to speak to you.' This was one of Henry's party-pieces: he made two growling sounds which could just about be taken for 'hello' at the other end.

'Tell you what,' said Vanda. 'That's cheered me up more than sex did.'

She seemed disinclined to discuss the matter further. She wouldn't even tell Joan the man's name. They just swapped odd bits of news until the trunk-call operator interrupted: 'Do you wish to pay for further time?'

'I've paid enough for this afternoon,' laughed Vanda Bell.

'Vanda, you never *bought* it?'

'It cost me sausage, egg and chips.' The line went dead. The operator had cut them off.

Joan returned to her interrupted task of sorting through today's manuscript pages before putting them in the safe. She had once written an article for the *Weekly News* which listed the items that famous people had said they would grab in a fire. She never got to talk to the celebrities, she just culled the information from their agents. But when the piece was typed up Joan had asked herself the same question. The answer came back loud and clear: in a fire she would grab Henry and the manuscript of her novel, *Sweet Mignonette*.

That was when she'd bought the fireproof safe, for four pounds, at Shawcross's Auction Rooms in Eccles. Everybody had been highly amused at her paranoia, but it hadn't been long before both Granny and Toby Eden had come to see the sense of the small cast-iron cupboard. In fact Joan was now custodian of Granny's mother's engagement ring and her opal necklace ('So many strangers at Ingledene these days'). She was also minding some dubious diamond shirt studs, which Toby had accepted as security against a gambling debt.

'I feel just like a pawnbroker,' she said as they tried to settle on a number for the combination lock. 'I'm hopeless at figures. I'm bound to forget it.'

'Use your phone number,' suggested Toby, 'you can't forget that.'

She had seen a lot of Toby Eden since she had lent him the five hundred pounds. Mr Adcock had been very dubious as to the wisdom of this loan. The people who only counted Toby's sins were the ones who were immune to his attraction; he was like an educated Irish gypsy, even though he was related to aristocratic Anthony Eden. And you only had to walk down the street with him to realise how attractive he was to other women. Queers would turn round too, and Peter had always assured her that they didn't give a second glance to anybody who was less than stunning.

As for Vanda Bell's claims that sex was a big swizz, Joan could only imagine that her friend must have gone at it like a clog dance. She knew, from her own experience, that Toby's kisses raised desires which were blocked by only one thing –

her lightly padded brassière. 'Undetectable' was the maker's claim. But it wouldn't be undetectable when it went thudding over the end of the bed. Thoughts of this eventual moment of truth always caused Joan's blood to run cold. But that telephone call from Dewsbury was drawing the moment nearer; the Sun was no longer a virgin, so the Moon would have to follow suit.

Vanda always got to the theatre a good hour before the curtain was due to rise. Other people only had to make up their faces, she had to paint her whole body. And because she spent so long in grubby, inhospitable dressing rooms, she travelled with a sheeting cover for the dressing table and another one to go between herself and the chair.

The first thing she had to do was remove every stitch of clothing. This was to allow any marks made by elastic to subside. Wandering around in a cotton housecoat, Vanda would cut the evening's piece of sticking plaster to size, then she would give her bust the cold sponge treatment. The water often had to be brought in a bucket from a tap on the landing. But her bosom was money in the bank, and the icy sponges were meant to make her capital last for as long as possible.

She always painted her body before she touched her face. Kimi Chow had taught her to use a weak solution of decorator's distemper, in a shade known as Armenian Bowl. But sinister stories about premature withering caused Vanda to change to a bottled preparation made by Leichner. Phyllis Dixey was always said to use a secret formula, based on ground silk.

Not only did every striptease artiste have to satisfy the official censor, the Lord Chamberlain, but each town had its own watch committee. On two occasions Vanda had successfully defended accusations of indecency by claiming that the Elastoplast and the paint meant that she was not totally naked. Oh there were so many rules! The ostrich-feather fans were not meant to reveal her breasts until the climax of the act, when she was obliged to freeze like a statue. She imitated classical statues again in the posing routines. Even on an awful night when a rat ran across the stage, Vanda had still had to go on pretending to be a plaster cast.

It was always difficult to be sure that the make-up was smooth on the middle of her back. She peered over her shoulder, looked into the mirror and said to her own reflection, 'That's the most I'm doing for a dump like Dewsbury.' Somebody was knocking at the dressing-room door. 'Who is it?' she called out. 'I've only just finished stoning the steps, I'm not dry.'

'It's Alma Tate.' She might think of herself as Alma but the rest of the company called her Old Mother Benali.

'Come in,' called out Vanda. As the middle-aged woman entered Vanda added, 'If you see anything you've not seen before, throw a towel at it.'

Mother Benali wore nearly as much make-up off the stage as she did for a performance. And her bunny-rabbit coat was dyed almost exactly the same shade of blue-black as her great mass of frizzy hair.

'What can I do for you?' asked Vanda.

Mother Benali held out a clenched hand and then opened it. 'Yours I believe.' Two kirby grips were lying across her palm. 'You can't expect a mother to be delighted. Not when her son goes and dips his wick in the scrag end of show-business.'

Vanda needed to think quickly. Things couldn't be allowed to come to blows or her body might get marked. Nevertheless, she felt obliged to say, 'There's nothing scraggy about me.'

'No, but there's something terrible about what you do. It's nudes and female impersonators who've wrecked this business. Absolutely wrecked it.'

Suddenly Vanda didn't care whether she ended up black and blue. 'And who do you think you are? The ghost of Marie Lloyd? You're the *real* scrag end. Mutton dressed as lamb, bursting on the stage yelling Allez-oop! I wouldn't exactly call you the saviour of the music halls.'

These words were enough to make Old Mother Benali look every minute her true age. But she was a game old wreck. 'I once had everything you've got. I had the lot.'

'And look where it got you!'

The old pro was ready for her: 'And where's all this nudity going to get you? When the show folds and we all go off into pantomime, where will that leave you? There's no place for bare tits in *Cinderella*.' Obviously recognising a good exit line, Mother Benali flew out of the room. Two seconds later, just her head appeared around the door. 'Allez-oop!' she cried triumphantly. And then she turned into the sound of heels clacking down the corridor.

Ankle straps at that age! But Vanda was forced to concede that Old Mother Benali had got a point. Pantomime took up almost a third of the touring year. Everybody else in the *Naught But Nice* company was starting to compare offers. Yet nobody seemed to want Vanda Bell. And when she'd tried telephoning Alf Blatt, all she'd got was a secretary saying he was in Glasgow. Three times he was supposed to have been in Scotland – three times. She was willing to bet he wouldn't be in Glasgow when she stormed her way into his office. Because that's what she was going to do: she was going to hand in her notice and head for the West End of London.

What the Sun had, the Moon would always want. Or, in Joan's case, want to lose. This was the December when 'Lay Down Your Arms and Surrender to Mine' seemed to be forever streaming out of the portable radio at Thistle Cottage. Either that song or another one called 'I've Got a Lovely Bunch of Coconuts'. And because Joan had *not* got a lovely bunch of coconuts she felt herself to be a walking lie. That wretched padded bra was still standing between herself and the fulfilment of her most passionate ambition. And now she was worried that she might have pushed Toby's hands away once too often, because he'd started talking a lot about platonic friendship and saying that she was like the sister he'd never had.

In Joan's stories the characters were always driven by the need for love or money. Toby was not the same: his whole personality had been sidetracked into a dead end. Joan thought of it as Gambler's Alley. Not that there was anything furtive about his gambling. 'It's more important to me than

437

food or drink,' he would enthuse. 'I only really come alive when I've got a bet on.'

Horses, dogs, football pools: if there was nothing else going he would settle for a penny wager on a steel ball flying around a slot machine. 'See those two bits of paper?' he said to Joan. They were walking along the side of the man-made lake known as Worsley Dam. 'I bet you sixpence that the white paper gets sucked into the whirlpool before that Cadbury's wrapper does.'

He lost. But he didn't always lose. On one occasion he'd come back from Chester races with over seven hundred pounds in his pockets. That was the evening when Joan had fully expected to have her loan repaid. Instead, he took her to dinner at the Midland, and then on to a big private house in Didsbury. There they were conducted into a dining room that only seemed to lack one thing, or rather one person – Edward G. Robinson.

Heavy velvet curtains blocked out all chances of the police spying through the windows. Roulette was still strictly illegal, but a wheel was spinning in the middle of a baize-covered dining table, and very large sums of money were changing hands.

In under an hour Toby was cleaned out.

'But that was my money,' protested Joan as they found their way back to Manchester on a bus.

'No it wasn't.' He seemed genuinely anxious to put her right. 'It was my winnings from Chester, and winnings are gambling money. Your five hundred will be paid back another way.' But when he lost, Joan was forever having to save him from dishonour. Nothing massive: ten pounds here and twenty there, but it all added up. On one occasion a cheque from her agent's office didn't even get paid into the bank. Joan just signed it on the back and Toby handed it straight over to a Salford bookmaker.

Why? Why did she do it? Because she loved him: it was as simple as that.

Their steps had carried them beyond the dam and now they were heading downhill, towards the village. The streetlights flashed on. It was already overcoat weather and

438

frost was forecast for the rest of the weekend. 'See that house over there,' he said. 'That's where James Brindley lived when he was drawing up the designs for the very first English canal.' In its time, the Bridgewater Canal had been a massive gamble, so she supposed that this was why it interested him.

As if in confirmation he said, 'They had to keep getting the shareholders to invest more and more. But in the end they reaped massive rewards.'

Toby fell silent and she had a good look at him. He was well over six foot tall and more than ever like Rodin's statue of a soldier, with broad shoulders and dark curly hair cut closely to his head. It was Peter Bird who'd first pointed out the similarity, after he'd seen him naked in the changing room. Peter had seen him with nothing on; Vanda had lost her virtue. I'm distinctly lagging behind, thought Joan. 'And why have you suddenly gone silent?' she asked.

'Have I? December always makes me moody. Our kid died in December.'

This was news. 'Your brother?'

'Yes, I only ever had just the one. Actually he was my twin.'

This was even bigger news. 'I never knew you had a twin. I always thought you were an only child.'

'I don't talk about him much. It makes me feel guilty that I'm alive and he's not here.'

Joan linked her arm through his as they crossed the green. 'When did he die?'

'Before I left London. It was infantile paralysis. They couldn't do anything about it in those days. Still, he went very quickly. Nobody ever bought a gravestone, though – that's the part that narks me.'

'What's to stop you buying one?'

'That's a nice idea, Joan.' He said it gratefully. 'And I will, when I've got some ready cash.'

She wasn't about to offer it to him. She wasn't that big a fool. Oh dear, was all this business of forever having to hand over bits of money making her hard? Joan certainly never thought to question the truth of his story, and at that moment a boy going over the grass on a bicycle yelled 'Legs!' and gave her a wolf whistle.

'Cheeky bugger,' said Toby. 'He's got good taste though. Your legs are amazing.'

It was the first time he'd ever mentioned them. Compliments belonged in the past. In fact, things had reached the stage where Joan was having the kind of relationship that Vanda craved – Toby Eden was rapidly becoming little more than a pal.

'Cheeky bugger,' he repeated. 'What time do we have to get Henry back?'

The retriever sometimes spent Saturday afternoons with Miss Lathom. Whenever he returned to his original home, Henry behaved so much like company arriving that Toby swore that once the Sunbeam Talbot had driven away Miss Lathom and the dog would probably be sitting down to a hand of whist. 'We should collect him by half past six,' said Joan.

'Two hours.'

Was it her imagination or had he sneaked a second glance at her legs?

He had. He'd been looking at them. But he could have chosen to whistle a more tactful tune than 'I've Got a Lovely Bunch of Coconuts'. That brassière has caused me to think of myself as deformed, thought Joan. And when I get in, I'm going to take it off. There may not be much there, but at least I can pass the pencil test. She put the key in the lock. 'It seems funny not to hear barking.'

'No chaperone, eh?'

There *is* such a thing as sexual telepathy, she thought. There is, there is. 'You put the kettle on,' she said. 'I've just got to go upstairs and do something.'

In her bedroom she caught sight of her own reflection in the looking glass. 'I don't care,' she said to the mirror. 'I'm taking it off.'

'What did you say?' he called from downstairs.

'Nothing,' she called back. 'I'm a writer, we all talk to ourselves.' By now she was stripped to the waist. Say today was the day when something did happen? What would he think of a girl who didn't wear a bra? It was no use, it would have to be an unpadded one. Except, when she tried it on, it no longer fitted.

I've grown, she thought in wonder. And this was a thought that did much more for her self-confidence than any cheque from her agent. Except nothing's going to happen, she told herself. This is all in my imagination. But he'd said 'cheeky bugger' – twice he'd said it – about the boy who'd looked at her legs. With sudden decision she pulled out her only pair of pure silk stockings.

When Joan got downstairs Toby asked, 'Is the safe still on the same combination? I need to get those studs out,' he explained. 'He's giving me cash for them tonight.' There was already a pile of money lying on top of his open wallet. 'I've just been having a Jew's roll call; we're going to be playing chemmy, only they're ritzy North Londoners so they call it baccarat.' And then the miracle happened. He stopped talking about gambling and looked at her, really looked at her. 'Joan? What's happened to your eyes? They're absolutely shining.'

Instead of answering she pointed to his wallet. Two purple and white packets were poking out of one of the flaps. 'What are those?' she asked. In truth she knew. Joan and Peter and Vanda had often seen similar packets lying discarded next to squashed grass in the bottom field.

Toby seemed embarrassed. 'It's the barber. I had my hair cut today and he always asks "Anything for the weekend?" And you don't like to say no. I hope you didn't think . . .' He must have suddenly registered the sheen of pure silk: 'Have you changed your stockings?'

It was now or never. 'Yes.' And that's as much work as I'm putting in, she thought. Joan was not like Vanda Bell: beyond a certain point she needed to be wooed, to be won.

'Come here,' said Toby.

'No. You come over here.' And now Joan wished she hadn't turned the bedcovers down. It was going to look so forward!

Number 26 Charing Cross Road was a solid, turn-of-the

century office block, and it reeked of rubber flooring. You could also enter the building from St Martin's Lane where it was known as Cranbourne Mansions. The whole place was a warren of lesser theatrical managements and agents. Alf Blatt's office was off the main corridor; it shared its own little staircase with Lytton's Dramatic Agency and Xcelsior Dance Bands Ltd.

Recalling her first visit, Vanda knew that getting through the front door was easy. You just pushed and you were in. It was admittance to Alf Blatt's inner sanctum which was more difficult. You had to get past a female gorgon who sat behind a green-painted tin desk.

'Do you have an appointment?' Anything less theatrical than this woman it would be hard to imagine. She had a perm that was growing out, and pink-rimmed National Health glasses, and an old tweed topcoat was flung over her shoulders like a cloak – the office was distinctly chilly. 'Is Mr Blatt expecting you?'

'No, but he'll see me, my name is Vanda Bell.'

'Take a seat.' The woman might have looked like one of Vanda's mother's customers but she made it obvious that she knew herself to be royalty. Her hopeful subjects were ranged round the waiting room on tubular steel and canvas chairs: two women and a man. They had 'out of work variety artiste' written all over them. If variety was on its last legs, six of them were in this room.

And I don't know of any garment sadder than a shabby camel overcoat, thought Vanda as she plonked herself down next to the man. He had tried to disguise the white bits in his eyebrows with burnt cork; she only knew this because Jack Vesta had always used the same trick.

'Not fixed for panto?' he said to her.

Before she could reply, one of the identically dressed women chipped in with, 'We were going to Jersey. Nice engagement, Prince and Dandini. But now we've found the management's blacklisted.'

'You're better off knowing where you stand,' sighed the old wraith in camel. 'Anything's better than getting stranded. Mind you, you've left it late to fix anything else.'

442

Much too late, thought Vanda. Both the 'sisters' were forty-five trying to look twenty years younger. This whole place is false teeth and chins held well up, and brave little bunches of artificial violets. Those poor cows shouldn't be tramping round the agents, they should be at home with their feet in soak.

In the background, behind a plate-glass door labelled *Private*, she could hear Alf Blatt on the telephone. 'You can have him for fifteen,' he was saying. 'But I'm not letting him go for a penny less. And you'd do me a favour if you took his wife for the Fairy Godmother . . . All right, don't do me a favour.' Slam. The receiver had plainly gone down with a bang.

But there had been enough energy in all this to charge Vanda with some of her own. Rising to her feet she marched past the seated tragedies and up to the desk. 'Uncle Alfred will see me now,' she announced importantly.

'Uncle?' The dingy secretary obviously didn't know what to make of this. 'Just a minute . . .'

But Vanda, in her new black coat, had already swanned past her and was pushing open the door marked *Private*.

'What the . . .' Alf Blatt had been caught behind his desk with a wooden toothpick in his mouth.

'You carry on picking,' said Vanda easily as she closed the door. 'I told her you were my uncle.'

'Just don't try yelling rape,' he said wearily. 'Nobody'd believe you, it's been done too often.'

'I need a job.' The office was lined with similar framed smiles to the ones on the staircase at her digs – Vanda was back in Paddington.

'Why did you leave *Naughty But Nice*? News travels fast in this neck of the woods.'

He was still as brilliantined as ever, and his sallow complexion made Vanda wonder whether, if you got close enough, he would have bad breath. But Alf Blatt was the only person she knew who could find her work. 'I left before it left me. It folds in a fortnight.'

'Not a clever thing to do. Not when the reports on you were so good. And they were, they were very good.' He donned a pair of horn-rimmed spectacles and pulled a heavy ledger towards himself; it looked as though it dated back to Dan Leno. 'This is not a good time of year.' He'd said the same thing on her first visit. 'And your end of the business is changing. They do want a dancing Cat at Chatham, but you're a bit exotic for that. How old are you now?'

How old was she supposed to be? She couldn't remember what she'd said last time. Vanda settled for the truth: 'Nearly twenty-one.'

'Christ, time does fly! It doesn't seem two panto seasons since you were stopping the traffic at that audition at Hulme. But you did stop the traffic,' he chewed his bottom lip thoughtfully, 'even at that age. The thing is, Amanda . . .'

'Vanda.'

'The thing is, I'm an extremely moral man.' Whatever could be coming next? 'And I'm not sure that I like what's happening to striptease. Phyllis and Jane were Art. But these clubs . . .' This time he pursed his lips; they were just a little bit blue.

'What clubs?' She was sniffing opportunity.

'They're mushrooming up all over the West End. An Indian found a loophole in the law. As long as the audience are club members the nudes can move.'

No more pretending to be a statue, no more trouble with the watch committee. 'Yes please!'

He still seemed at war with his conscience as he said, 'I suppose they do no more than you'd see in Paris . . .'

'Can you get me in?' she asked eagerly.

'You've not got an act, darling,' he sighed. 'All this goes way beyond floating around with a couple of fans. Still, I suppose you could always do that for an audition.'

'And can you get me one?'

'Without a proper act? Only at the very bottom end. And they're rough, Amanda. There's no point in pretending they're anything but dead rough.'

'That'll do,' she said, 'for a start. And when I find a choreographer and get an act together, will you book me into somewhere better? I invest in what I do. You'll see. I'll *make* you remember my proper name.'

*

This, thought Joan as she snuggled closer, is perfection. Snow outside and the sound of children going across the green to school, and here we are in bed – together and warm.

And why did anybody ever bother with nightdresses or pyjamas? Her obsession with the inadequacies of her own body had vanished months ago; lovemaking had dispersed it entirely. 'I've got to get up,' said Toby. But he didn't show any signs of moving.

'Don't say you're ready for another roller-coaster ride?' She had been surprised to discover that her own appetite for passion was stronger than his.

'I just like being close. Ouch, you're letting the cold in. What're you doing?'

'Looking at you. Did you know that you're beautiful?'

'Just look at your little bosom,' he laughed. 'The cold's got the ends sticking out like little organ stops.'

'It might not be the cold, it might be you.' Oh but there was luxury in just sliding down next to him, back in the warmth. Was he expecting her to start something? She hadn't expected men to like women to take the initiative; not that this was regularly expected of her. The first time she'd found herself on top had come as a great surprise. A surprise and a revelation. It had also been the first time that she had shimmered out of control. Well, shimmered at first, and then after that it had unfolded into something so amazing that she had never even tried to write down words to describe it. And for Joan Stone that was a miracle!

Another bit of magic wasn't about to happen because Toby really was getting out of bed. 'If I don't get to the newsagent's he'll have sold the last *Sporting Life*.'

Her five hundred pounds having been repaid, Joan had ceased to mind the gambling. She was starting to make a career out of unusual ambitions – why shouldn't Toby? 'I should get up too. I've got to develop "History in Your Own Home".'

'No, do your novel today,' he said. 'The kids have all gone back to school so it should be quieter.'

She never needed much encouragement to work on the novel. 'History in Your Own Home' was another project altogether. It was aimed at *Good Housekeeping*, a magazine which was known to pay handsomely. In the cause of this article, Joan had borrowed her own deeds to Thistle Cottage from Adcock's safe. They listed everything, from the original arrangements for the leasehold of the land from the Bridgewater Estates to the names and occupations of all the people who had lived there since. Now she was trying to trace their histories in parish registers. 'Today's a bit cold for hanging around church vestries.'

'Yes, you do your novel.'

'Anyway, Granny's coming round at eleven.' Even the thought made Joan reach for her dressing gown. Granny Briggs had no idea that Toby Eden ever stayed overnight. It didn't happen all the time, and he always left his car on the spare ground at the side of the pub across the bridge.

By now Toby was in the bathroom. 'That bloody dog's whining to go into the back garden,' he called out.

'He's not a bloody dog,' Joan called back defensively. The two males in her household were not over keen on one another.

Once Toby had gone she gave herself a quick shower with the bath attachment, which was really meant for rinsing hair. After she had mopped up the mess and dressed, she walked Henry as far as the post office. The baker already had scones in his window, and these would do to entertain Granny who had already announced on the telephone, 'I'll only be diving in and out.'

These days Granny Briggs was very much given to starting sentences with the words 'Since I got wheels . . .' The wheels in question belonged to a little motor scooter. It was an Italian model and Granny always mispronounced the manufacturer's name. 'My Vee-espa,' she called it.

This vehicle came phut-phutting along the icy track that bounded the green promptly at eleven. 'I have to be sure and lock the Vee-espa,' she called out. 'Otherwise the insurance is invalid.' Since she'd become a businesswoman Granny was very hot on things like insurance.

This morning, however, she seemed less enthusiastic than usual about her role of students' landlady. 'All Jewish people are not like the Morgensterns,' she observed. 'I sometimes wish I'd never advertised in the *Jewish Chronicle*. That way I would never have got Melanie Scott-Kline.' Joan could never hear enough about this young woman, who was the bane of Granny's life. 'I've made a new discovery about her this week, Joan. She doesn't own a single pair of knickers.'

'How can you be sure?'

'I've searched,' said Granny with satisfaction. 'These crash helmets play havoc with your hair. I've had that girl's room upside-down and she doesn't possess so much as one pair of drawers.'

'But that's terrible. You've no right to go searching their rooms.'

Olive Briggs struggled out of her old tweed shopping coat. 'I've every right to know what's coming in and out of my own house. She allowed a man up the fire escape. I did not spend three hundred pounds on that contraption for it to be a short cut to immorality. I'm just glad that you're a good girl, Joan.' Henry chose this moment to bound in carrying Toby's discarded underpants. Toby always brought a clean pair when he was going to stay. If Joan had a criticism of this behaviour it was that it lacked spontaneity.

'Whose are those?' asked Granny in horror.

She had to improvise quickly: 'He found them on the green.'

'It's a terrible world we live in,' said Granny piously. 'I hope those scones aren't meant for me, Joan. Last time, they tasted of patent baking powder. I'm not here for long, I'm on my way to town. I just hope that old sign on the wall outside Brissenden's is right, and that they do still buy diamonds. I'm finally going to part with Mother's engagement ring.'

'Why?' Joan began to pour the coffee.

A faraway look came into Granny's eye. 'I'm planning to dig. The front and the side rooms in the cellars could be deemed semi-basement if I dug down to let some light in. I might even get *three* extra rooms that way.'

Joan pushed across the milk jug. 'Sometimes I think you make work for yourself.'

'Then you would do well to remember that it will all be

447

yours some day.' She stirred her coffee thoughtfully. 'Anyway, it stops me thinking about Bruno.' She suddenly rapped a knuckle on the table. 'Come along, dear, time's money to me. Get that safe open.'

Joan and Toby had moved it into the bottom cupboard of the Welsh dresser. 'Just a minute.' Joan was crouching down. 'It's a bit difficult to see the dial.'

'I'm amazed you remember the number. You were always terrible at remembering your multiplication tables.'

'It's the same as the phone.' As she dialled it round she could hear tumbling clicking noises inside the lock, and then the door swung open. Joan could hardly believe what she was seeing. In fact she was so startled she said, 'Could you give me that little torch – the one by the cooker.'

'What's the matter?'

'Just give me the torch.' But it only illuminated what she'd already seen in shadow. Except for the manuscript of *Sweet Mignonette* the safe was empty. Toby . . . God, how the hell was she meant to protect him *this* time? 'Granny, could you come back later?'

'No, I could not come back later.' Old bones or not she was down on her knees and peering. 'Where are my things?' she cried. 'Mother's ring and the red leather case with the opals in it: where are they?'

'I don't know.'

'There are five stones in that ring, Joan, five. It's worth a lot of money. I clung onto it against a rainy day. Even when the lawyer's bills came in, I clung onto it. What've you done with my things?'

'I haven't done anything.' She was on the verge of weeping.

'What else has gone?' demanded Granny.

'The deeds of the house.' The minute the words were out she knew she shouldn't have said them.

'Have you had workmen in?' Joan shook her head. 'Then who? Nobody's just going to break in and head for the bottom of a Welsh dresser. Who else knows the right number?'

'Nobody.'

448

'You always were a rotten fibber,' scoffed her grand-mother. 'Somebody knew. It was that evacuee boy of the Fiddlers', wasn't it? That Eden.'

Joan's head was going in and out and she just wished she could faint dead away. 'I suppose he might have known the number.'

'Might have? Yes, and he might have left his underpants behind too. Come on, Joan, tell the truth and shame the devil.'

It was the fact that Toby seemed to have been discovered on two separate fronts which brought down Joan's defences. 'All right, he did know. But I'm sure there is some explanation.'

'There was "some explanation" at the tennis club. The explanation was that he'd made off with their money. Well, he's not a boy now, he's a grown man. I'm going to call the police.'

'Granny, no!' Diamonds, the deeds of a house . . . this was serious. 'They could send him to prison.' Joan sought wildly for words, any words, that might make Granny change her mind. 'Couldn't you try and show some Christian mercy?'

'Who showed mercy on my son?' Olive Briggs lifted the receiver and began to dial 999.

'Don't,' begged Joan. 'Put it down.' She tried to snatch the receiver from her grandmother.

Granny Briggs pushed Joan away and dealt her a stinging slap on her arm. 'Hello, operator? I want the police.'

8

It was more than five years since Vanda Bell had first left Manchester to look for fame. And in that time George Street had changed as much as Vanda had changed herself. Once the home of dozens of cotton merchants' offices, the first indications of the transformation were announced by a winking sign behind the Athenaeum. *Arthur Fox's Revuebar* – the words flashed on and off both day and night. And further up the street there was more neon, shaped to look like a woman's leg in a high-heeled shoe, kicking a shining star which announced that this was *Frenchy's . . . Frenchy's . . . Frenchy's*. But you had to go round the corner before you came upon the electric flames which surrounded the word *Sinerama*.

From midday onwards there were two bouncers on the door which led down into the basement theatre. Well, it called itself a theatre; in reality the members-only club was the cellars of an old warehouse, decked out with flocked wallpaper and plastic chandeliers.

But Sinerama did have a star dressing room. And at least I'm in that, thought Vanda. Half the light bulbs which should have been around the mirror were missing. But it was still one-up on that first communal dressing room in the club in Soho, the one the camp compère had always called 'the cow shed'.

Her first Soho job had led to two more, both of them in dumps. But as live musicians gave way to backing tapes, Vanda had begun to develop the act which would take her first to Hamburg and then on to Beirut. It was the German agent, the one who sold ostrich feathers as a sideline, who suggested that a big blonde like herself ought to be cleaning up in the Arab countries. And she had to get all the way to Casablanca before she learned what the 'consummation' clause in her contract really meant: if customers invited her to their table, she couldn't refuse to join them. And if they made a pass she just had to smile, smile, smile.

On some occasions she had been obliged to do more than that, mostly to further her career. It had never been any better, and sometimes much worse, than that first time in Dewsbury. If Vanda had one regret it was that right at the beginning she'd got shut of Toby Eden. And now the poor bastard was languishing in Strangeways.

Manchester or no Manchester, she was *not* going to get in touch with Joan Stone. The worlds of striptease and crime touched one another in many places: the one thing you didn't do was grass on your friends. She had only to think of Joan Stone going into the witness box to give evidence against Toby for her blood to boil.

And Joan had been so *secretive* about the whole thing. Tried to pass it off as 'a spot of bother' in her letters. But the tarot cards had told Vanda the whole tale. Long before the newspapers carried reports of the final court proceedings, Mr Midget had started whispering details into her ear. If only she could get him to whisper to order, life would be very much simpler. But she never could; Mr Midget still called the shots.

The box with the occult eye always sat on the dressing table, next to the pencils with the false eyelashes wrapped round them. These days Vanda didn't use greasepaint, she had graduated to Max Factor pancake. And the sticking plaster was a thing of the past, too. Why men wanted to see blonde or black or ginger muffs she could never understand; the finale of this present show always reminded her of a L'Oréal shade card.

'Come in.' Somebody had knocked at the door.

It was Leslie, the so-called stage manager. He was only about nineteen, with an unfortunate complexion and skinny forearms, and he was forever finding excuses to come into the dressing room. 'The barman says you've still got two glasses. They want them back.'

'I broke one.' She leant forward in her canvas chair and reached for the other tumbler, which was up against the mirror, on top of one of her wig boxes. 'Here.'

'They'll cut up rough. You know what they're like about glasses going missing.'

Why, when he'd seen her stark naked a dozen times onstage, did he still have to keep his eyes glued to the reflection of the cleavage of her dressing gown? In an attempt to recall him to his job she said, 'The broken glass is in the wastepaper basket. If the management feels so strongly about it, tell them I'll dance on the pieces for my second spot.'

'Aren't you doing enough in your second spot already?' His smile revealed discoloured teeth. 'The doorman says you're from Swinton.'

'So?' They shouldn't be allowed to employ people as oversexed as this youth, she thought. There should be a union rule against it.

'Aren't you scared somebody from your mother's street might come in and see what sort of tricks you get up to?'

'And aren't you scared I'm going to smack you across your spotty face?' Hamburg and Beirut had toughened her up. 'Nobody I know is coming in to see me, nobody at all.' And though one hand was resting on the tarot box, Mr Midget did not see fit to issue any warning.

On Wednesday afternoons Joan Stone always worked on her novel. She had been playing around with it for four whole years, ever conscious of the fact this was the manuscript that was meant to turn her into a proper author. And last week she had finally dared to send the first ten chapters of *Sweet Mignonette* to Molly Wainwright. She had asked the older writer to be absolutely frank in her opinion of its chances.

Eventually, Joan intended to publish the book under her own name; her increasingly successful output of romantic short stories always appeared under the pseudonym of Patsy Baker, and for her factual articles she changed sex and became Tom Fox.

But on Wednesday afternoons she was Joan Stone the novelist. With thoughts of 1920s American authors writing their hearts out in cafés in Paris, Joan generally took her pad and pencils to the Midland Hotel. There she would find a vacant table, order a pot of coffee and begin to scribble furiously.

The hotel lounge had a womblike quality; it was window-less and red-carpeted. And far from interrupting her writing, the tinkling pianist always seemed to ease Joan into the dream world where she met up with her characters.

Today the only vacant space was next to a table surrounded by businessmen who had obviously drunk too much at lunchtime and decided to make an afternoon of it. One of them must have been a resident because, even though it was after three o'clock, they were calling for more drinks.

Joan found herself thinking about a line from an Ernest Dowson poem, about the man who called for 'madder music and for stronger wine'. But even more she was thinking about the two unopened letters in her briefcase. There was one she wanted to read and one she didn't. The expensive blue envelope could only contain Molly Wainwright's reaction to her novel. Joan had made herself wait until she got to the Midland before she took it out and opened it.

'Is it a letter from your best boy?' called one of the men from the next table.

Joan ignored him. The *other* letter, the one on a carefully folded buff letter-form, was from somebody who had once been her 'best boy'. He was due out of Strangeways soon, and what the hell was she going to do then?

'I didn't mean to be intrusive.' It was the drunk again.

'That's OK.' Now then, what had Molly made of the novel?

My dear Joan,
This is not an easy letter to write. I have read your chapters of *Sweet Mignonette* (terrible title) twice. You seem to have fallen into the trap of telling yourself 'Now I am writing a novel,' and adopted a curiously high-flown and artificial style. I was on my guard from the moment I read that your hero was called Gervase and his ladylove Francesca. And I soon got very tired of that nursemaid spattering the pages with her eternal

453

cries of 'Miss Francesca'. You seemed to have over-dosed on John Galsworthy!

If these are hard words, I only write them because I believe you to have genuine talent. I want you to think right back to that very first story you sent me, when you were still at school. The one about the second-hand-clothes woman. It had its faults but it also had truth because you knew what you were writing about.

Begin again. And in going back to the beginning you could do worse than recall that first character. Ethel she was called. That's how good you *can* be because I remember her clearly.

Joan couldn't see the rest of it for tears.

'Oh Christ,' said one of the inebriated office truants solemnly. 'I hate to see a woman weeping. Fancy a brandy, love?' he called over.

'No thank you.'

'Have a whisky, have a gin, have what you want.'

'I don't want anything, thank you.' But she did want something, she wanted to throw her carefully sharpened pencils into the furthest corners of the room and never to pick them up again. A postscript to Molly's letter offered to return the manuscript but begged her not to show it to May Evans '. . . start again, *now*.'

With what? Terrible Ethel Bell? Vanda was more interest-ing than her boring mother! And that was when Joan was struck by a new idea. How about a story built around Vanda and Peter and herself? She could begin with measuring day at the grammar school . . .

A cockney cry of 'Where are we going, lads?' rose up from the next table.

'What about Arthur Fox's?'

'Been there, seen it. He's got nigger women and I don't fancy them,' yawned the one who had kept his hat on indoors.

The cockney one chimed back with, 'I used to like looking at them in geography books at school.'

She could put herself in the book as a girl who wrote lies in a diary. And Peter could be a boy who thought he was the only queer on earth. Since she was twelve Vanda had said she was going to be a stripper ... except Joan didn't really know anything about striptease. But what she didn't know she could research; at least she was still good at researching.

'Sinerama's the place,' roared one of the drunks. 'Off George Street S-I-N-erama.' He spelled it out. 'They say it's not just near the knuckle, it's the knuckle itself.'

'So are we off to this hot spot then, boys?' bellowed the one who had first spoken to Joan.

The man in the trilby let out a loud yawn, then he said, 'When you've seen one, you've seen 'em all. I'd rather have another double Scotch. Who's buying?'

When the waiter finally appeared he ignored the business-man. 'Hello there, miss,' he said to Joan. 'Your usual coffee?'

'No thank you. I'm just off.'

'I hope that lot haven't driven you away? Trouble is, one's a resident.'

'I'd already worked that out. They've not driven me away at all. In fact they've handed me a very good idea.'

Sometimes Vanda stopped thinking of the men in tip-up seats as the audience; they became the punters. Not all the girls had come into strip clubs via the stage, and the derogatory term had come from them. This kind of girl generally had a man in the background. And another word – ponce – was sometimes shouted around the dressing rooms.

At least these girls didn't go home to nobody, and some of the strippers went home to another woman. Vanda did not care to dwell on that. Not that she sat in judgment of any of them; if anything she was envious. Right back to her first days in the theatre she had known couples of whom it was said 'He's a bastard but she's a darling.' This generally meant that the man acted as mouthpiece and did the dirty work; the best of the darlings were very good at concealing the fact that it was really they who pulled the strings.

Yes, I could do with a bastard of my own, she thought as she waited for the curtains to part on her second spot. This was always the moment when Vanda was most conscious of working in something similar to a circus. Once those tabs opened she would have to step out onto a circular ground-glass floor, where banks of punters would surround her on three sides.

Suddenly she wasn't alone behind the curtains. Leslie, the creepy stage manager, had joined her. 'A word of warning,' he said, trying to sound efficient. 'Tone it down. There's a reporter out front. Tommy on the door thinks she might be from *The People*.'

Tone the act down? She most certainly would not. This was her last booking before she opened in London. And Vanda Bell could do with all the outraged publicity she could attract.

As usual the stage manager was standing too close and he was still muttering excitedly. 'We've warned Tilly not to go down on the electric light bulb. We don't want *The People* printing where she hides her batteries or we'll have the law in next.'

On the other side of the curtains, seated in the audience, Joan Stone had already made half a page of notes: 'Girls on the stage not the same as photos outside. First stripper took off clothes and pegged them to a washing line. Thin half-caste woman took snake into audience. Men hardly applaud at all . . .' There was the sound of more of this desultory clapping as a naked stripper carried her clothes off the stage in a suitcase labelled *Not Wanted on Voyage*.

The lights changed to mauve. 'And now, gentlemen . . .' The hidden announcer had a slight Birmingham accent and he sounded as automatic as a demonstrator in Lewis's basement. 'Direct from Beirut, where she received sundry proposals of marriage from Arab sheiks, that eyeful tower of glamour, Miss Vanda Bell . . . in Vanderella Fantasy.'

At the unexpected mention of that familiar name Joan was so startled that she dropped her pencil. By the time she retrieved it Vanda was in the centre of the stage in a huge white crinoline. The recorded music was Boccherini's minuet, and the vast lacy skirts and blonde corkscrew curls put Joan in mind of Bo-Peep. Except this had to be the most towering nursery-rhyme character on earth – Vanda appeared to be fully six feet tall.

Where could the height have come from? And surely this Vanda was too sweet and innocent for this kind of show? That was an illusion which didn't last. The dress must have had a trick bodice because two globes of breast suddenly burst into view. But even then the whole thing just looked like an eighteenth-century portrait of a shepherdess. Yet this figure wasn't a peasant, more like some courtier in fancy dress.

Vanda remained revolving in a white spotlight as the rest of the stage began to be bathed in crimson radiance. And another, smaller, spot picked out the girl who had pinned all her clothes to a washing line. This time she was dressed as a deferential French maid in powder-puff skirts and a little apron. She was carrying something on a black cushion, something covered with a black chiffon handkerchief.

Turning slightly upstage to tug on the concealed poppers that would release her frock, Vanda thought, If she drops that bloody cushion again with the press out front, they'll see a show they won't be expecting! She had already told the stage manager to bring the reporter round to her dressing room afterwards. 'I'm the star, just do it,' she had said. Only now the star couldn't get the metal poppers to burst. No, it was OK, here they came, just as the music crashed into 'The Ride of the Valkyries'.

Wagner in a strip joint? Joan Stone could hardly believe her ears. Her eyes were also being put to the test because the white dress had vanished, the blonde wig had been handed to the maid, and a severely raven-haired Vanda Bell was revealed in nothing but a pair of gleaming black, thigh-length, patent-leather boots, with platform soles and heels that were easily eight inches high.

'You thought you'd paid at the box office, didn't you?' Vanda said to the audience. Actually the words were pre-recorded over the soundtrack of the music, so she just mimed the talking. 'The truth is . . . you pay *now*.' The maid pulled back the black veil from the cushion and handed Vanda a vast plaited bullwhip.

Joan Stone, who had been thinking that her old friend had

457

taken off altogether too much too soon, suddenly realised that she was about to witness an act which would be as unusual as its music.

Just hurry up and carry that bloody cushion off the stage, never mind curtsying to the punters, thought Vanda. And then began the mental processes which always accompanied her second spot. As she bound herself up – almost ritually – within the leather thong of the whip, she recalled days and months and years of degradation. Dirty Ethel always went through her mind at this moment, and boys saying rude things about her figure on the top decks of buses as she travelled to school. And those awful months of covering herself in that gritty Armenian distemper to appear in *Naughty But Nice*. Then her thoughts would travel to the indignities heaped upon her in nightclubs in Athens, in Rio, in Agadir . . .

The elaborate knotting of the thong made it all look supremely painful but it wasn't, and all the knots were devised to come apart with one single tug. And now she tugged . . . The thong slithered free. As she seized hold of the plaited handle, Vanda systematically turned her mind to thoughts of revenge.

Crack! That slash of the whip was for Odette Ashworth – for daring to chuck her out of her school. Crack . . . Jack Vesta should never have told her that she would have to go to bed with a man to make herself into a proper artiste. Thwack . . . the tip of the thong just missed a man in the front row. He represented every man who'd ever watched with a raincoat over his knees. One silent one . . . one that just sneaked across the stage like a black adder. This was always difficult, but it was meant to highlight her own voice on the soundtrack. 'The kiss of the whip, the kiss of the whip.' The most massive slash so far was for vile old Mr Midget. And another for him, and another, and another.

I shouldn't be watching this, thought Joan. There's something dark and terrible here. No wonder she's got them on the edge of their seats.

One for Hamburg, thought Vanda. One more for the sex shop on the Reeperbahn where I bought these boots, and

458

another for the German who sold them to me, the man who said they were washable.

Then she started to do more with the whip than crack it. That was when Joan Stone closed her eyes. Left with nothing to do but listen to the music, she suddenly became very aware of its Nazi connotations.

At the end of the act the applause was genuine, and Joan uncovered her face to see Vanda holding the whip handle aloft. She was smiling like the best-natured girl on earth. The smile seemed to say, It was all an act, just a performance, but I had you lot kidded, didn't I?

'Excuse me, miss.' Joan was at the end of a row and one of the doormen was in the aisle. 'You're wanted.'

'Me?'

'She said to bring you round to her dressing room.'

Vanda had slipped into a clean white towelling dressing gown. This reporter woman, whoever she was, had seen the erotic side. Now she had to be shown Vanda Bell the tomboy, the good sport. And a few suggestions of intelligence wouldn't come amiss either; the stripper moved her copy of the new biography of Lawrence of Arabia to a more prominent position on the dressing table.

Vanda had been able to make out the outline of a female figure in the audience but she hadn't been able to see any details. What a good job she'd chosen today to buy herself a shilling's worth of tulips. Pity they were only in a jam jar, but you could only do your best with what was available. 'Hurry up, Miss Reporter, where are you?' As if in answer there was a knock on the dressing-room door. 'Do come in,' called out Vanda, putting it on a bit.

In walked Joan Stone.

'This I do not believe,' gasped the stripper. 'How long've you worked for the Sunday papers?'

'I don't.' Joan hadn't known what to expect, and the sight of the whip on the dressing table was already making her feel she was out of her depth.

'Then what are you doing watching a show like this? Are you a lesbian?'

459

'Course I'm not.' Joan found herself fishing around for something to say, which felt very odd when she considered what great friends they had once been. She settled for 'Do you want a cigarette? I'm afraid I dropped my matches in the theatre.'

Vanda had also been at something of a loss. 'Go on then, I'll have one. Not that I should be taking anything from somebody who sent Toby to jail.' As she fished in her vanity case for her lighter, Vanda wondered whether Joan would notice that it was a real gold one.

'Granny sent Toby to prison, not me. I had to be forced.' Joan had neither registered the artfully arranged biography nor the flowers; instead her eyes had come to rest on the old pokerwork tarot box. Accepting a light from Vanda, she blew out a cloud of smoke and said, 'Do you still do the cards?'

Here, at long last, might be the opportunity to be rid of them. 'Do you ever see Peter?' Maybe the three of them could get together and . . .'

'Never. I don't even know where he is.'

It was disappointment that caused Vanda to snap, 'Yes, but we all know where Toby is.'

Joan had taken enough. 'Look, Vanda, he didn't just rob us. There were six other charges, six.'

'I didn't know that. It all seemed to be you and those house deeds in the papers. I'm not used to visitors – unfold that other canvas chair and sit down. I don't suppose you ever hear from him either.'

Molly Wainwright's literary criticism had driven all thoughts of the other letter from Joan's head. It was still lying, unopened, inside her briefcase.

'That case and the dark green suit make you look like one of those women who go round cleaning phones,' said Vanda critically. 'What did you think of the act?'

Joan fished out the sealed letter. 'Very original. Not at all the sort of music I would have expected.'

'This queen called Roger did the choreography for me.' Vanda placed an ashtray at Joan's elbow. 'He's got great taste, he's gone to work for the BBC.'

'This is from Toby.' Joan was finally tearing the letter-form open.

'You can't have been panting for news.'

'They're always the same. They've been the same for years. Nothing but regrets, and he'll never do it again. And they're always full of impossible dreams for the future.'

'Can I see?' The hand which had cracked the whip was extended towards the buff form. The fingernails were very red. The last time Vanda had seen Toby's handwriting had been on the front of that envelope full of photographs taken at Barr Hill. She began to scan the contents of the letter.

There was a fine film of face powder on the wooden arms of the canvas chair, so Joan reached over and grabbed a tissue and used it as a duster. Fancy there being Johnson's Baby Lotion on a dressing table in a place like this! 'I could have told you what would have been in the letter without even opening it. Nothing but regrets and dreams.'

'This one isn't. Listen. "Dear Joan, I will be out next Wednesday. One gets out of the gate just after seven in the morning. If you are waiting for me, I shall be a very happy man. If not, I will know where I stand . . ." ' Vanda did not care to read out the closing protestations of undying love. '*Will* you be waiting?'

'I thought it was next month,' said Joan. 'I'd have staked good money on it.' And even that statement reminded her of his past influence and caused her to start imagining a future lined with bookies holding out their hands. 'I'll have to think about it. I don't know. I really don't know. I wish I could say more than that but I can't.'

The taxi had been making strange noises all the way from Worsley. And now they were at Irlams o'th' Height and the driver had pulled into the side of the road. He must have been expecting trouble because the bonnet was up and he was pouring water from a screw-topped vacuum flask into the innards of the old Rover; it wasn't a proper taxi, just a local hire car. And it had arrived late.

The bonnet went down with a rattle. As the driver settled himself back in the front seat he said, 'Bang go my chances of getting to the seven o'clock Mass.' Daylight was just beginning to break over Bolton Road. 'It's Ash Wednesday, a Holy Day of Obligation,' he explained.

Duty is a terrible thing, though Joan – terrible. Only a sense of duty would have got me up at this unearthly hour. 'Will we still make it to Strangeways by seven?' she asked.

'Just. That's if she doesn't start playing up again.'

Don't let him go into mechanical details, she prayed. My brain's not up to them this early in the morning. What was that hymn called, the one they always sang at Barton Grammar School on Ash Wednesdays? 'Day of wrath and doom impending', that was it. There'd be doom impending all right when Granny discovered that Joan had gone off to collect Toby.

But it's my life, I can do what I want with it. Granny does, she doesn't allow other people to influence her. Except, possibly, Herbie Morgenstern. Strangeways was just near to the Jewish quarter, but first you had to drop downhill and get past the racecourse.

I love Toby, she thought. I've tried not to and it doesn't work. And anyway I can't leave him to go off and end up penniless on the Thames Embankment. In this vision, a tattered Toby was always leading a dog on a piece of string – which was odd when you considered that Henry wasn't much struck with him.

'St Sebastian's Priory must have had an extra early Mass for the workers,' observed the driver. 'They're all coming out ashed.'

Through the window of the car Joan could see a procession of men and women emerging from the church with sooty marks on their foreheads. 'Aren't they allowed to wipe them off?' Her own High Church explorations had never led to anything as Catholic as this.

'Not for the rest of today. "Dust thou art and unto dust shalt thou return," ' he quoted gloomily. 'I'm going to have to watch my speed or else we'll be boiling again.'

By now it was five to seven and any doubts Joan might have had about the wisdom of this enterprise were transformed into fears that she would not be outside the prison gates on time. All her resistance had gone. She loved Toby, she was having him back, and Granny Briggs would just have to complain about it to her beloved lodgers.

The gaunt black Victorian prison was set on a high mound. The cobbled street up to the main gates was proving something of an uphill climb. 'Easy does it,' breathed the driver. 'But I'll get you there. We'll do it.'

Another taxi, a Manchester black cab, was parked outside the main entrance. A couple of men were already starting to leave the building through a small door set inside one of the huge studded ones. 'Stop,' she said, 'and wait. I'll run the rest.' By now she had caught sight of Toby. Carrying a brown paper parcel and a varnished fretwork firescreen, he was peering into the other cab.

But there had to be some mistake because he was opening the door and getting inside, and the taxi was already beginning to move downhill. As it passed Joan she realised she should have known what she would see. One of the passengers was Toby Eden and the other was Vanda Bell.

Peter was not recalling the same Lenten hymn as Joan. The one he was remembering from his own days at Barton Grammar School began 'Forty days and forty nights'. By now Lent was nearly over, and tonight was Peter's favourite feast of the whole church calendar. It was Maundy Thursday, a night which High Anglican churches celebrate with heavy drama.

After the final Mass of Lent, the doors of the tabernacle on the high altar had been left hanging open as the one last Communion wafer was processed round the church and then laid to rest on a side altar, in a simple wooden casket inscribed *Resurgam* – I will rise again. The casket was bathed in the light of dozens of candles, and the haunting smell of incense vied with the scent of all the spring flowers banked between the wax lights of this altar of repose.

The students at the college took it in turn to guard the Blessed Sacrament for an hour at a time, right through the night. For the past week a list had hung on a notice board inside the entrance to the chapel. You didn't write your name against a time, you drew a personal symbol instead. This was because it was between you and God, and there was not meant to be any spiritual pride in being the person who chose to keep watch at three o'clock in the morning.

Peter took his turn an hour after that, at four. The student already kneeling on the prie-dieu must have heard him coming because he rose to his feet and, without so much as exchanging a word or a glance with his replacement, left the chapel.

By now the candles had burned several inches down, and the silence had multiplied with itself in a way that only happens on the night which recalls Christ saying, 'Tarry ye here, and watch with me.'

If it's all true, thought Peter, God is inside that box. And he had every reason to believe it was true, because the silence was like an all-loving embrace; it reminded him of the angelic protection he had received at the height of the nightmare about the stinking tarot cards. It was another aspect of those loving arms which had gone around him on the appalling night when he had feared eventual exclusion from heaven. The silence was his friend.

But now there was work to be done, people to be prayed for: his mother, his father, uncles, aunts, cousins. Prayers for Miss Lathom, for the repose of the soul of Iris Parr, for Henry the dog ('And I hope that the Church of Rome is wrong and that animals do have souls'). For Vanda, for Joan and for Bruno Briggs. And there was a whole list of people whom he had met since he had come here. And then the saints, the martyrs, the angels. And for all those who had nobody else to pray for them . . .

Finally he felt free to pray for himself. Peter formed his silent words carefully: 'This is between you and me. It has nothing to do with Leviticus or St Paul or the Archbishop of Canterbury or the Pope, they were only mortals – they could have been prejudiced. I can't believe that all the people like me are your mistakes, you made too many of us. God bless us all.

'I'm lonely, God, I'm telling you straight. I'm lonely and you know what I need. And if it's what you want, please send somebody and let us be good at it. I'm not just talking about bed, I'm talking about a whole life together. But your will be done in this as in everything else.' And now Peter crossed himself as he murmured the familiar words: 'In the name of the Father and of the Son and of the Holy Ghost, Amen.'

Would the Worsley newsagent ever manage to sell all those Easter eggs by tomorrow? That was what Joan Stone was wondering as she bought one for Granny. Its metal foil wrapping was decorated with a portrait of a rabbit astride a motor scooter.

'Two shillings,' said the woman behind the counter. While handing over the money, Joan accidentally dropped a sixpenny piece onto a copy of *Sporting Life* which was lying with the other newspapers on the counter.

I must remember to put racing papers into the new novel, she thought. Since the morning of the shock at Strangeways, the plot of her second attempt at a full-length story had widened to encompass a character who bore more than a passing resemblance to Toby Eden. It had to be admitted that Joan was more than half in love with her semi-fictitious villain.

In the book, Vanda had become 'Nona'. And after the real-life events of Ash Wednesday, Nona had grown to be a less and less sympathetic character on the typewritten page. Joan Stone had been doing what she'd done ever since childhood: she'd been writing her troubles away. She had even got out of bed in the middle of sleepless nights to write letters to the real Toby and to Vanda. Harshly accusing letters, which had blazed with anger and threatened revenge. She never posted them, although she did once get as far as the pillar box with a coat pulled over her nightdress.

It was very silly of Vanda to give me that engraved visiting card with her address on it, very silly indeed. Because, sooner or later, I'm going to do something that'll make her sorry.

A brick through the window of the address in London W2 was one satisfactory thought that frequently rose to mind. But Pelican Court could have a lot of floors; she might not be able to aim that high. And could she be sure of smashing a window that belonged to Vanda?

This is stopping me from writing, thought Joan. I should really be thinking about Nona and Jane and David ... perhaps Pelican Court has a hall porter and I could ask him to point out the exact floor. But her next thought had the porter in the witness box: 'I immediately formed the opinion that the accused was of an unsound mind.'

And he'd be right. This is driving me mad. She's pinched what was mine. I need to steal something of hers. But what? What is as important to her as Toby was to me? Joan's mind threw up a mental image of Vanda curling her whip on the glass stage at Sinerama, and of the whip lying on the dressing able afterwards. In this moment of recollection, she suddenly knew what to steal. Six weeks, and only now had it occurred to her!

There was, however, an art to thieving, and she didn't possess it. 'But I know somebody who does,' she said to Henry. He had been watching her closely with puzzled eyes; Henry didn't like it when she got agitated. Joan's fretting had now turned to excitement, and he loved that. The retriever danced ahead of his mistress as she got up from her desk and made her way over to the khaki government-surplus filing cabinet.

The third drawer down contained all her notebooks from her days on the *Journal*. It took less than five minutes to locate the right pad. 'Mind your tail,' she said as she slammed the metal drawer. 'We're going to walk to Monton.' They could drop off Granny's egg at the same time.

In all her years at Barton Grammar, Joan had never known of the existence of the alleyway known as Sligo Street – she was looking for number 7. The houses were two-storeyed with overhanging roofs made of antique slate, and the window frames weren't wooden, they were stone. 'It's magic,' she said to Henry, who was busy sniffing an old brownstone sink filled with wallflowers. 'And you've even found the right house.'

She didn't have to knock on the door. It had already flown open to reveal the Thief of Baghdad in a scarlet dressing gown of artificial silk. He must have just finished shaving because he had a piece of toilet paper stuck over a bleeding cut on his blue chin. 'Have you come to put us in the papers?' he cried. Joan decided that the wild eyes were actually better than Hedy Lamarr's, so it wasn't too difficult to say 'Hello, Doris' to a man.

'How can they want to pull down this lovely little byway?' His sleeves were pushed up and the arms he held out dramatically wide were covered in fine black hair. 'Who says the only lady engineers are in Russia!' Doris was holding a rubber plunger, the kind used to unblock sinks.

'I'm afraid I'm not on the *Journal* these days.'

'But you must know people who are?'

'Oh yes.'

'Then come in. I've got a use for you.'

You walked straight into the living room. It's just like a magpie's nest, thought Joan. Every available surface was crammed with gleaming metal ornaments. The tops of the coffee tables were made out of polished silver trays, and even the photographs on the walls – the pictures of Dorothy Squires and Judy Garland and Sophie Tucker – were in big chromium-plated frames. 'Mind the crystal chandelier,' he said. It hung so low that you had to walk round it. 'I expect Waring and Gillow are still trying to work out where that went.'

Joan decided not to bother with preamble. 'I need a thief, Doris.'

'And I owe you a favour. So don't worry that I'll think of putting the black on you afterwards, because I won't. Is the doggie allowed ginger nuts?'

'Just one.'

'However,' the lustre-china biscuit barrel still had a price tag attached to its knob, 'Sligo Street needs saving. We want all the publicity we can get.'

'And you shall have it.'

'Then we're definitely in business. In which shop is the item you require?'

'It's not a shop, it's a flat, and it's in London. I'd pay your

467

rail fare,' she assured him. Having already sensed some
hesitation on his part, she added, 'First class.'

'The thing is,' he said cautiously, 'I don't do flats.'

Realising that she would have to think quickly, Joan settled
for throwing down a challenge: 'So the only lady cat burglars
are in Mayfair, are they?'

'Which is not to say I haven't *done* flats.' Suddenly 'the
Girl of Many Hands' was full of self-importance. 'What is it
you want? Letters, incriminting photographs?'

'No, nothing like that.'

The beautiful eyes had turned beady. 'Then what?'

Pelican Court always reminded Vanda Bell of a cut-price
British version of a Fred Astaire and Ginger Rogers movie.
Built in the 1930s, in that district where Bayswater loses its
name and becomes 'off the Edgware Road', the entrance hall
boasted four lifts and two porters. But when you got out at the
fourth floor and unlocked your way into number 402, you saw
what Pelican Court was really about. The hallway was small
and square, and it would have been impossible for two people
to pass one another on the corridor which ran the length of
the accommodation. Poky, that's what the flats were, downright poky with metal window frames.

But it's home and it's mine, thought Vanda. Or, at least, a
twenty-seven-year repairing lease is mine. She just wished
that thoughts of Frank Sinatra singing 'After You Get What
You Want You Don't Want It' would stop plaguing her. It
didn't apply to the flat, more to the man who was asleep in the
spare bedroom. Toby Eden snored, and that was the very
least of the accusations she could level against him.

Otherwise, life was good. She was appearing at the Casino
de Glamour in Dean Street. This was a strip club which was
not a dump. Of course Toby's ears had pricked up at the word
'casino' but the place was no gambling joint. Not that it had
taken him long to find his way to those. In next to no time he
seemed to have got himself on telephoning terms with young
men who boasted gossip-column surnames like Douglas-
Home and Elwes. It took less than a month for his own name

to turn up in the William Hickey column of the *Daily Express*. It referred to him as 'Toby Eden, the Mayfair gambler'.

And all done on my money, thought the woman who had been mentioned in passing as 'his unlikely companion'. Once she'd decided to take Toby on, Vanda had set aside a thousand pounds to do the job properly. This sum had outfitted Toby in a handsome wardrobe and still left him with several hundred pounds of capital. She knew he would gamble with it, she had no illusions about that. But Vanda considered herself to be giving him a fair start.

And what did she expect in return? Certainly not *that*! He was meant to be her dream pal. And he was meant to step in and speak up when some unpleasant situation might otherwise reveal her in a steely and determined light. In this new West End career she had every intention of being known as 'a good sport'. It was Toby's job to be Mr Tough.

In a matter of weeks the exact reverse had happened. Nancy Spain, the Fleet Street journalist, dubbed Toby 'Prince Charming' but described Vanda as armour-plated. It had seemed a poor return on a thousand quid. And not only on this sum of money, but also on breaking one of Gran'ma Dora's most inflexible rules. Dora had never minded making predictions about the stock market because these only dealt in positive and negative aspects, and not in specifics. But she had always refused point-blank to try to pick out winning horses. 'It's not fair on other gamblers,' she would say. 'And money won that way always has to be paid back at a higher price.'

Nevertheless, Vanda had spread the cards and begged Mr Midget for the name of a big winner. And he hadn't just given her one, he had given her two, on the same day at Aintree. Not just hints, the full names of the horses. Even these had been eerie – Other Voices and The Dwarf. It was the most convincing proof she had ever had that the personality within the tarot pack might actually be able to influence events.

There was barely room to turn around in the kitchen of the flat, so Vanda decided to carry her breakfast tray through into the lounge. The new cream leather three-piece suite had been a good buy, though she had never been able to bring herself to remove its clear plastic covers. The big gold drum lamp-shades were similarly encased. And another strip of plastic stretched over the cream carpet, all the way from the door to the low table in front of the sofa. The only unregulated thing in the whole room was a scarlet-sequined stage costume, hanging from the frame of Stephen Ward's new drawing of herself. The costume had follies-sleeves, made of ropes of beads. They would have to be changed: too reminiscent of a Christmas tree.

I've reached the age where the days are spinning by, thought Vanda. Time has become just like the string of beads Miss Parr said it would. And there's a repetitive sameness to my days. It wouldn't matter if Toby and I did sleep in the same bed, we'd never be in it at the same time. I wanted him because Joan had got him; and much good it's done me.

The white telephone on the wrought-iron shelf above the radiator started to ring. The caller turned out to be Eric Lloyd, the theatrical costumier, saying that the lemon dress 'for private wear' was ready for its final fitting.

Except where do I ever go? she wondered. This new offstage wardrobe had been ordered in the first excitement of a whole new life with Toby. The reality of green baize and roulette wheels had soon left her bored and disenchanted. It all went on so *late*, and she always had to be up and unmarked for midday. And the older Vanda got, the more a night's sleep seemed to crease her body. She had recently taken to sleeping flat on her back with her neck on a hard Japanese pillow.

The phone must have disturbed Toby. She could hear the lavatory being flushed, and now he wandered into the lounge with the *Sporting Life* off the hall table in his hand.

If she'd fancied that sort of thing, she supposed that all those lean muscles bursting out of a haphazardly tied silk dressing gown would have been quite appealing. 'Would you mind putting some slippers on, Toby? I don't like sweaty feet on my good carpet. I *have* told you before . . .' she called after him as, doglike, he got up and headed for the door. Feeling that pehaps she had been too hard she shouted, 'Did last night leave you up or down?'

No reply.

470

Down, she thought. Well, he needn't look to me for further finance because it won't be forthcoming.

Toby trudged back into the room with flip-flops on his feet. 'If I'd just had the sense to quit at two o'clock . . . But by then I'd got the red mist, and I was locked into the game.'

'So how much down?'

'It's not good.' The *Sporting Life* rattled open.

'And now I suppose you're looking for a horse to make it better?' This had come out more snappily than she had intended.

He did not rise to the bait. 'You know what I do for a living. You've always known.' Obviously feeling that he ought to make some greater contribution to the conversation, he pointed to her empty cereal bowl. 'Still dieting, still on the muesli?'

'I'm disciplined.' She said it with satisfaction. But she was thinking, I got myself into this, how the hell do I get myself out of it?

'Other Voices is running again. Vanda . . .?'

'No.' He didn't have to finish the sentence, she already knew what he was going to ask.

'If you could just work your abracadabra one more time, just to turn my luck around.'

'Yes, and if I did that you'd have me doing it every day.'

Perhaps the bead sleeves on that costume could be replaced with strip sequining – Eric would know what to do. Oh God, Toby had put on his little-boy-lost look. 'Well?'

'Just once,' he said. 'Just one more time and I'll never ask you again.'

'No.' Vanda got up from the sofa. It had suddenly occurred to her that Toby might try to consult the cards himself. They needed locking into her vanity case. Now that she had a permanent address, she seldom took them to the theatre; the tarot box lived on her dressing table in the bedroom.

'Where are you going?' he called after her. 'I thought we were talking.'

'I've got to get ready for work.' By the time she said this she were already through the bedroom door. Hollywood off the Edgware Road: peach walls, peach satin curtains, and a quilted bedspread which had been copied from one with Debbie Reynolds lying on it, in *Photoplay* magazine.

But no cards.

Where could the box have gone? When had she last seen it? Tuesday: she had definitely come home and spread the cards on Tuesday because a talent scout from Raymond's Revuebar was supposed to have been in the audience, and Raymond's was her ultimate British ambition. 'Toby,' she shouted, 'where are my cards?'

'I don't know,' came through the thin dividing wall.

Vanda stormed back into the living room. 'Where are they? Look me straight in the eye.'

'I've already told you. I don't know.' And he obviously didn't. Back she marched to the bedroom. The flat was a monument to tidiness; the box had only ever lived in one place. Where could it be?

Stealthily Vanda closed the bedroom door. 'Mr Midget,' she said, 'where are you?'

The answer inside her head was like one of those radio programmes which demonstrates what it is like to be partially deaf. Muffled and indistinctly, she could hear his voice saying, '*Stolen. I've been stolen.*' And then he got even more indistinct: '*Zar deef of Tagdad. Zar Teef of Baghdad. Get me pack. Vanda, get me back!*' And now he'd started, it seemed he couldn't stop. Muffled gibberish countinued to wail round Vanda's brain. She might have lost the cards but her life was more than ever haunted. '*Get me pack,*' he screamed. '*I lerve you, Fanda, I lerve you.*'

Joan opened the front door to find the Thief of Baghdad standing on the step, looking in the direction of the green. 'I'm just admiring the view,' he said. 'It's ever so picture-postcard.'

'Yes, but they want to build houses on that land opposite. So they'll see all this, and we'll look out onto bricks and mortar.'

'The council want to turn *us* into a car park.' He had turned round to say this and Joan noticed that there were dark shadows under his eyes.

'My friend from the *Journal* will be happy to come and see you with a photographer,' she assured him. 'They'll be round just as soon as you ring them.'

'And I've got what you want. My dear, don't look at me. I've been rattling through the night on a train.'

It was almost lunchtime. 'Would you like a glass of sherry?' She had already led the way into the sitting room.

'There's just a hint of Lady Bountiful about you, dear,' he said, not unpleasantly. 'I'd watch that if I were you. Mind you, Vanda's apartment is the least hospitable place I've ever visited – nothing but empty crystal decanters. Go on then, I will have that sherry.'

'I do vote Labour,' said Joan. 'Sit down and tell me everything from the beginning.'

'Where's the doggie? I've got a ginger nut for him in my pocket.'

'In the back. Let's leave him there for a minute or he'll only want to dominate everything. What's Pelican Court like?'

'Something a child could have built with Minibricks. And it's got the world's doziest porters. I went straight up in the lift, and I'd already sounded out the back, on the fire escape. Ta.' After accepting the glass of sherry he took a dainty sip. Joan just hoped that the story was not going to be let out in a hundred dribs and drabs.

'She's got two locks on the front door, and they are *not* of the best quality. The apartment is Joan Crawford and water, and she keeps him slaved-up in a little boxroom. I've seen things of Toby Eden's that she can have no idea of. Threatening letters from Crockford's Club, locked away in a little attaché case; and a very finger-marked envelope that's full of dirty picture postcards. But her bedroom is *sumptuous*. It seemed a shame to see all that peach satin going to waste: I was sorely tempted to nip down to the Victory Club and pick up a sailor!'

He took another sip before he said, 'Next time she goes along her dress rails, she's going to find herself short of one very beautiful cocktail gown. I'm sorry, Joan, but it was covered in black jet so I was just like a kiddie in a toffee shop. Beading? She's got so much it's a miracle she doesn't lacerate herself!' His voice became much more practical: 'Anyway, I've taken the label out of the frock and a queen called Sugar Lee's coming round to try it on tonight. She thinks it's fire-damaged stock from Paulden's.'

'The cards, what about the cards?'

He fished in his raincoat pocket, produced the box and placed it on a little piecrust table. 'All yours. And there's something funny about them – evil. That box may be made of wood but it's like touching dirty suede. Your doggie must be able to smell the biscuit in my pocket. Just listen to the noise he's making!'

'I'll only be a second.' Joan walked out of the room quickly; she didn't think the Thief of Baghdad would pinch anything of hers, but she couldn't be sure. As she opened the back door Henry shot past her, heading for the sitting room. She retraced her steps to find the retriever transfixed on the threshold of the room.

All the hair on the back of his spine was standing up, and he was growling at the box on the piecrust table in exactly the same way he would have growled at an intruder. Not content with that, he pulled back his lip and showed it his teeth.

'My sentiments exactly,' nodded the Thief of Baghdad.

'When you've finished looking at that silver ashtray,' said Joan, 'would you mind putting it back on the mantelpiece?' But her words were drowned out by Henry's frantic barking.

The bead follies-sleeves of the red dress were never changed, so every time Vanda climbed into this costume she was reminded of the passing of days and of the arrival of month ends – when Crockford's would present Toby with their account. This was ostensibly for games of bridge because playing poker for money was still illegal. Not that Vanda had to wait for their expensive handmade envelope to arrive to know the state of the game. Most nights Toby would barge into her bedroom and wake her up with a running commentary on the level of his fortunes.

It was either 'Christ, I'm ruined,' or else 'What do you want for a present?' But recently his nocturnal arrivals had been curiously silent, and she had noticed that he had taken to wearing imitation gold cuff links and a fake Cartier watch. These sometimes came out when the real things were in the custody of Sutton's, the posh pawnbroker's near Victoria Station. In the past, that had always been an almost lighthearted and certainly temporary measure; this time he seemed to have taken to wearing the imitations on a permanent basis, even though an assured front was of prime importance to a professional gambler.

Vanda could cope with everything but his self-pity. It was all the 'What have I done to deserve this run of bad luck' that drove her mad. And when he felt sorry for himself he would creep around the place with 'pardon me for being in the way' written into his every move. That was when she would have to remind him that his shoes needed heeling, and that a haircut wouldn't come amiss. It was almost as though Toby had redrawn himself as a loser.

Just occasionally he would get up enough of his old courage to ask, 'Why can't you get another pack of tarot cards? Just give me one big winner and I can refinance my whole operation.'

He was not to know the effect these requests had on her. The cards were gone, but a diminished and distant Mr Midget was still a part of Vanda's life. Some mornings, just as she was waking up, she could hear him trying to talk to her. At best, his voice sounded like that of a hopeless stroke victim; on other attempted visitations he had only succeeded in manifesting furious fluttering noises, like a bird trapped in a loft.

Sometimes she thought she was going mad; when Mr Midget failed in his attempts to communicate, her nostrils seemed to fill up with the stench of putrefaction. It was like standing outside an abattoir on a Sunday.

'If you'd just get another pack of cards . . .' Toby was at it again.

'If you must know, I got another pack. It didn't work. I slung them in the bin.'

Maybe she had thrown them away too hastily. Perhaps she should try again. Not for Tony Eden, for the sake of her own peace of mind. If she was going to spend the rest of her life haunted, at least she should try to do something to improve the quality of the soundtrack.

'I'm in a mess,' said Toby quietly.

'What sort of mess?'

'The kind that makes headlines.' He was dressed for out, and he went.

And you could see that he'd worn the trousers of the suit more often than the jacket, thought Vanda. But the word 'headlines' had stayed with her. What sort of headlines? And would they harm her own career? If I could just sit down with the tarot for ten minutes . . . She had only binned the last shop-bought pack because it had failed to tune her in to Mr Midget; there was nothing to stop her reading a spread by Gran'ma Dora's rules.

I'll go to that shop off St Martin's Lane, she thought. The one near Alf Blatt's office. I'll get myself a pack there.

But when she got to the esoteric bookshop in Cecil Court, they still didn't sell Black Mendoza's. 'Nor are we ever likely to.' It was the same critical assistant behind the counter, the man with the greyhound eyes.

'Let me look at some others.' Cups and Swords and Wands and Pentacles seemed to be available in an infinite number of designs. In the end she settled for a German pack because its Tumbling Tower looked for all the world like the present chaotic state of Toby's life – or as much of it as he had deigned to reveal to her.

'That'll be seventeen and sixpence. Shall I wrap them?'

'No, they'll go in my pocket.'

As the shop assistant made heavy weather of finding the right change, Vanda thought some more about Toby. Pal? Baldy Hogan would have thrown him off the team! It was months since they'd so much as shared a laugh. All the gleam had gone off Toby, and he'd turned into nothing more than a fucking liability. She never used that word out loud, but it was what she was thinking of him. Yes, a fucking liability.

As she walked down Cecil Court, Vanda noticed a woman with a man's haircut getting out of a sports car at the corner where the passageway met St Martin's Lane. Getting nearer, she recognised the owner of the car, who was wearing a brand-new sheepskin overcoat and denim jeans. It was Nancy Spain, the journalist who had described her as armour-plated.

'Good morning to you, Miss Vanda Bell,' smiled the famous columnist. She had an amused voice, which even on the radio had always sounded as though it was about to impart delicious secrets.

'I am *not* armour-plated,' said Vanda. A fortuitous gap in the traffic allowed her to sail past the journalist and over the road.

Finding herself outside Olmi Brothers' San Carlo Restaurant, which was just an Italian café much frequented by the theatrical profession, Vanda decided to go in and have a cup of coffee. She never put her make-up on before she got to the club, so she was hiding behind a big pair of dark glasses. But she always dressed like a star. My God, I even dressed like a star for Dewsbury, she thought as she strode past the counter, where her scarlet cashmere coat was reflected in the huge chromium-plated tea urns. The hair was black again because she had recently revived Vanderella Fantasy. But these days it no longer looked as though she'd done it with Zebo grate polish; these days she went to Phyllis Earle, in Dover Street, to have it coloured. Armour-plated? Bloody cheek!

She decided she looked good enough to allow herself to be seen on the upper tier, where you were very much on view. The tables were tile-topped and could have been designed for spreading tarot cards.

As she shuffled the pack, she listened for the inner voice. Silence. Absolute silence. And if silence could have a shade, this one was best described as reproachful. Oh well, you could only do your best with what you were given. She extracted Toby's card, the Tower, and began to surround it with one of Dora's favourite spreads.

Most of the other cards seemed to be coming from the Major Arcana, the ones her grandmother had always called 'the biggies'. Justice, Death, and then the card Vanda always thought of by its French name, *L'Homme Suspendu* – Dora's name for it had been Gallows Meat. Here was one from the

477

Minor Arcana but it was the Ten of Wands, the card for a man who had bitten off more than he could chew.

'Me oh my oh my,' said an interested voice. Miss Nancy Spain had stolen up on Vanda and she was pointing to the spread. '*Not* a very pretty picture. Now before you start getting cross with me, I want to explain something. May I sit down?'

Torn between the desire to be seen with somebody as famous as Nancy Spain and the worry of being caught on view with Britain's most famous lesbian, Vanda just said, 'You weren't very nice about me in print.'

'That's what I need to explain. May I sit?'

'OK.' If Miss Spain was a lesbian, it was in a very posh way – she was even said to fly to Paris to sleep with Marlene Dietrich.

'I wrote absolutely lovely things about you, but a beastly subeditor at the *Express* went and cut them out. I want to make up for it. Will you let me interview you about striptease for *She* magazine?' She managed to make it sound as though Vanda would be doing her the most tremendous favour. The intelligent brown eyes were raking their way through the cards on the tabletop. 'My God,' she breathed. 'I hope you're not telling those for yourself? I researched the tarot for one of my detective novels.'

'No, it's not for me, it's for somebody else.'

Now the brown eyes looked straight into Vanda's. 'You know what that lot means, don't you?'

Writers evolve their own rituals. Although Joan Stone always went upstairs to the office to type, she generally wrote the first draft of her work on a big lined pad, and she did it in the sitting room.

But first there were pencils to be sharpened. Always the same number – eight. And always Venus 3B. Sharpening the pencils was all part of the process; it seemed to crank up her brain.

This morning her creative abilities refused to spring into action. The new novel, *Timely Warnings*, was finished. Once again Joan had sent it to Molly Wainwright. And this time the reactions had been altogether more enthusiastic. 'I've forwarded it straight on to your agent,' she wrote back. 'And I've suggested to her that she should let my own publisher have a look at it.'

Molly's publisher had felt that Joan's style was a little too near that of one of his already established authors. 'I fear that the two of them could never sit happily on the same list,' was what he'd said in his letter to Joan's agent.

May Evans maintained that this was an entirely positive reaction. And now the manuscript was on offer to a publishing house called Yates. In the meantime, there was a potboiler of an article for *Weekend* to be drafted. Joan did not feel one bit like tackling it.

Henry also had his morning rituals. Once Joan's first pencil began to glide across the pad, he would sneak onto the room, place his paws on the windowsill and direct a single warning growl towards an ornamental rock in the garden.

The box of tarot cards was buried underneath it. And Henry's attitude was not the only thing that had prompted Joan to get them out of the house. She hadn't been able to work with the cards in the room. As she confided to her diary: 'I'll be in the middle of a paragraph and I suddenly get the feeling that somebody wants to speak to me. But when I look up there's nobody there – just that bloody box. I even wrapped it in a plastic bag before I buried it. I didn't want whatever-it-is seeping into the ground. These reactions make me feel very African.'

However often you told people not to ring until half past four – told them that telephone calls were worse than blackbirds or electric drills for breaking the bubble of concentration – they still did it. 'Yes?' she snapped into the receiver.

'One day you'll be rude to somebody who matters.' It was Granny Briggs. 'Anyway, never mind that. Have you seen the papers?'

'I'm trying to write.'

'Do you think I'd be ringing you if it wasn't important? It's obvious you've *not* seen the papers. Joan, I don't want you to open them till I get round there. Just don't do it. I'll be round in ten minutes.'

No, Granny wouldn't, it would take a quarter of an hour. And I'm certainly not going to leave the *Guardian* lying on the mat for that length of time, thought Joan.

A diligent search through the newspaper gave her no clue. Mr Khrushchev had been denied a visit to Disneyland 'for security reasons' but she could hardly see Granny Briggs climbing onto the Vee-espa for that. Except, suddenly, it became impossible to try to inject humour into the situation. Granny had sounded genuinely concerned: could it be something to do with Bruno? His disappearing act had been so thorough that he could have got himself involved in anything, anything at all.

Phut-phut-phut-phut coming nearer, and a happy bark from Henry, announced Granny's imminent arrival. What's more, she *had* done it in ten minutes.

Joan opened the door to an obviously agitated Olive Briggs. She was clutching a copy of the *Daily Express* and hadn't even bothered to put on her crash helmet. Without any preamble she said, 'You're going to have to be very brave. I never liked him, but I know he meant a lot to you. Toby Eden's taken an overdose.'

Joan's brain felt as though it was ventilating like a lung, and she had to steady herself on the hall table. 'Is he all right?'

'Dead. Apparently he went to the doctor for sleeping tablets. And then he went into Hyde Park in the middle of the night, sat down on a bench and took the whole lot.'

I should be feeling something, thought Joan. Why am I shaking like this when I'm totally cut off from my emotions?

'I'll put the kettle on,' said Granny.

'But why? Why did he do it?'

'Money again. It seems he owed a mint. This is Melanie Scott-Kline's *Express*. The boy on the top floor had the *Mirror* waiting for him, and you should read what *they've* dug up.' Because she was running the tap she had to raise her voice. 'Did you know that Toby Eden still had a real mother alive, and two sisters? They all live in a caravan on the Isle of Dogs. About the right place for them, I'd say!'

'Leave him alone.' Joan suddenly felt fiercely defensive. 'Just stop bad-mouthing him.'

'Might I remind you that he made off with my dead mother's engagement ring? We *are* talking about the man who pinched my opals. And you were very lucky to get your deeds back.'

'Things. You're just talking about things. He was flesh and blood.' And so beautiful, she thought wildly; and I flew to places in the sky with him. Her mind was no longer blank, it was unlocked to memories. Toby picking her up in the snow outside Belle Vue Pleasure Gardens, Toby betting sixpence on the fate of a chocolate wrapper heading for a whirlpool. And it went even further back, to Barton Grammar: in her mind's eye he was once again bathed in sunlight as he played the school piano on the platform. 'He never pretended to be anything but a gambler,' she shouted. And then she wondered why she was shouting.

'Where do you keep your sugar?' Once again the phone began to ring. 'I'll answer it.'

'I'll do it myself. Hello.'

'Wonderful news.' This was May Evans. 'Yates wants to buy your book. Not only that, they want another one.' There was a pause and then May said, 'Are you there? Aren't you excited? The money they're offering is very respectable.'

'Somebody just died.'

'Oh my dear.' The agent always treated her clients as friends. 'I'm so sorry. How awful. Just when this should be one of the great days of your life. Look, I'll leave you to cope, I'll put everything in a letter.'

'Thanks.' But even in her misery this news was shining into her brain like a shaft of brightness. 'May, it's amazing news – amazing.' As she replaced the receiver she said to Granny, 'My book's going to be published.'

'I just hope you've not put me in it. I don't want any publicity. You should see the *Daily Mirror*! They've printed a picture of Vanda, in tears, wearing nothing but a sarong. Wouldn't you think she'd have reached for a dressing gown?'

But Joan knew Vanda better than that. In time of crisis she would only ever have reached for one thing – the cards. And with Toby gone there was no reason why they should not be dug up and sent back to her. Joan would be only too glad to have them off her property.

Olive Briggs looked her granddaughter straight in the eye. 'Did you love him? I never asked you.'

'Oh yes, I loved him.' She said it gratefully. 'I really loved him.' And finally she allowed herself to weep, and Henry moved in to be her comforter.

Vanda never got to Raymond's Revuebar. Instead, she spent the next year midway between Eros's statue and the Ritz Hotel, at a Piccadilly nightspot called the Montmartre. This was not a strip club but a late-night restaurant with a lavish floorshow.

In the glossy souvenir brochure Vanda Bell was listed as representing Venus de Sade. Though the leather whip was on view again, she was far more covered up than she had been in Soho, and the act was very much less explicit. For the most part Vanda just strode round the stage cracking her whip in the general direction of champagne-swilling tourists, and of businessmen eating 'chicken in the basket' on expenses.

The show went into a second edition, and in this production she swanked around in a huge chinchilla cape as 'Venus in Furs'. Because there were almost as many women in the audience as there were men, Vanda was delighted to be allowed to add some light comedy to her performance. Along with the furs, she was handed a musical monologue entitled 'I Forgot Something'.

'It's not my diamonds all a-glimmer,
Nor the pearls, just see them shimmer,
It's not my Rolls, that's parked outside . . .'

Three choruses later she absent-mindedly dropped the cape to the ground and the audience finally got to see what it was she had really forgotten – her clothes.

This was the nearest Vanda had ever got to starring in a West End revue. The floorshow had ten girl dancers, four boys, an international conjurer, a comedian who had just finished his own television series . . . It also employed a small army of stagehands and its own publicist.

Whatever time of day you saw Eammon Boyle, he always wore a dinner jacket. It was as though he was perpetually planning on leaving you for somewhere more exciting. Boyle didn't just publicise the show at the Montmartre, he was also the press representative for two West End musicals, and he often undertook personal publicity for visiting American stars. Small wonder that the little Irishman's red hair had gone prematurely grey. But there was a merry twinkle in his boozy blue eyes as he stopped Vanda in the dressing-room corridor after the finale of the second show.

She had learned to mistrust this twinkle. It was entirely professional and generally meant that Eammon wanted something. Tonight was no exception. 'Business seems a bit slack,' he said. 'They're pulling in their horns for Christmas. We can do with all the publicity you can get us.'

'What is it you want, Eammon?' She could never decide whether he was gay or not. There was a wife somewhere in the background, but you occasionally saw him at the late-night coffee stall, in St Anne's churchyard, in Soho. And most people who went there had something or other to hide. Come to think of it, I go there myself, thought Vanda. 'Come on, Eammon, you're after a favour.'

'I just wish everybody was as co-operative as you. The thing is, this girl from Leeds or somewhere has written a book. And one of the characters is a stripper. They're having a do to launch it, tomorrow night. And we've been asked to provide a bit of the real thing.'

'Did they ask for me?'

He went straight into an imitation of stage leprechaun: 'You're a terrible sharp girl. I cannot tell a lie, they just asked me for a name-stripper.' More realistically he added, 'We should count ourselves bloody lucky they didn't go to Mr Raymond.'

The clever little swine knows that that's the one name guaranteed to put me on my mettle, she thought. 'What time and where?'

483

'The Ivy, in the private upstairs room. Six thirty. It's cocktails and bits. I'll squire you along myself.'

'There'll be no need. Jack will take me. Could you shift? I need to get into my dressing room.'

'It's just that . . .'

'What?'

'Are you wise being seen out with Jacko? The press will be there and . . .'

'Just let them dare,' she said levelly. 'Let them print two wrong words and I'll have them straight up in court. If you want me, you'll have to have both of us. Jack's my pal.'

This was only the third time that Joan had been to London. Once to meet the publishers, once to deliver the corrected proofs of *Timely Warnings*, and now she was here for the launch of the book. As on previous visits, she was staying with Molly Wainwright in Belgravia.

The guest room was right up at the top of the building. The rambling flat was on two floors, above a shop which sold handmade chocolates. Joan even had her own little bathroom. It was mildly ramshackle, and Molly always quoted from an Edward Lear poem when describing her guest quarters: 'Two old chairs and half a candle,' she would say. In truth it was much more comfortable than that. Comfortable was the best way of describing the whole flat. As Joan descended to the floor below, she paused to look at one of the original designs for book jackets which lined the walls.

I'll have to try and get the one for *Timely Warnings* from Yates's, she thought. Charles will probably see to it for me. Or was that being presumptuous? Charles Yates belonged to the third generation of the publishing family. And he was so *nice*. Miss Titheradge, at school, had always said that 'nice' was a nasty word. But Miss Titheradge hadn't met Charles Yates: all the fun of Toby at his best, none of the problems, and she was willing to bet anything that he'd be just as good at . . .

'Good morning.' Jessica, the housekeeper, had emerged from the drawing room. Jessica had grey hair like a barrister's wig and a stern face which belied an extremely kind heart. 'Excited about your big day?'

There could be no denying it. 'Yes, wildly excited. Is Miss Wainwright up?'

'I'm writing,' a voice called through the door.

Joan couldn't bear anybody near her when she was working; she had even been known to vow vengeance on a neighbour's creaking garden gate. 'Sorry. I'll leave you to it.'

'Not at all. Come in, come in.'

The drawing room led into the bedroom, where Molly was sitting up in bed wearing a pink dressing gown. A cigarette was already alight in her gold wire holder, and she was clutching a fountain pen and some loose manuscript pages. 'I've just had such a nice fan letter,' she said. 'A small boy heard me on the radio and he thinks that I sound like Mrs Tiggy-Winkle. I'm going to write back and tell him that I look like her too.' Mrs Robinson, the cleaner, was attacking the bedroom windows with a squeaking chamois leather and Jessica's wire-haired terrier was chasing his own tail round the room.

'Can you really write in the middle of all this?' asked Joan in wonder.

'I've done six pages since I woke up. Brenda should be in soon, to type them up. Flowers for me?' she said to Jessica who had come back in with an armful of roses in cellophane.

'No, madam, for Joan.'

'It'll be Charles Yates,' said Molly with satisfaction. 'I told you he was mad about her.'

'Don't!' protested Joan.

'He is. It's a fact. His father told my agent.'

Joan had been reading the card. 'Well he can't come tonight. He has to go to Edinburgh.'

'Yes, and he's spent a good ten pounds on saying so. He's batty about her,' she assured Jessica. 'And it's probably a very good thing that he's not going to be at the party. You'll have quite enough excitement as it is. That woman's been on the phone again.'

Joan didn't have to ask who Molly was talking about. 'That woman' was the girl who handled Yates's publicity.

'It's all a very different world from when I was starting out,' grunted Molly. 'In my day we just wrote books, and they were published, and then we waited for the reviews. If they were good the books sold, and if they weren't they didn't. I find all this publicity business a little bit common. But Yates must be really behind you, Joan, for them to go pushing out the boat for a party at the Ivy.' The whole time she had been talking her brain must have been working on something else because she further grunted, 'Just a minute,' and wrote down two more sentences. 'Your grandmother telephoned. She's gone shopping with the Morgensterns.'

Granny was staying at Brown's Hotel '(('And hang the expense!'). But she'd bought a special midweek ticket, which meant that she would have to hare straight from the Ivy to her train. 'We also had a telephone call from a gentleman who said his name was Doris. It was just to tell you that Henry's in the pink.'

'I'll put those in water.' Jessica took the flowers from Joan. 'Mr Coward's back,' she observed. 'Listen.'

Noël Coward's studio in Gerald Road backed onto Molly's building, and you could hear a piano playing the Chopin theme that somebody else had turned into a popular song called 'I'm Always Chasing Rainbows'.

'It's your day, Joan,' said Molly Wainwright. 'Your very first publication day. And if it's anything like mine was, it's got to be the most magical day of your life.' She paused, thought, and then added more realistically, 'Except it rained torrents and my hair had just been Marcel-waved. But enjoy yourself, my little love, you enjoy yourself. You've proved you can stick at it, and I'm very, very proud of you.'

In the taxi, on the short ride from the publisher's office to the Ivy, 'that woman' was giving Joan another lecture. 'Just remember, if anyone asks, you're twenty-one.'

'But I'm not,' protested Joan, 'I'm twenty-four.'

'But we have to give the press an angle.' Heather Swan was a fierce little blonde who looked as though she could have begun life as a redhead. 'Ever since that Delaney girl wrote *A*

486

Taste of Honey, the Cult of Youth has been on – so you're twenty-one.'

Charles Yates always spoke of Heather as somebody who was as focused on her work as a microscope. As the taxi rattled along ill-lit Garrick Street, she asked the driver to switch on the passenger light, then she began to run a finger down a guest list attached to a clipboard. 'My big fear is that the whole thing will look like one of those awful tarts and vicars parties. The thing is, Joan . . .' She used Christian names a lot, in the American manner. 'The thing is, I've taken the plot of your book and I've asked guests who are like the characters.'

'But there aren't any prostitutes in *Timely Warnings*.' Joan was remembering that Granny Briggs was also to be at this gathering.

'I was talking about the strippers. And Joan, watch what you're eating at the party; I've never forgotten a press photograph of lovely Elizabeth Goudge with spinach on one of her front teeth.' She continued fretting aloud with, 'Will the *Mail* send anybody from the Paul Tanfield column?' And then looking through the taxi window she observed, 'There's a vicar. I sincerely hope that old tart's not one of ours. I distinctly asked my contact at Faith House to try and get us well-groomed beauties.'

In *Timely Warnings*, the real-life Peter Bird had been translated into a character called David Barr. It had been easy enough to write about his schooldays, but once 'David' turned seventeen Joan had been obliged to invent. And she had turned him first into a divinity student, and then a clergyman.

'Christ, I hate these new shoes of mine,' moaned Heather.
'But you look very nice.'

Joan had invested in a blue silk suit, a Balmain copy – eight pounds from Woollands on Knightsbridge. As the taxi pulled up opposite the little theatre where *The Mousetrap* was playing, it was bumper to bumper with another cab, one that was already disgorging Granny and Sally and Herbie Morgenstern.

'Hi!' yelled Sally excitedly. 'You look great. Like mine?'

She was wearing a short green and white spotted flamenco frock. 'I got it off a gypsy dressmaker in Seville.' The outfit was a far cry from the sweater sets and the felt circle skirts of all those years ago. But Sally was still the same: blonde, elegantly assured and ever ready for the next new excitement. Nudging Joan she murmured, 'You're meant to notice that old Olive's finally had her fur cape remodelled.'

'Granny, how smart!'

'Yes, but I think that the furrier kept some of my pelts for himself.' Granny seemed quite pleased with this idea.

'I already read your book, Joan. I liked it,' said Herbie.

The Ivy's commissionaire was attempting to bow the party into the restaurant but Heather Swan motioned him to wait. 'Hello, Herbie,' she said. 'Hasn't your daughter got a coat?'

'It would squash her skirt,' protested Joan.

But the publicist was still talking to the American publisher. 'The thing is, Herbie, we've got a lot of money riding on this. That dress is just crying out to be photographed. And I don't want somebody else scooping Joan's publicity.'

'Wanna swap?' Sally asked Joan.

Heather Swan let out a sigh of relief. 'What a good idea.' And now she allowed them to enter the restaurant. 'I'll wait here while you two go to the ladies.'

Joan and Sally giggled their way to the cloakroom. 'She's a monster,' said Joan.

'But one hundred per cent right.' Sally was already climbing out of the dress. 'Dad will probably offer her a job on the spot. Here,' she thrust the flamenco frock at Joan, 'you'll need these petticoats too. And listen, I can only stay an hour and then I have to rush back to Oxford before they lock the college gates.' Sally was doing a postgraduate course at Somerville.

'So what do we do about swapping back?'

'Swapping back would look too tacky. We'll mail 'em. This is your night for being a big star.'

In 1960, the great days of literary launches were yet to come. But Heather Swan, always ahead of her time, had decided on a cocktail party to introduce Joan to both the press and the book trade. Her choice of the upstairs private room at the Ivy was a typically clever one. This room was a recent innovation, so everybody was curious to see it. And that had guaranteed a spectacular turnout.

Sipping champagne in a corner with Jack, Vanda Bell said, 'I'll kill Eammon Boyle, half the strippers in London are here. Look, there's Trixie Kent, and there's that Fiona woman who makes such a thing out of being middle-class . . .'

'Yes, but you're the only one in white,' Jack consoled her.

'Who's the bloody author of this book anyway?'

'There's a poster with a photograph over there.' Jack lit Vanda's cigarette: it was one of the many little tasks that validated Jack's presence. The pair of them moved across to examine the advertisement.

'I do not believe it,' breathed Vanda Bell. 'Joan Stone, of all people!'

Across the room, by the top of the stairs, Peter Bird had already seen the photograph. This cocktail party was something he had not been expecting to attend. It was the curate from St Mary's Bourne Street who had roped him in by saying, 'It'll only cost us the tube fare, and there's bound to be lashings of free champagne.' Now they were here, this same man asked Peter, 'Why don't you wear the Roman collar?'

'Because I'm an Anglican clergyman. Anyway, my vicar's very down on anything too Romish.' Without any explanation whatsoever he added, 'I think I'm seeing things.' He had suddenly noticed Vanda in a white dress like a second skin. And she had seen him. 'Excuse me,' he said to his companion.

Vanda was already walking towards Peter. As they got within earshot of one another, she blurted out what she was thinking: 'Is that fancy dress or are you really a parson?'

'I'm a curate at St Pega's Westminster.'

'And I'm in my second show at the Montmartre. Meet Jack.'

Peter looked round for a man, but the only person who seemed to be with Vanda was a tomboyish girl in a black velvet dinner suit and a bow tie. She was holding a set of white fox furs which were definitely not her own.

At just that same moment Heather Swan led Joan up the

stairs into the room. 'Oh my God,' she murmured. 'I should have guessed that some of those bloody strippers would be very eye-catching. Listen, I'm going to speak to Basil, we'll nip a bit more off your age – we'll make you nineteen.'

'No.' There came a point where you had to put your foot down. 'I'll stick with twenty-one.'

Heather looked dubious, and then she conceded: 'It does say that in the press releases.'

Sometimes it felt a bit as though you'd sold yourself into bondage. But who could grumble at a publishing house which had splashed out on such a lavish party? Joan waved over to Molly Wainwright just as old Basil Yates moved to the centre of the room and called out, 'If I could have your attention for a moment please . . . thank you.' Charles's father looked like a retired guards officer, tall with a countryman's complexion. 'I thought we would get the speech over now, so that everyone can get on with enjoying themselves.'

'Too soon, Basil,' Heather Swan muttered to herself, 'too bloody soon. The *Evening Standard* aren't here yet.'

But he was already in full flood: 'Joan, come here and let them have a look at you. This is Joan Stone, ladies and gentlemen. And we at Yates are delighted to welcome her to our list. This young writer of twenty-four . . .'

'I give up,' groaned a perfectly audible Heather Swan.

But Basil Yates hadn't given up. On he droned, and on, and on: 'Vivid new talent . . . rare insights into the minutiae of life . . . not since we first published . . .' All this gave Joan time to register Vanda Bell standing next to a clergyman. It couldn't be . . . but it was.

It's Peter. At long last it's Peter. And the sight of him in that dog collar makes me feel as though the plot of *Timely Warnings* is turning into reality. Peter, back in my life, but I mustn't cry with happiness – not with all these people watching.

And still Basil Yates continued to lecture the cocktail party. But now another voice had gone into competition with him. 'Too kind.' It was rising up the well of the stairs. 'Mind the wheelchair on that banister . . . Most grateful.'

In the same way that she had managed to get kippers

490

delivered in wartime from Scotland, Miss Lathom had got herself delivered to Joan's party. She was being carried up the last bit of the stairs in a wheelchair, by a commissionaire and a young woman in a navy raincoat.

'You came!' exclaimed Joan delightedly. 'Oh Miss Lathom, you came all this way for me.' And now she did burst into tears. And all the press cameras let off flashes.

'Perfect,' breathed Heather Swan contentedly. 'Only now you have to earn your keep, Joan. I'm going to take you round the room and introduce you to the Trade.' She always seemed to speak of them with a capital T. Indeed Yates's motto could have been 'First, Second and Third, the Trade'. They even had a special counter for them at their offices in Covent Garden. It had a wooden hatch with an old man sitting behind it, and his sole job was to parcel up books in brown paper and waxed twine.

Joan was introduced to somebody from Foyle's, and then to a frighteningly smart woman from Hatchard's, the Piccadilly bookshop with royal crests over its front door. That was the moment when it occurred to her that even the Queen could end up reading *Timely Warnings*. As she shook hands with the man from W.H.Smith she remembered the wonderful smell of their little branch in Eccles. And she thought, My own books will be part of that smell from now on. Joan shook hands with handsome booksellers and plain ones, and even with an oversexed one who tried to tickle her palm. By the time she'd finished doing her duty, Granny and the Morgensterns had already left.

'I hope I'm not outstaying my welcome, Joan.' Miss Lathom, still in her chair, already had Peter and Vanda round her. 'I shall be spending the night at the University Women's Club. It's been a most memorable evening but I can't pretend I'll be sorry to see my bed. I expect you three will want to run along together, just as you always did.'

'Why don't you all come back to me?' said Peter to his childhood friends. 'I'm only about a mile away. We could even walk.'

'Jack,' called out Vanda peremptorily, 'I need the furs and the vanity case.' The girl in the dinner jacket, who had been leaning against a wall, handed these items over. 'See you at home,' said Vanda.

Heather Swan detached herself from a group of journalists and came up and said to Joan, 'Who do you want to take to dinner? It's on us.'

Yates's youngest author had suddenly had enough of celebrity: 'I think we're going to walk to Peter's.'

'With no coat?' was the outraged reaction. 'I don't want you sneezing on *Woman's Hour* tomorrow. I'll lend you mine.'

In next to no time the three of them were outside on the pavement where Joan said, 'Would you believe that I walked into the Ivy in a completely different outfit? All I've got left of my own are my shoes and my underclothes!'

With Peter in the middle, the three of them strolled arm in arm down St Martin's Lane. Each girl was hoping that the other wouldn't mention Toby Eden. Crowds of theatregoers were beginning to stream through the night, towards the brightly lit entrances of the New and the Coliseum. As they walked past the end of Cecil Court, Vanda caught a glimpse of the esoteric bookshop. Not for nothing had she asked Jacko for the vanity case: the tarot cards were inside it, and the three of them were together again.

Joan was trying to work out how long it was since they'd last marched out as a trio. It was amazing to think that the other two had managed to get on with complete lives, with no help from her. There was no conceit in this thought; it was just that she was remembering the days when their lives had been as intertwined as the three strands of a plait.

Peter suddenly started to laugh. 'The only thing I've got in the fridge is three-quarters of a pound of mince.'

'Have you got basic essentials in your storecupboard?' demanded Vanda.

'Oh yes.'

'Then I can work miracles with your mince!' Vanda adjusted about five hundred pounds' worth of white furs and reflected that the other two were still posher than she was. Crossing the street beyond Trafalgar Square was dicing with

492

death, but eventually they ended up outside the Whitehall Theatre. 'Phyllis Dixey once owned this,' she said.

It was Peter who remembered: 'She was on the posters at Hulme. Phyllis Dixey was billed as a coming attraction on the night we went to see that drag show.' In the light of all that had happened since, he felt it was safe to say to Joan, 'Your uncle was there too.'

A small shadow had been cast across her happiness. 'Bruno's somebody who's vanished completely.'

'No he hasn't,' said Peter cheerfully. 'I can tell you exactly where he is.' He looked at his watch. 'At this precise moment, he should be taking his seat in the stalls at the Old Vic. Let's grab that taxi,' he suggested. 'I want the clergy house of St Pega's Westminster,' he said to the driver. 'The entrance is on Little Shotover Street.'

Joan had been adding two and two together: ever since Bruno's trial, Granny Briggs had always maintained that Peter Bird was somebody who had missed jail by inches. And now he even seemed to know her uncle's timetable. As the taxi rattled past New Scotland Yard she asked, 'Are you and Bruno . . ' Joan sought for a word and came up with 'friends.'

'Not said in that tone of voice,' laughed Peter. 'We're not lovers, if that's what you mean. Mind you, I have got a lover – a very nice one.'

It was Vanda who slid the glass partition across so that the driver couldn't hear what they were saying. 'Peter, I thought you were a parson!'

'I am,' he said. 'And I asked God to send me a man to love – and he did.'

'That's not a bit how I've written it in *Timely Warnings*.' Joan sounded almost indignant. In the days when they sat on the school wall they had been privy to every detail of one another's existence; yet here was Peter distilling whole years into a single sentence. Her author's mind simply had to ask one question: 'How can you be sure that the devil didn't send this boyfriend?'

'I know it was God.' Peter said this with absolute certainty. 'He sent somebody who was so right that there can be no mistake about it.'

'I can't even cross my legs in this frock,' groaned Vanda. 'And I need to go somewhere.'

'We're almost there.' Peter slid back the glass partition. 'Driver, can you pull up by that gate in the wall?'

Joan suddenly remembered something: 'I've got no money on me.' Sally had waltzed off to Oxford with a folded fiver in the pocket of the silk suit.

'I'll get it.' Vanda had never minded paying to get her own way, and tonight she was going to need help from both of the others.

Peter unlocked the Gothic door and led them across an enclosed courtyard, behind a church. 'Choir practice,' he said. Boys' voices were singing 'Panis Angelicus'.

'Doesn't that mean bread of angels?' asked Joan.

'I'm bursting and she's still got to prove that she's the cleverest!'

Peter unlocked another door. 'You'll find it at the end, on the right.'

Joan needed to ask more about her uncle, but first she wanted Peter's opinion on something else. She waited until Vanda had disappeared and then she said, 'Peter, did you notice that very butch girl she was with? You don't think . . .'

'I've learned that it's much better to wait until people choose to tell me these things.' He didn't sound pompous, he had just grown in authority.

'And you've got even better-looking,' she said.

'Let me show you something.' The walls of the corridor were painted bright orange and the woodwork was white. 'These engravings are the vicar's, they're real Rowlandsons.'

'He must be quite well-off.'

'He still has to take in lodgers – look.' A visiting card pinned to one of the doors said *Mr Arthur Farber M.P.* 'But you will find the next door much more interesting.'

There wasn't a visiting card on this one, just a postcard signed Bruno Briggs. The handwriting was much less taut than it had been in Eccles, and she was glad of that. 'But he doesn't want anything to do with us,' she said sadly. 'I expect he still thinks he's got to be ashamed.'

'When he's a hugely successful university lecturer? Give

him even half a chance and I promise you he'll come running with arms outstretched.'

A loud clanking sound, followed by a Victorian amount of flushing, announced Vanda's imminent return. 'Right,' she called out. 'I'm human again.'

'Let's go up to the kitchen.' Peter led the way up two flights of uncarpeted stairs. On the top floor the walls changed to turquoise, and the big old-fashioned kitchen was at the end of a corridor. 'This house was built in the days of armies of servants,' he explained. 'And now all this impoverished curate's got is a bit of mince in the fridge.'

'Have you got spaghetti?' asked Vanda. 'Have you got butter and onions?'

'All of that.'

Vanda placed her vanity case on the scrubbed kitchen table. You could hear the choir more clearly from up here. 'If you two do something for me, I'll make the meal.'

Peter lifted the metal lid off a boiler with an oven glove and threw in some coal from a cast-iron scuttle. 'Such as what? What is it you want us to do?'

She opened the vanity case and took out the box of tarot cards.

'My God, you carry them around with you,' cried Joan. And then she wondered if she should have said 'God' in a vicarage.

'I've carried them around ever since somebody pinched them. But they came back, through the post.' She looked Joan straight in the eye: 'All of that was you, wasn't it?'

'Yes. And you know why.'

Vanda was prepared to avoid discussion of those events in the cause of discovering something else. 'When you had the cards, did you hear him? Did he haunt you too?'

What on earth was she talking about? 'All I know is that I didn't like having the things in the house.'

Peter was just hoping that Vanda was not proposing to tell their fortunes. The Bishop of London had recently come down hard on the subject of divination. But what could she want? The only thing to do was to wait for her to come out with it.

495

Abandoning all fear of ridicule, Vanda began to try to explain. 'There's something in them.' Inside her head the midget was already crying out, '*I'm your friend, Vanda. I was always your friend.*' 'It's something I can hear – a voice. And it first got in that day at Magi House.' Vanda Bell had stopped being hard-boiled and uncaring. 'There were three of us when it started and now it's got to end. It must, it tries to wreck everything. It even managed to smear its way onto Toby and your Uncle Bruno. It's evil.'

Peter was ready with the official response: 'If all you say is true, and I'm not doubting you, then this is a case for the diocesan exorcist.'

'Don't be so fucking stupid!' Vanda could have been echoing the sound of the roaring and cursing voice which was ringing round her brain. 'Was the diocesan exorcist at Magi House? It was us, just us, and now we're here again. You're meant to be a priest, Peter. Do something, get something done.' And then she added a word that neither of them could remember her ever having used before: 'Please.' In that moment Vanda looked fully forty-five. 'Please,' she repeated. 'Please.'

Her need was so obvious that Peter swept aside all thoughts of the rules. First he crossed himself. And then, taking the box from Vanda, he used his finger to draw another cross over the pokerwork occult eye. 'In the name of the Father, and of the Son, and of the Holy Ghost, Amen.' But what was he supposed to do next? Remembering the full horror of his adolescent nightmare about these same cards, he said, 'May our Holy Guardian Angels draw near and protect us, and may Almighty God show us what to do, and give us the strength to do it.'

Vanda's hands were wrapped round her head and her fingers were digging into her scalp. 'He's screaming like somebody scalded. God, I think he's going to burst my brain!'

'Whoever you are,' Peter was improvising quickly, 'and whatever you are, go to a happier way of life than this. And if you have a soul, may it rest in peace.'

Vanda could hardly believe what was happening inside her

skull. 'He's crying,' she said in wonder, 'he's crying just like a little child. I never heard him sound so young before.'

Peter carried the box of cards over to the boiler. Lifting the iron lid again, he dropped the box into the flames. And straight away the room was flooded with the smell that had once haunted his dreams – the stench of putrefaction. The girl in the white dress screamed, the noxious odour flared up like a sudden and intense gas leak, and just as quickly it was gone.

When Vanda spoke it was with complete conviction: 'It's finished. It's over.' And no diet on earth had ever left her feeling as light as this.

'Praise God,' said Peter quietly. 'Praise God.'

Joan only hoped that he wasn't going to oblige them to sing the school hymn. Instead, life went straight back to normal as he added, 'I think I'd better just run my hands under the tap. The mince is in the big fridge, not the little one.'

'First I need an onion,' announced Vanda. It finally felt as though they were really together again.

Being together was always best when we were chopping onions, remembered Joan. It was good to be back amongst friends.